My K-Drama Life

The Complete Trilogy

Sara Martin

Published by
Westwell Press
New Zealand

Cover design by romancepremades.com

ISBN 978-0-473-61530-7

saramartinauthor.com

Contents

The Practice Kiss

Book 1

Chapter 1

As I stumbled through the neon-lit back streets of Seoul, I wondered whether I'd freeze to death if I had to sleep outside tonight.

My tired arms dragged my heavy suitcase over the rough pavement, the dizzyingly bright, colourful storefronts and signs becoming a blur as my head spun, drunk from the soju. I tried to focus, desperately grasping for some kind of solution.

I'd spent the last year dreaming and preparing for this…How could it all have gone so terribly wrong? *Should I call my parents and admit defeat? I couldn't even make it 24 hours...*I swallowed dryly, an uncomfortable lump in my throat.

Salty, spicy, pungent fumes drifted from the doorways of restaurants into the night air. My stomach lurched. In a haze of nausea, I staggered forward, hunger and exhaustion stabbing my body.

I stopped outside a convenience store and fumbled in my jeans pocket, retrieving my phone. I stared in disbelief at the low-battery warning displayed on the screen. Overcome with hopelessness, my eyes filled up with tears. I dropped to the ground feeling dizzy and lost, unable to think straight or to ask for help. Hurried passersby ignored my crumpled figure. Under the glow of a flickering, buzzing fluorescent sign, I leaned my head against my suitcase. *I give up.*

Chapter 2

Eight hours earlier

I burst through the arrivals gate at Incheon International Airport, brimming with excitement. *Today, my new life begins as an English teacher in South Korea.*

With a deep breath, I stepped forward, wheeling my suitcase over the shiny, tiled floor. Friends, relatives, and colleagues of arriving travellers gathered behind the barrier rails, a buzz of anticipation in the air.

The teacher placement agency, SK-Teach, had booked and pre-paid a driver to pick me up and take me to my accommodation—a studio apartment that the school was providing for me. I scanned the crowd, searching for someone holding a sign with my name on it.

Searching…searching…

Hmmm. No "Chloe Gibson" sign in sight. *How odd.* I had been assured that there would be someone to meet me at the gate.

I stood and waited a while longer, but fatigue quickly caught up with me. I hadn't slept on the flight. My ears were blocked, and my head was foggy. It felt like I was underwater. I moved to a nearby row of chairs, where I slumped down, suitcase in front of me and backpack on my lap.

I pulled my phone out from my jacket pocket. Using the free airport WiFi, I checked my emails in case I had been sent updated plans. Scrolling through my inbox revealed nothing but junk mail. I sighed heavily. Resting my head in my hands, I continued to watch the small gathering around the gate.

Several batches of arrivals came and went. At last, I conceded that no one was coming to pick me up. There must have been some kind of mix-up.

I'll just take a taxi, I decided, certain that I could be reimbursed for the fare. Before leaving the terminal, I called my contact at SK-Teach. An automated message played: "The number you have called is not available." *Gah.* I composed a short email instead, letting them know that I was leaving the airport.

As soon as I pressed send, I headed out the airport doors and into the fresh afternoon air. I spotted the rank of bright orange taxis immediately. I waved to the driver first in queue. He got out of the car.

"Good afternoon," he said in English.

"Afternoon," I replied.

He hauled my suitcase and backpack into the boot, then opened the door for me. I made myself comfortable in the back seat. The taxi was clean and smelled as if it had been freshly filled with petrol.

"Where are you going today?" the driver asked.

I handed him a printout of the location of my apartment in Mapo-gu, Seoul.

"First time in Korea?" the driver asked, pulling out from the rank.

"No. I lived here for a year when I was sixteen. I did a high school exchange trip."

"Wow. You must have been outgoing to do that at such a young age."

"It was hard at first, but my host family was so kind and welcoming."

"Can you speak Korean?"

"Yes."

"Oh, that's good."

I gazed out the window, watching the cars go by on the expressway—Kias and Hyundais in white, silver, and black. The driving style looked chaotic, with cars weaving in and out of lanes without indicating. This didn't faze the taxi driver, who engaged in the same behaviour himself.

"What brings you back to Korea?" he asked.

"I've been hired as an English teacher."

"Ah, I see. Lots of foreigners come here to do that."

The overcast sky lent a dreary atmosphere to the city and the monotonous view from the expressway caused me to yawn. I closed my eyes, only meaning to rest them temporarily, but when I opened them again, we were in the heart of Seoul.

I snapped upright, absorbing the sights and sounds of the bustling metropolis around me, a jumbled mixture of high-tech, futuristic skyscrapers, plus older, low-rise buildings, some of them rundown and dilapidated.

The streets hummed with activity, hordes of people walking the footpaths, past shops, restaurants, offices, and street food vendors.

We continued to drive, winding through side streets as the last rays of afternoon sunlight pierced a gap in the clouds.

Eventually we came to a residential neighbourhood composed mainly of houses and apartment blocks. There were fewer cars and people around. Grassy areas provided a more relaxed, suburban feel.

The car slowed, then pulled over. "Rose Tower" read the sign on the building up ahead. I recognised it from the pictures I had been sent. Around 20 floors high and with a peachy-pink exterior. A small courtyard and garden bordered its entrance.

"The fare is 62,000 won," the driver said.

"I'll pay by credit card."

He passed me the card reader and I inserted my credit card. An error message appeared on the screen. I tried again but it still didn't work.

"It's not working for some reason," I said. "I'll pay cash." I counted my money and offloaded a wad of notes, leaving my wallet considerably lighter.

"Thank you."

We got out of the car and he retrieved my luggage from the boot.

"Enjoy your time in Korea." He bowed.

"Thanks!"

Excited to finally get settled in my apartment, I crossed the road and approached the building. Glass double doors marked the entrance to the lobby. Raising a shaky hand, I reached out and pushed the door...but it wouldn't open. I tried to pull instead, but that didn't work either. *Hmmm...Is there something I need to press?* I noticed a panel at the side of the door and some kind of sensor. *Ah! I must need an access card to get in. How inconvenient.* I hadn't been told about this, and I hadn't been provided with one. Frustrated, I set my luggage down and took out my phone. I tried to call SK-Teach again.

"The number you have called is not available."

Is my phone not working? Maybe I should have bought a new sim card at the airport...

I checked my emails. A new message appeared at the top of my inbox, subject line: Message delivery failed. Clicking the email, I saw that the earlier message I sent had bounced. A deep unease unfurled in my stomach. *What's going on? Why can't I contact the agency?*

I took a few deep breaths to calm myself. It's okay, I assured myself. It was a big building. It wouldn't be long before a resident would come and open the door, and I could follow them in. I sat down on the edge of a planter box near the entry and assumed stake-out mode.

As time passed, I grew increasingly drowsy. I could barely keep my eyes open. *Please...someone come soon...*

Finally, my ears pricked at the sound of footsteps approaching. I sprang into action, swiftly moving in behind the female resident. She opened the door, and I followed her inside. The door swung closed behind me and locked with a clunk. I exhaled in relief. *I'm in.*

The small, plain lobby had white walls, a tiled floor, and three elevators. I followed the woman into the middle elevator. She swiped her access card and pressed six. I pushed ten, but it didn't activate without a card. The woman gave me a questioning look and I mumbled something about losing my card by way of explanation.

After the short ride up, the elevator doors opened at the sixth floor and the woman departed. I had no choice but to get out and take the stairs the rest of the way.

The windowless corridor was dark and narrow. I followed an illuminated green sign to the fire exit and pushed open the door. The steep flight of stairs rose up in front of me like a mountain. I groaned inwardly. Gathering all my strength, I lugged my suitcase up the staircase, step by agonising step.

By the time I reached the tenth floor, my arms ached and sweat soaked my top. I burst out into the corridor, gasping for breath.

As soon as I had recovered, I scanned the row of doors for my apartment number—10F.

There it is. I stood in front of the door to my apartment, almost crying with relief. Now, the only obstacle in my way was the digital lock. Luckily, I knew the code and had already memorised it off by heart. I reached for the keypad and typed the number in. 4910.

Nothing happened.

Did I type it wrong? I tried again.

Nope, still didn't work.

I groped in my backpack for my wallet, where I had stowed a slip of paper with the door code. I double checked it. *4910.* My heart dropped. *Something is seriously wrong here.*

Out of desperation, I knocked on the door. I heard movement in the apartment. A strange old man opened the door and looked at me with a surprised expression on his face.

"What is this?" he asked in Korean.

"Sorry! Wrong apartment!"

Flustered, I hurried away.

My head reeled. *What's going on? What should I do?*

I took the elevator back down to the lobby.

This must be a mistake...

Once again, I tried to contact SK-Teach. No luck.

Changing tack, I decided to call the school instead. *They might know what's going on.* I hadn't dealt with the school directly since my interview with the principal. I had to look up the school's phone number. I paced backwards and forwards as the phone rang, willing someone to pick up.

"Hello, this is Gongwon School reception."

"Yes, hello. My name is Chloe Gibson. I'm the new English teacher. I need to speak to Principal Choi."

"Chloe…Gibson…?"

"That's right."

"I can't find your name on our staff list."

"Maybe it hasn't been added yet?"

"That shouldn't be the case…Hold on. I will ask Principal Choi."

She put me on hold. My stomach undulated with nerves as I waited. *Principal Choi knows me. He should be able to sort out this mess…*

Eventually, she picked back up.

"I'm sorry. Principal Choi has not heard of you. There hasn't been a new English teacher hired this year."

My world came crashing down as reality hit me.

Chapter 3

The pieces slowly drifted into place. *It was all a scam.* The interview must have been fake. The job contract and the apartment lease too.

I felt sick to the pit of my stomach, frozen in shock, unable to move, unable to think straight. Completely numb.

I stood in a state of stupor until the elevator door suddenly opened, startling me. The young man who walked out threw me a curious glance but continued on his way.

I can't stay here. It was already dark outside. I needed to find a place to stay the night. I could decide what to do after a good, long sleep.

I checked Kakao Maps for the nearest hotel. Only a fifteen-minute walk away, but I couldn't bear to drag my suitcase that far. Instead, I walked to the nearest main street and hailed a taxi. A grey-coloured cab pulled over. The driver flung my luggage in the boot and I hopped in the back seat.

"Crane Hotel, please," I said.

A short drive later we arrived at the hotel. I paid the small fare with cash.

Standing outside the hotel, the rapid beat of my heart stabilised. I felt safe in the knowledge I would soon be resting in a warm and comfortable hotel room.

Warm light emanated from the hotel windows, inviting me inside. I stepped through the revolving door into a stylish, contemporary lobby, with a polished concrete floor, and plush, designer furniture. I approached the reception desk where a woman wearing a navy-blue suit and a silk scarf around her neck talked on the phone. When her lengthy conversation concluded, she finally turned her attention to me.

"Hello. How can I help you?" she asked in English.

"I'd like to check in. I don't have a room booked…"

"I see." She looked at her computer screen. "We have standard and deluxe rooms available."

"Standard is fine."

"How many nights?"

"Just one, for now."

The woman printed out a form. She handed it to me, along with a pen. "Please fill in your details."

I quickly scrawled down my information and slid the form back to her across the desk.

"Perfect." She took the form. "Now, I just need you credit card to confirm the booking."

I fished it out of my wallet. "Here you go."

She inserted my card and prompted me to enter my PIN on the keypad.

Processing…

Transaction declined.

I remembered how the card hadn't worked in the airport taxi either. "Sorry. Let me try a different card."

I used my debit card but received the same message. I started to sweat. *Why aren't my cards working?*

"I don't know what's wrong," I stammered. "Can I pay in cash?"

The woman shook her head. "We need a card on file to cover incidentals."

"Please? I really need to book this room."

"I'm sorry. Our system can't process the booking without a card. There's nothing I can do."

"I see…Then I'll have to go somewhere else."

Head hung low, I retreated from the desk. My body trembled with accumulated frustration and exhaustion. I sat down on a chair in the lobby and wearily opened my banking app. When the app loaded, my heart jumped in shock. My account balance showed I was in overdraft and my credit card was maxed out. *What the hell?*

I scrolled through the transactions, my hand shaking. Large withdrawals had been made from my account, all of them during the timeframe I had been on the plane.

Not only had my teaching placement been a scam, but they had also taken my money.

Freaking out, I called my bank. Music played as I waited in the hold queue.

"Your wait time is approximately 45 minutes," played an automated message.

"45 minutes!" I repeated in disbelief.

Sighing, I curled up on the chair and closed my eyes, phone pressed to my ear. The same song played over and over again until its tune was drilled into my brain.

I was practically dead by the time I was finally put through to a customer service representative.

"How can I help you today?" he asked, cheerily.

I blurted out my situation and he quickly cancelled my cards and filed a fraud report.

"We should be able to get these transactions reversed, but it could take a few days…" he explained.

"When will I be able to get new cards sent to me? I'm in South Korea right now."

"South Korea? I'll arrange express international delivery. Where are you staying?"

"Uh…actually…I don't have an address right now. I'll have to get back to you."

He gave me his direct line so I could call him back.

Ending the phone call, I realised my dilemma was only partially resolved. I should be able to get my money back and a new card, but for now I would somehow have to survive on the limited amount of cash I had left.

I counted my money. 103,000 won. That would have to pay for food and accommodation and whatever else I needed, possibly for a few days. Where could I stay that would accept cash and not cost too much? A hostel dorm? A *jjimjilbbang*?

Across the room at the lobby bar, two businessmen sat drinking beers and eating fried chicken. My stomach growled with a sharp stab of hunger. I hadn't eaten in hours. *I need food…*It would be easier to think about what to do with a full stomach.

I heaved myself up to venture outside. A blast of freezing air slammed into me as I stumbled out the door and I tightened my scarf, huddling closer into its warmth. My breath came out in puffs of mist as I walked the moonlit street, searching for a place to eat.

I halted when the delicious smell of fried food tugged at my nostrils. I followed a trail of wafting steam to a *pojangmacha*—rows of orange tents with transparent plastic windows, through which I could see tables and chairs, people, and a bar laden with trays of food.

The sound of meat sizzling, broth bubbling, and people chatting pulled me closer. Shivering, I entered the tent. Heaters inside provided immediate comfort.

I took a seat at the bar and ordered *tteokbokki* and soju. Speaking in fluent Korean was enough to deter the vendor from attempting to rip me off with inflated tourist prices, despite the enormous suitcase by my side.

The food and soju were promptly served, and I snapped apart a pair of disposable chopsticks. I popped one of the cylindrical rice cakes into my mouth, then another, and another. I ate too fast, launching a coughing fit. The dark red broth overpowered my weak stomach.

While I waited for my stomach to settle, I poured a glass of soju. I drank it in one gulp. The strong, slightly sweet, clear liquid warmed my throat.

I continued to drink while turning over my situation in my head. I could find a place to stay the night, but then what? Search for another teaching position at this late stage? Contact my old host family and ask them for help? Just give up and call my parents and ask them to book me on the next flight home?

I downed another shot of soju. My parents had been against me going to Korea in the first place. The thought of telling them I had failed was unbearable.

Asking my host family for help wasn't palatable either. They were poor and lived all the way in Tongyeong. I didn't wish to burden them.

No closer to a resolution, I drank until my worries numbed. I tried to eat more food, but my stomach rejected it despite my hunger. My head felt heavy. How I wished to lay it on a soft pillow…I had to peel my eyes open to keep myself from falling asleep at the bar. I hopped down, leaving the empty soju bottle and my half-finished meal.

Towing my suitcase behind me, I set out, stumbling along the back streets of Seoul. My head spun, and the bright, colourfully lit streets became a blur as I walked.

I willed myself to focus, but I couldn't.

I stopped outside a convenience store and took out my phone. The screen displayed a low-battery warning.

At that point, I lost it. I dropped to the ground, crying. *I give up.*

I'd have to call my parents and ask to come home. The thought made me wail even louder.

"Hello? Are you all right?" a female voice asked in Korean.

I looked up, wiping away tears.

A woman in corporate attire and her hair pulled back in a low ponytail stood watching me.

"No. I'm not all right. Everything has gone wrong," I replied.

The woman looked surprised. "You speak Korean well." She offered me her hand and pulled me up. "My name is Seo Minjung. I work for KAM Entertainment." She passed me her business card.

Seo Minjung

Talent Recruitment Executive

KAM Entertainment, Gangnam, Seoul

"I think I can help you," she said.

A wave of relief swept over me.

She took me to a nearby café. The dimly lit room was divided into comfy booths containing worn, brown couches and wooden tables. Shelves messily crammed with old books separated the booths. The air smelled of fresh coffee, chocolate, and pastry.

"Let me buy you something to eat and drink," Minjung said, approaching the counter.

"I'm fine," I stammered, taken aback by her kindness to a stranger she just met on the street.

Minjung scrutinised me, unconvinced. "No, you're not. Come on. What would you like to drink?"

"My stomach is a bit upset…" I clutched it tenderly.

"How about a chamomile tea? It's good for settling a sore stomach."

"Hmmm…That sounds nice."

Minjung ordered and then we sat down in one of the booths. She looked at me with concern, her big, round eyes sympathetic. "So… what's your story?"

My head continued to spin. I took a big breath to calm myself before answering. "I arrived in Seoul today to start an English teaching job…but it turned out the job didn't exist."

"Why is that?"

"I was scammed by a sham recruitment company."

Minjung gasped. "*Omo…*"

"The apartment lease they arranged was fake as well. They also took my money."

"So that's what happened. No wonder you were so upset."

"I don't have anywhere to stay. All I have is around 100,000 won in cash."

Minjung chewed her lip. "I see. You're in a tough predicament."

I nodded, wearily.

A girl in a black apron served us—a chamomile tea for me, an Americano for Minjung.

"Drink up," Minjung said.

I took a calming sip.

Minjung cradled her coffee cup, a thoughtful expression on her face. "Chloe…I think I can help."

"Really?"

She nodded. "But I have a proposal for you."

So, there's a catch...

"Okay. What is it?"

"Do you have any acting experience?"

Chapter 4

"Acting experience?" I repeated, bemused.

"Yes. Do you?" Minjung pressed.

"Well, I've been in school productions…I took drama lessons throughout high school too."

"That's something!"

"Why do you want to know?"

"The truth is, I had a motive for approaching you on the street…"

"Oh?"

"When I saw you, I thought you would be the perfect fit for a role."

"An acting role?"

"That's right. On a drama."

My mouth dropped open. "Me? Appear in a drama?"

"Exactly."

I couldn't believe what I was hearing. This couldn't be right, could it? It must be the alcohol, the exhaustion…*I'm delirious.*

I took her business card out of my pocket and looked at it again, focusing my blurry vision. "You work for KAM Entertainment."

"That's right. We specialise in sourcing and developing actors and models. There's a new drama due to begin filming on Thursday, but one of the actors pulled out at the last minute. There's been a desperate rush to fill her role."

"And you think I would suit the role?"

Minjung nodded. "A good-looking foreigner who can speak Korean fluently. You even resemble her. You're about the same size too, so wardrobe shouldn't need to make many adjustments…"

Is this real? Am I dreaming?

"Is this something you would be interested in?" Minjung asked.

My heart raced. "Are you kidding? It would be a dream come true!"

"Great! You'll still need to audition, of course. But it's a minor role, and at this late stage, I don't think they're going to be too picky."

I felt dizzy with excitement and disbelief.

Minjung continued. "I'll take you to KAM tomorrow and arrange a meeting with the director. As for tonight…I can't offer much, but I do have a couch you can sleep on. Would that be all right?"

Under normal circumstances I wouldn't go and sleep in a stranger's house, but these weren't normal circumstances, and what other option did I have?

"Yes. Thank you!"

I hastily slurped back my tea.

"Are you ready to go? It's a quick ride on the subway to my place," Minjung said.

I nodded. "Let's go."

We ditched the cozy café for the bitter cold street. Minjung pulled my suitcase for me, a relief to my aching arms. She led the way to the nearest subway entrance.

We entered a large station, bustling with workers heading home after a long day at the office. Through turnstiles and down an escalator, we reached the platform. The train had already arrived, and we managed to board just before the doors closed.

It was a short journey to Hapjeong station. From the exit, we emerged on a busy main street lined with shops and high-rise towers.

I followed Minjung down back roads with a quainter vibe, past coffee shops and small apartment buildings. We stopped outside a nondescript building the colour of concrete. She unlocked the door and let me in.

Minjung's apartment was on the third floor. She entered her passcode and pushed open the door.

"I'm home!" she said, taking off her shoes at the entrance.

The compact apartment had white walls and a wooden floor, with house plants, cushions, and art prints providing pops of colour to the otherwise minimalist interior.

A man sat at a small table by the window, a book in one hand and a coffee cup in the other. He lifted his head and peered at us through his thick glasses. "You're home late. Who's that?"

"Potential new talent."

"My name's Chloe," I said, removing my shoes.

"I'm Gong Dongsik, Minjung's husband."

"She'll be sleeping here tonight," Minjung stated.

Dongsik raised his eyebrows at this news but didn't push back.

"Sorry to intrude," I said.

"Sit down," Minjung said. "You must be so tired."

I made myself comfortable on the couch.

Minjung rummaged in a closet and retrieved a warm blanket and a pillow. She passed them to me.

"Thank you," I said.

"Feel free to have a shower. And help yourself to anything in the kitchen."

"Hmmm...I might use the shower." Although I was eager to go to sleep, I was more desperate to wash off the layer of grime which had accumulated on my skin and in my hair.

"Of course. Oh, but before that, can I take a couple photos of you? I want to send them to Mr. Kim at KAM. I'm sure he'll be very pleased that I found you."

"Okay. I don't look my best, though..." I ran my fingers through my messy hair, trying to comb it.

"You look fine," Minjung assured me. "Stand here."

I stood in front of the white wall.

Minjung snapped two pictures of me with her phone—one close-up and one full-length shot.

"There. You can go and have your shower now. I'll let you know what Mr. Kim says."

I grabbed my toiletries bag and a pair of pyjamas from my suitcase before heading to the bathroom. Minjung tossed me a clean towel on my way.

I quickly undressed and got in the shower. The hot water felt amazing on my bare skin. My aching muscles sighed with relief. *I've had the strangest day*, I reflected as the water flowed over me.

One year ago, I quit a soul-destroying job and moved back in with my parents. Depressed, I spent my days binge-watching K-dramas, not knowing what to do with my life. Eventually, those K-dramas gave me the idea to go to Korea and teach English. And now, I actually had the chance to *be in* a K-drama. Nothing could make me happier.

After scrubbing myself from head to toe, I emerged feeling thoroughly cleansed and refreshed. I put my pyjamas on and wrapped my hair in the towel.

As I left the bathroom, Minjung's phone started to ring.

"It's Mr. Kim!" she said.

Butterflies in my stomach, I listened as she answered the call.

Chapter 5

"He wants to meet you first thing tomorrow!" Minjung said excitedly when she had finished talking with Mr. Kim.

"That sounds promising," Dongsik said. "Is it for the part in Hidden History?"

"Yes."

"Should I do anything to prepare?" I asked.

Minjung shook her head. "Just try to have a good sleep. There will be time to look over the script tomorrow. We'll leave you to get some rest."

"Goodnight," Dongsik said.

They retreated to their bedroom.

Alone in the dark room, I lay on the couch and pulled the blanket over me. Thoughts swirled in my head, becoming more and more nonsensical until they turned into dreams. I slept heavily through the night.

In the morning, the smell of breakfast prompted me to open my eyes. Minjung prepared kimchi, rice, and soup. I sat up and breathed in the powerful aromas.

"Oh, you're awake," Minjung said.

"Do you need any help?" I asked, stifling a yawn.

"No. I'm just reheating leftovers."

"Morning," Dongsik said, emerging from the bedroom. He wore a dark grey suit and a striped tie. "Sleep well?"

"I did. This couch is comfortable."

"That's good to hear. Come and join us for breakfast when you're ready."

I got changed in the bathroom, then sat down with Minjung and Dongsik at the table.

"Looks delicious," I said.

Minjung shrugged. "It's nothing much."

I wolfed down the food, my stomach having fully recovered from the previous night.

"Ah! Look at the time," Minjung said. "We'd better get going."

"I can drop you off at the station," Dongsik said.

In a flurry, we got ready to leave.

"Let's go." Dongsik rallied us out the door.

We descended the stairs to an underground carpark where Dongsik unlocked a white SUV. I hopped in the back seat.

Early morning sunlight poured in as we surfaced from the carpark. Commuters in business attire crowded the roads and paths.

After a short drive, Dongsik pulled over near the subway entrance. "*Hwaiting!* I'm rooting for you."

"Thank you!"

We hopped out and Dongsik drove away.

I stayed glued to Minjung's side in the jam-packed subway station, terrified that we'd get separated as people pushed and shoved their way around us. Eventually, we managed to squish ourselves into a train carriage.

An uncomfortable forty-minute ride to Gangnam Station ensued. I sighed with relief when we finally made it.

In trendy central Gangnam, Minjung guided the way to the KAM building.

"Here we are," she said at last.

The large office building had light grey panelled walls and a border of planter boxes providing pretty greenery. A discreet plaque by the entrance read "KAM Entertainment."

Minjung swiped her employee ID to enter and I followed her in.

"Whoa," I said, looking around as we entered a spacious and modern reception area. Large screens displayed a rotation of glamorous shots of the talent. *They're gorgeous...I wonder if I'll get to meet any of them.* I stood transfixed until Minjung tore me away.

"We're going to Mr. Kim's office on the fifth floor." She steered me towards the elevators.

When we reached the fifth floor, the elevator doors opened to reveal a posh suite of executive offices. We walked into Mr. Kim's office. He stood up from his desk when we approached. Despite his age, he looked trendy, wearing a plain, white t-shirt under a blue blazer.

"You must be Chloe Gibson." He grinned enthusiastically.

"Yes, Mr. Kim," I said.

"Please, take a seat." He motioned to the leather couch at the side of the room.

"I'll leave you to it." Minjung flashed me a look of encouragement before slipping away.

I sat down. Mr. Kim pulled up his chair to sit opposite me.

"Now, as I'm sure Minjung explained to you, there is an urgent role to fill on the drama Hidden History. It's not a lead part, but it's crucial to the storyline, that's why the character can't simply be written out."

He reached over to his desk and picked up a comb-bound document. He tossed it into my lap.

Hidden History

Episode 1 script

"The character is Louise Sullivan. She's the only foreigner in the small town. She works at a bar and attracts a lot of customers due to their curiosity. Louise seems, how should I say this...*ditzy* at first. But it's an act. She's actually an undercover reporter for a foreign newspaper. In fact, Louise Sullivan isn't even her real name. She's in town to investigate a cold case—a string of disappearances, which seem somehow linked with her Korean friend back in the UK. Early in the series, Louise ends up dead."

"She found out too much?"

Mr. Kim snapped his fingers. "You've got it."

"She sounds like an interesting character."

"Right? An actress called Tamara Wilson had been cast to play her, but the poor thing found out her father's terminally ill. She pulled out so she could go back to England to be with him."

Mr. Kim pulled out his phone and brought up a photo. He showed it to me. "This is Tamara."

The woman looked to be in her mid-twenties, fair and blonde, with hazel eyes. I realised why I had caught Minjung's attention on the street. I looked just like Tamara.

"The resemblance is amazing, isn't it? I feel like you could slip right into her place. As long as you can act reasonably well, I don't think the director would hesitate to cast you. Minjung told me you've been in plays?"

"That's right."

Never in a lead role, though...

"The programme director, Im Nara, is coming in—" Mr. Kim checked his watch, "—just over an hour. She'll audition you. In the meantime, I want you to practice your lines from the first episode. There aren't too many."

"Okay." I clutched the script in my sweaty hands, suddenly feeling the pressure.

"I think Minjung has booked a practice room for you." Mr. Kim stood up. "Come with me."

I followed him to an open-plan area with rows of cubicles. Minjung sat at a desk overflowing with files.

"Seo Minjung-ssi, take Chloe to a practice room. Better send an intern as well."

"Yes, Mr. Kim."

"Chloe, we'll speak again if you pass the audition. Good luck."

I nodded. "Thank you, Mr. Kim."

He left me with Minjung.

One hour to learn my lines. I felt jittery all over, my insides twisting and turning with nerves.

"Are you ready?" Minjung asked.

I hesitated. "Uh, I need to use the bathroom…"

"Of course. It's down that corridor, on the left."

"Thanks. I'll be right back."

My thoughts swirled as I walked towards the bathroom. *What if I don't pass the audition? What if I end up back where I started—homeless and jobless?* I pushed open the bathroom door in a daze. *What's this?* A row of urinals. A man with a shocked expression on his face. *Oh crap.*

Chapter 6

The tall young man wore a denim shirt and slim black jeans. He had a mop of wavy, dark brown hair. Under straight eyebrows, two bright, smiley eyes, squishy cheeks, and a broad mouth.

So cute...I wonder if he's talent?

He looked at me with an expression of bewilderment on his face. I snapped to my senses.

"Sorry!" I stammered, before running out with my arms flailing.

In the safety of the women's bathroom, I took deep breaths and fanned myself with my hands.

"Calm down," I said to myself in the mirror.

I couldn't let an accidental detour into the men's bathroom faze me. I needed to focus on the task at hand. Passing the audition was crucial.

When I returned to Minjung, a petite young woman accompanied her. She had red-dyed hair worn half up in a high bun and a pair of circle-lensed glasses adorned her small face.

"Chloe, this is Intern Yang Bora. She'll help you practice the script," Minjung said.

"Nice to meet you, Intern Yang," I said.

"Actor Chloe, let's give it our best shot." Bora beamed.

One floor up, we stopped outside practice room D.

"Here we are," Minjung said. "All yours for the next hour. Unfortunately, I can't stay. I have work to do. I'll see you after the audition."

Bora showed me into the room. A TV screen was mounted on the wall at one end and a whiteboard at the other. A large table stood in the centre. We sat down opposite each other, scripts in front of us.

"Louise doesn't appear until page 15, so let's start from there," Bora said.

I flipped to page 15. Bora prompted me, acting as a drunk patron at the bar where Louise works.

I read my first line. "Another beer, Mr. Cha?"

Bora frowned, unimpressed.

"Did I say it wrong?" I asked.

"Well…not *wrong* exactly. I just think you need to come across a bit bubblier."

"Another beer, Mr. Cha?" I repeated, trying to sound more lively.

Bora grimaced.

I can't even say one line right...

"Do you know about the character of Louise?" Bora asked.

"Yes. A little bit."

"Well, she's an undercover reporter, right? Who do you think is her main source of information?"

"The bar patrons?"

"Exactly. And how does she get them to talk?"

"Alcohol?"

"Yes, but also her charms. She flirts with them."

"Ah, I see! You seem to know a lot about Louise…"

"I know this script back to front. I've been helping Shin Jinseung practice as well."

"Shin Jinseung?" The name sounded vaguely familiar.

"You don't know him? He's another actor from KAM who's in this drama."

"Who does he play?"

"Officer Park Minjoon. It's the lead male role."

"Oh…So if I get the part, I'll be working with him…"

"That's right." Bora sighed. "So lucky…In the third episode, there's a scene—"

Her phone beeped, diverting her attention.

"*Aigoo*! We've already wasted ten minutes. Let's get back to the script."

With Bora's advice, I nailed the bar scene and we moved on to the next scene featuring Louise.

"Oh! This scene has Officer Park in it," I said.

"Yes. There are quite a few scenes between Louise and Officer Park. They're friends. He's the only person who she shows her intelligent side. You can act more natural with him."

"Got it."

We read through the scene. Since I just had to act like myself, it came easily to me.

"That's good," Bora said. "Shall we try everything again? This time, try not to rely on the script."

I closed my script. "I'm ready."

We started over from the top. I repeated my lines over and over until they were drilled into my head. Fully focused on the script, I jumped when Bora's phone rang.

"Yes, Mr. Kim?" she answered. "…I see…Yes…Room D…" She put down her phone. "PD Im Nara is here. It's time for your audition."

The sound of high heels clicking on the floor intensified as Im Nara approached. I gulped, feeling apprehensive.

She appeared at the door—a woman in her forties, immaculately dressed in a beige pant suit, a designer bag tucked under her arm. Her fierce eyes locked onto mine. I stood up and bowed.

"You must be Chloe Gibson. I'm Im Nara—PD of Hidden History."

She offered her hand. I shook it firmly.

"Nice to meet you, PD-nim."

Nara turned to Bora. "And who are you?"

"Intern Yang Bora. Can I get you anything to drink, PD-nim? Tea, coffee…?"

"A glass of water will be fine, thank you."

"Yes. Right away." Bora hurried off.

Nara pulled out a chair and sat down. I followed suit, lowering myself into a chair, my heart pounding.

Nara studied me. Her red lips curled into a half-smile. "Well, you certainly look the part…But can you act?"

"I'll do my best, PD-nim."

"Your best is certainly expected."

Heat rushed to my cheeks.

Bora returned with two glasses of water. She placed one in front of Nara, and one in front of me. I drank, trying to bring my soaring temperature back down.

"Could I please watch the audition?" Bora asked.

"That's fine. Take a seat," Nara said.

Bora sat at the back of the room. She gave me a thumbs-up and mouthed, "*Hwaiting!*"

Nara retrieved a leather-bound notebook from her handbag. She opened it and jotted down a few preliminary notes.

"Right. Let's begin," she said at last. "Stand up there."

"Should I leave the script?"

"Yes. I'll prompt you if you get stuck."

I took my place at the front, standing as straight as my back would allow.

"Intern, I have a job for you," Nara said.

"Yes?"

"Could you please film the audition on your phone?"

"Yes, PD-nim." Bora tapped at her phone screen then positioned the camera lens towards me.

"All set?" Nara asked. "From your first line. Go."

I took a deep breath, then with all the confidence I could muster, I delivered my lines. I even added a little bit of movement to spice things up.

While I acted, Nara sat with her arms folded and a bored expression on her face. She read back to me in flat, monotone delivery. I pushed through, not letting her behaviour detract from my performance.

"Stop," Nara said, after just a few lines. "That's enough."

Did I do something wrong?

"Stop recording. Here." Na-Jung passed Bora her business card. "Email the clip to me."

Is that it? How could she reach a decision on just that?

"I've sent it," Bora said.

"Perfect. Excuse me for a moment."

"Wait!" I said, the word surprising me as it tumbled from my lips.

Nara stopped. "Yes?"

"I have something to say."

She tapped her foot impatiently. "Go on."

"The thing is, Louise and I have something in common. She's the only foreigner in her town. I know what that's like. When I attended Tongyeong High School for a year, I was the only foreign student. I can relate to Louise in this way. Maybe it will help me portray her."

"...I see."

I couldn't tell whether my little speech had helped or hindered my chances. Nara left the room, closing the door behind her.

I looked at Bora, confused. "What's happening?"

She shrugged. "I guess we'll just have to wait and see."

"Was my acting okay?"

"I think so."

"Hmmm..."

I sank into my chair, sighing. A little voice at the back of my head told me that I'd missed my chance. Why else did Nara seem so unimpressed?

Every minute which passed felt like torture. I practically jumped out of my skin when Nara swept back in.

"A decision has been made," she said.

Chapter 7

My muscles tensed. I couldn't read Nara's blank expression. Then, slowly, the corners of her mouth lifted into a smile.

"I want you to play Louise," she said.

I thought I must have misheard. "Sorry?"

"The producer agrees. He watched the clip."

"So…I passed the audition?"

"You look surprised."

"It just happened so fast…"

"Chloe, I've auditioned hundreds of people in my time. I can tell very quickly whether I want to work with someone or not."

"Congratulations!" Bora beamed. "I'm so happy for you! I'll text Seo Minjung the news."

Nara checked her watch. "I've got to run. Producer Kang will send the paperwork through to Mr. Kim. You'll need to sign it today."

"Yes, PD-nim."

"See you on set."

"See you."

She rushed away. I could hear her talking on her phone as she walked.

Bora squealed with delight and grabbed my hands. "This is so awesome! You're going to be great."

I was dumbstruck. The reality of the situation still hadn't sunk in.

"Oh! Minjung's calling." Bora answered her phone.

I'm going to be in a K-drama. My heart raced. *I'm actually going to be in a K-drama.*

Bora put her phone down. "Minjung invited us for lunch with her and Mr. Kim. We'll meet in the restaurant next door."

"Intern Yang, this is real, right? I'm not dreaming?"

"It's real. I can pinch you if you want."

I shook myself and let out a high-pitched yelp of joy. "Yes!" I yelled, punching the air.

"That's right. Let it all out." Bora watched on, amused.

After I had calmed down, I excused myself to go and make a call. I needed to tell my best friend, Han Seri, the news. She and I had known each other since we were thirteen years old. We had been host sisters twice—first, when my family hosted her on a three-month exchange, and again, when her family hosted me on my one-year exchange to Korea. Seri introduced me to K-dramas. The fact that I was going to act in one would no doubt blow her mind.

"Hello?" Seri answered.

"Seri, it's me, Chloe."

"Chloe! It's nice to hear your voice." She spoke in English. Her fluency had improved greatly since moving to Melbourne. "We haven't spoken in a wee while."

"I have big news!"

"Oooh. Well, what is it then?"

I paused for effect before letting it spill out. "I'm going to be in a K-drama!"

Seri took a moment to process what I said. "Wait, what? Slow down and explain. A K-drama?"

"A talent scout from KAM Entertainment spotted me last night and asked me to audition for a role in a new drama. I had the audition today and I passed. I'm going to be in a K-drama."

"Oh my God! This isn't a joke, is it?"

"I'm completely serious."

"What happened to teaching English?"

"Long story short, that didn't work out. But now I get to act in a K-drama instead!"

Seri let out a shriek of joy. "I can't believe it!"

"Neither can I!"

"This is like our childhood dreams come true."

"I know!"

"Which actors are in the drama?"

"I only know about one actor so far. Shin…" My mind went blank. "Shin something."

"That's helpful."

"I don't know very much, but I'll tell you everything as soon as I find out."

"This is so exciting!"

"It feels surreal."

"What's the drama called?"

"Hidden History."

"I'll look it up."

"You'll probably find out more than me. Anyway, I've got to go. Heading to a celebratory lunch."

"You lucky thing."

"Let's chat again soon."

"Definitely. Don't leave me hanging."

"Bye, Seri."

"Buh-bye."

After ending the call, I returned to Bora.

"Are you hungry?" she asked.

"Starving," I replied.

We made the short trip to the nearby barbecue restaurant. Its warm interior featured exposed brick walls and lights hanging low over wooden tables and chairs. The smell of sizzling meat permeated the air.

Minjung and Mr. Kim had already arrived. They beckoned us to their table, grins plastered on their faces.

"There's the star of the day!" Mr. Kim said. "Let's celebrate. Lunch is on me."

We ordered a vast array of delicious small dishes to share.

"I hear you passed the audition with flying colours," Mr. Kim said.

"She did!" Bora said. "I was there."

"I couldn't have done it without your help, Intern Yang," I said.

"Awww, I didn't do much."

"Both of you did a very good job," Mr. Kim said. "Intern, I'd like you to keep helping Chloe. You and Manager Bong will already be on set assisting Jinseung, so you can look after Chloe as well."

"Yes, sir."

Bora and I exchanged delighted looks.

Mr. Kim continued. "Chloe, the lawyers are putting your contract together as we speak. It should be ready for you to sign this afternoon. Shooting begins on Thursday. You'll receive a call sheet tomorrow which will tell you the location and the time you need to be there. I believe it will be mostly filmed at the production studio in Yongin."

I nodded along, although it was a lot of information to take in.

"Do you have a Korean bank account?" Mr. Kim asked.

"No, not yet."

"I'll get the lawyers to sort that out too. We can also give you a small advance. Minjung told me about your money situation."

"That would be great. Thank you. What about accommodation? I slept on Minjung's couch last night…"

"Oh! I've found an apartment which looks promising," Minjung said. "Hopefully you'll be able to move in today if all goes well."

"Thanks, Minjung! That's a relief."

My whole body relaxed, all of my doubts and concerns melting away. *Everything's working out…*

In high spirits, we tucked into the steaming dishes of *bulgogi*, *galbi*, *bibimbap*, and *samgyupsal gui*, plus heaping rice and vegetable side dishes. I hadn't eaten so well in a long time. I let out a satisfied sigh once full.

Mr. Kim's phone began to ring. He swallowed his mouthful before answering. *"Yeoboseyo?* Oh, Jinseung…you heard?…Uh huh. When?… All right…See you soon."

"Jinseung!" Bora whispered to me, sounding excited.

Mr. Kim set down his phone. "That was Actor Shin Jinseung. He heard about the casting and wants to meet you since you'll be working together."

"Shin Jinseung wants to meet *me*?" I said.

"Of course. He's at KAM. Meet him when we get back."

Shin Jinseung…Despite years of K-drama watching, I didn't think I'd seen him in anything before. I wondered what he was like. Young? Handsome? Cute?

I didn't have to wonder for long. Back at KAM, Bora took me up to a lounge on the eighth floor where we had agreed to meet Jinseung. A man was there, back turned to us—he was tall and a bit chubby, with short black hair. *Is he Shin Jinseung?* He turned around. He was a man in his forties with a soft, kind-looking face. I peered at him, confused. He didn't look like the typical lead K-drama star.

"Manager Bong, where's actor Shin?" Bora asked.

Ahhh…he's Jinseung's manager.

"He'll be back in a minute." He turned to me. "So you're Chloe? I'm Bong Changsoo, manager of Shin Jinseung." He shook my hand.

"Nice to meet you."

Something caught his eye behind me. "Oh, he's here."

I turned around and saw him approaching. *No…It can't be…*The wavy-haired, cute guy I had encountered in the bathroom earlier that day. He stared at me, looking startled. My face grew hot with embarrassment.

Chapter 8

Shin Jinseung's jaw clenched and unclenched as he studied me. He bit his lip. I shifted on my feet, nervous that he would bring up the bathroom incident.

"Shin Jinseung, this is Chloe Gibson," Changsoo said.

"Hello." I lowered my head.

Jinseung bowed back, grinning.

We sat down on the two large suede couches around a coffee table, Bora and I next to each other, Jinseung opposite us.

"Does anyone want a drink?" Changsoo asked.

"A coffee," Jinseung said.

"Me too," Bora said.

"And you, Chloe? Coffees all round?"

"Yes, please."

Changsoo got to work in the small kitchen area, pulling mismatched mugs from the cupboard.

"So, how come we weren't introduced sooner?" Jinseung asked, leaning towards me, head resting in his hands.

"She only came to KAM today," Bora explained. "Seo Minjung scouted her last night."

Jinseung raised a sceptical brow. "You were found yesterday, and you've already nabbed a drama role?"

I nodded. "It surprises me as well. I arrived in Seoul yesterday to be an English teacher. Now, twenty-four hours later, here I am."

"*Aigoo*. After years of formal acting training I didn't even get a role that big to start."

"You sound bitter, Actor-nim," Changsoo chided, filling the mugs with boiling water.

Jinseung laughed. "Not bitter. Just baffled."

"I'm just lucky," I said. "It's like the stars were aligned just right for this to happen."

"Must be fate," Bora said dreamily.

"Fate? Hmmm…" Jinseung had a faraway look in his eyes.

Changsoo brought a tray of coffees over and sat next to Jinseung. "Cheer up, Actor-nim. You never know, Officer Park could be your breakout role." He passed Jinseung his coffee.

"That's what I'm hoping for."

"Officer Park is Actor-nim's first lead role," Changsoo explained. "Before this he has only had second lead and supporting roles."

"But he's still really popular!" Bora said.

Changsoo sipped his coffee, then he looked up, a thought striking him. "Chloe, did you know that you're playing Officer Park's love interest in this drama?"

"What?" I spluttered, managing to spray coffee before I could cover my mouth.

"*Omo*." Bora handed me a napkin.

"Love interest might be going a bit too far," Jinseung said dismissively.

"Why? It seems like Officer Park likes Louise," Changsoo said.

"I think so too," Bora said.

I chewed my lip. *Are we really going to play love interests?* I made a mental note to ask for more episode scripts so I could see for myself.

"*Aigoo*. Look at the time. I need to take you to your hair appointment," Changsoo said to Jinseung.

"Hair appointment?" Bora said, wide-eyed.

"They want my hair short for the drama," Jinseung said as he got up, leaving behind his half-drunk coffee.

"Noooo!"

"It was nice meeting you, Chloe," Changsoo said.

I bowed.

"See you soon," Jinseung said.

"Goodbye Actor-nim, uh, *Seonbae-nim*," I said.

"His hair…his precious hair…" Bora lamented as Jinseung left the room. She withered on the couch, sulking.

I finished the rest of my coffee while I arranged my thoughts.

"So, what do you think of Shin Jinseung?" Bora asked, clearing the mugs from the coffee table.

"He's nice. He seems humble."

"Isn't he good-looking?" She sighed.

"Yeah, he's cute." I couldn't deny it.

"He's single too! Not that he's even considering dating anyone right now. Whenever he dates, his career slows down. 'The dating curse,' he calls it. Not to mention Mr. Kim would murder him if he ever caused a scandal—he's at such a crucial stage in his career."

"I've heard that most Korean celebrities won't date, at least not publicly."

"That's right. Such a shame…" She sighed again before changing the subject. "Say, why did Jinseung have that weird expression on his face when he first saw you?"

"You noticed that? It's, well…Actually, this wasn't the first time we saw each other."

"What do you mean?"

"I accidentally walked into the men's bathroom this morning…and I saw him…"

"*Omo*. Did you see his—?"

"No. I didn't see anything."

Bora pouted. "What a pity."

We looked at each other before cracking up with laughter.

Chapter 9

As I signed my name across the dotted line on the final contract, a thought crossed my mind that the company was taking advantage of me. *But what else can I do?*

It had taken me hours to go through the contract. Although my Korean language skills were good, my proficiency didn't extend to legal jargon. I used an app to translate as much as I could, but I would have preferred to get everything properly translated and looked over by a lawyer. Unfortunately, time was of the essence.

"Is that everything?" Mr. Kim peered across his desk.

"I think so," I replied.

"Excellent." He combed through the stack of documents, checking I had signed all the necessary pages. When satisfied, he straightened the pile and placed it neatly to the side. He stood up. "Congratulations, Actor Chloe. You're now signed to KAM." He shook my hand. "Your contract will last through the filming of Hidden History. Unfortunately, at this stage we can't promise an extension. Roles such as this are a rarity."

"I understand. Thank you, Mr. Kim."

"It's been a whirlwind day, hasn't it? You should go home and get some rest. You're probably still jet-lagged, right?"

"Home…"

"Ah. Talk to Minjung. She should have something arranged for you."

"Yes, Mr. Kim."

He showed me to the door. "You'll do well, Actor Chloe."

"Thank you, Mr. Kim."

"Do you remember the way to Minjung's desk?"

"Yes."

"Okay. See you around. Call me if you need anything."

I bowed to him before leaving to find Minjung. *Now, which way was it?* I looked from left to right, trying to recall the direction. I scratched my head. *Hmmmm…*Following my gut, I walked the corridors until I made it to the open-plan office where Minjung worked. I crossed the floor to her desk.

"Minjung-ssi…" I said.

She looked up. "Oh! Actor-nim. I have something for you." She searched her messy desk. "Where did I put it? Aha!" She held up a card hanging from a blue lanyard. "Here's your ID card. Now you can come and go from the building as you please."

"Thanks!" I took the card and stuffed it in my pocket. "Mr. Kim said I can go now. I was wondering if…"

"Don't worry. You won't need to sleep on my couch again. I managed to find you a place. It's a serviced studio apartment in Seocho-dong. The rent will be deducted from your pay. I hope it will suit your needs."

"I'll just be happy to have a roof over my head."

"I'll text Intern Yang. She can drive you there. I've already had her collect your luggage from my place."

She sent the message and a moment later Bora texted back.

"She'll meet you at the carpark. Let's go."

Minjung took me down to the underground carpark. Bora waved from a black SUV.

Before leaving, I said goodbye to Minjung. "Thank you for every-thing. I don't know how things would have ended up if I hadn't met you."

Minjung smiled. "It's thanks to you that the production of Hidden History can start without a hitch. I look forward to watching you."

"Hopefully I'll see you again before filming starts."

"Let's keep in touch anyway."

"That would be great."

"Take care. Hope everything's okay with the apartment. Call me if there's anything you need."

"I will. Thank you."

We bowed to each other then parted ways.

Bora stood impatiently outside the car. I rushed over to her. She opened the door to the back seat and ushered me in.

"Can't I sit in the front?" I asked.

"Oh? Okay."

We hopped into the car next to each other. Before I even put my seatbelt on, Bora zoomed away to the exit. She drove erratically through the darkening streets of Seoul. A sudden turn off made me lurch in my seat. "Gyaaa!"

"Oh. Sorry. I'm not a very good driver."

"I can tell."

"When I got this job, I realised that I needed a driver's licence, so I had to quickly learn and pass the test."

"How did you pass?"

"I don't know."

I clutched the edges of my seat for dear life as Bora drove.

I didn't catch my breath until we finally turned down the driveway to an apartment building and parked.

"This is it," Bora said. "Sapphire Apartments."

The high-rise building had a facade of shiny, blue-tinted glass. Several small shops occupied the ground level, including a convenience store, café, and a pharmacy.

"Your apartment is on the seventeenth floor. I'll go up with you," Bora said. She got out and grabbed my luggage from the boot.

"I'll take that," I said, reaching for my suitcase.

"Let me do it," Bora insisted. Despite her small size, she didn't seem to struggle with my heavy bags.

We proceeded to the lobby, classy and clean, with a small seating area, mailboxes, and a reception desk. Bora retrieved my access card from reception.

It was smooth sailing to the seventeenth floor.

"Here we are. Key code is 9409. Make sure to change it later." Bora typed in the code then pushed open the door.

The apartment was compact but perfectly adequate. Storage cupboards on the left, bathroom on the right. Farther down, a kitchen, and at the far end, a double bed by the window. The appliances and furniture looked modern and in good condition. The room was quiet, and the air felt warm and dry. I immediately felt at ease.

"It's probably smaller than you're used to, right?" Bora asked.

"No. It's cozy. I like it."

Truthfully, I was just glad to have a place to stay. It seemed comfortable and secure, and that's all that mattered after everything I had been through. I would be happy to call this apartment my home— at least until the end of my acting gig. I wouldn't be able to afford the rent after that.

"The location can't be beaten." Bora gazed out the window at the vast metropolis of buildings, their windows lighting up as night fell.

"Whereabouts do you live?" I asked.

"Gwacheon. I still live with my parents. They won't let me move out. Not that I could afford to, anyway."

"This is my first time living alone. I've only lived with my parents or with flatmates before."

"You're lucky. So much freedom!"

"Yeah. I guess I never really thought about it."

Bora sighed. "Oh well. I'll leave you to it. You must be looking forward to unpacking and getting settled."

"I would ask you to stay and have a drink, but I don't have anything to give you."

"That's all right. Next time!"

"Okay. Next time."

"See you soon!"

"Bora-ssi—"

"What?"

"Drive safe."

She stuck her tongue out at me as she closed the door.

Alone in the apartment, the first thing I did was collapse on the bed. Since the moment I had arrived in Seoul, it felt like I was on a rollercoaster. In just two days, more had happened to me than in my entire life. My body ached. My head reeled.

I lay like that for a while until I found the resolve to put away my stuff. Clothes into the drawers, books onto shelves, and everything else into cupboards.

With everything stored in its rightful place, I turned to another piece of life admin. I messaged my host parents in Tongyeong, letting them know I had arrived in Korea. I had already let my parents know I had arrived but left out all the nitty gritty details. I'd deal with that another day.

By the time that was done, my stomach growled. I popped down to the convenience store and bought instant *ramyeon* to eat for dinner. I slurped the hot, spicy noodles while reading articles and watching videos about Hidden History. To my delight, I learned that Baek Yena played the other lead character in the series. She was an actor I had admired for a long time. I couldn't wait to meet her.

Shin Jinseung also featured prominently in the Hidden History press coverage. I found myself browsing for information about him, and soon enough I fell down a rabbit hole of interviews and photoshoots.

I was midway through typing *Shin Jinseung shirtless* into the search bar when my phone rang, and I hurriedly closed the tab, feeling guilty.

"*Yeoboseyo?*" I answered.

"Actor-nim, this is Bong Changsoo. Shin Jinseung would like to rehearse with you tomorrow. Is that okay with you?"

"Yes. Of course," I stuttered.

"Great. I'll let him know. I'll book in a practice room. See you tomorrow."

Chapter 10

I sat alone in the practice room, fully absorbed in reading my script, when a deep male voice startled me.

"That's cute."

I looked up and saw Jinseung. His new short hairstyle lent him a more mature look. He wore jeans, a hoodie, and a pair of glasses with black wire frames. I recalled the pictures I had viewed of him last night and how handsome he looked, but he looked even better in real life.

"What's cute?" I asked, raising an eyebrow.

"You bite your lip when you're concentrating," he explained.

"I do?"

"You were just doing it."

"Oh, was I?"

"Have you eaten breakfast?"

"No."

He dropped a plastic bag on the table. "Eat."

"What's this?" I opened the bag and found a sandwich and a bottle of orange juice. "Can I have this?"

"Yes. I ate mine on the way here."

He took a seat next to me on the couch.

I nibbled on the sandwich self-consciously.

"Do you recognise me?" he asked, suddenly.

I felt my face turn red. *Is he really bringing this up now?*

"I walked in on you before," I mumbled.

Jinseung laughed. "I'm not referring to that."

"Oh."

"I mean, we know each other."

I stopped eating. "What? How could that be possible? We just met."

"Tong…yeong…" he said slowly.

No…Could it be?

"Tongyeong? You know me from Tongyeong?"

"You lived in Tongyeong for a while. Am I right?"

"Yes. How do you know that?"

"We went to the same high school. You probably don't remember me. I was your *seonbae*. We didn't interact much since we weren't in the same year group, but you stuck out as the only foreigner."

I went to high school with Shin Jinseung and I didn't even know it.

"*Aigoo*. What a coincidence," I uttered.

"It must be fate," Jinseung mused.

"Huh?"

"Intern said that, remember?"

"That's right! Little did she know."

"I got a shock when I saw you in the bathroom. Obviously, I didn't expect to see a girl there, but I also felt a stab of recognition. When I heard your name, it confirmed it."

"I can't believe it."

"It's insane, right?"

"Sorry I didn't recognise you."

"That's okay. My image has changed a lot since I started acting."

I chewed over this interesting development while finishing the sandwich. *So Jinseung knew me all along…What a strange turn of events.* Somehow it made me feel more comfortable about working with him. We had common ground.

"Shall we practice our first scene together?" Jinseung asked once I had finished eating.

"Okay. Let's do it."

"It's late at night in the town." Jinseung paced the room as he set the scene. "You've just finished up at the bar, and you're walking home. I'm out on patrol, when I notice you and pull over."

"The couch can be your car?"

"Good idea."

Jinseung sat down and grasped an invisible steering wheel. He pretended to pull over and wind down the window.

"Louise," he said, in character.

I stopped and turned to him. "Officer Park."

"It's late. What are you doing walking around by yourself?"

"I just finished my shift. I'm heading home."

"You're not driving?"

"My car's out of action. It's being repaired."

"Then let me give you a ride home."

"Really? Is that okay?"

"Of course. It's my job to make sure everyone stays safe in this neighbourhood. Hop in."

I mimed opening the passenger door, then sat down beside him.

"Are you okay?" Jinseung asked.

"It's been a long night."

At that point, there was a knock on the practice room door. It pulled us both out of the scene. Jinseung sighed. "Come in!" he barked.

It was Bora, holding two takeaway coffee cups. "Did I interrupt? Oh, sorry." She placed the coffee cups on the table. "Drink this and keep your energy levels up."

"Thanks," I said.

"Do you need any help with practicing?"

"I would have asked you to stay and prompt, but it doesn't seem like we need it," Jinseung said. He turned to me. "You know your lines perfectly already."

I shrugged. "I'm good at memorising."

"Well, just text me if you need me and I'll come right over," Bora said. She closed the door behind her.

"Now, where were we?" Jinseung said, flipping through his script.

After finding our place, we got back into character and continued rehearsing the scene, free from interruption.

When we finished, I looked to Jinseung, bracing myself for criticism. Instead, I was met by an intrigued smile.

"I have to admit, I was worried to hear PD-nim had cast someone with no drama experience. But it turns out I had nothing to worry about. You're a natural."

I exhaled, relieved. *So at least my acting is okay...*

Jinseung continued. "There's room for improvement, of course, but I think you can do a good job."

"Thank you, *seonbae-nim*. That's encouraging."

We ran through the scene a couple more times and Jinseung gave me some helpful pointers.

"Time to move on to episode two?" he suggested, satisfied with our progress.

"I only have the first episode script..."

"Here. Use mine for now. I can get by without it."

We rehearsed our scenes together in the second episode. I relied on the script while Jinseung read from memory.

Once we had exhausted those scenes, we decided to work separately for the rest of the day—Jinseung had many more scenes to learn that I wasn't involved in. I had offered to help, but he declined.

"I'll ask Intern or Changsoo *Hyung* to run through them with me," he explained. "It's better for you to focus on your own lines."

"Okay."

"You should get the scripts for episode two and three. That's all that's been released so far. Ask Changsoo. He'll be able to sort that out for you."

"All right. Thank you."

I was about to leave when Jinseung spoke up again.

"Chloe...do you know what happens in episode three?" he asked, a nervous edge to his voice.

"Louise dies, right?"

"Yes. But there's, uh, something else..."

"What is it?"

"You should read the script."

"Why? What happens in episode three?"

"You'll see."

* * *

CURIOUS ABOUT WHAT Jinseung was referring to, I called Changsoo to ask him to prepare the scripts for me.

"No problem, Actor-nim. I'll get them sorted," he said.

After eating lunch, I returned to KAM and met Changsoo on the third floor. He worked in a small office along with other staff in Jinseung's team. His clean and organised desk featured a framed photograph of him posing and making heart signs with Jinseung. *How sweet! Changsoo must care a lot for Jinseung.*

"Here you go," he passed me the scripts. "These were actually delivered yesterday, but reception didn't know who they were for."

"That's understandable. I'm new."

"In future, anything addressed to you will come to my office and I'll let you know."

"Thank you, Manager Bong."

"I've booked you practice room D for the rest of the afternoon. Off you go. Learn those lines." He shooed me away, grinning warmly.

"Manager Bong..."

"Yes?"

"What happens in episode three? *Seonbae-nim* said something about it..."

Changsoo scratched his head. "Episode three...Oh, that!"

"What is it?"

He chuckled. "You've got the script now. Read it and find out."

"So, you won't tell me either? Hmmm...what could it be?"

I made my way to the practice room, still pondering over the third episode.

Afternoon sunlight poured in the practice room window. It warmed my back when I sat down at the table. Not wanting to jump ahead and spoil things, I started reading from episode two, before moving on to the third episode.

By the time I had reached the halfway point of episode three, I still hadn't discovered what it was that Jinseung had warned me about. Then, finally, I saw what he meant. A kiss scene. A kiss scene between Louise and Officer Park.

Chapter 11

*N*o*...I must be seeing things.* I reread the passage to make sure my mind wasn't playing tricks on me, but it was there in clear print—*Louise kisses Officer Park. I have to kiss Jinseung.* Now his shy reaction made sense. *A kiss scene...I have to do a kiss scene... and with Jinseung!*

I couldn't concentrate. As I tried to learn my lines, my mind kept travelling back to the kiss scene...the thought of Jinseung's lips on mine...*It won't be too embarrassing, will it?* I recalled the usual K-drama kiss scenes. That weird, frozen, close-mouthed lip press. Completely passionless. *That's what it will be like. I wonder whether Jinseung has a lot of experience with kiss scenes...*

I remained curious for the rest of the day, and as soon as I got home, I grabbed my laptop and searched *Shin Jinseung kiss scene.* A few results popped up. *Let's see...*

I watched the first video intently. Jinseung and his co-star, Choi Miyoung, are walking along together when a downpour suddenly starts. They run for cover under the eaves of a temple. Soaking wet and panting, they look at each other, expressions turning serious. They start to kiss. A realistic, passionate kiss.

*Oh my...*I fanned myself, suddenly feeling hot.

I scrolled through the comments beneath the video.

"So romantic."

"He is a good kisser!"

"I love his kiss scenes."

I worked my way through the other video clips and none of his kisses were the stiff, close-lipped kind. *So, looks like Jinseung doesn't hold back...*

I stroked my lips unconsciously as I pictured how our kiss might unfold. *My character is assertive, so I must go for it without hesitation, in one swift movement. Our lips touch...*

A notification popped up on my screen, interrupting my train of thought. *Hidden History day 1 call sheet.* I opened the email, ready to see what the first day's shoot had in store for me. My call time struck me first. I needed to be at the production studio by 5:30am for costume, hair, and makeup. I groaned internally, before resolving to get myself tucked up in bed nice and early.

* * *

A LOUD NOISE pierced my dream and yanked me into consciousness. *Is it time to get up already?* Forcing my eyes to stay open, I groped in the darkness for my phone and turned off the alarm. 4:30am. *Ugh.* I heaved myself out of bed and hurried to get ready. While in the process of putting my clothes on, I received a text message:

Bora: We're nearly at your apartment.

Gah! I quickly piled on the rest of my clothes and grabbed the bag I had pre-packed the night before.

Still half-asleep, I took the elevator down and waited outside the building, huddled in a padded down jacket, beanie, and scarf. My breath came out in puffs of mist in the pitch black air.

A couple minutes later, a black van rolled up. Changsoo occupied the driver's seat while Bora sat in the passenger seat. Bora hopped out and opened the door for me. Jinseung sat in the back. He appeared calm and collected, studying his script while sipping from an extra-large cup of coffee. I slid in next to him and pulled on my seat belt, feeling shyer than usual in his presence.

"How are you feeling, Actor Chloe?" Changsoo asked as he drove. "Ready to take on the day?"

"Absolutely," I said, then failed to stifle a humongous yawn.

Jinseung put his script down. "Let me guess. You're not a morning person?"

"Correct," I admitted.

"You better get used to early mornings. And late nights."

"*Aigoo.*"

"He's winding you up," Changsoo said. "It won't be too bad for you since you're not in that many scenes. Actor Shin has it much worse."

"Here." Jinseung pulled another coffee from the cupholder and passed it to me. "There's an extra shot in there. It might help you wake up."

"Thanks." I accepted it eagerly.

The strong coffee warmed me to the core.

"Your call time is probably so early because you haven't been fitted for wardrobe yet," Changsoo explained. "They'll need to sort all that out before they can film your scenes."

"Ah. I see."

"It's going to be a long day." Sighing, Jinseung returned his attention to his script.

I watched him as I drank my coffee. He had a focused expression on his face, a small crease between his brows. I found my gaze wandering down to his lips, reminding me that I would soon have to kiss him. "*Seonbae-nim...*"

"Yes?"

"I read the third episode script."

He sniggered. "You did? Is that why you've been staring at my mouth?"

Damn. He noticed that? "I have not!" I retorted.

"You're so lucky," Bora piped up. "Lots of girls would kill to be in your position."

"That's right," Jinseung teased.

"I'm actually pretty nervous about the whole thing," I confessed.

"Don't worry. I've done it a few times before. You're in safe hands. I'll guide you."

"Such a gentleman!" Bora said.

Jinseung wiggled his eyebrows seductively at me, making me laugh.

"It's nice to see you two getting along so well," Changsoo remarked. "It will help your on-screen chemistry."

"Want to know something funny?" Jinseung asked.

"What is it?"

"Chloe and I went to high school together."

"How can that be? Are you joking?"

"It's true," I said. "I did a high school exchange to Tongyeong for one year."

"*Aigoo*. What are the chances?"

"What was Chloe like in high school?" Bora asked.

"All the boys liked her," Jinseung said.

"Really? So she was popular..."

"Only because I was the only foreigner in the school!" I retorted. "They probably thought I was exotic or something."

"What about you, Actor Shin? Did *you* like her?" Bora asked.

"Don't be ridiculous," he spluttered.

It was a thirty-minute drive to the production studio in Yongin. We passed through a gated area to reach a huge, windowless building which looked like a warehouse. Changsoo parked outside.

The four of us approached the building. Two production assistants flanked the main entrance, taking down the names of people arriving in a register. Changsoo announced our arrival.

"You're both due in wardrobe," the man with the register said. "Make your way to the dressing rooms." He pointed us to an external staircase at the side of the building.

We climbed the staircase and entered a door which led to a blue-carpeted corridor with small rooms off each side.

I noticed one of the rooms had Jinseung's name on the door.

"Oh! This is your dressing room," I said.

Jinseung pushed open the door and inspected the room. It contained a couch, dressing table, and clothes rack full of outfits.

"I guess I'll get settled in," he said. "See you on set later."

Changsoo joined him.

Bora stayed with me and we searched the corridor for my dressing room. Halfway down, we bumped into an *ajumma* with wild, curly hair, her neck and wrists piled with an abundance of jewellery.

"Are you Chloe Gibson?" she asked.

"Yes."

"Through here, my dear. I'll get you fitted."

She ushered us into a large room filled with racks of clothes and tables brimming with accessories. Then my eyes fell upon the other woman in the room. My heart skipped a beat.

Bora gasped. "*Omo*. It's Baek Yena!"

Chapter 12

Baek Yena looked just as cool and attractive in real life as she did in the dramas and movies I'd seen her in. She wore black from head to toe. Her blunt bob haircut and choppy fringe framed a round face with almond eyes and doll-like lips. She stood with her arms folded, an intrigued expression on her face.

"Hello," she said, eyebrow raised.

"Actor Baek Yena, I'm a big fan," Bora gushed.

"Oh? Thank you. Are you two actors?"

Bora giggled. "Do I look like I could be an actor?"

"I'm one of the actors," I said. "My name is Chloe Gibson. I'm playing Louise."

Yena's expression brightened. "So you're the replacement for Tamara? You're pretty! And you speak Korean so well!"

"Thank you."

She motioned to Bora who continued giggling away. "Is she your manager?"

"She's an intern from KAM Entertainment. Her name is Yang Bora."

"Ahhh…KAM. So you know Shin Jinseung then?"

"That's right."

Yena smiled. "I can picture it…"

"Sorry?"

"You and Shin Jinseung. I think you'll look good together on-screen."

"Really?"

"Yes. I can see why PD-nim cast you."

"You're too kind." I blushed profusely. "I can't wait to work with you. I love your dramas."

"I'm sure we'll have a few scenes together. It's gonna be great!"

The wardrobe *ajumma* approached Yena with a measuring tape and started wrapping it around her body and jotting numbers down on a notepad.

"My schedule's been so hectic," Yena said with a sigh. "I haven't had a chance to get fitted until now."

Once Yena's measurements had been taken, the *ajumma* turned the measuring tape on me.

"Take off your jacket," she said.

I shrugged it off and tried not to squirm too much as she coiled the tape around different parts of my body.

At last, she withdrew the tape and I relaxed.

"All done," she said. "Both of you, please try to maintain your weight—it will make my job a lot easier."

"*Aigoo*…You're asking the impossible there," Yena said under her breath.

"What was that?"

"Nothing!"

* * *

AFTER TRYING on an abundance of outfits, we were sent to hair and makeup. I emerged several hours later, completely transformed. Standing before the full-length mirror in my dressing room, I examined myself from every angle. The slinky black blouse, unbuttoned down to the middle of my chest, revealed a not-so-subtle glimpse of cleavage. It was tucked into a denim miniskirt—perhaps the shortest skirt I'd ever worn in my life. A pair of stiletto heels further elongated my bare legs, and a gold choker with a crystal pendant adorned my neck. I wore my hair out. Previously dry and tangled, it had been trimmed and tamed into glossy, loose curls. Makeup consisted of a pale wash of shimmery eyeshadow above kitten eyes, with soft, peachy lips and cheeks on a canvas of flawless glass skin.

"*Aigoo*," Bora said, watching from behind me. "You look incredible! Like, devastatingly, heartachingly beautiful."

I assessed my reflection self-consciously. I had never worn anything like this before and couldn't help but feel uncomfortable. To my eye, it seemed a little too much—even in the context of my character.

"You have a way with words, but don't you think you're over-embellishing?"

"I think she's spot on," Changsoo said, appearing behind my shoulder. "I admit I don't know much about these things, but you really do look beautiful."

I felt reassured by his kind and genuine words.

"Awww. Thank you, Manager-nim."

"How's Jinseung doing? Everything okay out there?" Bora asked.

"It's slow progress, but he's doing well. You two should come out and watch," Changsoo suggested.

"Really? Is that okay?"

"Of course. Just be sure to stay out of the way of the crew."

"You coming too, Actor-nim?"

My desire to see Jinseung and Baek Yena in action vastly overpowered my urge to stay back and study my lines.

"Yes. Let's go," I said.

Before leaving, Bora grabbed my jacket and held it out to me.

"Here. Put this back on, you must be cold."

"You're right. I'm freezing."

I pulled it on, relieved by its warmth. I also changed my shoes, unable to walk properly in heels.

Changsoo led the way down the corridor to a doorway guarded by a production assistant wearing a headset.

"Can we go through?" Changsoo asked.

"Yes. They're currently not recording. Just be quiet and stay out of the way," the assistant said. He opened the door for us.

We stepped into a huge open space with unpainted walls and a concrete floor. Moveable lights hung from metal rods running across the high ceiling. We walked carefully, dodging tripods and cords strewn haphazardly over the floor.

I gazed in awe as we passed rows of interior location sets boxed inside wooden board walls. They looked just like real rooms, furnished with impeccable detail.

Most of the crew were concentrated around one set. *That must be where they're filming.* We quietly approached.

The police station office set featured cream walls and a wood vinyl floor. Fluorescent ceiling lights shone above wooden desks topped with phones and computers. Filing cabinets and shelving units bordered the room.

Yena sat down on an orange office chair. Jinseung stood, leaning over the desk towards her. He wore a police uniform. A couple of extras sat at other desks.

A crew member stood with a clapperboard in front of the camera.

"Action," Im Nara said from the director's chair, a large monitor in front of her.

Yena and Jinseung sprang to life.

"What do you want? Can't you see I'm busy?" Yena said, eyes glued to the computer screen in front of her.

"I have a question," Jinseung said.

Yena looked up. "All right. What is it?"

"I was—"

He stopped abruptly. His eyes had wandered from Yena. He looked out past the crew, a dazed expression on his face and his mouth slightly agape.

He's looking at me, I realised. I locked eyes with him, and he snapped out of it.

"Cut!" Nara said. "Shin Jinseung, is everything okay?"

Jinseung rubbed his head sheepishly. "Sorry. I got distracted."

"Perhaps it's time we take a break…"

"Break time!" her assistant announced.

On that note, everyone promptly dispersed.

"What was that all about?" Bora asked.

"He's probably just tired. They've done so many takes," Changsoo said. "I'll go talk to him."

He hurried to Jinseung's side.

"*Aigoo*. Acting looks tough," Bora said. "But I'm sure you'll be fine!" she added, quickly.

I took a deep breath. Nerves began to set in as I contemplated the fact that it was my turn next.

"Let's get something to eat. I'm starving," Bora said.

I hesitated. "You can go on ahead. I'm going to go and read my script again. I'll be in my dressing room."

"Well, okay then. But make sure you have something to eat later."

"I will."

Bora joined the flow of cast and crew heading to the break room. I turned the opposite way, returning to my dressing room.

Alone in the small room, I studied my script, painstakingly reading, re-reading, and reciting my lines, drilling them into my brain. *I have to get this right. I can't embarrass myself.*

Deeply absorbed, I didn't even notice Jinseung enter the room until he loudly cleared his throat. He watched me, half smiling, with a knowing look in his eyes.

"Oh! *Seonbae-nim*," I said.

"Uh, sorry to interrupt. Intern told me I'd find you here. You haven't eaten yet, have you? I brought you some food."

He placed a wrapped Subway sandwich and a bottle of water down on the table.

"Thanks," I said.

"Can I sit down?"

"Go ahead."

He lowered himself onto the couch, then returned to staring at me in a way that made my skin prickle.

"You look...good." His eyes drifted down to my chest, but he swiftly averted them.

I wrapped my jacket tighter around me, self-conscious.

"Isn't it too much?" I asked.

"No."

I wondered if it had been my outfit that distracted him earlier. *Surely not...*

"I'm sorry if we broke your concentration before," I said.

"What?"

"When Intern Yang and I came to watch your scene."

Jinseung shook his head. "That was my fault. I shouldn't let myself get distracted so easily. I should be more professional as an actor."

"Well, apart from that, you looked amazing out there with Baek Yena."

"She's far more experienced than me, so I'm hoping to learn a lot from her."

"I'm looking forward to working with her too."

"How are your lines coming along?"

"Right now, I know them off by heart. But I'm scared that I'll forget them all as soon as the camera starts rolling."

"It's only natural to feel that way." He placed his hand on my shoulder. It felt strong, warm, reassuring.

"Just stay calm," he continued, "breathe, and forget everything else but the scene. Can you do that?"

"Yes, I think so. Good advice."

He lifted his hand away as if suddenly remembering himself. "I should get back on set. They'll start shooting again soon."

"Okay."

"Don't forget to eat."

I picked up the sandwich to appease him.

"See you later," he said, smiling broadly. He closed the door behind him.

I tried to resume where I had left off but found I couldn't concentrate. I touched my shoulder where Jinseung had grasped it and let out a small sigh. His cute grin flooded my thoughts...his lips which I would soon get to kiss...

I shook my head. *Be professional. Now's not the time to get feelings for my co-star.* I turned to my script again, but it seemed pointless. *Forget it.* I put the script aside. I had learned my lines as well as I possibly could. Reading them over again wouldn't help.

I ate lunch then went back to the set. Bora waved to me, beckoning me over.

"Have you got everything memorised now?" she asked.

"Yes."

"That's good." She retrieved a folding chair for me and set it down. "Sit," she urged.

I settled on the chair and watched the scene being filmed. Jinseung and Yena performed flawlessly this time, delivering their lines with full confidence. The subtle detail in their movements and facial expressions added a sense of realism. I studied them, entranced.

"Cut," Nara said, after a lengthy pause at the end of the scene.

The camera moved to shoot it all again from another angle.

As the minutes passed, I grew more and more uneasy. In the back of my mind, I worried whether I'd be able to act even half as well as them. *I'm not even a real actor*, I reminded myself. *I'm an imposter.*

During another change in camera angle, a production assistant approached me.

"Chloe Gibson?" she asked.

"Yes?"

"We're just about to wrap up this scene. You'll be up next. Please get prepared to go on shortly."

I gulped, my throat dry. *This is it.* I wobbled as I stood up. My stomach twisted into knots of apprehension. All the self-doubt which had been nibbling away at me now screamed loudly in my head.

What if I'm terrible?

What if I stuff up?

What's my first line, again?

I can't do this...

But I had no choice. I couldn't back out now.

Chapter 13

I shifted nervously on my feet, trembling as I stood in position behind the bar, waiting for the shoot to begin. A buzzing sound had started in my ears, drowning out the background noise of everything around me. The clapperboard came down.

"Action," Im Nara said.

What am I meant to do? I froze, mind completely blank. Everyone stared at me expectantly.

"Cut!"

"I'm sorry…"

"Let's try that again, shall we?"

The set was dimly lit. Black stools perched under the wooden bar. Shelves stocked with liquor bottles lined the wall behind me, and fridges on the floor below glowed with a blue backlight.

Two male actors sat at the bar—Cho Dongjoo and Kim Jaehyun, playing Mr. Cha and Mr. Lee, two middle-aged men living in the fictional neighbourhood. Extras filled the tables and chairs to create a lively atmosphere.

"Relax," Cho Dongjoo said. "You'll do fine." He smiled reassuringly.

Both he and Kim Jaehyun appeared completely at ease. They had years of experience in dramas.

"Are you ready?" Nara asked.

I nodded.

Deep breaths…

"Action."

I half-choked out my line. "Another beer, Mr. Cha?"

"You read my mind," Dongjoo said, grinning. He swayed slightly, feigning drunkenness.

I took a beer from the fridge, popped open the cap, poured it into a glass, and served it to him.

"Thanks, sweetheart."

I hesitated for too long before saying my next line. Someone prompted me, and I continued.

The scene carried on in a stop-and-start fashion, usually with me forgetting an action or a line. Take after take after take ensued.

I recalled Jinseung's advice: *Just stay calm, breathe, and forget everything else but the scene.*

Stay calm...

Breathe...

Focus on the scene...

I concentrated solely on my immediate surroundings, mentally blocking out the crew and the filming equipment.

"Action."

Everything around me dissolved apart from the characters in the bar.

At last, I managed to perform an error-free take.

"Cut."

The crew started setting up for a change in camera angle, affording me the chance to have a short break. I sat down on the fold-out chair. Bora handed me a water bottle. She massaged my shoulders. "You're doing great," she assured me.

A stylist hovered in my vicinity holding a comb and a cushion foundation compact.

"Where's Actor Shin?" I asked Bora, as the stylist patted foundation on my face and poked at my hair with the end of the comb.

"He couldn't stay and watch. He went to record some voiceover. Manager Bong is with him."

"I see." *At least Jinseung won't see me embarrass myself.*

The break was short-lived. I returned to my mark on set, prepared for the next take.

"Action."

We performed the scene over and over again. My legs ached. My head pounded. I could say my lines automatically, but my energy waned with each take, and I feared that my acting was becoming more and more lacklustre. Nara asked me many times to be bubblier, but each time it became more difficult to muster a bubbly persona. Even when I thought we achieved a good run through, Nara made us retake.

The shoot continued for hours, each take more demoralising than the last.

When we finally wrapped up the scene, I felt completely and utterly exhausted. Unable to repress how upset I felt, I fled to my dressing room, closed the door, and cried my eyes out.

Who am I fooling? I'm not cut out to be an actor. I should have just flown back home when I had the chance. These thoughts swirled in my head, mocking me.

A knock at the door made me jump. *I can't let anyone see me like this.* I tried to brush my tears away in time, but the door began to creak open.

Chapter 14

I desperately wiped at my eyes as the door inched open. Through my tear-blurred vision, I saw Bora step inside. Her mouth dropped when she locked eyes on me.

"*Unnie*, are you all right?" she asked.

"No," I sniffed.

"Oh dear." She sat down by my side and wrapped an arm around my shoulders.

"I messed up the scene and made everyone suffer through all those takes." Fresh tears rolled down my cheeks.

"You didn't mess up the scene! It's normal to do that many takes."

I lifted my chin, bottom lip quivering. "Really?"

"Of course. I think most people are surprised it didn't take longer. It was a hard scene for you."

"I made so many mistakes."

"Not from where I was watching. Besides, no one expected you to be perfect. Everyone already thinks you're a hero for stepping up and filling the role at such late notice. You were fine."

"Do you really think so?"

"Yes."

Her reassuring words calmed me down. Perhaps it really didn't go as badly as I felt it did. Maybe it was all in my head…

She rummaged in her purse and extracted a packet of tissues.

"Thanks," I said, accepting them.

"I've confirmed that you're not needed for anything else today. Actor Shin is just about ready to finish up too."

I dabbed at my eyes.

"*Aigoo.* You're too hard on yourself." Bora patted my back.

"I don't know what came over me."

"You're probably overwhelmed. It's understandable. Let's go to the bathroom and wash your face. There are streaks of makeup down your cheeks."

Bora accompanied me to the bathroom. She held my hair back as I splashed warm water on my face.

"I always carry a few supplies," she explained, fishing a pouch filled with mini-sized skincare products out of her bag.

She washed my face for me, making sure to remove every scrap of makeup. Her small, soft hands soothed and relaxed me.

"There. Looking much better. You have such beautiful skin." She beamed at me.

"Thank you. I don't know what I would do without you."

"It's so stressful being an actor. You need someone to rely on."

"You're like an angel."

Bora framed her face with her hands in a display of *aegyo*, which made me giggle.

Her phone started to ring.

"It's Manager Bong." She picked up. "*Yeoboseyo?*…We're in the bathroom…Okay…See you in a few minutes."

"Was he looking for us?"

"Yes. He's with Actor Shin. They're ready to leave. Are you okay now? Shall we meet them?"

"Yes, I think so. Let's go."

After a quick stopover at my dressing room to change out of my costume, we met Jinseung and Changsoo in the van. I slumped into the seat next to Jinseung. He turned to me and ran his eyes over my face, biting his lip. I looked away, scared that it was still obvious that I had been crying.

"*Aigoo*. What a day," Changsoo said, starting the van. "And that's just the beginning. Four months of this to come."

"I think it's exciting," Bora said. "Beats sitting in an office all day."

"Is waiting on set all day so different?"

"Yes, I think so. The atmosphere is energising. By the way, Chloe did an amazing job today for a first-time actor."

Changsoo smiled. "So I heard. Well done!"

"Thanks, guys, but I realised that I have a lot to learn," I admitted.

"It must have been tough," Jinseung mused. "That was a demanding scene for a first-time actor."

"Yes, it was. But I survived." I forced a smile.

"You did. Hey, what do you like to eat?"

"Huh? Ummm…steak is my favourite."

"So, you like steak? Intern, find the best steak restaurant in the area. We're going out for dinner, my treat."

"Yuss!" Bora pumped her fist.

"That's very generous of you," Changsoo said.

"Thank you, *seonbae-nim*," I said. "Sorry for choosing steak. It's too expensive."

Jinseung grinned. "What are you saying? You should take advantage. Order the most expensive thing you want."

"Well, if you say so."

Bora searched her phone for nearby restaurants. "Oh! This one looks good. Jin Steakhouse. It's not too far away, and it's got great reviews."

"Jin Steakhouse it is," Jinseung said.

Bora typed the address into the car's GPS, and Changsoo followed the directions.

Ten minutes later, we arrived at a small strip of restaurants on a quiet suburban street. Warm light glowed from the steakhouse's windows upon its red-brick facade. Jinseung led the way through the door into the restaurant's cozy, rustic-styled interior. A gas fireplace blazed in the corner. After battling the cold all day, I felt warmed to the core.

A waiter showed us to a table with four comfy chairs. I sat next to Jinseung and opposite Bora.

"Shall we get some soju?" Jinseung asked.

"Go for it," Changsoo said.

"Do you drink, Chloe?"

"Yes. But I won't have much. I'm a lightweight."

"Is that so? Well, I'll get two bottles. That will be more than enough. I can't have a hangover tomorrow."

He ordered the soju and started pouring it into shot glasses.

"Hold on. One of us needs to drive," I said.

"I don't mind. I'll keep driving. It's my job, after all," Changsoo said.

"Wait. I've got an idea," Jinseung said. "Let's play paper scissors rock for it. The loser has to be the sober driver. Okay? Can you drive, Chloe?"

"Yes. But I'm not used to the roads here…driving on the right-hand side and all that."

"Ah. I forget that it's different in the UK. You don't have to participate then."

"No. I'll play. I'll just have to not lose."

Jinseung laughed. "Okay, good plan. Is everyone in then?"

"I'm in!" Bora said.

"Me too," Changsoo agreed.

"Round one will be Intern versus Chloe and *Hyung* versus myself. The winners will then face each other. Best two out of three," Jinseung explained.

I faced Bora. "Are you ready?"

"I was born ready," she replied.

"Paper…scissors…rock!" we cried in unison.

I chose scissors and she chose paper. I won the next round as well, with a rock versus her scissors.

"Too easy," I said.

Meanwhile, Jinseung and Changsoo were still going since they kept tying. Eventually, Jinseung won.

"Final round," Jinseung announced.

Changsoo fired rock and Bora launched scissors.

"Tonight's not my night," Bora admitted.

After a tied round, Changsoo ended up defeating Bora on the third go.

"Looks like I'm driving," Bora said, pocketing the car keys.

My mind flashed back to the last time Bora had driven me and I grimaced.

"It's quite a long drive…" I said cautiously.

Bora pouted. "Don't you trust me?"

"No. Not really."

Jinseung frowned. "Ugh…you're right. I don't trust her either."

"Just let me drive then," Changsoo said. "Like I said before, I'm fine with it."

"All that for nothing," Bora grumbled.

"Don't complain. You get to have a drink now," Jinseung said, nudging a glass of soju towards her.

We clinked glasses and downed our first shot.

"Ahhhh…" Jinseung held his head back in pleasure. "Let's order the steak. I'm starving."

He called the waiter over and we placed our orders. Contrary to Jinseung's insistence that I order the most expensive thing, I decided not to be too greedy. Besides, I'd have to keep my weight in check now that I had been fitted for wardrobe.

Jinseung refilled my shot glass. "Drink up."

"Thanks." I tipped it back. The alcohol warmed my throat and made my head fuzzy. All my earlier worries about my acting seemed to dissolve.

Our steaks arrived shortly, perfectly cooked and succulent, with a heaped side of steamed vegetables. My mouth watered.

Jinseung peered at my plate. "*Aigoo*. Yours is so small. Have some more." He cut off a piece of his steak and put it on my plate.

"It's plenty for me, but thank you."

Partway through our meals, two young women approached our table.

"Excuse me, aren't you Shin Jinseung?" one of them asked.

Jinseung's face reddened. "Uh, yes. It's me." He shifted uncomfortably.

"I love you!" the woman gushed.

"Can we get a photo with you?" the other woman asked.

"Yes. That's fine," Jinseung said.

He stood up and posed between the two women. Bora snapped the photo for them.

After that, Changsoo politely, but firmly, asked them to leave, and the two women sheepishly retreated.

Word spread around the restaurant like wildfire, and Jinseung found himself having to dish out several autographs and photos. I admired the way he got on with it with a smile.

"Sorry about that. I can't usually eat out in peace, unfortunately," Jinseung said, returning to finish his meal.

"No need to apologise. It's all part of being a celebrity," Changsoo said.

"You're so good to your fans," Bora said, dreamy-eyed. "Such a gentleman."

After we finished eating, Jinseung paid the bill and we returned to the car.

"Thanks for the meal, Actor-nim!" Bora said.

"Thanks, *Seonbae-nim*," I echoed, certain he had shouted dinner to try and cheer me up.

"My pleasure," Jinseung said.

Bora looked at her phone. "*Omo*. Tomorrow's call sheet has come through."

"What does it say?"

"You're required all day again, Actor Shin. Actor Chloe…you're not needed."

Jinseung nudged me with his elbow. "That will give you some time to practice," he said. "Your next scene will probably be the one with me in it, so you better not mess up, okay?"

Even though I knew he was just winding me up, I felt a surge of emotion bubble up and spill over, and I couldn't hold back my tears.

Chapter 15

I still hadn't recovered from my mortification at crying in front of Jinseung when he called me out of the blue the next day.

"It's me, Shin Jinseung," he said. "Intern gave me your number."

Stunned to hear his voice, I found myself unable to speak.

"Are you there?" he asked.

"Yes," I squeaked. "Can I help you with something?" *Please don't bring up the crying incident,* I prayed.

"What are you doing tomorrow night?"

The question took me by surprise. "Tomorrow night? Nothing I can think of…"

"Would you be interested in attending an acting workshop with me? There's one I sometimes go to."

"Uh—"

"I mean, you don't have to. I just thought it might help with your confidence."

"I'll come."

"Really? Great. I'll send you the details."

He hung up before I could say anything else.

*An acting workshop…*I wondered what it would involve, and more pressingly, why Jinseung wanted me to go with him. *He must feel sorry for me*, I decided, sighing.

* * *

Is this the right place? I peered at the nondescript door tucked between a convenience store and a cosmetics retailer. After a moment's hesitation, I pushed open the door and entered a dark stairwell. Faint voices drifted down the stairs from the floor above.

I ascended the steps and arrived in a bright studio with floor-to-ceiling mirrors lining the walls. A small group of people sat chatting amongst themselves on the wooden floor. My eyes met Jinseung's and a warm grin spread across his face causing my heart to flutter involuntarily. I even forgot my embarrassment at crying in front of him the other day.

"You made it!" he said.

"Of course." I plopped down next to him. "Did you think I wouldn't come?"

"I couldn't be certain."

"Well, I figured you're right that I need to work on my confidence. Thanks for inviting me."

"No problem."

"What's the workshop about anyway?"

"Portraying emotions."

"Emotions, huh? Sounds useful."

A few minutes later, a boisterous man entered the studio. "Welcome, welcome. Lots of people today. I see some new faces. My name's Lee Hoon and I'm leading today's workshop. Newbies, could you please stand up and introduce yourselves?"

I stood up along with two others.

A tall, beautiful girl spoke first. "I'm Do Soomi. I'm an actor and model with Kyss Entertainment."

"I'm Kim Inho," the other person, a young man said. "I'm currently a student at Seoul University. I want to take up acting."

Everyone turned their heads to me expectantly. I cleared my

throat. "My name's Chloe Gibson. I'm from the UK and soon I'll be appearing in a K-drama."

"Wonderful to have you here," Hoon said. "I hope you'll get a lot out of today's workshop. If you didn't know, today we're focusing on emotions. First, as a warmup, we're going to play a little game. If you've played charades before, it's just like that, but you have to guess the emotion. Who wants to go first?"

Several hands shot up, including Jinseung's.

"Shin Jinseung? All right, you're up."

Jinseung stood up in front of the group. Hoon shuffled a stack of index cards and presented the top card to him. Jinseung squinted at it, thought for a moment, then the left corner of his lip turned up into a smile.

"You're not allowed to say anything," Hoon reminded him.

Jinseung mimed a wide-eyed, mouth-gaping look of shock.

The group of actors called out their guesses.

"Awe?"

"Shock?"

"Terror?"

"Fright?"

The guesses kept coming until someone said, "Horror," which was the correct answer.

Hoon picked the person to go next. Round after round, the game continued. Some emotions were more difficult to guess than others and some acting attempts were so hilarious that guessing paused until the fits of laughter subsided.

I pulled the next card on my turn. Heat rushed to my cheeks at the sight of the word. *Lust.* I froze, stuck at a complete loss as to how to act it out.

"Give it a go," Hoon urged.

Jinseung mouthed words of encouragement.

All eyes on me, I took a deep breath and shoved my embarrassment aside. I narrowed my eyes and bit my lip in the most lustful way I could muster.

Silence reigned. *How long will I have to keep this up?* I wondered.

"Hungry?" someone eventually guessed.

I shook my head. *Not even close.*

"Curious?" someone else ventured.

They'll never guess correctly at this rate. I had no choice but to take it further. I licked my lips seductively and twirled my hair around my finger.

Someone started to giggle, and it set off a chain reaction of laughter. I blushed even harder.

"Horny?" Jinseung asked.

Hearing him say that made me momentarily forget what I was doing, and I dropped my act.

"Sexy?" someone else said. "Is that an emotion?"

My attention snapped back to the game. They were getting close now. I pointed at her and nodded, letting her know she's on the right track.

Several more guesses rapidly ensued, each a variation of sexy or horny.

"Lust?" someone finally guessed.

"Yes!" I said, relieved. I collapsed onto the floor next to Jinseung. "God, that was embarrassing."

"Is that your sex face?" Jinseung teased. "If it is, I'm horrified."

I shoved him. "Shut up."

After the warmup, Hoon announced our first exercise. "Get into pairs, everyone. We're going to improvise some scenes."

Jinseung latched on to me. "Let's do this together."

I nodded enthusiastically. At least I wouldn't have to stand up by myself this time. I could feel more confident with Jinseung by my side.

Hoon went around handing out bits of paper with different scenarios written down.

"A lovers' quarrel," Jinseung said, reading ours.

We had no time to prepare at all.

Hoon called up the first pair to perform their scene, which was "Friends reuniting."

The pair acted out an airport scene, one of them arriving back after living abroad. They expressed their sheer joy at seeing each other again with hugging and crying.

Hoon stopped them after a few minutes and provided feedback, then he invited everyone else to comment.

Jinseung volunteered us to go next. My mind was blank as I stood up with him. Fortunately, Jinseung spoke first, setting up the scene. "Please don't leave me! I beg you. I'll do anything you want." His voice shook.

I crossed my arms and said the first response to enter my head. "It's too late. I've given you so many chances and every time you let me down."

"I'm sorry. I'm so sorry."

The desperation in his voice made me waver for a second, but then I shook my head. "I have to go. I can't do this any longer." I pulled an invisible bag over my shoulder and turned to leave. I took one step before Jinseung pulled me forcefully into a tight back hug, his arms around me, his body against mine. I fell out of character at once. All I could think about was how close we were and how nice it felt.

"Please don't go," he pleaded, then lips to my ear and with a voice soft and smooth as velvet he said, "I love you."

If he wasn't holding on to me, I would have melted to the floor in a puddle. I tried to speak but I could only stutter. "I...I..."

Jinseung kept hugging me until Hoon told us to stop. After that, the rest of the workshop was a blur. I didn't snap out of my stupor until the cold night air hit me when we left the studio.

"Did you have fun?" Jinseung asked.

"Yeah. I had a good time. We really covered a lot, and *seonsaeng-nim* gave us tons of great feedback," I said.

"You can come back any time. KAM will cover the expense since it will help your acting. I already told Changsoo *Hyung*."

"Thanks. I'll definitely go again."

"How are you getting home?"

"I'll take the subway."

"Okay. Well, enjoy the rest of your evening."

"You too. Goodnight."

"Night night."

We parted ways.

On the subway home, I mentally listed the reasons why I shouldn't fall for Jinseung.

1. We work together.
2. He's famous.
3. KAM wouldn't allow us to date.
4. "The dating curse."
5. I might not be able to stay in Korea.
6. Why would he be interested in me anyway?

No. The reasons were clear. I absolutely could not fall for Jinseung. I shouldn't even entertain the idea.

Chapter 16

"I'm disappointed in you."

Those were my mother's first words when she called me.

After skirting around the issue for a long time, I had no choice but to come clean with everything that had happened. Mum had been asking direct questions about what the school was like, and I couldn't lie to her.

"I'm sorry," I said.

"If you were having trouble in Korea, you should have let me know straight away," she continued. "It breaks my heart that you didn't think to confide in me."

I knew she would react like this. That's why I had been putting off telling her. But I couldn't avoid the subject forever.

"What could you have done to help? I only wanted to save you the worry," I said.

"I would have taken the next plane to Seoul and stayed with you while we sorted everything out."

"Well, I appreciate the thought, but you didn't have to do that. I'm not a little kid anymore. I can take care of myself."

As I said those words, doubt tugged at my mind. *Can I really take care of myself? What would have happened if Seo Minjung hadn't found me drunk and alone on the street?*

My mother exhaled a deep sigh. "You're okay. I suppose that's all that matters."

"I got my money back too."

"Have you spoken to the police?"

"No. I haven't had time."

"Well, I'm going to file a report on your behalf then. Those people should be punished for this."

"Thanks. It's not something I want to deal with right now. There's so much going on."

"I can imagine. Look after yourself, all right? I don't know exactly what being in a K-drama involves, but I don't want you to get taken advantage of again. If it all gets too much for you, come back home, okay?"

"Okay." Truthfully, going back home to the UK was very far from my mind. I had come to Korea to escape my life there. Nothing short of disaster would pull me back.

"Well, call me again soon. I want you to tell me *everything* from now on."

"Yes, Mum."

"Goodnight."

"Goodnight."

* * *

Immediately after our phone call, Mum set about hiring a lawyer to help us pursue a case against the culprits from SK-Teach. She kept me in the loop by cc-ing me in on her lengthy emails. As she dealt with that, I spent my time job hunting. Too bad that jobs with enough flexibility to work around my part-time acting gig didn't seem to exist. Feeling defeated, my job-hunting efforts dried up after a few days, and I dedicated myself to practicing acting instead—and watching K-dramas (It's research!).

Then, out of the blue, I was summoned for my next scene.

Changsoo dropped me and Jinseung off at the filming location on an overcast afternoon. Large detached houses and evergreen trees lined the charming suburban street. A section of the road had been cordoned off for filming, and several trucks and trailers were parked up on side streets.

Jinseung and I reported to separate trailers to get changed into our costumes before reconvening at hair and makeup.

When we emerged from the trailer, the crew was setting up on the street. The sun still shone in the sky, and filming wouldn't begin until nightfall. A production assistant directed us to one of the houses on the street.

"Im Nara's friend owns this house and she has allowed us to use its facilities while we shoot," she explained.

We walked a path across the lawn to a two-storey house, picture-perfect with its cream weatherboard exterior and burnt-orange-coloured roof. Inside, shoes were piled up on the shelves by the door. We added our shoes to the pile and ventured farther into the house.

The wooden floorboards creaked below us as we navigated the hallway to the lounge where a group of crew members lingered. Changsoo and Bora were seated there too, their laptops open, catching up on work.

Changsoo looked up, spotting us. "All ready for the shoot?"

"Yes. We're just waiting for the sun to go down, then we'll start," Jinseung said.

Changsoo looked out the window. "Shouldn't be much longer…"

"How are you feeling, Actor-nim?" Bora asked me.

"I've had more time to prepare, so I feel more confident this time. Plus, it doesn't seem as difficult as my last scene."

"And you'll be with Actor Shin. He'll help you."

"You're right."

"Don't rely on me too much," Jinseung teased.

Waiting for the sky to darken, we used the time to practice our lines together. Fortunately, I had memorised them off by heart.

As the last rays of sunlight faltered, a crew member called us back outside.

Coldness encroached us. Standing on the side of the road, Jinseung did star jumps to keep warm. I couldn't do the same in my tight miniskirt, but I had a long coat covering me which I pulled tighter.

"I'm so ready for this," Jinseung said, still jumping around.

"You're all hyped up," I said, amused.

He switched to jogging on the spot. "A bit of movement is good for the endorphins. You should try it."

"Really?" I joined in, although my range of movement was limited.

Jinseung began to punch the air, moving from foot to foot. I mimicked him, then he started play fighting with me—a pretend boxing match, which had me in a fit of laughter. Suddenly he launched a crescent kick at me.

"Hey, no fair. I can't kick in this skirt."

"I don't play fair," Jinseung taunted.

A crew member broke up our fight. "We're going to run through the first part of the scene. You need to take your places."

She directed me to my starting place farther up the footpath, while Jinseung made his way to the black sedan parked on the road surrounded by several crew members waiting for him.

I felt my nerves rise in my stomach, but I swallowed them back down.

Following a dry run-through of the scene, recording began.

I walked down the footpath, hands stuffed in my coat pockets. The biting cold made me shiver, serving to disguise my nervous trembling. I aimed to appear as though I were lost in thought.

Jinseung drove the car up to me, pulled over, and wound the window down. "Louise," he said, reaching his head out of the window.

I stopped in my tracks. "Officer Park."

"It's late. What are you doing walking around by yourself?" he asked, voice laced with concern.

"I just finished my shift. I'm heading home."

"You're not driving?"

"My car's out of action. It's being repaired."

"Then let me give you a ride home."

"Really? Is that okay?"

"Of course. It's my job to make sure everyone stays safe in this neighbourhood. Hop in."

I opened the passenger door and got in. Jinseung started driving again, just a short distance, then put the car into park.

"We stop here," he said. "Good job."

I exhaled with relief. One take down. "I must be getting the hang of it."

Filming continued from the top, shooting from another angle. Multiple takes later, Im Nara declared that we'd move on to shooting inside the car. As the crew set up, Jinseung and I were allowed a short break.

"That went much better than I expected," I said.

"You did great! I'm impressed," Jinseung said.

"Are you just saying that? You can tell me the truth. I won't cry again, I promise."

"No. I sincerely mean it."

I still didn't quite believe him, but it was enough to instill me with a smidgeon more confidence.

Bora scurried towards us, bearing two travel mugs filled with hot coffee.

"You're amazing," Jinseung said, eagerly accepting one.

Bora blushed profusely, momentarily forgetting about me until I cleared my throat.

"Here's yours," she said.

"Thank you!" I sipped the coffee down, delighting in the warmth spreading through my body.

Several sips later, we were herded back to the car, which now resided within a low trailer, towed by a small truck.

"So this is how a car scene gets filmed..." I mused, examining the set-up with intrigue.

"Yeah. It's pretty hard to do a dialogue scene in the car and drive at the same time, so they just tow the car along," Jinseung explained.

"The camera operator shoots while standing along the side of the trailer."

"Fascinating…"

When instructed to do so, we entered the car. As I pulled on my seatbelt, something caught my eye in the rear-view mirror. I jumped in fright, but quickly realised it was just the sound guy hiding in the back seat.

"Hello," he said. "Don't mind me."

I caught my breath again.

Filming began and the car moved forward. It felt so strange. Jinseung grasped the steering wheel as if he were really driving. Alone together in the car (with the sound guy tucked away out of sight), the scene felt very intimate. I could even ignore the cameraman pointing his lens at us.

"Are you okay?" Jinseung asked, glancing at me.

"It's been a long night." I sighed.

"It must be tiring…"

"Yeah. But I can't complain. What about you? Are you on patrol tonight?"

Jinseung nodded.

We continued to act the scene as the truck towed us in a loop around the block. After each loop, we'd reshoot the scene.

Partway through one take, spits of rain started splashing on the windscreen. A few seconds later, the sky opened up and raindrops pelted down on the car with incredible force. The cameraman desperately tried to shield his equipment from the rain.

"Ah, crap," the sound guy said, removing himself from his hiding place. "We'll have to stop the shoot. Hopefully they already caught enough material."

The crew ran around outside taking equipment under shelter.

"The rain isn't letting up. Shall we run for it?" Jinseung asked.

"Okay."

"On the count of three. One…two…three."

We simultaneously exited the car. Side by side, we ran to the house.

This reminds me of something...

We arrived at the doorstep of the house, soaked and panting. I watched Jinseung as he struggled to catch his breath.

Images flooded back to me—Jinseung's kiss scene where he ran for shelter with Choi Miyoung and they kissed under the eaves of a temple...I realised I was still staring at him. He looked back at me with a bemused expression on his face. I quickly turned away, blushing.

Drenched, we entered the house and removed our wet shoes and coats. Fortunately, the rest of my costume remained reasonably dry. We traipsed down the hallway, careful not to drip water behind us.

Everyone had gathered in the lounge, huddling around Im Nara who was preparing to make an announcement.

"We have decided to wrap up the shoot tonight," she said. "I believe that we shot enough footage to make the scene work, but if an issue arises in editing, a reshoot might be necessary. We'll keep you informed."

A woman who stood by Im Nara's side spoke. "Good effort today, everyone. I've been on set to observe, and I was so impressed with the shoot. I can't wait to see the first episode."

"Who's that?" I whispered to Changsoo.

"Kim Eunsook," he answered.

The name sounded familiar, but I couldn't remember from where. She was an older woman, petite with long black hair. She had a shrewd look in her eyes.

"She's the writer," Bora explained.

To my surprise, Kim Eunsook approached me.

"I don't believe we've been introduced. I'm Kim Eunsook, writer of Hidden History."

"Nice to meet you, Writer-nim. I'm Chloe Gibson."

"Are you really a first-time actor?"

"Yes."

"*Aigoo.* I can't believe it! You did so well."

"Thank you," I croaked.

"Can I speak with you and Shin Jinseung for a minute? There are some script changes I'd like to discuss."

"Of course."

We relocated to the dining room. Kim Eunsook sat opposite me and Jinseung at the table.

"I've decided to change part of the storyline from episode three going forward," she explained. "This involves the character Louise."

I snapped to attention, wondering what she had planned for my character.

Chapter 17

"An email will be going out tomorrow," Eunsook said. "But I thought I'd let both of you know in person, since I'm here."

"So what are the changes?" I asked, voice tinged with concern.

"Don't worry, it's nothing bad," she reassured me. "In fact, quite the opposite. You see, I was going to have Louise killed off in the third episode, but recently I've had second thoughts. Seeing your scene together tonight made it even more clear to me... I don't want to kill Louise."

"So, Louise will live?"

"She will live...but she will go missing. Once Officer Park and Detective Jung solve the case, she'll return."

"I see."

"You won't be required for too many extra scenes, just in the last couple of episodes when you make your reappearance."

"What changed your mind?" Jinseung asked.

Eunsook broke into a sheepish smile. "I like the Louise and Officer Park pairing too much, and I think the fans will too. That's why I want them to reunite at the end."

Jinseung chuckled. "So that's why."

"You two have great chemistry!"

Jinseung wiggled his eyebrows at me.

"Stop that!" I said, batting him away.

Eunsook laughed. "Too cute!"

* * *

A COUPLE DAYS LATER, three new scripts arrived at KAM for me to pick up—the amended third episode script, plus the scripts for the fourth and fifth episodes.

The KAM lobby bustled with busy employees. I watched a digital screen display a photo of Jinseung in a relaxed pose upon a couch, his shirt halfway undone, and a come-hither look in his eyes. My jaw gaped at the sight. *I can't believe I work with this gorgeous human…*

A voice came from behind me. "Actor Chloe?"

I swung around, startled.

It was Seo Minjung. She looked immaculate as usual, with her sleek low ponytail and beautifully tailored skirt suit.

"What brings you here? No filming today?" she asked.

I nodded. "No filming for me. I'm here to pick up some new scripts."

"Do you know where they were delivered?"

"Shin Jinseung's management office."

"I'll get them for you."

"Thanks!"

"Do you have time for a catch-up? Wait for me in the cafeteria and I'll buy you a coffee."

"That sounds great."

"Okay. I'll be back in a minute." Minjung dashed to the elevator.

I made my way to the staff cafeteria situated down the right end of the lobby. I took a seat at an empty table.

Minjung returned shortly, a thick pile of scripts tucked beneath her arm. "I hope you don't mind, but I had a quick flick through. I couldn't help it. It's so gripping. Writer-nim is truly excellent."

"I don't mind. I'm eager to read it too."

While Minjung ordered the coffee, I scanned my eyes over the scripts, looking for parts which involved Louise. I stuffed them in my bag when Minjung returned.

She pulled out a chair. "So, tell me everything. What's it like to act in a drama?"

I relayed my experience so far while we sipped the strong coffee. She listened intently, keen to hear every detail.

I was describing what it was like to act alongside Shin Jinseung when my phone started ringing—a call from an unsaved number.

"Go ahead, take it," Minjung said.

I swiped to accept the call. "*Yeoboseyo?*"

"Chloe Gibson?" a female voice asked.

"Yes."

"This is Baek Yena."

Baek Yena? Why would she call me? How does she even have my number? "Baek Yena!" I exclaimed, my voice breaking.

Minjung's mouth dropped open.

"Don't sound so shocked!" Yena said. "I got your number from Shin Jinseung's manager. I'm having a party at my house next week, and I wanted to invite a select few people from Hidden History. I thought of you and Shin Jinseung. What do you think?"

"Absolutely! I'll come."

I simply couldn't pass up an opportunity like this.

"Wonderful! I'll text you the details."

Still in a state of awe, I put my phone away.

"Baek Yena called you?" Minjung asked, gobsmacked.

"I'm surprised too. She invited me to a party at her place."

"*Omo.* That's so cool. I'm jealous."

"She's inviting Shin Jinseung as well."

"Exciting! What will you wear? How will you do your makeup?"

"I don't know!"

Minjung appeared more frantic than me.

A party at Baek Yena's place...I wonder what it will be like.

A text message from Yena came through shortly. "Join me for a casual dinner party," it read, followed by the address and timing.

"When is it?" Minjung asked.

"Next Friday."

"Let me see if I can arrange a stylist and something to wear through KAM. It's a business expense, right? This is a networking opportunity for you."

"Oh, really? That would be amazing if possible. It's just a casual event, though, so nothing too extravagant."

"I'll see what I can do."

Minjung seemed just as excited as I was. She saw me off, promising to do everything she could to help me look my best on the day.

As I rode the subway home, my phone buzzed.

Jinseung: Hi Chloe. Are you going to Baek Yena's party? Want to go together?

Chloe: Yes. Let's go 😊

Jinseung: It's a date!

A date?! I shook my head, telling myself it was just a turn of phrase.

Chapter 18

Face up close to my bathroom mirror, I touched up my lips with a thin layer of moisturising lipstick in a colour called Rouge Royale, which promised to be long-wearing and "kiss-proof". I pouted, admiring how juicy and kissable my lips looked. Not that I ever imagined I'd be kissed by anyone that night. That would be completely delusional. *Who would kiss me anyway? Shin Jinseung?* I scoffed.

I had already had my makeup done. Minjung had arranged a stylist and loaned me some designer clothes from KAM's extensive closet. I wore a black turtleneck beneath a slip dress with a leather jacket over the top. The combination looked very chic.

I was trying on different pairs of earrings when I received a text message.

Jinseung: Are you ready? I'm in the taxi outside.

I quickly settled on a pair of dangly silver earrings, grabbed my purse, and dashed to the elevator.

A fancy black cab with tinted windows awaited me at the entrance. A uniformed driver got out and opened the door for me.

I slipped into the leather interior next to Jinseung. He wore slim black pants and a chunky wool sweater with a white shirt collar poking out underneath. A pair of thick-framed glasses and a black face mask hid his features. He pulled the mask down to speak. "Why, hello there. Nice threads."

"Thanks. They're actually on loan from KAM."

"Ah…You've discovered one of many work perks."

"Thanks for taking me to the party."

"That's all right. I thought it might be kind of intimidating if you arrived by yourself. I'm sure you're not used to being around lots of celebrities. I think it will mainly be people from Hidden History, but still…"

"You're right. I'm really excited to go, but a bit nervous as well. I don't have much in common with celebrities."

"Well, you look the part anyway. And who knows? Once the drama starts to air, maybe you'll get a little bit famous."

I laughed. "No way."

"Why not?"

"I'm not even a real actor."

"*Aigoo*. Your acting looked real to me."

"You know what I mean."

Jinseung folded his arms. "Sounds like you've got a pretty serious case of imposter syndrome."

"Imposter syndrome?"

"Despite your success, you feel like a fraud. Take it from me, you need to get out of that mindset. It takes up far too much energy."

"Perhaps."

"Trust me. Have more self-confidence. And let me tell you something, I've worked with many 'real' actors who weren't half as good as you."

"Really?"

Jinseung nodded.

I sighed. "I guess you're right. My mindset isn't doing me any favours." I ran a hand through my hair, ruminating on Jinseung's advice. He had certainly given me some food for thought.

"Oh—" Jinseung said, his eyes on me.

"What?"

"Your earring fell out."

I felt my earlobes. The right earring was missing. "Where did it go?" I looked around, then spotted it in my lap, light glinting off its edges. I tried to put it back in but struggled without a mirror.

Jinseung reached towards me. "Here, let me."

He took the earring and moved closer. He brushed my hair back behind my ear. With a focused expression on his face, he threaded the earring into my lobe, still holding my hair back, his hand against my neck. I could feel his warm breath against my cheek, making my skin prickle.

"There," he said, leaning back to admire his handiwork.

"Thanks."

The taxi slowed upon entering a posh neighbourhood with enormous mansions lining the streets. The driver dropped us off outside a four-storey house, modern and minimalist in design, with a flat roof and each floor jutting out at different angles creating the illusion of a stack of boxes. The lights were on inside and jazz music drifted from an open window.

"Wow. Baek Yena lives here?" I said, as we approached the house. "Impressive."

"I wonder who designed her house. Some famous architect, I suspect," Jinseung said.

We ascended the stairs leading up the side of the house to the entrance.

Jinseung pressed the doorbell. The door clicked open shortly, and a young woman neatly dressed in black pants and a white shirt greeted us.

"The guests are in the lounge. This way, please," she guided us down the hallway.

The interior of the house had a lived-in feel. Framed artwork covered the walls—a mixture of professional pieces and what looked like kids' artwork. Stacks of worn books and vinyls overflowed shelves and took up residence on the floor and in boxes. I spied a family photo of Baek Yena, her husband, and her three young children, huddled together and smiling broadly. They looked like the perfect family.

We entered the vast lounge area, possessing beautiful views over park-like surroundings. A gas fireplace burned, and couches were arranged to maximise potential interaction between their occupants.

Guests sat on the couches and on cushions on the floor. Others stood in corners partaking in intimate one-on-one conversations.

I recognised most of the people there from Hidden History—actors, plus Im Nara and Kim Eunsook, but there were also a few unfamiliar faces.

"Chloe, Jinseungie!" Baek Yena waved us over to join them. She grabbed more cushions and signalled for us to sit down. "Did you two come together?"

"Yes," Jinseung said.

"That's so sweet! I'm glad you could make it."

"Hey, I'm Ko Dongwoo." the man sitting next to her said. He had long hair and rugged features. "I'm Yena's husband."

Other people around us also introduced themselves.

Before long, I had a glass of wine in my hand, and I was chatting away with several people—forgetting all about the fact that they were celebrities. An endless stream of canapés flowed from the kitchen, and my wine glass seemed to get refilled whenever I wasn't looking. I had to make a concerted effort to drink slowly.

Kim Eunsook and Baek Yena started gushing over how cute Jinseung and I looked together.

"It's like magic," Kim Eunsook said. "So little time together and you've already managed to achieve such good on-screen chemistry."

"And off-screen as well," Baek Yena jibed, lightly elbowing Jinseung.

"What's that for?" Jinseung asked, bemused.

"How on earth did PD-nim manage to find you at such short notice?" Kim Eunsook asked me.

"Well, it's actually a funny story." I relayed the whole tale of how I had been conned, and how Seo Minjung spotted me on the street at my lowest point.

"*Aigoo*. That's crazy."

"And here's the kicker," Jinseung said. "It wasn't my first time meeting Chloe."

"What do you mean?"

"I came to Korea as a teenager," I explained. "I did a high school exchange."

"The same high school that I attended," Jinseung continued.

Baek Yena gasped. "*Omo!* It's like you were destined to be brought back together."

Kim Eunsook seemed struck by a sudden idea. "Why don't you get KAM to write up a press release about this? The media would love it! It could drum up some interest in the drama too."

"That's not a bad idea." Jinseung turned to me. "What do you think?"

"Sure. I don't mind."

"Then it's settled. I'll ask Changsoo *Hyung* to organise it."

"There's going to be so much interest in this story!" Kim Eunsook said excitedly.

* * *

As the night wore on, the guests grew increasingly intoxicated—especially Baek Yena. She turned the music up and started dancing with her husband who didn't seem overly enthusiastic.

I had become separated from Jinseung, but Kim Eunsook took me under her wing as we talked and snapped photographs with various guests.

When Baek Yena tired of dancing she bounded towards me and pulled me aside.

"Guess what..." she said in a conspiratorial tone.

"What?"

"You and Shin Jinseung..."

"Yes?"

"...Have to kiss!"

Facepalm. "I know that! I've read the script."

She sidled up to me. "So...are you nervous about it?"

"Yeah, I guess so. More embarrassed than anything. I haven't even kissed a guy in real life for a long time, and now I have to kiss on-screen."

Kim Jaehyun, who had been nearby, slid into our private conversation.

"I've done plenty of kiss scenes in my day," he said. "I'd be willing to let you practice on me."

"Why would she practice with you? Dirty old man," Baek Yena snapped back.

"Who are you calling old?"

"So you don't deny that you're dirty?"

"Well, there's no denying that."

"She should practice the scene with Shin Jinseung. Hey! Jinseungie!"

Jinseung, who stood at the opposite end of the room, turned his head to us, eyebrows raised.

Baek Yena gestured for him to come over, a scheming look on her face.

He cautiously approached. "What is it?"

"Show Chloe how to kiss."

"What?" he spluttered.

"The kiss scene. You don't want it to look awkward, so you should practice and get comfortable with it."

"That's really not necessary..." I said, holding my hands out in protest.

Jinseung stroked his chin. "Should we?"

"Huh?" I squeaked.

"It's not a bad idea."

"Well..."

"See? He agrees," Baek Yena said. "You can use an empty bedroom if you like."

Is she serious? I suddenly felt very hot and flustered.

"I'm joking!" Baek Yena said.

"They'll work it out in their own time," Kim Jaehyun assured her.

"That's right," Jinseung said. He turned to me. "You have nothing to worry about."

"Oh! I love this song!" Baek Yena's attention snapped away and she resumed dancing, targeting an unsuspecting Im Nara.

I regained my composure in her absence. "I wonder what that was all about…"

Jinseung scratched his head. "Well, Baek Yena seems to think that we'd make a good couple. I don't know where she got that idea from, but she won't stop bugging me about it."

"*Aigoo…*"

Ko Dongwoo had overheard us talking. "Sorry about that. It's her hobby to play cupid. Either play along or just ignore it. She's harmless, really."

"Ah. That's good to know," Jinseung said.

* * *

MIDNIGHT DREW NEAR. Some of the party guests had already left, returning home to their families, or to get some much-needed sleep before busy schedules ahead. I had stopped drinking a long time ago, and the drunken antics of the remaining guests ceased to be all that amusing.

"Do you want to leave soon?" Jinseung asked. He must have sensed my rising boredom.

"Yeah. I think I will."

"Then I'll go too. I'll order a taxi."

"Are you sure? You can stay if you want."

"I'd rather leave with you."

I wasn't sure whether he genuinely wanted to leave, or if he was just being a gentleman, but I was happy either way.

We said our goodbyes to Baek Yena. She protested, but eventually resigned herself to the fact that we were leaving.

The taxi arrived and we clambered inside.

"So, what did you think? Was it all that you imagined it would be?" Jinseung asked.

"I had fun."

"Everyone seems to like you."

"I'm relieved."

"…I'm actually not that tired. Are you?"

"No. Not particularly."

He seemed to be angling at something.

I realised the taxi was heading towards the KAM office, rather than my apartment.

"Do you need to get something from the office?" I asked.

"Actually, I thought I might use a practice room."

"At this time of night?"

"Yeah. It wouldn't be the first time."

"Then…should I join you?"

Jinseung nodded. "That scene…it could be shot any day now."

"The kiss scene?"

"Yes. *That* scene. We haven't done any work on it apart from a dry read-through. I meant what I said before. It wouldn't be a bad idea to practice it properly."

My heart rate increased. *Does he mean it? Is he drunk or something?*

"So you…want to practice the kiss?" I asked.

He nodded.

Chapter 19

"This is the part where we kiss," Jinseung reminded me.

I had said my line and then frozen, overwhelmed by the prospect of having to launch myself towards him and press my lips to his.

"Oh. Right," I mumbled.

We stood together in a small, windowless practice room at KAM, possibly the only two people in the entire building. The air was so quiet and still, making me hyperaware of Jinseung's movements, the sound of his breath, and his scent—slightly sweet, a little bit sweaty.

"You have to take the lead on this," Jinseung pushed. "Louise kisses Officer Park, not the other way around."

"All right. Got it."

"Let's try again."

We started from the top, where Louise gets out of the car and Officer Park reprimands her for her crazy driving. He wants to know if something's wrong.

"I...can't say anything," I said.

"Don't be scared. Tell me," he urged.

"I..."

He stood patiently, watching me, waiting for me to do something.

My heart hammered in my chest. I took a deep breath. *Okay...Let's do this.* I closed in on him, tilted my head, and gently pressed my mouth up against his, my lips sealed tight. I didn't dare take it any further. I held the kiss for a moment before breaking away, then I looked at him expectantly.

He raised his eyebrow. "Was that it?"

I frowned. "How should I do it then?"

"Well...how should I put this? I don't think the kiss should be too polite. Louise needs to throw Officer Park off-guard, making him completely flustered so he forgets everything."

"So, I need to kiss you...*harder?*"

"Yes. And you're too stiff. Don't clench your mouth shut. Move a little bit."

*Oh my gosh...*My cheeks blazed with embarrassment. "Can you show me?"

Before I could mentally prepare myself, Jinseung flung himself at me and pushed my mouth open with his lips, eliciting a gasp I couldn't hold back. He moved his lips against mine, softly but purposefully. I didn't take a breath until he pulled away.

"More like that," he explained.

"I'll try to."

"Don't be shy, okay? You don't have to hold back with me."

"Right. Umm...What should I do with my hands?"

Jinseung thought for a moment, then he took my left hand and pulled it up to his shoulder, then my right hand to the side of his neck.

"Like this," he said. "I think that will look good."

"Okay."

"Now, let's try it again. This time you have to take the lead."

We positioned ourselves and ran through our lines again. I didn't hesitate this time. At my cue, I dove straight into the kiss, with my hand on his neck pulling his head down and making our lips meet.

Jinseung feigned shock but then started to engage, returning the kiss with vigorous enthusiasm. It felt warm and slightly wet.

*Is this real? It feels like a real kiss...*One slip of the tongue and we'd practically be making out.

Jinseung's hand clutched my waist, his fingertips digging in, massaging my lower back. I could feel a vein throbbing in his neck, faster and faster…

Lost in the kiss, I nearly forgot to break away, but Jinseung didn't let up until I remembered and detached myself from his lips.

We both had to take a moment to catch our breath.

"Was that too much?" I asked.

Jinseung shrugged. "I don't think so. But it will be up to PD-nim to decide."

"I hope it looks okay. What if I have a weird expression on my face when I kiss?"

"I'm sure you don't."

"But you couldn't see, could you?"

"Yeah. My eyes were closed. If you're worried about it, we should see what it looks like."

"How can we?"

"Let's record it. There's a tripod around somewhere. It might be in one of the other practice rooms. I'll look for it."

While he left the room to search for the tripod, I took slow breaths, trying to calm myself.

Shin Jinseung kissed me…He really kissed me…So what if he's acting? It didn't feel like acting…

Jinseung reappeared holding a tripod in his arms. He set it up in the corner of the room, balancing his phone on top.

Before we resumed, he took his sweater off, revealing the crumpled white shirt underneath. *So I'm not the only one feeling hot right now…*

We got straight into it. I grabbed onto him and kissed his lips, slowly at first, but building in intensity. Jinseung eagerly responded. He held me closer this time, and I could feel his hard abs up against me. It felt so good that I didn't want to stop, but eventually I had to tear myself away.

Jinseung opened his eyes. He stared at me, biting his lip. My face burned under his gaze.

"The recording," I croaked.

"Right!" He retrieved his phone. "Let's see…"

Standing next to me, he positioned his phone in front of us and played the clip.

I watched with bated breath. There I was, rosy-cheeked, and with a look of concentration on my face as I kissed him. Jinseung's face was more animated, conveying surprise, then delight, and then…*desire?* Anyone who didn't know that he was acting would have thought he was genuinely into it. It looked like a perfectly hot, romantic kiss scene.

"It looks good," Jinseung said, voice slightly hoarse.

"Your face looks so expressive…"

"Viewers love to see emotion."

"Can you send that to me? I want to study it more closely."

"No. It's too risky. I'm going to delete it. It would cause havoc if it somehow leaked out."

"Ah. I understand."

He was right. Something like this could cause a scandal if it ended up in the wrong hands.

He put his phone away in his pocket. "It's getting late. We should go home."

I agreed, even though I didn't feel tired. The kissing had flooded my body with adrenaline.

Jinseung booked a taxi. It arrived outside the building a few minutes later.

Seated in the back of the car, I stroked my lips. They felt puffy and dry. The "kiss-proof" lipstick had completely worn off. I applied a thick layer of balm with my finger and rubbed my lips together. I noticed Jinseung watching me as if hypnotised.

"Sorry if my lips felt dry before," I said.

"No, they felt…nice…" His voice trailed off. "Your seatbelt—"

"Huh? Oh." I had forgot to put it on. I tried to pull it down, but it was jammed.

Jinseung reached across to help, his body inches from mine. He also struggled, but one more try and he was able to ease it down

"There," he said, clicking it into place.

He lingered in front of me, so close that if I leaned forward just a little, our lips would brush. He swallowed, then as if remembering something, he suddenly pulled away.

I slumped in my seat, disappointed. *What was I thinking?* I reminded myself that he had only been acting before, and that he had no reason to kiss me in real life.

I watched the streets of Seoul go by out the window, a blur of colourful lights.

Chapter 20

"Looking forward to showing everyone what we've been working on?" Jinseung teased with a smirk.

I lightly punched him in retaliation. He gripped his arm and staggered in mock pain.

We occupied a cordoned-off section of road, waiting for our scene to begin. The kiss scene.

The cameraman set up to shoot from the part where Officer Park approaches Louise's car. Jinseung, dressed in police uniform, rocked on his heels as he waited.

Baek Yena watched attentively from the sidelines, laid back on a fold-out chair, sipping bubble tea through a straw. Her manager stood beside her, shading her with a sun umbrella. Bora and Changsoo also watched from nearby.

Thanks to our practice kissing, I didn't feel too nervous about the scene since I knew exactly what to expect. Nevertheless, my heartbeat sped up as our cue drew near.

"Starting positions please," Im Nara said.

I got into the car. Jinseung walked off camera.

"Action."

Jinseung approached my vehicle. I got out, acting irritated.

"Louise, what's gotten into you? Have you been drinking?" he asked.

"No."

"You ran a red light. You're speeding. You're driving erratically. I should give you a ticket."

"I don't have time for this."

Jinseung raised an eyebrow. "...Is everything okay?"

"I...can't say anything."

He softened. "Don't be scared. Tell me."

"I..." I searched his eyes, and then without hesitation, stepped closer, pulled his head down, and kissed his lips, just as we had practiced.

Jinseung acted surprised at first, then he kissed me back with a hungry urgency. It took all my effort to stay focused on acting and not lose myself completely.

Just as the kiss reached its peak, I broke away, and before Jinseung could react, I got back into the car, hit the accelerator, and sped off a short distance down the road. Jinseung watched on, completely dumbstruck, powerless to act.

When I returned for the next take, Bora and Changsoo stared at me, mouths agape.

"What?" I asked.

"That kiss..." Changsoo said, eyes wide.

"How did you do that? It's like you're already used to kissing each other..." Bora said, a hint of suspicion in her voice.

"They must have done a lot of practice," Yena jibed, appearing from nearby having overheard the conversation.

"Practice?" Bora squeaked. "Did you? When?"

"Well..." I said, awkwardly.

Jinseung cut in. "Since this was Chloe's first kiss scene, sharing my expertise was the right thing to do."

"*Omo*. Sharing your expertise?" Bora repeated, stunned.

"I knew it!" Yena said.

* * *

THANKS to our excellent kissing skills, we were able to wrap up the scene much earlier than anticipated.

"Good work today," Changsoo said, opening the van door.

Jinseung and I climbed in.

"I still can't believe you could kiss like that. Isn't it too risqué for a prime-time drama?" Bora said, pulling her seatbelt on.

"I like to push boundaries," Jinseung retorted.

"When it comes to kiss scenes, Shin Jinseung has a reputation to uphold," Changsoo said. "Don't you remember he won that 'best kiss' award for the scene with Choi Miyoung in Midnight Dreaming?"

"I remember," Bora said. "But still…"

"I'm more impressed that it was Chloe's first kiss scene, and she was able to hit the ball out of the park on the first take."

"I couldn't have done it so well if *Seonbae-nim* hadn't coached me," I admitted.

"Hey, Actor Shin, who's the better kisser, Chloe or Choi Miyoung?" Bora asked.

I shot up in my seat, startled by the intimate question.

"*Aigoo*. Don't ask him that," Changsoo said.

"It's all acting," Jinseung said. "I don't make comparisons like that."

"That's sensible."

"That's boring," Bora grumbled.

Further into the journey home, she finally dropped the subject of kissing and turned her attention to her iPad. "Oh? What's this?"

"What is it?" Changsoo asked.

"An email from Drama Day News. They're requesting an interview with Chloe and Jinseung."

"*Omo*. It must be regarding the press release we sent out."

"Yes. They want to write an article about your high school memories of each other."

"What do you think, Jinseung, Chloe?"

"I'm in," Jinseung said straight away. He nudged me with his elbow. "Up for a trip down memory lane, Chloe?"

*My high school memories of Jinseung…*Since he had revealed that we went to the same high school, I had racked my brain trying to remember him, but nothing surfaced. Perhaps the interview would help jog my memory? "Yes. I'll do it," I said.

Chapter 21

A young female journalist from Drama Day News entered the meeting room carrying a thick brown envelope marked *Tongyeong—Important*. I eyed it warily, curious about its contents.

"Hello, I'm Hwang Yura from Drama Day News," she said. "I'm here to conduct the interview." She handed us a business card each.

"Hwang Yura," Jinseung repeated, studying the card. "Shall we get started?"

"Yes. Is it okay if I record?"

"Go ahead."

She set her phone to record audio and placed it in the centre of the table. She kept the brown envelope safely on her lap as she seated herself.

"Chloe Gibson, you were cast in Hidden History after a chance encounter with a KAM talent scout who spotted you on the street," she said. "At what point did you realise you'd be working alongside Shin Jinseung?"

"I found out after I auditioned," I replied.

"And did you recognise him?"

"No, I didn't."

She turned to Jinseung. "Did you recognise her?"

"Yes," he said. "It took me a moment, but then I realised where I'd seen her. I was so shocked. I had never expected to see her again."

"It must have felt like a blast from the past."

"Yeah. It was crazy."

"So, what was Chloe like in high school?"

I blushed, feeling self-conscious about how he would answer. *What does Jinseung remember about me? What was my impression on him?*

"Ummm…well," Jinseung fumbled for words. "She was the only foreigner, so naturally, people were curious about her."

"You too?"

"Yes. Of course."

"Anything else?"

"Her Korean was terrible at first."

"Hey!" I interjected.

"But she seemed to become fluent pretty fast," he added. "She was a high achiever even with Korean as her second language."

"I'm a nerd," I confessed. "Actually, as a foreigner I was excused from having to study after school with the other students, but I still joined in a lot of the time, anyway."

I had been top of my class in my UK high school, but the competitive nature of Korean schooling still came as a shock to my system. I had to study really hard to keep up with everyone, but somehow, I made it work.

"Were you good at studying, Shin Jinseung?" Yura asked.

"No. Not at all," he said. "I barely passed high school. Not that I lacked intelligence, I just wasn't focused on school and had no aspirations to go to university, work a corporate job, anything like that."

"So you knew you wanted to be an actor, then?"

"I wanted to work in entertainment. I actually did idol training but ended up as an actor, not a singer."

I gasped. "You wanted to be an idol?" *This is news to me…*

"You would have made a great idol," Yura said, enthusiastically.

Jinseung rubbed his head, shyly averting his eyes. "You think so? Actually, I'm glad things worked out this way. The idol lifestyle is a bit too full on, I reckon."

"Ah, I can understand that."

The envelope on Yura's lap made a rustling sound.

"I've got something I want to show both of you," she said. "Perhaps it might jog some more memories." She produced the envelope and opened it, pulling out what looked like a magazine, some of its pages bookmarked with sticky tabs.

"What's that?" Jinseung asked.

Yura held it up so we could see.

The words *Tongyeong High School Yearbook 2011* emblazoned its cover.

I gasped. "That's our yearbook!"

"How did you get this?" Jinseung asked.

"I made some calls and found an ex-student who still had it in their possession," Yura replied.

"Can I have a look?"

"Yes. Check out the pages I have bookmarked." She passed it to him.

Jinseung pulled his chair up close to mine so we could both see. He flicked to one of the bookmarked pages. There I was, smiling in a class photo.

Jinseung grinned. "You still look the same."

I ran my finger across the glossy page, scanning the faces of my former classmates. "Yoo Mina...Han Seri..."

"Were you close with them?" Yura asked.

"Yes. We were best friends. We were inseparable, especially me and Seri. My family hosted her when she did an exchange at my intermediate school when we were 13, then her family hosted me when I went to Tongyeong High School. We're practically sisters."

"Have you kept in touch?"

"Yes. We still chat on social media and email...although, not as often as we used to." A hint of regret edged its way into my voice.

"Is she still in Tongyeong?"

"No. She's in Melbourne now, but she planned to return to Korea this year so we could meet." I made a mental note to follow up with her.

Jinseung turned to the next bookmarked page. He smiled. "My old class…"

"Where are you?" I asked. "Oh—" I spotted him.

He appeared slightly chubby, with an awkward bowl-cut hairstyle, caterpillar eyebrows, and a dorky grin, but the same handsome, mischievous face peered out underneath.

"That's you!" I looked closer, blinking as I studied his image. My brain was on the verge of a memory, but the harder I tried to recover it, the more it slipped away. "I think…I think I do remember you…"

"Of course. How could you forget a face like mine?" Jinseung said. "I've lost my baby fat since then, of course."

"Turn to the next bookmark," Yura urged.

Jinseung flipped through the yearbook, stopping at the final bookmark. On a spread titled *Community Service Day*, my eyes fell upon a photograph of a small group of students, Jinseung and I standing side by side, and in the background, a beautiful, sandy beach. The floodgates in my mind opened up, and a deluge of memories poured in.

"I remember this," I said. "I remember this day…"

I let the memory wash over me, transporting me back to that moment eight years ago.

It was a rare break from the usual crushing school day routine of back-to-back lessons and study sessions. Instead, the entire school spent a day doing volunteer work.

We were divided into small groups, mixing up the students from different classes and different year levels. Jinseung and I ended up in the same group. We were assigned the task of clearing litter from a beach.

It was a gloriously hot, sunny summer day. It felt so good to be out in the fresh air, away from the stuffy classroom. None of us minded having to pick up rubbish. But partway through the day, disaster struck…

I had removed my shoes to enjoy the warm sand against my bare feet. Walking along the beach, a piercing pain shot through my foot. The sand turned red with my blood. I shrieked.

It was Jinseung who had rushed to my aid. He asked the teacher looking after our group to bring the first aid kit, then he had tended to my wound himself, removing the shard of glass that had wedged itself in my foot, cleaning and sterilising the cut, and wrapping my foot in bandages.

When the beach cleanup finished, the other students in the group cooled off in the ocean. I couldn't due to my injury, but Jinseung stayed with me on the beach to keep me company.

Snapping back to the present, I turned to Jinseung. "You were really nice to me. Did I ever thank you?"

Jinseung shrugged. "Probably. I don't remember."

"What happened?" Yura asked.

I told her the story, with Jinseung interrupting now and then to add his own embellishments.

"Awww, that's sweet," Yura said. "And did you talk to each other at school after that?"

"No," I confessed.

"I saw her around at school, but we didn't have much of a reason to interact," Jinseung explained. "We weren't in the same year, we didn't have any mutual friends..."

"Ah. I see." Yura asked a few more questions before she began to wrap up the interview. "I have one more question. Do you have any plans to go back to Tongyeong?"

"Yes," I replied. "Part of the reason I came back to Korea was to visit my host family and to see Tongyeong again."

"And you, Shin Jinseung?"

"I would like to see my parents again soon, and my dog, Buster."

"Buster! How cute. Well, that's about everything. Thank you so much for your time today," Yura said.

"No problem."

"I'll send the article through to your manager to review before we hit publish." She got up from the chair, bowed her head, and said goodbye.

I stopped her before she reached the door.

"You forgot this." I picked up the yearbook she had left on the table.

"You can keep it," Yura said. "I've already got everything I need from it."

"Okay. Thanks."

She left the room.

"Do you want this?" I asked Jinseung.

"You can have it. I still have my copy somewhere at my parents' house."

"Thanks. Well, I guess I'll get going then."

"Hey—have you had lunch?"

"No."

"Then let's go to the cafeteria. I have something I want to ask you about."

"Oh? All right then."

Wondering what he had to say to me, I followed Jinseung down to the cafeteria on the ground floor of KAM headquarters.

We grabbed a table, and over bowls of *bibimbap*, Jinseung leaned in to speak.

"Are you really planning to go back to Tongyeong?" he asked.

"Yes," I replied.

"Soon you won't have too many scenes left to shoot. I'm sure you'll have time to go."

"What about you?"

"The pace of filming is only going to increase from now on. Once the first episode airs, I don't think I'll have much time off, so I want to go soon. As soon as possible, actually—if *PD-nim* allows it."

"I should go soon, too. There's no reason to put it off."

"It seems like we're both on the same page, so how about this? Why don't we go together?"

My eyebrows shot up in surprise at his proposal. "Really?"

"Now, I can't guarantee it so don't get your hopes up—"

"I'm not!"

"—but if we can both get a few days off together, let's do it. It would be nice to have company for the journey. I could drive us there. What do you think?"

A road trip with Shin Jinseung? How cool would that be. "I'm in. Let's go to Tongyeong."

Chapter 22

I should have heeded Jinseung's advice not to get my hopes up. One week after our chat in the KAM cafeteria, I rode a bus from Seoul to Tongyeong, alone.

He had called me the other night, apologetic that he couldn't come. He was required on set on what was supposed to be his day off. I tried to brush my disappointment aside—I could still enjoy the trip without him.

Face pressed to the bus window, I peered out as the picturesque seascape unfolded before me. I had arrived in the beautiful port city of Tongyeong, often called the Napoli of Korea for its attractive seaside charm.

The bus rolled into Tongyeong station. I slung my duffel bag over my shoulder and searched the waiting area for my host parents, Mr. Han and Mrs. Soo. My throat tightened when my eyes met theirs.

Mrs. Soo waved frantically, her eyes crinkling as she smiled, and Mr. Han stood with his arms folded, nodding his wispy-haired head. Both of them looked the same as I remembered, only slightly greyer. Seeing them again brought tears to my eyes. I hadn't realised how much I missed them.

"Eomeoni! Abeoji!" I ran to them.

"Chloe!" Mrs. Soo cried.

"My daughter!" Mr. Han called.

I hurtled into their arms.

"*Unnie*," a third voice said.

I turned to see Seri approach from nearby. I leapt back in surprise. "Seri-ya! I didn't know you would be here."

"When I heard you were coming, I expedited my travel plans," she explained.

I hugged her. "Thank you. It's so good to see you."

Seri looked just as pretty as she did in high school, but more mature with shorter, side-parted hair, and light makeup on a thinner, more angular face.

Mr. Han drove us to their house in Inpyeong-dong. I felt faintly nostalgic passing through the city which my sixteen-year-old self once knew intimately.

As we drove up the driveway, a golden retriever ran over to us, barking.

I opened the car door and the dog came over to sniff me, tail wagging with excitement.

"Who's this?" I asked, patting the dog.

"Her name's Snow," Mrs. Soo said. "Oscar is no longer around, I'm afraid. He passed away."

"Yes, Seri told me. I'm very sorry."

Oscar was the family dog when I had lived with them, and I had loved him very much.

"Come inside and have some tea," Mrs. Soo said. "We have a lot of catching up to do."

I followed the family inside the house. The interior hadn't changed one bit. Faded floral wallpaper lined the walls, and mismatched second-hand furniture stood on creaky wooden floorboards.

We sat on cushions around a low dining table. Mrs. Soo prepared fragrant herbal tea and served it using a traditional Korean celadon tea set.

"So Chloe, you're in a drama with Shin Jinseung and Baek Yena. I can't believe it!" Seri gushed.

"Neither can I," I admitted.

"What happened to teaching English?" Mr. Han asked, brow furrowed beneath his spectacles.

"Things didn't work out. But after I've finished the drama, I might try to get a job teaching again."

"A respectable plan."

"Won't you be able to get more entertainment work?" Mrs. Soo asked.

"I don't think so. The work available to foreigners is pretty limited."

"Oh, I see. Well, whatever happens, I wish you success."

"Thank you. How have things been here? Still working at GNU?" I asked Mr. Han.

"Yes. Still teaching at the university. My wife has a job now too."

"Really?"

"Yes," Mrs. Soo replied. "I'm working part-time at a clothing store. I found myself with more time on my hands after Seri moved out."

"It's good to keep busy. Seri-ya, how's Melbourne?"

"It's wonderful! I still work for the same company. I do miss Tongyeong, though."

"Me too. It feels good to be back."

"*Unnie*, do you want to go out tonight? I'm meeting some old school friends at a restaurant in Gangguan. Kind of like a mini school reunion."

I brightened at the thought of seeing old friends. "Yes. I'd love to come."

"Great. I'll let them know you're coming. They'll be thrilled."

* * *

IN THE EVENING, Seri and I started getting ready to go out. We sat side by side at the makeup table in her bedroom.

"So tell me, is it true that Shin Jinseung and Choi Miyoung are dating?" Seri asked while applying false lashes.

I dropped my lipstick on the floor, startled. *Shin Jinseung and Choi Miyoung?* "Eh? That's the first I've heard of it," I blurted.

"There were rumours flying around while Midnight Dreaming aired that they were a couple in real life."

"I don't know about that. I don't know much about his personal life, but he hasn't mentioned Choi Miyoung at all."

I flashed back to Bora asking, "Who's the better kisser, Chloe or Choi Miyoung?" Based on Jinseung's reply, "It's only acting," it didn't sound as if he had kissed her outside of filming. That was only conjecture, though.

"I hope it's not true…" I murmured.

"Why? Do you like him?"

"No!"

Seri looked at me through narrowed eyes.

"Maybe a little," I admitted.

"*Aigoo.* I'm so jealous. If you do like him, you could actually be in with a chance. You're so beautiful—plus loads of actors fall in love while filming a drama."

"Really?"

"Yeah. It happens all the time."

"Do you remember that he went to Tongyeong High School?"

"Yes. He didn't stand out much back then. If only we'd paid more attention…" She paused in thought before we both cracked up laughing.

When we were ready, we took a taxi to Gangguan Port. The sun melted down over the harbour and lights started switching on, illuminating the area and cascading off the rippling sea in brilliant hues. The fish markets and restaurants bustled with patrons.

We entered a cozy restaurant with a dark wooden interior and enchanting views of the harbour where fishing boats bobbed at their moors.

I spotted a couple of familiar faces at one of the tables. Seri and I approached.

"*Omo.* Chloe Gibson, what brings you back to Tongyeong?" a woman with long brown hair and high cheekbones asked.

"Kim Hana?" I ventured.

She nodded.

"I'm here to visit my host family," I explained.

"And you're in a drama. How cool is that?" a man said. I recognised him but couldn't remember his name.

"What? You're in a drama?" Hana asked, shocked.

I nodded.

"*Aigoo*. Don't you keep up with entertainment news?" the man said. He turned to me. "I'm Do Hanjae, by the way. I was your *seonbae* at Tongyeong High School."

"Is anyone else coming?" Seri asked.

"Bae Yoojin and Hyun Taewoo said they would come. I'm sure they'll be here soon."

"I spread the word on social media, but it seems very few of us are currently in Tongyeong," Hana said.

The remaining guests arrived later, bringing the total to seven of us around the table. Food and drinks included a plenitude of beer and soju, plus seafood dishes and various *banchan*.

We chatted as we ate, talking about our lives since leaving Tongyeong High School. Only a couple of them still lived in Tongyeong, the rest were just visiting like Seri and myself. Everyone seemed the most interested in me, and I spent a large portion of the conversation fielding questions about what it was like to act in a drama.

"My part is not that big," I assured them.

"But you have scenes with Shin Jinseung and Baek Yena, right?" Tae-woo asked.

"Yes. A few. Anyway, enough about me. I want to hear all about what you guys have been up to."

I successfully redirected the conversation away from me, so I could lay back and listen to everyone else's stories.

As the hours passed and the beer and soju flowed, we were starting to get pretty drunk.

"I've got an idea," Hana drunkenly announced.

"What is it?" Seri asked.

She paused for effect. "...Let's go to a *noraebang!*"

"Great idea!"

Others chimed in with approval. We agreed to finish our drinks then head to the karaoke place next door. We were about to get up and leave when a tall man wearing a beanie and a black face mask entered the restaurant and walked over to our table. *Is that...*

"Sorry I'm late," he said.

Shin Jinseung!

"*Omo!*" Hana gasped.

Chapter 23

Jinseung introduced himself to the group. "Hi, I'm Shin Jinseung. I was at Tongyeong High School from 2009 to 2011."

Everyone stared at him, mouths gaping, too starstruck to say anything.

"*Seonbae*," I said. "I thought you weren't coming."

"My scene was cancelled at the last minute, so I could make it after all."

"How did you know to come here?"

"News of this little reunion was all over my social media."

"Oh. Well, sit down."

He took the last empty seat at the table.

"*Seonbae...*" Hana said.

Jinseung turned to her. "Yes?"

"You really came..."

"Of course! I'm a former Tongyeong student, after all."

"We were just about to go to karaoke," I said.

"That sounds good. It will be a little more private too." He looked around nervously at the other patrons.

"Do you want a drink before we go?"

"Nah. It's fine. I'll have something when we get there."

We headed next door to the karaoke place where we booked a large private room. Jinseung ordered and paid for more food and drinks.

The room had black walls and faux leather seats around its perimeter, with a large screen at the end, and a low table in the centre. A mirror ball hung from the ceiling, making specks of light dance around the room.

"Who wants to go first?" Jinseung asked. He turned to me. "Chloe?"

Even though I had drunk a lot, it still didn't feel enough to sing in front of Jinseung.

Seri offered to go first instead. She chose the song "Palette" by IU. It really suited her. She even resembled her a bit.

Jinseung took the stage next, singing "Genie" by Girls' Generation, complete with sexy dance moves. Despite his joking tone, I was pleasantly surprised by his singing voice.

"You could have been an idol," Hana gushed.

I grinned with the secret knowledge of his idol training.

"I could have been in a girl group, right?" Jinseung quipped.

After everyone else had had a turn, I couldn't put it off any longer. I had another shot of soju before grabbing the mic.

Everyone whistled and cheered as I sang, feeding my confidence. I looked Jinseung in the eyes and he grinned back at me, nodding along to the beat of the song.

Several drinks later, we were all singing and dancing together, no concern for how awful we sounded or how stupid our dance moves looked.

Hana had her sights set on Jinseung all night long, and partway through one of the songs, she slipped her arm around him and started to dance with him. Jinseung reciprocated, to Hana's utter delight. I watched on, sick with jealousy. The room spun around me. *I've had waaay too much to drink...*

"Whoa there. You okay?" Jinseung asked. He had broken away from Hana and held out a hand to steady me as I stumbled drunkenly.

"I'm fine," I assured him.

"Doesn't seem like it. Do you want to go outside and get some fresh air?"

"All right. That sounds good."

He told everyone we were heading out for a minute, then donned his face mask and beanie again. I could sense Hana glaring at us as he guided me outside.

We walked across the road to the harbourside, where I leaned against the railing, inhaling the salt air, trying to sober up a bit and stop my head from spinning.

"Feeling better?" Jinseung asked.

"Yeah. I think so."

He stared out at the ocean. "You saved me."

"Huh?"

"You helped me get away from Kim Hana."

"Oh. Did you want to get away from her?" It hadn't seemed as if he weren't enjoying the attention.

"She's a bit full on."

I sighed. "You must get hit on all the time, being a celebrity and all..."

"Yeah. Not that I like it, or anything. Actually, I find it too much."

"I get it."

"Hana didn't take any interest in me in high school, so why now? Because I'm famous. That's all people like her care about."

I didn't take any interest in him in high school either, I thought regretfully.

"Are you cold?" He offered me his jacket.

"No. Not really."

We stood in calm silence, watching the waves crash against the shore.

"Why did you come out tonight?" I asked.

Jinseung smiled. "I might be famous but I'm still an ex-student of Tongyeong High School. Sometimes I want to do ordinary things like go to reunions."

"Ah...I see."

The wind blew my hair in my face. Jinseung held it back, his fingers caressing my face as he did so. He took his beanie off then pulled it onto my head, which kept my hair out of my eyes.

"Cute," he said, grinning.

"Don't you need that?"

He looked around. "There aren't too many people around. It's fine."

The cold ocean wind continued to whip me, drawing a shiver, and I suddenly regretted refusing his jacket. As if reading my mind, he removed his jacket and draped it over my shoulders.

"*Aigoo*. I'm taking all your clothes," I said.

"I don't need them." He gripped the railing, his knuckles pale.

Not thinking what I was doing, I reached out and placed my hand on his. His skin felt cold to the touch. He turned to me, eyebrow raised, and a mildly disapproving look in his eyes. I quickly snatched my hand away, realising I was crossing a line, just like Kim Hana.

"You're cold," I stammered. "We should go back inside."

"I don't want to."

"You can't avoid her all night."

"Oh yes I can. The time in the karaoke room will be up soon, anyway."

I thought they might add some time on, but Jinseung was right. A couple minutes later, the group emerged from the building.

"Chloe!" Seri called out from across the road. "We're leaving now. Are you coming?"

"Uh, yes. Just a minute!" I turned to Jinseung. "I should go with Seri. I'm staying at her parents' place."

"Okay. Maybe I'll catch you around."

"How long are you here for?"

"Until Sunday."

"Okay. Well, I'll still be here. Maybe we'll bump into each other." I returned his jacket and beanie.

"Goodnight. Drink a big glass of water before bed. You need it."

"Thanks for the advice. Goodnight."

Seri stood waiting, arms folded.

"Coming!" I said, crossing the road back to her.

Jinseung stayed by the harbour, looking out at the fishing boats.

"What was that all about?" Seri asked when we were safely inside a taxi on our way home.

"What?"

"You and Shin Jinseung having one-on-one time."

"Oh, he just wanted to get away from Kim Hana."

"Get away from Hana, or be alone with you?"

"Huh? It wasn't like that."

"Are you sure? You were standing so close to each other. And back at karaoke, he couldn't keep his eyes off you."

"Really? Are you sure you're not imagining things?"

"I'm not. Trust me."

I sighed. Even if that were true, he probably gravitated to me simply because he knew me better than everyone else there.

When we arrived back at Seri's house, the lights were off and her parents had already gone to bed. We did our bedtime routines then retired to her room together—the same room we had shared while in high school. Seri used to sleep on the bed, while I slept on the ground on a thin mattress called a *yo*. I actually found it very comfortable, especially since the floor was heated.

Now, the room had been cleared of most of Seri's belongings, and the bed was gone.

"My parents got rid of the bed when I moved out to create more space," Seri explained.

Yos and blankets had already been laid out for us. Her parents must have done so knowing we'd come home tired and drunk.

I slipped beneath the heavy blanket and pulled it up to my chin.

"Goodnight, Chloe," Seri said, before turning off the lamp, engulfing the room in darkness.

With the weight of the quilt on top of me, and my head fuzzy from alcohol, I swiftly fell asleep, deep and dreamless.

I didn't wake up until morning light seeped through the gaps in the curtains. The sunlight stung my pupils when I opened my eyes, causing me to clench them shut again. My head felt like it was going to explode, and my mouth and throat were like sandpaper. I let out a deep groan.

When I could finally open my eyes, I rolled over to see if Seri was still in bed. Her *yo* was empty, the quilt pulled down in a wrinkled pile at its foot. *She must have gotten up already.*

Gathering all my strength, I peeled myself out of bed and marched directly to the kitchen to get a glass of water. A hearty, beef-flavoured smell wafted in the air growing stronger as I approached. The source of the fumes became apparent when I saw Mrs. Soo boiling a pot on the stove.

"That smells wonderful. What is it?" I asked.

"Hangover soup," she replied.

"That's exactly what I need."

"I thought so. It'll be ready in a few minutes."

I poured myself a glass of water, then walked over to the table. Seri sat there, texting someone on her phone. She looked up when she noticed me approach. "Oh, you're up," she said. "I was just about to go and get you. How are you feeling?"

"I've been better," I admitted. I sat down and chugged the tall glass of water, relieving my dry mouth.

Mrs. Soo served us the steaming soup, ladling it into large bowls.

"*Eomma* makes the best hangover soup," Seri said. "You'll feel better in no time."

After two bowls of delicious soup, it was as if my internal battery had been recharged. I was ready to face the day.

"It worked!" I exclaimed.

"Told ya," Seri said.

Snow came up to me, sniffing around my feet. I gave her a pat and she wagged her tail, panting.

"Would you like to go for a walk, Snow?" I rubbed her furry tummy.

Snow let out a delighted bark.

"Can I take Snow for a walk?" I asked Mrs. Soo.

"Oh, would you? That would be great. She'll love it."

"Okay. A walk will help clear my head too. Where's her lead?"

Mrs. Soo retrieved the lead which made Snow jump up and down with excitement.

"Settle down, Snow," Mrs. Soo said, as she attached it to her collar.

"All right. I'm going now," I said.

"When you come back, do you want to go to the *jjimjilbbang* with me?" Seri asked.

"Sure. I shouldn't be too long."

I set out with Snow. She ran so fast ahead that it was like she was walking me, not the other way around. Eventually she settled into an easier pace. The fresh sea breeze woke up my senses as we followed a walking trail around the coastline. Sunlight gleamed off the gentle ocean waves. *Ahhhh...this is the life. Maybe I should try to get a teaching job in Tongyeong once I'm through with the drama?*

While I ambled along, lost in thought, Snow started whining and going crazy. She pulled at the lead and I lost my grip. I was powerless to stop her as she bounded into the distance, disappearing from my line of vision.

Chapter 24

"Snow!" I called after the runaway dog. "Snoooow!"

I ran and ran until I finally caught sight of her. She was playing with another dog—a cute little Maltese.

"There you are!" I said, relieved.

A voice came from nearby. "Looks like we had the same idea."

I shot up, startled. It was Shin Jinseung's lovely deep voice. He stood watching me, an amused expression on his face.

"*Seonbae*, is that your dog?" I asked.

"His name's Buster," Jinseung said.

"He's adorable." I picked up the fluffy white dog and cuddled him. He licked my arm with his tiny pink tongue.

"He likes you." He petted Snow. "Good boy."

"It's a girl. Her name's Snow. She belongs to my host family."

"Good girl, Snow."

I let Buster down and he immediately went back to playing with Snow.

"They get along," Jinseung said. "Shall we walk them together?"

"Okay."

We walked along the quiet trail, side by side, bathed in morning sunlight.

"It's a beautiful morning." I inhaled a deep breath of fresh air.

"Do you have a hangover?"

"Yes, but I'm getting over it. What about you?"

"No. I don't think I drank as much as you since I arrived late."

The dogs kept criss-crossing around each other causing their leads to tangle.

"*Aigoo.*" Jinseung got down on his knees and unwound them.

We had arrived in a picturesque park area overlooking the sea, so we slowed down to take in the views.

"Could you take a photo of me and Buster?" Jinseung asked. "I want something to post to social media."

"Sure."

He passed me his phone, then posed holding Buster.

I took several photos while gushing about how cute they looked. "Your fans will love this," I said.

As I reviewed the photos, I noticed something in his gallery. The video of our practice kiss. "Huh? I thought you were going to delete that video."

"What? Oh that." Jinseung's face reddened. "I forgot about it. I should delete it." He grabbed his phone and did so, right in front of me.

My heart sank as I watched the file disappear. I wished I had a copy. I'd play it over and over again. That kiss, although pretend, had been so amazing, it made my knees weak just thinking about it. The way he held me up close, the softness of his lips…

"You okay?" Jinseung asked.

"Oh? Yes. Sorry. I zoned out for a second there."

We carried on walking, passing by a café on the marina surrounded by outdoor seating bustling with people enjoying a morning coffee.

"Jinseungie!" a female voice called.

Uh oh. Someone has recognised him.

Jinseung stopped in his tracks and watched the woman wave to him.

"*Eomma,*" Jinseung said under his breath.

"That's your mother?" I asked.

"Yes. I should go say hi."

I went with him to his mother, a glamorous-looking woman with short hair, wearing a dress and a pearl necklace. She sat opposite another, similarly glamorous woman.

"*Eomma*. Don't call out my name like that in public," Jinseung said.

"Oh, I'm sorry." Her eyes switched to me. "*Omo*. Who's this? Can it be? Does my Jinseungie have a girlfriend?"

I dropped Snow's lead in shock at the word "girlfriend."

"This is Chloe Gibson, *Eomma*. My co-star in Hidden History. I told you about her, remember?"

"Didn't you go to Tongyeong High School?" the other woman asked.

"That's right," I replied.

"I think you were in the same year as my daughter, Gu Eunjae."

"Yes. I remember her. She was in my class."

"So you went to Tongyeong High School? I thought you looked familiar," Jinseung's mother said, her eyes still narrowed in suspicion. "Are you sure you're not dating? I'm quite modern, you know. I wouldn't mind a non-Korean daughter-in-law."

"*Eomma!* Leave her alone," Jinseung said.

"We're not dating," I said, shuffling my feet in embarrassment.

Her eyes continued to scan me up and down. "Dating or not, you two seem very close. Chloe Gibson, why don't you come over for dinner tonight? I'd love to have you over."

I gaped at her suggestion, unable to respond.

"We already have dinner plans," Jinseung said quickly.

My eyes widened in surprise. Jinseung threw me a look which said to play along.

"*Omo*." Jinseung's mother clutched a hand to her chest. "Dinner plans? Alone together? And you say you're not dating."

"We're friends," Jinseung said. "Can't two friends eat alone together?"

"Can you be friends with such an attractive girl?"

"*Eomma!*"

"Okay, well, whatever you say. Have fun tonight."

I gave the pair of women a bow before Jinseung led me away.

"Sorry about that," he said once safely out of earshot of the women. "My mum can be a bit extreme. I've never introduced her to a girl before. She's always asking when I'll bring someone home to meet her and my dad."

"What did you mean by dinner plans?" I asked. "Did you say that just to get me out of having dinner with your parents?"

Jinseung shook his head. "Actually, I was planning on asking you to have dinner with me anyway."

"Really?" I raised a sceptical brow.

"Not as a date or anything!" he quickly added. "I mean, you know how I went to the reunion last night?"

"Yeah…"

"Well, I liked going out and feeling like a normal person for once. It feels that way when I'm in Tongyeong. I don't get to experience it often."

"I…kind of get that."

"So what do you say? Will you go out with me tonight?"

I mulled his proposal over. There was just one detail which made me hesitate. "I know you say it's not a date, but won't it look like that? What if it fuels dating rumours?"

"I know the owner of the restaurant. He'll make sure we're seated privately and that no one bothers us. And besides, it's not a date. We're friends and colleagues. Why shouldn't we have dinner together?"

"I guess I'm overthinking things."

Jinseung gave my shoulder a little squeeze. "I appreciate your concern."

The two dogs yapped at another passing dog. I held tightly onto Snow's lead, worried that she might escape again. My arms were starting to tire from holding her back.

"I better get going," I said eventually. "I've already stayed out far longer than I intended."

"I'll walk you back," Jinseung said.

We turned to follow the trail back in the other direction. He walked me all the way to my host family's house.

"So this is where you lived," he said, surveying the property from the bottom of the driveway.

"Yup."

"We lived so close to each other. It's crazy how things turned out."

Snow whined, sticking to Buster's side longingly.

"The dogs don't want to part," I said.

"Sorry, Buster. We have to go now." He tugged him away. "See you tonight, Chloe. I'll pick you up, say, around seven-thirty?"

I nodded.

"I'll see you then. Come on, Buster."

* * *

"You're going out for dinner with Shin Jinseung?!" Seri said loudly while we sat together, naked, in a public bath.

"Shhhh…keep it down," I said.

"*Omo.* Sorry."

I looked around, making sure the other bathers weren't paying us any attention before I replied. "Yes. I'm going tonight."

"Wow. Is it a date?"

"No. It's just as friends."

"Oh really?"

"Yes. Really."

Seri pouted. "That's too bad."

"Jinseung's mother seemed convinced we were dating too. I met her while we were out walking."

"His mum? Shin Jinseung's ideal type is someone who gets along with his family, you know."

"Is it? How do you know that?"

"That's what the internet says. I think he said that in an interview one time."

"They always answer something like that. 'Someone who gets

along with my family', 'someone who's mature and respectful.' Do you think they'd say 'someone who has a sexy body'?"

"So cynical. Anyway, you do have a sexy body."

I folded my arms to cover my boobs. "*Aigoo*. I shouldn't go bathing with a pervert."

She ignored my comment. "When we get home, let me help you get ready. I want to live this night vicariously through you. Text me updates throughout the night."

"No."

"Please? Not even a couple of short messages?"

"…Maybe."

"Yes!" She pumped her fist.

* * *

JINSEUNG'S CRISP, freshly ironed white shirt and the upscale restaurant we arrived at made me question if it really were a date, because it felt suspiciously like one.

Suddenly I wished I'd put more effort into my appearance, feeling self-conscious in jeans, when a skirt or dress would have been more appropriate. A bit more makeup also wouldn't have hurt.

The owner of the restaurant greeted Jinseung as an old friend and directed us to a privately located table. Large windows presented a view of the sky, scattered with thousands of twinkling stars, and the Tongyeong landscape: buildings with illuminated windows and signs surrounding the placid harbour, lush green hills, and dark islands in the distance.

I looked out, absorbing the beautiful sight. "It's stunning…"

"It's a nice spot, isn't it?" Jinseung said, standing next to me.

"Makes me feel like I want to live here again."

"In Tongyeong?"

I nodded. "Maybe I could look for a teaching job—"

"Why don't you stay in Seoul?" Jinseung interjected.

I shrugged. "I will if I can make it work."

"This is a nice place, but it does get boring."

"Well, that's true I suppose…"

"You should stay in Seoul."

"You think so?"

"I do."

"Hmmm…" I continued looking out the window, deep in thought. *Should I really stay in Seoul?* I had come here to experience the vibrant city I had witnessed in countless K-dramas, but since my arrival I'd felt continually on edge and way out of my comfort zone. I sighed, ruminating on the fact that my life would be one big question mark after Hidden History wrapped.

"Take a seat," Jinseung urged, tearing me from my thoughts.

He pulled out a chair for me, and I sat down, peeling my eyes away from the view to open a menu.

"You like steak, right?" he said. "It's great here."

"I'm in Tongyeong. I should get seafood."

"Get whatever you like, and as your *seonbae*, I'm paying."

"You don't have to—"

He raised his hand. "Not another word. I insist."

I sheepishly returned to examining the menu.

After an inordinate amount of time deciding, we finally placed our orders.

The waiter brought out the wine first and poured us each a glass.

"Hey, Chloe," Jinseung said after downing a generous sip.

"Mmm?"

"We're friends, right?"

"Yes. Of course."

Jinseung rubbed the stem of the wine glass between his fingers. "I don't mind if you use *banmal* with me outside of work."

My mouthful of wine went down the wrong way and I coughed. *Banmal? He's asking me to get closer with him…*

"You okay?" Jinseung asked.

"Yes," I said, regaining my composure. "So…You want me to speak casually with you. I think I can do that."

"And why don't you drop the *seonbae*?"

"What should I call you then? Jinseung-ssi?"

He shook his head. "Too polite."

"Jinseung-ah?…*Oppa?*"

The left corner of his mouth lifted into a charming lopsided smile. "I like *Oppa*. Call me *Oppa*."

My cheeks flushed with warmth. "Okay, *Oppa*."

"I like it, *Dongseang*."

A giggle escaped my mouth.

"What's so funny?" he asked, amused.

"I don't think anyone's called me a *dongseang* before."

"You look cute when you laugh."

"You say that a lot."

"What?"

"Cute," I said, mimicking the deadpan way he said it.

"I don't sound like that."

"Yes you do."

"No, I don't." He lightly kicked me under the table.

"Hey!"

He did it again.

"Cut it out!"

We didn't notice the waiter approach with our meals until he placed them on the table, interrupting our flirty exchange. We bashfully reverted to acting like adults.

A grilled mackerel lay on the large white plate in front of me, skin lightly salted and charred to form a golden-brown crust.

I picked up a piece with my chopsticks and deposited it into my mouth, where it practically melted on my tongue.

"How is it?" Jinseung asked.

"Delicious!" I exclaimed.

We ate in silence, revelling in the delectable flavour of the fish until Jinseung stopped suddenly, a thought appearing to strike him as he toyed with his chopsticks. "Chloe, can I ask you something?"

"Sure, what is it?"

"Why did you come back to Korea?"

I paused, wondering how much to tell him. "To escape," I said eventually.

"What is it that you wanted to escape?"

"Various things…"

"What exactly?"

"It's a long story."

"I'm happy to listen."

"Well, all right then. If you insist."

Jinseung leaned in ready to listen attentively.

I took a moment to get the story straight in my head before start-ing. "Just a couple years ago I had everything going for me," I began. "I was fresh out of university with a business degree. I had an amazing boyfriend, and a job offer from a cool new startup company, but within a few months everything fell apart. The job wasn't the dream job I thought it would be. I was a 'customer experience specialist'—a fancy name for customer service rep. I quickly realised the company was short-staffed. Customer calls and emails piled up at a rate faster than my team could answer them. This meant working nights, week-ends, public holidays…sometimes weeks would pass without having a day off. We weren't paid overtime."

"That's horrible."

"That's not all. Our boss micromanaged us, and if anyone made a mistake they would be singled out and shamed in front of the whole company. It happened to me several times. The pressure was relent-less. To top it all off, I learned from a friend that my boyfriend was cheating on me. While I worked late, he was meeting up with another girl. We had a huge argument and split up. I had to move out of the flat we shared and into a grotty house with five flatmates and one bathroom."

"Did you quit the job?"

I nodded. "I ended up fainting at work one day. I was hospitalised. The diagnosis—too much stress. I decided then and there that I wouldn't return to work. I quit the job, left my flatmates, and moved back in with my parents."

"Sounds like that was for the best."

"Yeah, but after my experience at the startup, I developed an anxiety around working, which stopped me from applying to new jobs. Instead, I stayed at home all day lazing around watching K-dramas. "

"You deserved some time to relax and recover."

"That's what I kept telling myself. My parents were supportive at first too, but as the months passed, it was no secret that they were growing frustrated by my reluctance to work or to contribute to the household in any way. They told me that I would have to start paying rent if I wanted to stay at home, and that would mean getting a job."

"An ultimatum."

"Exactly, and I hated them for it. Fortunately, it wasn't long before I had an epiphany, and it came from watching K-dramas of all things."

"The decision to teach English in Korea?"

"Right. I had always wanted to go back anyway."

"I see. So that's how it happened. Chloe…"

"Hmmm?"

"You've revealed a lot to me. Now I feel like I have to come clean about something."

Chapter 25

What is it? What is he going to say? My mind reeled with possibilities.

Just as Jinseung was about to open his mouth to speak, a shrill voice pierced our bubble.

"Jinseungie! Chloe!"

Jinseung gritted his teeth in annoyance.

His mother, and a man I assumed to be his father, now occupied the only table visible from ours. She walked over to us.

"What a pleasant surprise," she said.

"Why are you here?" Jinseung asked, irritated.

"Since you weren't home for dinner, we decided to go out to eat as well."

"To the same restaurant?"

"You never told us what restaurant you were going to. It's just a coincidence we're all here. Maybe I should ask if we can join our tables together?"

"There's no need. We're nearly finished eating and we'll be leaving soon."

"*Yeobo*, leave them be," Jinseung's father said.

"This is the girl I was telling you about," Jinseung's mother explained to him. "They look good together, don't you think?"

"*Eomma!*" Jinseung said.

"Okay, okay. I won't bother you anymore. Finish your meal." She retreated to her table in a huff.

"Sorry about that," Jinseung said, returning his attention to me.

He ate another piece of fish, appearing to forget what we were talking about before the interruption.

I couldn't let it pass. I needed to know what he had to come clean about.

"What were you going to tell me?" I asked.

Jinseung swallowed his mouthful. "I can't say it with my parents right there, spying on us."

I sighed. "Fair enough. Tell me later, when we're alone."

He nodded and continued to eat.

I played with my food, suddenly losing my appetite.

"Are you finished?" Jinseung asked when he had emptied his plate.

"Yes. It was a bit too much for me."

We polished off the rest of the wine before getting up to leave. I gave his parents a quick bow as Jinseung tugged me to the counter. He tried to pay the bill, but they said his parents had already paid. Jinseung heaved a sigh.

"They didn't have to do that," he murmured.

The cool night air hit us as we exited the restaurant. Jinseung put his hoodie on and pulled the hood over his head.

"Come on," he said. "I'll walk you home."

He cast a cautious glance around before we set out, walking side by side down a quiet route through residential streets, dimly lit by street-lights and the glowing full moon.

"Sorry about my mother," Jinseung said. "She has a habit of trying to get involved in my relationships."

"I don't mind. Anyway, I'm sure she didn't intend to crash our evening."

He scoffed. "I'm sure she did."

My thoughts drifted back in the direction of our conversation over dinner. Now was my chance to bring it up again. "*Oppa...*"

"Yes?"

"What were you going to tell me before?"

Jinseung paused and rubbed the side of his broad neck. "About that...I've changed my mind."

I froze in my tracks, stunned. "What?"

"I don't want to tell you because it might put ideas in your head."

"But now that you've mentioned it, you have to tell me."

"Is that a rule?"

"Yes."

"I don't think it is."

"You're seriously not going to tell me?"

"Hmmm...Not right now."

"This is going to drive me crazy, you know that?"

"*Aigoo.*" A smile crept onto his lips. "Then how about this? Let's play a little game."

My interest was piqued. "Game?"

"If I win, I get to keep my secret. If you win, I'll tell you everything."

He's loving this. He has me right under his thumb. I pursed my lips in frustration.

"What? You don't want to play?" he teased.

I crossed my arms. "Fine! Whatever you want. Let's do it."

"Okay...First person to run to that tree over there, wins." He pointed to a large tree in the distance.

"No fair! You're faster than me."

"I'll give you a three-second head start."

"Hmmm..." *Will that be enough?*

"You in?" he asked.

"All right. Let's go."

"On the count of three. One...two...three...go!"

I sped off towards the lone, tall tree across a field of grass. I didn't look over my shoulder to see how far Jinseung was behind me, but I could hear his breath when he had just about caught up. The tree was just a few metres away.

So...close...

Jinseung grabbed me by the waist and flung me backwards. *Oh no you don't!* I caught the back of his hoodie and pulled him with me. I didn't let go even when I lost my footing. I fell down on my butt, and Jinseung came tumbling down on top of me, our legs interlaced, his panting body covering mine.

His right hand landed on the ground. His left hand was on my chest. I froze, unable to process the compromising position we had ended up in.

Jinseung's intense, charismatic eyes locked onto mine and he swallowed hard. We stayed fixed in that position until he suddenly realised where his left hand was.

"*Omo!*" he snatched it back, then hurriedly detangled himself from me and got up.

Back on his two feet, he reached out, held my hands, and pulled me up. "Sorry," he stammered. "I didn't mean to do that."

"I know. It's okay."

"Are you hurt?"

"No. I don't think so. You?"

"I'm fine."

We brushed blades of grass off our clothes.

"No one won. What do we do now?" I asked.

"You didn't win, so I'm not telling you."

I eyed the tree. *Who said the game was over?*

Jinseung noticed what I was looking at, but it was too late to stop me.

I jumped over and touched the tree. "I win."

"*Aigoo.* You want to know that badly, huh?"

"Yes!"

"Okay. Here goes..." He suddenly turned shy, colour rising in his cheeks. "...I had a huge crush on you in high school."

"Huh?"

"There. It's out in the open."

Chapter 26

I could feel my cheeks turn red. *Jinseung liked me in high school? I can't believe it...*

"Say something," Jinseung urged.

"I'm shocked," I spluttered.

"Is it really that surprising? Lots of guys liked you. I pretended not to care, but in reality, I was no better than them, fawning over a girl because she looked different. I've grown up a lot since then, of course."

I turned this new piece of information over in my mind, unsure what to make of it. "Why didn't you want to tell me?" I asked at last.

"I didn't want you to get the wrong idea. I liked you in high school, but it's not like I'm gonna date you now just 'cause of something like that. I'm completely over it."

The snark in his voice made my blood pressure rise. "I wasn't thinking that," I bit back.

"Good."

An awkward silence lingered over us as we walked the rest of the way to the house. Try as I might, I couldn't hide my annoyance at Jinseung's comment.

"Are you angry with me?" he asked when we reached the bottom of the driveway.

"No," I said, my tone bitter.

"It seems like you are."

"I'm not."

"Well, okay…" He didn't sound convinced.

"Thanks for dinner."

"That's all right."

"Goodnight."

"Goodnight." He turned away and disappeared into the shadowy night, not glancing back even once. I slipped inside the house with a sigh.

"*Unnie,*" came Seri's voice out of nowhere, startling me.

She appeared in the hallway, wrapped in a fuzzy pink dressing gown, her hair held back by a cat-ear hairband.

"Why do you have dirt all over you?" she asked, brow furrowed.

"I, uh, fell on the ground."

"*Aigoo*. So clumsy."

"Yeah."

"So…how did it go?"

"I don't know. Good and bad."

"Hmm? Come here and tell me what happened." She ushered me into her bedroom.

I explained what had happened as I changed into my pyjamas and did my nighttime skincare routine.

"I was beginning to let myself believe that he might actually like me," I admitted, as we lay on the *yos*, moisturising sheet masks adhered to our faces. "Then he comes out and says something like that. *It's not like I'm gonna date you now,*" I imitated his tone.

"Hmmm…" Seri fiddled with the edge of the blanket. "Could it be that he does like you, but he doesn't know if it will be possible to date you?"

"What do you mean?"

"Well, dating is so hard for celebrities. There's a lot he would have to take into consideration. It would no doubt harm his career, not to mention the hordes of jealous fans that could go after you."

I sighed, knowing she talked sense. "I suppose so. But still…"

"Don't jump to any conclusions. That's my advice."

We removed our sheet masks and tucked ourselves back into bed.

With the lights off, my mind raced, analysing the night's events over and over. Could Seri be right? Maybe he does want to date me, he just…*can't*. Either way, it was frustrating.

My phone screen lit up with an incoming message, distracting me from my thoughts.

Bora: Breaking news. The air date of Hidden History has been brought forward two weeks. Not much time to go now! PS. Check the mail tomorrow. I sent you a package.

Chloe: What package?

Bora: You'll see. Goodnight!

Chapter 27

The powerful stench of raw fish filled my nostrils making my stomach churn. I tried to breathe through my mouth instead as I walked around the fish market with Seri and Mrs. Soo.

"This is just like old times," Mrs. Soo said, linking arms with us. "You two used to come with me to the fish market every week."

"I've missed it," I said. "But I haven't missed the smell."

"What are you talking about? There's nothing better than the smell of fresh fish." She breathed in a great whiff of air. "Ahhhh!"

Seri and I exchanged amused looks and giggled.

All around us, *ajummas* wearing sun visors and rubber gloves crouched over colourful buckets of squirming and flopping live fish.

Mrs. Soo stopped at a stall selling shellfish and bartered with the vendor for a large box of oysters.

After purchasing the oysters, a nearby sweet stall caught her eye. "Let's have a treat," she said. "You girls used to love eating *kkoolbbang*."

She bought three *kkoolbbang*—balls of sweet red bean paste, encased in deep fried dough and smothered in sticky honey syrup, topped off with a light sprinkling of sesame seeds.

I took one small bite and its sugary sweetness exploded in my mouth. I ate slowly, savouring the rest of the *kkoolbbang* as we walked back to the house.

Upon returning home, Mrs. Soo stumbled over a package on the doorstep. She bent down and examined the label. "It's for you, Chloe."

"Oooh…What's that?" Seri asked.

"I'm not sure," I replied, picking up the package.

I could feel a thick document within the padded courier bag and understanding dawned on me.

I grabbed a pair of scissors from the kitchen and opened it up. Sure enough, it was a Hidden History script. Episode 10.

Bora had attached a fluorescent-pink post-it note to the front with some page numbers scrawled on it. I flicked to the pages she had noted—flashback scenes involving my character.

I had already filmed several flashbacks in advance, but these were new scenes. I'd need to go back to Seoul soon, I realised. I could be called on set at any time. My stay in Tongyeong would have to come to an end sooner than I anticipated.

"What is it?" Seri asked, leaning over my shoulder.

I cradled the script to my chest. "It's confidential."

"Let me see!"

I loosened my grip. "Okay. I'm not really supposed to share this, so you have to promise to keep it secret."

"I promise."

I passed the script to her outstretched hands.

She flipped through its pages, intrigued. "So this is what a drama script looks like…Need any help practicing your lines?"

"Yeah, if you're offering."

"Let's do it."

We sat down together and read through the scenes featuring my character. Seri gave it her best effort, altering her voice and actions for each character she portrayed.

"You're much better at this than Yang Bora," I commented.

"Who's she?"

"An intern at KAM. She's kind of like my manager now."

"Oh, I see."

After several run-throughs, Mrs. Soo brought in a tray of freshly made rolls of *gimbap*. "Have something to eat," she urged. "You can't work well on an empty stomach."

"Thanks, *Eomma*," Seri said.

"Thank you," I echoed, helping myself to one of the rolls.

We were about to get back to work when my phone buzzed. My heart skipped a beat at Jinseung's name. I opened the message.

Jinseung: Want a ride back to Seoul tomorrow?

I started to type a reply then promptly deleted it.

"Who are you texting?" Seri asked.

"No one." I shielded my phone screen from her.

"It's Shin Jinseung, isn't it? Gimme." She grabbed my phone and read the message. "Are you going to go?" she asked.

"I haven't decided yet."

"Won't you need to film these scenes soon? You'll need to go back to Seoul."

"Yes, but I was hoping to spend a few more days here first." I stroked my chin in thought. "Then again, it would be very convenient to have a ride home…"

"And a convenient excuse to be alone with Shin Jinseung."

I rolled my eyes. "I'm still mad at him, remember?"

"Just go with him. I know you want to."

"Are you that desperate to get rid of me?"

"You know I'm not. But let's face it, there's not much to do here. It's too boring to stay for more than a few days. Besides, I'll definitely be heading to Seoul soon as well. We'll see each other again."

I sighed. "I guess you're right. Then should I just tell him I'll go with him?"

"Of course."

I can't stay mad at him forever, I decided. I replied to his message, agreeing to the ride.

Jinseung replied almost instantly:

Jinseung: I'll pick you up tomorrow afternoon 😁

* * *

THE NEXT MORNING, I walked Snow along the coastline one last time. I took my time absorbing the sights and sounds, as if trying to imprint the city in my mind. *Goodbye, Tongyeong. I hope to see you again soon.*

When I got back to the house, I started to pack my things. I hadn't brought much with me, so it didn't take long.

I ate lunch with my host family, then we said our goodbyes.

"If things don't work out in Seoul, you're always welcome here, and you can stay as long as you need to," Mrs. Soo said.

"Thanks. I appreciate that," I said.

Right on cue, Jinseung's car rumbled up the driveway.

"He's here," I said, looking out the window.

"Have a nice drive back," Mr. Han said.

I hugged the family members one more time before leaving.

Jinseung came out of the car, wearing a white t-shirt, blue jeans, and a cap on his head.

"Are you ready?" he asked.

"Yes," I replied.

"Let's go."

He took my bag from me and hurled it into the boot of his black SUV.

I said few words as I got seated in the car, Jinseung's comment from the other day still heavy on my mind.

"Are you still mad at me?" Jinseung asked, picking up on my icy demeanour.

I shook my head.

"So you admit you *were* mad at me."

"I wasn't—" I sighed, unwilling to start an argument. "I'm sorry."

"It's okay."

"Thanks for offering me a ride back."

"No problem. We're going to the same place anyway. It would have been rude not to offer." He reached his arm behind my seat and turned his head to look out the rear window as he reversed. I bit my lip, admiring the tantalising curvature of his bicep until he snapped away to put the car into drive.

"Let's put some music on. What do you like to listen to?" he asked.

"K-pop," I answered. "Astro, Got7, B1A4."

He sighed. "Not that."

"BtoB? ShiNEE?"

"I'll put something else on." He scrolled through the tracks on the LCD screen on the dashboard.

I crossed my arms. "Why even bother asking my opinion?"

"I thought you might have good taste in music," he chided. "Ah, let's listen to this." He turned the volume dial up and Korean rap music started to blast out.

"Agghh! My ears." I covered them in mock horror.

"Would you rather sit in silence?"

"Yes."

"Okay. That's all right with me. Silence it is." He turned the music off, much to my relief.

Before long, we were out of Tongyeong and cruising along the highway. I felt comfortable in the car with Jinseung driving. He handled his car with ease, steering smoothly and paying attention to the road.

"You're a good driver," I commented.

"*Aigoo*. You know how to stroke a man's ego. To be honest, I'm used to Changsoo *Hyung* driving me everywhere. I rarely go on outings by myself—or with a passenger. It's nice to go for a drive. I've missed it."

"Sorry I made you turn the music off before…You can put it back on again if you like."

"It's okay. It gives me a headache after a while anyway."

Partway through the journey, I let out a large yawn.

"Are you tired?" Jinseung asked.

"Long car rides always make me feel drowsy."

"You can have a nap if you want."

I snorted at the idea, but eventually I let my head flop against the window, and the rhythmic vibrations of the car began to lull me. *Maybe a nap isn't such a bad idea.* I reached under the seat, wondering how to recline it.

"What are you doing?" Jinseung asked.

"How do I recline the seat?"

"Going to have a nap after all?"

"Yes."

"There's a lever at the side."

"Ah. Found it." I adjusted the seat into a comfy position, lay my head down, and soon enough I drifted off.

Bizarre dreams played in my head, punctuated by moments of waking in confusion whenever the car hit a bump.

The next time I woke up, the car had stopped. Jinseung hovered over me, so close I could feel his breath on my cheek.

"Am I still dreaming?" I asked.

"No," he replied.

"What are you doing?"

"Wiping your drool off the seat."

"I don't drool!"

"Oh yes you do!" He dabbed at the seat and my mouth with a tissue. "There."

"I didn't drool," I said again, pouting.

"I have photographic evidence, you know."

I gasped. "You didn't!"

"Look." He thrust his phone in front of me, a photo of my sleeping form on the screen. I had a stupid look on my face, and yes, a tiny bit of dribble trailed from the corner of my mouth.

"Delete that!"

Jinseung snatched the phone away from me. "No. It's cute. Should I make it my screensaver?"

"Don't!"

"Then I'll make it your photo on your contact." He tapped away on his screen. "Done."

"You're so mean."

"I'll delete it if you let me take another photo of you…"

"Forget it."

"Come on."

I sighed, exasperated. "All right then. But you have to let me check if it looks good."

"Okay." He aimed his lens at me, and I posed with a V sign next to my face.

"Gimme," I said, after he had taken the photo.

He passed me his phone and I checked the image. "That's better. You can keep that one and delete that sleeping one."

He did so, and made the other picture my contact photo, a pleased grin on his face.

For the first time since waking up, I looked around, taking in our surroundings. We appeared to be in an underground carpark.

"Where are we?" I asked.

"In the carpark of my apartment building," Jinseung said.

"We're here already? You didn't take me home."

"I don't pay much attention when Bong Changsoo is driving, so I don't know the exact address of your place. I didn't want to wake you up to ask. You looked so peaceful."

"Oh, I see. Well, I'm awake now, so will you be able to drop me at my place?" My stomach growled with hunger and I clutched it in embarrassment. "On second thought, do you happen to have any food in your apartment? I'm starving."

"Even if I did, I can't let you in my apartment."

"Why not?"

"I never take girls up to my apartment."

"Never?"

"Well, I try not to make a habit of it. The other residents will gossip, and I don't want to get a reputation."

I sighed dramatically. "Fine. Just take me home then."

Jinseung started the car and drove to the carpark exit. The gate slowly rolled open. It poured with rain outside.

"Huh? What's going on here?" Jinseung asked.

A truck blocked the street. Jinseung honked his horn, but then realised there was no driver in the truck.

"Fantastic," he said. "We're stuck."

Chapter 28

"Under no circumstances will I let you stay the night in my apartment," Jinseung said. "Understood?"

"Under—wait, what?" I paused, confused. "Who said anything about staying the night? I wasn't even thinking about that."

"Uh…Just trying to cover my bases. You can come in and have something to eat. That's it. And if the truck still hasn't moved after that, you can take a taxi home."

"Okay."

I followed Jinseung to the elevator, where he swiped a key card and punched the button for the 20th floor. Standing side by side, alone together in tight proximity made my skin prickle and my heart speed up. *He's actually taking me up to his apartment. Reluctantly, but still…*

The elevator stopped at the ground floor. Jinseung instantly pulled away from me before the door opened.

A man entered and pushed the button for the sixth floor. He didn't so much as glance at us, but Jinseung didn't speak or look at me while he was there.

When the man exited, Jinseung visibly relaxed, his posture drooping.

"Pretending not to know me?" I asked.

"I have to be careful," he explained.

We arrived at the 20th floor. Jinseung led me to his apartment door, entered the code, and let me inside.

I took off my shoes and looked around. The apartment was large, but by no means extravagant. A small entranceway led through to an open-plan lounge, kitchen, and dining area decked out with high-end furniture and appliances.

Framed art and photographs hung on the walls, and house plants added a splash of greenery to the decor. Floor-to-ceiling windows provided an expansive view of metropolitan Seoul.

"Nice place," I said, wandering around and taking everything in.

"Thanks," Jinseung said.

I peeked through an open door into another room where a king-size bed dominated the floorspace, and dark walls gave a masculine vibe.

"That's my bedroom," Jinseung said from behind me with an unamused tone.

"*Omo!* Sorry. I was being nosy." I averted my gaze from the room and followed him to the kitchen.

I sat down on a bar stool at the bench while he inspected the fridge and cupboards, which appeared to be empty.

"*Aigoo…*" Jinseung said, scratching his head.

Eventually he located a lone packet of *ramyeon*.

"Is this all right?" he asked.

"Yes. I like *ramyeon*."

"I would have cooked you something proper, but I don't have any ingredients."

"You can cook?"

"Well, more or less. What about you?"

"Yes, I can. I don't know how to cook Korean food, though."

"What can you cook?"

"I can cook a roast meal."

"Ah, very British. I'd like to try that some time."

"I can make it for you if you like."

Jinseung smirked. "I might take you up on that one time."

He put a pot on the stove. While waiting for the water to boil he grabbed a beer from the fridge.

"Would you like something to drink?" he asked.

"Yes please. I'll have a beer too, if there's another one."

He opened two bottles of beer and passed one to me. I took a swig and let out a groan of satisfaction. I probably got dehydrated during the car trip. I gulped down more of the drink.

"Take it easy," Jinseung teased.

Right on cue, I launched into a coughing fit. Jinseung spun me around and patted my back until I stopped.

"Glass of water?" he offered.

"Yes please," I rasped.

The glass of water calmed my angry throat, but then my stomach started making rumbling noises from hunger. I blushed with embarrassment.

"The *ramyeon* won't take long to cook," Jinseung said.

"*Aigoo.*"

"You're cute when you make that face."

"There it is again."

"What?"

"Cute," I mimicked.

"Can't I say that?"

"I can't tell whether you mean it or if you're making fun of me."

"It's a bit of both," Jinseung said, grinning.

I scrunched up my face in frustration.

"That's not so cute," he chided.

"Whatever." I stuck my tongue out at him.

Jinseung added the dry cake of noodles into the boiling water, then rummaged in the fridge again.

"I wonder if these are still okay?" He sniffed at a bunch of green onions and an open packet of mushrooms. "I think they're fine…"

He chopped them up and added them to the pot along with a couple of eggs.

He brought the steaming pot to the table, then ladled the noodles and bright red broth into large bowls. My mouth watered. I grabbed my chopsticks and ate with fierce hunger.

Jinseung watched me in amusement. "You look like you're enjoying that."

"It's good," I said, mouth half full.

"I'm glad."

When I finished eating, it hit me that Jinseung would make me leave soon. The rain continued to pour—even more heavily now. I wished I could stay longer—at least until the rain let up.

Jinseung ate his noodles slowly.

"It's still raining…" I said, head tilted towards the window.

"Yes. It is."

I sighed. "I guess I should order a taxi now."

He didn't say anything or even react.

It seems he really does want me to leave now. I retrieved my phone from my pocket and pulled up the taxi app. "What's the address of this building?"

"It's…" Jinseung put his chopsticks down. "Wait."

"Hmmm?"

"Since you're here now, do you want to hang out a bit longer? I mean, it doesn't really make a difference whether you leave now or in a couple of hours."

"Well, if it's okay with you…"

"It's okay."

"As long as I don't stay the night?"

"Right." He coughed slightly.

I couldn't contain my smile. *He wants me to stay after all.*

"I'll take these." I cleared our bowls and the pot, taking them to the kitchen. Jinseung followed me to help.

"So…Do you want to watch a movie or something?" he asked while washing the pot.

I pictured us snuggled on the couch watching a romantic scene on the television. My face grew hot from the mental image.

"What do you think?" he asked again.

"Uh, okay then," I stammered.

"What kind of movies do you like?"

"I like anything that's not too scary or violent."

"Hmmm…" He stroked his chin. "What's the most scary and violent film I own?"

"Very funny."

Dishes cleaned, dried, and put away, we relocated to the lounge area. Jinseung sat down on the couch. I hesitated, wondering if I should sit next to him, or on one of the other chairs, but he made the decision for me, patting the space next to him. I awkwardly took the spot.

Jinseung scrolled through a selection of movies on the screen. We eventually settled on the romantic fantasy film, Midnight in Paris— one of my favourites.

As the opening credits began, I became hyperaware of Jinseung next to me. I could hear him breathe, feel him adjust his position. I tried to concentrate on the movie.

Shortly into the film, I felt Jinseung's eyes on me. When I looked at him, he averted his gaze, but a few minutes later, I could tell he was staring at me again.

I turned to him and caught his eyes. He didn't look away this time, and neither did I. He chewed his lip in thought as his eyes searched me. My heart pounded on overdrive. He tentatively leaned closer.

Chapter 29

My gaze trailed down to Jinseung's lips, which were parted enticingly. Every muscle in me tensed. He moved closer still. I had no doubt about it now—he was about to kiss me. I closed my eyes. Oh so gently, Jinseung's lips brushed against mine.

The sound of the doorbell pierced the air, and I jumped in shock. Jinseung grimaced.

"Who is that?" He paused the movie and got up to view the intercom screen. "Oh? Changsoo *Hyung.*"

He opened the door and Changsoo entered balancing several food containers in his arms.

"*Hyung*, what brings you here?"

"Didn't you get my message? I thought I'd bring you some food seeing as you just got back and probably don't have anything to eat."

"I've already eaten."

"Eat some more." His eyes met mine, and a look of shock washed over his face. "*Omo*—Actor Chloe…Why are you here?" He looked at me, then Jinseung, then at me again, eyes narrowed.

"I gave her a ride back from Tongyeong," Jinseung explained, casually. "Now we're just hanging out, watching a movie."

"But you never bring women up here..."

"I don't see her that way. She's my colleague, my friend. Can't I bring her here?"

"Hmmm...I suppose so." He didn't look entirely convinced. "What are you watching?"

"Midnight in Paris."

"I love this movie!"

Changsoo put the food containers on the coffee table and plopped himself down next to me on the couch. "You're not very far through. Mind if I watch it too?" He didn't wait for Jinseung's reply, grabbing the remote to resume the movie.

With gritted teeth, Jinseung sat down on another chair.

Changsoo helped himself to the food he brought over, eating noisily while watching the movie. Meanwhile, Jinseung and I exchanged exasperated glances.

If Changsoo hadn't arrived when he did, what would have happened? This thought kept playing through my mind, distracting me from the movie.

As soon as the movie ended, Changsoo announced he would be on his way. "Do you need a ride home, Chloe?" he asked.

"Uh, yes please," I replied.

I couldn't turn his offer down, it would only increase his suspicion, and I didn't want to get Jinseung into trouble.

I said goodbye to Jinseung and followed Changsoo down to the carpark. I hopped into the passenger seat of his rundown car. Changsoo didn't start the engine straight away. Instead, he turned to me and his cheerful demeanour rapidly dissolved, replaced by a side of him I'd never seen before.

"Don't get involved with him, Chloe," he said sternly. "It will only end in tears."

Chapter 30

I replayed our brief kiss over and over again in my head while I lay in bed, allowing myself to fantasise about what would have happened if we hadn't been interrupted. Eventually my fantasies blurred into dreams.

When I woke up in the morning I reached for my phone, hoping to see a message from Jinseung. As I had wished, a new message awaited me, but my heart dropped as soon as I opened it.

Jinseung: I'm sorry about what happened. The kiss was a mistake.

* * *

I DIDN'T MAKE eye contact or say hello to Jinseung when I got in the van. I sat silently in the back seat, arms folded tightly across my chest, seething with fury.

"You're awfully quiet," Bora said. "Everything okay?"

"I'm fine, thank you," I said curtly.

Bora let out a loud sneeze.

"Are *you* okay?" I asked.

"I think I'm coming down with something."

"That's no good."

"You shouldn't be working today," Changsoo said.

"I'm sure I'll be fine," Bora said, right before another sneeze.

I could feel Jinseung's eyes on me the entire car trip, but I ignored him.

Bora interrogated me as soon as we were alone in my dressing room. "Are you mad at Actor Shin or something?" she asked.

"It's…nothing," I said.

She opened her mouth to question me further but started sneezing again.

Jinseung appeared at the door, bearing a box of tissues. "Want one?"

"Oh! Yes, please."

He passed her the box. "Do you mind if I speak with Chloe alone for a minute?"

"Uh…sure." She hesitantly left the room.

"What do you want?" I snapped.

"I can't stand this," Jinseung said in a tone which made it seem like I was the bad guy.

"What? How were you expecting I'd react?"

"I thought you'd be a little more understanding of the situation."

"I was so happy when you kissed me…and then you take it all back. How can I be understanding of that? Was it really a mistake?"

"Yes—I mean, no—I mean…I don't know."

"Did you mean it or not?"

Jinseung's demeanour softened. "I really care about you, Chloe."

I paused, feeling my heart stir with the sincerity of his words. *No. I can't let him off the hook so easily.* "That doesn't answer the question. Was the kiss a mistake?"

He rubbed his neck. "Perhaps I didn't word it so well. What I meant was, I wanted to kiss you, but I probably shouldn't have done it. At least, not yet. I acted rashly in the heat of the moment. I didn't think things through."

I considered his explanation since he sounded so earnest.

"There's a lot I have to think about. Give me some time." He looked at me with pleading eyes.

My anger slowly melted away. "...Okay."

He pulled me into a hug. "I shouldn't have sent you that message. I'm sorry. Can you forgive me?"

"...Yes. I forgive you."

Chapter 31

I hummed a song absentmindedly, walking across the house to the bedroom. I pushed open the door. That's when I saw it.

I dropped my bag to the floor with a heavy thud, a deafening scream escaping my lungs.

There on the bed, a dead dog, lying on blankets stained crimson with its blood.

I hyperventilated, back against the wall, unable to tear my eyes from the gruesome scene.

"Cut," Nara said. "Thank you. That's all the shots we need."

Slowly, my breathing returned to normal, and I morphed from Louise back to Chloe.

"Bravo!" Jinseung made his way past the crew surrounding me, clapping and cheering. "That was great. Your acting skills have come a long way."

"Thanks," I said, my voice hoarse from all the screaming.

Jinseung stared at the model dog, grimacing. "*Aigoo*, that looks so realistic. It's creepy."

I looked around. "Where's Intern?"

"She wasn't feeling well. I made Changsoo *Hyung* take her home."

"Ah. She did seem sick."

"Since *Hyung* isn't back yet, I guess you'll have to keep me company instead."

I smirked. "Will I just?"

"I left something in my dressing room. Come on, let's go." Before I could protest, he tugged me away from the set and towards the dressing rooms.

Once safely inside his room, he closed the door firmly behind us. I wondered whether he really needed to get something or if he just wanted to get me alone for some reason. Changsoo's warning replayed in my head. "Don't get involved with him, Chloe." Plus, I still hadn't fully forgiven him for telling me the kiss was a mistake.

"Perhaps I should go," I said. "I don't have anything else to shoot today. There's no point in sticking around."

"Stay, please?" He pouted. "It's too boring waiting around by myself."

Damn him and his cuteness. I can't resist that face. "What was it you left here?" I asked.

"Huh? Oh, these." He grabbed a pair of handcuffs off the table.

"Handcuffs? Is that what you need?"

"I have to arrest someone in my next scene." He snapped one of the cuffs closed around his wrist.

"What are you doing?" I asked, laughing. "I hope you can get that off."

Before I could react, Jinseung snapped the other handcuff on my wrist, linking us together.

"Now there's no escape!" he said. "Muahahaha…"

"Arrggh. What have you done?"

I tried to manoeuvre my wrist out of the handcuff, but it was too tight. We were well and truly stuck together.

Jinseung tugged me by the wrist, causing me to stumble. I half shrieked, half laughed.

We continued to mess around, stumbling up and down the room. When Jinseung flopped down on the couch I came tumbling on top of him, right into his lap. "*Omo…*"

Jinseung made no effort to wriggle away. Instead, his lips slowly curled into a wide grin. "No wonder I kissed you. You're so hard to resist…"

I turned my head away. "I won't let you make another mistake."

A loud knock sent us scrambling up from the couch.

"Shin Jinseung, please report to set," an assistant said.

Jinseung sighed. "I guess they're ready for me now. I should go."

"What about the handcuffs?" I asked.

"Hmmm…I wonder how to get them off."

"You don't know how?!"

"I don't have a key. I wonder if there's a button or something." He felt around the cuff.

I also tried to work out a way to open the handcuffs, but my attempts were futile.

At last, Jinseung admitted defeat. "We'll have to go to wardrobe and ask how to get them off."

"Oh, great," I said, dreading the impending walk of shame.

Sure enough, crew members threw us odd stares and chuckles as we made our way up the corridor to the wardrobe area.

The wardrobe *ajumma* looked at us with her eyebrow raised.

"We're stuck in these," Jinseung said.

"I can see that. How did—never mind. I'd rather not know. There should be a spare set of keys around here somewhere…" She rummaged in a drawer and fished out a pair of tiny metal keys. "Ah, here we are."

Jinseung eagerly accepted the keys, but before we could free ourselves, someone spotted us.

Baek Yena stopped in the doorway. She burst out laughing at our predicament. "If you want to play with handcuffs, they have pink fluffy ones designed for that."

I blushed furiously as Jinseung released me.

Chapter 32

"I can't believe you managed to talk me into this," I lamented.

Bora stood outside the door to my apartment armed with beer and snacks.

"You'll thank me later," she said, removing her shoes and coming inside.

I hadn't planned on watching Hidden History. The very idea of seeing myself on-screen made me cringe with embarrassment. Yet here we were, about to watch the first episode as it aired.

We made ourselves comfortable on the couch. Bora pulled her laptop out of its sleeve.

"Why did you bring your laptop?" I asked.

"To monitor people's reactions online, of course," she replied.

"Ohhhh."

She fired up her laptop and brought up a dashboard of various stats and charts on the screen.

"The search term 'Hidden History' is already trending," she said.

I peered at the screen in bemusement. "Did you set all this up yourself?"

"Yep."

"That's cool."

Bora shrugged. "It's all part of the job. I've got to keep tabs on these things."

As the previous show started to wrap up, I grew increasingly jittery. Teasers for Hidden History played in the ad breaks.

"I'm so excited," Bora squealed.

Meanwhile, I felt like I was going to throw up. *My acting's terrible, I know it is. How can I watch this?*

"You look like you're about to faint," Bora said. "I'm sure it will be fine."

Her words did nothing to reassure me.

The episode began. I watched through squinting eyes, ready to squeeze them closed as soon as I appeared.

Jinseung and Yena lit up the screen as Officer Park and Detective Jung investigating a murder, but I couldn't fully focus being so apprehensive about seeing my scenes. I couldn't even follow the storyline despite my familiarity with the script.

During the ad breaks, Bora opened her laptop and refreshed her dashboard, looking for updated stats and comments. "People seem positive so far," she said. "Lots of Jinseung's fans are watching."

I glanced at the stream of comments coming in through the feed.

"Shin Jinseung is so hot!"

"*Saranghae* Jinseungie! Fighting!"

"🤍 Shin Jinseung 🤍"

While reading the comments, I didn't realise the ad break had already ended. I returned my attention to the television.

We reached the halfway point in the episode and I still hadn't appeared.

"When is your scene going to play?" Bora asked.

I shrugged. "Maybe I was so bad they cut the scene?"

"Don't be silly—" She gasped. "There you are!"

The bar scene played. I held my breath the entire time, waiting for my poor acting skills to be exposed. But it never happened. The scene had been cut in a way that disguised my errors. Eventually the butterflies in my stomach dissipated. Before I knew it, it was over.

"You were so good," Bora said, clapping.

"It wasn't as bad as I thought it would be," I admitted.

"It wasn't bad at all! You're way too hard on yourself."

With my first scene out of the way, I allowed myself to relax and enjoy the rest of the episode.

"Our Jinseungie is so good-looking in police uniform," Bora mused, crunching into a *tteokbokki*-flavoured snack.

"He sure is…" I agreed, thoughts turning to our recent handcuff escapade in the dressing room.

"What are you smiling about?" Bora asked.

"Oh, nothing!" I snapped out of my daydream.

My next scene came up sooner than I expected and I momentarily cringed, but like before, I eased into it, realising it wasn't so bad.

It felt strange to watch myself with Jinseung. The way he looked at me, or rather, the way that Officer Park looked at Louise, made me blush.

"Your chemistry with Jinseung is amazing!" Bora gushed.

"You think so?"

"Definitely. I'm so glad that writer-nim decided to include a loveline."

"I wonder what the viewers will think…"

"We don't have to wonder." Bora brought up her dashboard again and scanned through the comments. "Hmmm…not much to go off yet, but people are searching 'Hidden History Louise'. They must be curious about you."

After a few more scenes, a cliffhanger marked the conclusion of the episode. An immense sense of relief washed over me as the credits rolled. I wasn't terrible. I hadn't made a complete fool of myself with my attempt at acting. Everything was okay.

"There. That wasn't so bad, was it?" Bora said.

"I shouldn't have gotten myself so worked up," I admitted.

I walked to the kitchen and unplugged my phone from its charger. The screen turned on, and I nearly dropped it in astonishment.

"What the…?"

Notification pop-ups filled the lockscreen. I swiped my thumb to unlock it and scrolled through a long notification list of friend requests, new followers, and private messages.

"What's wrong?" Bora asked when I returned to the lounge.

"I've got so many new followers on social media all of a sudden."

"That's to be expected. People were looking you up during the episode."

"What should I do?"

Bora stroked her chin in thought. "Don't respond to anyone right now. There are loads of staff at KAM who help with the actors' social media accounts. I think someone will be able to help you."

I nodded. "Good idea."

"Come to KAM tomorrow and I'll sort you out."

* * *

ON MY WAY to the KAM headquarters the next morning, something strange happened.

I left the subway at Gangnam station and walked along the street minding my own business when a stranger approached me from out of the blue.

"Are you Louise?" the woman asked.

My first instinct was to say no, then I realised she meant my character in Hidden History.

"Yes," I said. "I play Louise."

"Can I take a photo?"

"Sure."

She quickly snapped a shot, thanked me, and walked away grinning.

*That was weird...*I continued on my way, bemused by the experience. I didn't imagine I'd get recognised just from a couple short scenes in the first episode. It was both exciting and unnerving.

When I arrived at KAM, the atmosphere in Jinseung's management office buzzed.

"Overnight ratings are in," a male staff member said. "Hidden History picked up 9.5."

"What does that mean?" I asked.

"It's doing well."

"That's good news!"

Bora waved me over to her computer.

"Check this out," she said.

She loaded a webpage titled "Chloe Gibson Fans."

"*Omo*. What's this?"

"A fan page."

"I have a fan page?"

"Pretty cool, huh?"

The poorly made website featured screenshots of me from the first episode of Hidden History paired with a few other photos of me scraped together from various sources.

"That's kind of cool…kinda creepy too," I said.

"Right?"

After we'd had our fix of the strange website, Bora suggested we head to the PR department to get their intern to help me with my social media. We were about to leave when Changsoo and Jinseung entered the office.

"I didn't expect to see you here," Bora said. "Aren't you supposed to be at an audition?"

"We're heading there shortly," Changsoo said.

"Audition?" I asked.

Jinseung nodded. "I'm up for the lead role in a romantic comedy called Love Apprentice."

"That's fantastic!"

"PD Song has Jinseung specifically in mind," Changsoo explained. "His heartthrob image and young female fanbase makes him a perfect fit for the role. The audition is just a formality. He practically has it in the bag already."

"Don't mess it up by being late!" Bora reprimanded.

Changsoo checked his watch, before running to his desk and grabbing a few bits and pieces. "Right. That's everything. We're leaving now."

"Good luck!" I said.

Chapter 33

I *can't live in this prison cell*, I thought, examining the tiny bedroom. Dust particles floated in the sliver of dull light cast through the dirty window. A single bed took up most of the floorspace, and although my arms weren't long, when I extended them, I could easily touch the opposite sides of the wall.

"Rent is 800,000 won per month," the property manager said.

"800,000 won?" I repeated in disbelief.

"You won't find better value in this part of town."

I sighed. "No. I suppose not."

Maybe it wouldn't be so bad. It would be a temporary situation, after all. Once I had secured a teaching job, the school would provide me with an apartment.

A rhythmic banging noise started up and the paper-thin walls vibrated.

"What's that sound?" I asked.

The property manager's face turned red and he rubbed the back of his neck nervously. "I'm not sure. It's usually very quiet, I assure you. Anyway, that's all there is to see." He hurriedly ushered me away from the room. "So…are you interested?"

"Hmmm…I'm going to have to say no."

"Okay. Well, if you change your mind, you know how to contact me."

I left the building, dejected. Another failed apartment inspection to add to my list. At this rate, I'd be homeless when I needed to move out of my current place. *Maybe I have to lower my expectations. Maybe I'll have to move out of Seoul.* The prospect of leaving Seoul saddened me, or more accurately, the prospect of leaving Shin Jinseung.

On board the subway home, I checked my phone. A notification of a new email popped up on the screen and I absentmindedly tapped it open. My heart sped up when I saw it was about one of the teaching positions I had applied for. I quickly scanned the message and one sentence jumped out at me. *Unfortunately, you have not made it through to the next round of the application process.*

Disheartened, I slid down in my seat and stuffed my phone back in my bag. The rejection was upsetting but not surprising. Hiring season wasn't for a few more months. Jobs were limited and competition was fierce, particularly for jobs in Seoul. The little voice in my head repeated my previous thought. *Maybe I'll have to move out of Seoul...*

Hidden History would wrap up soon. Even if I managed to get a job in Seoul, my life would change dramatically. Jinseung and I would be on completely different paths. I might not even get to see him again. And even if by some miracle he decided to risk his career to date me, we wouldn't be able to spend much time together.

Negative thoughts plagued me as I walked home from the station, home to my apartment I would soon be kicked out from.

Crossing the lobby to the elevator, a familiar face stopped me in my tracks. I rubbed my eyes. *Seri?* She sat on a chair by the post boxes, hunched over with her eyes glued to her phone screen.

"Seri-ya," I said.

She lifted her head at the sound of my voice. Her face brightened.

"*Unnie!*" she cried.

I stared at her in confusion. "What are you doing here?"

"I was just trying to call you. I recently arrived in Seoul and thought I would stop by."

"It's good to see you again."

Her face contorted into a look of concern. "Are you okay? You look totally worn out."

"It's a long story."

* * *

IN A SMALL *JAJANGMYEON* restaurant decorated with hanging red lanterns, I relayed my various dilemmas to Seri. She listened intently while slurping her noodles.

"You're in a tough situation," she said. "If only Jinseung could be more clear about his feelings for you."

"I feel like I can't move on with my life until I know what he's thinking. Do I have a chance with him or not?"

"Maybe dating a celebrity isn't such a good idea anyway. Think about it. You'd have to deal with jealous fans, relentless media scrutiny, and being in the public eye, not to mention the resentment he might feel if it negatively impacted his career."

"I know all that…and yet, I still think it would be worth it. Am I crazy?"

"No. It's Shin Jinseung after all. I don't blame you."

I rested my head in my hands. "*Aigoo*. He's constantly on my mind these days. I don't know what to do."

"I know what to do."

"What?"

"Let's get drunk."

I couldn't help but laugh. "That's your solution to everything."

Seri ordered a bottle of soju. She poured the clear liquid into shot glasses.

"Cheers," we said, clinking glasses.

I downed my shot. "Ahhhh…I feel a bit better already."

"See. Told you."

We continued to drink, the strong alcohol numbing my incessant thoughts. When we finished our first bottle, Seri ordered another. It didn't take long to polish that off either, and before I knew it, Seri had ordered a third bottle. By our fourth bottle, I was well and truly inebriated.

"You know what?" Seri slurred. "You should just ask him. Ask him straight up whether he wants to date or not."

"I can't do that!" I said. "If I put pressure on him, I'm sure he'll just say no."

Seri frowned. "Yeah…that could be true."

I let out a wistful sigh. "I wish I could see him right now. He lives in this area, you know."

"Hey! I've got an idea!"

"What is it?"

"Pass me your phone."

I unlocked my phone and handed it over. She started to tap at the screen with a conspiratorial look on her face.

"What are you doing?" I asked.

"Shhhh!" She pressed the phone to her ear, a mischievous smirk on her face.

"Who are you calling?"

She didn't answer me. And then, whoever she had called must have picked up.

"*Oppa!*" Seri said.

My face grew hot. "Is it Jinseung?"

Chapter 34

I tried to grab the phone away from Seri, but she evaded.

"It's Seri, Chloe's friend," she explained to Jinseung. "We're drunk!"

I tried to snatch the phone from her again, but she deflected me and I fell off my chair with a crash.

Seri continued her conversation while I gathered myself. "Look, we need a ride home, okay? We're too drunk. Chloe's practically passed out right now. I'm worried about her. Come soon, okay?… We're at Masitda Jajangmyeon restaurant…Okay, bye!" She hung up and passed my phone back to me. "He's on his way. You know what his car looks like, right? He'll call you when he's here."

"He's actually coming?"

"Of course!"

I fanned myself, suddenly dizzy. We went to the counter to settle the bill, but I was so drunk I couldn't even count my money.

"Don't worry," Seri said. "I'll pay."

"But I'm older than you," I spluttered.

Seri laughed. "You sound like a Korean." She paid the bill.

"Thanks."

"No problem. Have a good night, okay? Bye!"

"Bye—wait a minute! You're leaving?"

"I'm not going to be a third wheel."

"How are you getting back to your accommodation?"

"It's just down the road. Don't worry about me!"

"Wait, don't leave me!"

Seri ignored my plea. She smiled and waved before exiting the restaurant.

I slumped back down onto a seat to wait for Jinseung's call. Although I expected it, the sound of my ringtone still startled me. I picked up.

"I'm outside," Jinseung said.

"Coming!"

I hurried out the door and saw Jinseung's car waiting out front. I stumbled into the passenger seat. Jinseung stared at me with a mixture of concern and amusement.

"Are you okay?" he asked. "Where's Seri?"

"She left." I hiccupped and covered my mouth in embarrassment.

Jinseung studied me. "I've never seen you this drunk before." He pulled out into the flow of traffic.

"I'm sorry, *Oppa*."

"What for?"

"You didn't have to come get me. I tried to stop Seri from calling. Are you annoyed?"

"Not at all. I want to make sure you get home safe and sound. In fact, I'm glad she called me."

I broke out into a smile. "Really? You're so sweet!"

Jinseung smirked. "Am I?"

I nodded.

We approached an intersection.

"Now, how do I get to your place?" Jinseung asked.

I gave him directions as best as I could, but we did end up making a few wrong turns along the way.

Finally, we arrived outside my apartment building. That's when I reached for my bag and discovered with a sinking feeling that I didn't have it. I groaned.

"What's wrong?" Jinseung asked.

"My bag. I must have left it at the restaurant."

"Can you go back and get it tomorrow, or do you need it now?"

"My key card is in there. I won't be able to get into the building without it. Reception is closed at this time of night."

Jinseung sighed before making a U-turn and heading back in the direction of the restaurant.

"I'm sorry," I repeated.

When we arrived back at the restaurant, a closed sign hung on the door.

"Maybe you could knock. There must be staff still inside," Jinseung said.

My body swayed as I opened the car door and I nearly fell over on the road.

"Never mind. Stay in the car." He tugged me back inside before pulling out again.

"But my bag!" I wailed. "Where are we going?"

"My apartment."

"Oh! Your apartment is so nice."

"Uh, thanks."

A short drive later, we arrived in the underground carpark of Jinseung's apartment building.

"Wait there," Jinseung said, getting out of the car. He opened the door for me and let me lean on him like a crutch as I got out. He guided me to the elevator, his arm around my waist.

I looked around confused when we entered his apartment.

"Why are we at your apartment?" I asked, dazed.

"You can stay the night here, since you're locked out of your building."

I gasped. "But what about the rule? You can't break the rule!"

"What rule?"

"No staying the night. Remember?"

Jinseung sighed. "Under these circumstances, the rule doesn't apply."

"Ooooh…So we're spending the night together?"

"Uh, well, not—"

Suddenly, throwing myself at him seemed like a great idea. I flung my arms around him.

Jinseung gently peeled me away. "You're drunk."

I pouted. "You're no fun."

"Sit down. I'll get you a glass of water."

He settled me on the couch then brought over a large glass of water. "Drink up."

I gulped it down in no time flat, then lay my head down, yawning.

"Do you want to go to bed?" Jinseung asked.

I had never heard him say anything so erotic.

"Bed?" I repeated suggestively.

"Don't get any ideas. I'll sleep on the couch. You can sleep in the bedroom."

He opened the door to his room and ushered me through.

I marvelled at the space I had caught a glimpse of only briefly on my last visit. Dark wooden bedside tables, a desk, and a bed with a quilted headboard, grey linen, and black silk pillowcases furnished the classy room. A framed abstract art print hung on the wall.

Jinseung closed the window and pulled the curtains. "Sleep well, Chloe. Goodnight."

"Goodnight."

He left the room, closing the door behind him.

I crawled under the blanket fully clothed. His bed felt incredibly soft and warm, and it smelled just like him. I fell asleep quickly.

Later in the night, something strange happened. A noise jolted me awake and I saw the door open. *What's going on?*

Jinseung walked into the room and got into the bed next to me.

Chapter 35

Is this a dream? I wondered. *I like where this dream is going...*But as he got into the bed, I realised that it wasn't a dream.

"What are you doing?" I asked.

Jinseung grunted. His eyes were closed, and he didn't appear to be lucid. I shook him several times, but he was completely out to it. I gave up trying to wake him. *Maybe I should go sleep on the couch...*

I stared at Jinseung's sleeping form, transfixed. He was only half covered by the blanket. He wore nothing but a thin grey t-shirt and black, form-fitting boxer shorts. My eyes trailed down his enticing figure. *He won't notice if I just cuddle up to him for a bit.* I cautiously edged closer, but at the slightest movement, Jinseung turned over with a groan and draped his arm across me. *This is nice...*I let him hold me in his sleep and soon enough I drifted back to sleep as well.

I didn't wake again until the sound of a blaring alarm in the morning. My head pounded and my throat was dry. "Ow, my head," I murmured.

"*Omo!*" Jinseung jumped out of bed, then realising he was just in his boxers and t-shirt, shielded his crotch with a pillow. "How did I get here?" he asked groggily.

"You walked in during the night. You must have been half asleep."

"Ugh. I must have instinctively walked back to my room after getting up to use the bathroom. I'm sorry…But why didn't you wake me up?"

"You sleep like a log. I tried to wake you up, but I couldn't, and I was too tired and drunk to get up."

Jinseung ran a hand through his hair. "I didn't do anything…weird, did I?"

"No." *Apart from putting your arm around me...*

He exhaled a relieved sigh.

"What time is it?" I asked.

"Five o'clock. I need to get ready for today's shoot."

I staggered out of bed. "I'll leave you to it."

"Help yourself to whatever's in the kitchen if you want something to eat or drink."

"Thanks."

I walked to the kitchen and halfway through pouring myself a glass of water, the intercom buzzed. I froze in panic. No one could know I was here.

Jinseung emerged from his room, flustered. "It must be Changsoo *Hyung*. Why is he so early? Quick, hide in the ensuite."

I hurried through the door on the left side of the bedroom, past a walk-in wardrobe, to the ensuite bathroom. I locked myself inside.

The bathroom was sparkling clean, and the bathtub and shower were huge and fancy-looking. A glass display cabinet housed a wide array of skincare products—bigger than my own collection. I supposed that as a celebrity, he must have to take good care of his appearance.

I examined myself in the mirror, grimacing. I hadn't removed my makeup the night before and its remnants were smeared all over my face. I splashed some water on my face and tried to clean it off.

I sat down on the toilet seat with a sigh. I recalled with embarrassment how I threw myself at Jinseung last night. I wondered if his opinion of me had gone down. My drunkenness couldn't have been at all attractive.

I waited several minutes, unsure whether Jinseung and Changsoo had left yet or not. When I pressed my ear against the door, I couldn't hear anything and decided it was safe to leave. I carefully opened the door and ventured through the wardrobe, back into the bedroom. Again, I pressed my ear to the door. Silence. Slowly, I turned the doorknob and peered through the crack into the living area. *They're gone.*

Alone in Jinseung's apartment, I made myself a coffee.

As much as I wanted to go back to bed, I couldn't risk it. What if someone else showed up at the apartment? A cleaner, or someone from work? Besides, I needed to get my bag back from the restaurant. Someone could be trying to contact me.

I set out, not one hundred percent sure of the exact location of the restaurant, but with enough wandering I found it. It was still closed, but I figured there must be staff inside preparing for breakfast. I knocked on the door.

An elderly lady answered after my second knock. "What can I do for you, *Agassi?*"

"I left my bag here last night," I explained.

"I see. Can you describe it?"

"It's a black leather crossbody with silver hardware."

"Oh! I think I have seen it. I'll go get it for you."

She disappeared then re-emerged holding the bag. "Is this it?"

"Yes! Thank you."

Once she had handed over the bag, I checked through it to see whether everything was still there. I relaxed when I discovered that nothing had been stolen. But my luck ended there. Jinseung called me later in the day with a shocking announcement.

I was in my apartment, scrolling through a job board on my laptop, when my phone started ringing. When I saw that it was Jinseung, a fresh wave of embarrassment washed over me, thinking about how I behaved in front of him last night. I nervously picked up the call. "*Yeoboseyo?*"

"Changsoo knows," Jinseung said, voice solemn.

"Huh? What does he know?"

"That you were in my apartment this morning."

"What?! But how?"

"In my rush, I forgot to hide your shoes. He must have seen them. We had a huge row. He thinks we're dating. I explained what really happened, but he didn't believe me."

"Oh no…What does this mean?"

"Well, he's not happy about it, but I managed to convince him not to tell Mr. Kim."

"That's a relief."

"He says we have to keep our relationship a secret."

"Perhaps we should stop seeing each other outside of work. I don't want to get you into any more trouble."

He reacted swiftly to my suggestion. "No."

"…No?"

"I want to keep seeing you. In fact, as soon as I have some time off, I want to meet up with you. There's something I want to tell you."

"Can't you tell me now?" I implored.

"No. This is something I want to say in person."

My pulse sped up. *Could it be?*

Chapter 36

've been stood up, I finally realised, sitting alone in the private room of a bar with two empty cocktail glasses in front of me.

My hopes had been so high for this meeting with Jinseung. I had spent the last few days fantasising, dreaming, praying, wishing, hoping that Jinseung would confess his feelings to me. But it had all been for nothing. *He's not even coming.*

I tried to call him, but it went straight to voicemail. I texted him again, but he didn't reply. *Did he forget? No, that can't be it...*

Ready to give up, I exhaled a deep sigh and peeled my eyes away from my phone, tucking it away in my bag. I slumped over, laying my forehead on the table in defeat.

"What are you doing?"

I shot up, startled.

Jinseung had arrived. He appeared windswept and flustered, colour in his cheeks.

"You're here," I croaked.

"I'm so sorry. I would be banging my head against the table too if I were you. I know it's no excuse, but I got held up. First, Changsoo decided to engage me in a lengthy conversation I couldn't get out of, and then, I got accosted by fans on the way here. And my phone is dead. You must have been trying to reach me."

My annoyance dissolved. Just seeing him again was enough to warm my heart and erase all my concerns. "It's all right. You're here now."

Jinseung sat down opposite me. "Thanks for waiting. I wouldn't have blamed you if you'd left already."

"I was about to."

"I'm glad you're still here. Can I buy you another drink?"

"Yes please. But better make it a mocktail." Getting drunk and making a fool of myself in front of him again was not on my agenda for the night.

He called over a staff member and ordered a beer for himself and a virgin raspberry mojito for me.

Drinks on their way, Jinseung leaned in across the table and ran his eyes over me. "You look very pretty tonight."

I blushed and pulled my hair back behind my ear. "Thanks. So do you."

Jinseung smirked. "I look pretty?"

"Cute, I mean. Handsome."

"...Sexy?"

"That too."

His smirk widened into a hearty grin. "So...I have some good news."

I raised an eyebrow. "What is it?"

"I found out this morning that I've been offered the lead role in Love Apprentice."

I gasped. "That's brilliant!"

"It's a pretty major step up in my career."

"Congratulations. I'm really happy for you."

"It still hasn't quite sunk in, to be honest."

"One day soon you'll be getting more offers than you can accept, I just know it."

"Thanks. I really hope so."

Our drinks arrived. I took a sip, the sweet, fruity mixture cooling my throat.

"Can I try some?" Jinseung asked.

"Sure." I pushed the glass towards him.

He sipped the drink. "Tastes like raspberry."

I rolled my eyes. "No kidding."

"Refreshing." He slid the glass back to me. "How are things with you, anyway? How's job hunting?"

I sighed. "Well, I hate to be a downer, but not so great. There's a lot of competition for positions in Seoul, and I've only managed to get one interview. It seemed promising, but I didn't end up getting the job. I'm starting to get worried. Soon, I'll have to move out of my apartment, and I don't know where I'm going to live or what I'll do."

"Can't you just stay on at your current place?"

"No. It's too expensive. I can only stay a few more weeks at most. It's funny, but I didn't actually make much money from being in Hidden History."

Jinseung crossed his arms in outrage. "That's not funny! KAM probably gave you terrible terms."

"I know. I didn't have time to go over the contract properly."

"KAM have treated me well over the years, but they'll still rip you off if they have the chance. Just like all the other entertainment companies."

"There's nothing I can do about it now."

"I suppose not, but maybe I can help you on the accommodation front. I own another apartment and it's going to be vacant soon. You could stay there for a while until you sort yourself out."

I considered Jinseung's offer, but it didn't feel right. "That's very generous, but it's too much for me to accept."

"Let me help you."

"I don't want to have to rely on anyone."

"Ah, I see. I can respect that. But if you change your mind, let me know."

"Thanks. Sorry for making you listen to me whine."

"Not at all. I want you to be able to share everything with me. The good and the bad."

I rubbed my fingers up and down the stem of my glass in thought. I couldn't wait any longer. The suspense was killing me. "*Oppa...*"

"Yes?"

"What was it that you wanted to tell me?"

Suddenly he was tongue-tied. "I...hmmm...I don't know how to say this properly."

"It's okay. Just say what's on your mind."

He scratched his head. "So, we kissed a while ago..."

"Yeah..."

"And I still wasn't quite sure if that was a mistake or not. I mean, I loved it, but—"

"I know. Things are complicated for you."

He nodded. "But I've been thinking it over and..."

"And?"

"I've made up my mind. After filming finishes, if it's okay with you, I want to keep on seeing you."

My heart did a somersault in my chest. "That's okay with me. More than okay."

"I'm feeling more open to the prospect of dating now. But let's take it slow. Let's wait until after Hidden History and things are more settled."

I nodded. "Let's take it slow."

Jinseung smiled. "I'm glad you agree."

So, he wasn't going to date me *yet*, but the fact he had warmed up to the idea was more than I ever expected. *It's only a matter of time*, I decided.

"Does this mean you like me?" I asked coyly.

Jinseung reached below the table and took my hand in his. The affectionate gesture made my heart pound.

"Yes, I like you," he said.

"Didn't you say you were over your high school crush?"

"I am over it, but now I have a new crush. This time I know you much better. I'm attracted to you in a completely different way. I really like you as a person."

I smiled, blushing. Jinseung grinned back.

"Do you like me?" he asked.

"Yes, I do."

"I'm so happy to hear that."

We spent the rest of the evening drinking, chatting, laughing. Time flew by and eventually we had to call it a night. We left through a private back exit into a quiet carpark. A single streetlamp shone down on us.

"When will I see you again?" I asked.

"I don't know. As soon as possible." He glanced around the carpark. Upon determining that we were completely alone, he pulled me into his arms and hugged me. I relaxed my head against his solid chest and breathed in his scent.

Just as we were breaking away, I thought I saw movement out of the corner of my eye. "What was that?"

"Huh?"

"I thought I saw something."

I looked around, but there was nothing there. "Never mind."

Jinseung squeezed my hand. "Goodnight, Chloe."

"Goodnight."

Chapter 37

Bora: How could you do this?

I had just woken up and reached for my phone, only to be confronted by this strange message. I rubbed my bleary eyes and read it again, confused. Unable to make sense of it, I texted her back.

Chloe: What are you talking about?

Bora: Don't play dumb.

Chloe: ???

I waited for Bora to respond, but in the meantime, I received a call from Changsoo.

"You need to come to headquarters and talk with Mr. Kim," he said, voice stern.

"Is something wrong?" I asked.

"Have you not seen the news?"

"What news?"

"I'll send you a link. Read it and report to Mr. Kim's office as soon as possible. Jinseung is already on his way."

Jinseung? Did this have something to do with him as well? A sense of panic unfurled in my stomach.

Changsoo hung up. I received a message from him shortly, containing a link to an entertainment news website. I opened it, hand shaking, wondering what I was about to see. The headline struck me first.

Shin Jinseung Dating Scandal? Exclusive Photos

My heart dropped from my chest to the pit of my stomach. I took a deep breath, bracing myself before I read the article.

Exclusive new photographs show actors Shin Jinseung and Chloe Gibson, co-stars in currently airing drama Hidden History, leaving a bar in Gangnam after a romantic date together.

The couple were caught on camera sharing a hug and holding hands outside the bar. Exclusive photos below.

Shin Jinseung and Chloe Gibson are both represented by KAM Entertainment. A statement has yet to be made on the status of their relationship.

I remembered our hug the night before and how I had seen movement nearby. There must have been someone there, hiding. I wondered whether a worker at the bar might have tipped off a reporter, then the reporter could have hidden and waited for us to leave, camera at the ready. *We should have been more careful.*

Several photographs accompanied the article. They showed Jinseung and I leaving the bar, talking with one another under the streetlamp, hugging, and Jinseung holding my hand. In the Korean entertainment world, this was very incriminating evidence of secret dating—a betrayal of the trust of thousands of possessive fans.

My stomach twisted with nerves as I made my way to KAM headquarters, wondering what Mr. Kim had in store for me and Jinseung. Would he ban us from dating each other? Ban us from even seeing each other? I had heard stories of such things before. My mind reeled with endless horrible possibilities.

When I arrived at Mr. Kim's office, Jinseung and Changsoo were already there sitting on the couch with heavy expressions on their faces. Mr. Kim looked grave, a stark contrast to his usual chirpy persona.

"You're here," he said.

His serious tone sent a wave of fear through me.

"I got here as fast as I could, Mr. Kim," I stammered.

"Do you understand the current situation?"

I nodded.

"While neither of your contracts stipulate no dating, it has always been made clear that relationships should only be pursued with utmost discretion. We cannot tolerate this kind of public behaviour. It may be good publicity for Hidden History, but it's not good for the development of Jinseung's career at this crucial juncture."

"I understand."

"I have already heard Jinseung's explanation for those photographs, but I'd like to hear your side of the story."

Jinseung eyed me nervously, his face pale. I had to be careful with my words for his sake. "Jinseung and I have become close friends. We met up for a few drinks, that's all."

"And the hug? The hand holding?"

"Where I'm from, those things aren't a big deal. Friends hug and hold hands all the time. It doesn't mean anything."

Mr. Kim thought this through for a moment then visibly eased, his posture slackening. "I believe you. But in Korea, people will get the wrong idea. You're a foreigner and you don't understand how things are done around here, so I'll let you off the hook this time."

"Thank you, Mr. Kim."

"But this cannot happen again in future."

"Yes, Mr. Kim."

He turned to Changsoo. "Manager Bong, get your team to prepare a press release explaining that Chloe and Jinseung are friends, nothing more."

Changsoo nodded and made a note in his diary.

Mr. Kim continued, eyes on me and Jinseung. "From now on, you two are strictly not allowed to see each other outside of work, and at work, you will not be left alone together. And one more thing. Jinseung, hand over your phone."

Jinseung reluctantly passed Mr. Kim his phone.

Mr. Kim put the phone in his desk drawer and locked it. "This phone is confiscated. You'll be provided with a new phone with a new number. You are not to share numbers with each other. You have no need to contact each other directly. If you need to get in touch, then Manager Bong and Intern Yang can pass on your messages."

I flinched at the swift and heavy blow. Jinseung looked devastated too, his face drawn and his eyes downcast.

Mr. Kim dismissed us from his office, but we weren't free yet. Changsoo took us aside to continue scolding us.

"I knew this would happen!" he spat. "I should have told Mr. Kim as soon as I started getting suspicious."

He went on and on yelling at us, cursing us for our stupidity.

"Mark my words, I'll be strictly enforcing Mr. Kim's conditions," he said.

Jinseung and I sat in silence, absorbing blow after blow from Changsoo until a phone call finally interrupted his lengthy tirade.

"I have to take this," he said, calming himself.

Jinseung and I exchanged relieved glances, welcoming a moment of reprieve. But reprieve quickly turned to apprehension. As he listened to the mystery caller, Changsoo's features twisted into a look of severe distress.

Chapter 38

"No..." Changsoo's voice quavered. "You can't do that. We were about to reach an agreement...The rumours aren't true. We're about to release a statement."

My stomach turned at the mention of rumours. Did this have something to do with the dating scandal?

"Please," Changsoo continued. "This will all blow over. Can't you just give it a few more days' thought?"

His pleas didn't seem to convince the caller. Eventually he hung up in defeat.

"I need to speak with Actor Shin alone," he said.

"Of course." I bowed before leaving the room.

As Changsoo and Jinseung privately conversed, I paced up and down the hall, wondering what the call was about. I had an extremely bad feeling about it. Lost in thought, I bumped straight into Bora.

"Intern—" I started.

"Actor-nim," she said coldly, glaring at me with rage-filled eyes.

"I—"

"I hope you have learned your lesson. Jinseung's fanbase is up in arms over what you've done." Her voice shook. "But worst of all, you kept it all from me. I thought we were friends, but maybe I was wrong."

"Look," I began, then shook my head. Now was not the time to try and explain myself. I had a much more pressing concern. "Do you know what's going on? Manager Bong just got a phone call which made him very upset."

Bora softened. "No. I haven't heard anything."

"He's in there talking with *Seonbae*."

"Hmmm..."

Curious, Bora moved closer and turned her ear towards the door. I joined her but couldn't hear anything except snatches of conversation.

"...Knee-jerk reaction..."

"...I'll try to reason with them..."

"...No use..."

We leaned in closer, pressing up against the door, then quickly backed away when it swung open. Jinseung stormed out of the room, face pale and eyes red.

"*Oppa!*" I called after him, but he ignored me.

Changsoo appeared in the doorway, a heavy look on his face.

"What's wrong, Manager-nim?" Bora asked.

He drew a deep breath. "I suppose you'll find out sooner or later, so I'll tell you now... His offer for the lead role in Love Apprentice has been withdrawn."

I stumbled backward in disbelief. "W-what? They can't do that, can they?"

"I'm afraid it's entirely within their rights. We were still in negotiation and no contract had been signed yet."

"Why would they do that?" Bora asked. "Actor-nim is the best fit for the role. PD Song specifically had him in mind—"

"PD Song doesn't want a lead actor who has recently been involved in a dating scandal."

His words exploded like a bomb ripping through every cell of my body. I started to hyperventilate.

Bora looked at me, concerned. "Are you okay?"

I apologised then ran to the bathroom, too upset to hear anything more.

Locked in a toilet cubicle, tears cascaded from my eyes and sobs heaved from my throat.

Jinseung lost his part in the drama and it was all my fault. If we didn't meet on that day... If we hadn't stood outside the bar together...

It finally sank in why Jinseung couldn't, shouldn't date me, or anyone else. His career was his priority right now. He had made that abundantly clear.

The dating curse is real.

* * *

"You're not good enough for Jinseung!"

"Shin Jinseung should be with a Korean girl."

"What gives you the right to think you're entitled to Jinseung?"

"Give Shin Jinseung back!"

"Whore."

The nasty comments poured into my social media channels through the night. An unstoppable flood. Unable to bear it, I deleted all the social media apps off my phone then tried to go to sleep.

I couldn't get out of bed the next day. When the intercom buzzed, I ignored it. When it buzzed a third time, I slowly staggered out of bed and made my way to answer it. I saw Bora on the screen and let her in.

"You look terrible," she said, looking me up and down.

"I feel terrible."

"I came to deliver these." She held up two scripts. "The final two episodes. I thought you might not be up to coming into work today—nor should you. There's a mob of angry fans and reporters outside KAM HQ. It's best you lay low for a while."

"*Omo...*"

"Don't worry about it too much. It will all die down in a few days. Just wait and see."

I sighed. "You're probably right."

"The social media team is in the midst of deleting the negative comments off your accounts too."

"That's a relief. Do you want to come in? I'm going to make some tea."

She nodded and stepped into my apartment. "So...how are you holding up?"

"Not very well," I admitted, flicking the kettle on.

"The news about Actor Shin...it really hit you hard, didn't it?"

"I feel so bad for him. It's all my fault."

"No one blames you—"

"Manager Bong does. It was written all over his face."

"That...may be so, but only because he's very protective of Actor Shin. Overly so. He's been his manager for so long. They're like brothers."

As I prepared two cups of tea, Bora shuffled on her feet. "*Unnie...* I'm sorry about the things I said to you. I was just so angry..."

"You have every right to be angry."

"But I never sought to listen to your side of the story."

"If you want to know the truth, I'm willing to share it now."

"So, what is the truth? You're dating him, right?"

"Let's sit down."

I brought over the two cups of tea and set them down on the coffee table. Bora and I sat side by side on the couch.

"I'm not dating Shin Jinseung," I said.

"Really?"

I nodded. "But I can't deny that we're not interested in each other. I really hoped that we would start dating soon after Hidden History. He said that he was open to it, but he wanted to take things slow."

"I wish you had told me."

"I was only just coming to terms with it myself. And then this happened..."

"What are you going to do? Have you spoken with him?"

I shook my head. "I'm probably the last person he wants to speak to right now."

"I'm sure that's not the case—"

"I cost him a job. I got in the way of his career. This was the reason why he said he doesn't date. How can we possibly be together now? He won't want to continue seeing me. We'll have to break things off."

"Is that what you want?"

"No, but I can't see any other option."

"You should discuss this with him."

"How? We can't see each other alone right now, or even talk on the phone."

"I can help you." She took out her phone and sent me a message. "It's his new phone number. Don't tell anyone that I gave it to you."

"I won't. Thank you." I saved the number under a code name —Buster.

"Give him a call when you're ready."

I nodded.

When we finished our tea, Bora prepared to leave. She paused before reaching the door, a thought striking her. "I almost forgot." She rummaged in her bag and fished out a cap, a pair of sunglasses, and a face mask. "Take these. Like I said before, it's best you lay low for a while and call me if there's anything you need. But if you absolutely must go out, keep a low profile."

"Thank you."

"If you need someone to talk to, remember that I'm here."

"I'll let you know how everything goes."

"Bye, *Unnie*."

"Bye."

On Bora's advice, I didn't leave my apartment for the rest of the day. I attempted to call Jinseung several times, but each time I picked up my phone I felt sick. *I can't do it.*

I didn't work up enough courage to try again until the evening, but just as I picked up my phone it started to ring. The caller was "Buster." Jinseung. *How can it be?*

Chapter 39

Heart racing, I answered the call. *"Oppa..."* My voice was weak.

"Hi, Chloe," Jinseung answered. He sounded surprisingly calm.

"How did you get my number back?"

"Did you think I didn't write it down anywhere? I knew something like this could happen."

"Oh. I see."

Jinseung paused. I could hear his steady breathing. Eventually he came out with it. "You know I lost the role, don't you?"

Tears gathered in my eyes again. "Yes. I'm so sorry."

"It's not your fault. It was my fault. I let my guard down. I should have known better."

"I feel terrible."

"Don't. Please don't."

"I can't help it. I know how much you value your acting career. I can't bear to think I'm getting in the way..."

"Chloe...It's going to be hard for us to keep seeing each other, you know that, right?"

"Yes."

"That's why I'm starting to wonder if it's better that we don't."

My blood turned cold. I didn't say anything. I *couldn't* say anything.

Jinseung continued. "All the sneaking around, all the secrets...I don't want that for you. You deserve better."

I blinked back tears.

"Chloe? Say something."

"I know," I spluttered. "It won't work. As much as I want it to, it won't work. I won't be happy if your career gets ruined because of me."

"Don't cry. Please don't cry."

"I'm not crying," I lied, though he could definitely hear me crying.

He waited on the other end of the line until my sobs quietened. "Are you okay?"

"Yes."

"Good. I'm really sorry about this."

"It's okay."

"Then...I'll let you go. Goodbye, Chloe."

"Goodbye."

I held back from bursting into tears again until he hung up, then I buried my head in my pillow and wailed. *It's over.*

Chapter 40

Staring into the empty fridge, my stomach growling, I realised I had two options: leave my apartment or starve. At first, starving seemed like the more palatable option, but eventually the hunger pangs won out. I put on glasses and a face mask to obscure my identity, then made the trek down the hall to the elevator. I had my finger poised on the button, but the door lurched open before I pressed it. Bora stood in the elevator, grasping a large shopping bag bursting with groceries.

"Oh, *Unnie*! Heading out?" she asked.

"Not anymore." I said. "That for me?"

"Yep! I got your message. Sorry I didn't reply. I've been in meetings all day and I only just managed to slip out now."

"That's all right." My stomach rumbled.

"*Omo*. Sounds like you need to eat something right away. Let me prepare you a meal."

"That would be amazing, but are you sure you have time?"

"I can spare the time. After all, looking after you is the most important part of my job."

"You're an angel."

Bora beamed.

Back in my apartment, Bora set about preparing me a ham sandwich and a berry smoothie. "You know," she said, "It's about time you started venturing outside again. The anti-Chloe mob has dissipated and everyone seems to have moved on to the next scandal. Did you hear about it?"

"I haven't been keeping up with entertainment news."

"The idol, Jasper, has been accused of filming secret sex tapes and distributing them amongst his friends. Makes your scandal seem insignificant in comparison, doesn't it?"

"You're right. Thank God I haven't been involved with anything like that. So you think it'll be safe for me to go outside?"

"Yes, but it still pays to be discreet. Hidden History has been growing in popularity—in no small part due to the dating rumour. There's no doubt you will get recognised in public. Avoid crowds, take taxis, not public transport—things like that."

"Okay. Thanks for the advice."

Bora served the meal and sat opposite me at the table. She looked at me with empathetic eyes. "How are you, anyway?"

Her sweet voice, full of concern, was enough to make me crack. Tears welled in my eyes before sliding uncontrollable down my cheeks.

"Oh dear," Bora said, going to my side and wrapping an arm around my shoulders. "Everything will be okay."

"I'm going to have to film my final scenes soon," I blubbed. "I don't know how I'm going to cope seeing Jinseung again."

"Be strong. I know you're capable."

"Thanks," I sniffed.

Be strong...I repeated her words in my head. They would become like a mantra to me over the next few days, preparing me to face him again.

* * *

DESPITE MY EFFORT TO be strong, seeing Jinseung felt like ripping the band-aid off a wound which hadn't closed up yet. I couldn't bring myself to look him in the eyes as we sat in the van, on our way to film some scenes for the penultimate episode of Hidden History.

An uncomfortable silence reigned, eventually broken by Bora. "What about that whole sex tape saga, eh? That cute little *maknae*... who would have thought?"

None of us responded to her insight.

"Just trying to make conversation," she grumbled. "Sheesh."

As much as I tried to avoid looking at Jinseung I couldn't help but notice the strained expression on his face and the way he kept clutching his stomach. I wondered if he was ill.

"Are you okay?" I asked. "Does your stomach hurt?"

"I'm fine," he said.

He was obviously unwilling to talk about it so I didn't push the subject any further.

* * *

Filming faced significant delays. Camped out in Jinseung's dressing room, we practiced our lines together, chaperoned by Changsoo and Bora at all times.

"Shall we try it once more from the top?" Jinseung asked.

I nodded meekly and flipped back to the start of our scene.

Despite all that had happened between us, Jinseung's ability to act hadn't suffered at all. Meanwhile, I could only summon the energy to dredge up a mediocre performance at best. Having spent the last couple of weeks sick with grief, I had barely practiced my lines, nor had I even managed to *look* at the final episode's script.

Over and over again, we practiced episode 15 with no improvement on my part. Eventually Changsoo suggested we move on to episode 16—the final episode.

"Shall we?" Jinseung asked.

"Okay. I haven't practiced any of it yet, though," I warned.

"All the more reason to start working on it now," Changsoo said.

I read from the episode 16 script in my hands, every line completely new to me. The slow-paced episode answered lingering questions and tied up loose ends to create a satisfying conclusion to the series.

With only a few pages remaining in the script, my final scene appeared: Louise meets Officer Park after the criminals have been sentenced and they take a walk together.

"Now that the criminals have been reprimanded, and my story has been published, I don't really have a reason to stay here," I read.

"You do have a reason to stay here," Jinseung said.

"…What is that?"

"Me. Please don't go. I'm asking you not to go." He had a pleading look in his eyes.

Real tears welled in my eyes. I brushed them away. "I've been waiting for you to say that."

The next words in the script were a stage direction: *Louise and Officer Park kiss.*

I froze. *How can I kiss him now after everything?* I anxiously lifted my gaze to read Jinseung's reaction, but just as I met his eyes he groaned and doubled over, clutching his stomach again. This time his discomfort did not escape the notice of Changsoo and Bora.

"What's wrong?" Bora asked.

"Do you have an upset stomach?" Changsoo asked.

Jinseung winced. "I don't know."

"Where exactly does it hurt?"

He motioned to his lower abdominal area.

"This is no good. We should get you to a doctor."

Jinseung shook his head. "Let's wait until the shoot is over. I'm sure it's nothing."

Bora rummaged in her bag and retrieved a packet of tablets. "Take these," she said, popping two tablets out. She served them to him with a glass of water. "Painkillers."

Jinseung swallowed the pills.

"Are you sure you're okay?" Changsoo asked.

"I'll be fine."

Changsoo didn't seem convinced, but he had no time to persuade

Jinseung to leave. A production assistant came to the dressing room to call us onto set.

We relocated to the police station set to prepare for the shoot. A stylist accosted me and Jinseung, fixing our hair and makeup while the crew set up the camera and lighting.

Baek Yena, who was also appearing in the scene, sat on a chair while her manager aimed a mini electric fan at her face to keep her cool.

I kept a wary eye on Jinseung until the shoot was ready to begin. He gave no sign of illness away to the cast and crew.

On Im Nara's signal, the actors took their positions on set.

"Action!" she called.

With the camera following me behind my shoulder, I approached the police station reception. The actor playing Officer Do looked up and his face dropped in shock.

"I'm back," I said.

He called out to his colleagues. Yena and Jinseung as Detective Jung and Officer Park came running. They stared at me, speechless.

"Surprised?" I asked.

"Cut," Nara said. "Shin Jinseung, someone you love, someone who you thought might be dead, has just returned. You should be overflowing with emotion."

Jinseung nodded.

"And please walk normally. Looks like you're limping slightly? Let's try again."

We started the scene again. At the point when Jinseung's eyes locked onto me, his face turned white. Everyone waited for him to say his line, but he didn't say anything. He had a spaced-out look in his eyes and his forehead was slick with sweat. It seemed like he was about to say something, then his whole body went limp and he collapsed with a loud thump on the floor.

Chapter 41

"Jinseung!" I screamed, before flinging myself towards his unmoving body. I laid a hand on his cold, clammy forehead. His eyes briefly flickered open and then closed again.

"Stand back!" A crew member wearing a fluorescent vest and holding a first aid kit shooed me out of the way. He crouched down and checked Jinseung's pulse. Upon determining it was okay, he bundled up a jacket and put it below Jinseung's legs to raise them slightly. He also loosened Jinseung's clothes by removing his belt and undoing a few of his buttons.

A siren in the distance grew louder while I watched on helplessly. I shifted anxiously on my feet, heart pounding, eyes wet with tears. Bora stood beside me whimpering.

Murmured questions filled the room.

"What happened to him?"

"Is he okay?"

"Is he dead?"

When the ambulance arrived, paramedics rushed to Jinseung's side.

"He's been experiencing stomach pains in his lower abdominal area," Changsoo explained.

"Thank you. That's useful information," a young female paramedic said.

After checking his vital signs, the paramedics lifted Jinseung onto a stretcher and carried him to the ambulance waiting outside.

"I'll go with him in the ambulance," Changsoo said.

"Can I come too?" I asked.

"Me too," Bora said.

Changsoo shook his head. "There's only room for one person to go. Take the van and meet us at the hospital." He hopped into the back of the ambulance and strapped himself into the chair.

As the ambulance zoomed off, siren blaring, Bora and I bundled into the van. A determined look in her eyes, Bora started the engine and haphazardly sped away. For once, I didn't care about Bora's terrible driving. All I cared about was getting to the hospital as quickly as possible.

"He's going to be okay. He's going to be okay," Bora said over and over like a mantra as she drove.

I desperately wanted to believe her.

At the hospital, Bora didn't park properly and didn't care to correct her mistake. We hopped out and ran towards the accident and emergency entrance.

"We're looking for Shin Jinseung. He just arrived by ambulance," Bora said to the receptionist.

"Are you family?"

"We're colleagues."

We showed her our KAM employee cards.

"Yang Bora and Chloe Gibson..." She checked something on the computer. "I see that you're both approved visitors. You'll find him in room 12. Through those doors, then follow the signs."

Bora and I hastily made our way through the linoleum-floored corridors which smelled of disinfectant.

A security guard stood outside the door to room 12. We explained who we were, then he let us inside.

The immaculate private room had beige walls and a polished wooden floor, a large television, a couch and two armchairs. Jinseung lay on the hospital bed, awake but weak, while Changsoo stood talking to a doctor, an anxious look on his face.

I immediately went to Jinseung's side. "*Oppa.*"

Jinseung turned and ran his eyes over me but didn't say anything. His face was pale.

"Is he going to be okay, Doctor?" Bora asked.

"It's suspected appendicitis. We just need to run a few tests to be sure."

"And if it is appendicitis?"

"He'll need to have surgery straight away. The longer it's left, the more likely there could be complications."

Bora joined me at Jinseung's bedside.

"We're here, *Oppa*," she said. "Everything's going to be okay."

Jinseung's pale lips curved into a weak smile.

Bora, Changsoo, and I stayed with him in the room while he underwent various tests. As suspected, the diagnosis was appendicitis. After a brief wait, Jinseung was taken through to surgery.

We sat nervously in the waiting room.

"This is a routine operation," Changsoo assured us, but his voice shook with a tinge of worry.

Time crawled at an agonisingly slow pace while Jinseung's appendectomy was underway. I wasn't someone who usually prayed, but this time I did. I closed my eyes and silently begged God that Jinseung would be okay. I even promised that I would forget all notions of ever dating him—I'd be happy just to see him alive and well again. That's all I could ever ask for.

I didn't get up from the hard plastic chair. My legs were beginning to fall asleep by the time the waiting room doors finally opened. I jumped up to attention as a doctor emerged. My heart thudded in my chest and my hands were tight fists at my side.

"How did it go?" Changsoo asked.

"I'm pleased to announce that the surgery was a success," the doctor said.

The tension in my body slowly drained as relief washed over me.

"But thank goodness he got here when he did," the doctor continued. "His appendix was severely inflamed, and rupture was imminent."

"But he's okay now?"

"He's in a stable condition. He's still asleep from the anaesthetic. We'll keep him in hospital overnight to recover."

"Thank you, Doctor."

A nurse wheeled Jinseung's bed back to his room.

Mr. Kim arrived later with a bunch of flowers. "How is he?"

"The appendectomy was a success," Changsoo said. "He should fully recover in a couple of weeks."

"That is good news indeed."

Bora fetched teas and coffees and we chatted between ourselves while waiting for Jinseung to wake up.

After finishing his tea, Mr. Kim excused himself. "I'm needed back at the office, but let him know I stopped by."

"Will do," Changsoo said.

"Don't stay here all day. You need your rest too."

We all agreed, though I had absolutely no intention of going home. I wanted to stay with Jinseung through the night if I could.

Changsoo and I flanked Jinseung's bed on armchairs at each side, while Bora lay on the couch opposite the foot of the bed. We all jolted when Jinseung made a groaning sound. Changsoo and I leaned over him. He opened his eyes. The first word to come out of his mouth was "Chloe."

Chapter 42

"Yes, it's me," I said.

Jinseung turned and reached his hand out to stroke my cheek. "You're cute."

I blushed furiously at the display of affection in front of Bora and Changsoo. Clearly the drugs were still affecting him.

Before Jinseung could say anything else, the door opened and his parents entered the room.

"My Jinseungie!" exclaimed his mother as she rushed to him.

His father stood at the foot of the bed, arms folded. Considering how quickly they had arrived from Tongyeong, they must have dropped everything to race here as soon as they got the call.

"He's okay," Changsoo explained. "Just recovering from the surgery. I don't think the drugs have fully worn off yet."

"My poor Jinseungie!"

"Changsoo-ssi, Chloe, thank you for staying with him through all this," Jinseung's father said. He turned to Bora. "I don't believe we've met."

Bora bowed to him. "Yang Bora. I'm an intern at KAM. I've been working with Jinseung for nearly a year now."

"Thank you, Bora-ssi."

"Now that you've arrived, perhaps we'd better leave. It's a bit too crowded in here for five…" Changsoo said.

I didn't want to leave, but he had a point. Jinseung's parents might want some privacy. Bora and I reluctantly agreed.

"C-Chloe…" Jinseung said.

"Oh? Is there something you want to say to Chloe, dear?" Jinseung's mother said. "Do you want to stay here a bit longer, Chloe?"

I looked to Changsoo for permission. He nodded, giving me the go-ahead.

Changsoo and Bora left the room. I stayed with Jinseung, while he vaguely tried to speak to me, but didn't make much sense. Eventually he fell back to sleep.

"I suppose I'll get going then," I said, turning towards the door.

"Wait—I want to ask you something," his mother said.

I stopped.

"Are you dating my son?" she asked.

"No," I said, flustered.

"Is that so? Jinseung denied it too. What a pity. I kind of hoped the rumours were true."

"Really?"

"I look forward to the day Jinseung introduces me to his girlfriend."

"But what about his career?"

"Some things in life are more important, don't you agree, *yeobo*?"

Her husband murmured in vague agreement.

Feeling bashful, I once again edged towards the door. "I should go. I hope his recovery goes smoothly."

"We'll stay in Seoul and look after him until he's better," Jinseung's mother assured me.

"That's good to hear."

With Jinseung left in good hands, I went home.

* * *

I SPENT the rest of the evening not quite sure what to do with myself. Seeing Jinseung sick like that had been a shock to my system, and I couldn't shake the memory of him collapsing from my mind.

After a cup of tea, I managed to calm myself down enough to open my laptop and check my emails. Mass emails from KAM and the Hidden History production team had been sent around about Jinseung's appendicitis. Farther down my inbox, another subject line caught my attention—"English Teacher Job Interview". I read the email.

Dear Chloe Gibson,

We have read your resume and would like to interview you for a position at BT Academy in Busan. Could you please confirm a time for a phone call?

Kind Regards,
Alice Kim

My initial reaction was to decline the interview and say I was only interested in jobs in Seoul. Then I remembered that I no longer needed to stay in Seoul since I didn't need to stay near Jinseung.

I heaved a large sigh. *Busan*...A nice city, by all means. Close to Tongyeong, so I could see my host parents more often. It wouldn't be so bad to leave Seoul. With this in mind, I confirmed a time for the interview.

Chapter 43

I didn't see or hear from Jinseung again until filming resumed two weeks later. All remaining scenes of Hidden History involving Jinseung had been delayed until his recovery, and then all shot at once over a hectic three-day period.

Bora had teased him about the way he said my name when he woke up in the hospital, but Jinseung couldn't remember anything from that afternoon.

On the final evening of filming, Jinseung and I stood in our starting positions for the last scene to be shot for Hidden History—the kiss scene between Louise and Officer Park.

Golden hour bathed the leafy park in warm evening light. I shuffled my feet on the concrete pathway, my thoughts heavy with the prospect of leaving Hidden History, leaving KAM, and perhaps never seeing Jinseung again.

"Are you okay?" Jinseung asked. "You look concerned."

"I was just thinking about how this is my last day as a K-drama actor. It's bittersweet."

"Ah, I see. But I'm sure there will be many more opportunities for you in the future. Changsoo said you had an interview for a job at a *hagwon* in Busan?"

"Yes. I've been offered the job. I'm starting next month."

"That's good."

The steadicam operator positioned himself so we were correctly in frame, and an assistant shone light onto us with a reflector. Everyone readied themselves for the first take.

"Action," Im Nara called.

The scene began with Louise and Officer Park taking a walk through the park, chatting about everything that had happened. It had a bittersweet feeling, just like my mood.

We came around a bend in the path then took a seat at a park bench. My heart rate increased, knowing the kiss drew near. We hadn't practiced it at all. My lips tingled in anticipation.

"Please don't go. I'm asking you not to go," Jinseung said, his eyes were fixed on mine.

My face broke into a relieved smile. "I've been waiting for you to say that."

"…I like you."

"Me too."

Jinseung swallowed, studying me with an intensity which made me flinch. Slowly, he moved towards me, the space between us disappearing. He planted a brief kiss on my lips. It felt awkward. Both of us blushed.

"Cut!" Im Nara yelled. "Shin Jinseung, this is the moment viewers have been waiting for. It looks like you're holding back for some reason. Put some more enthusiasm into it."

"Yes, PD-nim," Jinseung said.

I could understand his hesitation. Kissing was difficult in our situation. But we had to put that behind us to make the scene convincing.

We began again from the point where we sat down at the bench.

"I like you," Jinseung said, his breath shaking.

"Me too," I said.

My heart pounded as he leaned in. Slowly, softly, he pressed his lips to mine. This time, he didn't break away so fast, spending time to build and deepen the kiss. Completely mesmerised, I forgot everything else, becoming oblivious to the filming, oblivious to the fact that we were acting.

When Jinseung finally pulled away, reality came crashing back. I could see the crew around us in my peripheral vision, even as I tried to focus only on him. He stared into my eyes with an expression of longing. I couldn't tell whether it was Jinseung longing for me, or Officer Park longing for Louise. We stayed with our eyes locked on each other until Im Nara called cut.

"That's more like it," she said.

We had to kiss several more times so the camera could capture it from multiple viewpoints. I applied lip balm between takes because my lips were starting to get raw and dry. Each time we dove in for another kiss, I felt Jinseung's resistance wear further away.

"And…cut! That's a wrap. Good job everyone," Im Nara said at the end of the last take.

Cheers and whoops erupted all around.

Changsoo and Bora came rushing to us, smiles on their faces. We embraced in a group hug.

"Congratulations, guys! A brilliant end to a brilliant drama," Bora said.

"Good work, both of you," Changsoo said. "I'm so proud."

"Are you crying?" I asked, noticing the tears well in his eyes.

"No. Some dust just flew into my eyes." He wiped his face with his hand.

"Dust?" Bora asked incredulously.

An awkward pause ensued before we burst into a fit of laughter.

"Everyone's heading to a bar now to celebrate," Changsoo said once he had caught his breath.

"Then what are we waiting for?" Jinseung said. "As soon as we're out of these clothes and makeup, let's go."

* * *

THE ENTIRE BAR had been booked for the event and drinks were free. Cast, crew, managers, and assistants piled inside.

"Shin Jinseung! Chloe Gibson!" Baek Yena called, inviting us to her table. We pulled up a few more chairs to join her, Cho Dongjoo, Kim Jaehyun, and their managers. Yena filled our shot glasses with soju.

"Cheers," she said, clinking glasses with us. "Another drama under wraps."

"Did you hear about last episode's ratings?" Cho Dongjoo asked. "Nearly double digits!"

"It's going even better than I expected," Kim Jaehyun said.

"What's next for you, Chloe? Have you heard of any other roles?" Yena asked.

"I think Hidden History is probably my first and last drama," I replied. "There aren't many roles out there for foreigners like me."

"I keep forgetting that you won't be with KAM anymore..." Bora said. "That's so sad."

"Yeah. We probably won't see each other again."

She shook her head.

"No. Let's stay in touch, no matter what."

"I would like that."

"We're friends, *Unnie*."

"Yes, we're friends."

"I'll visit you in Busan."

We exchanged warm smiles. Yang Bora would no longer be my colleague, but the idea of our continued friendship filled me with joy.

The voices around us began to hush, and heads turned in the direction of Im Nara, who stood on top of a chair to draw everyone's attention.

"I'd like to make an announcement," she said. "I hope you have all kept Friday evening free as requested. In celebration of the success of Hidden History, we will be holding a party at the Domain Hotel for all cast and crew members."

Cheers and applause rang through the venue.

"It's a strictly private event. No press will be in attendance," Im Nara continued. "And the dress code will be formal, so dress up!"

"Chloe, Jinseung-ah, I trust I will see both of you at the party?" Yena asked.

"I'll be there," Jinseung replied.

"Me too," I said. "I wouldn't miss it."

Chapter 44

Jinseung's jaw dropped when his eyes fell on me across the crowded hotel ballroom.

I had arrived at the wrap party, feeling confident in a long, strapless red dress and high heels.

"C-Chloe," he stuttered. "You look…"

"She looks stunning," Baek Yena cut in, gliding over in a sparkly gown and oversized earrings.

"Thanks," I said. "You look great too. And Jinseung…I haven't seen you in a suit before."

I looked him up and down, admiring the charcoal-grey suit and navy tie, perfectly tailored to his tall, slim form.

"It looks sexy," I said.

"Oh—thank you," Jinseung said. He ran a hand through his hair, suddenly flustered.

A waiter appeared, bearing a tray of wine glasses and an expensive-looking bottle of champagne.

"Would you like some wine?" he asked.

Jinseung and I took a glass each. Yena already had a drink in hand.

"I wonder where we're sitting," Yena said, casting a sweeping glance over the round tables covered with white tablecloths. She checked a sign which showed who was seated where.

"Oh! There we are. We're all sitting at the same table."

People began to take their seats. I joined Jinseung and Yena at a table up front which we shared with several other main cast members.

Prior to dinner being served, Im Nara took to the stage to make a speech. She said thank you to all the main contributors to the series and handed out several flower bouquets and gifts to the important people involved. I had started to zone out when my ears pricked at the sound of my name.

"I'd also like to make a special mention of Chloe Gibson, who stepped up at the last minute, with no acting experience, and did a brilliant, convincing job of Louise," Nara said. "She impressed Writer Kim so much that she wrote her a bigger part than initially conceived. I don't know what we would have done without you, Chloe."

Baek Yena nudged my shoulder and cheered.

I sank into my chair, embarrassed by the mention. I didn't feel like I had done anything particularly special.

Im Nara continued. "Now onto a more solemn note. The actor Tamara Wilson, who was originally cast as Louise, left us to be with her father who she learned was terminally ill. It is my regret to inform you that her father has since passed away. So I'd like you to join me in a minute of silence." She closed her eyes and lowered her head in respect.

Silence fell over the venue.

*Poor Tamara. I was only offered this opportunity thanks to her misfortune...*I couldn't linger on that thought for too long. *It's the work of fate,* I decided.

At the conclusion of Nara's speech, entrees were served—a mouthwatering collection of Korean and Western small dishes.

Between courses, more speeches ensued from people including Kim Eunsook, producers, and executives from the TV network.

After three dinner courses, the music turned up and people began getting up from their seats to mingle and dance.

I stared at Jinseung, who chatted with Cho Dongjoo beside him.

This could be the final night I spend with him…I had better make the most of it.

"You should ask him to dance," Yena said, noticing my stare.

"Who? Cho Dongjoo?" I quipped.

Yena laughed. "You know who. Hey! Jinseungie!"

Jinseung turned to her. "Yes?"

"Go on," Yena said, winking at me.

"*Aigoo*," I uttered, exasperated.

Jinseung eyed me expectantly.

I had never asked a guy to dance with me before, but what the hell, there was a first time for everything.

"*Oppa*, will you dance with me?" I asked.

Jinseung's lips curled into a radiant smile.

"Sure. Let's go." He took my arm and led me towards the other dancing guests.

"Have fun!" Yena shouted after us.

We danced holding hands to an upbeat song. He twirled me around and did all kinds of funny dance moves, making me smile so hard my face hurt. I allowed myself to forget all that had happened between us and just enjoy the moment. We danced together for another two songs before a male guest I didn't recognise swooped in and stole me away from Jinsueng. He was good-looking, tall, and oozed charm.

"Hey Chloe, my name is Lee Chiwon," he said.

"Chiwon-ssi," I repeated.

I looked over my shoulder back at Jinseung, but he had disappeared into the swarming crowd. Not wishing to be impolite, I stayed dancing with Lee Chiwon until the song ended. By then, another girl had caught his attention, and he left me alone.

Wishing to spend more time with Jinseung, I went in search of him, but got sidetracked by Kim Eunsook who engaged me in a lengthy conversation.

Once I had finished talking with Eunsook, I spotted Yena thanks to her eye-catching dress. I approached her.

"Baek Yena-ssi, have you seen Jinseung?" I asked.

"Yeah. He was chatting with one of the producers," she said. "Probably trying to find out about upcoming projects."

"Ah. I guess I better leave him to it then. It must be important for him to network."

"Chloe, I've booked a suite at the hotel for the night, and I've invited a few people up for some drinks later on," Yena said. "Do you want to come? I'll ask Jinseungie too."

"Yes, I'll come," I replied without hesitation. If Jinseung would be there, I had to be there too.

"Great. You looked so cute dancing with Jinseungie before. You two look so good together. The rumours are true, aren't they? There's something going on between you. I can tell."

"Well, actually…"

"No need to say anything. I understand. Come to my suite at midnight, okay? Room number 1208."

"Got it."

* * *

At midnight, I exited the ballroom and took the closest elevator to the 12th floor. Down a maze of corridors, I located room 1208. I pressed the doorbell. Yena opened the door, a grin on her face.

"Come in, come in," she urged.

The gorgeous suite contained a large bed, a sitting area, and floor-to-ceiling windows with magnificent views of the Han River. No one else was in the room except the two of us.

"There's no one else here…" I said. "Am I the first person to arrive?"

"Yes," Yena replied.

She poured me a drink while we waited for Jinseung and others to arrive. A doorbell ring shortly followed. Yena shot up to answer.

"Jinseungie, you made it!" she said.

Jinseung entered the room, his eyebrows knitted with confusion.

"Where is everyone?" he asked.

Yena bit her lip.

"Actually..." she began.

"What?"

"I only invited you two."

"Oh?"

"And I'm just about to head home. You two can use the suite. I know how hard it can be to spend quality time alone together when you're dating. It was the same when I was dating my husband."

"We're not—"

"No need to thank me!"

Before we could do anything, Yena slipped out of the room, leaving us alone in stunned silence.

Chapter 45

Realisation sank in. *We've been set up.* Jinseung and I stood frozen in the centre of the fancy hotel room, acutely aware of the huge bed looming behind us. We couldn't even meet each other's eyes.

"I wasn't expecting this," Jinseung said at last.

"Neither was I," I said.

"I suppose I should leave…"

"No!"

Jinseung lifted an eyebrow. "What? Do you want me to stay?"

"Well…that's not what I meant. But this could be the last time we see each other. I just wanted to say a proper goodbye."

"I hope things work out well for you in Busan."

"Thank you. I hope your acting career picks up again."

"Then…I guess this is goodbye."

I nodded weakly.

Jinseung opened his arms and beckoned me to him. I stepped closer and he enclosed me in a tight, warm hug. We stayed in that position for what felt like several minutes. I wished he would never let go, but eventually, he dropped his arms.

"Well, I guess I'll be going now," he said.

"Goodbye, *Oppa*."

"Goodbye."

I could have been imagining it, but it looked like his eyes were full of regret.

I felt a painful knot in my stomach as Jinseung reached for the door handle. He turned to me one more time before leaving.

He left me alone in the room. I waited for his footsteps to dissipate before allowing myself to cry. *He's gone. Gone from my life.* The finality hit me hard, destroying the facade of strength I had built up around myself.

Still crying, I walked to the bathroom, stripped the suffocating red dress off my body, and pulled open the glass door to the enormous shower. I turned on the water and submerged myself beneath the powerful flow from the waterfall showerhead.

Why does it have to be this way? Why? I reminded myself that having a girlfriend would hold Jinseung back from reaching his full potential, but for some reason, that idea seemed weak to me now. Jinseung's mother's words echoed in my head: *Some things in life are more important.* I couldn't help but feel that I'd made a huge mistake. *I should have tried harder. I shouldn't have given up on him.* But now it was too late. Jinseung had departed from my life. I cried and cried, letting the shower water mix with my tears and wash them down the drain.

When my skin began to feel tight, I reluctantly turned off the water and stepped out into the steamy room. White towel wrapped around my body, I wiped a hole in the misted-up mirror.

I can't let the night end like this, I thought sombrely, staring at my pale reflection, eyes red and puffy. Then and there, I made up my mind.

Still in my towel, I rushed back into the bedroom and grabbed my phone. I trembled as I pressed the call button. Phone to ear, I waited. *Please pick up.* It rang several times then went to voicemail. I tried one more time. On the first three rings, he didn't answer. Then I heard something strange. The faint sound of a phone ringing outside the hotel room door, and then the doorbell.

I rushed to the door and opened it, forgetting I was just in a towel.

Jinseung stood in the corridor.

"You came back," I said, voice wobbling.

He looked me up and down. The corner of his lips quirked into an amused smile.

I blushed realising I hadn't dressed and pulled the towel tighter around me. "Why are you here?"

He swallowed. "I know it's selfish, but I don't think I can give you up."

My heart leapt. "Then don't."

He stepped forward into the room, pushing me back as he did so. Door closed behind us, he kissed me.

His lips felt warm and soft against mine. I pulled back a little in surprise, and he ran his eyes over me, gauging my reaction before diving in again with more force. He coaxed open my mouth and tasted me with his tongue, drawing shivers up my spine. One of his hands cupped my head, the other held my waist. Deeper, faster, we kissed until we ran out of breath and I broke away, panting. "Jinseung-ah…"

He nuzzled me and said, voice low, "You don't have any clothes on."

"I was so flustered…I wasn't thinking when I answered the door."

There were so many questions I wanted to ask him. Had he changed his mind? Could we be together after all? But I was silenced as he kissed me again. I succumbed immediately, my knees weak. He held me tight against him while vigorously making out with me. His hands explored my body. I dug my fingers into his back and deepened the kiss. Jinseung groaned and pulled off my towel in one swift movement.

I blushed, feeling exposed.

He pulled back to get a better view.

"Beautiful," he murmured, before kissing me again.

As we kissed, I kept my hands occupied by unbuttoning his shirt. My heart beat faster with each opened button revealing more of his muscular chest. When I reached the bottom, he took it off. I ran my hand down his torso. It felt every bit as good as I imagined it would. The body of someone who takes extremely good care of it.

"Let's go to bed." Jinseung's voice was gruff and low.

I nodded, completely at his mercy. He guided me to the bed.

Chapter 46

Bright sunlight burned my eyes when I opened them in the morning.

"Morning, sleepyhead," Jinseung said, his arms still around me.

So it wasn't a dream. Last night really happened.

"Morning," I said, smiling sheepishly. I extracted myself, desperately needing to stretch. My back clicked.

"Did you sleep well?"

"Yes. You?"

"Mmm. I had pleasant dreams for once."

"Did you dream about me?"

"Yes, actually."

"You did? So what happened in the dream?"

Jinseung smirked. "I don't want to corrupt your innocent mind."

"You know I'm not innocent," I retorted.

He chuckled and pulled me closer into his arms. I rested my head on his chest, feeling the rise and fall of his breath. I would be completely relaxed if it weren't for the niggling little question in the back of my mind.

"Are you okay?" Jinseung asked. "You seem a bit tense."

"I…" I wondered whether to bring it up or not. It might spoil the mood.

"What's wrong?"

"I need to know. Where do we stand now? What's next for us?"

"Don't let those things worry you. Let's just enjoy the moment." He glanced at the alarm clock on the bedside table. "There's still enough time."

"Enough time for what?"

"You know…" He leaned in seductively. "We've got this beautiful hotel room for another hour. It would be a shame to waste it."

Despite the concerns plaguing my thoughts, I was unable to resist his magnetic pull. "Well, okay. If you insist."

"I do insist."

He moved closer still. All my muscles tensed in anticipation. Jinseung's eyes bored into me, half-lidded in desire. His lips touched mine, soft and welcoming. He parted his lips and ever so slowly sank into the kiss. His tongue brushed against mine, making me tremble with delight. He groaned and pulled me tighter to him.

Beep beep beep beep.

What the—? I broke away and reached across to the bedside table to grab my phone. I had set a check-out reminder the night before and now it popped up on the screen: Check out 11:00am. *But that's still ages away…*I looked between my phone and the alarm clock and back again.

"*Omo*," I said.

"What's wrong?" Jinseung asked.

"This alarm clock's wrong. Check out is in ten minutes."

"Wait, are you sure? How could we have slept that long?"

"I don't know."

He checked his own phone. "Gah!"

We scrambled to get up and ready ourselves to leave.

Dressed at last, we only had a few minutes to spare.

"Go home," Jinseung said. "I'll go and check out." He kissed me on the cheek. "Let's meet tomorrow and talk things through, okay? I'll be in touch."

* * *

FEELING SLIGHTLY self-conscious in my evening wear, I took the elevator to the lobby then hailed a taxi from outside the hotel.

"Where to?" the taxi driver asked. My head was in the clouds, replaying all the delicious moments in the hotel room, and in my blissed-out state I had forgotten to tell him. I gave him my address.

During the ride home, I sent Yena a text message thanking her for the hotel room. A short moment after I pressed send, my phone started to ring. Yena was calling me back.

"*Yeoboseyo*," I answered.

"So you had a good night, huh? Did you make good use of the room?"

"Uh, yes."

She cackled with glee. "I'm glad to hear it. You and Shin Jinseung make such a cute couple!"

"Heh. Thanks."

"So, are you going to keep your relationship a secret?"

I paused, caught off-guard by her question. "Actually, we haven't discussed anything yet." *Does he even want a proper relationship with me? Was it just a one-night stand?*

"Ah. So you haven't had that conversation."

"I'm a little nervous."

"Don't be. Jinseung's a good guy. I'm sure you'll both come to a sensible solution."

"I hope so."

"If it helps, my husband and I are living proof that a relationship can work between a celebrity and a non-famous person."

"Then…can I ask you something?"

"Fire away."

"When you started dating your husband, did it impact your career? Did you resent him?"

"*Aigoo*. Such heavy questions. Are you worried about Jinseung? The scandal must have hit you both hard. I'm not going to lie, it was hard sometimes. But Dongwoo and I are obviously still together. I have no regrets."

"And your career?"

"I'm still acting, aren't I? Sure, I don't get the same kind of roles as I did when I was a single, hot young thing, but I actually prefer it this way. I'm recognised for my skills as an actor, rather than my looks and single status. I'm taken far more seriously now."

Yena's thoughtful answer lifted an invisible weight off my shoulders. "Thanks. You've clarified things for me."

"I'm glad to be of help. When will you see him again?"

"Tomorrow. I expect we'll discuss things then."

"Good luck."

Chapter 47

A surprise announcement came from Changsoo the next morning.

"Yang Bora has been promoted!" he said excitedly over the phone.

I was so surprised I fumbled with my phone, nearly dropping it. "*Omo*. For real?"

"Yes. Mr. Kim gave her the good news last night."

"That's wonderful. So what's her new title?"

"I'll leave it to her to explain everything. I'm sure she'll want to tell you the news herself. Are you free tonight? I'm taking her out to celebrate. It would be great for you and Shin Jinseung to come along too."

"Of course! I'll be there."

I was too happy to care that it would disrupt the plans I had already made with Jinseung.

* * *

I ARRIVED at a dark underground bar with graffiti art on the walls and Korean hip hop music pumping through the speakers. At a table situated in a corner largely hidden from view, Changsoo, Jinseung, and Bora occupied a small table. I met Jinseung's eyes first and blushed, then quickly diverted my eye contact to Changsoo and Bora.

"Am I late?" I asked.

"Not at all," Changsoo said. "We only just got here."

I took a seat. "Yang Bora-ya, congratulations on your promotion."

She grinned from ear to ear. "Thank you, Chloe."

"So I take it you're no longer an intern, but a fully fledged staff member now?"

"That's right. It's a full-time, salaried position."

"*Daebak*! You deserve it."

"Doesn't she?" Jinseung said. "I've never seen an intern so hard-working and dedicated."

"Just remember to work on your driving skills," Changsoo jibed. "She pranged the van yesterday."

"Thanks again for covering for me!" Bora said sheepishly. "I promise I'll work on my driving."

Changsoo waved over a waiter and we ordered beer, soju, plus a few small dishes to share. Changsoo filled our glasses.

"To Yang Bora," Jinseung said, raising his glass.

"Cheers!" We clinked glasses and downed our drinks.

"Tell us more about your promotion," Changsoo said, leaning in to speak with Bora. "You'll be a manager, right?"

"Yes. I'm going to be a manager for a freshly recruited actor," she explained.

My mouthful of beer went down the wrong way and I started coughing. "Hold on. That means you won't be working with Jinseung anymore," I said when I had regained my composure.

"Correct."

"*Omo…*"

"I know. It's the one thing I'm upset about. But I can't be Jinseung's manager when he has Bong Changsoo."

"Who's the new actor? I don't think I've heard anything," Jinseung said.

"Her name is Go Yoojin," Bora explained.

"Ah yes, Go Yoojin…" Changsoo said. "I think you'll be a good fit for her."

"I guess I'll get to meet her soon," Jinseung said.

"I hear a congratulations are in order for you too, Chloe," Changsoo said.

"Oh?" I wondered what exactly he was referring to.

"Did you not snag a teaching job in Busan?"

"I did." I smiled weakly. The job was yet another thing which stood between Jinseung and I being together, but I decided not to let my thoughts linger on that right then. In the meantime, I refilled my glass. Things would be clearer once I'd talked to him, and I could decide what to do after that.

When we finished our drinks, Changsoo ordered more. Bora filled our glasses, a deliriously happy look on her face.

Should I tell her about Jinseung and I? I promised I would tell her everything, after all.

When Bora got up to go to the bathroom, it was the perfect opportunity. I waited a couple of minutes then excused myself from the table and headed to the restroom. I caught Bora as she left the stall.

"Chloe! How was the party last night? I'm so bummed I didn't get to go."

"I had a great time. Actually…"

"Did something happen?"

I nodded.

"Is it to do with Jinseung?"

I nodded again.

"Tell me!"

"Well, uh, things have progressed in our relationship."

Bora gasped. "Does that mean what I think it means?"

"I think so, yes."

She shrieked with joy. "I'm so happy for you!"

"We still haven't talked everything through yet."

"Busan…"

I nodded. "Among several other considerations."

"You'll work things out with time."

"Yeah. I hope so."

"Anyway, it's fantastic news. I'm so glad you told me. No one else knows anything, right?"

"Yeah. Apart from Baek Yena. She's the one who kind of gave us the final push."

Bora giggled. "She's so meddlesome, but cute. And don't worry about me—I won't tell anyone."

"I know. I trust you."

Bora squealed again, unable to contain her sheer excitement. She had to make a considerable effort to gather herself before we rejoined the others at the table. Apart from a few glances back and forth between us, she managed to conceal her knowledge.

"Another drink, *Seonbae-nim?*" Bora asked Changsoo.

"Yes please."

She refilled his glass.

Later in the evening, Bora suggested we head to a *noraebang*. Within the confines of the karaoke room, she continued to ply us all with drinks, especially Changsoo. I had never seen him so drunk. In fact, I don't think I'd ever seen him drunk at all—he was always the sober driver.

Bora got me up to sing a pop song with her, then Changsoo and Jinseung entertained us with a soppy ballad.

"It's getting late," Changsoo said woozily. "Perhaps I'll leave soon."

I thought Bora would protest, but instead she agreed that was a good idea. After one more song, we said goodbye to Changsoo.

Shortly after his departure, Bora announced she'd be heading off too.

"Are you sure?" Jinseung asked. "We haven't even used up all our time."

"I'm sure. But you two stay here, okay? Make good use of the time left." She flashed me a cheeky grin before leaving.

"What was that about?" Jinseung asked. "Does she know something?"

"Yes," I admitted.

He chuckled. "I suppose that's okay. It's Yang Bora."

"I trust her."

"Yeah, me too."

Our eyes lingered on each other. Jinseung looked so tantalising, biting his lip and surveying me, but we had an important topic to discuss.

"So, about us…are we…" I couldn't get the words out properly.

"Are we a couple now?" He finished for me. "I want you to be my girlfriend. It's as simple as that."

I want you to be my girlfriend. His words echoed in my head and spread a warm, dreamy feeling through my body—but one thing still bothered me. "Why the sudden change of heart?"

He paused in thought. "When I was in hospital I realised something…Ever since I left school, I've been working so hard. I've put work above everything else: my health, my family, my relationships…I don't want to do that anymore. I don't want to deny myself a relationship with you just because my popularity with fans might go down, or I might not get the same kind of acting roles anymore…You're more important to me." He took my hand in his and stroked it tenderly. "In saying that, if you don't want to be my girlfriend, I'd completely understand—"

"I do want to!"

"It's not easy to date someone like me. It won't be a normal relationship. We'll need to keep it a secret—at least in the beginning—and I'm so busy. I won't always have time to see you—"

I always knew there would be downsides and I was prepared to obey all the conditions. "I still want to try."

"You were against it not too long ago."

"I couldn't stand knowing that you lost that role because of me."

"You don't need to feel bad about that."

"Talking to Baek Yena eased my concerns. Once upon a time, she was in a situation just like ours. She and Ko Dongwoo made the choice to be together and she's never regretted it. That made me feel like we have a chance to make this work."

"And Busan? I don't want to stand in your way…"

I shook my head. "There's still time. I can back out of the job and keep looking for a position in Seoul."

"If you're sure."

"One hundred percent."

"Then let's do this. Let's make it work."

Before I could verbalise my agreement, he kissed me. It caught me off-guard and I took a moment to close my eyes and reciprocate, but by then he was already breaking away.

"Chloe…" he said, lips by my ear.

"Hmm?"

"When would you like to go on our first official date?"

Chapter 48

Our first official date. That's what Jinseung had promised, yet he cancelled our plans and days passed with no further word on that front. Just as I was beginning to get dispirited, a surprise flower delivery arrived to my apartment.

"Chloe Gibson?" the delivery man asked when I answered the door.

"Yes, that's me."

"These are for you." He presented me with the huge bouquet. Beautiful, bright pink peonies.

I accepted it, bemused. "Thanks." I brought the flowers inside, placed them on the table, and fumbled for the message card.

Meet me at Cinema Lumiere, 5pm.

* * *

When I arrived at Cinema Lumiere, a note on the locked door read "Closed for a private booking." I stated my name over the intercom and the door clicked open.

Classic movie posters in skinny black frames lined the corridor leading to the lobby which featured leafy indoor plants, a well-stocked bar, and a small sitting area. A large blackboard displayed screening times written in white chalk. A lone woman stood behind the counter flipping through a magazine. Her eyes met mine. She was tall, lithe, and beautiful, with brown dyed hair and green contact lenses, probably in her late twenties.

"So you're Chloe Gibson," she said, a twinkle in her eye. "Nice to meet you. I'm Shin Jina, Jinseung's sister."

"Jinseung's sister!?" I spluttered. I had heard a sister mentioned before, but for some reason it had never occurred to me that I might meet her.

"That's right. He has told me all about you."

"Really?"

She nodded.

"Do you work here?" I asked.

"Yes. I do this part-time and I'm a part-time model."

"So you work in the entertainment industry too…That's cool."

"Yeah, though I'm hardly as successful as *Dongsaeng*—not that I envy him at all. Anyway, go on through to the cinema. He's waiting for you." She motioned to a pair of double doors.

I entered the cinema and gazed around in awe, absorbing my surroundings. The room had been decorated with fairy lights strung across the walls, and candles glowed softly inside cup holders. Jinseung sat in the centre of the back row, a delighted expression on his face as he watched me look around.

"Wow…It's so pretty…" I gushed.

"Do you like it? *Noona* helped me with the decorating."

"It's beautiful. You organised all this for me?"

"Of course. Come here and take a seat."

I ascended the steps to the back row and sat down next to him on the fancy recliner seat. "Comfy!"

Jinseung held my hand in his. "Sorry it's been a while. Things have been busy, as you know."

"I was beginning to think you had forgotten," I admitted.

He shook his head. "How could I? I've been so excited for this."

"Sorry for doubting you. It's clear you put a lot of thought into this date."

"I wanted to make it special for you. I know that the idea of dating in secret is hard, but I wanted to show you that we can still go on proper dates. We just have to improvise a little."

"Thank you. And thank you for the flowers as well. They're lovely."

"I'm glad you liked them. Are you cold?"

"A little."

He reached to his left and grabbed a blanket off the chair.

"Thanks." I draped it over myself and snuggled into its warmth.

"What would you like to watch?"

"What are the options?"

He handed me a programme of new releases, plus some old classics.

"Hmm…"

"What are you in the mood for?"

"Something funny."

After some deliberation, we settled on a recently released romantic comedy. Jinseung notified his sister and brought back an armload of drinks and snacks. As he settled down beside me, the lights turned off and the big screen lit up. He lifted the chair arm between us so we could snuggle up close under the blanket.

The movie started to play. Jinseung wrapped his arm around me and I leaned my head on his shoulder.

"This is nice," he said.

"So nice," I echoed, savouring the closeness between us.

Throughout the movie, our eyes constantly wandered from the screen to gaze at one another.

"Not enjoying the movie?" I asked.

"You're more interesting," Jinseung replied. He pulled me even closer.

"You're distracting."

"Don't you like it?"

"…I do."

"See." He nuzzled me and kissed my neck.

We spent the rest of the movie only half watching. When the credits rolled, a sense of disappointment swelled up inside me. *I should have picked a longer movie, I don't want this night to end.*

"What would you like to watch next?" Jinseung asked, snapping me from my discontent.

"...Next?"

"I have the cinema booked out all evening. There's still time to watch another two movies if you want."

"It seems neither of us can really concentrate on watching movies."

"You know that's not the point. We get to spend all this time together."

I grinned. "Give me the programme."

We watched two more films over the course of the night, and following that, we hung out in the foyer of the cinema. Jina brought us over dinner from the restaurant next door.

"Delicious!" I exclaimed after swallowing my first mouthful. Despite constant snacking during the movies, I somehow felt ravenous. Jinseung didn't eat much of his own meal, seemingly preferring to watch me eat instead.

"Not hungry?" I asked.

"Must have eaten too much popcorn."

"But it's so delicious!"

"I'll take it home and eat it later."

"Okay, suit yourself."

He continued to watch me eat for a few more minutes, head resting in his hands. "Chloe..." he said tentatively.

"Hmmm?"

"You're not going to Busan anymore, right?"

"I'm staying here."

"Then are you still looking for somewhere to live?"

"Yeah. I mean, there are a few options I could take. None of them great."

"The vacant apartment...please take it."

The offer was tempting, but it was overly generous. I didn't want to be a burden on Jinseung, nor did I want to rely on him too much. "I don't know…"

"Please. I want to help you."

His insistence was so earnest that it didn't take much to wear my resistance down. "Well…Okay. But only until I have a job."

"I'm not going to be able to convince you to stay there longer than that, am I?"

"No."

"*Aigoo*. I like your independent streak. And you're stubborn, just like me."

I checked the time. "It's after midnight."

"Should we call it a night then?"

"But I don't want to."

"Then perhaps…should we head back to my apartment?"

"Is the no-sleepover rule still in play?"

Jinseung laughed. "No. That was recently abolished."

Chapter 49

A pang of guilt hit me as I looked around the lavish apartment, box of belongings in hand. I wondered how much income Jinseung was sacrificing to let me live here rent-free.

Putting my feelings of guilt aside, I released the heavy box from my arms onto the living room floor. As I stood back up, I noticed a bottle of wine wrapped in purple ribbons on the dining table, a note alongside it. I unfolded the small piece of paper.

See you tonight x

It had been a little while since I last saw Jinseung and this reminder that we would shortly see each other again filled my heart with joy.

Feeling reenergised, I started to unpack my things. It didn't take long to find a place for everything in the spacious apartment. With that done, I needed to go to the supermarket to stock the pantry for the evening's meal. I grabbed my bag and headed out.

An hour later I returned, arms aching from lugging two shopping bags brimming with produce.

As I prepared dinner, my lingering sense of guilt started to be overshadowed by the satisfaction of getting to cook in a full-sized kitchen with all the bells and whistles. I turned some music on and sang at the top of my lungs while I chopped vegetables.

My singing aloud continued while the food cooked in the oven and I almost didn't hear my phone ringing. I quickly turned down the music and ran to pick up my phone on the last ring. "*Yeoboseyo?*"

"Chloe, I'm afraid I have some bad news," Jinseung said, voice sombre.

I braced myself, fearing I was about to be let down. "What's wrong?"

"…I have to cancel tonight."

There it is. "Why?" I croaked. My throat was dry and tight. *All this dinner preparation. All for nothing.*

"I'm sorry. It's work. I can't get out of it."

Before I could express my disappointment to him, the doorbell rang.

"Hold on a sec," I said. *Who's ringing the bell if it's not Jinseung? I* answered the door, bemused.

Jinseung stood outside, handsome as ever, crooked grin on his irresistibly cute face. He bore a bouquet of flowers and a box of fancy chocolates.

I gasped in outrage. "You're evil!"

"Did I take that joke too far?"

"Yes! How could you say that?"

"But aren't you relieved I'm here?"

"Incredibly relieved. But don't do something like that again!"

"All right, all right." He sniffed the air as he brought the flowers and chocolate inside. "Wow, smells delicious! What's cooking?"

"A traditional British roast. Well, as traditional as possible with the ingredients available here."

"*Daebak.*"

"I told you I would make it for you."

"I remember. Thank you." He looked around. "I like what you've done with the place."

I laughed. "It doesn't look any different. I don't have enough stuff to fill up a space as big as this. I shouldn't get too comfortable here anyway. Soon, the school will rent an apartment for me."

"So you heard back?"

"Yes. I got the job!"

He hugged me. "That's great! I knew you wouldn't struggle to find something."

"And the good news doesn't end there. Remember how I got scammed by that teaching placement company? They have been fined for their actions, so I'll be getting some compensation."

"Good. Compensation is the least you deserve for going through all that."

"It definitely helps."

"I have some good news too."

"Oh yeah? What is it?"

"My latest audition went really well, and I've already been invited back for a screen test. If I get it, it'll be my biggest role yet."

"That's amazing! It seems like you've landed back on your feet."

"A good excuse to celebrate, don't you think? Shall we crack open that bottle of wine?"

"Good idea."

He opened the bottle and poured us each a generous glass. As I drank, I mused on how far I'd come in the last few months—from the clueless girl who got scammed, to an actor in a K-drama with wonderful friends in the entertainment industry, and even a famous boyfriend who seemed to adore me. Even though I would be dropping acting for teaching soon, the future excited me.

"What are you smiling about?" Jinseung asked, lips quirked in amusement.

"Oh, I was just thinking how lucky I am."

He shook his head. "I don't believe in luck. Good things happen when you're a good person."

"That's—" Suddenly all of the lights turned off, leaving the room in darkness. "Huh? What's going on?"

"Must be a power cut." He looked out the window. "Yep. It's affecting this whole area."

I felt a surge of panic. "Oh no! What about dinner?" I rushed to open the oven. "It hasn't finished cooking."

"Hopefully it will come back on soon, but for now, let's light some candles and just enjoy it."

I sat back down, arms folded, feeling bitter about my dinner being ruined if the power didn't come back on. Meanwhile Jinseung placed some candles around the room, lit them, then pulled the throw off the couch and laid it out on the floor.

"What are you doing?" I asked.

"It's an indoor picnic. We can sit on the floor, drink some wine, and eat some chocolate while the candles flicker around us. Isn't it kind of romantic? Come here."

Still pouting about dinner, I reluctantly joined him. He pulled me into his arms, my head leaned back on his chest.

"See, isn't this nice?" he murmured into my ear.

I had to admit, it was pretty romantic.

He began to kiss my neck, light and fluttery, mixed with his warm breath making my skin prickle. The candles glowed softly in the background. We sank low onto the floor, limbs tangled. He kissed me slowly, taking his time to draw out each glorious sensation. I was completely at his mercy.

"Chloe," he said between kisses. "Let's go public with our relationship…"

I pulled back in surprise. "Huh?"

"…In one year."

"Oh."

"If you can put up with me for that long."

The power came back on, and everything started up again with a whirr and buzz.

One year. I couldn't possibly know what would be in store for us. The only thing I knew for sure was that I was willing to put my heart on the line to be with him.

I nodded. "Okay. One year."

The Dating Drama

Book 2

Chapter 1

The last time I saw my boyfriend was on a gigantic digital billboard prominently displayed in the middle of Gangnam, Seoul. Funny how I saw him more in advertisements than in real life—but that's just the way it is when you're dating a celebrity. His hectic filming and promo schedule were to blame. But today was the day we would finally see each other again.

Sweet daydreams filled my head as I floated in a haze of bliss towards the reunion with my love. Nothing could spoil my good mood. Absolutely nothing.

I skipped and twirled along the route to Shin Jinseung's apartment building, headphones blasting feel-good K-pop in my ears. In my daydreamy state, I stepped out onto the street to cross the road, oblivious to the fact that the pedestrian signal had turned red. A screech of car brakes followed, then the long, loud honk of a horn. The irate driver rolled down his window and yelled at me. "Oi! Watch where you're going, *oeguk saram!*"

"Oops. Sorry," I said sheepishly. I brushed the incident off and continued on my way. *Nice try, but you can't ruin my mood that easily.*

The gleaming tower of luxury residential apartments where Jinseung lived entered my view, and I hurried my pace, winding through the crowded footpath. When I reached the main entrance, I reminded myself that it was safer to slip in through one of the hidden side doors. After four months as a couple, we were still keeping our relationship a secret, and I couldn't enter and leave his apartment building willy nilly lest we get caught.

I took a roundabout path to the other side of the building, carefully surveying my surroundings, checking no one was watching me. When the coast was clear, I entered a nondescript door marked "no entry" with a swipe of my key card—Jinseung had gifted me his spare one.

The door led into a narrow, windowless corridor which eventually opened out to the elevators in the lobby. From there, I made my way to the twentieth floor.

Butterflies in my stomach, I quickly checked my appearance in my compact mirror. Jinseung was around gorgeous actors and models all the time, so I had to look my best. After touching up my lipstick, I took a deep breath and told myself not to worry. *You've got this. He's not interested in anyone except you.* The relationship was doomed if I allowed myself to be the victim of poor self-esteem.

I took a calming breath before pressing my finger to the doorbell. Jinseung opened the door immediately. You would think I'd be used to his amazing good looks by now, but my jaw still dropped at the sight of him. In fact, he looked even better than I remembered. His bright, smiley eyes scanned me while he bit his lip, and his lean, toned body dressed in a slim-fitting black t-shirt and jeans leaned up against the door frame, arms folded. I felt myself falling for him all over again.

"What are you standing around for?" Jinseung asked with a charming smirk. "Come in."

I shook myself out of my lovestruck stupor and followed him inside. He turned on some music—a quirky acoustic love song which suited my mood.

"Would you like something to drink?" he asked, walking towards the kitchen.

"Sure. What have you got?"

He held up an expensive-looking bottle of wine. "Would this lovely little bottle of exquisite French wine suffice, my lady?"

"That will do nicely."

He poured two glasses then beckoned me to sit down with him on the black leather couch. "God, I've missed you," he said. "It feels like forever since I last saw you."

"I've missed you too. Dating you feels like I'm still single half the time," I admitted.

"Thank you for being so patient."

"Even for the small snatches of time we get to spend together, it's worth it."

"I'm glad you think so. Still, you put up with a lot to be with me. I'm well aware of that. Not everyone would do it."

I shrugged. "It's all part of the package of dating someone famous. How is your schedule looking now, anyway?"

"You'll be pleased to know that I've finished all my scenes for Love's Awakening. Apart from a couple auditions coming up, I'm a free man."

"That's a relief." An invisible weight lifted from my shoulders. I could have him all to myself—at least for a little while. I recalled the promise he made to me six months ago—we would go public with our relationship in one year. We had already made it half-way through. If I could just hold on for six more months, we wouldn't have to sneak around anymore. I couldn't wait.

Jinseung took a sip of his wine. "How's teaching going? Are the kids still keeping you on your toes?"

"Well, they've finally stopped asking me questions about my time on Hidden History, but I still wish they'd focus more."

"I'd be distracted too, if you were my teacher." He sidled up to me, a mischievous look on his face. "It's been so long I've forgotten what it's like to kiss you. Help me remember?"

I grimaced at his corny line but still found him irresistible. I leaned in to kiss him, but stopped short to observe the cute, slightly ridiculous look on his face—his eyes closed tight and lips puckered in anticipation. I couldn't help but giggle.

He opened his eyes. "What? You tease." He pulled me to him with an aggression that thrilled me. His lips found mine, hot and sweet. He wasted no time in deepening the kiss, tongue exploring my mouth with fervour. His body pressed up against mine. I had to pull away for breath. He turned his attention to kissing my neck before returning to my lips and pulling me into his lap. I squirmed to get into a comfortable position, but ended up kicking my wine glass over and spilling it on the floor. I turned my head to check the damage.

"It doesn't matter," Jinseung mumbled, fumbling with my buttons.

I returned my focus to him, settling in his lap, feeling his body rub up against me. He was in the process of pushing me down onto my back when another disruption arose—the doorbell. "Ignore it," he implored.

"But—"

"Please."

"Who could that be? What if they're waiting outside? What if they can *hear* us?"

"It's probably just Changsoo. No one else can get up here anyway, except the cleaner."

"He might let himself in if you don't answer. He knows your door code, right?"

"Ugh. You're right."

Changsoo knew about our relationship, but it would still be awkward if he barged in on us during such a private moment.

We quickly untangled ourselves, tidied our outfits and hair. Jinseung went to the door. He peered through the hole to check who was there. "Huh? They've gone."

"That's weird."

He opened the door and glanced around the corridor. "No one's here. Oh—" Something caught his attention. He bent down and reemerged holding a cardboard box.

"What's that?" I asked.

"I don't know. It was outside the door."

"Not expecting any deliveries?"

"I don't get packages here. They come to my private post box or to the agency."

"Ah. Does it say anything?"

"Nope. No label or anything."

"Could a fan have put it there?"

"I hope not. So far I've managed to avoid fans finding out my home address."

"Are you going to open it?"

"Yeah. Maybe I'll be able to find out who it's from and how it got here."

He brought the package to the dining table where he opened it with a knife. He peered inside the box, rummaged a little, then suddenly recoiled with a look of distaste.

"What? What is it?" I asked.

"It's…nothing. Never mind." He closed the box.

"I can tell that it's not nothing. Let me see."

"I'd rather you didn't."

"Don't hide things from me."

Jinseung reluctantly stood aside and let me open the box. Heart pounding in my chest, I pulled one cardboard flap open, and then the other. What I saw made a shriek escape my throat. There, lying atop a pile of shredded paper, was a mutilated Barbie doll—its limbs twisted and disfigured. Its eyes stabbed out. Its plastic body stained red. *Human blood?!*

"What the heck! Who would send you something like that?"

"Probably a *sasaeng* fan or something. Don't worry about it. Stuff like this happens all the time when you're famous. Occupational hazard." He closed the box again and put it by the rubbish bin.

"How can you take this so lightly? This *sasaeng* fan must know where you live!" I knew all about *sasaeng* fans and the crazy stuff they were capable of—extreme stalking, letters written in blood, breaking into a celebrity's house in their underwear, poisoning their idol's drinks, to name a few.

Jinseung chewed this over. "You're right. That does present a problem. I'll let the security team know tomorrow."

"Tomorrow? But this crazy person could still be in the building this very moment! You should call the police."

He shook his head. "That would be a vast overreaction. If I called the police every time a fan did something disturbing, there'd be no end to it."

I sighed helplessly. "I suppose you're right."

"Please don't let it worry you. I've had fans do weird shit in the past and it's never amounted to anything. Come on." He led me back to the couch and placed a comforting arm around me. "Everything will be okay."

"Well, if you're sure…"

"Absolutely." He massaged my shoulders, trying to put me at ease.

My tension began to dissolve. Celebrities dealt with stuff like this every day. Besides, the security in this building was top-class. They would be able to catch the culprit through checking the CCTV footage as soon as Jinseung told them what happened.

He turned my head towards his and kissed me again, tenderly stroking my cheek. I tried to get into it but couldn't. My thoughts kept turning back to the doll. The image of the blonde-haired, blue-eyed, blood-stained toy seared in my mind. A frightening idea began to take form, and I broke away from the kiss with a gasp.

"What's wrong?" Jinseung asked, concern flashing in his eyes.

"The doll…" I croaked. "What if it represents me?"

Chapter 2

Silence reigned as twenty-five faces stared up at me with blank expressions. I repeated my question and not a single person raised their hand to answer.

Teaching at the *hagwon* was like speaking into a void a lot of the time. I found it difficult to get the kids to engage with me. They all just sat silently with their exercise books open in front of them, happy to listen but unwilling to say a word, or even to express a grain of interest. At first, I didn't mind this behaviour, but as the months wore on, it began to frustrate me. *Perhaps I'm not cut out to be a teacher.*

The only thing which seemed to excite my students was the fact that I used to star in a K-drama with Shin Jinseung and Baek Yena, but by now we had thoroughly exhausted that topic.

I clicked through to the next slide in my presentation on the large LED screen adjacent to the whiteboard at the back of the classroom. The topic was "text language" and common acronyms used in online forums, which I thought was a fun topic for teenagers. but before I could begin, a short bell ring signalled the end of the lesson, and the students quickly dispersed.

During the five-minute break between classes, I checked my phone, hoping for an update from Jinseung regarding the doll incident, but there were no new messages. Jinseung had convinced me that the doll didn't represent me—it was just the most common kind of doll available to buy. Still, I had hoped for some progress regarding identifying the culprit. Jinseung said he would speak to the building staff, but I didn't know the outcome. Before I had time to type a message, the next batch of students began to filter into the room. My eye was drawn to a new student in the group. She was tall, with long hair pulled back in a high ponytail. Thick-framed glasses gave her a studious look, along with the overstuffed leather satchel on her hip and the large ring binder hugged to her chest. She was wearing a school uniform I hadn't seen before—a cream-coloured sweater over a white shirt with a neat bow tied below the collar. On the bottom, a red-plaid pleated skirt and white over-the-knee socks. I wondered which high school she went to.

When everyone had settled down in the bright orange ergonomic chairs behind their desks, I asked the new student to introduce herself. To my surprise, she got up and stood in front of the class. "My name is Kim Sungmi," she said. "I am eighteen years old. I am joining your class from now on." Her voice was quiet but assured. She spoke English well.

"Thank you, Kim Sungmi."

As was tradition, I asked her to pick an English name for her to use in the class. She picked Sophie.

When Sophie had returned to her seat, I put up my slides for the day's lesson. We would be going over some common homonyms, and I had prepared a little game. The slides displayed multiple sentences, but only one sentence on each was correct. I tasked the class with telling me which were right, and even threw in a bribe of candy.

At the beginning of the first round of the game, I was fully prepared to be met by bored expressions as usual, but to my surprise, a hand shot up. It was Sophie.

"Yes, Sophie?"

"Number three," she said.

I clicked to the next screen and a red tick mark animation

appeared beside the third sentence. "That's correct. Well done." I put a small wrapped candy on her desk.

Sophie answered correctly twice more, and then something unexpected happened—another couple of tentative hands rose into the air. And after a few more rounds, other members of the class started to join in. Sophie's enthusiasm seemed to be contagious.

After the game, keeping the class engaged was a breeze. The entire lesson flew by, and before I knew it, class was over. The classroom slowly emptied until the only student who remained was Sophie. She approached my desk. "Excuse me, Ms. Gibson."

"How can I help you?" I asked, a little taken aback. No one had stayed behind to talk to me before.

Sophie blushed. "I was wondering if you could recommend some English books to read."

"Of course. What kind of books?"

"Novels. But ones that are simple to read."

"What is your English level?"

"Around B2."

I opened my notebook and compiled a short list of titles, before tearing out the page and passing it to her. She accepted it eagerly.

"And if you can't find any of these, I'd be happy to bring some books from home for you to borrow."

"Thank you," Sophie said, glowing with gratitude. She carefully folded and stowed the piece of notepaper in the front pocket of her satchel.

"Have a good evening," I said.

"Good evening." She bowed.

What a breath of fresh air, I thought, watching her leave the classroom.

* * *

Drip. Drip. Drip. Streetlamps illuminated clusters of raindrops in the darkness.

I had just left work. Like most *hagwons*—a.k.a cram schools, students attended in the late afternoon or in the evening. My teaching hours were four through nine, but normally I arrived earlier to prepare, and left later to mark student work. On this night, I had stayed around an hour late.

I opened my umbrella—a cheap transparent one, and set out at a quick pace, dashing through puddles which splashed up my ankles. The bus was already at the stop, route number 76 displayed on its back in orange digits.

I ran as fast as I could, but the bus started to indicate, and it pulled out into the flow of traffic before I could reach it. I sagged in defeat, puffing.

After I had caught my breath, I checked the schedule affixed to the back of the glass bus shelter. To my dismay, the next bus wouldn't be for another forty minutes. I made up my mind to walk home rather than wait, hopeful that the rain wouldn't intensify.

Normally I stuck to main streets as much as I could whenever I walked home from work, but in my desperation to get back as quickly as possible, I decided to take a shortcut.

The steep, narrow side street had no footpath and cars were parked haphazardly along one side. I carefully made my way down the road, avoiding slippery smooth parts. As I walked, my ears pricked at the sound of footsteps following me. Panic surged through my body— I was still on edge after the doll incident. I turned around just to check who was there and put my mind at ease. All was still and quiet on the empty street, not a soul in sight. I shrugged and moved on. *It must have been my imagination.*

A few steps later, I heard the sound again. Without pausing to think, I turned my head. I caught sight of a figure, but before I could process anything about the person, they had entered a shop and disappeared, the door swinging shut with a bang behind them. I was alone on the quiet road again. I admonished myself for being so paranoid.

Chapter 3

"Ewww, that's disgusting!" Yang Bora said, face screwed up in revulsion.

I had just finished relaying a graphic description of the mutilated, bloodstained Barbie doll delivery. We were in the kitchen of my apartment, getting food and drinks ready for an afternoon binge-watching K-dramas.

"Do you think a *sasaeng* fan could have done it?" I asked, turning the electric kettle on to make tea.

Recovering from her initial disgust, Bora adjusted her circle-framed glasses. "Sounds like the work of a *sasaeng* fan, all right. Though what could be their motivation? A warning perhaps. Don't date anyone?"

"I was afraid that the doll might represent me."

Bora shuddered. "Now that's a scary theory. I truly hope that's not the case. Has the culprit been ascertained?"

I shook my head. "They were caught on the security cameras bribing the concierge to find out Jinseung's apartment number. Unfortunately, they were wearing a black motorcycle helmet and dark clothing. Don't even know if it was a man or a woman."

"So they could still be at large…Has anything else happened since then?"

"No. Nothing." Except a strange feeling that I was being followed, but I had no concrete evidence and put that firmly down to paranoia.

"Well, I'm sure that concierge was sacked, and no one will be let up to Jinseung's apartment again."

"Yeah. No doubt."

"And if something like this happens again, KAM will definitely up the ante on his personal security. So I wouldn't worry too much if I were you."

"You're right. Though I feel I should be careful."

"You should always be careful anyway—dating someone so high-profile." She sighed. "After all this, I think we should watch something nice and comforting."

"I couldn't agree more. How about a family drama?"

"Good idea."

I prepared a pot of English breakfast tea and opened the seven-eleven shopping bag Bora had brought over with her. "Nice selection," I said, examining the variety of colourfully packaged treats inside. I arranged them on the bench.

"I know you're addicted to those honey butter chips."

"They're my absolute favourite. Thank you."

We relocated to the lounge—a nook in the open-plan living area containing a small cream-coloured sectional topped with a mountain of soft cushions, and a fluffy faux-fur rug at our feet. I laid out the tea and snacks on the coffee table. Bora had already gained control of the TV remote and proceeded to browse the catalogue of shows on the large screen opposite us.

Meeting regularly to binge-watch K-dramas and chat had become a regular activity for me and Bora, vastly favoured over going out to restaurants and bars, plus more frugal as well. I was so happy that we had managed to maintain our friendship despite our busy schedules. She hadn't changed a bit since we worked together—apart from the more sophisticated wardrobe and designer handbag she had procured after her promotion.

After some deliberation, we picked Ojakgyo Family, which seemed to fit the bill of a warm and cosy family drama. Neither of us had watched it before.

"Joo Won is so hot," Bora said with a wistful sigh, sinking lower onto the couch. "I suppose you can't relate to celebrity crushes anymore. You're already dating one."

I hit her lightly with a cushion. "I still think Joo Won is hot. Don't tell Jinseung."

Joo Won aside, as I watched the episode, I couldn't help but think about my time on Hidden History and the amazing experience of being part of a K-drama. A surge of longing flowed through my veins, a melancholy feeling that I'd never get to experience that same thrill again.

"I miss it…" I murmured.

"What?"

"Acting. Being in Hidden History was the best time of my life. And not just because I met Shin Jinseung."

"I get that. Teaching must feel boring in comparison."

"It does."

Bora nudged me playfully. "Why don't you get back into entertainment?"

I shook her off. "It's too difficult as a foreigner."

"There's gotta be something else out there for you."

"I'm not that optimistic. No. I think I'll stick to teaching. It's solid work. It pays the bills."

She rolled her eyes. "Solid work that pays the bills…so boring."

"There's one good thing. A new girl started recently, and she's been making teaching worthwhile for me. Her name's Kim Sungmi."

"Sounds like you've found your star student."

"Yes. I think so too."

We returned our attention to the episode and refilled our mugs with tea.

"Uee is funny looking, isn't she? But still pretty." Bora assessed the female lead, nibbling on a bar of Ghana milk chocolate.

Partway through the third consecutive episode, her phone began to ring in a tone which got progressively louder until she fished it out of the depths of her handbag.

She grimaced as she looked at who was calling her. "Can you pause it? I need to take this. It's Go Yoojin."

"Sure."

Go Yoojin was the teenage actor Bora was managing. She had a reputation for being a major drama queen, and Bora had confirmed this to me on a number of occasions.

Bora answered the call. Go Yoojin spoke in a shrill, high-pitched voice which I could hear despite my distance from the phone. She seemed to be having some kind of a crisis.

"Stay calm," Bora told her. "I'll be there in a minute." She ended the phone call. "I've got to go. Yoojin's having another one of her little meltdowns. On my day off too. Ugh. Sorry, Chloe."

"No problem. Hope she's okay."

"It's probably something trivial. Last time she called me like this it was because she couldn't find her favourite top."

"I'm sure she's grateful to have you to rely on."

"Yeah, I guess. Anyway, I better get going." She grabbed her leather jacket and put it on. "Don't watch any more episodes without me, okay? I'll try to come back later."

"Okay, buh-bye."

The door shut behind her with a click.

I put the remaining snacks away before they could tempt me, then flung myself in a heap on the couch, wondering what to do for the rest of the afternoon.

My eyes wandered to my diary which lay atop the coffee table. If there were any errands or tasks I needed to get done, they would be listed within its pages. I reached for the leather-covered notebook and opened it to the thin, red ribbon bookmark. Scanning the page, a note I had scribbled down a few days ago caught my eye—*English books for Sophie*. It reminded me to check my bookshelf for something that might interest her.

I ran my fingers along the spines of the titles housed in my book-shelf. I did not have a large collection, since I left most of my books behind in England, and I hadn't procured many new titles since moving to Seoul. Out of the few books I did possess, I pulled out any which looked promising. I settled back on the couch with the small pile of books on my lap and proceeded to read a few pages of each to determine whether they would be appropriate for someone still learning the language.

After deciding the first book was too difficult, I started a stack of rejects on the coffee table. As I checked each book, the reject stack grew. I held out hope for the last book in my hands, but quickly realised that it too would be inappropriate. I put the books back on the shelf, annoyed that my chance to do something nice for a student had been dashed. *Or had it?* A new idea popped into my head. There was a bookshop not too far from my place and it stocked a few English books. I had nothing else to do that afternoon, so why not go and have a browse? Besides, I was short on reading material, and if I ended up buying something for Sophie to borrow, I could read it after her.

Before leaving my apartment, I put on a woollen hat and scarf—it was early spring, but the weather was still wintery. I decided to walk to the bookshop rather than taking the subway, pushing my recent paranoia about being followed to the back of my mind. I needed the exercise, and I hadn't been outside all day, so the fresh, crisp air was welcome—despite the hint of pollution.

The brisk walk quickly warmed me up, especially as there were a lot of steep roads to climb. After winding through the network of narrow backstreets dense with houses, convenience stores, and small restaurants, I emerged in a busy shopping area. The bookshop was located between a chain coffee shop and a pharmacy. "Ginger Books," read the sign above a large window peering into the warm and cosy interior.

I removed my hat and scarf upon entering the shop and tucked them away in my bag. Like most indoor spaces in Seoul during cold weather, the shop was well-heated, necessitating the removal of layers.

Tall shelving units formed aisles with display tables around the border. A few patrons quietly browsed. I headed straight for the English-language section. Running my eyes over the shelves, I realised there were fewer books than I had hoped. I examined them one by one, looking for something easy to read, but with subject matter appealing enough for someone in their late teens.

As I spent my time perusing, I felt the eyes of the shop assistant behind the counter watching me. I suspected that he wasn't used to seeing foreigners in the shop. I simply ignored him and continued with my task.

After a thorough assessment of all the titles, I ended up selecting three and took them to the counter. The shop assistant continued to stare at me even as we were face to face during the transaction. His brow was furrowed slightly. He looked like he was trying to place me.

"Do we know each other?" I ventured.

He looked at me with surprise, possibly at my ability to speak Korean, and he averted his gaze as if suddenly embarrassed by his behaviour. "Maybe," he said. "I'm sure I've seen you somewhere before."

I looked him up and down. "I'm sorry. I don't recognise you."

"Is that so?" He hummed as the receipt printed out. He slipped it inside the cover of one of the books, then placed them in a plastic bag emblazoned with the store's logo—a curled-up ginger cat.

I put away my wallet and grabbed the bag.

The shop assistant snapped his fingers. "Ah! I've seen you on television. You were in that drama."

So that's what he recognised me from. I was surprised. It had been several months since the drama aired and no one had recognised me since. "Yes. I was in Hidden History."

"That's the one!"

"Well, I'll be going now…"

"Wait! Can I take a picture? I like to show the other staff members whenever someone famous visits the store."

I scoffed slightly. "I'm not famous."

"Please. My colleague was obsessed with that drama."

"Oh, all right then."

He whipped out his phone and took a couple of photos.

I relaxed again when the phone was back in his pocket.

"Thanks," he said. "Enjoy the books."

I departed the bookshop feeling slightly perturbed. I thought my days of being recognised were behind me, but it appeared I was mistaken.

Chapter 4

I hadn't been expecting to see the mangled doll again, yet there it was, exactly where Jinseung had left it the last time I visited his apartment—in the cardboard box next to the rubbish bin.

I had almost tripped over the box on my way out of the kitchen, then jumped back in fright, catching a glimpse of the creepy doll under the flimsy cardboard flap. Shuddering, I hurried away to confront Jinseung. "You didn't get rid of the doll?" I asked, aghast.

He sat on the couch, hunched over playing a video game on the TV. He put the controller down and rubbed the back of his neck sheepishly. "Oh that. I haven't gotten around to it. Changsoo said I should keep it as evidence, in case something like this happens again and I need proof, but I can't bring myself to go near it...to touch it... I've just been ignoring it. Helps that I haven't been home that much lately."

"Still, you can't just leave it there! How can you even live with that thing right there!"

"I know. Perhaps I should tackle the job now."

My gut clenched. I'd feel better if he got rid of the doll, but I didn't want to watch. "You should. I won't be able to think of anything else knowing that it's still sitting in that box, right where you left it before."

"Then I'll do it."

"I don't want to look, though."

"Close your eyes."

"That's not enough to detract my attention from what you're doing."

"Shut yourself in the bedroom while I take care of it then."

"Now?" I hummed in consideration. "Okay. Come and get me when you're done."

I crossed the living room to his bedroom and closed myself inside. I sat on the end of his bed while I waited. The process seemed to be taking some time, so I lay back and stared up at the ceiling, trying not to think about it.

Jinseung opened the door a few minutes later. He seemed flustered, his ears and cheeks tinted bright pink. "It's taken care of."

I snapped upright. "What did you do with it?"

"I wore rubber gloves and put it in a ziplock bag. I stored it in a drawer for now. Maybe I'll get Changsoo to take it off my hands…"

"Good idea. I'd feel better if it wasn't in this house, but for now, I'll tolerate it."

"I got rid of the box too."

"Good."

Jinseung shuffled on his feet, an anxious look upon his face.

"Is something wrong?" I asked.

He shook his head. "No…it's nothing. Don't worry."

I raised an eyebrow, unconvinced. Before I could press him further, he extended a hand and tugged me off the bed. He drew me into his arms and kissed my forehead.

"I'm sorry this happened," he murmured, lips against my skin.

"It's not your fault."

"You've seen one of the ugly sides of fame now. I should have protected you from it."

"There was nothing you could do."

"I suppose not." He sighed. "Anyway, let's not dwell on that anymore. Come on. I've got a two-player game we can play." His arm around me, he walked me back to the living room.

* * *

"I WIN AGAIN," Jinseung teased, after beating me what must have been the tenth time in a row.

"Ugh," I grumbled. "I suck at these kinds of games!" I tossed the controller to the side in frustration.

He chuckled. "Perhaps we should take a break. You hungry?"

"Famished."

"Shall we go get something to eat then? There's no food here."

"You mean, should *I* go and get something to eat." It seemed trivial, but one of the things I disliked about dating him was that I always had to be the one to go out and pick up food.

He flashed me a sympathetic look. "I know it's a pain. Sorry. I'll make it up to you later."

I huffed. "Fine. I'll go. That Chinese place you like?"

"Yep. Sounds good."

I called the restaurant to place an order, then got ready to leave a bit later.

"Don't forget to get some of that yummy sauce they have," Jinseung reminded me on my way out the door.

"Got it." I made a mental note.

On my way to the nearby Chinese restaurant, I stuffed my hands in the fleece-lined pockets of my jacket. My breath came out in puffs of mist in the night air. The streets were busy, and I could hear music in the distance. I remembered that there was a lantern festival on at the park. I would have gone if I hadn't made plans to spend the evening with Jinseung. *If only we could go together.* I tried to shrug off my disappointment.

The restaurant looked like nothing special from the outside. An LED sign flickered and buzzed above the door, two of the characters missing due to the bulbs having died. Fragrant ginger, garlic, and cooking oil assailed my nose when I entered. The takeaway area was packed with customers, all the waiting seats were taken up, and a line trailed from the counter. A door on the left led to a dining area with plastic chairs, tables lined with paper tablecloths, and faded posters on the walls. The restaurant was much busier than usual thanks to the festival. All of the tables were full with hungry patrons, the noise of their loud chatter mixing with the clanging and splattering sounds from the kitchen.

I waited in the queue at the counter only to be informed that my order would take at least another ten minutes due to how busy they were. Feeling cramped in the small waiting area, I went outside and sent a message to Jinseung saying I would be a while. I stood leaning with my back against the wall, watching the crowds of people on their way to and from the festival. Many cute couples passed by, holding hands or with their arms around one another. A lot of them were dressed in *hanbok*. A wave of longing washed over me. Would I ever be able to do that with Jinseung in public? Those couples looked so carefree. I couldn't help feeling a pang of jealousy.

After waiting ten minutes, I went back inside. Soon enough, my order was ready. The man behind the counter passed me three large polystyrene takeout containers in a plastic bag. I asked for an extra punnet of the sauce Jinseung liked and threw that in as well.

Bag swinging from my hand, I made my way back to Jinseung's place, walking quickly so the food wouldn't get cold.

"That smells good," Jinseung said as I entered.

"Hopefully it was worth the wait."

He relieved me of the bag and unloaded the containers onto the table. "Why was it so busy?"

"The lantern festival is on tonight. The whole area is busy."

"Ohhh. I didn't realise. I should have made alternate dinner plans."

"Never mind. It didn't take *that* long. Let's eat. I'm starving."

We tucked into the overflowing containers of fried rice, dumplings, and sweet-and-sour pork. Despite how basic the restaurant appeared, the food really was delicious.

As we ate, my mind wandered back to the couples on the street. I imagined how romantic it would be to lay out a blanket and sit under the stars, surrounded by lanterns glowing in the moonlight. There would probably be fireworks as well. I was starting to get a major case of FOMO.

"What ya thinking about?" Jinseung asked, pausing between mouthfuls.

"Oh, nothing really." I gathered some fried rice with my chopsticks.

"Is there anything you want to do tonight? I told you I would make it up to you since you had to go out and get the food."

I wish we could go to the festival. "No. Not particularly." I couldn't help the note of melancholy in my voice.

Jinseung frowned, lines appearing on his forehead. "You want to go to the festival, don't you."

Damn. He's a mind reader. "Yeah, but I know that's not possible."

"You can go if you want. You don't have to stay here with me. I won't be offended if you go."

"But I want to go *with you*. It wouldn't be any fun by myself."

Jinseung smiled, his cheeks dimpling. "That's real sweet. Maybe if I disguised myself enough…"

My heart leapt with hope. "Wait—really?"

His smile slowly faded. "Perhaps not. It's kinda risky."

I returned my attention to my meal, disappointed.

"Unless…" He toyed with his chopsticks. "There will be fireworks, won't there?"

"I think so."

"I have an idea."

"What is it?"

"I'm not one hundred per cent sure if this will work, but I'll give it a shot."

I had no idea what he was talking about, but it sounded promising.

"I'll have to go and ask someone," he explained. "So, let's finish eating first."

My curiosity was well and truly piqued, but he wouldn't answer any of my questions, telling me to wait and see.

He slipped out of the apartment after dinner. Several minutes later, he returned, a triumphant look on his face.

"Well?" I asked.

"I just need to grab a few things, then we'll go."

"Go where?"

He didn't answer me. Instead, he disappeared into his room and re-emerged with a backpack slung over his shoulder. Then he went to the kitchen and filled a thermos with boiling water and grabbed something from the pantry. I watched him, bemused.

"Come on," Jinseung beckoned. "Bring your jacket."

Were we going to the festival? How was it possible?

Confusion reigned when Jinseung took me to the stairs rather than the elevator. "Aren't the elevators working?" I asked.

"We can only get to the top floor by the stairs."

"The top floor? Why are we going there?"

"You'll see."

Fortunately, there weren't too many flights of stairs to ascend since Jinseung's apartment was situated on one of the higher floors. At the very end of the staircase, there was a door which read "no entry." I realised that it led to the rooftop, and I understood Jinseung's plan. From the roof, we would be able to see the park and watch the fireworks. Too bad it didn't look like we'd be able to go through the door. I tried the handle, but as expected, it didn't relinquish. "It's locked," I said, frowning.

"Lucky I have the key then, isn't it?" He produced a green lanyard with a key attached from his pocket.

"How did you get that?"

"Had to work my charm on the building staff. Probably felt they owed me a favour too, since they let that crazy doll person up to my apartment. Anyway, I have the key for the night. I'll return it tomorrow morning." He unlocked the door, and we stepped out onto the rooftop.

I gazed around, absorbing my surroundings. The rooftop was utilitarian—ventilation units, aerials, and satellites on a concrete surface. However, the view was incredible. I leaned up against the fence and peered out over the city, Seoul in all its metropolitan glory—a dazzling array of multicolour lights, sprawling towers, bumper-to-bumper traffic, and thronging pedestrians.

"We're so high up…" I mused, feeling a little dizzy.

"Not scared of heights, are you?" Jinseung asked, standing beside me.

"I'm okay as long as I don't look straight down for too long."

"I know what you mean. It's a big drop."

"Where's the park?"

"Let's see…We're facing east right now, so the park should be somewhere over there." He gestured to his right. "Ah, I see it. Can you?"

I followed his gaze to a large patch of green, swarming with tiny people. The lanterns were reduced to glowing dots, but the sight was still magical.

Jinseung took off his backpack and opened it. He pulled out a blanket and lay it on the ground. He sat down and patted the space beside him. The fence around the perimeter of the rooftop was transparent, so we could still see well from our new viewpoint. I lay on my back and looked up at the sky. It was washed out due to the light pollution, but if I squinted enough, I could make out the stars.

"Want a coffee?" Jinseung asked. He procured the thermos from his backpack and a handful of flavoured coffee sachets.

"Yes, please."

He prepared me a cup and handed it to me. "So, what do you think? I know it's not as good as being at the festival for real…"

I shook my head. "It's perfect."

He smirked. "You're just saying that."

"No, truly. I've never been up on a rooftop so high like this before. It's pretty special."

"I'm glad you think so. Come 'ere." He lifted his arm, beckoning me to snuggle up to him. "Comfy?" he asked when I had wedged myself by his side, his arm around me.

"Very."

"Are you cold?"

"I'm fine. The coffee was a good idea." I cradled the warm cup in my hands.

Jinseung stroked his hand up and down my arm. "I feel kinda bad…not being able to take you to the places you want to see…do the things you want to do. I'm a bad boyfriend. I know it."

"You're not," I argued unconvincingly.

"You don't have to lie to me. It can't be fun being in your position. Sometimes I think you're too patient for your own good. Making sacrifices and compromising…those things aren't my strong point."

"Your ambition is part of what makes you so attractive to me." That was the truth. His work ethic was something I looked up to. Something I wanted to emulate. Just being around him was energising. "I wish I could be more like you."

"Ha! Why would you want to? You have plenty of attractive qualities, yourself."

"Such as?" I sidled up to him, fishing for compliments.

"You're so smart and courageous, coming here and learning the language when you were so young. You're talented, acting in a drama without any training and doing an excellent job at it. You're beautiful without much effort. You're kind and caring and intelligent. Oh, and I can't forget how fiercely independent you are. You never try to take advantage of my fame or my money, preferring to work things out on your own. I strongly believe that you could achieve anything if you set your mind to it. You just haven't decided what you want to do yet."

His words made me feel all warm and mushy. "You flatter me."

"You deserve all the praise you get."

I threw my arms around him, overwhelmed by his sweet compliments.

We spent the next hour talking about our hopes and dreams, our worries and our fears. It was the most he had ever opened up to me. This whole side of him was most endearing. The invisible barriers between us broke down. We were no longer a famous star and an ordinary young woman, we were simply two humans, sitting side by side on the rooftop.

Jinseung looked so dreamy, the moonlight caressing his skin, illuminating his features in a soft blue tone. His bright eyes sparkled as they looked down at me, full, soft lips quirking at the corner as he noticed me stare. He brushed my cheek with his thumb before catching my lips with his. He kissed me tenderly, but thoroughly, fingers laced in my hair. A soft whimper escaped my mouth when he broke away, and three words came tumbling out before I could help it. "I love you."

Jinseung's forehead wrinkled, an inscrutable expression on his face. He looked into my eyes but didn't say anything. My cheeks were beginning to burn. *Perhaps I shouldn't have said anything...*A loud screech pierced the air followed by a crackling sound, drawing my attention. Fireworks burst in the sky, shooting colourful sparks through the air.

Chapter 5

I had a feeling I was forgetting something as I left for work the next afternoon. Halfway to the bus stop, I froze in my tracks, realising what it was. The books I had purchased to lend Sophie were still at home, and it wasn't the first day I had forgotten to bring them with me. Fortunately, I had enough time to turn back if I walked quickly.

Dodging the pedestrians in my way, I made it back to my apartment and grabbed the plastic bag with the ginger cat logo containing the books. I returned to the bus stop in the nick of time.

I rode the bus with the bag resting safely on my lap, thinking how happy Sophie would be to receive the books. Lending them to her was important to me. Until she joined my class, teaching was an uninspiring task. Thanks to her, I was beginning to engage more with the subject and the students. This little favour was my way of thanking her.

The books sat on my desk until my last class of the day, when Sophie and the other final-year high school students took their seats in the room.

As she always did, Sophie emptied the contents of her satchel and arranged the items tidily on her desk. I walked around the classroom handing out homework I had marked. When I reached Sophie, I asked if I could speak with her after class. "I have some books for you," I explained.

"Okay," she said, looking pleased.

Once everyone had left at the end of class, I placed the books on Sophie's desk. "I know that you were struggling to find English books to read. I found these and wanted to lend them to you."

Sophie eagerly picked up one of the books and turned it over in her hands, scanning the blurb. "This is wonderful. Thank you so much."

"I wasn't sure what kind of books you usually read. I hope you enjoy them."

"I'm sure I will!"

"You can borrow them for as long as you need, and if you have any questions, let me know."

"Thank you."

"Are you in a hurry to get home?"

"Not really."

I pulled out the chair from the desk beside hers and sat down. "I wanted to ask you how you're getting on, being new to the class and all."

"Oh. Everything is fine. I'm enjoying it."

"Your English is good."

She blushed. "Thanks."

We had mainly been speaking in English. She only reverted to Korean every now and then when she didn't know how to say something. Compared to most other students her age, she was advanced in her skill.

"I never did ask you what school you're from," I said. "I haven't seen that uniform before."

"Horim High School."

"Never heard of it."

"You wouldn't. It's a small school."

"What subjects are you taking?"

She thought for a moment. "There are a lot. Korean, English,

Japanese…history, mathematics, science…technology. There are more."

"Gosh. You have a lot on your plate."

"On your plate?" She crinkled her brow.

"It's an expression," I explained. "It means you're very busy."

"I see." She jotted the phrase down in her notebook, filing it for later.

"Are you taking any other *hagwon* classes besides English?" I enquired.

"No. Just English. It's my most important subject since I want to go to university overseas."

"Oh? Which country?"

"You're from England, aren't you?"

"Yes."

"I'd like to study there if possible. If I can get into a good university."

"I can tell you a lot about universities in England, if that's useful."

"Really? That would be so helpful!"

"It's no problem. We can talk about it another day."

"I look forward to it." She beamed.

"Anyway, I'll let you get home now."

"Thanks for the books!"

"You're welcome."

She stowed them in her satchel. "See you tomorrow."

As Sophie left the classroom, I glowed with the happy feeling of doing something nice for someone. I resolved to try harder with my other students as well.

I didn't have anything else I needed to get done that evening, so I packed my briefcase and headed out. I was on the bus when a call came from Jinseung.

"Hey, Chloe. Are you free?" His voice sounded strange. "There's something I need to tell you. Can you meet me at Cinema Lumiere?"

"When?"

"As soon as possible."

"What's this about?"

"I'd better tell you in person. I'll see you at the cinema."

He hung up before I could say anything else.

* * *

MAKING my way through the fluorescent-lit subway station, something caught my eye and stopped me in my tracks. An entertainment news bulletin played on a small TV above the waiting area. A montage of Shin Jinseung photographs and video clips graced the screen with the words "breaking news" in large red characters.

I moved in closer, determined to find out what it was about, but I had just caught the tail end and the sound was muted. The next item started to play before I could decipher anything.

I wondered if the news story was connected with what Jinseung wanted to tell me. Automatically, I pulled out my phone and started typing "Shin Jinseung news" into the search bar, then rapidly backspaced. *I should give him the chance to tell me himself,* I decided.

I hopped on the next train, rode three stops, and emerged from the station on a busy six-lane street buzzing with late-night activity.

Through a maze of dark little backstreets, I arrived at Cinema Lumiere, the tiny boutique movie theatre that had become the de facto meeting place for me and Jinseung. His sister worked there and would let us come in after closing, or other times Jinseung would book the entire theatre for a private date.

I announced my arrival via the intercom. The door unlocked. The warm foyer smelled of buttery popcorn. Shin Jina stood wiping down the bar with a yellow cloth. Jinseung didn't seem to have arrived yet.

"Chloeeee!" Jina rushed towards me to give me a hug. "So good to see you. Feels like ages since you last came here." She looked gorgeous as usual, wearing a crisp white shirt over black skinny jeans, hoop earrings, and her hair in a cute pixie cut.

"It has been ages," I replied.

"You should visit even when you're not meeting *Dongsaeng*. I've missed you."

"Then I'll come and watch a movie." I picked up a printed schedule from the bar.

"I'll even let you in for free."

"Really?"

"Of course. Giving my friends free tickets is a perk of the job. I'm going to make myself a coffee. Want anything?"

"Oh, a hot chocolate, please."

"Coming right up." She prepared the hot drinks, tinkering away with the espresso machine.

I pulled up my sleeve and checked my watch. *Jinseung must be running late.* My mind wandered back to the news bulletin. *What could the news possibly be?* Temptation rose in me. *How simple it would be just to do a quick search...*

"Here you go." Jina passed me a mug.

Does Jina know? It doesn't look like she's holding anything back from me.

Determined not to give in to the temptation, I left my phone in my bag, not even allowing myself a quick glance.

Jina and I chatted at the bar, cradling our mugs in our hands, helping me take my mind off Jinseung and whatever it was he had to tell me.

Twenty minutes later, the intercom buzzed. Jina unlocked the door, and Jinseung came in at the same time as a large gust of wind. He looked tired and dishevelled, but still wore a warm smile. "Hey," he said. "Sorry I'm late. Hard to get away. It's been crazy."

"Something to drink?" Jina asked.

He shook his head. "I can't stay long."

He ushered me to a couch below a wall of black-and-white portraits of famous directors.

"You look exhausted," I said, looking him up and down.

"A lot has happened."

His condition tugged at my heartstrings, and suddenly I wasn't so desperate to know what he wanted to tell me. "I think you need to go home and sleep. Maybe we should have this talk another day..."

He shook his head. "It's now or never."

It sounded serious. "What is it?" I held my breath.

"I thought you might have already found out. It's already been leaked to the media."

"I saw something on TV but didn't quite catch what it was about."

"You know the actor, Kim Jimoon? He has been having medical issues and had to drop out from his role in Love in Flames. Now I've been offered the part."

My muscles relaxed. It wasn't bad news after all. "Well, that's great! —Except for Kim Jimoon and all. You were so upset that you missed out on that one."

"Yeah. But the thing is, it's so last-minute."

"Oh? How much time do you have?"

"Filming begins in two days."

I recoiled, startled. "Two days?!"

"And it's set on Jeju Island. They want me to go there tomorrow."

"Jeju Island?! Does that mean—"

He nodded. "They have a house rented for me for four months—I'll still be able to visit you from time to time, on my days off," he added, as if a consolation.

"I'm happy for you." My cracking voice betrayed my bitterness.

"Four months will go by before you know it," Jinseung assured me.

"Yes, I'm sure it will." *No, it won't. Four months is forever.*

Before embarking on this relationship, Jinseung and I had agreed that I wouldn't purposely interfere with his career, and I was more than happy to oblige. But now, faced with yet another prolonged period apart, it was difficult to keep my emotions reined in. As selfish as it was, I wished that he felt strongly enough about me that he would turn down the role. But who was I kidding? Acting was his first love, and I couldn't compete. Still, I didn't want to lose him, so I was required to put on a brave face and bear it.

"Are you okay?" Jinseung asked.

I forced a smile. "Of course. Why wouldn't I be? You've got the role you really wanted. We should be celebrating."

He squeezed my shoulder. "Thanks. I knew you'd understand. That's why our relationship works so well."

"What time will you leave tomorrow?"

"First thing. I'm off to Gimpo Airport at six o'clock."

"Then can I stay the night with you so I can say goodbye in the morning?"

"Sorry, but it would be more sensible if you didn't. I've got packing to do, and I need a good night's sleep tonight."

I pouted, unable to hide my disappointment. My bottom lip quivered. "Then this is the last time we'll see each other for a while…"

"Yeah." He stroked my cheek, a sympathetic look in his eyes. "Look at it this way, all this time apart will make our relationship stronger."

"I suppose so." *Or it could break us up…*

"I better head home. I need to prepare for tomorrow."

"But—"

He hugged me, muffling my protestation. "Be a good girl while I'm gone, okay?"

I sighed. "Don't worry. I won't get into any trouble."

"Good. I'll be in touch. Maybe not every day, but as often as I can."

"I'll be waiting to hear from you."

"I'm gonna miss you."

"Me too."

"Then…I'll head off now."

I bit back the urge to say, "I love you." He hadn't responded last time, and I couldn't face the same reaction this time.

Hands on my shoulders, Jinseung kissed me on the forehead one last time.

Jina coordinated his departure, checking that the coast was clear before permitting him to exit.

"Goodbye," Jinseung said, dropping his arms.

"Bye," I said weakly.

He turned, and without looking back, he left the building. I watched the door swing behind him and close with a firm click.

I was unable to control the tears that suddenly leaked from my eyes. Jina caught me in her arms and let me cry into her shoulder.

"Don't tell Jinseung about this," I sobbed.

"I won't," Jina said, patting my back.

Chapter 6

454 kilometres—the distance which now separated me and Jinseung. He had only been gone for a few hours, yet I could feel his absence in my very bones.

I didn't feel like doing anything that morning, not even getting out of bed. I pulled the covers up over my head to block out the sunlight and tried to fall back to sleep, but sleep didn't come. Begrudgingly, I pulled myself up and ate breakfast—cornflakes and milk.

After breakfast, I tried to do some prep work for my upcoming lessons, but my brain wasn't cooperating. I closed my laptop, deciding to go for a walk instead. Perhaps that would snap me out of this funk.

It was a clear day, the air brisk. I walked to a small neighbourhood near mine, where standalone houses replaced apartment buildings, some of them in a traditional Korean style with panelled walls and sloping roofs. I had always been fascinated by *hanoks* and had visited the *hanok* villages in Seoul many times. The houses in this neighbourhood weren't quite as impressive, but I still admired them. I wondered who lived in them. I imagined you'd have to be very rich to afford to live there. I watched the windows of the houses as I passed, hoping to catch a glimpse of their residents. I didn't see anyone in the houses, but a cat on top of a roof caught my attention—

midnight black with vibrant yellow eyes. He looked like he was watching me.

"Here, kitty," I cooed, trying to get him to come down.

He didn't move. A sparrow landed on the roof next door and the cat's head snapped to attention. He leapt across to the other roof, but the bird flew away. I followed the cat for a while as he hopped from rooftop to rooftop until he eventually disappeared from view. At that point, I decided to head home.

When I reached my apartment building, I turned to the group of locked metal mailboxes beside the main entrance, deciding to check if I had any mail. I inserted the small key that I kept on a cute *Pororo* key chain.

My friend, Han Seri, and I had been writing each other letters, and I was expecting her latest piece of correspondence. We had been pen pals throughout high school to practise our language skills—I wrote in Korean, and she wrote in English. We had picked the habit back up in the last few months. It helped us to keep in touch, seeing as I wasn't going on social media often these days. After the "scandal" that occurred when the media released pictures of Jinseung and I together before we were even officially dating, I received a lot of hateful comments and DMs. The experience had put me off social media, and I rarely checked my accounts.

Sure enough, inside the metal mailbox was an envelope. I fished it out, recognising Seri's handwriting immediately. Envelope in hand, I went up to my apartment. I made a cup of tea before sitting down to read it, tearing open the envelope. The letter was written on thick, cream-coloured notepaper.

Dear Chloe,

Thanks for your letter. I'm so happy to hear that you're doing well. Seems like you have settled into teaching life quite well by now. I can't blame you for feeling uneasy at first. It's a big change from acting.

I have been watching Shin Jinseung's drama. I'm addicted! And he's soooo cute. I still can't believe that you're actually dating him. You lucky thing. In your letter you complained that you don't get to see him much due to filming. That must really suck. By the time you receive this I suppose filming will have already wrapped, so you'll get to see more of each other—for the time being, at least. Let me know how he's doing.

I have quite a bit of news to share this time. Guess what? I'm dating someone! He's an Australian guy, tall, good-looking. He works for an IT company. His name is Adrian. I've never felt this way about a guy before. It's only been a month and I'm already fantasising about marrying him! But there's a problem...

Remember how I told you last time that I was thinking about quitting my job and moving back to Korea? Well, now that I'm with Adrian, I'm not sure if I still want to. I can hardly ask someone I've only been dating for a month to go back to Korea with me, so we would have to have a long-distance relationship—or break up. I'm not too keen on that and I'm sure he wouldn't be either. That's why I'm having second thoughts about the whole idea.

I already told my parents that I wanted to come back to Korea, and they were so happy and excited. I'm not looking forward to telling them I've changed my mind. They'll be devastated. Then there's you, of course. We were thinking about moving in together if I came to live in Seoul. I still think that would be awesome, but it doesn't seem like that will happen now. I'm sorry.

Even if I don't leave Melbourne, I'll want to look for another job. Part of the reason I wanted to leave was that I'm not enjoying it. Don't know how much longer I'll be able to stick it out. Thank goodness I didn't already give my notice, though. Much like you, I need a job or I'll lose my visa.

Hope everything's okay with you. Give Jinseung a kiss for me! Ha! Just because I have a boyfriend now doesn't mean I'm not jealous.

Write back soon.

Your friend,
Seri Han

I folded the letter up and stuffed it back into its envelope. So, Seri had a boyfriend. I was happy for her, yet a little melancholy. Our plans to live together didn't look like they would pan out. *Never mind.* She hadn't had a boyfriend in a long time, so it made sense that she wanted to give their relationship a proper chance.

I sent a text message to Seri telling her I had received her letter. We always did so in case our letters ever got lost in the post.

My phone pinged a little while later, and I picked it up expecting to see Seri's reply. Instead, I saw a message from an anonymous sender. My breath caught in my throat.

Unknown: BREAK UP WITH SHIN JINSEUNG.

Chapter 7

I was too overwhelmed by the mysterious text message to begin to try and make sense of it. The only thing I could think to do was to reply. Hand shaking, I composed a message.

Chloe: Who is this?

I watched anxiously as my message turned from "unread" to "read," then as the three little dots indicated the person was typing their reply. Even though I was expecting it, the pinging sound of a new message still gave me a fright.

Unknown: YOUR ENEMY

My blood turned cold. *My enemy?* Not knowing what else to say, I replied with a single question mark. Silence followed, and I didn't try texting them again.

Who could possibly send me such a message? No one knew about my relationship with Jinseung apart from a few close confidantes, and I was sure none of them would claim to be my enemy. Unless someone else had found out—a possibility I couldn't ignore. We had been very careful, but perhaps not careful enough...

I wondered whether I should tell Jinseung. He would surely be very busy preparing to shoot the drama, and I didn't want him to worry about me. Maybe this was all nothing—a disgruntled fan who still believed the old dating rumours and somehow got my number. *Yeah, that could be it.* Satisfied with my conclusion, I decided to ignore the message, block the number, and not tell Jinseung. I hoped the incident would be a one-off.

Only it wasn't a one-off. Similar messages started flowing in over the next few days. All of them a variation of "Break up with Shin Jinseung." Whenever I blocked the sender, they came through from a different number. I could no longer ignore them. I needed to confide in Jinseung and hear his opinion on the matter. Should I be concerned or not?

Predictably, I couldn't get through when I tried to call him. I left him a message instead.

Chloe: Call me when you get the chance. I have something to tell you.

I waited for several hours, but he didn't reply. *Is he ignoring me?* I wondered, beginning to get frustrated. More "break up with Shin Jinseung" messages appeared in the meantime. I tried to call him once again, pacing the room while I listened to the dial tone. To my surprise, someone picked up, but the person who answered wasn't Jinseung. "Bong Changsoo here," the voice said.

"Changsoo-ssi, it's me, Chloe. Why do you have *Oppa*'s phone?"

"I took it from him. He needs to be completely free of distractions today."

"Oh. I see." *So that's why he hasn't been replying...*I berated myself internally for believing that Jinseung was wilfully ignoring me.

"It seems like you're desperate to get hold of him. Is something wrong?"

"Yes. A situation has come up."

"I'm all ears."

I told him about the text messages and asked for his advice, praying he wouldn't be angry that the relationship might have somehow leaked out.

Changsoo paused. He breathed heavily down the line, apparently thinking the situation through. At last he spoke. "How likely do you think it is that this person could know you're dating?"

"I don't think it's very likely. We've done everything we can to keep it a secret."

"You haven't told them anything, have you? You haven't been replying?"

"I sent one message asking who they are, but that's it."

"In that case, I think the best course of action is to ignore the messages. Block the sender."

"I tried blocking them, but more messages come through from different numbers."

"They'll stop eventually if you don't engage with them. You've heard the expression 'don't feed the trolls,' right? This person sounds like a troll, trying to provoke a reaction from you."

"What if they really know about me and Jinseung? What if they leak it to the media if I don't respond to them?"

"We'll just have to take that risk."

It wasn't the reassurance I was hoping for, but I knew he was right. "Okay." I sighed. "I'll do as you say and ignore them."

"Good. Don't delete the messages, though. Keep them as evidence. Unlikely as it is, you might need to show them to the police if the harassment escalates."

"Yes. Good advice."

"Thanks for letting me know about this."

"I'm just glad to get it off my chest. I wasn't sure what to do. Thank you."

"No problem. If anything like this happens again, let me know. It's best not to get Jinseung involved. He needs to focus right now and doesn't need this kind of stress."

I agreed with him. Jinseung was working hard and I didn't want to upset him. I'd deal with it myself, and with the help of Changsoo if necessary.

I left the phone call feeling a bit better about the whole situation, but not much clearer on the intention of the person behind the messages—*my enemy.*

Sticking to Changsoo's advice, I blocked the latest number that the messages were coming from but didn't delete them. *Keep it as evidence.* Where had I heard that before? *That's right.* Changsoo had advised Jinseung to keep the doll as evidence. The doll...the text messages. I wondered if there could be a connection between the two. What if the person in the motorcycle helmet who delivered the box to Jinseung's apartment was the very same person who was sending me these messages? Almost as soon as the idea entered my head, I dismissed it. *Don't be ridiculous.*

Chapter 8

One evening at the *hagwon*, I noticed something on my desk that wasn't there before. The three novels I had recently lent Sophie had been stacked in a neat pile. *Has she finished them already?* On closer inspection, the stack was topped with a note written on rose-patterned stationery and a tiny pale blue box wrapped in a brown ribbon branded La Maison du Chocolat. My mouth dropped open a little. *Is this for me?* I unfolded the note. A message was written in beautiful handwriting with a blue-ink pen.

Dear Ms. Gibson,

Thank you for letting me borrow these books. I had a very nice time reading them. Slowly I am getting better at reading in English. Thank you for teaching me.

Yours sincerely,
  Kim Sungmi (Sophie)

Tears sprang to my eyes and I shielded my face, blinking them away before anyone could notice. I was so touched by Sophie's sweet gesture. It was the first time I had ever felt valued as a teacher. I lowered the note and met Sophie's eyes across the classroom. She swiftly averted her gaze, her cheeks pinkening.

I taught with much enthusiasm that day, and I was sad when class was over.

The students filtered out, leaving me alone to my thoughts. I had been avoiding checking my phone over the last couple of weeks, worried I'd see more anonymous text messages, but I couldn't stop looking altogether. What if someone was trying to contact me? I held my breath as I checked my messages, expecting to see a bunch of new ones. But nope. Not one. None from "my enemy." None from Yang Bora or Han Seri. None from Jinseung. I put my phone down feeling vaguely disappointed. Sure, the creepy text messages had stopped, but so had the texts from the people I cared about. The lack of contact from Jinseung hurt me the most. He had barely talked to me at all since he left. I knew he was busy, but still…

His words echoed in my head. "I'm a bad boyfriend." I had denied it at the time, but if he kept this up, perhaps I would start to agree with him.

I went to the staffroom, where I turned my attention to the latest batch of marking I needed to complete. Red pen in hand, I got to work. It took my mind off Jinseung, at least.

After an hour engaged in correcting and commenting on student work, I began to get drowsy. I stopped and gathered my papers up into my briefcase, calling it a night.

I felt a rush of cold air as I left the building. A lone student stood outside in the dark. It was Sophie, huddled in her jacket and rocking on her heels, glancing at her phone every few seconds. I approached her. "Everything all right?"

She lifted her head. "Oh, Ms. Gibson. I'm okay, but it doesn't seem like my mother will be able to pick me up."

"How will you get home?"

"Don't worry. I can take the bus."

"I'm just about to head to the bus stop myself. Which bus do you take?"

"76."

"Same as me! Do you want to walk together?"

"Yes, please!"

We left walking side by side along the footpath, bathed in the light from shop windows and glowing signs. The area bustled with groups of salarymen letting off steam after a long day's work.

"I want to thank you for the note and the gift," I said. "I wasn't expecting anything in return for lending you those books."

Sophie shrugged. "I just wanted to show you my appreciation. I've never had a teacher like you before."

"Really? You're the only student who seems to pay attention to me. I often wonder whether I'm any good at teaching at all."

"Don't mind the other students. They're just worn out from all the studying. There's so much pressure."

"Yes. You're right. It's very tough being a student in Korea. I studied here for one year on a high school exchange, but as a foreigner, I didn't face the same kind of pressure as the other students. How do you cope, Sophie?"

She thought for a moment before answering. "Ever since I was in primary school, I've been focused on my goal to study abroad, so I've never been concerned with the competition to get into Korean universities."

"Ah, I see. Though it can be challenging to get into overseas universities as well."

"I know. That's why I think you can help me."

We reached the bus stop, but the number 76 bus was already pulling away from the curb, indicator flashing.

"Wait!" I yelled, flailing my arms, but it was too late. I had missed the bus many times recently. It was starting to become a habit. "The next one won't be for a while..."

"I will wait," Sophie said, unfazed.

I would have walked home, but I didn't want to leave Sophie

waiting at the bus stop by herself at this time of night. Instead, another solution entered my head. "Sophie, do you like cake?"

Her eyes lit up. "I love it."

I took her to a nearby dessert café. Its interior was warm and inviting, softly lit, with framed poetry decorating exposed brick walls. An array of decadent cakes and pastries was displayed in a vast glass cabinet.

"What would you like?" I asked her.

"Hmmm…" She scanned the cabinet, her finger tracing her gaze across the glass. "Mont Blanc, please."

I ordered and paid for a slice of Mont Blanc cake for Sophie, and a slice of red velvet cake for myself

We crossed patterned rugs to a two-person table by the window, overlooking the hustle and bustle of a busy pedestrian square.

"Now, what were we talking about before?" I asked. "Oh, that's right. Studying abroad. Do you have a particular university in mind?"

"Yes," Sophie replied. She looked down at the table, blushing. "It's my dream to go to Oxford."

Although it was an obvious choice, her answer still surprised me. "Why Oxford?" I asked after taking a small bite of moist cake.

"My parents took me to visit England when I was little. I fell in love with Oxford, and it's been my dream to go there ever since. Think I just find the whole idea very romantic. The history, the architecture, the library, and the gardens…" She let out a little sigh of longing. "Have you been?"

"Yes. Several times. I even applied to study there, but I didn't get in. Ended up going to the University of Sussex instead."

"I know it'll be tough to get in. That's why I need to think about other universities as well, just in case."

"I could recommend some, depending on what you want to major in."

"I care more about where I study, rather than what I study. Certain programmes are easier to get into than others. That will influence my choice."

"I get what you mean. Picking something unpopular could make it more likely that you'll get into your preferred school."

"Exactly. What did you study?"

"Business."

"Oh?"

"A boring, practical option, which I'm not sure I'll ever make proper use of," I lamented. "If I could go back in time, I'd choose something else. Maybe Asian studies due to my interest in South Korea. Or possibly Korean language. Or maybe even acting…"

"Acting?"

"Didn't you know? I had a small part in a K-drama last year."

Sophie's jaw gaped. "Wow! That's so cool! What's it called?"

"Hidden History."

"I'll check it out."

Due to the small nibbles we took while conversing, we still hadn't finished our cake by the time we had to leave. A kind staff member boxed up our leftovers to take with us.

We walked back to the bus stop and joined the crowd of waiting passengers. The bus rolled up shortly. I found a free seat near the front, and Sophie sat down beside me. Just before the bus was about to leave, an elderly lady slowly climbed on board. Sophie readily gave up her seat to her. "Thank you, child," the *halmoni* said with a crinkled smile.

I gazed out the window throughout the short journey, watching the colourful storefronts and crowds of pedestrians go by in the night. When my stop neared, I pressed the red button. "Bye, Sophie. See you tomorrow," I said before hopping off.

While I made my way home, I thought about how Sophie reminded me of myself when I was her age—but a touch more romantic, intelligent, and sophisticated. I wondered whether she'd truly be able to get into Oxford. One thing was for sure, I was determined to help her succeed in her dream.

Shortly after arriving home, I rummaged through the fridge looking for something to cook for dinner and emerged with a pack of minced beef and some leftover chopped vegetables. I heated some oil in a frying pan then tossed everything in. As I prepared the stir fry, my phone started to ring. An unknown number, but I answered it anyway, pressing the phone to my ear with my shoulder. Due to the splattering, sizzling sound of oil, I couldn't hear properly. I removed the pan from the heat and listened more intently. What I heard disturbed me greatly. A computer-generated voice repeated the same message over and over again in a loop: "I'm warning you. Break up with Shin Jinseung or else."

Chapter 9

I woke in a hot sweat during the night, a loud, piercing sound reverberating in my eardrums. Feeling dazed, I couldn't work out where the noise was coming from. Then I noticed my phone lit up on the bedside table. I rubbed my blurry eyes and focused on the screen. It was the same number calling me—the one which played the weird looping message: "I'm warning you. Break up with Shin Jinseung or else."

I groaned. *Not again.* I swiped to decline the call.

No sooner had my head touched the pillow than the ringing started again. I sprang back up and rejected the call. Fed up with the rude interruptions, I navigated through various menus and options to place a block on the number, then lay my head down again.

The rest of the night went uninterrupted, but I tossed and turned, unable to sleep. My mind raced. The doll, the text messages, the looping phone call…Were they connected? Was the same person behind all of these incidents? I was beginning to believe they were.

I had let Changsoo know as soon as I received the first phone call. His belief was that the person was trying to provoke me. He advised me not to do anything—yet. *Easier said than done.* I was starting to get scared. What else was this person capable of? A deep shudder trailed down my spine and I turned over, hugging the blankets around me more tightly.

A strong mug of coffee helped awaken my senses the next morning, sipped while I prepared a pot of Scottish-style porridge on the stove—a comfort food which I craved. How I wished I could confide in Jinseung about everything that had been going on. But Changsoo was right, he didn't need the stress right now. In the wake of these unusual events, I missed him even more. My whole body yearned for him. I texted him a simple message: "I miss you."

No reply came through all morning. It was like Changsoo said—he was too busy to pay me much attention.

Despite feeling less than stellar, I had to get on with my day. My cupboards were bare, and I needed to buy groceries. I grabbed my handbag and two reusable shopping bags and set out.

The sun beat down on the footpath filled with noisy groups of shoppers and tourists. Thanks to the anonymous messages and phone calls, my paranoia about being followed had returned. I stuck to the main streets, feeling safer among crowds.

I had just about reached the grocery store when a large digital screen on the side of a bus shelter caught my eye. I stopped. There was Jinseung, and alongside him was a devastatingly beautiful young woman. She had long wavy brown hair and a wispy fringe framing an angelic face with doe eyes and plump pink lips, a cute button nose, and a pointed chin. I realised she must be his costar in Love in Flames—Ahn Jieun. They posed together, eyes locked on each other. Jinseung had a mischievous smirk on his face, and Jieun met him with a determined stare. The sexual tension between them was palpable. Below the image was the text: "Love in Flames—Coming soon to J2CB."

I felt a stab of jealousy through my heart. Unable to look at it anymore, I tore myself away.

* * *

I LOST myself down a rabbit hole that afternoon.

Curious about Jinseung's hot costar, I typed her name into a search engine. A host of stunning photographs and video thumbnails popped up on the results page. The familiar stab of jealousy pierced my chest. *Damn. She's absolutely gorgeous. I'm seriously up against this? No man would be immune to her good looks...*

Scanning through the rest of the search results, I quickly learned that she was more famous as an idol rather than an actor. She was in a girl group called "Bad Grlz." I had heard of them before but didn't know anything about them. I clicked through to a profile of the group and found out that it consisted of five members, and Ahn Jieun was the leader. All of them were drop-dead gorgeous, not to mention talented. They wrote and produced all their own songs, as well as running a small clothing line and beauty brand.

After reading their profile, I found myself watching their music videos. Catchy pop songs with a slight hip-hop edge, featuring lots of sexy dance moves. Leading on from those videos, I watched interviews and dance practice clips. Next thing I knew I was on V Live watching the girls chat to their fans—a group called "Dollz."

Hours passed as I consumed Bad Grlz content in a trance, envy seeping through every pore in my body. *Why do I have to torture myself like this?*

When I finally couldn't take any more, I shut my laptop and put it away in a drawer. I marched to the pantry and took out a jumbo bag of chocolate chip cookies which I proceeded to binge-eat. Between every few bites, I checked my phone, hoping that Jinseung would reply to me.

At last, my phone pinged.

Jinseung: I miss you too.

A wave of relief swept over me and I resolved to stop eating, but when I looked in the bag, I saw that it was empty. I had eaten all the cookies. A deep sense of shame replaced my relief as I brushed the crumbs off my sweater.

Chapter 10

Dear Seri,

Sorry it has taken me so long to reply! I ran out of letter stationery and kept forgetting to buy more.

So you have a boyfriend now. Congratulations! I totally understand why you would want to stay in Melbourne to be with him. It sucks that we won't live together after all, but I'm still really happy for you.

By now I'm sure you know that Jinseung has left me to go film Love in Flames on Jeju Island. Once again, I find myself in a situation where I hardly see or hear from him. I know he's working hard, and I'm really proud of him, but it's still difficult. Then there's the fact that his costar, Ahn Jieun, is incredibly gorgeous. Have you heard of her? She's an idol in the group Bad Grlz. Everyone online is commenting on their chemistry. I'm not usually the jealous type, but this time I admit I'm feeling jealous.

There's another thing. I've been getting anonymous text messages and phone calls telling me to break up with Jinseung. It's pretty freaky. I'm not sure there's much I can do for now except ignore them. I haven't told Jinseung about them because it could distract him. There's nothing he could do anyway, so why bother him with it? I'm trying not to let the messages get to me, but I can't help feeling a bit paranoid. Sometimes I even feel like I'm being followed, but I have no solid proof of that.

There you have it. You have no reason to be jealous of me. In a way, I envy you for having a "normal" boyfriend. Things would be so much easier.

Hope everything is going well with Adrian and good luck job hunting.

-Chloe Gibson

* * *

I pushed the envelope through the post box slot and watched it disappear, wondering if its contents would still be relevant by the time it arrived in Han Seri's hands. Corresponding by letter was a bit like time travel, I mused. My life would move forward while the letter stayed the same. It landed inside the box without a noise, never to be seen by my eyes again.

With that taken care of, I walked down the subway station steps to board a train. I had arranged to meet Yang Bora at Cinema Lumiere.

A handful of moviegoers occupied the cinema lobby. Though there weren't too many people, the small space felt lively. The sound of chatter and the smell of popcorn filled my senses. I spotted Bora looking at the "coming soon" movie posters.

"Hey," I said, going to her side.

A smile spread across her round face. "Movie date time!" She linked her arm with mine.

We joined the short queue for tickets where Shin Jina manned the counter wearing a white blouse and bright pink lipstick.

"Hi, Chloe," Jina said when we reached the front. "Two complimentary tickets for The Strangers?"

"Yes, please!"

"Who's your friend?"

"Oh! This is Yang Bora. She works at KAM."

"Ahhh. The intern, right?"

Bora shook her head. "I'm Go Yoojin's manager now."

"Go Yoojin? Wow. That's cool."

"Yeah. She's great. A handful at times, though."

"I can imagine." Jina passed us the tickets. "Can you both stay a while after the movie? Let's chat."

"Sure," I said. "If it's okay with Bora."

"Yep," Bora said. "I don't need to be at work early tomorrow."

"Great," Jina said. "Enjoy the film!"

Tickets in hand, Bora and I entered the darkened movie theatre.

* * *

WE EMERGED from the theatre two hours later and sat at a table while the other moviegoers slowly filtered out of the cinema. Once everyone had left, Jina joined us at the table with a bottle of white wine and three wine glasses. She filled them up.

Bora and I accepted a glass each, thanking her.

"So, Yang Bora, how long have you been working at KAM Entertainment?" Jina asked, sipping wine.

"Just about two years now," she said.

While Bora and Jina acquainted themselves, my phone buzzed. I checked it, groaning internally at the sight of another "break up with Shin Jinseung" message. I slipped it back into my pocket, but every couple of minutes, it buzzed again. I pulled it out to turn it off.

"So, who's texting you?" Jina asked before I could press the power button. "My brother?"

I shook my head.

"Who is it then?"

"Actually…"

Bora and Jina stared at me, suspicion in their eyes. If I lied about the messages, they'd be able to tell. There was little use in hiding the truth from them anyway, so I showed them the messages.

Both of them squinted at the screen, shocked looks dawning on their faces.

"*Omo!*" Jina gasped.

"How long has this been going on?" Bora asked.

"A few weeks now," I admitted. "I've been getting phone calls too."

"You don't think…" Bora trailed off.

"What?"

"Is it the same person who delivered the doll to Jinseung?"

She was much sharper than me, making that connection almost instantly.

"The doll?" Jina's eyes widened in confusion.

"Some *sasaeng* fan delivered a mutilated Barbie doll to Jinseung's apartment," Bora explained.

"Yikes. That's disturbing."

"It might be the same person," I said. "I'm not sure."

"Does Jinseung know about the messages?" Bora asked.

I shook my head. "Bong Changsoo knows. He told me not to tell Jinseung."

Jina looked startled. "Eh! Why?"

"He'll be distracted from his work if he gets worried about me. Besides, it's not like there's anything he can do about it."

She pursed her lips. "Hmmm…I guess you're right. Though I'm sure Jinseung wouldn't agree with that."

"Please don't tell him."

"I won't."

"Same," Bora said. "I can see Changsoo's point. Jinseung's got enough to deal with as it is. I assume you've seen that recent article."

"What article?" I asked, concern in my voice.

"You don't know? The one about Ahn Jieun."

Ahn Jieun…My heart started to pound. What was this all about? "I haven't seen it."

"I'm sure it's nothing to be worried about. Just the media trying to stir things up, as per usual." She brought the article up on her phone. "Here, see for yourself."

I grabbed her phone and read the title. "Ahn Jieun and Shin Jinseung: Lovers Reunited." I gulped, my worst suspicion confirmed. I read on.

Ever since actors Ahn Jieun and Shin Jinseung started working together on upcoming drama, Love in Flames, fans have been abuzz about the sizzling chemistry between the pair.

An exclusive source reveals that their chemistry might not just be good acting. It turns out that Ahn Jieun and Shin Jinseung share some history— they used to date!

Will their reunion reignite their passion? Our source on set thinks so. The pair have been spending a lot of time together, both on set and off.

Judge for yourself if their love is real when Love in Flames starts to air in June.

Several photographs of Jinseung and Jieun together behind the scenes accompanied the piece, as well as a photo that looked like they were having dinner together in a restaurant.

I set Bora's phone down on the table, unable to look anymore. The rational part of my brain agreed with Bora—it was just the media trying to stir things up and create publicity for Love in Flames, but the irrational part of my brain screamed louder, jealousy bubbling up inside me. I tried not to let it show.

"Like I said, it's nothing to be concerned about," Bora said, taking back her phone.

"Is it true that they used to date?" My voice wobbled.

"I don't know," Bora said with a shrug.

Both of our gazes turned to Shin Jina. If anyone knew, she would.

"It might be true," she admitted. "They used to spend a lot of time together. That was before either of them became famous. They were both trainees at the time. If they did date, I'm sure it was nothing serious. You shouldn't worry about it."

But I was worrying about it. Ahn Jieun was absolutely gorgeous and leagues ahead of me in talent and accomplishments. I gulped my wine down so fast I started to cough.

Bora rubbed my back soothingly. "Jinseung would never cheat on you."

"Yeah. He's not that kind of guy," Jina agreed.

"I know, but he's practically been ignoring me since he left for

Jeju," I grumbled. "How does he have time to spend with Ahn Jieun off set when he doesn't even have time to contact me?"

"I'm sure the article's exaggerating. I know he's busy. He hasn't been responding to my messages either."

"You know what the media's like, Chloe," Bora said. "Just ignore it."

I did know what the media was like, but that did little to reassure me. When photographs of me and Jinseung hugging and holding hands came out last year, we weren't *officially* dating, but we weren't just friends either. *There's no smoke without fire.*

Chapter 11

I took a deep breath before stepping on the scales in my bathroom. The number on the display shot upwards, then moved erratically up and down before settling on a final figure. I gulped down a lump in my throat. I was the heaviest I'd ever been. Thanks to the stress of the anonymous messages and the jealousy and worry about Ahn Jieun, I had been engaging in a lot of comfort eating lately. I stepped off the scales, making a promise with myself to cut back on the junk food. If Jinseung saw me like this, I'd be so ashamed. I needed to get back in shape before the next time we met.

I was about to leave the bathroom when I caught my reflection in the mirror and did a double-take. *Ugh. My skin.* I peered closer at the mirror. There was a massive lump on my forehead—a pimple under the skin that was threatening to burst forth at any moment. I supposed this was also a result of my unhealthy eating habits. *Don't touch it*, I told myself. *Do...not...touch...*I touched the spot, just lightly, but it was enough to turn it from skin-coloured to light pink. I lowered my hand. *See what you did?* Restraining myself from touching it again, I covered the spot with a light layer of foundation. It wasn't completely invisible, but no one would notice from a distance.

I got changed for work in my bedroom, pulling on a pair of smart grey trousers and a silky light pink blouse. Perhaps it was just my imagination, but the clothes did seem much tighter than usual. The waistband of the trousers cut into my stomach causing a muffin top, and the fabric between the buttons of my blouse gaped slightly. I realised I might need to buy more clothes, which would prove a challenge. By British standards I was small, but certainly not by Korean standards, so it would be difficult to find nice clothes that fit me properly. All the more reason to lose weight, I decided.

Ready for work, I grabbed my bag and headed to the door to leave when my phone started to ring. *Don't tell me it's another call from that weird stalker.* My hopes weren't high when I glanced at the screen, but to my surprise, the caller was Shin Jinseung. I couldn't believe it at first. When the shock wore off, I scrambled to answer the call before the ringing stopped. "Hello?"

"Hey, Chloe." His voice was raspy. He sounded worn out.

"*Oppa...*"

"How are you? I'm sorry I haven't been in contact. This has honestly been the most hectic drama I've ever worked on. You wouldn't believe how understaffed and overworked we are. I haven't had one day's break since we started. I'm not getting paid enough for this."

I didn't realise quite how busy he was until he divulged this. He gained my sympathy immediately. "That sounds tough."

"Are you okay? I have some time to chat with you a bit if you want. I've been missing you like crazy."

"Really?" Due to how busy he was, and how little he contacted me, I found it hard to believe he missed me.

"Of course."

"Thought you might be too busy to miss me."

"Even if I'm busy, I miss you."

I still wasn't convinced. The photographs of him looking cosy with Ahn Jieun surfaced in my mind. Before I could help myself, the question I had been desperately holding back surged forth. "What about Ahn Jieun?"

He paused. "Huh? What do you mean?" His tone of voice shifted from calm to irritated.

"It seems like you're close. Is it true that you used to date?" I tried to sound calm and reasonable, but it came out sounding more accusing than I intended.

He hesitated. "What have you heard?"

His reaction didn't comfort me at all. "I read it online. I wasn't sure if it was true or not."

He was silent, breath slow and steady.

"Say something," I urged, growing worried. "Tell me it's not true."

"That would be a lie."

His words hit me like a physical blow to the stomach, knocking the wind out of me. I had to sit down. "So, it's true," I said, voice cracking.

"Yes. We dated. It was a long time ago. I hadn't even debuted at that point—"

His protestation did little to soothe my flaring anger. "Is she the reason why you don't answer my messages?"

"What? Chloe, you've got the wrong idea."

"She's very pretty…"

Jinseung raised his voice. "Do you think I'd cheat on you? Is that what this is about?"

"I don't know," I bit back. "You don't love me. Maybe you love her?"

Fury laced his voice. "Ugh. I can't believe I'm hearing this. Perhaps I was wrong about you. I thought you could handle this relationship."

It was the first time I'd heard him this angry. I opened my mouth to try and take back the things I said, but I could only splutter unintelligibly.

"I've had enough of this," he said.

The call cut out.

* * *

AFTER HOLDING back my tears all evening, the dam finally burst. Before any students or colleagues could see me, I rushed to the bathroom and hid inside a stall, tears rolling uncontrollably down my cheeks. *Have I ruined everything? Is this the end? Jinseung must hate me now.*

Sitting on the toilet seat, I bent over my knees and buried my face in my hands. I wished I could retract the things I'd said. By revealing my insecurity and distrust to Jinseung, I had shown him that I wasn't fit to be his girlfriend. If he didn't have an excuse to leave me for Ahn Jieun before, he did now. A loud whimper escaped my mouth at the onset of a fresh round of tears.

The bathroom door creaked open, and I quickly covered my mouth with my hand to stifle the whimpering. I heard footsteps across the lino floor and a stall door open then close with a thunk. I bit my tongue, trying to be silent. If the girl heard me cry, she might ask me what was wrong, and I had no intention of revealing my vulnerability to a student.

I waited for the telltale signs of her leaving—the sound of the tap running, the rustle of a paper towel, and the clack of the door shutting behind her. Breathing a small sigh of relief, I emerged from the stall to wash my tear-streaked face. Standing before the mirror, I groaned at my reflection. The monster of a pimple on my forehead was angry and inflamed. I could even feel it throbbing. No amount of foundation or concealer would cover it up now. I gritted my teeth, bent down over the basin, and splashed my face with cold water, washing away my tears and soothing my burning cheeks.

In the midst of my second splash, the bathroom door swung open again. There was no hiding now. I lifted my head and saw Sophie walk in. Her eyes fell upon me at once, a wrinkle of concern appearing between her brows. "Ms. Gibson! Are you all right?"

"I'm fine, thank you," I croaked.

The line between her brows remained, a sign that she was unconvinced. "Are you sure? You looked unwell during class."

"Maybe I'm coming down with something."

"Well, I hope you feel better soon." Her gaze lingered on me and I felt totally exposed. She knew I had been crying, I was sure of it.

"Good job on your homework, by the way," I said, trying to change the subject.

"Oh, thank you." She looked away, blushing.

We stood in awkward silence for a moment before she remembered herself and disappeared inside a stall.

I splashed my face one more time then patted it dry with a paper towel. Reviewing my appearance in the mirror, I decided that would have to do. Perhaps the massive pimple would serve as a distraction to the fact I looked like I'd been crying. Then again, I wasn't sure if that was better or worse.

I managed to make it through the bus ride home without crying again, merely sniffling a few times as if I had a cold. No one seemed to notice anything amiss, and if they did, they ignored me anyway.

At home, with no energy to cook a proper meal, I forgot all about my resolution to eat healthier and grabbed a packet of instant ramen from the cupboard. While the noodles boiled, I checked my phone, hoping to see a message from Jinseung. Hoping to see an apology. Surely he was feeling as guilty as I was. But nope. No new messages. I swallowed my pride. *Looks like I'll have to be the one to make the first move.*

I spent several minutes trying to draft a text message that conveyed the depth of my remorse. While I worked on it, I forgot about the noodles until I heard hissing sounds indicating the pot had boiled over. I rushed to attend to it, removing it from the heat immediately.

I prepared the noodles and ate them while I continued a cycle of writing then deleting text messages. Nothing sounded right. At last, I settled on something simple: "I'm very sorry." I held my breath as I pressed send.

I kept checking my phone throughout the night, aching to see him accept my apology and forgive me. But he didn't reply. Not that night, the next day, or the rest of the week. My sadness turned to anger, and with each day that passed without a response, the anger simmered away until it threatened to reach boiling point.

Chapter 12

Of all people, I thought Yang Bora would understand my situation and offer her sympathy. Turned out to be a different story.

We sat on the couch in my apartment, cups of tea in hand. A K-drama played in the background, but we weren't really paying attention. Instead, I spilled my guts to her, telling her all about my fight with Jinseung and bemoaning his treatment of me.

She listened with a neutral expression on her face. Her reaction confused me since I expected her to be more fired up about this, the same as I was feeling. "So, what do you think?" I asked when I had finished my rant. "Is Jinseung totally out of line or what?"

Bora thought for a moment, her face still inscrutable. "I'm afraid I'm going to have to side with Shin Jinseung," she uttered at last.

I was taken aback by her statement. How could she side with him? "What do you mean? I apologised to him and he hasn't even acknowledged it!"

"He probably still needs time to process his feelings. I'm sure he'll come around eventually."

"It's been days!"

She spoke calmly. "Can I be frank with you?"

"Of course."

"Low self-esteem, jealousy, clinginess…those traits are unacceptable in a relationship between a celebrity and a non-celebrity. I don't blame Jinseung if he's still angry at you."

I tensed up in reaction to her harsh words. "I'm not usually that kind of person."

"But you have to admit that your outburst was a bad look."

"I couldn't control myself. All the stress of what's been happening piled up and I snapped. The lack of contact from him hasn't helped. Since the doll incident, I would have thought he'd be checking up on me, making sure I'm okay. And I'm not."

"You can hardly blame him for that. He doesn't even know what's been going on."

"If he had kept in touch, I probably would have told him."

"You know how busy he is with the drama."

I slumped forward, feeling defeated. "I don't know what to do."

Bora placed a comforting hand on my back. "I'm sure he'll forgive you. Just wait and see. My advice would be to stop worrying so much and trust him. Stop trying to contact him and get on with your own life."

"Easier said than done," I mumbled.

"Well, if you can't do that then I don't think you should be together."

Her words stung. "You really think so?"

She nodded slowly. "That's the way it is."

I started to cry. I couldn't help it. Bora wrapped her arm around my shoulders to try and console me, but I pushed her forcefully away. She dropped her cup of tea and it spilled all over her. She sprang up, her expression dark.

"Oh no! I'm so sorry." I grabbed a fistful of tissues from the box on the coffee table and tried to dab at her shirt.

"I should go," Bora croaked.

"I didn't mean to—"

She flung on her jacket and walked out in a huff, door slamming behind her.

I wept into my hands. Fighting with Jinseung was bad enough, now I had turned Bora against me as well. Worst of all, deep down I knew she was right. If I couldn't handle Jinseung acting alongside a beautiful costar, if I couldn't handle jealous fans sending me threatening messages, how could I continue to date him? But the thought of ending our relationship hurt even more than those things combined.

Only one thing could numb my state of mind—junk food. I scoured the pantry for any sweet or salty snacks I could get my hands on, coming away with a packet of honey butter chips, a bag of macadamia nut cookies, and a bar of milk chocolate. Oh, and I couldn't forget the tub of salted caramel ice cream in the freezer.

Arms full with my haul, I relocated to the couch and spread the goodies on the coffee table. With a mindless reality TV show blaring in front of me, I proceeded to eat my way through all of the treats.

Only a few minutes after I had finished stuffing myself, my stomach groaned. A wave of nausea swept over me. I ran to the bathroom as fast as I could, flung open the toilet seat, and puked into the bowl. I purged over and over until there was nothing left in me.

Trembling on the bathroom floor, I realised I had reached a new low. *I can't go on like this.* Something had to change—and the most obvious answer was me.

Chapter 13

I was ready to apologise to Bora, but she wasn't ready to listen to me. Much like the situation with Jinseung, my calls and messages begging for forgiveness went unanswered. Determined to see her and apologise face to face, I resorted to catching her unaware. I went to KAM HQ one day, hoping she'd be there rather than out on a shoot.

Standing in the sleek, glitzy lobby, surrounded by screens playing video clips of the agency's star talent—including Shin Jinseung, Go Yoojin, and another young actor I recognised called Jung Jen. An overwhelming feeling of nostalgia took hold of me. It wasn't that long ago that I used to be signed to KAM as an actor, but now that short period of time felt like a distant dream.

As I stood lost in thought, many familiar faces passed me by. I felt self-conscious. *They're wondering what on earth I'm doing here...No. They probably don't even remember who I am...*

Shrugging off my embarrassment, I strolled up to the reception desk.

"Can I help you?" the receptionist asked, her tone clipped.

"I would like to see Yang Bora if she's available."

She narrowed her eyes. "Is she expecting you?"

"No."

"Then I'm afraid I can't help you."

"But—"

"Due to her busy schedule, Yang Bora does not meet anyone without prior arrangement."

I dropped my head in defeat. "I see. Thank you."

Now what should I do? Wait in the lobby and hope she comes out? I couldn't stay all day since I had work that afternoon. Besides, it would look suspicious if I hung around too long. What if I got mistaken for a fan trying to catch a glimpse of one of the agency's stars? I cringed at the thought. Heaving a sigh, I started towards the exit.

"Chloe?" came a voice over my shoulder.

I turned to see Seo Minjung—the talent scout who originally spotted me all those months ago and set my acting fate in motion. She looked beautiful as always, with her polished hair and makeup, and a Chanel handbag tucked beneath her arm.

"Minjung-ssi…" I spluttered, lost for words.

"Haven't seen you for a while. What brings you here?"

"I was hoping to see Yang Bora."

"Oh. Does she know you're here?"

I shook my head. "If she knew then she'd avoid me. We had a fight, you see. I'm here to apologise. Have you seen her today? Is she in the office?"

"Yes, I've seen her. I can go get her if you want. She might be busy, though."

"I'm not sure if she'll agree to see me."

"I'll tell her there's someone waiting for her, but I won't say it's you."

"All right, then. Thank you."

"Just wait right here. I'll message you what she says."

"Perfect."

With that, she whisked herself away to the elevators.

I paced the floor, phone glued to my hand. Eventually, it pinged with a new message.

Minjung: She'll come down in a minute. Good luck!

I hovered around the elevators, watching for any sign of Bora. At last, she emerged. Our eyes locked and she froze. "What are you doing here?" she asked. "Wait—did you send Seo Minjung up to get me?"

"Yes. Sorry to bother you. I just wanted to apologise again. Face to face."

She pursed her lips. "I can't discuss this right now. There's so much to do." She turned on her heel.

Before she could fully turn around, I dropped to my knees in front of her to beg her forgiveness. "Please!"

Her steely facade melted away, replaced by a sheepish smile. "All right, all right! Get up." She pulled me up off the floor, flustered by my embarrassing display.

"You're a true friend, you know. I needed someone to be brutally honest with me like you did."

"I'm glad you realised that."

"I really want to talk with you. Have you got time? Are you about to have a lunch break?"

"No. I'll be eating lunch at my desk. But I can meet you after work. There's a *pojangmacha* nearby. What time do you finish work?"

"Nine or so."

"Meet me at around half-past, then."

* * *

MY POST-WORK MEETING with Yang Bora couldn't come soon enough. The minute the last student left my class, I disappeared as well, taking the train back to Gangnam.

I located the *pojangmacha* easy enough. Bora, draped in a trench coat, stood outside waiting for me.

"Hey!" I said, walking up to her. "Hope you haven't been waiting long."

"Nope. Just got here."

We entered the bright orange tent filled with the fumes of salt and oil. It bustled with workers drinking alcohol and eating crispy, spicy, fried foods.

"What would you like?" I asked.

"*Sundae*," Bora replied.

"You eat that stuff?" I shuddered at the mere mention of the blood sausage dish.

"Of course."

"It makes me gag."

"You don't have to eat it."

"I'll get *tteokbokki* then. Anything to drink?"

"A beer, please."

I ordered the food and drinks, then we sat at one of the plastic tables. We were served two cold cans of Cass beer. I opened the cap on mine, and it made a "tsst" sound.

"So, what did you want to talk about?" Bora asked.

"Let's talk about you first. I've been so wrapped up in my own little world. I haven't been listening to your problems. How's everything with Go Yoojin?"

"She's started table reads for her next drama. Apart from that we're not too busy."

"Still giving you a hard time?"

"Always." She chuckled. "But I feel like she's grown to trust me now. We have a good relationship."

"I'm glad to hear it. Not missing working with Shin Jinseung?"

"Surprisingly, no."

Our food came—a bowl of rice cakes in spicy red broth, and the gross blood sausages I despised.

We snapped apart our chopsticks and began to eat.

"It's good," Bora said, mouth half-full. "Want to try some?"

I screwed up my nose. "No, thanks." I picked at my food, playing with it more than eating it. "I actually shouldn't be eating this. My diet has been terrible recently. I've put on so much weight and my skin is constantly breaking out."

"Not to be rude, but I've noticed you haven't been looking your usual self."

"I haven't been taking care of myself properly."

"All that stress, huh?"

"Yeah. I could really use your advice. I'm ready to listen to your opinions properly this time."

"You want me to be brutally honest?"

"Yes. Please go ahead."

"Promise you won't get angry at me?"

"I promise."

She came out with it at once. "I think you should consider breaking up with Jinseung."

My heart sank. It was not what I had wanted to hear, but I held back my gut reaction of defensiveness. "Why do you think so?"

"Think about it. Your relationship with him is the cause of all your problems. Breaking up with him would be the simplest solution."

"But not the only solution?"

"No, but the other way is more difficult. You'll have to overcome all your issues. Are you strong enough to do that?"

"I always believed I was a strong and resilient type of person, but now I'm not so sure…"

"Regardless of what you choose to do, I think you should come clean to Jinseung about the messages you've been getting."

"But Bong Changsoo—"

"Pfft. Forget about him. He doesn't have your best interests at heart. He only cares about preserving Jinseung's career for the sake of his job. Ignore him and come clean."

"That's not what you said before."

"The situation has changed. Jinseung needs to understand the stress you've been under and why you snapped at him."

"Then he might take pity on me…"

"Well, that's one way of putting it."

"…Or he might break up with me."

"He might break up with you either way, and this is the better option."

"Ugh. You're right. I guess I'll have to take the risk."

Bora's eyes fell upon the largely uneaten dish in front of me. "You gonna eat that?"

"Nah. You can have it." I pushed it towards her. My appetite had disappeared. If I had any chance of keeping my boyfriend, I'd need to quit my binge-eating habit.

"Man, I'm stuffed," Bora said, after managing to polish off a lot of what I didn't eat.

"You taking the subway home?" I asked.

"Yeah."

"Then let's go to the station together."

We stepped out of the warm tent and into the brisk night, navigating the streets to the nearest subway entrance. Our paths diverged inside the station, where escalators to the left and right led to separate train lines.

"I'm going left here," Bora said.

"Well, thanks for the chat. It's given me a lot to think about."

She beamed. "No problem. Any time."

"I don't know what I'd do without your friendship."

"Let's never fight again."

"Agreed."

We exchanged smiles, expressing contentment with our reconciliation, then headed our separate ways. I might not have been any closer to making up with Shin Jinseung, but at least I had Yang Bora by my side.

Chapter 14

A chorus of groans reverberated through the classroom. I had expected such a reaction. No one likes a surprise test. "Don't worry," I said, trying to be reassuring. "There should be nothing unfamiliar on the test. Just give it your best shot. You have until the end of class to finish."

I walked around the room passing out the test papers. Some students accepted theirs with glum expressions, others with determination—including Sophie. After handing out the last paper, I returned to the front of the room. Everyone stared at me expectantly, pens at the ready, waiting for me to tell them they could start.

"You may begin," I announced.

A flurry of rustling paper and scratching pens took over the class. I sat down behind my desk and relaxed, my shoulders drooping. One good thing about tests was that I didn't have to do any actual teaching. I kept one eye watching the students at all times, making sure no one was cheating, but my mind wandered. I found myself absent-mindedly reaching for my phone. One new message. Could it be from Jinseung? I swiped the screen, then deflated a little upon seeing Han Seri's name.

Seri: I got your letter. Hope everything is OK. My reply is already in the post.

I typed a response.

Chloe: I'm okay. I'll tell you everything in my next letter. Can't wait to read yours.

I returned my attention to the students. Their heads were down, faces etched with concentration. Sophie looked the most confident out of everyone, her tongue poking out slightly as her pen raced across the page. She was the first to lower her pen. After a couple of minutes reviewing her answers, she raised her hand.

"Are you finished?" I asked.

"Yes. What should I do now?"

"You can study quietly until the end of class."

I collected her paper. From a brief glance while carrying it to my desk, I could tell that she had done well. *I wonder if this class is too easy for her.* She was clearly leaps and bounds ahead of her peers.

A full fifteen minutes passed before the next person finished their test. Only a handful of other students managed to finish before I called "time's up."

I collected the rest of the papers then dismissed the class. As the room emptied, I regarded the intimidating stack of test papers on my desk. *This will take some time to mark.* I remembered the chicken and fresh vegetables I bought earlier that day, intending to prepare a healthy meal for dinner. If I stayed late marking, there was no chance I'd be bothered to cook when I got home. *The marking can wait,* I decided. If I made a big dinner tonight, I could bring the leftovers to eat tomorrow while I did the marking. Satisfied with this plan, I headed home.

Arriving at my apartment building, I checked my mailbox as usual. Seri's letter probably wouldn't arrive for another week or so, but I was expecting a credit card bill.

I reached my hand inside the mailbox—empty, apart from a folded piece of notepaper. *Hmmm, what's this?* I retrieved the piece of paper and carefully unfolded it. As soon as I read the note it slipped from my grasp as I reeled in shock.

I'M WARNING YOU AGAIN. BREAK UP WITH SHIN JINSEUNG.

A startling realisation dawned on me. *The stalker knows where I live.*

I stood frozen, head spinning. A gust of wind almost sent the note flying into the air, but I pinned it down with my foot just in time. I bent down to pick it up and tucked it away in my pocket—I needed to keep it as evidence.

Still in a state of shock, I wearily made my way up to my apartment. Once inside, I carefully looked around for signs of a break-in. Since this person knew where I lived, it was entirely conceivable that they might have tried to gain entrance. They could even be hiding inside at this very moment...

So far, nothing looked out of place, but then a noise from the bathroom made me jolt to attention. I armed myself with a knife from the kitchen, then slowly approached the bathroom door. Hand shaking, I tightened my grip around the doorknob and twisted. I held my breath as I pushed the door open in a swift motion, expecting to catch a startled intruder. But the room was empty. I was alone. I let out my tension in a long relieved sigh.

Before doing anything else, I set about changing my door code— the simplest safety measure I could take. I input my old combination into the keypad, then proceeded to set a new four-digit code. The digital lock played a short confirmation tune. *There.* Safe and secure.

* * *

IF ANYTHING WAS GOING to reveal the identity of the culprit, it was the security footage from the camera at the building's entrance. I called the building manager the next morning, whose number I had saved on my phone in case of emergency.

"*Yeoboseyo?*" a pleasant-sounding woman answered.

"Hello. This is Chloe Gibson. I'm a resident of the Saimdang building, apartment number 4C."

"What can I help you with?"

"I received a threatening note in my mailbox today. I wondered if you could review the security footage for me and see who placed it."

The woman hesitated. "Usually we only accept this kind of request from the police."

My resolve deflated. *Of course. They wouldn't just share the footage with anyone.* "I understand, but I don't know if this is serious enough to involve the police."

"Could I see the threatening note you speak of? You could send me a photo of it."

I considered whether or not to show her the note, after all, it did reveal my secret relationship. I had no idea whether I could trust the woman I spoke with. "It's…of a personal nature. I would rather not share it if possible."

"Then I'm not sure if there's much I can do. Sorry."

I didn't have time to change my mind. The woman promptly hung up.

I collapsed on my bed, groaning in frustration. *What should I do now? Contact the police?* I had evidence of harassment, but would it be enough? After all, no physical harm had befallen me…*yet.* There was also the risk of revealing my relationship in the process. *No.* The police should be a last resort, I decided. For now, I had to remain vigilant.

I spent the rest of the morning re-organising and backing up my file of evidence—screenshots of the text messages and call log, a recording of one of the phone calls, and a photograph of the note.

Maybe I should look into security systems as well. I checked out a website selling cameras, locks, and alarms. *This shit's expensive. What if I'm overreacting…*

My phone started to ring. *The building manager?! Did she have a change of heart?*

"Are you the person who called earlier about the security footage?" the woman asked.

"Yes."

"I had some time, so I decided to take a quick look."

My heart thudded in my chest. "Oh? Did you see anything?"

"There *was* a suspicious individual."

"Who was it? What did they look like?"

"It's clear that they don't want to be identified. They were wearing all black, and a motorcycle helmet over their head."

The significance of this development was not lost on me. "A m-motorcycle helmet?"

"That's correct. Is that useful information?"

"Yes. It is. Thank you."

'I'm glad I was able to help you. Sorry I can't provide any more details."

"That's all right. Thank you very much for letting me know."

A black outfit and a motorcycle helmet. That was enough to confirm my suspicions. My stalker was the same person who delivered the mutilated doll to Jinseung's house. A disturbed and possibly dangerous individual.

Chapter 15

The tower of test papers leaned precariously in front of me, threatening to topple and cascade around the room. I deftly restrained the stack and rearranged it into three smaller piles.

Working kept my mind off the stalker, and I felt safe within the confines of the *hagwon*. I needed to get this marking done, anyway.

My last class for the day was over. I sat at a messy, overflowing desk in the staffroom, surrounded by utilitarian office furniture, shelves bursting with books and files, and equipment cords like snakes lying hazardously over the floor. I was alone, my only light source a desk lamp, plus the streetlight coming in through the gaps in the blinds.

I reached for Sophie's paper and opened it. Her handwriting was beautiful as usual. I read her answer to the first question and awarded her a red tick.

With each tick, I felt a growing sense of disappointment. Call it selfish, but I hoped she would get at least a few questions wrong. My hopes diminished as I neared the end of the paper. On the last page of the booklet, I wrote 100% and circled it. Time to face up to the reality of the situation—Sophie couldn't stay in my class any longer. She was finding it too easy and needed to be moved up to the advanced level. That meant I would no longer be her teacher. I let out a sigh, thinking how much I'd miss her. *It's for the best*, I told myself. Sophie needed to excel to get into Oxford, and that meant pushing her capabilities.

Over time, the piles in front of me dwindled, and at last, I left the building. I made my way to the bus stop, never straying from the main streets and always keeping a wary eye tuned in on my surroundings. I no longer considered it paranoia. There really was someone out there targeting me, possibly planning to harm me. I had to tread carefully.

I was near the bus stop when something caught my eye, sending a wave of fear surging through my veins. A person who fitted the exact description of the culprit. They were riding a scooter, dressed in black, and with a black motorcycle helmet over their head. *Could it be?*

Before I could react, the scooter driver zoomed off and turned down a side street. My legs unfroze, and with a sudden spike of adrenaline shooting through my body, I ran after them. Now was my chance to possibly catch and identify my harasser.

The side street was long, dark, and narrow. I could see the scooter driver in the distance, tail light shining.

"Wait! Stop!" I cried. I ran as fast as I could, but the gap between us widened. Nearly out of breath, I was about to give up the chase when a traffic light at the end of the road turned red and the scooterist stopped. *Now's my chance.* I ran as fast as my legs would take me. *Almost there...*

My foot landed funny on the pavement. My leg gave out and I fell down with a smack. I lay helpless, head dizzy and my body throbbing with pain. When I finally gathered the strength to lift my head, I saw the helmeted individual walk towards me. Closer...closer...

"No!" I whimpered, shielding myself with my hands.

They reached out their hand to me. "Are you okay?" He lifted his visor, revealing a baby-faced young man—or boy—with big, wide eyes full of sincere concern.

The tension drained out of me as I let him help me up. "Yes, I'm okay." I brushed myself off.

"Were you following me?" he asked in heavily accented English.

"Yes. I thought you were someone…I must have been mistaken." It seemed unlikely that this boy could be my harasser.

"Be more careful, okay?"

I nodded and limped away, head hung in embarrassment. Emerging back onto the main road, I looked around and realised there were many people on scooters and motorcycles in the surrounding area—and several wearing black outfits and the same, generic helmet. I cursed myself for being so stupid. Of course I wouldn't be able to pick the culprit on that information alone. It wasn't nearly enough to go off.

I managed to get to the bus stop on time—barely. The driver had just closed the bus door, but I rapped on it, and it jerked back open. I hopped on board, panting, and dropped into the closest available seat.

My face stung. I gingerly touched my cheek. The skin felt rough and sore. I pulled a pink compact mirror out of my bag and examined my reflection. Sure enough, my face was grazed and tender along the left side, matching the state of my palms. I resolved to put some ointment on it as soon as I got home.

I got off the bus at my stop and walked briskly to my apartment building. When I reached my door, I input the code on the digital lock. An error sound played. Thinking I had mistyped, I re-entered the code. It didn't work. Eventually, I remembered that I changed the combination the previous night. I closed my eyes and searched my brain, willing for the new code to surface in my memory. My mind was completely blank. It was no use. I was locked out.

Chapter 16

There was a trick to opening locked doors that I had learned from movies. I pulled out my wallet and selected a random card. Not entirely sure what I was doing, I inserted the card into the narrow crack between the door and the frame and tried to run it through the junction where the lock bolted across. As soon as the card met resistance, I lost my grip. It slipped out of my hand and disappeared into the crack. *Damnit. Why did I use my main credit card?!* I didn't dare attempt the "trick" again, lest I lose another important card.

On to the next tactic. I tried a few different codes which I had used for other things in the past. No luck, and after several incorrect attempts, the digital lock wouldn't let me try again. "Arrggggh," I groaned.

Pacing the corridor, I racked my brain for what to do. I could call the building manager again, but I'd get charged a hefty lockout fee plus an after-hours surcharge. Besides, I was sure that given time, I would remember the combination.

I made up my mind to stay the night somewhere else, and if I still couldn't recall the code by morning, I'd call the building manager and stump up the fee.

The most obvious place to crash was Jinseung's apartment, but could I risk going there when there was a crazy stalker bent on breaking us up on the loose? Not to mention they knew where it was and had managed to get up to it before. No, it would be more prudent to stay at a friend's house.

I scanned my eyes down the list of contacts on my phone, wondering who to call. My first choice was Bora, but she lived quite far away and with parents I had never met which made things awkward. I kept scrolling until another name jumped out at me—Shin Jina. I called her.

"Hello?" Jina said.

"*Unnie*, it's me, Chloe."

"Oh, Chloe! How are you?"

"Actually, I'm in a bit of a predicament."

"Is that so?"

I explained my situation to her, and she was more than willing to help.

"I'm at work right now," she said. "But if you meet me at the cinema, I'll take you to my place when I'm finished. Does that work for you?"

"Yes, it does. Thanks so much!"

"All right, see you soon."

"See you."

Continuing to exercise caution with my movements, I reached Cinema Lumiere by subway.

Jina was alone in the foyer when I arrived. She sat behind the counter, flipping through a glossy magazine, a bored expression on her face.

"Hey," I said, approaching her.

She looked up. "Hey!" Her dark eyes fell upon my cheek and she frowned. "What happened to your face?"

"Oh, this? I fell over."

"Ouch."

"Yeah."

"Falling over, then getting locked out of your apartment. Things aren't going well for you today, are they? How did you manage to lock yourself out, anyway?"

"I changed my door code yesterday and forgot what I changed it to. Stupid, I know."

"Why did you change it?"

"It's a long story."

"I'm intrigued. Tell me when we get back to my place, okay?"

"Okay." She was letting me stay the night at her house, the least I could do was give her the truth of the situation.

"The last screening is in session," Jina explained. "Once that's over, I just need to do a quick clean-up, then we'll go."

"Okay, no problem."

"Coffee?"

"Yes, please."

Jina prepared us a hot cup of coffee each, then she joined me at a table. By the time we had finished our drinks, the movie had finished. The moviegoers slowly filtered out while the credits rolled. I helped Jina tidy up. Cleaners would be in later to do a more thorough job.

At last, Jina turned off all the lights, set a security alarm, and locked the door. We walked to the subway station.

"I live in Hongdae," Jina explained. "It won't take long to get there."

I was very familiar with the young and trendy area of Seoul. At this late hour, the streets were still jam-packed with young people heading to bars and clubs. The lively atmosphere re-energised me.

Jina's apartment building was located near Hongik University. The low-rise building was a bit decrepit looking, but the interior had a lovely traditional Korean style with wooden floors, panelled walls, and sliding doors. The charming little apartment was cramped and a little messy, with piles of fashion magazines littering the floors and tons of clothes and papers strewn about

"Sorry, it's messy," Jina said, hastily removing the dirty dishes off the coffee table and dumping them in the already overflowing kitchen sink.

"That's all right. It's a cute apartment."

"Thanks. My flatmate lives here too. Her name's Scarlett. She's a model at the same agency as me." She knocked on Scarlett's bedroom door, but there was no answer. "Looks like it's just the two of us. Probably staying at her boyfriend's place. Make yourself comfortable."

I sat down on the living room couch. Jina disappeared for a second, then reemerged holding a tube of ointment. She bent down in front of me. "This will help your face heal." She squirted a little ointment into the palm of her hand, then gently applied it to my face. "There. That should do the trick."

"Thank you."

She put the tube away then entered the kitchen. "Would you like a beer?" She pre-emptively took two cans out of the fridge.

"Oh, yes, please. If you're having one."

She joined me on the couch and handed me a cold beer.

"So, I'm curious." She opened the tab on her can. "Why did you change your lock?"

I stroked the side of my neck, carefully thinking through how I would phrase my plight, but when I opened my mouth the words came tumbling out. "You know that person I told you about who's been harassing me with the phone calls and messages? I have a feeling they've been spying on me as well. Today they left a note in my letterbox, which means they know exactly where I live. I changed my door code as a precautionary measure."

Jina raised a hand to her lips and chewed her nails. "That's really freaky. They're like a stalker or something. I think you should tell my brother, if you haven't yet. He's involved in this. It's probably one of his fans doing it. He would want to know."

"I'm planning to tell him, but there's a problem. We recently had a fight. He hasn't been answering any calls or messages, and I don't want to pester him too much right now. I'm scared it's annoying him."

"A fight, huh? Was it about Ahn Jieun, by any chance?"

"Ugh. You guessed it."

"I figured you were probably jealous. Not to mention the stress of the stalker mixed in. It's no wonder you fought. But *Dongsaeng* doesn't know the whole story. If you told him about the stalker, I'm sure he'd be more understanding."

"That's what Yang Bora said too."

"He's not answering your calls, but maybe he'll respond to me. I can try my best to get through to him."

"You mean, you'll tell him what happened to me?"

"Yeah. If that's okay with you."

I chewed my lip, unsure. "I don't know…wouldn't it be better for him to hear it from me?"

"I'll just tell him the basic details and prompt him to call you. Then you can explain everything."

I still wasn't quite sure how involving Jinseung would help the situation, but for some reason it felt like the best way forward, and I knew Jina would handle the conversation with tact. I made up my mind. "Okay. Agreed."

Jina brightened. "Good. I'll try to contact him tomorrow. For now, you better get some rest. You look super tired."

"I feel super tired."

"You can sleep in my room."

"Are you sure?"

"Yup. I'll sleep in Scarlett's room. She won't mind." She led the way to her room and slid open the door.

Jina's bedroom was girly to the extreme. Her canopied bed overflowed with cushions and stuffed toys, and a string of fairy lights decorated the headboard. Opposite the foot of the bed was a dressing table covered with cosmetics and perfume bottles. A large mood board hung on the wall, made up of cuttings from magazines featuring beautiful women and inspirational quotes. The room smelled like hairspray, flowers, and scented candles.

Jina quickly scooped away a pile of clothes off the bed and threw them inside her wardrobe. "You have nothing to wear to bed, do you?" She ducked down and opened a drawer, rummaged a bit, then emerged with a pair of silky pink pyjamas. "Here you go. They're clean." She gave them a sniff just to double-check, then passed them to me.

"Thanks."

"Have a good sleep. See you in the morning."

"Night night."

She closed the door. I changed into the pyjamas, flicked off the light, and climbed into the bed, careful not to disturb her collection of plush toys.

Like most epiphanies, it hit me in the middle of the night as I was waking from a dream: the door code. I repeated it in my mind, willing myself not to forget it until I could write it down. I grabbed my diary, turned to a blank page, and quickly recorded it. I knew that it wasn't a good idea to write down your passwords or secret codes, but it's all I could think to do in the moment while sleepiness threatened to let the number slip from my mind again.

Chapter 17

I held my breath as I input the door code, praying that my memory hadn't betrayed me. After I punched the last digit, a lengthy delay ensued until finally the door unlocked with a click. *Phew.* Home sweet home. My credit card was lying upside down on the floor. I bent down to recover it and slipped it safely back into my wallet.

I tried to keep busy that morning to stop myself from constantly checking my phone, wondering when or if Jinseung would contact me. The few times I did allow myself to take a peek, there were no new messages.

I still hadn't heard from him by the time I left for work. During my lessons, I kept my phone on my desk and occasionally glanced down to check it inconspicuously. A call came through mid-lesson, Jinseung's name on the screen. For obvious reasons, I couldn't answer. My break couldn't come soon enough.

At the end of the class, I looked for a private spot on the premises to call Jinseung back. After a quick look around the building, I decided that the balcony off the staff kitchen would suffice. I nipped out and closed the sliding glass door behind me. The balcony was very exposed, and the wind whipped at me. I pulled my hair back into a ponytail to keep it from blowing in my eyes. Without further hesitation, I made the call and pressed the phone hard to my ear so that I could hear through the street noise below.

Jinseung answered immediately. "Chloe..." His voice sounded husky with exhaustion.

I opened my mouth to respond but was unable to summon any words.

"Are you there?" he asked.

"...Yes."

"I don't know what to say except I'm sorry. *Noona* told me what you've been dealing with since I've been gone. I'm so sorry."

His sincerity quickly melted my icy facade. "I'm sorry too."

"What for?"

"Ahn Jieun—"

"Oh. Never mind that. It's understandable. You would have been so anxious and insecure with those messages hounding you. All the while I had no idea what was going on. I should have been more attentive—"

"It's not your fault," I cut in. "You're not psychic. How could you possibly know?"

"I need to come clean about something."

"What is it?"

"That day that I removed the doll...I found something else in the box. Something we didn't see before."

"Huh?"

"A note. It said 'Break up with Chloe Gibson.'"

I paused for a second, letting this new piece of vital information sink in. "What the hell? Why didn't you tell me?"

"I honestly thought it was just some jealous fan being a pain. I didn't want to concern you because I thought you'd overreact."

"It's not overreacting if it's a legit threat! This person could be really dangerous! You should have told me."

"And you should have told me about this too! Why didn't you?"

"I wanted to, but it's been hard to get hold of you. Plus, Changsoo told me not to."

"Changsoo did? Why would he?"

"He didn't want to cause you any stress."

"That's not his decision to make! Agggh I could murder him!" Rage coursed through his strained voice.

"I understood his point of view, though. What good does it do now that you know? You'll just worry and fret."

"I can help you."

"How?"

"I'll do something."

"What?"

"I don't know right now, but there must be something I can do. Perhaps a serious message to my fans. Perhaps…" He trailed off, then after a thoughtful pause he continued. "If you wanted to end things right now, I'd understand."

My throat turned dry. This was the line of thinking I was afraid he'd take. "No," I said resolutely. "I don't want to break up. No matter what happens."

"No matter what happens?" he repeated, voice tinged with uncertainty. "Okay…If you're sure."

"I'm absolutely sure."

He sighed deeply. "Chloe…I wish I could be with you and protect you, but I can't. I'm simply too deep into this project to quit now. I'd be letting everyone down—"

"I'm not asking you to do that."

"I know, but I've been asking myself if it's the right thing to do. At the moment it doesn't seem like you've been seriously threatened, but who knows what will happen. Be careful, okay? I've asked *Noona* to check up on you regularly and make sure you're all right. Also, I'd like you to stay at my apartment. The security is much better—"

"The security has already failed us once. The stalker knows where you live and knows how to get up to your apartment. It might make them angry if I stay there. I don't think I should risk it."

"If you're sure—"

I glanced at my watch. There was no more time to talk. "Jinseung-ah, I've got to go. My next class is starting in a minute."

"Promise me you'll be careful, and if anything else happens, you'll let me know?"

"I promise."

I ended the call and tucked the phone away in my bag. Was letting him know the right thing to do? I still wasn't sure, but at least we were both on the same page now.

The rest of the day's classes passed uneventfully until I saw Sophie arrive, and I remembered that I'd have to break the news to her—she would move to a different class from next week. I felt sad to lose her. We had formed a close connection somehow, and I couldn't imagine reverting back to pre-Sophie days at work.

At the end of class, the students began to leave in a flurry. I caught Sophie as she stood up and hauled her bag over her shoulder. "Sophie, can I have a word with you?"

"Of course." She put her bag back down.

I waited until we were alone, then took a seat near her. "You got 100% on the test. Well done."

She shrugged awkwardly but couldn't conceal her smile. "It wasn't difficult."

"This class must be too easy for you…"

She shook her head. "I'm still learning."

"I'm sure that's true, but it's clear to me that you would be better off in the advanced level. From next week, you'll move up a class."

"But…"

"You need to be in a more challenging environment. If you really want to pursue Oxford—"

"I'm leaving the *hagwon*," she interjected.

I paused, wondering if I had heard her correctly. "What?"

"My parents want me to have private tutoring instead."

"…I see." I rubbed my neck as I slowly absorbed this new piece of information.

"Will you do it?"

"What do you mean?"

"I want you to tutor me."

"That's—"

"My parents will pay you well."

Foreign English teachers weren't permitted to undertake private tutoring in Korea, but that didn't stop many from doing it since it was such a lucrative side gig.

"Think about it at least," Sophie urged.

I didn't need to think. I had already made up my mind. "I'll do it."

Chapter 18

Jinseung took action against my harasser using the most powerful weapon he had at his disposal—his platform. He posted a sad-faced selfie accompanied by a short message composed like a letter.

My dear fans,

How are you all? I hope you are eating well, staying fit, and getting plenty of sleep.

Unfortunately, I have some sad news. It has recently come to my attention that a so-called fan has been harassing someone close to me.

It makes me feel very upset that someone would do this—especially someone who is my fan.

My message to you is this: If you truly love me then you would never cause harm to my friends or family in any way—physically or mentally.

So I ask all of my true fans to leave my friends and family in peace, and to step in and stop anyone who behaves in such a horrible way.

It would make me so happy if you could support me with this.

Thank you for understanding.

Yours always,
   Shin Jinseung

A long list of comments followed the post. I read the first few.

"That's awful. A true fan would never do this!"

"As fans we have to protect Shin Jinseung!"

"Nooooo. Poor Jinseungie."

"Whoever does this is not a real fan."

"Sasaeng fans are evil."

"Who dares to hurt Shin Jinseung?"

The post quickly became viral, being shared across K-drama groups and forums worldwide. If the person who was harassing me really was a *sasaeng* fan, then they definitely wouldn't miss it. Would it make them second-guess their behaviour? I could only hope so.

Several days passed with no new anonymous messages, and gradually I began to relax and let my guard down.

On a rainy Sunday afternoon, I walked to Booksea—the bookstore where I had agreed to meet Sophie for our first tutoring session. The huge, multi-floored bookshop housed soaring shelves full of titles in a vast number of genres and formats. Chandelier lighting suffused the store with a soft, warm glow, and the air smelled of coffee and fresh paper. An adjoining café furnished with mismatched chairs and tables served up fresh pastries, cakes, and hot drinks. Sophie waited for me there, head bent down over a book, steaming mug on the table in front of her. Absorbed in her reading, she didn't notice me until I had taken the seat opposite her. Her face lit up when she saw me.

"Hi, Sophie," I said cheerfully.

"Hello, Ms. Gibson." She beamed at me.

"Oh—since we're not in the classroom anymore, it's okay if you call me Chloe."

"Okay...*Chloe*." She made a strange face as she said my name.

"And what do you prefer, Sungmi or Sophie?"

"I don't mind. You can keep calling me Sophie."

"Were you waiting long?"

"Not really. I came early just to have a look around the bookstore. This might be my favourite shop in all of Seoul."

I chuckled. "I love bookstores too. I didn't know about this one. Shall we get started?"

"Yes. I'm ready." She positioned a notebook in front of her and pulled a pen from her case.

I hadn't met Sophie's parents, but I had spoken to her mother on the phone. She didn't have any particular expectations for what I taught her, as long as I could help bring her language level up to what was required to study at an English university. This allowed me a lot of free rein over what to teach her. First, I wanted to assess Sophie's skill level more thoroughly, and I had devised an activity which would truly put her knowledge to the test. I pulled two books from my bag. One, a Korean novel, the other, an English translation of the same novel. I explained what I wanted her to do. "I'm going to choose a passage from the Korean book. I'd like you to try translating it to English as best you can, not word-for-word literally, but taking into account the nuances of the language. Once you've done that, we'll compare it to the professionally translated version."

Sophie's brow creased with concern. "Sounds difficult."

"That's the point. I don't expect you to be up to the level of a professional translator. Far from it. But it will show me your lapses in comprehension."

"Okay. I'll try my best."

I turned to the first bookmarked page where I had marked a section out in pencil. Sophie bit her lip in concentration as she pored over the passage. After reading it through twice, she slowly began to translate it in her notebook. I was very curious to see what she'd come up with.

Being the perfectionist she was, Sophie took her time, but at last she set down her pen. "Okay. I think I'm done. That was tough." She wiped the back of her hand across her forehead.

I opened the English version of the book where I had bookmarked the same passage. Sentence by sentence, we compared the two translations. This was when it became apparent that there were many gaps in her grasp of the language. Idioms, metaphors, and various other constructions were tripping her up.

I had her repeat the exercise once more using a different passage of text. Sophie tried even harder this time, and I allowed her to consult her Korean-English dictionary to help her. The result was the same. Her ability to translate was only surface level. She didn't understand the deeper intricacies of the language.

Disappointment reigned on Sophie's face. "Looks like I still have a lot to learn..."

"That's only natural—but your level is still outstanding for someone who has never lived in an English-speaking country," I said, trying to cheer her up.

For the rest of our allotted one-and-a-half-hour time slot, we simply conversed in English, and I would correct her every time she said something that didn't make sense. Eventually our conversation turned personal.

"Ms. Gibson—I mean, Chloe—can I ask you a personal question?" Sophie asked.

"Uh, okay. What do you want to know?"

"Do you have a boyfriend?"

My eyes widened in surprise at the sudden enquiry. "I...No. I don't." It was simpler just to say no.

"Oh."

"Why do you ask? Is there someone you like?"

Sophie's cheeks turned red. "Yes. But I don't know how to make him notice me."

I smiled, thinking she sounded just like a typical teenage girl. "You are a lovely person. Just be yourself and I'm sure he'll notice you."

She didn't look convinced. "But what if he's much more popular than I am?"

"All you can do is to try and be his friend and see if anything develops out of that."

"I see." She chewed her lip, absorbing my advice.

Checking my watch, I realised we had already gone well over the time limit of our session.

"Is the lesson over?" Sophie asked, frowning in disappointment.

"Yes. But I'm not in a hurry to do anything else. If you want to hang out a bit longer."

"I'd like that."

We browsed the bookstore together until evening.

* * *

"Maybe she has a crush on you," Yang Bora mused, finger to her chin.

"What? A crush on *me*?" I spluttered. "Don't be ridiculous." The very notion that Sophie might like me in that way seemed ludicrous.

Shin Jina looked equally surprised at Bora's conclusion.

We were seated around a table at Cinema Lumiere, chatting while we waited for the next film to start. Jina wasn't working, so she could watch it with us. I had come straight from Booksea, carrying a bag with my purchases. I told them how the tutoring session had gone and briefly mentioned Sophie's boy problems.

"Is it so ridiculous?" Bora asked. "You two seem to have grown quite an attachment."

I shook my head. "No. I don't think that's it. Surely not."

"She blushes around you, she gave you a gift, she asked you to be her personal tutor, and now she's confiding in you about her love life."

"That doesn't necessarily mean anything," Jina said, coming to my defence.

Bora pushed her glasses up the ridge of her nose. "Well, just sayin'. I'd be careful if I were you. It never pays for teachers to get too close to their students."

"True, but this is different," I said.

She cocked a brow. "How so? Because you're both female?"

"No..." Perhaps I had made a big mistake by talking too much about Sophie. I had given her the wrong impression.

"Proceed with caution, that's my advice. Keep things strictly professional."

"Hmmm. I'll keep that in mind."

The movie was about to begin, so we took our seats in the theatre. As the film played, I couldn't pay attention. My thoughts lingered on Bora's surprising analysis. Was I really too close with Sophie? Could our relationship be misconstrued? Was the boy Sophie had a crush on not actually a boy? Was it actually me? She did blush a lot in my presence, but that was the only thing which stood out. I tried to concentrate on the movie and block out the niggling feeling that Bora was actually right.

* * *

WHEN I GOT HOME after the movie, I prepared a healthy home-cooked meal for dinner—a vegetable stir fry and rice. Since re-discovering cooking, I realised that I found the experience rather pleasant and relaxing.

After dinner, I sat on my bed with a hydrating sheet mask attached to my face, humming along to a catchy pop song while painting my toenails a vibrant shade of purple. My phone started ringing, interrupting my concentration, causing me to overrun my toenail and get nail polish on my duvet cover. I licked my finger and tried to rub it out which, unsurprisingly, didn't work. With my other hand I answered the phone without even looking at who was calling.

"Hey, it's me," Jinseung said.

I shot bolt upright at the sound of his voice. "Hey!"

"How's things?"

"Oh, you know, the usual. Actually, I'm tutoring one of my students privately now."

"Wow. That's great!"

"How's filming going? You sound tired."

He stifled a yawn. "It's progressing. I'm finally getting a break tomorrow. I plan to spend all day sleeping."

"Good plan."

"So, uh," he lowered his voice as if bringing up something secretive. "Have you had any more anonymous messages?"

"No. Not since you put up that letter to your fans. It seems to have done the trick. For now, at least."

He exhaled a sigh. "I'm relieved."

"Me too."

"Hey, your birthday is coming up soon, isn't it?"

"Yup. In two weeks."

"Keep the day free—no, the whole weekend. I want to arrange something."

My eyes widened. "Arrange what?"

"I can't tell you. That would spoil the surprise."

I overflowed with curiosity. "Come on, just tell me."

His firm answer was, "No."

"You're no fun," I muttered under my breath.

He abruptly changed the subject. "Hey, can you turn your camera on? I want to see you."

I did so, forgetting I still had the sheet mask on and the fluffy bunny headband holding my hair back.

Jinseung appeared on my screen too. He was sitting on a bed, propped up by a pile of pillows. His usual chubby cheeks were replaced by a gaunt and pallid visage, but dimples still appeared when he grinned upon seeing me.

I hastily peeled off the mask and removed the headband, cheeks blushing with embarrassment.

"Keep it on. I don't mind," he said, amused.

"I look silly."

"You look cute. But you always look cute."

I smiled sheepishly.

He was silent for a while, just gazing at me, his eyes drinking me in. Then he began to chew his lip in thought. "What have you got on under that robe?" he asked tentatively.

"Oh? My pyjamas."

"Can I see?"

I undid my waist tie and let the robe fall open. I wore a pair of classic blue plaid pyjamas. Comfortable and cute.

"Those are my favourite." He leaned back with an arm behind his head, admiring the view. "I haven't seen you in such a long time... Could you...?"

I knew what he was angling at. Despite my self-consciousness I decided to indulge him. I undid the first few of my buttons, revealing the plunging cleavage between my breasts.

He watched appreciatively. "Keep going," he breathed raggedly.

"I'm not wearing anything underneath."

"Show me."

I slowly undid the rest of my buttons. Jinseung watched on with a look of strained concentration.

When I got to the bottom, I edged my top open until my chest was fully exposed.

"You look so good."

"Now it's your turn."

"Is it just?"

I nodded.

He pulled off his black t-shirt in a swift motion. His physique was just as delicious as always, broad, toned, and hard. I wished I could reach through the screen and touch him. Jinseung displayed a similar look of yearning. "I wish you were here with me," he said.

"Me too."

That night, although separated by hundreds of kilometres, we regained some of our lost intimacy.

Chapter 19

I received an unexpected visitor in my classroom one evening—
Linda Choi, the principal/CEO of the *hagwon*. She was a
middle-aged, half-Korean woman, short and slightly over-
weight, streaks of grey through her hair. She had a dour expression on
her face. "Chloe, can I have a word with you after class?" she asked.

Her presence unnerved me, and I wondered what she wanted to
speak with me about. "Yes, of course," I politely replied.

"Come to my office when you're ready."

I nodded and she left the room. Her request distracted my
thoughts throughout the lesson. I couldn't help but jump to conclusions. Would she question my relationship with Sophie or, worst-case
scenario, had she somehow found out about the private tutoring? She
wasn't exactly a sympathetic woman, and she'd probably ask me to
cease immediately or threaten to report me. Most likely I'd be let off
with a warning first, but getting deported was a possible outcome I
couldn't ignore.

I walked to Linda's office after class feeling extremely apprehensive. When I reached her door, I knocked before entering. The room
reeked of her perfume—a sickly sweet artificial rose scent which

made me gag. She sat behind a desk decorated with framed photographs of her cat—a hairless sphynx. I recoiled at the sight of the rat-like creature and tried to avert my eyes.

"Pull up a chair," Linda urged.

I sat down, fidgeting with my hands in my lap nervously.

"Kim Sungmi was in your class until recently, correct?" she asked, peering at me sternly through her spectacles.

I gulped. "Yes, that's right."

"You don't happen to have her contact details, do you?"

I hesitated. Was this a trap? Was she trying to find out if I'd been in touch with Sophie since she left? "No," I lied.

She tapped her nails on the desk, sighing. "That's too bad."

"Do you need to contact her?"

"Yes." She leaned closer to me and lowered her spectacles. "Kim Sungmi may have left us, but it doesn't excuse her from paying the term's fee. Her tuition is well overdue. I have been trying to contact her parents to recoup the outstanding payment, but I can't seem to get through to anyone."

So that's what this is about. I felt a mixture of relief for myself and concern for Sophie. It seemed strange that her parents were capable of paying a private tutor but not her overdue *hagwon* fees.

"Well, never mind," Linda said relaxing back into her chair. "I'll just have to switch tactics. Perhaps I'll get a debt collector involved at some point…"

A debt collector! I made a mental note to warn Sophie or her parents.

"You may go home," Linda said with a gentle shooing gesture of her hand.

"Sorry I wasn't of any help."

"That's okay. Enjoy your evening."

"Goodnight, Linda."

I had no further work to do that night, so I left straight away and walked to the bus stop. Usually, I had my transit card ready before I boarded, but I wasn't thinking straight. I held up the queue while I fumbled in my bag searching for it. At last I gripped the card at the bottom of my bag. When I retrieved it, something else fluttered out and onto the floor of the bus. Before I could react, someone behind me picked it up. "You dropped this."

"Thanks." I accepted the small piece of crumpled light pink paper, though I didn't recall what it was.

Curious, I unfolded the piece of paper once I sat down. It was a note, and as soon as I read it, a loud gasp escaped my throat.

LAST CHANCE. BREAK UP WITH SHIN JINSEUNG OR ELSE YOU'LL PAY.

The *ajumma* next to me turned my way, alarmed by my sudden outburst. "Are you okay?"

"Yes," I said quickly, recovering my breath. "I'm fine."

I stuffed the note back into my bag, hands trembling. My thoughts were a scrambled mess, but as soon as I had calmed down, I tried to think through the situation rationally. *What does this mean?* The stalker must have been in close proximity with me at some point—close enough to slip a note in my bag undetected.

How long had it been there? Maybe it had been put there a while ago and I didn't notice until now—its crumpled appearance certainly suggested that it wasn't new, and I didn't regularly empty out my bag, letting the receipts and other miscellanea build up instead.

"OR ELSE YOU'LL PAY." *How will I pay? Am I in danger? Would the police take this seriously or not?*

Caught up in these thoughts, I nearly missed my stop. The door had already closed, but I called to the driver and he opened it again to let me off.

Alone at the bus stop, a cold wind swirled around me, making the hairs on my exposed neck stand up. I cautiously walked the short distance home, constantly glancing around, making sure no one followed me.

I slumped with a sense of relief when I reached my apartment building unscathed. The stalker might have known where I lived, but I still had faith in the security of my building.

I entered my code and pushed open the door to my apartment. It quickly dawned on me that I wasn't alone.

Chapter 20

I dropped my bag in shock. Its contents scattered over the floor. A woman I didn't recognise stood in the middle of my apartment. She was young and pretty with long dark hair and glasslike skin. She had an innocent look except for a pair of shrewd eyes which were piercing in their intensity.

"Who are you?" I stammered.

The young woman just stared at me for a bit, then her lip slowly curled up at one corner. She started to approach me. I impulsively backed away.

"Are you all right?" she asked as if I were the strange person and not her.

"What are you doing in my apartment?"

The woman raised her perfectly groomed eyebrows. "Didn't Manager Yang tell you?"

"Yang Bora?" *What does she have to do with all this?*

I heard the toilet flush, the sound of running water, then Bora emerged from the bathroom. "Oh! Hello, Chloe. You're home."

"What are you doing here?" I asked.

"Didn't you get my message? I tried calling you as well, but you didn't answer."

"Who is this?" I pointed to the young woman accusingly.

"Don't you recognise her? It's Go Yoojin."

I calmed myself, breathing slow and steady. It was only the actor who Bora managed. If I wasn't completely flabbergasted, I'd be starstruck. "Why did you bring her here?"

"There's a ghost in my apartment," Yoojin said simply.

A ghost? This makes no sense. Am I dreaming?

"Actor-nim is very superstitious," Bora explained. "She refused to go to her apartment. I didn't know what else to do so I brought her here in the meantime. Sorry you didn't see my message. It must have been a shock."

"Shock is an understatement."

"I'm sorry."

"How did you get in?"

"You gave me your door code for safekeeping, remember?"

"Oh yeah."

In fact, I had let Bora go to my apartment when I wasn't there a few times in the past, so it was no wonder she thought it would be all right this time.

"Speaking of ghosts, it looks like *you've* seen one," Bora said, eyeing me with concern.

"I thought…"

"What?"

"I thought that my stalker had gained entrance. I found this in my bag just before." I took out the note and showed Bora.

"*Omo!*" She clutched a hand to her chest. "That's serious."

Yoojin caught a peek at the note as well. "Yikes! Are you dating *Seonbae?*"

"Yes," I admitted, too depleted to come up with a convincing lie. "But it's a secret, okay?"

"I won't tell anyone."

"You need to sit down." Bora guided me to the couch. "I'll get you a glass of water and clean up the stuff you dropped."

I slumped down, my heart still pounding on overdrive. My hand shook as I drank the water.

When Bora had finished picking up my things, she sat down next to me. "Do you think…you could be in danger?" she asked, a slight tremor in her voice.

"I did think so when I read the note. But then again, I don't know when it ended up in my bag. It could've been days or weeks ago. I thought that Jinseung's announcement had worked, and I'd just been going about totally carefree. Obviously nothing happened to me."

"Perhaps they're just trying to scare you and don't actually intend to 'make you pay'?"

"Yes. That's a possibility…But I'm still scared."

"I think you should get the police involved. Better to be safe than sorry."

"I'm worried they won't take this seriously."

"Maybe so, but it's worth it just to bring it to their attention."

"Yeah, you're right. It couldn't hurt to try and explain the situation. Maybe there's something they can do."

Yoojin had been hovering around us listening in on our conversation. "Is this person a fan of Shin Jinseung?" she piped up.

"That's what we suspect," Bora said.

Yoojin stroked her chin in thought. "How strange. Usually, the goal of *sasaeng* fans is to get noticed by their idol, but this person seems to be hiding in the shadows."

Bora contemplated this. "True, but at the moment it seems their only aim is to get Chloe and Jinseung to break up. Perhaps he or she plans to 'come out of the shadows' once they've broken up?"

"I don't know. Something seems off about this…"

"I don't disagree, but it's impossible to try and guess their exact motive right now. Best put this in the hands of the police. Chloe, I'll go with you to the station if you want."

"Oh? That would be a big help," I said, grateful for her support.

Bora turned her attention to Yoojin. "Actor-nim, I better take you home…"

Yoojin crossed her arms and shook her head. "No way. I'm not going home until it has been thoroughly cleansed of ghosts."

"The paranormal agent can't come until tomorrow, and you can't stay here. I'll book you into a hotel tonight, would that suit?"

"Make it the Four Seasons and you have a deal."

Bora let out an exasperated sigh. "Mr. Kim won't like this one bit…"

Yoojin looked at her with puppy-dog eyes.

"Fine. I'll make a booking." She grabbed her iPad off the dining table and started tapping away. At the payment screen, she whipped out a platinum business credit card and typed in the details. "There. All done. Let's go. Chloe, you're coming too."

"I am?"

"Once I've dropped Yoojin off, I'll take you to the police station."

Before leaving, I quickly saved my electronic file of evidence onto a flash drive. I also grabbed the pieces of physical evidence I had and stowed them safely in my bag.

We left the apartment. Yoojin covered the lower half of her face with a surgical mask and pulled a hood over her head to disguise herself as we walked the short distance to where the van was parked.

I took the passenger seat next to Bora, while Yoojin climbed in the back. My muscles tensed as Bora started the engine. Past experience of Bora's driving taught me not to get too relaxed. Fortunately, her driving seemed to have improved a great deal. We made it to the hotel without incident.

"You okay to check in by yourself?" Bora asked Yoojin when she had stopped outside the main entrance. "I booked you under the pseudonym Do Minha."

"Sure. Hope you get along okay at the police station."

"Thanks," I said.

Yoojin disappeared into the luxurious hotel through the revolving door.

"Right. Off to the police station," Bora said, pulling away from the hotel.

"Wait. We need to make a stopover somewhere."

She looked at me questioningly.

"There's more evidence I should bring with me," I explained.

"Oh right. The doll."

"Yes. And the other note."

"There's another note?"

"Jinseung was holding back from me. It turned out that there was a similar note with the doll."

"It certainly would have been handy to know that before."

"You're telling me."

"Okay. Let's go to Jinseung's place."

We drove to his apartment building. Bora parked nearby and I ran out, up the elevator, and into his apartment, praying that the evidence was still there and he hadn't given it to Changsoo like he said he would.

All was quiet and still. The air smelled faintly of cleaning detergent, which told me that his cleaner must have recently been in to freshen up the place.

Now, where did he say he kept the doll? In a drawer? It couldn't be a drawer in the bedroom, closet, or en suite, as I had waited on his bed while he put the doll away.

That left the kitchen or his office room, and I doubted that he kept it in the kitchen so close to where he prepared food. The office was the most likely contender. There were few drawers in the small room —just a small set inside a cupboard, and his desk drawers. I searched his desk first, pulling out each drawer one by one until I got to the bottom. Most were filled with random papers and folders, but the last drawer contained what I was looking for. The doll, sealed in a plastic bag, along with the note: "BREAK UP WITH CHLOE GIBSON."

I grabbed what I had come for and rushed back down to Bora's van.

"Did you find it?" she asked.

I nodded.

"Good. The more evidence we have, the better, and that doll is quite compelling."

As she drove me to the police station, my stomach clenched with nervousness. What if the police couldn't do anything to help me? What if they thought I was making things up? Thank goodness Bora was with me for support. I didn't think I'd be able to do this on my own.

We pulled up in the carpark outside the police station—a large, generic-looking office building with a flat blue roof. Flags fluttered in the wind above the entryway. Bora and I walked side by side up the steps to the main door. Cold, harsh fluorescent lights lit the reception area. Bora explained my situation to the person at the desk. The receptionist handed me a clipboard with a blank police report attached. She asked me to fill out the report while I waited to be called up, then we would be referred to an officer we could speak to.

An eclectic group of individuals milled around the waiting area. Bora and I sat down on hard plastic seats. An old man wearing dirty, tatty clothes leered at me in a way that made my skin crawl. I would have felt unsafe if we weren't inside a police station.

The hours dragged on. People came and went from the station. I had already filled out the report and checked it over twice, making sure I hadn't left out any important details. Bora took it up to the receptionist.

I had almost nodded off to sleep in my chair by the time my name was finally called. Bora gently shook my shoulder, making sure I was awake. "Chloe? We're up."

A staff member took us through a door to an open-plan office area where police staff were stationed at desks around the room. We were guided to a young man. He had defined cheekbones and closely shaved hair. The bulging biceps visible below his rolled-up shirt sleeves announced his athletic body. He couldn't have been older than thirty.

"Good evening, I'm Officer Bae Sangwook," he said. "I have had a brief read of your report, but could you explain everything to me from the beginning?"

I was silent for a moment, unable to process my thoughts into a coherent sentence. Bora nudged me. "The doll," she mouthed.

"Right." I explained everything starting from the doll incident.

All the while, Sangwook listened intently, taking notes while I spoke. I covered everything that had happened up to the discovery of the note in my bag. I also handed him the flash drive, the physical notes, and the doll. Sangwook perused the evidence. To my relief, he appeared to be taking everything very seriously.

"You were right to report this," Officer Bae said.

His reassurance instantly soothed me.

"However…" he continued.

My heart plunged. I already knew what was coming next.

"…I'm afraid a case like this is low priority. There has been no concrete threat of physical harm. From what I can tell, you aren't in any immediate danger. Your situation must be stressful, I'll give you that, but stress is not enough to start a police investigation. I will, of course, open a case file, though."

"What about a DNA test?" I asked.

"We would need a suspect's DNA to run a comparison."

"Then what should we do, Officer-nim?" Bora asked, frowning.

"Keep gathering proof and send it to me. The culprit could slip up at one point and reveal something about their identity. Once we have something to go on, maybe then we'll be able to do something. And if at any point, you feel physically threatened, contact me immediately."

He gave us each a copy of his card which listed his contact details.

We went back to the car, a sombre mood hanging over us.

"I knew it. They won't investigate," I grumbled, pulling on my seatbelt.

"It wasn't all for nothing," Bora said.

"Oh?"

She waved Bae Sangwook's business card. "We have someone who we can contact now. Who knows when this could come in handy."

"That's true. But still, I feel like a sitting duck."

"Don't worry. I'll keep in touch with you and help you with whatever I can."

"Thanks. I appreciate that."

Chapter 21

As I approached Sophie in the bookshop café, Bora's warning replayed in my head. "I'd be careful if I were you. It never pays for teachers to get too close to their students." While I still didn't believe there was anything wrong with my friendship with Sophie, I made a mental note to keep things professional during our session.

The café was pleasantly quiet with only a few solo patrons present, calmly sipping drinks while reading books or working on laptops. Sophie sat at a small table by the window, carefully writing in a notebook, a look of deep concentration etched on her face. She was casually dressed in jeans and an oversized sweater. I pulled out the chair opposite her. "Hello," I said, sitting myself down.

Sophie closed her notebook. The smile on her lips faded as she examined me. "Are you okay?"

"I'm fine, thank you."

"You look out of sorts."

"Oh? I guess I'm just a bit tired." Exhausted, more like. The stalking and the police's unwillingness to investigate weighed heavily on me, but I wasn't about to go into that with Sophie. She didn't seem convinced, but she didn't press the matter.

As I prepared my teaching materials, a niggling feeling developed in the back of my mind. There was something I had to tell Sophie about, but I couldn't remember what. No matter how hard I tried to grasp the memory, it kept slipping away. I had no choice but to let it go and move on.

I took out my phone to set a timer. "I'm going to time today's lesson," I explained. "Hope you don't mind."

"No, go ahead."

I was about to press start when she stopped me.

"Wait. I'm going to go get another drink. Want anything?"

"Ah, no thanks."

She went to the counter. When I saw her open her wallet to pay, it hit me. The debt collector. I had called Sophie's mother not long after my meeting with Linda, but I hadn't been able to get through to her, and with everything that had been going on, it had completely slipped my mind. When she rejoined me at the table, I didn't hesitate to bring it up. "Sophie, there's something I need to warn you about."

Her eyes widened. "What's that?"

"I had a chat with the principal of the *hagwon* a few days ago. She told me that your fees haven't been paid and she's been unable to get hold of your family. She was seriously considering hiring a debt collector."

The news appeared to throw her off-guard. She seemed flustered, unable to hold eye contact with me. "Thank you for warning me."

I had intended to keep my distance from her, but in this situation, I couldn't help getting personal. If Sophie was in some kind of trouble, I wanted to help her. "Sorry to pry, but is everything all right? Is your family having any financial difficulties?"

She shook her head and summoned up a smile. "No. Don't worry. I'm not sure why my parents haven't paid. They're very busy and they must have forgotten. I'll remind them."

"Okay. But just so you know, you can tell me if anything's wrong."

"Thanks."

* * *

When the timer went off, I wondered if I had set it wrong since it felt like hardly any time had passed at all. But no, one and a half hours had really gone by and our lesson was over. "Looks like our time's up," I said regretfully.

Sophie frowned. "That went quick."

"I know. Must have achieved a flow state."

"Flow state?"

"When you're so involved in what you're doing that time just flies by."

"Oh, I get it. That happens to me all the time."

"It means you have a great deal of focus. No wonder you're such a good student."

Sophie's cheeks glowed red. "It doesn't usually happen during a lesson, though. Must be your teaching."

I chuckled. "Maybe, but I can't take all the credit. Let's finish up now."

We quickly wrapped up the activity we were engaged in.

Sophie packed her notebook and pens away. "Do you want to have a look around the bookshop again?" she asked hopefully.

I was tempted but thought better of it. "No, I need to head home."

"Oh. Okay." She drooped in disappointment.

"But don't let me stop you from browsing."

"Nah. That's okay. I'll head home too. Why don't we walk together? Part of the way, anyway. It's nice weather."

Since the latest threatening note, I hadn't been walking around by myself very much. I had planned to take a taxi home, but if Sophie was offering to walk with me, then perhaps it wouldn't hurt if I went with her. It seemed safer than going alone. "All right," I agreed. "Let's walk."

We set out. The evening was warm and still. Birds twittered in blossoming trees. The sky was pink as the sun descended below the horizon. I kept an anxious eye out as we walked. Sophie called out my odd behaviour. "Something wrong?"

"No. It's nothing."

Eventually, I relaxed. We chatted as we walked, discussing the latest English books that Sophie had read.

Further into our journey, our chitchat began to peter out. Sophie seemed a bit distracted, constantly checking her phone. I wondered who she was texting. We turned onto a quiet backstreet with an office building along one side, and the rear side of a strip of shops on the other. The last remnants of sunlight were beginning to fade, plunging the street into shadow. Our pace slowed. I heard something from above—the swish of an opening window. Sophie let out a scream. It all happened so fast that my brain didn't register what was going on.

Chapter 22

An object whooshed past me, missing me by mere centimetres. It shattered loudly on the concrete, sending shards of glass flying at every angle. I sprang out of the way, heart thumping wildly in my chest.

"Are you all right?" Sophie asked, eyes wide with shock.

I brushed myself off. "Yes. It missed me. Just."

A man came running from a nearby shop, startled by the noise. "What happened?" he asked.

Neither Sophie nor I replied, too shaken by the event. Once I had caught my breath I looked up. All the windows were shut, and I couldn't see anyone there. Whoever did it would have run away by now.

"What is that, anyway?" Sophie asked.

I bent down to inspect the remains of the object. "Looks like a vase."

"Someone threw that at you?" the man asked, bewildered.

"They dropped it from that window," I said, pointing up.

He held up a hand to his mouth and gasped. "*Omo*. Who would do such a thing?"

"I don't know," I replied.

"A random attack?" Sophie suggested.

"There are crazy, dangerous people out there," the man said, shaking his head. "Are you okay?"

"Yes, I think so." I examined and flexed my limbs. If I had been hurt, the adrenaline coursing through me covered up the pain.

The man took a notepad from his pocket and scribbled something down. He tore off a page and handed it to me. "Here," he said. "My contact details in case you need a witness. You will report this, won't you?"

"Yes. I'll report it."

"I'll check the shop's CCTV footage in case it shows anything useful."

"That would be a big help."

"I'll clean up this mess too. Don't want anyone to hurt themselves."

"Thank you, *Ajussi*," Sophie said.

"You better leave. The attacker might still be lurking around somewhere."

"Yes, we'll go," I said. "Thanks again."

"That was scary," Sophie admitted as we left the scene.

I didn't share with her what I was thinking—that it wasn't just some random attack. That perhaps I was intentionally targeted. The stalker warned me that I'd pay, and maybe that vase wasn't meant to miss me.

* * *

As soon as I was home safe and sound, I pulled out Officer Bae Sangwook's card from my wallet. I called him to report the incident. The line was busy at first, but I tried again a bit later and managed to get through.

"Officer Bae Sangwook speaking," he said.

"Hello, this is Chloe Gibson. I saw you at the police station a few days ago. I reported being harassed by someone trying to break up my relationship."

"Ah, yes. I remember. Is everything okay?"

I explained to him what had just occurred and my strong suspicion that the attacker was the same person who had been sending me the notes.

"Are you completely sure about that?" Sangwook asked.

"I can't be one hundred per cent sure, but that's the way it seems. They warned me I'd pay, and then this happens."

"Hmmm…"

"You're not convinced?"

"How could they position themselves to drop the vase without knowing in advance that you would walk by that exact building?"

"Must have been following me, or tracking me somehow, and saw me turn onto that street."

"It would have been difficult to get into the building and up several floors in time."

"True…" Now that he said that, it did seem like a stretch. Doubt edged its way into my mind.

"Is it not possible that this was, after all, a random attack? Unrelated to the messages?"

"It's possible," I admitted.

"Rest assured, we will investigate this. You could have been seriously injured, or worse, killed."

"Thank you. Oh—there were witnesses too." I gave him the phone numbers of Sophie and the man from the shop—Lee Haneul.

"That's helpful. Be careful, okay? Give me a call if anything else happens."

"Yes. I will."

The next person I called was Yang Bora.

"That's really scary, Chloe," she said. "I hope you're all right."

"Officer Bae doesn't think it's the same person. But it seems like too much of a coincidence if it's not."

"I agree with you."

"I don't know what to do."

"I've been thinking about your situation lately, and I think I've come up with a plan."

"Oh? What is it?"

"I don't know why I didn't think of it before. You don't need to break up with Jinseung, you just need to make the stalker believe that you have."

"And how would I manage that?"

"You and Shin Jinseung are actors. Time to put those acting skills to use and stage a breakup scene."

"A breakup scene? Interesting…"

"And if we play our cards right, we might just be able to catch the stalker at the same time."

Chapter 23

Chloe: I will break up with Shin Jinseung.

My finger hovered over the send button, hand shaking. Is this the right thing to do? Will it work? I wasn't even sure if they would be able to reply. I hadn't received a text from the stalker in a while, and I was relying on them receiving my message at the last number they contacted me on.

I held my breath, and before I could talk myself out of it, I hit send. This was my best shot at ending the torment I had been going through once and for all.

I waited for the status of my message to turn to "read." To my surprise, it happened quickly, then three dots in the bottom corner showed that the recipient was typing. Their message popped up with a ping.

Unknown: How will you prove it?

I quickly typed my answer.

Chloe: Meet me and I will make a call to break up with him.

I gritted my teeth and waited for the reply.

Unknown: I will not meet you face to face, but make the call somewhere I can see you.

Fortunately, I had anticipated such a response.

Chloe: How about a coffee shop? You can watch from a distance.

Unknown: I need to hear the call too. There is an app that will let me listen in. I will send you a link to download it.

I wondered why watching would be necessary if they could simply listen to the call from any location.

Chloe: You need to see me and listen in as well?

Unknown: Yes. I need to get a good sense that the call is genuine. I will watch you and listen. That's the only way I'll believe you.

So they were already suspicious that the call might be fake. This could be trickier to pull off than I had anticipated. Plus, downloading something that the stalker sent me seemed seriously risky, but what choice did I have?

Chloe: Fine. Let's do as you say.

Unknown: You better go through with it.

* * *

BORA and I had named our plan "Operation Breakup," and it was finally time to put it into action.

The coffee shop bustled with late-morning patrons. It was much busier than I had anticipated. As I stood in line to purchase a drink, I scanned the large room, trying to identify anyone who looked suspicious. The clientele was varied—businesspeople in suits, casually dressed creative types, and university students. No one in particular stood out, but I knew that my stalker, my *enemy*, must be among them. I tried not to think about it too much.

"What would you like?" the staff member behind the counter asked.

I had been so preoccupied I didn't notice that I was at the front of the queue. "I'll have a white chocolate mocha, please." I wanted something sweet to sip to keep me going through the arduous task ahead.

After a short wait, I picked up my coffee and sat down at a small table in the centre of the room. I had downloaded the app on my phone which would allow the stalker to listen in on the call at 11:00 am. I checked the time. 10:57 am. My whole body was tense with anticipation. Could I really pull this off? Could I make this breakup look realistic enough to be convincing?

I kept checking the time, but it seemed frozen. Finally, the clock ticked over from 10:59 to 11:00. I cleared my throat, took a deep breath, then I called him.

"Hi, Chloe. What did you want to talk about?" Jinseung answered, a note of apprehension in his voice.

He was in on the act, I reminded myself.

"*Oppa*...there's something I have to tell you."

He took a sharp intake of breath. "What's wrong? Has something happened?"

"I...I..."

"I'm listening. Tell me what's the matter."

I paused, gathering my words. "This might come as a shock, but...I think we should break up."

The line went silent for a moment. "Are you serious?" He sounded bewildered and upset.

"Yes. I'm serious."

"I don't understand...Why? Why would you do this to me?"

Although we were only acting, the agony in his voice was difficult to listen to. I continued on, explaining my situation. "I think I'll be in danger if I keep on seeing you. That stalker…it's all getting too much for me to bear. I can't keep doing this. I can't go on."

"There must be some other way to work this out…I'll think of something, I swear I will."

"No. I'm afraid this is the only way. We have to break up. I'm so sorry."

"But—"

"Please don't try to contact me again."

"Wait—"

I ended the call, feeling overwhelmed with emotion. Tears welled up in my eyes. I didn't realise that a fake breakup could be so genuinely heartbreaking. On the plus side, looking miserable helped my act.

Several people in the coffee shop stared at me, and I felt painfully self-conscious. Wiping tears from my eyes with my sweater sleeve, I quickly deleted the spying app from my phone, then got up and left without finishing my drink.

In the public bathroom of the subway station, I cleaned my face with a wipe and reapplied my makeup. *Deep breaths*, I told myself, looking at my reflection in the dirty mirror. My heart was still racing. *I've done my part. Now all I have to do is wait.*

Unable to sit still, I paced up and down the length of the waiting area with my phone clutched tightly in my hand in case Bora or Sang-wook tried to contact me. My mind reeled with possible outcomes and I felt so nervous I could be sick.

"Chloe!" came a voice across the station. Yang Bora rushed towards me. I ran to her and we met in the middle by the ticket vending machines.

"What is it? What happened?" I asked, grasping her by the shoulders.

She grinned. "The operation has been a success. The stalker has been caught."

* * *

My role in the operation was probably the easiest part. Yang Bora and Officer Bae Sangwook had the hard job. While I staged the breakup, Bora and Sangwook were watching, trying to identify the stalker.

Bora explained that Bae Sangwook had indeed spotted someone acting suspiciously. "After you left, Officer Bae showed him his police badge and asked him whether he had been listening in on a call. He denied it at first, but when asked to see his phone he confessed."

"What happened? Where is he now?"

"Officer Bae took him to the police station for further questioning."

"Has he been arrested?"

"No. I don't think so."

"What did he look like? Has he admitted to the stalking? Gosh. I have so many questions…"

"He was young and kinda dorky-looking. Skinny, tall, and wearing glasses. I don't know much more than what I've already told you. Let's go to the police station. I'm sure we can find out more."

"All right. Let's go."

We rushed up the steps out of the subway exit and hailed a taxi. I twitched with impatience in the back seat as we travelled at a snail's pace in the traffic. All the while, I kept my eyes glued to my phone in case Sangwook contacted me.

"No need to fret," Bora said. "The interview will probably take a while. I'm sure we won't miss anything."

Her words of reassurance did little to calm me down. I was anxious for the whole ride.

When the police station eventually came into view, we were still stuck behind a queue of cars.

"Driver, we'll get out now," Bora said. "It'll be faster to walk from here."

I handed him some cash and we hopped out in the standstill traffic.

"Nearly there," Bora said, as we dodged pedestrians on the footpath.

Through the gate, the carpark, then up the steps, we arrived at the entryway, Korean flags flapping overhead. It hadn't been all that long since our last visit to this police station, but everything looked somehow different in daylight.

Bora spoke to reception. "Could you please let Officer Bae Sang-wook know that Yang Bora and Chloe Gibson are here?"

"Sure, please take a seat." The receptionist gestured to the waiting area.

We sat down at the row of chairs by the window. Apart from an elderly couple, we were the only ones there. I fidgeted, rocking my heels back and forth on the floor as we waited.

"I'm sure everything will go fine," Bora said. "The police already have all the evidence."

"But what happens next? What if I'm asked if I want to press charges? Will I need a lawyer?"

"Don't get too ahead of yourself. I'm sure Officer Bae will explain what you need to do."

"I'm so nervous."

"Just think, all this stalking business will be over soon, and your life can return to normal."

"I hope so."

The elderly couple were called in before we were. Bora got up and poured us each a cup of cold water from the dispenser in the corner.

"I wonder what's taking so long?" I asked as she passed me a cup.

"I'm sure they have to be very thorough with their questioning."

Just then, someone emerged from the office door. I stood up in reaction, expecting it to be Bae Sangwook, but it wasn't him. It was a lanky guy, maybe a few years older than me. He had floppy black hair and wore silver wire-framed glasses. He matched Bora's description. I froze, staring at him in shock. *That's him. He's my stalker.* He glanced back at me with an inscrutable expression. It looked like he was about to say something, but he shrugged it off and walked straight to the exit.

"What's going on?" I asked Bora. "Why did he get set free just like that?"

"I have no idea." She looked just as confused as I was.

Bae Sangwook entered the room.

"Officer Bae!" I cried. "What happened?"

"Come through and I'll explain." He ushered us to the office.

My legs were shaking as I took a seat opposite him. "Who was that man? Why did you let him go?"

Sangwook scratched his head. "Your stalker is much smarter than we anticipated."

"So…it wasn't him?"

"Unfortunately not."

"Then who was he?"

"A journalist."

"What?"

"Your stalker didn't come. He or she tipped off a journalist instead."

Bora's expression morphed into a look of dawning comprehension. "Oh, that *is* smart."

"I don't get it!" I said. My brain was too frazzled to make sense of anything.

"Rather than going there and risking being exposed, they sent a journalist," she explained. "The stalker would get confirmation that the breakup happened, and the journalist would get something juicy to publish in return."

"That's right," Sangwook said.

"Then does the journalist know who the stalker is?" I asked.

"Unfortunately not. The tip-off was sent anonymously through an encrypted email service."

"Damn. Does that mean we're no closer to catching them?"

"Not necessarily. I asked Yeo Chul—the journalist—to continue contacting them via email to try and wheedle out more information. He will pretend that everything went smoothly and that an article about the breakup will be published."

"There won't really be an article, will there?" Bora asked, a hint of panic in her voice.

"Don't worry. I made him delete his recording of the phone call, and he swore he wouldn't publish anything."

"Phew."

I drooped in my seat, still in the process of absorbing everything. *So, we didn't catch the stalker after all, but at least the fake breakup part was a success.*

"Thanks for everything, Officer Bae," Bora said. "Our plan wasn't as foolproof as we thought, but thank you so much for helping us go through with it."

"I don't usually get involved in harebrained schemes like this, you know. I only helped because I thought you'd try to catch them on your own otherwise."

"Well, you're right about that."

Sangwook chuckled. "I'll be in contact with Yeo Chul about the emails and I'll let you know if I find anything else out."

Bora and I thanked him again before leaving. We walked side by side to the subway station, the afternoon sun glowing faintly through a gap between skyscrapers.

"We didn't catch the stalker after all," I said, head bowed in disappointment.

"It wasn't all for nothing," Bora said. "We have Yeo Chul on our side now, and the stalker must think you've broken up with Jinseung. Hopefully, they'll stop harassing you, but be careful, okay?"

"Huh?"

"I'm just saying not to let your guard down too much. If they manage to work out that you didn't really break up, then you'll be back at square one."

"Yes. You're right. I didn't think about that."

"Best play it safe. Keep contact with Jinseung to a minimum until you're sure the stalking has stopped."

I let out an exasperated sigh. "And here I was thinking that my life would return to normal…So much for that."

Chapter 24

I cringed in embarrassment as Yang Bora sang at the top of her lungs outside my door. The whole floor of apartments could no doubt hear her off-key rendition of the Happy Birthday song. "Happy Birthday to yooouuuuuu!" she bellowed. "Happy Birthday to yoouuuu! Happy birthday dear Chloeeeee. Happy Birthday to you!"

"Shhhh! Come inside," I beckoned.

Bora stepped into my apartment and produced the object she held behind her back—a present wrapped in shiny purple paper with a pink ribbon attached. "Open it," she urged, thrusting it at me.

I gratefully accepted the gift, giving it a little shake to see if I could determine what was inside.

"Don't do that!" Bora said. "Just open it."

I began the painstaking task of unwrapping the gift, trying not to damage the beautiful paper. "What is it?" I asked, still in the process of unwrapping.

"Wait and see."

"The anticipation is killing me." I managed to slide the wrapping off, revealing a lidded black box.

"Go on. Open the box."

I carefully removed the lid. A pair of pretty silver ballet flats lay nestled in white tissue paper inside. I ran an appreciative hand over the dainty shoes. They were just my style.

"Do you like them?" Bora asked.

"They're so cute! Thank you!" I slipped them on, trying them for size. "Perfect!"

After gushing over the shoes a while, I put them back in their box and added it to the pile of gifts I had accumulated on the table: A beautiful handmade wooden jewellery box from my parents, a set of Amore Pacific skincare products from Shin Jina, a small bottle of Givenchy perfume from Han Seri, and a box of loose-leaf teas—each one with a different healing property—from my host parents in Tongyeong. Even Seo Minjung had sent me a card with a heartfelt birthday message inside. Too bad the one person whom I most wanted to acknowledge my birthday hadn't done anything at all.

"What did you get from Jinseung?" Bora asked.

"Ah…well…" I twiddled my fingers.

"I bet it was something really expensive."

I shook my head, eyes downcast. "Actually, he hasn't given me anything."

Her mouth dropped open in outrage. "What?"

"And I haven't heard from him at all today."

"I know you guys have been keeping your distance because of the whole fake breakup and stalker thing, but surely he could have found a way to celebrate your birthday in secret."

"He told me to keep the weekend free, but it seems like he's forgotten."

Bora tightened her hands into fists. "That jerk! I'll call him and give him a piece of my mind."

"No! I mean, I'd rather give him the benefit of the doubt. There's still the rest of the day."

"You're much more tolerant of this than I would be."

"Yeah, well, I have to exercise a great deal of patience in this relationship."

"I sure hope he comes through with something."

"Me too."

Bora squeezed my shoulder. "Anyway, I've got to go. I have appointments I need to attend with Go Yoojin. Sorry I can't stay."

"That's all right."

"Hope your birthday improves! I'll organise a party for you another day if it doesn't."

"I might just hold you to that. Thanks again for the shoes!"

Bora left humming the Happy Birthday tune. It was too bad she couldn't stay. I really could have done with some company.

Hours passed with no word from Jinseung. I should have been out celebrating, not moping around the house all day.

As night fell, I came to terms with the fact that he had forgotten me, or was otherwise too busy to even wish me a happy birthday. I dropped to the couch with a sigh, holding my head in my hands. *I can't believe this.* Since we made up after our fight, I thought things had improved between us. Obviously I was wrong. *He doesn't care much about me after all...*

Before I could stop myself, I was at the pantry searching for junk food to consume. I had been good for so long, preparing healthy meals and refraining from too much sugar and salt, but this latest injustice had pushed me to my limit.

I rummaged the shelves in a frenzy, but since I had stopped buying junk food a while ago, there was nothing unhealthy to be found. I decided to walk to the convenience store and buy something.

Outside the building, I was greeted by the view of flower petals blowing across the footpath in the wind. A discarded bouquet lay on the ground, all messed up and trampled upon. *How sad.* I wondered how it got there. I was about to reach down to look at the attached notecard but thought better of it. It was dirty and probably illegible at this point.

Leaving the ruined flowers behind without a second thought, I walked to the convenience store. A bell sounded upon my entrance. Row after row of bright and colourfully packaged goods stood out beneath stark white lighting. I traipsed through the aisles, loading up my arms with junk food until I couldn't carry any more.

As I approached the counter with my extra-large haul, a deep sense of shame descended upon me. *I shouldn't be doing this. I've come too far to undo all of my hard work now.* Weighed down with guilt, I slowed to a halt then turned around, making up my mind to put everything back bar one small treat—it was my birthday, after all.

On the way back up to my apartment, my phone started to ring. I immediately stopped in my tracks to answer it, thinking the caller was Jinseung. But it wasn't Jinseung who answered. It was a male voice I didn't recognise. "Ms. Chloe Gibson?"

"Yes?" I answered, bemused.

"Your taxi has arrived."

Huh? I never ordered a taxi..."Sorry?"

"The taxi is waiting at the entrance."

"There must be some mistake…"

"The booking was made by a Mr. Shin. Does that sound correct?"

Jinseung booked it for me? Why hasn't he told me anything? "Oh…okay. I'll be down in a minute." *What's this all about?*

Chapter 25

The classy black limo awaiting me gleamed luxuriously under the streetlight. A driver stood by the door wearing a dark suit and driving gloves. I tentatively approached, bewildered by this strange turn of events.

"Good evening, Ms. Gibson." The driver bowed politely then opened the door for me.

I stared at the empty back seat before hesitantly climbing in. The sleek interior smelled of freshly cleaned leather. Before pulling on my seatbelt I leaned forward to ask the driver a question. "Excuse me, but, where are we going?"

"Gimpo Airport," he replied, adjusting the rear-view mirror.

"*Omo!*"

"The booking indicated that you have a flight to Jeju Island at nine o'clock this evening."

"Oh! I see."

"Is everything okay, Ms. Gibson? Gimpo is correct, is it not?"

"Yes. Thank you."

So, I was going to Jeju Island. To think I ever doubted Jinseung. He had planned the best birthday present ever—I would get to see him again. The only downside was that I had nothing with me apart from my wallet, phone, and keys, and the chocolate I had bought from the convenience store. I wasn't wearing nice clothes or any makeup. The trip was a wonderful surprise, but being told in advance would have been more practical. *Oh well.* I relaxed back into my seat and helped myself to the complimentary bottle of sparkling water in the door compartment.

Anticipation and excitement brewed as we neared the airport. Soon I would be enjoying a romantic night in Jeju with my love. I never dreamed of a birthday gift so special.

I knew we were close when I heard planes flying low overhead. We entered the airport carpark and came to a stop at the drop-off section in front of the departures terminal. "Do I need to pay?" I asked awkwardly. A taxi like this wouldn't come cheap.

"No. It has already been taken care of." The driver exited the vehicle and opened the door for me. "Goodnight, Ms. Gibson. Have a pleasant journey."

"Thank you. Goodnight."

Check-in was a painless procedure despite not having the ticket on me. Only my name was required to print the boarding pass. Holding it in my hands made the reality of the situation sink in. "Jeju Island— Departure time: 21:00. Gate 17," read the smooth white slip of paper. I tucked it into my bag.

Stomach rumbling, I ate the chocolate while I waited for my flight, watching planes take off and arrive through the window. I had butter-flies in my stomach.

It occurred to me that I had no idea what to do once I arrived at Jeju Island, since I didn't know where I was supposed to meet Jinseung. He wouldn't meet me at the airport—that would be much too public. *Why hasn't he contacted me yet?* I wondered with a sigh. Right on cue, my phone started to ring, Jinseung's name on the screen. *It's about time.*

"*Oppa?*" I answered.

"Please tell me you're at the airport," he said wearily.

"Yes, I am."

"Thank goodness! I was worried since you didn't reply to my

message. I've been on set all day and only managed to check my phone just now."

"What message?"

"You didn't get it? Damn. It must not have gone through for some reason. But you got the flowers, right?"

"Flowers?"

"Are you joking?"

"No, I'm not."

I flashed back to the flower bouquet lying on the street outside the apartment building. *Was that meant for me? What happened to it? How strange...*

"Damn. Everything has gone wrong today, hasn't it? At least you made it to the airport."

I decided not to bring up the fate of the flowers. I didn't wish to cause him any more frustration. "What should I do when I get to Jeju?"

"A taxi will meet you and take you to the hotel. I'll let you know what the room number is, and you can collect a key from reception."

"Got it."

"I'm sorry nothing worked out like it was supposed to."

"That's okay. At least I know now."

"I'm going to head to the hotel. See you later tonight. Oh—and happy birthday!"

I smiled at the words I had been longing to hear from him all day. "Thank you. See you tonight."

As I put my phone away, an announcement played over the speaker. "Flight 172 to Jeju Island is now boarding."

* * *

It was nearly 11:00 pm by the time I arrived at the hotel. My jaw hung agape as I entered the magnificent building. The lobby was huge, with a high ceiling and wide French windows with white frames. Lush green indoor plants contrasted the cream walls. Elegant couples sipped cocktails around small tables, and a pianist played classical music on a grand piano. I felt very out of place and self-conscious in my jeans and hoodie. It felt like everyone was staring at me, wondering what I was doing there.

I picked up the key card for room 73 from reception, as per Jinseung's instructions. My heart pounded as I rode the elevator up to the seventh floor. Once I emerged, I quickly located the room and knocked on the door. I had to make a focused effort to control my breathing and calm myself down. Jinseung opened the door at once. He stood there in jeans and a white t-shirt, his hair slightly mussed, bright eyes absorbing me. "Hey, you. Happy birthday," he said, lips turning upward into a broad grin.

Seeing him again made my heart feel like it was going to burst. I was so overwhelmed that I broke down and wept. Jinseung pulled me inside, straight into his arms. He closed the door behind us. "Shhh…" he said, stroking a large hand through my hair. "Everything is going to be okay. We're together again. I'll look after you."

"Thank you," I spluttered, voice muffled by his chest.

"You've been through a lot while I've been away. Sorry I couldn't be there for you."

"I'm fine, really…"

"No, you're not, and that's okay." He rubbed my back tenderly in a soothing rhythmic motion. "Let it all out."

I sobbed into his broad, hard chest until his t-shirt was damp with my tears.

When I finally stopped crying, I slowly peeled away from the warmth and safety of his muscular arms. "I'm sorry," I said, wiping my wet cheeks. "It's just—"

"No need to apologise," he said, brushing an errant tear from my chin. "Sit down and relax. You must be tired."

I removed my shoes, slid on a pair of slippers, and crossed the spacious hotel room to the sitting area where I slumped into a comfortable armchair. I gazed out the pair of French doors where a balcony overlooked an enormous pool with dazzling blue water. "Too bad I didn't bring a swimsuit," I lamented.

"It's no problem. I'll buy you one tomorrow," Jinseung said. He stood behind me, massaging my shoulders.

"Mmm…that's nice," I said, relaxing into the pleasure of his touch.

"Anything else you need?"

"Yeah, probably. This was all such a big surprise, I didn't think to bring anything with me."

"It wasn't meant to be quite so surprising. If only you got my message…"

"I spent practically all day thinking you'd forgotten my birthday."

Jinseung grimaced. "That's terrible."

"I shouldn't have doubted you."

He shook his head. "I would have thought the same if I were you."

"Never mind. I'm just glad to be here with you."

"Me too. Are you hungry? Have you had dinner?"

"Nope."

"I haven't eaten either. How about I order room service?"

"Sounds good. I'm starving."

We flipped through the menu together and chose what we wanted for our very late dinner.

"I'll call and put the order in," Jinseung said. "You just relax. Would you like something to drink? Would you like to have a bath?"

"Yes and yes."

He chuckled. He poured me a generous glass of wine and I brought it to the bathroom. The room had a Japanese-style design with wooden furniture and marble-tiled walls. A large soaking tub stood by a window overlooking the lush green hillside. I poured a scoop of bath salts into the tub as it filled, infusing the water with a soothing lavender scent and turning it a milky colour.

I undressed and sat on the wooden stool by the bath, washing myself using the provided bucket to scoop up bathwater. After a quick clean, I slowly submerged myself in the tub, my muscles instantly relaxing as the hot water covered my body. Wine glass in hand, I gazed out the window at the starry sky. Life was perfect in that moment. Even after everything I had been through, being with Jinseung was one hundred per cent worth it. I doubted anything could change my mind. Nothing could come between me and Jinseung.

Nothing. I lay back my head and sank deeper into the water with a sigh.

Between the heavenly warm bath and the delicious wine, I just about dozed off in the tub, but the mouthwatering smell of dinner brought me to my senses. My stomach growled. I quickly dried off and threw on the fluffy robe hanging from the hook on the door.

Jinseung had already set the table. He pulled out a chair for me. "How was the bath?"

"Wonderful."

"You smell nice." He sniffed the air around me appreciatively.

I was more focused on the smell of the food. My tummy rumbled again.

Jinseung snickered. "All right. Let's eat." He served the food and refilled our wine glasses.

I stabbed gnocchi dripping with sage butter sauce with my fork. It burst with flavour in my mouth.

"So, I've been thinking..." Jinseung said, toying with his chopsticks.

I swallowed my mouthful. "Mmm?"

"After Love in Flames wraps, I might take a bit of a break from acting."

"Fair enough. You worked on two dramas practically back to back. Anyone would need a break after that."

"Yes, but not just because of that. After what happened...I need to think about what's best for you."

I stopped eating, pleased by this announcement, but a little wary about what exactly he meant. "I see. And what do you think that is?"

"I think we should go public with our relationship sooner rather than later."

It wasn't the answer I had been expecting. I was intrigued. "Oh?"

"I know I said one year, but I don't think things can go on like this. I can't give you my full support if we're creeping around in secret."

One immediate problem jumped out at me. "The stalker—"

"Are we going to hide our relationship forever?"

"No. I suppose not. But what about your agency? Won't Mr. Kim frown upon this?"

"He sure will, but ultimately there's little he can do. It's not against my contract to date someone, and he can't keep us apart. He'll just have to deal with it."

"And your fans? They'll hate me if we announce our relationship."

"Yes. That's unavoidable. But there are also the good fans, and they will protect you. And I'll be able to protect you more too. You won't have to be alone. We'll be able to deal with everything together, as a couple."

"Hmmm…I do understand where you're coming from."

"No need to make a rush decision. Let's at least wait until I'm done with this drama. Then we can decide our next step."

"Okay. I'll think about it." I returned to eating my meal. Each buttery bite helped keep me focused on the present moment. I could worry about everything else in the future.

"How's the gnocchi?" Jinseung asked.

"Divine."

"Can I try some?" He leaned in and opened his mouth with a coy look on his face.

I fed him a tender piece of gnocchi.

"Mmmm! Delicious." His eyes rolled back with a look of utter pleasure.

I giggled at the exaggerated expression.

"Try some of this." Jinseung lifted a small piece of fish with his chopsticks.

I received the fish in my mouth and swallowed it down. "Yummy!"

After finishing our mains, we shared a small dessert. I felt downright spoiled. "This is my favourite," I murmured.

"I know you like sweets."

"Perhaps a little too much."

"It's okay to give in to temptation now and then," he said seductively before snatching the last piece of dessert.

I pouted. "No fair."

"Open your mouth."

I obliged and he fed me his spoonful. I ate it with a satisfied sigh. "That was delicious." I leaned back in my chair and stretched.

"Agreed. So…would you like your present now?"

I raised a brow. "Wasn't the trip here my present?"

"That was part one."

"So it's a multi-part present?"

"Exactly." He grinned mischievously.

"Now I'm intrigued."

"Close your eyes."

I did so, curiosity and anticipation welling up inside me. I heard a rustling sound.

"Okay. Open your eyes." He presented me with a gift bag, matte black and slightly velvety to the touch with a thick cord handle. It looked very chic and expensive. "Open it," he urged

I opened the thick paper gift bag. Inside was a small black box tied up with a thin piece of silver-coloured ribbon. I gripped the box, heart thudding. It felt surprisingly weighty and substantial in my hand.

Jinseung watched on in amusement as I struggled with the ribbon, but I eventually managed to undo it. I carefully lifted the lid off the box. Inside was yet another box—unmistakably the kind which houses jewellery. My heartbeat intensified. I had never received jewellery as a gift before, except from my parents. The box made a heavy click as I opened it. The velvet interior housed a delicate white-gold necklace with a small round diamond pendant. The exquisite gift had me lost for words. Eventually I gathered my thoughts enough to express my gratitude. "It's lovely…"

"Shall I put it on you?"

"Yes, please."

He removed the necklace from its box then moved behind me. I felt his soft fingers brush my neck as he pulled my hair aside. He carefully fastened the necklace around my neck. Hands on my shoulders, he turned me around to face him.

"Beautiful," he murmured, appraising me.

I smirked. "Me or the necklace?"

"You." His breathing hitched. He brought his hands up to cradle my face, then bent down and pressed a deep kiss on my lips.

It had been so long that kissing him felt entirely new. His mouth moved against mine in an urgent manner, enticing my lips apart so he could flirt with my tongue. I wrapped my hands around his neck and tilted my head, willing him to kiss me deeper, harder. I desperately wanted more of what I had been denied for so long. Jinseung gladly obliged, his tongue clashing with mine in broad, sensual strokes which made me shivery and weak all over.

Just as our kiss was about to reach a crescendo, he broke away, leaving me panting. "You have no idea how much I've missed this," he growled. His teeth grazed my bottom lip and I let out a strained whimper. From there his lips traversed my jawline and then my neck. He kissed and nipped along the sensitive flesh so lightly that my skin prickled.

Unable to endure the teasing sensations any longer, I yanked him back into a kiss. Jinseung responded with a throaty groan. He lifted me from the chair and pulled me flush with him, grabbing my bare backside under my robe. Through the thin fabric of his t-shirt, I ran my hands over his firm, perfectly sculpted body which tensed wherever I touched. It pleased me to no end to have such an effect on him. We sank into another kiss which quickly became hot and frantic with need.

"Do you want me?" Jinseung asked, his breath hot against my neck.

"Yes," I croaked.

He bent down and scooped me up, hooking his hands under my knees and pulling my legs around his waist. He walked me to the bed and laid me down, my thighs still wrapped tightly around his hips. "Are you tired?" he purred, grinding against me.

"Nope."

"Good. I'm not planning on letting you get much sleep tonight."

Chapter 26

Needless to say, any lingering doubts about Jinseung's continued attraction to me had completely dissolved by morning. True to his word, he didn't let me sleep at all. We made love until sunrise, then spent several lazy hours entwined in each other's arms, chatting, cuddling, and lightly dozing.

Beams of warm sunlight burst through the window and caressed my bare skin. I gazed at Jinseung's impressive naked form beside me, relishing the thought that only I could see him like this. My eyes trailed down his broad, muscular chest slowly rising and falling with his breath, to his firm, well-defined abs, then the tantalising stretch of skin below his bellybutton which disappeared beneath the duvet draped across his lower body. I snuggled closer, completely enamoured. Jinseung wrapped an arm around me and gently stroked his fingertips up and down my back. The comforting motion almost lulled me to sleep. A sudden thought stopped me from drifting over the edge. I rose up on my elbows. "Jinseung-ah?" I prodded his side.

"What?" he grunted.

"We don't need to check out, do we?" The last time we stayed in a hotel, a perfect morning just like this was ruined by rushing to leave on time.

Jinseung rubbed his eyes. "Oh, shit. What's the time?"

I sprang up onto my butt and stretched towards the bedside table.

Jinseung grabbed my arm. "I'm joking!" He tugged me back down. "I already booked the room for another night. You can stay right up until when you need to leave."

I lightly jabbed his shoulder in mock annoyance. "You had me there. What a relief. I don't feel like going anywhere or doing anything. Just hanging out with you right here." I rested my head on his chest.

"Sounds perfect."

I shut my eyes again and pulled up the duvet.

"What about the swimsuit?" Jinseung asked.

"Hmmm?"

"Didn't you want to have a swim today?"

"Oh. Nah, that's okay. Besides, there's a spa, right? No swimsuit required. I prefer a hot spa over a cold pool any day. Maybe I'll splash out and get a massage too."

"Go for it. Just add it to the bill."

"You're the best!" I held his face in my hands and kissed him on the forehead.

Completely oblivious to the time, I had no idea how long I snoozed, but it was early in the afternoon before I finally rose from bed. Dressed in a pair of the hotel's pyjamas and robe, I made myself a green tea. Jinseung was already up, sitting reading a book on the balcony. I joined him outside. The sun shone bright, but the wind had a cold bite to it. I tightened my robe.

Jinseung lowered his book. "You're finally up. Did you catch up on missed sleep?"

"Yes. I did actually. I feel quite refreshed."

"Sorry for keeping you up last night."

"Ha! You're not sorry for that."

Jinseung smirked. "You're right. I'm not."

"I might head down to the spa soon."

"Okay. Have fun."

When I finished my tea, I took the elevator to the spa on the basement floor. The entrance for males and the entrance for females were situated at opposite ends of the hallway. I made my way to the female spa.

Having visited *Jjimjilbbangs* a few times, I was familiar with the routine of public bathing in Korea. I stripped off in the changing room, shoved my clothes in a locker, showered, then headed to one of the spa pools which was designed to emulate a hot spring, complete with faux rocks and a trickling mini waterfall.

Soaking in the hot water, my thoughts drifted to the conversation with Jinseung the previous night, and his suggestion that we go public with our relationship sooner than planned. I was both excited and nervous by the prospect. Excited that I would finally be able to show off my boyfriend to the world. Scared of all the repercussions.

After my role in Hidden History, it had taken a while to regain my anonymity (well, most of it anyway). Dating Jinseung in public would thrust me back into the limelight.

The breakup ruse would be shattered, and the stalking might start up again. I couldn't rely on the police—their investigation had come to a dead-end as soon as the stalker stopped replying to Yeo Chul's emails.

I wouldn't be able to continue teaching. The students would be too interested in my personal life to take me seriously. Jinseung and I would be able to go out together as a couple, but we'd still need to be wary of the media. Then there was the serious issue of jealous fans and my security.

As I mentally listed all the pros and cons, it became clear to me that deep down I already knew what I wanted to do. I wanted to go public with our relationship, and there was no longer much point in waiting the rest of the year if Jinseung agreed to it. Feeling comfortable with my decision, I lay back and sank deeper into the hot water.

After indulging in the spa pool, the sauna, steam room, and a lengthy back massage, I returned to the hotel room in a completely blissed-out state.

Jinseung lay on the bed with headphones on, nodding his head to the beat of the music with his eyes closed.

"Hey, I'm back," I said, trying to get his attention.

He took his headphones off and looked me up and down. "You're all red."

"The steam makes me flushed."

"It's cute."

I sidled up to him on the bed. "I've been thinking about what you said last night…"

"What did I say?"

"You know. About dating in public."

"Ohhhh that. So tell me, what are you thinking?"

I fiddled with the edge of the duvet. "I would have to quit teaching…"

"Not necessarily."

"Are you serious? Have you worked with teenagers?"

"I see your point. Could you teach children or adults instead?"

"Perhaps, but it still wouldn't be easy. People would come to my class to try and find stuff out about you."

"Ugh. That's true."

"And there's another problem. Some of your fans can be overzealous."

Jinseung sniggered. "That's putting it lightly."

"I'd need some form of protection."

"That goes without saying. Anything else?"

"Apart from that, I don't have any other objections."

"So, if we can sort those things out, you're fine with it?"

I nodded, and he squeezed me tight with a hug.

"What about you?" I asked, extricating myself from his arms. "Are you sure you're ready to face the backlash you're bound to get?"

"I made a promise to you that we would go public in a year. That's only a few months away now. Backlash now or backlash a little bit later? It doesn't make much difference in the long run."

"But you'll be able to cope with it?"

"It's something I've been coming to terms with since I started having feelings for you." He grasped my hands in his. "I'm ready to date you no matter the impact on my career."

Now it was my turn to hug him, and I did it with such force that I fell on top of him.

"Whoa there," Jinseung said, grinning at the compromising position we'd landed in. "You're eager."

Taking advantage of the situation, I snatched a kiss.

"I like where this is going," Jinseung murmured, grabbing my hips.

I pulled back. "Actually, we don't have much time. I need to go to the airport soon—"

"It won't take long." He flipped me over onto my back, pressing himself between my thighs.

* * *

I KNEW this moment was coming but it was still gut-wrenching. As we stood by the door exchanging our goodbyes, I wondered how long it would be before I saw Jinseung again.

"Cheer up," he said with a smile. "Didn't you have a nice time with me?"

I lifted my head and summoned some positivity. "I did. Thank you for the wonderful birthday. I couldn't have imagined a better day."

"Have a safe trip back, okay?"

"Thanks."

"Got everything?"

"Yup. Not like I brought much with me anyway."

"The necklace?"

"I'm still wearing it." I pulled it out from under my collar. "I have the box too."

"Okay, good. Hmmm…why don't you take this?" Jinseung grabbed the book he was reading off the table. "I've finished it now. Something to keep you occupied on the plane."

"Good idea. Thank you." I accepted the well-worn paperback and tucked it into my bag. Some light reading material would make the trip go much faster.

"Give me a kiss." Jinseung leaned in and puckered his lips expectantly.

He looked ridiculous, but I obliged. His lips were still warm from all the previous kissing. I savoured the feeling.

"I'll see you again soon," he said, his forehead still pressed to mine.

"As soon as possible?"

"Yes. I promise."

"Then…goodbye."

"Goodbye."

We hugged once more then parted. I took one final glance at him before the door swung closed.

The journey home was a simple ordeal. The novel kept me entertained for the duration of the flight. Even though it was the Korean translation, I didn't have too much difficulty keeping up. I was already familiar with the plot, and I used my phone to translate anything I didn't understand. Before I knew it, the plane was preparing to land at Gimpo Airport.

I arrived at my apartment building just after eight in the evening. When I reached my floor, I knew something was amiss. The door to my apartment wasn't fully closed and the lock hadn't activated. At first, I wondered if I had left it like that, but that thought was quickly superseded by something more sinister. I reached a shaky hand to the handle and cautiously opened the door, heart hammering. My jaw dropped as I witnessed the scene in front of me.

Chapter 27

A strangled gasp escaped my throat, eyes widening in shock at the devastation in front of me. My apartment had been completely trashed. Chairs were tipped over. Objects had been pushed off the table. The cupboards were wide open and their contents strewn on the floor. I stood, jaw agape, unable to process what had happened.

Once the initial shock wore off, I dropped to the floor and sobbed. *What's going on? Why did this happen to me?* I was so overwhelmed that I couldn't make sense of anything.

At last, the fog in my brain lifted. *The stalker did this.* The stalker found out about my trip to visit Jinseung and went berserk. *The flower bouquet!* They must have intercepted the delivery, read the message, and overcome with fury, decided to take revenge by trashing my apartment. Convinced of this version of events, I pulled myself off the floor. I cautiously walked through my apartment to check the other rooms. It was much the same story. My bedroom was a mess of clothes and upended furniture. The bathroom floor was littered with bottles and jars pulled out of the cabinet and the mirror had been smashed. I winced at the carnage. It would take forever to clean up and cost a fortune to replace everything that had been broken. Worst of all was the feeling of complete and utter violation. I didn't think I'd ever feel safe in this apartment again.

I carefully made my way back to the living area dodging the scattered items on the floor. Unsure what else to do, I called the one person I knew I could count on no matter what.

Yang Bora answered straight away. *"Unnie?"*

I was so relieved to hear her sweet voice. "Bora-ya…something terrible has happened."

"Omo. What happened?"

"Everything's all over the floor!" I blurted, unaware of how nonsensical that sounded.

"Okay. Calm down and explain it to me from the beginning."

I took a deep breath and organised my words into something logical. "I just got home from Jeju Island. My apartment has been broken into. It's a huge mess. I think it was the stalker."

Bora gasped. "Oh my God! Are you okay? Have you called the police?"

"I'm all right, well, all things considered. I haven't called the police yet."

"Okay, first thing's first, call Officer Bae and tell him what happened. While you do that, I'll be on my way."

"You're coming here?"

"I can't leave you there to deal with all this on your own, can I? I'll be there as soon as I can."

"Thank you. You're always there for me," I said, tearing up again.

"It's no problem. Just hold tight, okay? Try not to touch or move anything. I'm sure the police will want everything left as it is."

"Okay, I'll try."

"See you soon."

Knowing Bora was coming over to help me eased my mind considerably. Now onto the next task at hand. I called Officer Bae and anxiously waited for him to pick up. After several rings, I began to think he wouldn't answer, but on what must have been the tenth ring, he finally picked up. "Hello, Officer Bae speaking."

I spoke as slowly and surely as I could manage. "Hello, it's Chloe Gibson."

"What can I do for you, Chloe?"

"Something else has happened."

"I'm listening."

I explained the situation to him, and he promised to come over to look at the scene sometime within the next few hours. I sat on the floor, hugging my knees to my chest as I waited. There was little else I could do without disturbing the crime scene. My thoughts turned to the stalker, seething with rage at the knowledge that I had visited Shin Jinseung. If they were capable of this attack on my apartment, capable of throwing a large and heavy vase at me from a window, what else would they do? I shuddered. Now I knew for certain, this person was incredibly dangerous and I wasn't safe. I prayed that the police would be able to catch them because I didn't know what else I could do to protect myself.

As time passed, I grew increasingly tense. Who would get here first? Bora? Officer Bae? Or perhaps, the stalker. I trembled uncontrollably, my body covered in cold sweat.

When I heard a knock on the door I just about jumped out of my skin. "Hey, it's me," came Bora's muffled voice.

I exhaled in relief and opened the door. She stood in the doorway silhouetted by the bright light behind her, an angelic glow emanating from her outline.

"My angel!" I exclaimed, hand clutched to my heart. "I'm so glad you're here."

"All right, all right. What are friends for?" She held up a plastic bag full of food containers. "I brought some food. My mum insisted. Hope you're hungry."

"I am! Although I must admit that food has been far from my mind."

Bora stepped into the apartment. As she looked around, the colour drained from her face. "It's even worse than I thought."

"I told you it was bad."

"Now I know why you sounded so distraught. Poor thing, you're shaking." She rubbed my shoulder soothingly.

"I'll be okay, now that you're here."

"Let's eat, shall we?"

We sat on the largest clear patch of carpet we could locate.

"Did you call Officer Bae?" Bora asked as she unpacked the food containers.

"Yes. He's going to come over tonight. I don't know exactly when."

"I'll wait with you until he gets here." She handed me a pair of disposable chopsticks.

"Thanks."

We began to eat from the open containers of rice, kimchi, and bulgogi.

"What were you doing on Jeju Island?" Bora asked, mouth part full. "Visiting Jinseung-ah?"

I nodded. "He flew me there to see him on the night of my birthday."

"How romantic!"

"It was, but I'm regretting it now."

"Do you think the stalker found out, and that's what made them do this?"

"Yes. That's exactly what I think."

I told her about the flowers Jinseung sent me that I never received, and the mangled bouquet I saw outside the building that evening.

"This is getting really serious now," she said. "The police will have to act."

"That's what I'm counting on. I don't know what else I can do. Even if I broke up with Jinseung for real, I doubt that would be enough to stop them now. They're obsessed."

"Maybe the police will be able to find some evidence of their identity this time."

"Yes. Good point."

Bora kept me chatting through the night, lifting my spirits and keeping my mind off the fact that the stalker might come back to my apartment before the police got there. I felt much safer with her.

As another hour passed, my butt began to hurt from sitting on the floor. I shifted onto my knees. Bora let out a yawn and stretched her arms above her head. "It's getting late," she said.

"Perhaps you should go home," I suggested, although I really didn't want her to go.

She shook her head. "No. I won't leave you on your own. I'm staying put right here."

"You have work tomorrow morning."

"I'm used to getting by without much sleep."

"Well, all right then. Thank you." I smiled, relieved with the security of her continued company. "Hopefully the police will get here soon—oh!" A text message came through and I fumbled with my phone trying to check it. "Officer Bae is on his way."

"Thank goodness."

The young police officer arrived shortly with a partner in tow—another young cop, but much shorter and pudgier. He introduced himself as Officer Cha. Officer Cha took some photographs around my apartment while Officer Bae interviewed me in the corridor.

"The door wasn't fully shut when you got home?" he asked, a chunky notepad and ballpoint pen in hand.

I nodded. "You can't tell from a quick glance, but if the door's not shut properly it won't lock. It wasn't locked when I got home."

"Do you remember if you shut it properly when you left?"

"I think so. I've never left it unlocked before. I think someone broke in and left the door like that."

"What makes you say that?"

"There's a trick to closing the door properly. You have to pull it hard until it clicks. Someone who hasn't visited my apartment before wouldn't realise, especially if they were in a hurry to leave."

"Sounds plausible, yet there's no sign of forced entry. If you locked it as you say, then someone could have only entered if they knew the code. Does anyone apart from you know the code?"

I shook my head. "Just me. Oh, and Yang Bora," I motioned to her standing farther down the corridor, leaning against the wall and texting on her phone.

"Did you tell anyone the code?" he asked Bora.

"Of course not," she snapped.

"Then, Chloe, perhaps you wrote it down somewhere."

"Yes. In my diary."

"Could someone have accessed your diary?"

"I keep it in my bag. But I suppose it's possible that someone could have peeked while I left it unattended."

"Do you leave it unattended often?"

"No," I admitted.

"And the code wasn't something that's easy to guess?"

"No, I don't think so. Even I forgot it once."

Officer Bae scribbled something down in his pad before continuing. "Has anything gone missing in your apartment? Could this be a burglary?"

"Not that I've noticed."

"All your valuables are still there?"

"Yes."

"Interesting." He stroked his chin. "So, this isn't a usual break-in, then."

"No. Like I said, I think someone wanted revenge."

"Or it might be possible that you left your door unlocked, and someone who passed by noticed. On the spur of the moment, they decided to have some fun by trashing the apartment."

"But I don't think that's what happened—"

"It is odd that nothing was taken. I'll give you that. The messages, the vase, the break-in…It's a lot to happen in such a short space of time."

"Exactly!"

"Still, we must consider all possibilities." He flipped his notepad closed. "I think I have enough. Officer Cha, how are you getting on?" He poked his head around the doorway.

The chubby officer rose to his feet after examining something on the floor. "I'm just about done here. I'll look for prints then we can wrap things up."

"Prints!" Bora whispered to me excitedly.

I mentally crossed my fingers that he would find something.

"Even if we find prints, we'll only be able to compare them to prints found on the evidence you brought in before," Officer Bae explained. "That should tell us if it's the same person, but we won't be any closer to identifying them, since we have no suspects. We'll need to take your prints as well, to rule them out."

Bora and I shared looks of vague disappointment. "At least it would be better than nothing," she said.

The two officers worked together in my apartment while Bora and I waited in the corridor. We were tense with anticipation, praying that the stalker had left sufficient evidence behind to lead to their capture.

"They'll find something," Bora assured me. "They have to."

The officers took their time. I was anxious to know what they had found, but I was glad that they seemed to be doing a thorough job investigating the scene.

Finally, the two cops emerged. "Right, we're done for now," Officer Bae said, removing a pair of rubber gloves.

"Did you find anything?" I asked.

Officer Cha shook his head. "Whoever did this was very careful not to leave any evidence behind."

"Oh…" I hung my head in disappointment.

"Seems it wasn't a spur-of-the-moment incident after all," Bora commented, sly eyes fixed on Officer Bae.

He smiled. "Yes. Seems that way. We'll call in again tomorrow to interview the building staff and your neighbours. In the meantime, if you realise something has gone missing, let me know."

I nodded.

"Stay vigilant. Make sure to change your door code."

The police officers left.

Even though it seemed as though they would conduct a thorough investigation, I couldn't help but feel disappointed. There still wasn't any evidence pointing to the culprit's identity. Meanwhile, they were still out there, capable of harming me.

"I don't think I can sleep in my apartment tonight," I told Bora. "I'm too scared."

"I don't blame you."

Chapter 28

Dear Linda Choi,

I am writing to inform you of my resignation.

I paused, staring at the blinking cursor on my screen. Now that I was typing it out, it felt real. I swallowed a lump in my throat and set my fingers back down on the keys.

My decision to resign had come after a recent call with Jinseung. As expected, he had reacted strongly to the news of the break-in. "I'll quit," he had said, voice shaking with emotion. "I'll quit working on Jeju Island and come back to Seoul for you."

I was stunned. "Really? You'd do that for me?"

"Yes. I would."

But he retracted this assertion later on. "I'll be dropped from the agency and Changsoo will lose his job if I quit now," he explained, having had more time to think it through.

I was disappointed, but I couldn't blame him. No agency would touch him, no director would cast him after quitting partway through a drama over a girl. Then there was Changsoo who was like an older brother to him. Destroying his own career was one thing, bringing

Changsoo down with him was another. Jinseung quitting now for my sake was asking too much, even I believed that. Besides, there was another option.

"Chloe? What are you still doing here?" came a voice behind me. The unmistakable Scottish accent belonged to Jake Mackenzie— another English teacher at the *hagwon*.

Startled, I quickly minimised the window with my resignation letter so he wouldn't see. "I'll head home in a minute."

Jake raised an eyebrow. "Everything okay?"

"Yes. Fine, thank you. What about you? Why are you still at work?"

"I taught an extra class tonight."

"Oh."

"Anyway, I'll be leaving soon. Just grabbing this." He reached for a folder on his desk. "See you tomorrow."

"See you." I exhaled a small sigh of relief as he left the staffroom. I didn't want anyone to learn of my plans to resign. Not yet. I would give it a few more days. If the police caught the stalker soon, I wouldn't need to leave, but if the police failed, Jinseung and I agreed that it would be best for me to return to the UK until my safety in Korea could be guaranteed.

I re-enlarged the Word file, saved it, then got ready to leave. In the days since the break-in, I hadn't been walking around or using public transport, taking taxis door to door instead. I caught one outside the *hagwon* and it took me directly to the underground carpark of Jinseung's apartment building.

Bora and Jina had helped me clean up my apartment, but I was still too scared to sleep there on my own. On Jinseung's advice, I had moved into his apartment for the time being, along with Jina so I wouldn't be on my own. I still didn't feel one hundred per cent safe due to the fact that the stalker had managed to get to Jinseung's apartment once before. On the other hand, a new security system had been installed since then and extra guards were stationed in the building. It certainly felt safer than my own apartment.

"Welcome home," Jina said when I arrived. She was sitting on the couch with the TV on, drinking a beer, feet up on the coffee table.

"Hey. No work tonight?" I asked. Normally her shifts at the cinema didn't finish until midnight or later, and I would stay up until she got home before going to bed as I was too scared to sleep alone in the house.

"Nah, it's my day off. How was the *hagwon*?"

"Fine. Teaching seems to take my mind off everything at least."

Jina muted the television. "Have you heard anything else from the police?"

"Nope. Not a word since the last time I spoke with them."

According to the police, the culprit didn't leave any clues. Security footage showed that they were wearing a hood and surgical mask to hide their identity. But one thing has been revealed. From the body shape of the culprit, the police were almost certain it was a woman.

"That sucks," Jina said. "I thought they would have figured something out by now."

"Apparently not. It's looking more and more likely that I'll have to leave."

"When will you decide?"

"In two or three days perhaps. I'll still need to give notice as well. Can't just leave those kids with no teacher. Hopefully, Linda will find a replacement quickly."

Jina rested her head in her hands and let out a sigh. "I feel so sorry for you and *Dongsaeng*. I never imagined something like this would happen."

"Tell me about it." I walked to the kitchen to look for something to eat.

"There's nothing to eat here. I already checked."

"*Aigoo.*"

"I can run down to the shop if you want. I'm feeling kinda peckish too."

"All right. Thanks."

Jina rose from the couch and got ready to leave. "Back in a minute," she said, slipping on her shoes at the door.

I went to my room to change out of my work clothes and into comfy pyjamas. I was staying in Jinseung's bedroom and Jina used the office as her room. Everything in the modern, masculine bedroom reminded me of Jinseung: the chair where he liked to sit and read, the colourful abstract print on the wall by his favourite local artist, and the bed where I had slept in his arms whenever we had the rare chance to spend the night together. I missed him dearly, but being surrounded by his belongings made me feel close to him.

Thinking it would be nice to wear one of Jinseung's t-shirts, I stepped through to the walk-in wardrobe which separated the bedroom and en suite bathroom. Clothes hung from a rail along the left side of the wall, and on the right, open shelves displayed shoes and accessories. Below the shelves were several drawers. Jinseung preferred to dress casually when he could—jeans, t-shirt, hoodie, and sneakers, but he still had an extensive wardrobe due to all the events he had to attend, and all the freebie items he received from brands. The drawers stored most of his casual clothing, and he hung up his dressier pieces.

I pulled open a drawer to begin my hunt for a t-shirt. As I rummaged, I quickly forgot my objective and lost myself in admiration of his lovely clothes, running my hand over the fabric and trying to remember if I'd seen him wearing each particular item. When I opened the next drawer, something caught my attention—a picture frame with the picture side facing down. I picked it up and turned it over in my hands. The frame held a photograph of me and Jinseung, his arm around my shoulder and his cheek resting on my head. We were smiling. I remembered that day. Jina had taken the photograph after Jinseung and I watched a film at Cinema Lumiere. I brushed my fingers over the glass to stroke his image. The fact that he had printed and framed this photograph brought happy tears to my eyes. He must have hidden it in the drawer until he could safely display it in his room once our relationship was no longer a secret.

After spending several minutes gazing admiringly at the picture, I reached out to return it to the drawer, but a sudden idea made me stop short. As many K-dramas had taught me, there was often something else hidden in a picture frame: another picture, a note, or some other special document. Curious, I carefully removed the back of the frame. Sure enough, I found a message written on the back of the photograph.

7.11.18 - A date with my beautiful girlfriend, Chloe. I am falling in love with her.

Now the tears fell freely down my cheeks as I hugged the picture to my chest. Suddenly, leaving Korea felt like it would be a big mistake.

Chapter 29

"I have some bad news," I said.

Sophie looked at me across the table with wide, round eyes full of concern. "What's wrong?"

"I won't be able to teach you for much longer. I'm leaving Korea."

The news appeared to hit her like a punch to the gut. The colour drained from her face and her mouth gaped.

"You must be surprised," I said. "It's all very sudden, I know."

The police still hadn't caught the stalker, or even come close to revealing her identity. As much as it pained me, I felt I had no other choice. Jinseung agreed too. It was for the best.

"I thought you would stay until the end of the year at least, like most of the foreign teachers do," Sophie stammered. "Why are you leaving? Did something happen?"

So far, I had kept my personal issues under wraps, and I wasn't about to divulge them now. "I have my reasons. It's complicated."

She frowned but had the good sense not to push the subject. "Oh. I see."

"I'm planning to come back! I just don't know when. Everything is up in the air at the moment. If you want, I can try and find another tutor to fill in for me while I'm gone, or we could continue our lessons online. Do you have a good internet connection?"

"It's not the same. I need to do this in person. I can't concentrate properly at home."

"Sure, I get that. Then, another tutor?"

She shook her head. "I only seem to click with you."

"Is that so? Well, you're a smart girl. I'm sure you'll be okay studying on your own, and if you ever need help, you can always contact me."

Sophie relaxed her hunched shoulders. "Thanks. That makes me feel a bit better."

"Sorry for leaving you in the lurch like this."

"It's okay. I'm sure that whatever reason you're leaving, it must be important. I hope you're okay."

I managed a smile. "Yes. I'm okay."

"That's a relief."

Her concern touched me, and I knew I'd miss her while I was gone. Maybe that was inappropriate, but I didn't care. We had advanced beyond a student-teacher relationship—we were friends, and I was completely fine with that.

"Chloe?" Sophie asked, snapping me from my thoughts.

"Hmm?"

"I still owe you money for the last couple of lessons…"

"Oh? I forgot about that. You don't have to pay me right now."

"It's fine. I have the money." She opened her purse and emerged with a fistful of bills. She counted out the correct amount and passed it over.

Taking money from her felt strange, but I accepted it none-theless. "Thanks." I tucked the cash into my wallet. "This reminds me, there's something I wanted to ask you about—"

I was interrupted by the server behind the counter. "Kim Sungmi," he called.

"I'll get it," Sophie said, rising from her seat.

I glanced at my lesson notes while she went to fetch our order. She returned with an iced tea for me, an americano for herself, and two cupcakes with purple frosting. "This is for you," she said, passing me a cupcake on a small white plate.

"Awww, thanks. Looks yummy." I took a bite and washed it down with a large gulp of iced tea.

Sophie didn't touch hers. She watched me with a faraway look in her eyes.

"Are you okay?" I asked.

She snapped to attention. "Sorry. What were you going to say before?"

"Oh yeah. Hope you don't mind me asking, but were your parents able to pay your overdue fees?"

"Oh, that." Sophie blushed crimson. "I believe it's been sorted."

"That's good. I was so worried that Linda would get debt collectors involved. What a nasty business."

"It was nothing really. My parents are busy people. They just forgot, and all the reminders got sent to the wrong place."

"Yes, I was sure that was the case." I drank more tea then set down the half-empty glass. "Shall we get started on our lesson?"

Sophie nodded and readied her books and pens, arranging them neatly on the table.

"Did you manage to get all the homework done?" I asked.

"Uh-huh."

"Then let's go through that first."

She opened her workbook to the correct page. Red pen in hand, I began to read her first answer.

"What about your timer?" Sophie interrupted.

"Huh? Oh, I completely forgot. It doesn't matter if we go over time today anyway. I want to help you as much as possible before I leave. You don't have anything else planned after this, do you?"

"No."

"Then let's take as much time as we need."

"Okay." She smiled and sipped her coffee.

I returned to marking her homework, discussing what she did right and wrong as I progressed. Partway through, I began to feel a little strange. Tired and foggy-brained. On several occasions, I stumbled with my words, unable to express myself properly. Sometimes I forgot where I was on the page. My mind drifted from the task at hand. I felt dizzy.

"Are you all right?" Sophie asked, brow furrowed.

"Yes. I'm just a bit tired. Not sure why."

"Do you want to take a break?"

"No, that's fine. Let's continue." I forced my heavy eyelids wider open and drank more tea.

We finished reviewing her homework and moved on to the next part of our lesson. I had devised a little activity with flashcards. Each card displayed a word, and Sophie had to think of as many synonyms as possible to earn points. I tried to explain the concept to her, but I couldn't form coherent sentences in either Korean or English. For some reason, I felt drunk.

"You're acting strange," Sophie said. "Are you ill?"

"I'm sorry...don't know...what's wrong."

"Let's end the lesson here. You need to go home."

I didn't argue with her. I really did feel sick and knew we had to stop. We packed up our things and left the partially consumed food and drinks on the table.

"Come on, I'll walk you out," Sophie said, offering me her arm.

I swayed when I got up from my seat, the room spinning around me. Sophie guided me out onto the street. The cool breeze momentarily brought me to my senses.

"I'm going to hail you a cab, okay?" Sophie said.

Good. I'd be able to get home and rest. *Sleep...I need sleep...*My surroundings began to blur. Next thing I knew I was in the back seat of a taxi and being driven off. I faded quickly, losing consciousness.

Chapter 30

I woke up in a dark room, seated upright and unable to move. Woozy-headed, I struggled frantically against the bonds which restrained me, no idea what was going on. Something in my mouth muffled my cries. A piece of fabric. A gag.

As my eyes adjusted to the dark, I saw my feet were bound with rope, and knew my hands must be tied behind the back of the chair. I was in an unfamiliar room, sparsely furnished. A few posters were taped to the walls, but I couldn't make out what was on them. Just below the ceiling was a single dingy window, a clue that I was in a basement room. An overwhelming sense of panic surged through me. I tried to wriggle my hands free from their binding, but it was too tight. I tried to shuffle forward on the chair, but tipped it over instead, sending me tumbling to the hard floor with a loud smack. I couldn't do anything but squirm and moan in desperation.

Where am I? How did I get here? The last thing I could remember was arriving at the Booksea café to meet Sophie. Everything after that was a blur.

Footsteps approached.

It dawned on me that the stalker must have brought me here. I started to panic, breath coming in short and sharp gasps, heart pounding on overdrive. Whoever was on the other side of that door meant to harm me, and I was completely defenceless—a writhing heap on the floor.

The door opened and harsh light spilled into the room. I clenched my eyes into slits, pupils stinging.

"You're awake." A silhouetted figure stood in the doorway.

*That voice...*I didn't think I had heard it before, yet there was a hint of familiarity.

She flicked the light on, fully illuminating the room. I clamped my eyes shut, then slowly reopened them, taking her appearance in bit by bit. I couldn't immediately place her, but it hit me soon enough. I tried to deny it, telling myself that it wasn't possible, it couldn't possibly be her. But it was. The girl I knew as Sophie, or Kim Sungmi, stood there, crazed eyes upon me. She looked so different from all the times I had seen her before. The girl I knew must have been fake—an identity designed with a wig, glasses, makeup, contact lenses, and more. The young woman in front of me was the real Sungmi. She had fine, shoulder-length hair, soulless black eyes, and thin lips which curled in a menacing smile. A dark aura surrounded her.

"Surprised, are you?" she drawled. "Yes, it's me, Kim Sungmi, although that's not my real name. Nor am I a high school student. Have the drugs worn off yet?"

I just stared at her in complete and utter disbelief. I had been such a fool. The person I had been searching for had been right in front of me the whole time.

"You must have a lot of questions on your mind right now, like why I went through all that trouble to get close to you, how I could change my appearance so drastically, how I got you here, and what I plan to do with you." She smirked, eyes glinting. "It was I who sent you the messages telling you to break up with Shin Jinseung. I'm sure you've worked that much out at least. The woman you spoke to on the phone who claimed to be my mother was a friend from work. She owed me a favour. The vase—a low-life thug I paid to do the job. I happen to meet a lot of thugs in my line of work. The person who broke into your apartment—that was me. I couldn't resist."

Craning my neck, I saw now that the posters on the walls were pictures of Jinseung. So she really was an obsessed fan.

Sungmi closed in on me. I flinched as she reached out and pulled the chair back up with me on it. "All you had to do was break up with Shin Jinseung and I would have left you alone," she said, stroking my cheek. "But no. You wouldn't listen. You spent a night with him in Jeju. That was the final straw. After that, I knew I couldn't just leave you to roam free." She pulled her hand back then slapped me with such force that I nearly toppled over again. I could feel the blood rush to my face, cheek burning with pain. I could only whimper against the gag.

"You never suspected me. I had gained your trust. You know the saying, right? Keep your friends close and your enemies closer. Kidnapping you was a simple task, really. I drugged your tea. I gave the taxi driver an address near this place. By taking shortcuts and dodging traffic on my scooter, I made it here first and quickly ditched my disguise, changing my appearance enough that the taxi driver wouldn't recognise me when I picked you up. I carried you here. You're heavy, you know that?"

I had absolutely no recollection of any of that happening, yet I knew it to be true.

"By the way," Sungmi continued, "don't expect your wee friends to come looking for you." She pulled something from her pocket—a mobile phone. *My* mobile phone. "I've sent them all a message, saying you took an early flight back to the UK." She twirled the phone in her hands. "This is great, you know. Now I have Shin Jinseung's number and everything. Such fun!"

I twitched with anger, wondering what exactly she intended to do.

"I'm going to undo this so you can speak," Sungmi said, reaching for the fabric tie around my mouth. "I'm sure you have many questions."

I nodded, eager for a chance to regain my voice. She untied the gag, and as soon as I had been released, I let out a loud cry for help. She refastened the tie so tight that it hurt. "You want to die, bitch? I thought you were smart."

Tears of frustration and helplessness rolled down my cheeks. Would she really kill me?

A beeping sound came from another room, catching Sungmi's attention. "Hmmph. I'll be back."

The mouthwatering smell of cooked meat and vegetables drifted in through the door. My stomach rumbled. I needed to eat, and I desperately needed to use the bathroom. Things I couldn't do unless Sungmi released me from my bonds. Perhaps screaming had been rash. Would she dare untie me again now?

She returned to the room shortly, a plate of food in her hands. She pulled up a chair, then proceeded to eat her meal in front of me—a subtle form of torture. My stomach growled audibly. Sungmi smirked. "Hungry, are you? If there's leftovers I'll let you have them, but you'll have to be on your best behaviour."

I watched her eat, praying she would save some food for me. She would have to undo the ties around my mouth and hands to let me eat, which would provide me with another opportunity. But what should I do with that opportunity? Try to escape? Or simply do as I was told and eat, biding my time until a better chance presented itself?

When she had finished, Sungmi took her empty dish away without a word. I waited, tense with anticipation, for her return. I still hadn't made a decision, but my mind was made for me when she reappeared, a plate of leftovers in one hand, a large, gleaming knife in the other. She held the plate beneath my nose, taunting me. "Want some?"

I nodded weakly.

"If you scream again, you're done for. Got it?" Light flashed off the knife blade in her hand.

I nodded again. She set the plate and knife down, and carefully undid the gag. I opened and closed my mouth, exercising the muscles which had become stiff from restraint. I didn't say a word.

Sungmi seemed hesitant about undoing my hands. Perhaps she was still deciding whether to feed me or let me feed myself. Eventually, she unbound them and used the rope to tie my waist to the chair instead. She handed me the plate and a pair of chopsticks. I ate silently. The food tasted bland, but it settled my stomach. Sungmi watched me the entire time, clutching the knife, turning it over in her hands. I bided my time, eating as slowly as possible, trying to formulate some semblance of an escape plan.

"I'm finished," I said at last.

Sungmi retrieved the plate.

"Uh—may I use the bathroom, please?" I asked.

She considered my request for a moment. "All right, but don't even think about trying to escape." She removed the rope from my waist but retied my hands in front of me. Next, she freed my feet. My joints made a clicking sound as I stood up. I took the opportunity to stretch a little. Still clutching the knife, Sungmi directed me to the bathroom. On our way there, I looked around, absorbing as much information about my surroundings as possible. We appeared to be inside a small basement apartment. It was shabby and unkempt, with peeling wallpaper, worn carpet, and a mould problem. The hallway led to a kitchen on the left and a bedroom to the right. The bathroom was near the entryway.

"In there," Sungmi said. She shoved me in and closed the door behind me.

The bathroom was tiny and windowless with a revolting orange colour scheme and a mouldy shower curtain. As I relieved myself, I tried to think calmly about the situation although I trembled uncontrollably. Sungmi didn't seem intent on killing me, or she would have done so by now. She must be plotting something else, I decided. Hopefully, she would leave me alone at some point, then I would try to make an escape. The front door seemed to be the only way out. The windows I had seen were too high and too small. I wondered whether the door needed a key from the inside, and whether there might be a spare one hidden somewhere in the house. In the mirror, I noticed that my necklace was gone. *She must have stolen it from me.*

"Are you done?" Sungmi asked, impatient outside the door.

"Just a minute."

She gave me precisely one minute then opened the door, unable to wait any longer. She yanked me out of the bathroom and guided me away, hand clamped like a vice on my wrist. She sat me back down on the chair and retied me.

"I've got to get ready for work," Sungmi said. "I'll be right back."

I didn't know what the time was, but it seemed to be late at night. I wondered where Sungmi worked that required her to go out at such a time.

I wasn't left wondering for long. It became clear what industry Sungmi worked in when she reentered the room with a face of heavy makeup and wearing a tight mini dress, fishnet stockings, and high boots. "I'm leaving now. Don't try anything stupid while I'm gone," she warned.

I heard a heavy clunk as she locked the door on her way out. This was my chance to escape. Perhaps my only chance.

Chapter 31

I had a trick up my sleeve, literally and figuratively. My bathroom break wasn't just to pee. I had used those precious few minutes to search the drawers and the medicine cabinet, hoping to find something sharp which I could use to cut the rope or as a weapon for self-defence.

"Are you done?" Sungmi had asked from outside the door.

I could tell she was getting impatient. I quickly pulled out the next drawer. That's when I spotted a pair of manicure scissors nestled among the rest of the drawer's contents. *Aha!* I fished them out with my bound hands, and hastily tucked them up my left sleeve. I pushed the drawer shut just as Sungmi opened the door. She didn't seem to notice anything amiss.

Now that Sungmi had left the house, I attempted to retrieve the scissors. With my hands tied behind the back of the chair, the task was a very delicate operation indeed. My constant nervous trembling didn't help either. One false move and the scissors would be on the floor rather than within my grasp. I carefully twisted my wrists until my right hand had access to the bottom of my left sleeve. I strained my fingers trying to grab the scissors, and at last, I managed to catch the edge of the handle and ease them down into my hand. Holding them was awkward, but I was able to slowly hack away at the thick rope.

Progress was much slower than I had hoped, and my hand was beginning to get sore from its awkward grip on the scissors. When my right hand could take no more, I transferred the scissors to my left hand and continued. My aching wrists felt like they were going to sprain, but I couldn't give up now. There were only a few weak strands left holding the rope together. *Just a little more...*I heard a snapping sound and felt the tie around my hands weaken considerably. There was now enough give that I could pull my hands apart, loosening the rest of the rope. Finally, my hands were free. I quickly undid the gag and the tie around my ankles.

I stood up, bones creaking. With no idea when Sungmi would return, I had to act quickly. I ran to the apartment door, praying that I could unlock it from inside. I grabbed the door handle in my sweaty hand and pulled. No luck. I searched the door for some kind of latch or button which would release it but found nothing bar the keyhole. It was no use. The door required a key. I backed away, heart sinking in my chest.

My hopes weren't high for my chance of escaping through a window, but it was my next best option. I checked every window in the house, which didn't take long because there were so few of them. They were all too high and too small. Some were even barred. I crossed that off my list.

With my immediate options of escape dashed, I had no choice but to change tack. I had to search the apartment for either a key, or a means of communicating for help—a phone or a computer.

I checked the kitchen first, thinking a kitchen junk drawer could be a likely place to store a spare set of keys. The kitchen was a shabby room with dated appliances. Several drawers were missing their handles and cabinet doors hung loose on their hinges. The sink was piled high with dirty dishes. I pulled out each drawer in quick succession. Cutlery...utensils...tea towels and oven mitts....*bingo!* A junk drawer. I rummaged through the overflowing drawer searching for a hint of silver or gold metal. My heart leapt when I spotted a likely looking candidate amongst the miscellanea. I snatched it up—a heavy, dull grey key. Holding it tight in my hand, I ran back to the door and tried to insert it in the keyhole. No matter how hard I tried to force it in, it wouldn't fit. It was the wrong key.

I returned to the kitchen, deflated. There were more junk drawers, but no more keys. I couldn't waste more time searching the kitchen. Sungmi could return any minute. I decided to try the bedroom next. The room creeped me out with its Shin Jinseung memorabilia plastering every surface. I approached the cluttered desk and spied a laptop hiding under a stack of papers and magazines. I pushed the clutter aside and opened the laptop. If I could access the internet, I'd be able to send an SOS message. I held my breath as the computer loaded. "Come on…" I muttered. "Please work." A password screen appeared, shattering my hopes. I tried some possible passwords involving "Shin Jinseung" but nothing worked, and after five tries I got locked out.

With every passing minute, I grew more desperate. I searched the room top to bottom in a frenzied state, looking for anything that could help me. Finding nothing but useless junk, I realised I'd have to resort to cruder methods. Desperate times called for desperate measures. At the front door I braced myself, then charged my weight against the door. Even if I couldn't break it down, the noise might attract a neighbour's attention. I rammed myself against the door over and over until my body was aching and bruised. It wouldn't budge. Time for my last resort. "HELP!" I screamed. "HEELLP! I'M TRAPPED." I yelled over and over at the top of my lungs until I had no voice left.

I heard movement outside. There were only two possibilities. Someone coming to my rescue. Or Kim Sungmi.

Chapter 32

I armed myself with a kitchen knife and waited, tense with apprehension. The clunk of a key being inserted and twisted in the lock was confirmation that Kim Sungmi had arrived home.

I stood next to the kitchen door with my back pressed to the wall, ready to pounce as soon as she entered the room, knife gripped tight in my trembling, sweaty hand. I heard Sungmi walk towards the room she had held me, and her gasp upon seeing that I had escaped my bonds. I held my breath.

"Chloe!" Sungmi yelled. "I know you're in here. Show yourself and I won't punish you!" The floorboards creaked as she moved about the house, checking each room.

Her footsteps approached. Adrenaline pumped through my body as I readied myself to strike. She appeared in the doorway and I immediately lunged at her. My knife pierced the air as she dodged the attack. She knocked the knife from my hand with ease and brought her own knife to my neck. I gulped.

"You've shown me that I can't leave you alone," Sungmi snarled. "I guess that leaves me no choice." She pressed the cold steel blade up against my throat.

"Wait!" I whimpered. 'Please…"

"What?"

"I can give you information about Shin Jinseung. That's what you want, isn't it? That's why you brought me here." It was a shot in the dark, but I had to try to buy more time.

"True. I did want to extract information before getting rid of you. I just didn't realise you'd be so tricky to keep under control."

"I'll tell you everything you want to know."

"How can I trust you after you tried to attack me? You'll do it again as soon as you get the chance. I can't risk it."

"I won't. I can't overpower you. I know that now."

"Hmmm…"

"Wouldn't you like to know more about Shin Jinseung? His most private information?"

I could tell that I was wearing her down. How could an obsessive fan resist such a tantalising offer?

"Sit down." She kept her knife pointed at me as she guided me to the kitchen table. "Keep your hands in front of you where I can see them."

I did so. Sungmi sat opposite me and finally lowered her knife but didn't release it from her grasp. "Go on. Tell me about Shin Jinseung. You better be able to share something good. Something I don't already know."

My plan now: keep Sungmi talking until she got tired. Perhaps then I could have a chance at overpowering her. "Is there anything in particular you would like to know?" I asked.

"Anything that could help me win his heart," she said, completely serious.

I tried to keep a straight face, knowing how ridiculous she sounded. A girl like her could never win his heart, no matter how good she was at presenting a fake version of herself to the world. Nevertheless, I'd have to go along with it. I wasn't good enough at lying to simply make everything up, but I was sure Jinseung wouldn't mind if I shared a few genuine personal details. My life was at stake, after all.

"What does he like in a woman?" Sungmi asked.

"Well…he prefers non-famous women because he desires as much normality as possible in his home life."

"I see."

"He likes someone who is independent. Someone who doesn't need to rely on him."

"Go on."

"I don't think he has a specific type when it comes to looks—he admires beauty in a wide range of forms. Most of all, he cares about personality. Someone who he can share a laugh with, someone who has similar interests."

"And what are his interests?"

I listed everything I could think of. His favourite books, movies, food, bands, games, and more. Even if I didn't know, I tried to make something up. Anything to keep on talking.

Sungmi listened intently but without displaying much enthusiasm. She tapped her fingers on the table impatiently. "I already know most of this. I want to know the *juicy* stuff."

My face reddened, realising I would need to delve deeper if I wanted to maintain her attention over a longer period. Much deeper. I hated to expose such intimate details, but honestly, I had no choice. "Let's see…"

"What does he look like naked?" Sungmi asked, eyes gleaming.

I came up against a wall of inner resistance at the question, but forced through it. I answered in great detail, starting at his chest and proceeding all the way down to his toes. Sungmi was absolutely enthralled, listening with rapt attention, hanging on to every word.

When I ran out of things to say on the subject of Jinseung's body, I talked about what it was like to kiss him and described him as a lover. I kept going on, providing detail after painstaking detail, drawn out to fill as much time as possible.

I don't know how much time passed as we talked, but Sungmi was obviously getting sleepy. Her eyelids drooped and she yawned. My gaze darted between her and the knife. *When should I make my move?*

"As much as I'm enjoying listening to your insider knowledge, I really must be going to bed," Sungmi said with a yawn.

"I can tell you more when you wake up," I suggested hopefully.

She sniggered. "I don't think so."

"But there's so much more—"

"If I fall asleep, you'll try to escape again, and this time you could succeed."

"I won't—"

"Don't lie to me." She lazily rotated the knife in her hand. "You have two choices. A: cooperate with me and take the drugs I offer you, or B: resist me and you'll meet your end by much more violent means. I suggest you be smart about this and pick option A. It's easiest for both of us."

My eyes were fixed on the knife. *Should I go for it?* No, I decided. It would be far too risky. I needed to distract her somehow...

"Well?" Sungmi snapped. "Make up your mind or I'll do it for you."

"Option A," I spluttered.

"Good. Now get a glass of water." She yanked me from my chair. Knifepoint at my back, she directed me to the sink to fill up a glass. My shaking hands caused water to spill on the floor as I brought the glass to the table. Sungmi produced a vial and poured the contents in, swirling the glass to mix the deadly concoction. Knife aimed at my throat, she pushed the glass towards me. "Drink," she urged.

I wrapped my hand around the glass, heart pounding. "Before I do this, would you answer me something?"

"What is it?"

"Just what are you hoping to achieve by killing me? Do you think you can win Jinseung's heart?"

She smirked. "Tragedy has a way of bringing people together, don't you think? Shin Jinseung will be grieving at the news of your death—so will Kim Sungmi. It's my chance to bond with him. He'll be vulnerable. It's the best chance I'll ever have."

"He won't fall for you."

"That's what you think. Now, drink up."

I trembled violently as I brought the glass's edge to my lips. *This better work...*

Just as Sungmi relaxed her grip on the knife, convinced that I would drink, I threw the glass at her with all the force I could muster. As I had hoped, she dropped the knife on the table. I lunged for it.

Sungmi shrieked with rage. "Now you've done it!"

No time to hesitate, I slashed at her. The knife tore the fabric of her top, but barely grazed her skin. "Give me the door key or I'll kill you," I said, voice shaking.

"You won't kill me. You don't have it in you," she spat.

"Don't underestimate me." I thrust the knife directly at her heart.

Sungmi ducked and launched a devastating kick at my ankles. I came tumbling down. The knife fell from my grasp and went skidding across the floor. Sungmi came down on top of me, pinning me to the ground. I struggled beneath her, but she had me locked down and completely at her mercy. I knew it was game over.

Chapter 33

Sungmi wrapped her clammy hands tight around my neck. "You're dead," she sneered.

I squeezed my eyes shut. *This is it. This is the end.* I didn't pray to God often but felt a strongly compelling need to do so at this moment. *Dear God—my friends, my family, and Shin Jinseung—please make sure they live long and happy lives without me.*

Sungmi increased the pressure on my throat. I couldn't breathe. White spots danced behind my eyelids, and the sound of rushing blood filled my eardrums. My strength was rapidly draining. I was beginning to lose consciousness.

A loud smashing sound ripped through the air and plunged me back to the world of the living, coughing and spluttering. In a moment of confusion, Sungmi had faltered, losing her hold on me just long enough that I could break free. I scrambled to my feet. So did Sungmi. She was first to grab the knife—but it was too late. Police officers in bulletproof vests stormed inside, guns trained on Sungmi. I recognised one of them—Bae Sangwook. "Drop your weapon!" he yelled.

Sungmi hesitated, but seeing she had no other choice, she released the knife. It clattered to the floor.

"Put your hands up!"

She slowly raised her hands above her head.

At once, Officer Bae descended on her, locking handcuffs around her wrists. "Oh Sejung, you're under arrest. Anything you say can be used against you. You have the right to remain silent."

I watched Sungmi being taken from the scene. I was too overwhelmed to feel relief, my legs like jelly, and my heart pounding so hard I thought my chest would burst. My surroundings became a blur. Figures approached me. "Chloe…Chloe Gibson…" Those were the last words I heard before I fainted.

* * *

"Chloe…"

"You're okay…"

"It's me…"

"It's safe…"

I heard the fragmented speech of a familiar voice before I came to with a start, gasping for breath. My gaze fixed upon Yang Bora, who leaned over me with a cautiously expectant look on her face, eyes wide beneath her circle-lens glasses.

I grabbed at her sleeve. "What happened? Where am I?" My voice came out in a rasp. It hurt to talk.

Bora stroked my head with her small, warm hand. "Shhhh. Everything's going to be all right."

I had a strange feeling that we were in motion. I heaved myself up onto my elbows and looked around. I was on a stretcher in a small enclosed space surrounded by medical equipment. An ambulance, I realised.

"We'll be at the hospital soon," Bora explained. "Doctors will take care of you, make sure your injuries aren't serious. The police will want to speak with you as well, I'm sure."

One question stood out in my mind, something I couldn't figure out at all. "How did they find me?"

Bora smiled faintly. "I'll explain everything in due time. For now, you just rest."

"Jinseung-ah?"

"He's on his way."

I flopped back down onto the stretcher and relaxed, my heartbeat slowing to an even tempo.

* * *

No one was allowed to see me until I had finished being examined, both by doctors and police. My injuries were minor, but it was determined that I should stay in the hospital for a while due to my fragile state.

I was in a private room, small and modern with blue walls, seating for guests, a TV screen opposite the bed, and a small station in the corner for making hot drinks. A humidifier sprayed a fine mist into the air.

For the first time since I had arrived in the hospital, I was left alone. My emotions were too mixed up for me to think properly. Grief for what I had been through. Happiness that I had survived. Terror from vivid flashbacks. Sadness that my life would never be the same again.

A soft knock on the door made me stir. Yang Bora and Shin Jina entered the room. According to the police, it had been thanks to those two that I had been rescued.

"Hey," Jina said gently. "How are you doing?"

"Not too bad." I still couldn't speak much, though the strain on my throat was beginning to dissipate.

The pair came to sit at my bedside. Shin Jina held a large fabric tote bag. "I brought you some essentials," she said. "Magazines, books, pyjamas, skincare products...Everything to make your stay here a bit more comfortable."

"Thank you."

"Is there anything else you need?" Bora asked.

"Not really."

"Jinseung will be here soon."

I tensed at his name. I didn't know how I'd be able to face him after this, or what would become of our relationship. It was all too much for me to process right now.

"Your host parents are also on their way," Bora said, sensing my unease.

"Ah, good." I had listed them as my emergency contact, rather than my real parents back in the UK.

"If you want to rest, just let us know. We can leave," Jina said.

"No," I said abruptly. I couldn't rest properly. Not until I had answers. "Please, tell me. How did you work out what had happened to me? How did you help the police?"

"Are you sure you're ready to listen to this?" Bora asked. "It's a long story."

"I'm ready."

Chapter 34

Jina made hot drinks at the mini espresso machine in my room while Bora helped me adjust my bed to a more comfortable position. Propped up with pillows and a warm mug in my hand, I was ready to listen to the story of my rescue.

"The first strange thing was the text message," Bora began. "The fact that you would make a rush decision to go back to the UK without even saying goodbye seemed out of character. I called Jina and she agreed with me."

"I saw you earlier in the day," Jina said. "But it didn't seem like you were planning to leave. I was sure you would have told me."

"Yes, I would have," I agreed.

"I tried to call you, but you wouldn't answer," Bora said. "There were a couple more texts from your number—vague reassurances, and then your phone was turned off. Perhaps you had really boarded a plane, but I was suspicious. I thought to go to your apartment—I knew the code since I was there when you changed it after the break-in. It was as I suspected: Everything was still there. If you were going to the UK, surely you would have gone back to your apartment and packed some stuff to take with you. Your suitcase was still in the closet. At that point I knew something was seriously wrong. I called

Officer Bae to voice my concerns. He didn't seem worried, but said he'd check with the airport to see if you had really left the country."

"If you hadn't gone to the airport, I could only think of two other reasons why you'd leave the apartment—work or tutoring," Jina explained. "I had been running your errands for you because you were scared to leave the house. I didn't think you'd suddenly decide to go wander out on your own for any other reason."

"That narrowed things down considerably," Bora said. "It was unlikely you had gone to work—unless your class schedule had changed. It seemed more likely that you'd gone to tutor your student. You had mentioned her a few times before—Kim Sung-mi. The more I thought about it, the more I suspected her. She was close to you. She could have accessed your bag when you weren't looking. I'm sure she could have worked out your address. However, there were a few things that didn't add up, the vase incident being one of them—she was there with you when it happened. But I realised that she could have had someone working with her."

"You must have wondered why I never suspected her," I said. "I feel like such an idiot."

"Not at all! She was clearly a master manipulator. Anyone would have been fooled."

"Perhaps, but it's so obvious in hindsight."

Bora shook her head. "I still had doubts, it was just all I had to go on."

"So, what happened next?"

"I contacted the *hagwon* to try and get her phone number, but they wouldn't give it to me. 'It's confidential,' they said." She rolled her eyes. "In the meantime, Officer Bae came back to me. He confirmed that you hadn't left Korea. Said he'd try and track you down. I was feeling suspicious of Kim Sungmi. I told him as much, but I had no evidence. I didn't know if he would take it as a serious lead or not. I decided to do my own investigation with the help of Jina *Unnie*."

"We needed to find out where you were having the tutoring sessions," Jina explained. "You hadn't mentioned it to either of us before."

"But *Unnie* remembered something—a detail that seemed completely insignificant at the time."

"When we met at the cinema you came straight from tutoring. You were holding a bag from Booksea. I've been there before and remembered the café. It clicked as a possible location where you could tutor someone."

"It was a strong enough lead, so we jumped on it. We didn't have much time. Booksea was about to close. We raced there to ask the staff if anyone had seen you. They were in the process of closing up when we arrived—wiping counters and telling the last patrons to get ready to leave. They tried to turn us away, but I insisted that we needed to speak to someone concerning a missing person. That piqued their interest and we were invited to speak with the manager. I showed him a photo of you on my phone and asked if you had been there earlier that day."

"He recognised you straight away! Knew your name and everything."

"Makes sense," I said. "I had been going there regularly and I gave my name whenever I ordered."

"I asked if he had noticed anything strange happen," Bora said. "My hopes weren't high, but to my surprise, he said yes. Something strange did happen. You left much earlier than usual. You looked unwell—like you were going to faint. Kim Sungmi led you out of the building. This was the crucial information we had been searching for. I called Officer Bae straight away. He agreed it was suspicious and said he would come to investigate. We stayed there with the manager past closing until Officer Bae arrived.

"From there, things pretty much fell into place. Security footage showed you getting into a taxi and Kim Sungmi leaving on a scooter. The motorcycle helmet fit in with past evidence. Officer Bae got the taxi company to trace where you had gone."

"So that's how you found me…"

"There's more. The police had to work out which house you were in as it wasn't clear based on where the taxi had dropped you off. Officers in plain clothes were dispatched to search the area. They had to be discreet—if Sungmi knew that police were hot on her tail she could have killed you and fled. Luckily it didn't take long to locate you. Screams were heard coming from a basement apartment. That's when Officer Bae and his colleagues got ready to storm inside and arrest Kim Sungmi, or I should say, Oh Sejung."

"How did they work out her name?" I asked.

"It's the name the scooter was registered under, the name on her driver's licence."

Listening to Bora, I hadn't noticed that a fourth person had entered the room. Shin Jinseung stood there in the doorway watching on in silence.

Chapter 35

Jinseung looked like a ghost—pale-skinned and hollow-eyed. "Please, don't let me disturb you," he said in a faltering voice.

He had obviously been hit hard by the news of my kidnapping. My heart ached for him. "You're not disturbing anything," I said. "Come in."

He hesitantly walked over. Jina and Bora's eyes met, and they nodded at each other. "We'll leave you two alone," Jina said. They scurried away, leaving us in privacy.

A heavy silence engulfed the room. Jinseung fell to his knees at my bedside. He didn't say anything, just burrowed his head in my blanket. His shoulders shook. I realised he was weeping. "*Oppa…*" I said softly, laying a hand on his back.

He lifted his head but avoided my gaze. His cheeks were wet with tears. "I can't believe what you've just been through," he rasped.

"It's a lot to process."

"I could have lost you."

"Yes."

"None of this would have happened if I had paid more attention to you and made sure you were completely safe."

"It's not your fault."

"Not directly, but I played a part. I don't think I'll ever be able to forgive myself."

I didn't push back because part of me really did blame him. He had ignored me when I needed support. He had brushed the seriousness of the threats aside, thinking them nothing more than an occupational hazard. He had failed to take care of me the way a partner should. I silently watched him grieve, unsure what to do or what to say.

Not long ago I had been convinced that I would never break up with Jinseung, no matter what, but now our future was a mystery. Could I realistically stay with him after what happened to me? Being with him was dangerous—more dangerous than I ever imagined. If we stayed together and went public with our relationship, there would be unrelenting media scrutiny. What's worse, there could be others out there just like Oh Sejung—fans who would stop at nothing to keep me away from Jinseung.

I wouldn't be able to continue the independent life I'd been living, doing my own thing while Jinseung disappeared for long periods of time filming. He would have to stay by my side and support me so I could feel safe through my recovery. That meant big changes for him career-wise. Playing second fiddle to his burgeoning acting career would no longer be in the cards. Would he be willing to accept that without resentment? Could I ask so much of him?

My head ached from the painful thoughts swirling in my head. I groaned and groped for the glass of water and paracetamol tablets on the bedside table.

"Are you okay?" Jinseung asked.

"I have a headache." I swallowed a pill with a large gulp of water.

"I'm sorry," he sniffed, wiping his tears with his sleeve. "You have more right to be upset than me. I should be the one comforting you, not the other way around."

"I have cried enough already. I don't think I have any tears left."

"But you must be hurting."

"Of course I am."

"Can I give you a hug?"

I nodded, smiling weakly. Jinseung stood up and leaned over me, then wrapped me up in his arms. I let my body relax against him, revelling in his warmth and his scent. My ear to his chest, I could hear his steadily beating heart. I lost myself in the hug, letting my head empty of all the negative thoughts so I could be content in the moment.

Jinseung stayed holding me for several minutes, stroking my hair, caressing my back, gently kissing my cheek. He seemed afraid to let me go, like I'd drift away and never come back. Perhaps I would.

"I'll stay here with you as long as you want me to," he murmured.

"Thank you, but my host parents will be here soon. They'll take care of me."

"I see. Then, can I wait with you until they get here?"

"Yes, of course." I lay back on my bed with a sigh.

Jinseung took my hand in his. "Chloe...I don't know what you're thinking—about us, I mean...But just so you know, I'll fully support you no matter what you decide to do."

"I haven't decided anything. I need to think things over."

"I understand."

"What about you? What are you thinking?"

He shook his head. "My thoughts don't matter. I will accept whatever you decide."

"I don't know. I just don't know right now."

But I did know one thing for certain. Being with Jinseung wasn't worth the traumatic experience I had been through.

Chapter 36

I dreaded being discharged from hospital. Leaving would mean having to face the world again. I'd have to look after myself and start making decisions about my life going forward. Big decisions, such as whether I'd continue to live and work in Seoul, and small decisions, like what to wear and what to eat. Both kinds seemed difficult to make right now. I was probably suffering from post-traumatic stress disorder.

My host parents, Mrs. Soo and Mr. Han, sat on the couch in my hospital room. Mrs. Soo was a short, plump woman, with a kind, crinkly face. Her husband was tall and thin, bespectacled and wispy-haired. The old couple rarely left Tongyeong these days, so I greatly appreciated that they came all the way to Seoul to see me.

Mrs. Soo got up and prepared a mug of the herbal tea she had brought for me as a gift. "It promotes mental wellbeing," she explained.

"Ah, just what I need," I joked, managing a faint smile.

As the tea brewed, Mrs. Soo settled herself down next to me. "Chloe, my husband and I have been thinking a lot about your situation and we have a proposition for you."

"Oh? What is it?"

"If you're not planning to go back to the UK straight away, stay with us in Tongyeong for a while," she implored. "The fresh air will be good for you."

"It's the best place for you to relax and recover," Mr. Han said. "Seoul is not a restful place."

I hadn't considered going to Tongyeong until their suggestion, but the idea certainly had merit. "Would that really be okay?" I asked. I always felt hesitant to impose on them.

"Of course. You are like family to us," Mrs. Soo said. "We want to help you."

My eyes welled up. "That means a lot to me."

"Consider it, okay?"

"You don't have to decide right now, just know that it's on the table," Mr. Han said. "We're not leaving Seoul until you're settled again."

Mrs. Soo offered me the mug of tea. "Here. Hope it's not too hot."

"Thank you."

I mulled over the possibility of going to Tongyeong as I sipped the hot tea. If I accepted their offer I wouldn't have to go back to my apartment. I'd be well looked after. I'd be away from Seoul and the bad memories of what happened here. On the other hand, I wouldn't be able to go to work and serve the rest of my notice. All my stuff was still at my apartment, and there were still repairs that needed to be taken care of. I'd be away from Bora, Jina, and Jinseung, and the rest of my support network in Seoul.

I sighed deeply, rubbing my temples. Staying put was probably the more practical decision, but my heart wanted me to go to Tongyeong, and after all I'd been through, perhaps giving my heart priority wouldn't be such a bad idea. Some time away from Seoul would give me some much-needed headspace. The more I thought about it, the more the decision became clear. "I think I will," I said. "I'll come to Tongyeong."

"That is wonderful news!" Mr. Han said, beaming.

"I'm so glad!" Mrs. Soo said, grasping my hand in hers. "It will do you a world of good, you'll see."

* * *

I AWAITED the result of my latest psychiatric evaluation with nervous apprehension—pass or fail? The outcome would determine whether or not I could be discharged from hospital.

Pass, the doctor eventually determined. I was cleared to leave, handed meds for PTSD, and sent on my way. Mr. Han and Mrs. Soo met me at the hospital to drive me directly to their home in Tongyeong. Yang Bora met me as well, wheeling along two large suitcases with her. "I packed as much as I could," she said.

"Thank you for doing this for me," I said. "To be honest, I'd been dreading going back to that apartment. Such a relief that I don't have to."

"It's okay. Besides, the fact that you're letting me stay there for free more than makes up for it!"

Since I wouldn't be living at the apartment but still had to serve the notice period on the contract, I had asked Bora if she wanted to live there in my absence. She had jumped at the chance. The apartment was much closer to her workplace than her current residence, and she had always wanted to live by herself. In exchange, she had tidied up and packed my belongings for me. She would also deal with the repairs which still needed to be taken care of. My insurance would cover the cost. As for my job, Linda Choi had been informed that I wouldn't be able to return to work. She was understanding of my situation. With all of the practicalities taken care of, I felt reassured of my decision to go to Tongyeong. The only loose strand was Shin Jinseung, but it hurt too much to think about. I needed time and space to reflect on that issue.

Mr. Han drove his car from the carpark to the pick-up spot outside the hospital. He hopped out. "Are you all set?"

"Yes, I think so," I replied.

He hauled my luggage into the car boot.

"Have a nice time in Tongyeong," Bora said. "Keep in touch."

"I promise I will," I said, giving her a hug.

I wound the window down and waved to her as Mr. Han drove

away from the hospital. Bora waved back, smiling kindly. She had done so much for me. Letting her use the apartment was the least I could do in return, and wouldn't even begin to pay back her unlimited kindness. I watched her until she faded from view then closed the window.

Mr. Han was a slow and cautious driver, and that fact wasn't helped by the small, old car he drove. I had a feeling the journey to Tongyeong would take much longer than it should. Not that I minded too much. Watching the world go by outside the car window soothed me.

Leaving Seoul, the landscape slowly morphed from high-density tall buildings to green countryside, sparsely scattered with small houses. At one point we stopped to eat the lunch boxes Mrs. Soo had packed—yummy *gimbap* with boiled eggs and pickled radish on the side.

Back in the car for the final leg of our journey, Mrs. Soo nodded off to sleep in the passenger seat. I was growing drowsy too. Long car rides tended to have that effect on me. The rest of the journey passed quickly, and the next time I looked out the window, I realised we had arrived in Tongyeong. The calm, seaside town quietly bustled with locals going about their daily lives. Even with the window closed, I thought I could smell and taste the crisp, salty air.

My host parents lived in an area called Inpyeong-dong—a small neighbourhood near the Gyeongsang National University Tongyeong campus where Mr. Han worked as a professor. We drove up the winding driveway through a large, slightly overgrown section to a ramshackle yet charming cottage.

I took one suitcase, Mr. Han took the other. Returning to this cottage strangely felt like coming home. The interior hadn't changed one bit since I lived there as a teenager, except that the wooden furniture was even more shabby, and the wallpaper more faded. I still recognised the framed family photographs (including some of me), stacks of well-worn books, and sentimental ornaments which dotted the rooms' surfaces.

Mrs. Soo and I drank cold barley tea as a refreshment while Mr.

Han went next door to pick up their golden retriever, Snow, who the neighbour had been looking after while they were gone.

As soon as Mr. Han returned, Snow came rushing to me, wagging her tail and panting. She even let out a little bark of joy as I petted her. She got up on the couch with her front paws and licked my face.

"She's missed you." Mr. Han chuckled.

"Good girl," I said, ruffling the sweet dog's soft fur.

After catching up with Snow, I brought my suitcases to the room I would be staying in—Seri's old bedroom. I opened a dresser drawer so I could start putting my clothes away but saw that it was still full of Seri's old things.

"Let me help you," Mrs. Soo said, appearing behind me. "I can move my daughter's stuff to another room."

"Are you sure? I can just keep my things in my suitcases."

"Don't be silly. It's not a hassle. I want you to feel like you're at home." She started removing the items from Seri's drawer.

Once adequate space was made, Mrs. Soo helped me unpack my things away and made up the *yo*, our conversation turned to the subject of my parents. "How are they holding up?" she asked. "They must have been devastated to hear what happened to you."

I squirmed, embarrassed to tell her the truth. "Actually, I still haven't told them."

Her mouth dropped. "*Omo*! You need to tell them. It is a parent's right to know such things."

"I know…but I can just imagine how they'll react. It makes me feel sick."

"I would call on your behalf if I could, but my English is too poor."

"I'll call them. Just not today."

Mrs. Soo fixed me a stern look. "All right, but don't leave it too long."

I wished that I could keep it a secret, yet I knew Mrs. Soo was right. They had to know, and I would have to be the one to have to tell them.

Chapter 37

The time had come. I couldn't put it off any longer. My parents needed to know the difficult truth: They had almost lost their daughter. My hand trembled as I picked up my phone and opened my contact list. I took a deep breath as I tapped on my mother's name, and before I could talk myself out of it, I pressed the call button.

I held the phone to my ear. My stomach churned as I waited for her to pick up. Secretly I prayed that she wouldn't answer so I could put it off again. But she did answer. "Hello, my dear," she said cheerfully.

"Uh, hi, Mum," I squeaked.

"It's so good to hear your voice. You should call more often."

"Yeah, sorry about that."

"How are you getting on? Everything okay?"

"Um...is Dad there?"

"Yes, he's around somewhere. Do you want to speak to him?"

"I want to speak to both of you. Could you grab him and put the call on speakerphone?"

"Sure. Just a minute."

There was a rustling sound, and I could hear my mother

consulting with my father in the background. "It's Chloe…She wants to speak to us…How do you turn the speaker on?…Ugh!"

The call cut out and I knew she must have hung up by accident. She called back a few seconds later. "Sorry about that. Think I've got it working now. Here's Dad."

"Hi, sweetie, how's things?" he asked.

"Actually…" My voice wavered. "I need to tell you something."

My parents were silent for a moment as if contemplating the seriousness of what I was about to tell them. "We're listening," Dad said solemnly.

I came out with the truth of what happened, starting with my kidnapping, then expanding to explain the background series of events which led to it. Telling them was painful. Having to relive the trauma through recounting it and hearing the reaction of my parents made me feel utterly sick to my stomach. I was crying on the phone. My mother was absolutely hysterical and partway through booking the next plane to Seoul before I stopped her. "I'm not in Seoul. I'm in Tongyeong with my host parents. I already have a flight booked back to the UK. I'll come home," I said.

"When will you come?" she asked.

"Later this month."

"That's not soon enough. You need to come home now!"

"I don't have the energy for a long-haul flight right now. I want to relax and rest some more first, but perhaps I could bring the flight forward a bit."

"Yes. Please do. We'll cover any change fees—just do it."

"Okay. I will." Anything to appease her and get her off my case.

As we spoke at length on the phone, she continued to fuss mixed with a healthy dose of victim-blaming for good measure:

"You let yourself go through all that for a boy?"

"Why didn't you just leave Korea?"

"If you told us what was going on, we wouldn't have let this happen to you."

Meanwhile my dad didn't say much, but I knew he must be heartbroken. He was the type to grieve in silence.

After a multitude of "I love yous" and "Take cares," I was finally allowed to hang up. I felt relieved to have gotten the call out of the way, but at the same time anxious and upset about what my parents must be thinking. I drooped down on the couch, exhausted. Snow came sniffing around me. As if sensing something was wrong, she jumped up on the couch and rested her head on my lap—her version of a cuddle. Her presence calmed me considerably. I stroked her head. "Life is so simple for a dog, isn't it? I envy you."

I could have moped around all day but resisted the urge. "How about a walk?" I asked Snow. Some fresh air would do me good.

"Woof!" she replied, getting off my lap and running excitedly to the door.

The sun had yet to rise when we left the house, but soon enough the first rays of light began to burst from the horizon, painting the sky pink and gold. I took Snow for a walk around the neighbourhood, passing many familiar landmarks as we went—the park with the view of the ocean, the walking track, the seaside café. I remembered walking this route with Jinseung the last time I was in Tongyeong. *Jinseung.* My heart stirred and an unbearable sadness washed over me. I hadn't even said goodbye to him.

"Come on, Snow. Let's turn back," I said.

Snow suddenly started going crazy. Yapping and tugging hard on the lead.

"What is it?" I asked.

I followed her to the source of her excitement. I couldn't believe my eyes.

Chapter 38

I froze, completely stunned. *Am I dreaming? This can't be possible...* Yet there he was. Shin Jinseung. A vision bathed in dappled sunlight. Tall and lean in a thin white button-up shirt and jeans, the wind ruffling his dark hair. His lips parted slightly, intense eyes taking me in. He looked just as shocked to see me as I was to see him.

"Jinseung-ah! What are you doing here?" I stammered.

His shocked appearance wore off, replaced by a fond gaze. "Visiting my parents," he said. "But I must admit I had an ulterior motive. I thought I might see you here. Still, I didn't expect to run into you so early in the morning. I was just taking a walk to clear my head. I'm not prepared."

I opened my mouth to speak but couldn't think of anything to say. I was too stunned. Too mixed up with my emotions. I didn't know how to react to his presence.

His eyes flitted down my throat. "You're wearing the necklace I gave you."

I touched it unconsciously. "I always wear it." Thankfully, the police returned it to me, along with the other possessions Oh Sejung had taken—my bag, wallet, and phone.

"I'm glad." Smiling, he took a step towards me and placed a gentle hand on my arm. "Well, I guess now's as good a time as any. I know you came here wanting space. Forgive me for the intrusion, but I have to get something off my chest. Will you listen?"

"Yes," I said without hesitation. He had come all the way here to see me. The romance of the gesture wasn't lost on me. I would hear him out.

His grip on my arm tightened. "Chloe..." His voice was soft and low, almost a whisper. "I know I said that my thoughts don't matter, and that's still the case, but I want to express them to you anyway. The truth is, you mean the world to me. I want you to stay. I want you to continue being my girlfriend and I want you to stay here with me."

My heart fluttered at the sincerity of his words. "Really?"

"Yes. That's my wish."

I felt a blush creep onto my cheeks. "Thank you for telling me." Hearing his feelings removed an invisible burden from me. Now I knew where he stood and I could move forward without any confusion.

"If you decide to stay, I'll put all my projects on hold to be by your side until you have fully recovered. I'll buy another house, one with the best security possible, and you can live there with me. I'll make sure you're safe, no matter the cost."

"What about Love in Flames?"

"I've come clean to the director about my relationship with you and what happened. He took pity on me—or perhaps he thought I'd walk out if he didn't accommodate me. Anyway, all non-essential scenes involving my character have been scrapped and the schedule has been reorganised so I can take a little bit of time off. After that... I'm not sure. It will depend on what happens with you and me."

"I see..."

"I won't pressure you, Chloe. Do whatever you think is best."

I looked down at the ground, the hopelessness of the situation heavy on my shoulders. "I can't stay here even if I wanted to. I quit my job. My visa will expire, and I'll be kicked out of the country."

"I'll find a way around that."

"I already have a flight booked. My parents are waiting for me to come home."

"Go home. See your parents. I won't stop you."

"And then?"

"You can come back here when you're ready. I'll wait for you. As long as it takes."

The offer was tempting, I couldn't deny it. But still...there was so much to take into account. "I...I'll think about it."

Jinseung dropped his hand from my arm. "I've said all I had to say. I'm glad I got it off my chest."

"I'm sorry I can't promise you anything."

He smiled faintly. "Don't worry. After everything you've been through, I don't blame you one bit. To put myself in your shoes...I don't know what I'd do."

Snow was beginning to get restless, tugging on the lead and whining.

"I should get going," I said.

Jinseung nodded.

"Come on, Snow."

"Wait." Jinseung reached out again. "Can I hug you?"

I stopped. "What if someone sees?"

"I don't care. Let them see."

Public displays of affection had always been forbidden territory for us, so his nonchalance took me by surprise, but at the same time I was happy. I opened my arms to him, and he stepped into my embrace. He felt so perfect. Warm and solid and strong. He smelled like a mixture of spice and sea salt. He pulled me closer, one arm wrapped tight around my waist, the other around my shoulders. My head was tucked under his chin. We stayed hugging each other as if it would be our last embrace. Perhaps it would be. He brought his lips down to my ear and said something I wasn't expecting. Three words he had never spoken to me before. "I love you."

Chapter 39

I woke up in my childhood bedroom and for a few minutes it felt like the events of the past year had been a dream. I looked around the room in a daze then reality sank in. Everything really had happened. Starring in a K-drama, dating a famous actor, being stalked, kidnapped, and nearly killed. I groaned and pulled the covers up to my chin.

The artefacts of my childhood surrounded me—books which I had read until the spines cracked, toys I played with as a little kid, photographs of me and my high-school friends, posters of bands I used to enjoy. I lay in the same bed with the floral duvet cover I slept on throughout my teenage years. I didn't feel a pleasant sense of nostalgia. The room didn't comfort me at all. Instead, it felt oddly surreal. Like I was frozen inside a time capsule, but with an eerie sense of detachment—like the items in the room belonged to me in another life.

Ultimately, I had little choice but to leave Korea. My parents would have been unbearably upset if I hadn't come home, not to mention my visa was expiring anyway. And Jinseung? I asked him to wait for me. Our relationship was on hold until I could decide whether I wanted to stay with him or not. That would depend on whether or not I could get over the trauma of being kidnapped, and my willingness to go back to Korea and put up with the downsides of dating a celebrity—crazy fans and all.

A soft knock startled me from my snooze. My dad pushed the door ajar and popped his head into the room. "Breakfast is ready. I made your favourite."

The smell wafted in—the rich, mouthwatering scent of butter, fresh bread, fried egg, and real maple syrup. That was enough to rouse me. I stumbled out of bed, wrapped myself in a dressing gown, and staggered to the dining room. The table was set with plates piled high with French toast, fresh fruit, strips of fried bacon, and fresh pastries.

"Wow. That looks amazing," I said, snapping out of my morning drowsiness. If there was one thing I missed while I was in Korea, it was a good, hearty western breakfast.

Dad brought in a jug of fresh orange juice. He was wearing a novelty apron which read "King of the kitchen."

"Eat up," he said. "A nice big breakfast will make you feel better."

"Come and take a seat," Mum said, motioning to the empty chair next to her.

I piled up my plate and filled a glass with juice. My first bite of French toast made me sigh with satisfaction.

"How is it?" Dad asked.

"Delicious."

"What are your plans for the day?" Mum asked.

"I don't know. I might just read a book or something."

She frowned. "I know you just got here, but maybe it would be a good idea to discuss some ground rules."

I groaned internally. "Rules?"

"Like doing your part around the house, searching for employment, and becoming independent again. You can't spend all your time wallowing. It's not good for you."

I pushed a piece of toast around my plate, suddenly losing my appetite. "I'm not sure I'm ready to discuss things like that yet."

"Fair enough. But we don't want to make the same mistake as last time, do we?"

"What mistake?"

"The last time you moved back in with us. Your father and I were much too lenient. What was meant to be a temporary safety net turned into months of looking after you."

It was something I didn't want to be reminded of. That was a painful time, made more painful by the lack of unconditional support from my parents. I lowered my knife and fork and pushed my plate aside, then stood up, tears in my eyes. "I'm going to read in my room."

"You've barely eaten," Dad said, concerned.

"I'm not hungry."

"Don't be silly," Mum said. "Sit back down and finish. I'm sorry for what I said. I've spoken too soon."

"I for one don't mind however long it takes for you to recover," Dad said.

Mum glared at him but said nothing.

I hadn't even spent 24 hours home with my parents and there was already tension in the air. I wondered if I had made a mistake coming back.

Chapter 40

The sky was dark in the middle of the afternoon. Flashes of lightning and rumbles of thunder accompanied the rain drumming against the windowpane. The raging storm outside made the therapist's office feel even more warm and cosy than usual. I sat on a plush couch, an overstuffed cushion behind my back, and a soft rug underfoot. My therapist sat on the couch against the opposite wall, a small notepad and pen in hand. A coffee table divided the space between us, a tray of tea and biscuits on top. On the other side of the room, framed certificates decorated the wall behind a large desk, clear apart from a single slim laptop and a phone. A bookcase stuffed with psychology textbooks and self-help paperbacks took up the remaining space.

My therapist, Lisa Keaton, was a woman with long silver hair and glasses, tall and elegant, dressed in a crisp white linen shirt, slim beige pants, and brown leather loafers. She didn't wear any makeup but still looked perfect, wrinkles and all. I fancied the idea of looking like her when I was older.

"What would you like to talk about today?" she asked, in her deep yet soft tone.

"I had another argument with my parents," I said.

"What was it about this time?"

"My mum wanted to introduce me to a friend who might have a job for me, but I turned the opportunity down. I told her that I still wasn't sure if I would stay here or go back to Korea, so there was no point in taking a job right now. She completely lost it. She can't understand why I would even consider going back to Korea—or she thinks I'm using that as an excuse to be lazy."

"And your father?"

"He agrees with her. Thinks I should be focused on re-establishing myself here. In the end, I did go to meet the friend for a job interview, but it only made things worse. No matter how hard I tried, I couldn't muster the energy to fake enthusiasm. The woman could see right through me. She knew I had no interest in the job. She rejected me and that made things awkward between her and my mum. My mum blames me, of course—'you should have put more effort in.'" I mimicked her nagging tone. "She thinks I embarrassed her on purpose to spite her. Called me ungrateful."

Lisa gave me a sympathetic look. "I can see how that situation was difficult for you, but I'm sure your mother thought she was genuinely helping by getting you a job lead."

"I know, but her way of helping is messed up. She puts her interests above mine and completely dismisses my feelings."

"She could have lost you. Does it seem reasonable to you that she might be trying to hold onto you, keep you close to her?"

"I suppose so," I said with a sigh. "But it's not her right to make that decision for me."

"How seriously are you considering going back to Korea?"

"My life, everything I care about, is in Korea."

"But there's something holding you back…"

"I'm not over the trauma of what happened there. I think I'll have flashbacks and panic attacks. I think I'll be paranoid about something similar happening all over again."

"You feel safer here?"

"Yes, I do."

"What if you were just as safe in Korea as you are here?"

"Then it would be a no-brainer. I would go back."

"So, you're left with two options: staying in a bubble of safety or facing your fears."

"When you put it like that it seems obvious that I should face my fears, but how can I when the fear is so paralysing? Meanwhile, I'm stuck in limbo, unable to move forward with my life, testing my parents' patience to the limit."

"Your only reason to stay here is that it feels safe, correct?"

I nodded.

"Logic tells us that bad things can happen anywhere," she explained. "One place isn't necessarily safer than another, yet fear overrides this logic. You are not any safer here than in Korea. Your sense of safety is a construct of the mind."

She spoke sense and I understood what she was getting at, but I had a special case. "I told you I was dating someone famous in Korea, right? That made me a target. If I want to keep dating him, there will be other crazy people out to get me. That's what my fear tells me, anyway."

Lisa's face brightened as if she had an epiphany. "Ah, so perhaps it is your relationship that scares you more than the location."

"That could be the case," I admitted.

"It seems like we're getting to the heart of the issue. How interesting."

Another flash of lightning lit up the room. Booming thunder rattled the window frames. The storm matched the tumultuous state of my mind. I sat silent for a while, ruminating.

"Tea?" Lisa offered.

"Yes, please."

She poured me a small cup. A few sips of the soothing chamomile tea and I managed to voice what I was thinking. "I would probably be fine going back to Korea if I broke up with my boyfriend, but I don't want to lose him. I really don't. I love him."

Lisa nodded with understanding. "It's not easy. Your only way to hold onto him is to face your fears. You have to decide whether he's worth it or not."

"I feel completely frozen. My brain tells me one thing, my heart tells me another."

"It's your love and your fear fighting for dominance."

"What can I do?" I looked at her hopefully, wishing she could give me all the answers, but knowing she could not.

"Deep in your heart, you know what you truly want. My advice would be to figure that out, then start taking baby steps to get there."

*What I truly want...*A life with Shin Jinseung and all the positives and negatives that go along with it? Or something else? A regular life with a regular partner? An exciting life with its ups and downs, or a stable, if boring, life? I would need to do a lot of soul searching to come up with the answers, but I didn't have much time. Jinseung wouldn't wait forever. Take too long and I could lose him.

"Have you been using the journal I gave you?" Lisa asked.

"Yes, I have." I kept the thick, softcover notebook on my bedside table, thinking I'd pick it up when I was in bed and couldn't sleep.

"Try to write an entry every day. It's a good place to reflect. Perhaps you'll find the answers you're looking for."

"Thanks. I'll do that."

Lisa glanced at the clock on the wall. "I'm afraid our time is up."

That went fast. I stood up and grabbed my bag and jacket.

"Will I see you again next week?" Lisa asked, walking to her desk to set her notepad down.

"Yes. I think so."

"Hope you don't get too wet on your way home."

"It's okay. I borrowed Mum's car."

"Then drive safe."

"Thanks. See you next week."

Outside, the rain continued to pour down. The car was parked right by the front of the building, but I feared that even walking the short distance to the car door I'd get drenched.

I waited a few minutes, standing under the eaves of the building, hoping the rain would ease. I checked my phone and saw a new message from Yang Bora. I read it once, then twice, bewildered by what I saw.

Chapter 41

Bora: I'm going to visit Oh Sejung. Would you like to join me?

*H*ow can I visit Oh Sejung when she's in Korea and I'm here? The question baffled me until I called Bora later that day. She explained that it was possible to set up a video call and talk with her remotely. *Ah, the wonders of technology.* With that mystery solved, I still wondered what made her think I would want to see or talk to Sejung again.

"I just thought that it might help you on your road to recovery," she said. "You know, it might help you get a sense of closure or something."

"I'm not sure…" I replied. The thought of seeing Oh Sejung again, even through a computer screen, made me feel incredibly anxious. She was the woman who attempted to murder me, after all.

"You don't have to if you don't want to, but I'm still going to go," Bora said.

"Why do *you* want to see her?"

"I'm a naturally curious person. I wanted to talk to her to find out more about her motivations and her methods. I find it simply fascinating. You know how much I enjoy true crime documentaries and stuff like that. I'm sorry if that bothers you, though."

I drew a long breath. "I guess I don't mind. It's just weird."

"If you want to join me, let me know soon. I need to book the visit in advance."

I wasn't going to dismiss the option entirely. Perhaps it really would be a positive step to overcoming my fear. "I'll talk to my therapist about it," I said.

"Good idea. Let me know what she says."

After that conversation, I called Lisa Keaton and left a voice message. She got back to me quickly. "It could be good for you, and there's nothing stopping you from leaving the call if you start to feel uncomfortable," she said.

So I gave Bora the go-ahead and a date was set.

* * *

WE WERE PHYSICALLY SEPARATED by thousands of kilometres, yet I still felt sick to my stomach when I saw Oh Sejung on my laptop screen. She sat in a small, windowless room, empty apart from a table and a few chairs. Yang Bora sat near her at the table, and a police officer stood by the wall, watching on with his arms folded.

The connection wasn't great, so the image was a little grainy, but I could still make out the beady, pitch-black eyes on Sejung's sallow face, framed by limp strands of thin hair. A far cry from the Kim Sungmi I used to know. Her current appearance gave me the creeps—she looked like a character straight out of an Asian horror film.

"I didn't expect to see you again until the trial," Sejung said, a sinister smile upon her lips.

I didn't respond. Bora and I had agreed in advance that she would do the majority of the talking. I didn't have much I wanted to say to her.

"It was my suggestion," Bora said. "I wanted to see you, but I thought I should offer Chloe the opportunity to be involved as well."

Sejung lifted an eyebrow. "And why would *you* wish to see *me*?"

"Simple curiosity. I want to understand you, and why and how you do the things you do."

"You'll never understand," she sneered.

"I also have a work-related interest in this case. I'm the manager of an actor, and it would be helpful to know more about people like yourself."

"People like me…" she repeated. "You work at KAM, don't you? You used to be on Shin Jinseung's team."

"Yes. How did you know—never mind. I'm here to question you, not the other way around. So I'll start with this: When did you start stalking Shin Jinseung?"

"I don't like the word stalking."

"When did you start *avidly following* him?"

Sejung hesitated. According to Officer Bae, she had already admitted to her offending, but I wondered whether she would be so forthcoming with Bora's questions.

"Well?" Bora pushed.

"I've been a fan since his debut," Sejung said, apparently deciding she would play along. "When I met him in person at a fan meeting, I became addicted to seeing him in real life. It started after that."

Since we had limited time, Bora moved straight onto her next question. "And how did you learn that Chloe was dating him?"

"I saw Jinseung pick her up in his car. I saw her coming and going from his apartment building. There were rumours online too. I could tell they weren't just friends."

"Why did you start following Chloe?"

"Initially I didn't plan to. Thought I would scare Jinseung into breaking up with her, but then I decided that Chloe would be an easier target. She seemed more vulnerable. Once Shin Jinseung left Seoul, that settled it. I focused all my attention on her."

"I see."

"These questions are boring," Sejung said, crossing her arms and yawning exaggeratedly. "When are you going to ask me something interesting?"

"Then what about how you were able to track Chloe."

Sejung perked up, stimulated by the new question. "A number of means. I've followed her and had her followed. I slipped a tracking device in her bag while she left it unattended—"

This was news to me. "What tracking device?" I interjected, confused.

Sejung laughed. "You still haven't found it? But I suppose that bag has a lot of pockets, and you don't use all of them regularly. I purposely put it in the pocket which looked least used too."

I resolved to check my bag as soon as this meeting was over.

"How were you able to get into Chloe's apartment?" Bora asked.

"Easy peasy. She keeps a diary and has a terrible habit of writing down important private information such as passwords and her door code. I was able to take a peek whenever she left her bag alone—which was quite often. She would leave it in the staffroom at the *hagwon*, or whenever she went to use the bathroom during our tutoring sessions."

I groaned at my stupidity. So much of this could have been avoided if I hadn't been so lax, leaving my bag around and writing things down that I shouldn't have. *I'm never keeping a physical diary again.*

Bora fired her next question at her. "Who threw the vase at Chloe, and how did you arrange it?"

"Paid a guy to do it. I'm not gonna say his name and get him involved. He was just desperate for the cash. I had Chloe walk with me, and the guy was tracking my phone to see when we would pass the building." Sejung smiled brightly as she spoke. She seemed awfully proud of her exploits. "I had only meant to scare her, but I wouldn't have cared if she did get hurt. Maybe that would have been for the best."

Bora winced, the first sign that she was uncomfortable being so close to Oh Sejung, attempted murderer.

"Two minutes," the police officer announced.

She hurried up with her next question. "What exactly were you planning to do after getting rid of Chloe?"

I braced myself, dreading her reply, but Sejung didn't answer. Instead, she turned her attention to me, looking straight down the camera lens. It felt like she was staring directly into my soul. I shivered.

"You know what, Chloe," she said. "You may have gotten away from me, but in the end, I've still won."

"What do you mean?" I asked, voice shaking.

"I succeeded in my goal to tear you away from Shin Jinseung, and that's what really matters." Her sneering, derisive tone made my blood boil, and I clenched my hands into fists. Something in me snapped and I no longer felt scared; instead, a fierce burst of determination sparked within me. I wanted to tell her that she hadn't won. That I was still together with Shin Jinseung and there was nothing she could do about it—but the police officer cut in before I could respond. "Okay, time's up."

The video disconnected, the screen turning black. I was still shaking with pent-up fury. *You haven't won. You'll never win.*

Bora had been right that seeing Oh Sejung would help me. It turned out to be the final push I needed. I spoke to Jinseung as soon as I could get hold of him.

Chapter 42

My life had changed completely and irrevocably since the last time I walked through the arrivals gate into terminal one, Incheon Airport. Yet there I was again, rolling a suitcase over the polished floor towards the crowd of waiting loved ones, under vastly different circumstances than before. I was a little anxious. Bad memories resurfaced about the job scam, and how lost and scared I had been on that first day in Seoul. I reminded myself that was in the past and everything was going to be okay this time. *Deep breaths.*

It had been three months since I announced to Jinseung that I wanted to go back to Korea and continue my relationship with him. Three months of planning, applying for a visa, and waiting for my application to get processed. I had used the time to physically and mentally prepare for my return. Jinseung had also been productive, getting everything in order and communicating his plans with his agency. He had sold his apartment and bought a new house where we would reside away from the city, away from the landmarks of my trauma.

I scanned the faces in the crowd and saw Bong Changsoo. He looked the same as always, tall and pudgy, wearing jeans and a striped shirt. Jinseung had sent him to pick me up since he couldn't meet me himself for obvious reasons—getting mobbed by people who recognised him being the main one.

Despite our tenuous relationship, I was glad to see Changsoo's chubby, unshaven face, and he seemed glad to see me too. He gave me a small wave, and I approached him.

"Hey, Chloe," he said, smiling. "You made it."

"Yup. I'm here. Hopefully for the long term."

"How was the flight?"

"It was great!" I never usually said that about a flight, but Jinseung had insisted on buying me a business-class ticket. I spent the flight in comfort, watching movies and napping interchangeably.

He grabbed the handle of my suitcase. "Let me take that for you."

We headed towards the exit.

"Are you tired?" Changsoo asked.

"Not too bad since I managed to sleep on the plane."

"Ah, that's good."

"How's Jinseung?"

"He'll be so glad to see you. He hasn't been the same man since you left."

A pang of regret hit me. The time apart must have been hard on him. I had been so focused on my own recovery that I had neglected him. I resolved to make up for everything I had put him through.

"I heard that there's going to be a cast reunion for Hidden History," Changsoo said. "Are you going to go?"

"Of course! I wouldn't miss it." An email about it had come through several days ago, and I was so happy that my flight arrived in time for me to attend. I looked forward to catching up with all the actors I had worked with, especially Baek Yena.

Changsoo led me through the massive carpark and located his car among the sea of vehicles. I recognised the black SUV at once. It was Jinseung's car, not Changsoo's. He advised me to sit in the back seat. I wondered why I couldn't sit in the front. Then I opened the door and jumped with shock. There was Jinseung. He had a wide grin plastered on his face, eyes shining brightly below his unruly head of hair. Every cell in my body lit up in his presence. I stared at him, wide-eyed. Seeing him again felt more wonderful than I ever imagined.

"Surprised to see me?" he asked teasingly.

"Jinseung-ah!" I cried, launching myself into his arms. "I wasn't expecting you to come."

"Why wouldn't I? I've been looking forward to this moment for so long. You're finally here!"

I basked in the glorious feeling of his strong arms around me. He stroked my hair and kissed my forehead. "Thank you," he said softly, breath warm against my ear.

"For what?"

"For coming back. For choosing me."

"Thank you for waiting. I'm sorry I took so long."

"You're here now. That's all that matters." He released me from the hug so I could put my seatbelt on.

We couldn't stop looking at each other and grinning as Changsoo drove us away.

"Excited to see my—*our* new place?" Jinseung asked.

"Yes! I've been dying to see it."

He had sent me photos of the house, but I couldn't wait to see it in person. *Our house.* I sat on the edge of my seat the entire trip, barely containing my excitement.

We eventually arrived in an upmarket suburb just out of Seoul. Large, standalone houses with high fences lined the perfectly maintained streets.

"It's on this road," Jinseung said.

Curiosity piqued, I looked out the window, wondering which house was ours.

Changsoo finally turned down a driveway. He used a little remote control to open the tall gate blocking the entrance. It swung open automatically. The house came into view. Not overly huge. Simple and modern with sharp angles and large windows with dark grey frames on a white facade. Tall trees surrounded the edges of the section, providing tons of privacy.

"What do you think?" Jinseung asked.

"It looks fantastic."

"Just wait till you see inside."

When we got out of the car, I heard a yapping sound from near-by. "Is that…?"

A cute white dog came running towards us, tail wagging furiously.

"Oh! Buster!" I said and bent down to pet him when he stopped at my ankles and pawed at my shoes.

"Since I have the space now, I brought him back from Tongyeong. He's going to live with me now."

"Weren't your parents disappointed?"

"Yeah, but he is my dog after all. My parents are getting a new dog and they're pretty excited about it."

"So, I'll be living with Buster too…"

"Is that all right? I wanted it to be a surprise."

"It's great! I love dogs. This is wonderful." I hadn't had my own pet since I was a kid, so I was bursting with joy at this revelation.

"I'll leave you two—*three* to get settled," Changsoo announced, watching on with a grin.

We thanked him and said goodbye. He swapped over to his own car and drove away. Jinseung took my hand and we walked to the front door together, Buster hot on our heels. He pointed out the secu-rity features—an intercom, camera, and alarm. The door was heavy and required a special key that was difficult to copy. The systems in place helped put my mind at ease. I was glad Jinseung had taken this into consideration when choosing the property.

The door unlocked with a clunk. Once inside, I looked around in awe at the place I would call my home. Spacious and light-filled, with walls in neutral tones and squishy new carpet underfoot. There wasn't much in the way of furniture, but I could visualise how it would look with a few tables and shelves, and with art and photographs on the walls.

"I haven't done much to it yet," Jinseung explained. "I thought you would want to help decorate. Make it your own."

"Yes, I would love to." I liked Jinseung's taste in design, but being able to inject some of my own style would make the house much more comfortable.

Jinseung took me on a tour of the rest of the rooms—three bedrooms, three bathrooms, a home office, living and dining area, and kitchen. I had never lived in such a nice place before. I wandered from room to room, the reality still sinking in.

Once my new house excitement began to subside, Jinseung and I settled down in the living room with drinks and snacks to chat and catch up. Buster lay quietly on the rug by our feet.

Jinseung wrapped an arm around me, and the conversation turned from lighthearted banter to something deeper. "You never told me before," he said. "What made you decide to come back?"

I rested my head on his shoulder and sighed.

"You don't have to tell me if you don't want to," he said.

"It's okay. I owe you an explanation."

"No, you don't."

"Well, I want to be honest with you. I want you to know everything."

"Okay. So tell me."

"Part of it was Oh Sejung," I explained. "Even though she's locked up, she looked so smug and happy with herself. Told me that she had succeeded in tearing us apart, and therefore she had won. I was furious."

An angry vein throbbed in Jinseung's forehead. "The nerve of her."

"Right? But I realised that, in a weird way, she was right. If I gave up on our relationship, I was letting her win, and I couldn't stand that thought. So that's one reason."

"And something else?"

"Something that Yang Bora said. She told me that I had made it through the worst thing possible, and that I'd be able to survive anything now. That made me think, why quit now? There will be more hurdles in the future, but I've already made it through the worst part. Things should be much easier from here on out."

Jinseung nodded, a look of understanding on his face. "I get it. Rather than letting yourself be defeated by what happened, you're choosing to become stronger and better equipped to fight the challenges in your future."

"That's a good way of looking at it." I snuggled closer to him. "But I can't deny that a little voice is still there, telling me that I could get hurt again, and making me want to run away and hide. I have to confront that voice every day and put it out of my mind."

"It must be difficult. Will you keep going to therapy?"

"Yes. I'll probably need it for a very long time. Hope I can find a good therapist here."

"Whatever I can do to support you, let me know." He kissed my hand.

I smiled, relieved to be back with him. Everything I had been worried about had melted away, leaving me with a feeling of contentment.

"There's one thing I think we should talk about," Jinseung said, voice turning grave.

My stomach tightened. I already knew what he was going to say, but I still felt wary.

"Word will spread quickly now that we're living together," he continued. "We'll need to come clean about our relationship soon."

We had already discussed this but still hadn't put an exact date on it. "When were you thinking?" I asked.

"As soon as possible. The Hidden History cast reunion is in two days. I thought we could announce it there."

I put on a brave face and nodded. "Good idea."

"So you agree? Are you sure you're ready?"

"I'm ready."

As ready as I'll ever be.

Chapter 43

Tonight is the night. As I stood in front of the bathroom mirror doing my makeup, all I could think about was how my life was about to be plunged into complete and utter mayhem. My hand shook so much that I messed up my eyeliner and had to wipe it off and start over. I was a bundle of nervous energy pumped full of adrenaline. *I won't back out now,* I told myself, determined to face the night ahead with confidence and composure.

We were about to embark on our first official appearance as a couple. From this point on, the cat would be out of the bag. KAM Entertainment had already prepared a statement confirming our relationship to be released as soon as word started to spread.

"Are you nearly ready?" Jinseung called from another room. "The taxi is here."

I quickly finished blotting my lipstick, flung on my coat, and grabbed my purse before meeting him at the door. He eyed me appreciatively. "You look stunning."

I blushed. "Thanks. You look good too. Is that a new shirt?"

He looked down at the rose-coloured shirt he wore tucked into straight black jeans. He looked hot, as usual. "Yeah. You like it?"

"It suits you."

He burst into a smile and grabbed my hand. "Come on. Let's not leave the driver waiting." We walked out to the car.

Stars glittered in the dark sky, soon to be replaced by the bright, multi-coloured lights of central Seoul.

"How are you feeling?" Jinseung asked during the ride.

I ran my hands up and down the top of my legs. "Nervous, excited, kinda nauseous."

He grimaced. "Better not drink too much then. Don't want you to be sick or something."

"I won't."

He rubbed my shoulder. "Just relax and have fun tonight. I don't think anyone's going to be gossiping about us straight away. Most likely nothing much will change—at least for a while."

"You're probably right." I sighed, letting out some of my pent-up tension. "I don't expect the other actors will spread gossip. The staff, though—"

"Yeah. One of them could leak it, but it's going to be okay if that happens. That's exactly what we're prepared for. Bit by bit, we want the secret to come out. That's the whole point."

"True. I guess I'm overthinking things."

For the longest time, I wanted so badly to reveal our secret to the world. Then the kidnapping happened and changed everything. I still wanted to go through with it, but I felt much more hesitant. I reminded myself that I chose to be with Jinseung, and keeping our relationship a secret forever wasn't an option.

We arrived at the restaurant—a trendy little bistro in Apgujeong-dong. A sign on the door read, "Private function". A velvet rope cordoned off the entrance and a guard stood outside.

Heads turned and eyes landed on us when we entered. I recognised the faces of my old costars—Cho Dongjoo and Kim Jaehyun, who played middle-aged residents of the fictional town in Hidden History, Baek Yena, the lead female who played a detective, and several others who played roles as police officers and townspeople. Yena called us over to the table with a grin and shuffled over so there was room to sit beside her. I reminded myself that she was one of the tiny few who already knew Jinseung and I were dating.

"You made it! I was beginning to think you wouldn't come." She poured us each a glass of soju.

"It's called being fashionably late," Jinseung quipped.

"A traffic jam made us late, that's all," I explained.

Kim Jaehyun eyed us suspiciously. "Did you two come together?"

"Yes, we did," Jinseung replied without skipping a beat.

"So you're still in touch with each other then? And very friendly by the looks of it."

Yena scoffed involuntarily. Jaehyun turned to her and raised an eyebrow. She pretended to cough.

"We're actually dating," Jinseung said casually.

He said it before I could even brace myself. A random silence in the room fell just in time for the words to leave his mouth, and now they hung heavily in the quiet air. It seemed like everyone in the restaurant could have heard him.

Yena gasped, bringing a hand to her mouth. "*Omo!*"

"You can drop the act," Jinseung said. "She already knows," he explained to the others at the table.

"How long has this been going on then?" Dongjoo asked with an amused grin.

"Must be over a year now," Yena said. "So it's no longer a secret, I gather."

I nodded. "No longer a secret as of tonight, actually."

Dongjoo slapped Jinseung on the back. "Congrats, man. Wonderful news."

Jaehyun pouted. "It's a pity. I had been looking forward to this evening because I was planning to make my move on Chloe."

"You perv!" Yena shot back.

Jaehyun chuckled. His dirty old man schtick never failed to rile her. "Only teasing," he said to me with a wink.

"This deserves a toast, don't you think?" Yena said. She lifted her glass. "To the first official Hidden History couple!"

Everyone raised their glasses and cheered. I cracked a smile at their enthusiasm while Jinseung beamed and blushed beside me. With step one of our "go public with our relationship" scheme complete, I indulged in a shot of soju. The alcohol soothed my jitteriness and I stopped worrying so much about the future.

We fielded questions for a while, but eventually, everyone's attention moved from us and onto other people present, catching up with each other, chatting about their families and their work.

During a brief moment we weren't occupied in a conversation with other attendees, Jinseung put an arm around me. "This is nice, isn't it? Not having to hide."

I was about to express my agreement when something caught my eye—a sudden flash of bright light. "What was that?" I asked.

"What?" he looked around, bemused. He obviously hadn't noticed, but a few others had. A group went to the window to investigate. More flashes quickly followed.

"Paparazzi," someone said. "They've located us."

Jinseung and I exchanged meaningful looks.

The security guard went outside to try and shoo the paps away. They were resistant at first, but after a while he succeeded in getting them to leave.

"They'll be back," Jinseung said. "As soon as people start to leave, I'm sure they'll swoop in to get their photographs."

"What should we do?" I asked.

He locked eyes with me. "Let's take this opportunity."

I swallowed the lump in my throat then nodded.

* * *

JINSEUNG WAS RIGHT. The paparazzi did come back as the event came to an end and the guests began to exit. The guard had given up trying to get rid of them and shifted his focus to escorting everyone safely from the restaurant into taxis.

"So, you're okay with this?" Jinseung asked again as we prepared to leave.

I nodded. "Yes. Let's do it."

Before I could change my mind, Jinseung took my hand and we walked out of the restaurant together. We faced a barrage of camera flashes. The security guard tried to get us to move on, but we purposefully lingered, letting the photographers get all the snaps they wanted as we held hands. To make the message even clearer, Jinseung kissed me. It took me by surprise, but I went with it, closing my eyes as he pressed his lips to mine. My heart pounded throughout our display and didn't slow down until we were safe inside a taxi.

We looked at each other and grinned sheepishly before bursting into laughter.

"It's going to be fun to read the news tomorrow," Jinseung said, wiping his eyes.

"Fun? That's one way of putting it."

"Not having regrets, are you?"

I shook my head. "You?"

"No. Absolutely not."

"Good, because there's no way we can turn back now."

"I wouldn't want to. I love you, Chloe Gibson, and I want the world to know it."

"I love you too."

He reached over and kissed me again.

The Superstar Scandal

Book 3

Chapter 1

In one swift motion, the attacker clamped his hand around my wrist like a vice. The contact caused a shockwave through my body. I tried to move but my feet were frozen to the ground. Towering walls surrounded me in every direction and I was trapped, helpless, as they started to close in on me.

Then, a voice. Soft at first but becoming clearer.

"You can do it, Chloe!"

Shin Jina?

That's right! The walls crumbled as I hurtled back to reality, remembering why I was here and what I had to do. A spike of adrenaline thrust me into action—a set of moves as practised as a dance choreography.

Step one: I lifted the arm the attacker was attached to and held it upright, palm facing my chin.

Step two: My other hand came up and grabbed him under his wrist.

Step three: I abruptly rotated my hips, breaking his grip.

Step four: I swung my foot towards his groin.

I came dangerously close to actually making contact with his crotch, but he dodged and stumbled backwards, falling on his butt with a smooshing sound on the thick foam mat beneath us.

I did it. I really did it. Maybe I wouldn't have been able to without Jina's encouragement, but still…

Applause and cheers erupted from the group of women around the mat. A surge of pride lit me up. I beamed, chest puffed out, shoulders back.

Damn. That actually felt pretty good.

The attacker got to his feet and faced me.

"Well done," he said with a smile. "You'll get the hang of this in no time. Keep up the good work."

"Thank you, *Seonsaeng-nim*." I tilted my head in polite acknowledgement before stepping down from the mat.

Jina welcomed me back to my spot beside her, grinning. "Yay! You did so well. I'm proud of you."

Despite the active nature of the self-defence class, she was wearing full makeup and was doused in a flowery perfume. At least she had the good sense to wear appropriate clothing—a loose sweater over high-rise leggings. Her hair had grown out of its pixie-cut style, and she wore it pulled back in a tiny ponytail, though many short strands escaped confinement. Despite the messiness of it, she still managed to look super chic.

"Thanks for suggesting this," I said. "It's not easy, but I can already tell that it's going to help me a lot."

Even if I never had to confront a physical attack from one of Jinseung's *sasaeng* fans again, knowing how to defend myself would give me much peace of mind.

We were inside a large Taekwondo studio with white walls and a red-and-blue-squared floor. Various pieces of fitness equipment lined the perimeter, along with wooden cubby holes and a picture of the Korean flag. Squishy foam mats in various colours lay strewn across the floor. The teacher stood in the middle of the largest mat, his arms folded across his chest. He was a small, slim man, but the muscles rippled in his arms, betraying his strength. He had hair down past his ears, and a short, wispy beard. His face was youthful except for his eyes which looked ancient and wise. I had no idea how old he was.

"Who's up next?" he asked, scanning the room.

None of the women made a noise or even moved. Many of them actually shrank backwards, as if to minimise themselves so they wouldn't get noticed.

"No volunteers? Then I'll have to pick someone at random. Hmmm…"

He pointed his finger and moved it in the direction of his gaze around the room, eliciting nervous jolts from everyone it passed.

I placed a hand on Jina's back and gave her a slight nudge forward.

"Hey!" she snapped.

"Come on, *Unnie*," I whispered. "You should have a turn. It will make you feel good. Promise."

She grimaced at her freshly manicured hand. "What if I break a nail?"

"Trust you to get your nails done right before a self-defence class."

She pouted. "I had a standing appointment and left it too late to reschedule. Do you know how difficult it is to get an appointment at Haejung's salon?"

"Jina-ssi, are you volunteering?" the teacher asked, drawn by the noise of our whispered conversation.

She cringed and covered her face with her hands. "No, no."

"He's going to make everyone come up and do it eventually," I said. "Might as well get it out of the way."

"That's right," the teacher said. "Come on up. I don't bite. I *will* grab you, though."

"That's not very reassuring," Jina grumbled. She reluctantly made her way forward.

They stood at opposite ends of the mat, then without warning, the teacher lunged at her. Jina flailed her arms, but he still managed to grab onto her wrist. She let out a high-pitched "Eep!"

"Do you remember what to do?" he asked.

"Uh, I think so." After taking a breath, she proceeded through the practised movements, up to raising her foot to strike.

The teacher had already relinquished his grip. He backed away from her.

"Good. Well done."

Everyone clapped as she hopped down from the mat. She turned to me.

"I was pretty good, wasn't I?"

"Now who's all confident?" I chided.

The same process continued until every student had had a turn. Some struggled more than others, but everyone eventually managed to break free. Many of the women in the class had dealt with physical assault in the past, so I knew better than anyone how difficult this was for them. That's why I yelled my support from the sidelines at the top of my lungs.

"That's it for today's lesson," the teacher said, stepping off the mat. "I'll see you all next week. Keep practising in the meantime."

The students bowed and thanked him then began to filter out of the studio.

Jina dabbed her hairline with a pink hand towel from her gym bag. "Whew. That was a tough sesh. I think we deserve a treat. D'you want to grab a tea?"

"Sounds good."

I'd never turn down an opportunity to hang out with Jina for a little longer.

We threw our winter coats and scarves on over our exercise gear and headed to a nearby bubble tea outlet. The interior had a pastel colour scheme and walls decorated with pictures of its cartoon giraffe mascot. We sat on high stools at a wooden bar by the window, looking out through the rain-speckled glass onto the dreary street.

"How's work going?" Jina asked, sipping her honey milk tea. "You've barely told me anything about what it's like to work at KAM Entertainment."

I shrugged. "What's there to tell? I don't work there much. It's pretty much a ruse arranged between me, Jinseung, and Mr. Kim, to get me a visa. I wouldn't have been able to come back here without it."

"Yeah, but you still get to teach English to Jung Jen and Go Yoojin, right? That must be so cool." She had a dreamy look in her eyes.

"I guess it's pretty cool. Though the dazzle did wear off after a while. Now they're just like regular people to me."

"What's Jung Jen like? I haven't seen much of her on TV since...*you know.*"

Jung Jen had been one of the top actors under management at KAM Entertainment...until she got involved in a big scandal. She got caught dating San Seung, the most popular male idol in South Korea. Then it came to light that she was also dating Lee Changho, his number-one rival, at the same time. There was a huge furore, with fans from both sides turning against her. Her own fans didn't like it either.

Jung Jen's argument was that she was seeing them casually, and that she hadn't agreed to dating either of them exclusively. San Seung and Lee Changho remained tight-lipped on the subject. Neither of them were seen with her again.

While the male idols' entertainment careers continued to flourish, Jung Jen's took a major nosedive, going from lead roles to bit parts at most.

"It's a shame she got so much backlash," I mused, resting my head in my hands. "She's actually a lovely person. I think I believe her side of the story."

Jina swirled her straw in her drink. "Fans can be so brutal."

"Tell me about it." I sighed. "Anyway, what about you? Been getting many modelling jobs lately?"

"I have. Surprisingly."

"Why surprisingly?"

"Well, you know how old I am."

"You're hardly old."

"Old in the modelling world."

"I suppose."

"Just a little while ago I thought my contract wouldn't get renewed, but now I'm busier than ever. I've had to cut back my shifts at the cinema."

"That's good, isn't it?"

"Yeah, I just wonder how long this will last."

"A long time, I'm sure. You're still drop-dead gorgeous, and I don't see that changing anytime soon."

"Really?"

"Absolutely."

My phone dinged, interrupting my little pep talk. I swiped at the screen.

Jinseung: How was the class? When are you getting home?

"Who's that?" Jina asked. *"Dongsaeng?"*

"Mmhmm."

"Meeting's over then?"

His meeting. I had been so preoccupied with the self-defence class that I had completely forgotten. I cringed. "Oh. The meeting."

Jinseung had been on hiatus for the past few months to support me through my recovery, but he still had weekly meetings with Mr. Kim. They always made me anxious for one reason in particular.

"Don't look so worried," Jina said. "I'm sure it's just general admin stuff, as per usual."

"I hope so."

"Finish your tea and go home. I'm telling you it will be fine, but you should talk to him and see."

"Yes. You're right."

I picked up my phone and replied to Jinseung.

Chloe: I'll be home soon. Talk then?

Jinseung: OK. See you soon.

I finished the last gulp of my peach green tea and hopped down from the stool.

"See you at the next lesson." Jina slung her gym bag over her shoulder.

We shared a brief hug before parting.

As I drove the short distance home in Jinseung's car, I couldn't help fixating on the meeting. I had a terrible feeling about it. The meetings were usually on Thursdays, so why was this one on a Tuesday? Something must have been different about it, that was why, and if my suspicions were correct then my life was about to be thrown into turmoil.

Changsoo's work van was outside the house when I arrived. This escalated my fears since he didn't usually stick around after dropping Jinseung home. I parked in the garage and opened the door into the house, a vortex of trepidation whirling in my stomach.

When I entered the living room, I saw Jinseung and Changsoo sitting with tensed-up shoulders and serious looks on their faces. That was all the confirmation I needed.

Chapter 2

Jinseung immediately lit up at my presence, though I could tell his cheerful smile was forced. Changsoo didn't make a similar effort, sitting there with a heavy scowl on his face.

"Hey," I said meekly, approaching.

Jinseung patted the space next to him on the couch. "Hey. How was the self-defence class?"

I swallowed the lump in my throat and sat down. "Good. Difficult, but good. I'm glad *Unnie* talked me into it."

"I'm happy to hear that."

A moment of awkward silence hung in the air. Both Jinseung and Changsoo didn't seem to want the job of bringing it up first, but if I had to wait a minute longer, I'd explode with pent-up tension.

"So, how did the meeting go?" I asked, keeping the tone casual though my anxiety must have been written all over me.

Jinseung's smile abruptly faded. "About that…"

"We need to talk to you about something," Changsoo said, crossing his arms. "Though I'm sure you've already worked it out."

I nodded solemnly, hands clasped together in my lap.

"Mr. Kim wants me to resume a full schedule of work," Jinseung explained, "starting tomorrow."

Just as I feared. Even so, tomorrow was much sooner than I expected.

"We all knew this day was coming," Changsoo said. "It'll be difficult to put it off any longer. It's already been three—almost four months. The fact that we've gotten away with it for this long astounds me."

"Mr. Kim pretty much gave me an ultimatum," Jinseung explained. "Get back to work or else my contract won't get renewed. I haven't said yes yet, but he wants an answer by tonight."

"Surely he should give us more time," I stammered. "There's a lot to consider..."

"I agree, but you know what Mr. Kim is like."

"I...I don't know what to say." My brain was mush. I couldn't process my thoughts.

"How do you feel about me going back to work?"

"Well, not good, obviously."

Jinseung frowned. "I know it will be hard for you. You're still recovering. You still have nightmares, panic attacks..."

I sighed, staring down at my lap. "I suppose you don't really have a choice."

"He'll be forced out of the agency if he doesn't agree." Changsoo glared at me with a look which told me not to screw things up.

I groaned, face in my hands. What could I do? If Jinseung went back to work I'd be left alone for long periods while he went on shoots. I wasn't ready for that, but I couldn't ask him to say no, could I? I'd be asking him to sabotage his career, and I had already done far enough damage as it was.

"*Hyung*, could you please leave us to discuss this in private?" Jinseung asked.

Changsoo's mouth narrowed to a thin line. "Certainly." He stood up, pulled his messenger bag over his shoulder, and closed his coat buttons. "Call me once you've made a decision." He caught my eyes on the way out, sending me a silent warning.

My posture slouched when he left. At least I didn't have to contend with him anymore.

Jinseung moved closer and laid his hand on my shoulder. "So, anything you want to say now that Changsoo's gone?"

"I...don't know." Head bowed, I anxiously twiddled my fingers in my lap. *Mr. Kim wants an answer by tonight.* My mouth was dry. My heart thudded in my chest.

Jinseung silently reached for my hand and stroked it soothingly. The gesture did little to comfort me.

Perhaps I should just be honest. *I don't want you to go back to work yet.* I wouldn't make him say no, I wouldn't give him an ultimatum like Mr. Kim had, but he would be free to make the decision knowing exactly how I felt.

I spoke up. "Jinseung-ah."

"Hmm? What's on your mind?"

"I..." *No. I can't do it. I've already asked so much of him.* "Never mind."

"It's okay, tell me."

I looked him in his deep, dark eyes, trying to work out what he was thinking. "You're going to say yes to Mr. Kim, right?"

He wore an inscrutable expression on his face. Several seconds passed before he nodded slowly.

Chapter 3

A pair of malicious black eyes glared at me, penetrating my soul, filling me with a deep sense of dread. I couldn't move. She had me pinned to the ground, her hands pressed hard on my wrists, sharp fingernails digging in, my back flush with the floor. I thrashed beneath her, completely powerless.

"You can't escape," she said, voice cold and laced with malice.

I opened my mouth to scream but no sound came out.

Her thin lips curled into a smirk. "You will die now."

Pressure built on my neck. Her eyes were blown wide, the pupils dilating as my throat began to constrict. I couldn't breathe. Everything became a blur except the beady pair of eyes, ablaze with determination to end my life.

Wake up. I know this is a dream. Please, wake up.

I tried to wrench my heavy eyelids apart, but they were sealed shut.

Wake up!

With a burst of focused effort, I cracked my vision open a sliver. A battle between the real world and the dream world ensued, flashes of my bedroom interior interlaced with the scene of my ongoing nightmare. The mental tug-of-war continued until I finally awoke with a sharp gasp, snapping into a sitting position, hands grasping fistfuls of the duvet, heart pounding.

The bedsprings creaked and the sheets swished as Jinseung rolled towards me. His warm hand came down on my arm which was clammy with cold sweat.

"You okay?" he asked. "You're shaking."

I couldn't reply until I regained my breath.

"A nightmare," I said at last.

The nightmares were far less frequent these days but just as vivid. Going to bed was a game of roulette—would I have pleasant dreams or nightmares?

Jinseung heaved himself onto his butt and wrapped me in his arms.

"Everything is okay," he murmured, rocking me gently. "Oh Sejung is locked up. She can't harm you. No one can harm you, not as long as I'm here with you."

His words rang hollow despite the sympathy in his tone.

"But you won't be here with me, will you?" I spluttered. "You're going to go back to work, and you'll be so busy that we'll hardly see each other."

Jinseung clenched his jaw and didn't say anything. Spurred by his lack of reassurance, I burst into uncontrollable, heaving sobs.

He tightened his embrace and stroked my hair. "Shhhh."

The truth I had kept pent up inside came gushing out. "I don't want you to go back to work. I want you to stay here with me. It's selfish, I know, but I can't help it. I'm sorry. I'm so sorry."

He wiped my tears. "It's okay. Shhhh. It's okay. I'm glad you told me. You don't always have to put on a stoic front for my sake. I completely understand what you're saying."

"But what will you do?" I choked between sobs. "Are you really going to go back to work?"

"I'll try to negotiate something with Mr. Kim. Maybe we can come to some kind of compromise."

"But you already called and told him yes, didn't you?"

He shook his head. "I had a feeling this might happen, so I said I needed an extension."

I looked at him doubtfully. "That worked?"

"He hasn't given me long, twenty-four hours. I'll meet him again tomorrow evening—tonight, I mean. He wants my final answer then."

"What will you say?"

"If he won't let me continue my hiatus, I'll tell him I don't want to come back to work full-time...a lighter workload...modelling, commercials, nothing more strenuous than that."

I perked up a bit but still had my doubts. "Do you think he'll agree?"

"I don't see why not. He's strict, but I know he doesn't want to lose me. That's why he let me go on hiatus in the first place and why he helped get you a visa. He wouldn't do all that if he considered me expendable."

"Good point."

"Then it's settled. I'll ask to extend my hiatus, and if he says no, I'll try to get him to compromise with part-time work. I know it's not ideal, but—"

I threw my arms around him and kissed him on the cheek. His solution was so much better than I had hoped for.

"No, that's perfect. I couldn't ask for more. Thank you."

"You should've spoken up sooner."

"I didn't feel like I could."

"Please don't feel that way. We should be able to tell each other anything—*everything*. I love you, Chloe."

"I love you too."

He continued to hold me for several minutes, riding out the last soft wave of my sadness. When my eyes and cheeks had dried and my shoulders stopped shaking, he gently let me go.

"I know it's hard, but try to get some more sleep. It's still early. You have teaching in the morning."

I glanced at the digital alarm clock on the bedside table. 3:04 a.m. I lowered myself with a sigh, my head sinking into the feather and down pillow. Jinseung draped an arm over my waist and snuggled against me, his chest to my back. Sleep tugged at my eyelids, but I kept them open, just in case I drifted back into the same nightmare and it continued where it had left off.

At some point, Jinseung rolled away from me and dozed off, one arm curled above his head, the other resting on his stomach. His hair was mussed and his crumpled white t-shirt was askew, half exposing his abs. I watched his broad chest rise and fall in the even rhythm of his breath.

What did I do to deserve a boyfriend as kind and understanding as you?

I resolved never to hold back my true feelings from him again.

My body began to ache. I groaned and turned onto my tummy, planting my right cheek firmly on the pillow. I continued to hold my eyes open, resisting sleep until pale morning light seeped into the room, illuminating the dust particles in the air. Birds chirped in the camellia tree outside the window.

Jinseung awoke with a grunt and stretched his arms above his head. He turned to check the time, rubbing his eyes.

"Good morning," I said.

"Mornin'," he replied groggily. "Did you—" he yawned "—manage to get more sleep?"

I shook my head. "I didn't want to."

"Because of the nightmare?"

"Mmhmm."

He gave me a sympathetic look. "You're gonna be tired today."

"Maybe I'll have a nap when I get back from work."

"Okay. Well, I'm gonna get up now. What about you?"

"I'll get up."

"I can make breakfast while you shower, if you want."

"Yes, please." I pulled back the covers and hopped out of bed, bare feet finding the soft, springy carpet.

Despite my lack of sleep, I felt much better. Talking with Jinseung had settled my fears. He wouldn't abandon me. Everything was going to be okay.

By the time I emerged from the bathroom and got dressed, Jinseung had already set the table and served breakfast—a vegetable omelette with side dishes of rice, seasoned tofu, and radish kimchi. The savoury scent of soy sauce, fried egg, and chilli pepper tingled my nostrils. My stomach growled.

"Wow. What's all this?" I asked.

"Since I might have to work a little bit from now on, and we might not get to eat together as often, I thought I'd make a proper breakfast today. Hope you're hungry."

"You know me. Always hungry in the morning." I grabbed my chopsticks, cut off a small piece of omelette, and tucked it into my mouth. "Delicious!"

Jinseung smirked. "You're easy to please."

"You're a good cook."

"Only you think that."

Buster whined at my heels as I ate, begging for food.

"*Ya!* You've had your breakfast already," Jinseung scolded.

Seemingly chastised, Buster gave up and trotted to the corner where he circled twice then lay down.

When I finished breakfast, I got ready for work.

"Take my car," Jinseung said. "Changsoo will drop me off later."

Since revealing our relationship, I no longer took public transit for fear of getting recognised, so Jinseung let me use his car whenever I needed, and at some point I would probably get my own. I still wasn't used to driving in Seoul, and the icy winter roads were difficult to navigate, but I needed the privacy more than anything.

I took my coat down from the hook by the door and put it on, closing the tie tight around my waist.

"Don't forget this," Jinseung said, coming towards me with my wool scarf.

"Thanks." I reached for it, but he snatched it away.

"Allow me." He stood close as he coiled the thick, warm scarf around my neck. "There. Feeling better today? Any more concerns you wanna share before you go?"

I shook my head. "I think I'm okay. Knowing that you're not just going to give in to whatever Mr. Kim says is reassuring."

"I can't promise anything, but I'll do my best."

I believed him with all my heart.

* * *

THE FIRST TIME I met Jung Jen, I was completely starstruck. She looked every bit as beautiful as I had seen her in countless K-dramas, magazines, and advertisements. She was tall and slender with long, straight black hair and creamy, blemish-free skin. Bright blue contact lenses and soft pink lipstick completed her trademark look. I had hearts in my eyes when I looked at her.

Despite her recent fall from grace, I had still blushed and stammered my way through my first lesson as her English tutor. Since then, I had become used to her presence, and I learned to treat her just like anyone else. Both of us were more comfortable that way.

She entered the lesson room late—as usual, casually dressed in faded black jeans and a baggy sweater, hair thrown back in a messy low ponytail.

"Good morning, Jen," I said in English.

"Good morning, Chloe," she replied with a weak smile, lowering herself into the seat opposite me.

I noticed the dark rings under her eyes, the hollows in her cheeks, and the grey cast of her skin. I didn't ask if she was feeling okay, because I knew she wasn't. A combination of overwork, extreme dieting, and lack of sleep would make anyone sick. Jinseung used to get similar bouts of exhaustion. Even so, Jen looked quite a bit worse than usual. I decided not to push her too hard this lesson.

We started by reviewing the English lines in her latest script. She was playing the small part of a doctor in an ensemble drama, and she had a few scenes with a patient who spoke English. I worked through the lines with her, making sure she understood the meaning of each sentence, then checking her pronunciation.

Going through the script took much longer than I anticipated. Jen kept yawning, she was scatterbrained, and I often had to repeat myself.

"Sorry," Jen murmured as she massaged her temples. "I just can't think today."

"Stressed out?"

"Yeah."

I didn't think there was much I could do to help but offered to lend an ear anyway. "Anything you want to talk about?"

She hesitated. "No."

"Okay. Well, take as much time as you need."

After going over the script several more times, we reached a point where I didn't think I'd be able to squeeze much more improvement from her, so we put it aside.

"How about a listening exercise?" I asked.

"Sure." She didn't sound very enthused.

I couldn't blame her. Regardless, I handed her the sheet of paper with a list of pre-prepared questions. "I'm going to read a short story aloud. I want you to write the answers to the questions, in English. Got it? I'll read the story three times and pause so you have plenty of time to write. On the first read, you can just listen."

"Okay."

Jen chewed the tip of her pen as I read the story. She had a blank expression on her face, and I wondered how much she was taking in. Not much, it turned out. By the end of the third read-through, I glanced at her paper and saw that she had only answered two questions out of ten.

"Could you read it one more time?" she asked.

"Of course."

I cleared my throat and began again. Jen concentrated on the question sheet, her forehead wrinkled from the strain. This time she managed to answer a couple more questions.

I had started going through the answers with her when someone knocked sharply on the door. Her manager, Jeong Daeshim, walked in —a short, stylishly dressed man in his mid-forties. He was neatly groomed and smelled like grapefruit-and-ginger-scented cologne. I didn't like him. Not sure why. Something about him just rubbed me the wrong way. He didn't acknowledge me when he came in, speaking directly to his charge instead.

"Dermatology appointment in fifteen minutes," he said brusquely. "We better get going."

Jen gave me an apologetic look. "Sorry, *Seonsaeng-nim*. I'll see you next time."

"No problem. Hope you manage to get some rest."

This kind of thing happened more often than not. English lessons weren't considered a top priority on the actors' schedules so they usually ended up missed, rescheduled, or cut short.

Jen got up and followed Manager Jeong out of the room, closing the door behind them. I sagged in my chair.

Jen was taking English lessons to improve her chances in getting roles overseas. Her reputation was damaged in South Korea, but in America she could start fresh. Unfortunately, she'd never make any progress in English at this rate. *Oh well.* At least I got to go home early. I packed up my teaching materials and went on my way.

As I walked across the concrete floor of the basement carpark, I didn't realise that someone was following me. I unlocked the car, hopped into the driver's seat, and was in the process of pulling on my seatbelt when there was a sharp rap on the window, making me jump. I let go of the seatbelt in shock and it retracted with a whoosh. *What the heck?* I looked out the window and saw Changsoo standing there. His face was red and shiny with sweat. He was puffing. He must have chased me. What did he want that was so important? I'd never known Changsoo to *run* before. I wound down the window.

"Manager Bong, everything okay?"

"Thank goodness I caught you," he huffed. "Jinseung is on his way for an emergency meeting with Mr. Kim."

I screwed up my face in confusion. "Emergency meeting? Is this about Jinseung going back to work?"

I thought he had twenty-four hours...

Changsoo shook his head.

"Then what?"

"He just received his draft notice."

Chapter 4

I always knew this day would come, but I never expected that it would happen so soon and so out of the blue.

Just like every young man in South Korea, Jinseung would have to serve in the military. And the worst part? There was absolutely no way he could get out of it. End of story. Even famous people had to enlist. The whole dilemma of him going back to work or not was moot. This was worse. Much worse.

I opted to wait at KAM HQ until the emergency meeting concluded. Changsoo had gone in with Jinseung and left me sitting at his desk in an office which smelled of weak coffee and warm printer paper. The framed photograph of him and Jinseung making a heart-sign pose still took pride of place on his neat and tidy desk, now joined by two other similar shots. All of the other desks in the room were unoccupied except for two where a very young man and woman worked. I hadn't seen them before. *Interns?* The pair kept stealing covert glances at me. They definitely knew I was Jinseung's girlfriend.

I caught the young woman's eye and she averted her gaze, blushing.

"Do you happen to know what's going on in the meeting?" I asked her. "I don't know anything except that Jinseung got his draft notice."

She grimaced. "Wish we could help, but we honestly don't know more than that either."

"You're Chloe Gibson, right?" the man asked.

"Yes."

"*Aigoo.* You're so pretty."

"Um, thanks."

I wasn't in the mood for flattery. My head whirred with the consequences of the latest turn of events. Jinseung would be away for around twenty months, leaving me to fend for myself. There would be no one to comfort me when I woke from a nightmare. No one to share the house with so I wouldn't be all alone, feeling paranoid about stalker fans breaking in. No one to notify the police if I got kidnapped again and didn't come home. I knew my fears were irrational, but that's what trauma does to your head. Although I had come a long way in the last few months, I still hadn't fully recovered and wouldn't for a long time yet. I sighed into my hands.

This is terrible. What am I going to do?

I wasn't keeping track of the time, but the painful hunger pangs in my stomach told me it had been hours since Jinseung and Changsoo entered the meeting room with their colleagues and Mr. Kim. What were they discussing that could possibly take so long?

My ears pricked at the sound of movement in the corridor. The office door swung open. I got to my feet as Jinseung, Changsoo, and their cohort entered the room, all of them straight-faced and speaking quietly or not at all.

At first glance, Jinseung looked calm and untroubled, but then I noticed one telltale sign of distress—his tightly clenched jaw, which clenched even further when his gaze met mine. I didn't want to make a scene in front of his colleagues, so I restrained myself from running over to ask all the questions racing through my mind.

Everyone returned to their seats, apart from Jinseung and Changsoo who remained standing. The sounds of typing and mouse-clicking seemed amplified in the otherwise quiet office. A phone rang, but no one answered it.

Changsoo was first to break the uneasy silence. "Why don't I take you two home? I'm sure you have a lot to discuss—in private."

"Chloe has the car," Jinseung said. "I'll drive us home, you take care of things here."

"Right. Call me if you need anything."

Jinseung turned to me. "Let's go."

He didn't say anything else until we sat down in the car. He crumpled in the driver's seat, deflating like a balloon.

"I'm sorry," he murmured. "I thought I had more time. Next year...several months, at least... That's why I never said anything."

"You think I didn't know this might happen? Of course I did. I just didn't want to think about it. I pushed it to the back of my mind."

Jinseung sighed, smiling wearily. "Talk about bad timing."

"Do you have to serve in the army? Can't you do public service work instead?"

I had heard of some men being able to work as public servants if they weren't capable of participating in the army.

Jinseung raised an arm and flexed his bicep. "Look at me. Do you think they'd let me go to waste as a public servant? I'm far too fit and healthy."

"Can't you just, I don't know, get an injury or something?"

Jinseung laughed.

"Hey! I'm serious."

"No. I can't just get an injury or something. How bad would that look?" He abruptly started the engine.

The heater came on, thawing me out. I pulled on my seatbelt. "What did you talk about in there, anyway?"

"Well, my contract is going to expire while I'm away, for one thing."

"Ah. So what's going to happen with that?"

"I'll make a decision when I get discharged. So will Mr. Kim. For now, he wants me to work up until I leave."

I snapped my head around to face him. "What? He won't let you stay on hiatus?"

"No. He was firm about that."

Damn. How could Mr. Kim be so harsh? Expecting him to work, with such limited time to spend with family and friends before joining the military.

"But it won't be too much," he stressed. "I obviously can't take on any big projects at this stage."

Well, that was true, but still…

One question remained. The biggest question of them all. *Do I dare ask?*

I swallowed the lump in my throat and forced it out. "How long until you leave?"

"Four weeks."

I gasped. "Four weeks!"

There's much less time than I thought.

"I'm lucky to get that much notice, to be honest."

I absorbed the news in silence while Jinseung drove out of the carpark. *Four weeks. Just four weeks.* Then we'd be separated for nearly two years. *How am I going to cope?*

Jinseung's gaze flicked back and forth between me and the frost-bitten road, a wrinkle of concern deepening between his eyebrows.

"*Jagi,* don't be sad. I know it will be hard, but we'll get through this. Together. Look at it this way: once it's over and done with, we'll never have to worry about it again."

His calm reason fell on deaf ears.

"Why, oh why did this have to happen now?" I wailed.

"Would it be any easier in a few months or a year's time?"

I opened my mouth to respond but didn't know what to say. He had me there.

"No. It wouldn't," I admitted.

"You see."

It would take a lot more than a few months or even years before I recovered from my trauma—if I ever did. Deep down I knew Jinseung was right. Better to get it over with now instead of living with an undercurrent of low-key anxiety, knowing that he could get sent away at any moment. The twenty months apart would be a short, sharp, shock to the system in the long-term scheme of things. Like a vaccine jab—once taken, I'd be protected.

"I've got an idea," Jinseung said, steering carefully on the icy road. "Why don't you consider going back to the UK while I'm gone? It might be easier—"

My answer came before I even gave the notion a brief thought.

"No. No way. Uh-uh. I'm not going back."

"Okay. It was just a suggestion."

I didn't know why I was so averse to the idea. Perhaps I equated it to a giant step backwards when I wanted so badly to keep moving forwards.

"I'll stay and wait for you here," I said with resolve.

Jinseung smiled, obviously relieved. "Then I'll visit you as often as I can."

"And you'll keep in touch?"

"Of course. One good thing is they're not so strict on phone usage in the army anymore."

"Really? Whew. That's comforting."

We continued our homeward journey, discussing the ins and outs of his pending military service. The more we talked, the more reassured I began to feel. It wouldn't be so bad. We'd chat on the phone every day, and he would visit me whenever he had a break. Twenty months would fly by before I knew it. In the meantime, I had my friends—Shin Jina and Yang Bora. I knew I could rely on them to keep me company and make sure I was okay.

I heard Buster before we even drove into the garage. How could such a tiny dog yap so loudly? He came running to us as soon as we walked in the door. I wasn't in the mood for petting him.

"Shush," I said, lightly batting him away as he pawed at my leg, whining.

I barely made it to the couch before collapsing in a heap.

What an overwhelming day.

Jinseung sat by my side and placed a steady hand on my knee. He said nothing. The lines etched on his face told me he was deep in thought.

It suddenly struck me how self-centred I was being. All I had done was worry and complain about my end of the bargain. What of Jinseung's plight? He'd have to leave his comfortable lifestyle behind for the drudgery of the army. I had heard stories of the hazing that goes on—the harsh treatment of new recruits. I wondered if he would be okay.

"Are you scared?" I asked.

He snapped out of his solemn trance and smiled his usual heart-warming smile, the corners of his eyes crinkling, dimples in his full cheeks.

"No. I'll be fine. If I can survive the entertainment industry, I can survive the army. Don't worry about me. Focus on taking care of yourself."

I had heard that idols and actors usually did okay in the army since they were already highly self-disciplined and used to rigorous training, but I still felt wary. Would he really be okay?

"Hey," he said, shuffling closer to me. "Cheer up. I don't like to see you sad."

"But I'm going to miss you."

"Me too." He lifted my chin and stroked my cheek. "But don't you think I'll look good in army fatigues?"

So this was his tactic for changing the subject and taking my mind off the bad things. The mental image invaded my thoughts before I could stop it. I pictured him in a camouflage uniform, looking tough, strong, and undeniably sexy.

"Now that you mention it, that does sound kinda hot," I said with a smirk.

He grinned. "Oh yeah?"

"I can't wait to see it."

"There, now you're smiling."

My smile turned to a pout just to tease him.

He wasn't having any of it. He grasped my face in his hands, pulled me to his lips, and kissed me roughly. I closed my eyes and let all the unhappy thoughts dissolve as I reciprocated, wrapping my arms around his waist and drawing him closer. He deepened the kiss, tasting my tongue, turning me weak and unable to think straight.

A ringtone suddenly assaulted my ears. I pulled away but Jinseung brought me back to his lips, insistent.

The ringing seemed to last forever, and when it finally stopped, only a few brief seconds passed before it started up again. It was far too distracting to simply ignore.

Jinseung reluctantly broke away, growling in annoyance. He grabbed the offending phone off the coffee table and checked who was calling. "Damn. I better take this."

I presumed it was Bong Changsoo or Mr. Kim calling—but the shrill female voice I heard definitely wasn't either of them.

"*Eomma*, is everything okay?" Jinseung asked.

So, the caller was his mother…

He tensed up in reaction to what she was saying.

"What?…You're in Seoul?…You're coming here?…Now?"

My wide eyes met Jinseung's.

Chapter 5

Half an hour later, Mrs. Woo and Mr. Shin arrived on our doorstep with luggage in tow.

Oh my gosh. Do they plan on staying the night? I tried not to let my horror show. Judging by his grimace, Jinseung was equally concerned.

"My dear son!" Mrs. Woo said, smiling fondly. The tall and elegant woman enveloped him in a hug, bracelets jangling on her wrists.

When she finally let go, Jinseung turned his attention to his father —a kind-looking man of average build, who wore round spectacles which looked far too small for his large face. They nodded wordlessly at one another.

I hid behind Jinseung, but Mrs. Woo's keen eyes found me.

"Chloe, my dear," she cooed. "How lovely to see you again. We haven't seen each other since you visited Tongyeong all that time ago."

"Uh, hello."

Jinseung hadn't told his parents the he was dating me until we had already moved in together, though Mrs. Woo had been suspicious about the nature of our relationship since I met her in Tongyeong. The fact that we were an unmarried couple living together had initially upset her, but she quickly got over it and had since accepted me as her precious son's girlfriend.

Something that Mrs. Woo and Mr. Shin weren't aware of was the kidnapping and attempted murder I had gone through. They knew I had suffered an altercation with a *sasaeng* fan, but that was the extent of their knowledge. I hadn't wanted them to make a fuss over me. We would have to tell them at some point, though, or they would learn the full story from the media once it inevitably got out. *That can wait,* I told myself.

"No need to be shy, dear. Come and give me a hug." Mrs. Woo held out her arms and I awkwardly stepped into her embrace. She smelled strongly of floral perfume. I held my breath to stop myself coughing from the sickly scent.

"*Eomma, Appa,* what brings you to Seoul with so little notice?" Jinseung asked. The tinge of annoyance in his voice went unnoticed by his parents.

"You could say it was a spur-of-the-moment decision," Mrs. Woo said. "We thought it would be a nice surprise."

"Does *Noona* know you're here?"

"Yes, we called her too. She'll come to dinner with us tonight."

Jinseung eyed the luggage warily. "Are you going to stay here?"

"*Aigoo.* What's with all the questions? You have plenty of room, don't you? Your sister doesn't have a spare room and lives with a flatmate, so naturally we should stay with our dear son."

"Naturally," he repeated with a forced smile. "So, how long do you intend to stay?"

"Just a few nights."

A few nights! I thought one was bad enough.

"Won't you invite us inside? It's cold out here." She wrapped her arms around herself and shivered exaggeratedly.

"Of course. Come in and make yourselves comfortable." He stood aside so they could get past.

Mrs. Woo shed her fur coat and I hung it up on the rack of hooks by the door. She studied her surroundings with her nose wrinkled in a mild look of distaste.

"How long have you lived here now? Looks like you could use the help of an interior decorator."

"There's no need. We like it how it is," Jinseung said, brushing her comment off.

Playful barking filled the hallway as Buster bounded towards Jinseung's parents. His tail wagged with furious excitement. He used to live with the couple so no wonder he was so thrilled to see them.

"Buster, my sweet puppykins!" Mrs. Woo bent down and scooped the little ball of white fluff into her arms. She kissed him all over, and he licked her with his tiny pink tongue.

"Let me take your luggage to the spare room," Jinseung said. He relieved his mother of her many bags, most of which were emblazoned with luxury designer logos—Louis Vuitton, Prada, and Gucci.

Not wanting to be left alone with the couple, I took Mr. Shin's single plain black suitcase and followed Jinseung away.

As soon as we were alone in the guest room and out of earshot, Jinseung threw me a look of sympathy.

"I'm so sorry about this."

I drew a weary breath. "Don't worry. It's okay."

It wasn't really okay with me, but what could I do? It would be totally inappropriate to kick them out. Such concepts as filial duty and respecting your elders were a big deal in Korea, and I didn't want to make a bad impression.

Jinseung squeezed my shoulder. "Thanks. I know this isn't ideal. I'll make it up to you. I promise."

"You better," I teased. "Well, at least you get to break the news of your conscription in person now."

"Yeah. I better tell them."

Once we were all sitting down together in the living room, Jinseung brought it up as soon as there was a lull in his mother's constant stream of chatter.

"*Eomma, Appa,* I have something to tell you." He spoke in a neutral tone which gave little away.

Mrs. Woo's face brightened. "Oh, let me guess! You two are going to get married!"

My mouth gaped in shock and I felt my face turn red. *Where did she get that idea from? Wishful thinking?*

"No. That's not it," Jinseung said, unruffled by her outrageous assumption.

"Then…you're going to have a baby? You should get married first."

A baby! It just gets worse.

This time her remark provoked a stronger reaction from him. "*Eomma*! It's nothing like that."

Mr. Shin spoke up, a serious look on his face. "You're going to the army."

At least one of his parents has sense.

Jinseung nodded.

Mrs. Woo's mouth snapped shut, all the brightness fading from her features. "Of course that's it. I should have known."

"I just found out," Jinseung said. "Got my draft notice this morning."

"Well, every man must do his duty. It's about time you went to the army. It will be good for you. Besides, just think how handsome and manly you'll look in your army fatigues!" she gushed, hands clasped together under her chin and a dreamy look in her eyes.

"I hope I live to see the day conscription gets scrapped," Mr. Shin grumbled.

"What are you talking about?" Mrs. Woo said. "The army is an excellent opportunity for young boys to become men. Of course they should enlist."

"You wouldn't say that if women were drafted too."

Mrs. Woo waved her hand and tutted. "Nonsense."

He dropped the subject, unwilling to argue with her. "Have you told your sister yet?" he asked Jinseung.

"No. Not yet."

"You can tell her at dinner tonight," Mrs. Woo said.

"Dinner? Are we going somewhere?"

"I booked us a table at a lovely Japanese place. Since we now have good cause to celebrate, you should eat and drink as much as you want. Our treat, of course." She turned to me. "You've met our Jina, haven't you?"

"Yes. We're good friends, actually."

"Wonderful!"

With a couple of hours left before we would leave for dinner, the four of us filled the afternoon discussing army life. Mr. Shin recounted grim memories of harsh toil and bullying which sometimes bordered on torture. The knot in my stomach tightened with each word.

"Stop it. You're frightening them," Mrs. Woo scolded.

Mr. Shin attempted to ease up on the negativity. "Fortunately, things have improved since then. I'm sure you won't have the same experience as I did. You're a strapping young lad too, so that's in your favour."

On the other side of the coin, Mrs. Woo's memories were rose-tinted and nostalgic. Her days as fiancée to the active-duty solider were full of romantic correspondence and wedding planning, longing for the day that he would return so they could finally marry.

"It was well worth the wait," she said, taking her husband's hand and giving it a gentle squeeze.

The gesture caused Mr. Shin to break into a shy smile. "Knowing you were waiting for me helped me get through it."

At seven o'clock, we piled into Jinseung's car and headed to dinner. Jina planned to meet us at the restaurant.

Haru was not your typical Japanese ramen or sushi joint, but a classy and modern establishment with minimalist decor in subdued tones, soft lighting, and floor-to-ceiling windows providing expansive views of metropolitan Seoul. All around, smartly dressed couples and small groups dined on fancy sushi platters while sipping drinks and making quiet conversation.

A waiter led us to our table—the most privately positioned in the restaurant.

"Nice place," I commented, taking a seat next to Jinseung and opposite Mrs. Woo.

"I dined here a few years ago and have wanted to come back ever since," Mrs. Woo said. "I hope it's still as good as I remember."

Jina arrived and joined us shortly. She looked stunning with her short hair tucked behind her ears, false eyelashes on, and her signature fuchsia lipstick which would look over-the-top on most people yet suited her to a T. Somehow her simple ensemble of slim black trousers and a cream sweater looked ultra stylish. I supposed with her model figure anything would look good on her. She greeted her parents then took a chair at the end of the table.

"It's been a while since we all got together as a family like this," she commented.

"We should do it more often, as I'm always saying" Mrs. Woo said.

"Well, now that we're all here, shouldn't we order soon?" Mr. Shin asked.

Mrs. Woo touched his sleeve. "Aren't you forgetting something?" She directed a meaningful glance towards Jinseung.

He coughed. "Right. Jinseung-ah, why don't you tell your sister the news."

"Oh?" Jina turned to him, brow raised. *"Dongsaeng?"*

"I received my draft notice today," he said.

Her mouth dropped open slightly, eyes widening. "Oooh."

"I'll enlist next month."

"Funny how something so expected can still take you off-guard." She reached out and squeezed his hand. "You'll do great."

He smiled. "Thanks."

"But what about Chloe? And I wonder what will happen with the trial and everything. Will they let you take leave to be a witness, or even just to watch?"

My stomach tightened. The confusion radiating off the siblings' parents was palpable.

"Trial?" Mrs. Woo asked, brows knitted.

An awkward silence descended before Jina gasped and brought a hand in front of her mouth.

Damn. The cat's out of the bag. Now I'll have to tell them...

"Oops," Jina said. The wide-eyed frowny look she gave me said, "My bad."

"Could someone please explain?" Mrs. Woo demanded, eyes flicking between me and her son. "What's this about a trial? And witness? Did something happen?"

Jinseung spoke up before I did. "This is between me and Chloe—"

"It's okay," I cut in. "We should have told them after it happened. I just...don't like explaining it over again."

Recounting my ordeal and having to answer a million questions about it was the bane of my existence. I had already done it enough in my lifetime to be completely over it.

"What is it, dear?" Mrs. Woo asked, face softening into a sympathetic expression.

"I'm not sure this is something we should discuss over dinner," Jinseung said. "Let's at least wait until we get home."

"That sounds fair to me," Mr. Shin said.

Mrs. Woo sulked and pouted but didn't say anything.

"Enough chitchat. I'm going to order." Mr. Shin pressed a button which alerted a waiter that we were ready.

A man in a crisp white shirt and black trousers arrived at our table momentarily. Mr. Shin placed an order for the priciest sushi platter on the menu, along with a vast array of side dishes and some premium-label sake.

Jina leaned in towards her brother, head resting in her hands, elbows on the table. "So, *Dongsaeng*, when will you be having a goodbye party?"

"Hmmm. Haven't thought about that yet," Jinseung said. "Not even sure I will have one."

"Of course you will! You must!"

"That so?"

"You haven't even had a housewarming party yet, have you? You should invite everyone over."

Jinseung rubbed his chin in thought.

"I think it's a good idea," I chimed in. "I haven't even met most of your friends yet. You should introduce me."

We rarely had guests over to the house or visited other people. I think Jinseung was trying to be considerate and not stretch me too much while I was still recovering, which was sweet but a bit unnecessary. I actually wanted to meet his friends.

"See? Chloe thinks so too," Jina said.

A grin spread across Jinseung's mouth. "Well, in that case…"

"You'll do it?"

He nodded.

"Yes! Can't wait. I *will* be invited, won't I?"

"Absolutely."

"And what about your parents? Will we get an invite?" Mrs. Woo asked.

Mr. Shin shot her a warning look. "Don't be ridiculous. He won't want his parents there spoiling the fun."

"No offence, but I think I'll just have my friends over," Jinseung said. "But you're welcome to come and see me off on the day I leave for training camp."

"We wouldn't miss it for the world," Mr. Shin said.

Dishes began arriving at the table, fragrant with the mingling smells of sesame oil, soy sauce, and wasabi.

"Let's eat," Mr. Shin said, grabbing a pair of chopsticks.

I looked over the spread of options, trying to decide what to eat first. Too bad my appetite wasn't all there. My stomach twisted into knots with anxiety. First, the news of Jinseung's conscription and now this. The thought of having to dredge up the details of my horrible experience yet again made me feel sick to my stomach. The feeling only intensified throughout dinner. At one point I had to excuse myself and go to the bathroom, thinking I might throw up. Fortunately, as I leaned over the toilet bowl, nothing came out of my mouth except my heaving breath.

When I emerged from the bathroom cubicle, Jina was standing with her back to the row of basins and mirrors, frowning with concern.

"Are you okay?" she asked.

"It's just…It's been a long day."

That was truth enough.

"Hey, I'm sorry about…you know."

"Don't worry about it. We should never have kept it a secret this long, and it's better they heard it from you than the media."

I leaned over a basin to splash my face with water. Jina held my hair back. The cold water refreshed me.

"Feeling better?" Jina asked.

I dabbed my face with a paper towel. "Yep. Good to go."

I stepped towards the door, but Jina grabbed my arm.

"Before we go back in, I want to give you something," she said.

"Oh?"

She fumbled in her Kate Spade handbag and emerged with something small, wrapped in fuchsia paper that matched her lipstick.

"I was going to give it to you after dinner, but since we're here, might as well give it to you in private."

I took the gift-wrapped object, wondering why she'd buy me something when it wasn't my birthday or any other special occasion.

"What is it?" I asked.

"Go ahead. Unwrap it and see."

Curious, I tore open the bundle.

Chapter 6

I *don't know what I expected but it sure as hell wasn't this.*

"Cool, isn't it?" Jina asked, beaming.

I stared at the object in my open hand. A keychain with two items attached—a mini flashlight and a small spray canister. I had a general idea what it was supposed to be but didn't know the specifics.

"So, er, what is it exactly?" I asked.

"A self-defence kit. The flashlight doubles as a stun gun. The other thing is pepper spray."

"Oh, I see. I thought it might be something like that. Did the self-defence workshop give you this idea?"

"Uh-huh. I asked *Seonsaeng-nim* which one to buy."

A strange gift, but it made a lot of sense. I didn't know why I hadn't thought of it myself.

"Thank you. I'll carry it with me whenever I go out on my own."

"I got one for me and one for Yang Bora too. I'll give it to her the next time I see her."

"She'll love it."

"I know, right? Though I can't help thinking she might be overzealous with it."

I cracked a smile. "I know what you mean. She'd use it without hesitation. Some poor guy might get hurt for no good reason."

"I better tell her to be careful. Come on, let's go back out. They'll start to think you really are sick."

With the kit safely stowed away, I followed her out.

The rest of the dinner carried on without incident. I barely touched the food but hoped everyone was too focused on their own meals to notice.

After Mr. Shin paid the bill, we said goodbye to Jina and left the restaurant.

Mrs. Woo's cheeks were puffed out as if she were holding her breath. She barely lasted one minute in the car before she burst.

"It's the *sasaeng* fan, isn't it? I didn't know you pressed charges. You should have told me, I could have recommended a good lawyer."

"We have a good lawyer, thank you," Jinseung said. "Let's talk about this when we get home." He turned to me and mouthed, "Don't worry."

But I did worry. Very soon I'd have to open up my wound again so they could leer at it. That was what it felt like, anyway.

At home, Jinseung managed to sneak a quiet word with me while his parents were in another room.

"Let me take care of this," he said. "I'll tell them everything while you go and have a relaxing bath then go to bed."

I stared at him in disbelief. He made it sound so easy. Was it really so?

"Go on," he urged. "They'll understand why you don't want to talk about it."

I stood on my tiptoes and planted a kiss on his cheek. "Thank you."

"And I'll tell them not to make a fuss the rest of the time they're here."

"You're wonderful, you know that?"

"Go. Enjoy your bath." He playfully shooed me away.

I didn't feel guilty hiding out in the ensuite bathroom. I felt relieved. *What a crazy day.* I sank into the hot bathwater loaded with epsom salts and tried not to think about the conversation going on in the living room or Jinseung's imminent enlistment. The meditation techniques my last therapist taught me came in handy. Focusing on nothing but my breath, I watched my belly expand and contract with each intake of air. Slowly, I began to relax, my muscles loosening, body slipping further under the water.

I didn't want to come out while Jinseung's talk with his parents was still in progress. I stayed submerged until my skin was wrinkled up like a prune.

Finally satisfied that the talk would be over, I stood up, water dripping off my naked body, and pulled the plug. I dried off in the steamy room and slathered myself in body cream. Before doing my skincare routine, I had to wipe the misted mirror with a cloth so I could see my reflection.

Hair pulled back with a pink bunny-ear headband, I got to work. My regimen had become a lot more extensive than it used to be, thanks to recently implementing the ten-step method.

A plume of steam rushed into the air when I emerged from the bathroom wrapped in a fluffy robe. The bedroom was empty— Jinseung hadn't come to bed yet.

Would it be rude to go straight to bed without saying goodnight to his parents? I contemplated this a moment before deciding that yes, it would be—at least his mother might think so. Just a quick "Goodnight," then I'd disappear to safety again.

I opened the bedroom door and tentatively stuck my head out into the hallway. All was quiet and still. I made my way to the living room, but the lights were off and the curtains drawn. Did they retire to their room? Where was Jinseung?

I walked up the hallway and saw light coming through the open door of the spare room they were staying in.

I'll just walk by and say goodnight.

As I approached, I heard voices—Jinseung and his mother.

"Please, take it," Mrs. Woo urged.

"I don't know," Jinseung said. "Won't *Noona* want it?"

"Don't worry about her. She'll be taken care of as well."

"...Are you sure?"

"It's my mother's ring and I want *you* to have it."

I stopped in my tracks before I reached the door. I didn't mean to eavesdrop, but before I could turn and walk away, I caught a few more words of their private conversation.

"All right," Jinseung relented. "I'll take it."

"Wonderful!"

I quickly tiptoed back to my room.

What did I just hear? My head fell on the pillow. *This is more than I can process right now.*

* * *

AN AWKWARD SILENCE reigned at breakfast the next morning. Jinseung, his parents, and I sat around the table avoiding eye contact as we ate the pastries Mrs. Woo had bought from a nearby bakery. The sounds of chewing food, sipping drinks, and crumpling page turns of the newspaper Mr. Shin was reading filled the void. I noticed Mrs. Woo taking furtive little glances at me. She practically trembled with the effort of self-restraint. I knew it would only be a few seconds before she erupted.

Five...four...three...two...one...

"I can't take this anymore," she snapped.

Here we go.

"Why are we being so quiet?" she asked. "Someone needs to say something."

"*Eomma,*" Jinseung warned.

She ignored him. "Chloe, you poor dear...If I had known...Oh, it just breaks my heart. All that you've been through...We could have done something. If you ever need anything, we are here for you. If you ever want to talk about it—"

"I went through this with you last night," Jinseung said firmly. "She doesn't like to talk about it."

"But I just can't ignore it. I can't."

I knew this would happen if we told them. Mrs. Woo wasn't the kind of person who could just leave things alone, she had to get herself involved. That didn't make her a bad person, but being smothered in pity was the last thing I wanted.

"Thank you for your concern, Mrs. Woo," I said, "but I have all the support I need and I'm recovering well."

"Is that so? What about when Jinseung leaves? However will you cope?"

"I have my friends."

"Friends who will always be available to look after you when you need them?"

"Yes." I wasn't going to let her make me second-guess the quality of my friendships.

"Well, you have us too. Right, *yeobo*?" She tugged her husband's arm.

He glanced up from his newspaper. "Yes," he grunted.

"Thank you," I said. "I appreciate that. I'll let you know if I need anything."

Mrs. Woo shook her head and clucked her tongue. "You poor, poor thing…"

Oh, great. Was the rest of their stay going to be like this? If so, my patience was going to wear through very quickly.

When we had finished eating, I took the dishes to the kitchen just to get away from everyone. Jinseung followed me inside and massaged my shoulders from behind as I rinsed the plates.

"I'm so sorry about my mother," he said. "She can't help it."

"I know she's just trying to be nice, but…Just how long are they planning to stay?"

"I'll tell them I'm going to be too busy to spend any time with them, so there's no point staying very long."

"Do you think that will dissuade them?"

"I'll put my foot down if I have to."

I bent over and put the dirty dishes in the dishwasher.

"Changsoo *Hyung* will be here in a minute," Jinseung said.

I straightened and faced him. "Are you going to work?"

"Yes. Like I said, Mr. Kim wants me to work up until I leave, and I should at least go in today and find out what he's planning for me.

Not too much can get arranged at this late notice. It's not like I'll have to be out on shoots all day or something."

"I suppose that's okay."

As much as I hated it, perhaps seeing less of Jinseung in the lead-up to his departure would help ease me into daily life without him. Or that was how I justified it to myself, at least.

"I know it's not ideal," Jinseung said, caressing my cheek. "I'd like to spend as much time with you as possible before I leave, but I don't want to argue with Mr. Kim and find out that I no longer have an agency when I return."

"I do understand. Just…please don't take on too much."

"I'll do the minimum required. Enough to keep Mr. Kim happy, and that's it."

The rumble of a car engine outside pulled my eyes to the window. Changsoo's work van rolled up the driveway.

"He's here," I said.

"Then I better get going."

We emerged from the kitchen. Mr. Shin was still absorbed in his newspaper. Mrs. Woo looked at us expectantly.

"Are you off somewhere?" she asked.

"I need to go into KAM," Jinseung replied.

"And leave us alone here? The whole point of coming over was to spend time with you. I thought you were on hiatus?"

"Not anymore. If you had given me notice of your visit then maybe I could have arranged something."

Mrs. Woo hung her head and let out an over-the-top sigh. "What will we do? Our trip is spoilt."

Mr. Shin folded his newspaper in half. "Don't be so dramatic. I'm sure we can find something to do. We're in Seoul, after all."

Mrs. Woo suddenly lifted her head, face brightened by a spark of inspiration. "Oh, I know! Chloe, let's go shopping together."

I shot Jinseung a panicked look. No way could I survive a day being dragged around expensive shops with his high-maintenance mother.

"Uhh..." Jinseung flicked a nervous glance back and forth between us.

Changsoo honked the horn outside, making my chest jump. I had forgotten he was already here.

"Why don't you come to KAM with me?" Jinseung asked her. "I'm sure someone can give you a tour. You've always wanted a tour of my workplace, haven't you? Potentially spot some of the other talent..."

This idea seemed to pique her interest. Her thin eyebrows shot up, mouth forming an O shape. "Well, I wouldn't say no..."

"Sounds good to me," Mr. Shin said, abandoning the newspaper and rising to his feet.

Whew. Nice save.

Changsoo knocked on the front door now. Jinseung normally didn't make him wait this long.

I answered the door while Jinseung and his parents got ready to leave. Changsoo stood on the doorstep, poking his head in, forehead furrowed in curiosity.

"Is something going on?" he asked. "There's another car here."

"His parents are here," I explained.

"Ohh..."

"They'll be with you in a minute."

He cocked a brow. "They?"

"Yeah...He kinda told his parents they could have a tour of KAM HQ."

"He *what?*" Changsoo threw his head back in disbelief, hands clenched into fists at his sides. "I s'pose I'll have to be the one to arrange this tour," he grumbled.

"Sorry, Changsoo-ssi, but someone needs to keep them entertained. Better you than me."

"*Aigoo...*"

Chapter 7

Two days later, Shin Jina and I said goodbye to Mrs. Woo and Mr. Shin. Jinseung was at work, so Jina had come over in his stead. She had also spent the previous day with her parents, kindly taking them off my hands.

The sky was overcast and misty rain wet us as we helped load her parents' luggage into the back of their car.

Mr. Shin closed the car boot with a thunk when we were done.

"Take care," he said, bowing his head to each of us in turn. "We'll meet you in Hwacheon County next month to see Jinseung off to the training centre." He removed his glasses, wiping a speck of rain off the lens with his coat sleeve.

"Goodbye, my darlings!" Mrs. Woo said, eyes shining with dramatic tears. She hugged each of us, lingering on me in particular.

"You poor dear," she repeated for the millionth time. I wondered if she'd always call me that from now on.

"Let's go," Mr. Shin said, opening the car door.

Mrs. Woo slowly backed away from us with a melancholy smile. Jina and I stood on the doorstep waving them goodbye. I held my breath until the iron gate clanged closed across the driveway exit and their car disappeared down the street. My shoulders drooped with the release of pent-up tension as I exhaled.

Jina chuckled. "You look relieved."

"I admit I am."

We went back inside, closing the door on the gradually worsening weather.

"I'm not used to surprise visits," I said.

"Sorry they imposed on you like that. If I had known, I swear I would have warned you."

"Don't worry. It wasn't too bad. Thanks for looking after them yesterday. You really saved me."

"No problem. They're my parents, after all. Now, since I'm here, let's talk party arrangements." She rubbed her hands together with glee.

"Party arrangements?"

"You know, the housewarming-slash-goodbye party. There's so much to organise—the guest list, food, music, security…"

"I haven't even thought about it yet."

"*Dongsaeng* isn't going to have time to plan it himself, is he?"

"Of course, you're right. I'll have to plan it."

"And I'll help you!"

"Thanks. Event planning isn't really my forté."

"Well, I looove planning parties. Let's start brainstorming some ideas, shall we?"

"Okay."

We moved to the living room. Jina took a sparkly pink notebook and pen from her bag which she had tossed on the couch.

"Before we get started, want something to eat?" I asked.

"I *am* feeling a little peckish. Anything's fine."

On my way to the kitchen, I checked my phone to see if Jinseung had answered the text I sent him a while ago. Still no reply. I sighed and slipped my phone back into my pocket. After months of Jinseung's hiatus, I had almost forgotten what it was like to be unable to contact him. Oh well, at least he *would* come home. All of his upcoming activities were based in Seoul, so I wouldn't have to spend any nights alone.

I scoured the pantry shelves for snacks and emerged with a packet of honey butter chips then grabbed two cans of Diet Coke from the fridge.

When I returned to the living room, Jina's head was bent down as she furiously scribbled in her notebook. I placed a small wooden bowl on the coffee table. The packet rustled as I poured the chips in.

"What are you writing?" I asked.

"Names of some people I could contact about music and catering."

"Good thing you know so many people."

As I sat down next to her, my phone pinged. *Jinseung?* I checked it again.

Bora: Hey, Chloe. Thought you'd want to know that the press release is out.

Intrigued, I clicked the link she sent. A web page loaded.

"Here it is," I said, registering the subject of the press release.

"Here what is?" Jina glanced over my shoulder.

"KAM has sent out the press release about Jinseung's conscription."

I read it aloud. "'Hello from KAM Entertainment. Today we confirm that Shin Jinseung has recently received his draft notice and will be enlisting as an active-duty soldier to fulfil his obligation as a male citizen of South Korea. There will be no public send-off as per Jinseung's request for privacy when he enters the training facility on the twenty-third of March. We ask for your patience during Jinseung's absence from all promotional activity until he returns from military duties. Please wish for Jinseung's safety and personal growth during his time with the military. Thank you.'"

"So, we can talk about it freely now," Jina said, reaching a manicured hand into the chip bowl.

"Yeah. As long as we keep the time and location of his entry to the training centre under wraps."

"That goes without saying. Now, back to party planning. Let's make a checklist of all the things we need to organise."

"Sounds good."

We got to work. Thank goodness I had Jina's help, because this would be a much bigger party than I had ever organised before.

After a couple of hours, the sun began to set underneath thick grey clouds.

"I better get going," Jina said, checking the time. "I'm meant to be going out with Scarlett for dinner tonight."

"Your flatmate?"

"That's the one."

"I see. Well, thanks for all your help today."

"You're welcome. I'll be in touch with more party ideas as they come up." She wound a pink cashmere scarf around her neck and grabbed her bag. "See ya, Chloe."

"Wait, have you got an umbrella? Looks like there's gonna be a storm. Maybe I should give you a ride?"

"Don't worry about me. I've got an umbrella and I'll catch a taxi. Oh—is that a car coming up the drive?"

We turned our heads to the window. Sure enough, Changsoo's van had entered the gate. The automatic light turned on outside the house, illuminating the driveway.

"Nice timing," Jina said. "I'll ask Manager Bong if he can drop me off."

She bounded to the front door. I followed. A blast of frigid air swept inside.

Jinseung was halfway out of the van when he paused, seeing his sister emerge from the house.

"*Noona*, you're here."

He was wearing makeup. Must have come straight from a photo shoot.

"Yep," Jina said. "Keeping your girlfriend company."

"Are you leaving? Why don't you stay for dinner?"

"Can't sorry, I'm meeting Scarlett."

"Oh. Maybe next time." He closed the van door.

Jina tapped on the driver window. Changsoo wound it down a smidge.

"Are you heading back to town?" Jina asked.

"Yes," Changsoo replied impassively.

"Can I have a ride, Changsoo *Oppa*? Pretty please." She fluttered her false eyelashes at him.

A snicker escaped my mouth. If she thought flirting with Changsoo would work, she was sorely mistaken. That man was totally immune to womanly charms.

"Go on, *Hyung*," Jinseung said. "It's going to pour down any minute."

Changsoo relented. "All right. Get in." He brusquely gestured to the passenger seat.

"Yuss!" Jina hopped inside the van.

Lightning flashed in the sky. We didn't linger outside. As soon as I shut the door, heavy rain started to pelt down and thunder rippled through the atmosphere, making the walls vibrate.

Jinseung headed straight to the living room couch where he slumped with a groan of exhaustion, his coat and scarf still on. I came to his side and gently helped him remove the excess clothing, which I folded and placed on the adjacent armchair. He wore a silky, black shirt and tight, black jeans underneath. His fingers were decked out with rings of various thicknesses and colours, and chains hung around his neck. The flashy outfit wasn't his normal style, so it must have been what he wore for the shoot.

I didn't bother asking if he was tired—that much was clear. Even under the heavy makeup I could see the shadows below his eyes.

"Three months off work and I seem to have lost all my stamina," he growled into his hands. "All I did today was photo shoots for the fan meeting merch and I'm exhausted."

"What else is on your schedule?" I asked.

"Apart from the fan meeting, let's see…I'm going to have a variety show appearance, a magazine interview, and I'm going to be a guest DJ on NCD Music…and probably some other things I'm not aware of yet."

"You work so hard," I murmured.

I wasn't crazy about him spending so much time working in the lead-up to his departure, but I understood he had little choice in the matter.

Another thunderbolt pierced the sky, lighting up the living room like an X-ray. A fresh downpour pounded on the roof and windows.

"Romantic, isn't it?" Jinseung said.

"The storm? Only when I'm safe and warm inside with you."

"Come here." He beckoned me to his open arms.

I enthusiastically obliged.

"Thanks for putting up with my parents," he said, hugging me and stroking my back, "and for being so good about everything else."

"I've even surprised myself how well I'm holding up," I admitted.

"You need to give yourself more credit." His hand travelled from my back, up my side, and to my cheek, which he gently caressed. "I'm so lucky to have you."

I basked in the warmth of his affection. Once upon a time I doubted his love for me, and now I couldn't fathom why I ever felt that way.

He took my hand, guided it to his lips, and kissed it. Just this small action had me release a little sigh of pleasure. Spurred on, he pressed his lips to the inside of my wrist, then, pushing my sleeve up, to the underside of my arm, and in the crease of my elbow, which was surprisingly sensitive.

"Oh," I mumbled.

"Do you like that?"

"Y-yes."

He pressed another kiss into my elbow, this time sucking and biting a little. I squirmed in my seat. This was driving me crazy.

"Chloe," he rasped. "Let's go to bed."

Chapter 8

Jinseung's best friend, Young Jae, had a wicked grin on his face as he held an electric razor above Jinseung's head.

A mixture of laughter, gasps, groans, and cheers filled the room, blending with the music pumping from the sound system. One of the groans came from Yang Bora, who stood next to me, watching on with trepidation.

"I can't look," she said, lifting her hands to shield her eyes.

"I'm sure it won't be that bad," I consoled.

Jinseung had worn very short hair for his role in Hidden History, but this would be even shorter. The shortest it had ever been. I wasn't worried, though. He would always look good to me—short hair, long hair, no hair.

It was the night of the farewell party for Jinseung, and shaving his hair off was the main event. He sat on a chair in the middle of the living room, a sheet draped around his shoulders to keep the hair off his clothes. The carpet would inevitably get messy, but a vacuum cleaner stood nearby at the ready.

The audience's anticipation intensified as Young Jae flicked the razor on, emitting a loud buzzing sound. He brought it closer to Jinseung's head. Bora took a sneak peek then quickly re-covered her eyes.

"Just tell me when it's over," she said.

The first tuft of black hair fell to the floor.

Then another.

And another.

Soon enough, hair was flying everywhere.

Young Jae chuckled away with a look of pure delight. Meanwhile, Jinseung grimaced, eyes clenched shut, hands gripping the sides of the chair. Perhaps he didn't trust his friend not to cut him or do something else stupid, like shaving a pattern into the back of his head. Seemed like the kind of thing Young Jae would do based off my first impressions of him.

After a while, there was more hair on the floor than on Jinseung's head. A few more strokes with the razor and the haircut was over. Young Jae turned the razor off. Military buzz cut complete.

Jinseung's boyish good looks had disappeared along with the hair. He looked much older now. Older, but no less handsome. I didn't mind the new style at all. The less hair he had, the more his impressive facial features stood out. He looked sexy.

"Is it over?" Bora asked, lifting a finger so she could peek through her hands.

"Yep."

She slowly lowered her hands and fully opened her eyes. She frowned at the sight of him. "Poor Jinseungie!"

"Come on. It's not that bad!"

"You know how I feel about his hair!"

"Yeah. You're weirdly obsessed with it."

"I just like his usual image. That so bad?"

Another one of Jinseung's friends held up a mirror. Jinseung examined his reflection. He eased up, apparently satisfied with his new look. He fist-bumped Young Jae.

"Thanks, man. Looks good."

Bora could barely look at him. "Ugh. I need a drink."

"I'll have one too," I said.

We walked to the kitchen. There were two staff waiters circulating the party, but food and drinks were mostly self-service, laid out on the kitchen island and stored in the fridge.

"What would you like?" I asked.

"Anything. A beer, maybe."

I grabbed two cans from the fridge and two clean glasses which were set out atop the bench.

While I poured our drinks, Shin Jina walked into the room. She approached the island, reaching for an open bottle of sparkling wine to refill her empty glass.

"Hey, guys," she said. "What you think of the buzz cut? Looks smart, doesn't it?"

"All his cuteness is gone," Bora complained.

Jina scoffed. "You would say that. What about you, Chloe? Your opinion matters most out of all of us."

"Well, I think it looks quite good, actually," I said. "He has the head and face structure to pull it off."

"I agree. He suits his hair in any style. Did you know that as a kid, he went through a phase of really long hair? He looked like a girl."

"Really? I would've liked to have seen that."

"I'm sure my parents have photos. Next time you visit them, ask to see an album."

"Ha! I might just do that."

"*Dongsaeng* will be so embarrassed. Tee hee."

"Won't there be embarrassing photos of you in there as well?"

"Oh yeah. Didn't think of that! I don't mind if you see them, though."

As we chatted in the kitchen, a male guest whom I hadn't been introduced to sidled up to us.

"Hey, girls, what you drinking?"

He seemed a little out of it, whether from alcohol or something else. I didn't like his vibe.

"The drinks are in the fridge," I said simply. "Help yourself to whatever you want."

He ignored me and focused his attention on Jina. "So, *Noona*, Dowoon tells me you're a model."

"Uh, yeah."

"I've always wanted to hook up with a model."

She screwed up her face in distaste. I was equally grossed out by him. *Who even says something like that?*

"Wanna go somewhere?" he asked, seemingly oblivious to Jina's discomfort.

"Can't you see she's in the middle of talking with her friends?" I shot back.

"Whatever," he grumbled.

"Hey, *Unnie*, let's go." I pulled her and Bora away with me towards the hallway. I took them to my bedroom, closed the door, drew the curtains, and turned on the lamps by each side of the bed. Now we could drink and chat in peace.

"Thanks, Chloe," Jina said.

"Who invited *him?*" Bora asked. "What a loser."

I shrugged. "Don't know. Jinseung wrote the guest list, but surely that's not one of his friends. He has better taste than that."

"He mentioned Dowoon," Jina said. "Maybe Dowoon brought him here."

"Should've stipulated no plus-ones." I sighed.

Too late now. If he kept behaving badly, I could ask the security guard to kick him out of the party.

The three of us sat on the bed together, sipping our drinks.

"It's funny," I mused. "Part of the reason we planned this party was so I could meet Jinseung's friends, yet I've spent most of it hanging out with you two."

I wasn't complaining. Jinseung had taken his time introducing me to everyone, but it had been overwhelming, surrounded by all these celebrities and cool and fashionable people, so I gravitated back to Jina and Bora.

"You can go back out there, if you like," Jina said. "Don't worry about me."

"Nah. I'm enjoying myself. You guys are the only company I need."

"What about *Dongsaeng?*"

"I'm sure he just wants to catch up with his friends. It's been a while since he's seen them."

I didn't think he would miss me. We had been lavishing each other with attention every spare moment over the last few weeks. Now he had time to focus on his friends for once.

Jina held her head in her hands, elbows propped up on the plump pillow in her lap. "Just over a week to go…"

"I know. Don't remind me. I'm kind of dreading it."

"Still feel scared to be on your own after what happened?"

I nodded.

"You know, you can always rely on me and *Unnie*," Bora said. "If you ever have flashbacks, start to panic, or anything at all, let us know and we'll do whatever we can to help you. Just 'cause Jinseung's not around, doesn't mean you have to go through this alone."

"Awww. Thanks, guys. It's not just that, though. I'm also worried about Jinseung. I'm scared about the abuse that goes on in the army, scared that he'll actually have to fight…"

"I know what you mean. I'm scared about that too," Jina said with a frown. "But we shouldn't underestimate him. He's smart, fit, and strong. If anyone can survive the army, it's *Dongsaeng*."

"*Unnie's* right," Bora said. "He's tough, physically and mentally. Besides, he wouldn't want you to worry about him. He'd want you to focus on taking care of yourself."

I cracked a faint smile. "That's exactly what he said."

"See? Don't worry so much. Let's all take care of each other while he's gone."

"Agreed," Jina said.

Their little pep talk really did make me feel better. I was so glad to have them on my side.

"Thanks, guys. You two are the best."

They beamed at me, blushing slightly from both the compliment and, I suspected, the alcohol.

"Shall we head back out to the party?" I asked, grabbing my drink off the bedside table.

"Wait—" Jina said. "There's one thing I wanna ask while we're here in private."

I paused. "Okay. What is it?"

"Has *Dongsaeng* been acting strange or anything lately? Like he's got some kinda secret?"

"No. Why?" Now I was intrigued.

"Well…" She suddenly became reluctant to spit out whatever she was going to say.

"Well?" I repeated.

"Oh, never mind. It's probably nothing. I shouldn't have said anything."

"Come on. You have to tell me now."

"You've got me curious too," Bora said. "Tell us."

With a little cajoling, Jina relented. "Okay. This is kinda silly, but I've been thinking about how my father proposed to my mother just before he entered the army. It made me wonder if *Dongsaeng* might be planning something similar."

My eyes widened. "You mean…do I think he's gonna propose?"

The thought had occurred to me. Mrs. Woo had given him a ring, after all. I just hadn't wanted to jump to conclusions, nor did I even think I was ready for such a big step in the first place. I doubted Jinseung was either.

"I know, it's silly," Jina said. "That's why I didn't want to say anything."

I rubbed my chin in thought. "We haven't been together that long. I can't imagine him making a big move like that."

"Yeah," Bora agreed. "And why would Chloe know anything if he was planning to do that? Maybe you should ask him yourself if you suspect something."

"Nah," Jina said, shaking her head. "We're not that close. He wouldn't tell me. None of my business, anyway."

I didn't tell them about the conversation I overheard in the spare bedroom. I wasn't even supposed to know about it.

"Let's go back out," Jina said. "He's probably wondering where we all disappeared to."

"So will Dowoon's friend," Bora commented. She stuck out her tongue and made a face like she was going to puke.

"It'll be okay," I said. "If he tries that again I'll get him kicked out."

Back in the living room, the party was still in full force—music blasting, lively chatter, the sound of drinks being poured and snacks being munched on.

"I've been looking for you," came a voice behind me. Not Jinseung —his friend, Young Jae. *Why would he be looking for me?*

"Oh. I was just with my friends in another room," I said casually.

"Wanna go outside for a minute and talk?"

"Um…"

"I feel like we should get to know each other a bit better. You're my best friend's girlfriend, after all."

"Sure, why not?"

Separating from Bora and Jina, I grabbed a jacket from the coat rack by the front door then met Young Jae out on the deck. The pretty garden was bathed in moonlight. It felt secluded, tucked away from the street behind tall zelkova and maple trees.

"Mind if I smoke?" he asked, pulling a pack of cigarettes from his jeans.

"Go ahead."

He lit up. The end of his cigarette glowed orange-red in the night air.

Young Jae was an attractive guy. Same age as Jinseung. He had a bulkier physique and an edgier appearance overall, wearing a baggy white t-shirt over his low-riding jeans, his hair dyed brown and spiked up a little, a tattoo on his arm, and a pair of gold earrings in his ears.

"So how'd you and Jinseung meet?" he asked. "I've heard his perspective, now I wanna hear yours."

I told him my story—how I came to Seoul to teach English but ended up acting in Hidden History instead, how Jinseung took me under his wing, and how we became friends, then more than friends. One thing I left out was the whole saga involving Oh Sejung. As always, it was something that I didn't want to dredge up again.

"Jinseung said pretty much the same thing," Young Jae said, taking another puff on his cigarette.

"And what about you? How do you know Jinseung?"

"We did idol training together. For a while I thought we were gonna debut in the same group, but Jinseung ended up getting dropped at the last minute."

"Wait—are you an idol?"

"Nah. Well, I was one, briefly. A rapper. The group wasn't successful. We disbanded after one album."

"Oh. That's a shame. What was the group called?"

"X-Tream. You wouldn't have heard of it. Like I said, we weren't successful. Jinseung was lucky he didn't end up in the group. Took an acting opportunity instead and look how well that turned out."

"So, what do you do now?"

"I'm still a musician, but I'm in production now. Sound mixing and all that."

"Sounds cool."

"It's a pretty sweet gig. I get to work with a lot of top groups."

"You must get to meet idols all the time then. I'm jealous."

"I'm sure you've met a few famous people too. Some are even at this party."

"Yeah, that's true."

Young Jae leaned back against the wall, exhaling a cloud of smoke.

"Have you done your military service yet?" I asked.

"Uh-huh. Ages ago. I enlisted after X-Tream split up."

"How was it?"

"After the stress of trying to make it as an idol, it didn't feel that bad in comparison. Not everyone has such an easy time of it, but Jinseung should be fine."

"Ah. That's good to know."

"Worried about him?"

"Of course. How could I not be?"

Young Jae grinned. "Must be nice to have a girlfriend to worry about you."

"Are you single?"

"Yep."

"I'm surprised. I would've thought a guy like you would be popular with girls."

Young Jae smirked. "You could say that. Unfortunately the kind of girls that like me aren't the ones I want to date anymore."

"Why not?"

"Well, this might sound kinda lame, but—" He shuffled awkwardly on his feet. "I'm looking for something authentic. You know what I mean. The kind of connection you and Jinseung have. Seriously, I've never seen him so in love."

I blushed so hard I felt sure he could see my red cheeks even in the dark.

"Jinseung is a lucky guy," he said.

"I'm just an ordinary girl. What's so special about me?"

"The fact that you would even say something like that, for one thing."

"There are plenty of girls out there like me. You just need to expand your horizons."

"Is that so?" He said it more like a statement than a question.

A chill wind suddenly picked up. Young Jae noticed me shiver in my jacket. "You're getting cold. Go back inside if you want."

"I think I will. It's been nice chatting with you."

"Hey, can I give you my number? So you can call me if you need anything while Jinseung's away."

"Sure. That's so nice of you. What's your number?"

The more allies I had during Jinseung's absence, the better.

I typed his number into my phone as he said it aloud.

"Thanks," I said. "Well, see you around."

"See ya. I'll tell Jinseung I approve."

"Approve?"

"Heh. Never mind." He lit up another cigarette.

The front door swung open. I could hear a commotion from the hallway. Young Jae and I exchanged confused looks. Someone got shoved out of the door. Dowoon's friend—the guy who had made that inappropriate comment to Jina.

"It was an accident!" he wailed, squirming and clutching at his nether regions, practically in tears.

Jinseung cut an imposing figure, arms folded across his chest, dark eyes glaring with fury.

"You groped my sister's butt by accident?" he spat. "I don't think so."

"Is everything okay here?" The security guard stationed outside, tall and broad, wearing all black, approached the scene.

"This guy's just leaving," Jinseung said. "Right?"

The man briefly considered his options before turning his back on Jinseung.

"Fine!" He marched away in a huff. "Your sister's not so hot, anyway."

Jinseung swore after him.

Young Jae and I approached the open door where Jinseung continued to stand, seething with rage.

"Is *Unnie* okay?" I asked.

"Yeah. She had the good sense to kick him right in the nuts as soon as he copped a feel."

Young Jae winced. "Ouch."

"He deserved it."

"Wow. I can't imagine her doing that," I commented. "Those self-defence classes have really come in handy."

Chapter 9

If the weather could match my mood, it would be gloomy, dark, pouring with rain. The weather gods had other plans, however.

Glorious sunshine descended from the heavens. Birds twittered in the trees and puffy white clouds like candy-floss drifted across the azure sky. The grass was lush and bright green, glistening with dew. Plump-budded plants threatened to burst into flower at any second.

Too bad I couldn't appreciate the beauty of my surroundings. All my effort went towards stopping myself from breaking down in tears.

The congregation in front of the training centre entrance in Hwacheon County, Gangwon Province, consisted of a small number of Jinseung's colleagues, friends, and family. No media present—the time and exact location of the gathering had been a closely guarded secret.

Jinseung, dressed casually in sweatpants, hoodie, and a puffer jacket, mingled and took photographs with his group of close companions. I wanted to be glued to his side but had to give him space so he could properly say his goodbyes one-on-one with each member of the congregation. Jina stayed with me instead.

"This doesn't feel real," I lamented. "I can't believe he's leaving today."

"Me too," Jina said. "It happened so fast. He seems cheerful, at least."

"I'm sure he's nervous on the inside."

"I'm sure you're right." She sighed wistfully. "It's a shame Yang Bora couldn't come."

"I know. Too busy with work. She did call him and said goodbye on the phone, though."

"Sweet of her."

I watched Jinseung talk with his parents, exchanging plenty of hugs and kisses. When he brushed a hand over his eyes, I knew that he was crying. My heart lurched.

"Want a tissue?" Jina asked, holding out a small packet.

"Yes, please." I grabbed one and wiped my eyes.

"You can have the whole pack. Plenty more where that came from."

"Thanks. Should've brought my own supply. Wasn't thinking."

Changsoo offered to take a photo of Jinseung with his parents. The trio arranged themselves in front of him—Mr. Shin on the left, Mrs. Woo on the right, and Jinseung in the middle. He aimed his phone and snapped a few shots. Checking the results, he appeared satisfied.

It looked like they were done, but Mrs. Woo stopped her son and husband from dispersing, tugging on their arms. She waved to me and her daughter. "Jina-ya, Chloe! Come here."

I reluctantly approached, feeling like I might look out of place in a family photo. I wasn't exactly a bonafide Shin family member. Mrs. Woo must have sensed my hesitance. She gently pulled me into position by Jinseung's side, making it very clear that she wanted me in the photograph. Jinseung wrapped his arm tight around my waist and tilted his head close to mine. I glowed with pride at how willingly he claimed me as his partner in front of all his closest companions.

Changsoo stepped back until we were all within frame.

"Say kimchi," he said.

"Kimchiiiii!" We all grinned stupidly.

After numerous shots, we broke apart. Changsoo showed Mrs.

Woo the photos. She looked delighted and asked him to send them to her straight away.

"I'll get one framed and put it up on the wall," she announced, beaming with glee.

Jinseung had already moved on to chat with others. As I watched him interact with his friends, I became aware of someone else on the periphery—a man wearing a cap and sunglasses, partially hidden behind a leafy tree. He wasn't a member of our party as far as I could tell, but he watched with immense interest.

"What are you looking at?" Jina asked.

"Do you see that man?"

"No—ah! I see him. Just what is he up to?"

The answer was clear when out came a camera lens behind the tree.

Jina's eyebrows shot up. "A paparazzi all the way out here?"

"I don't think so. Probably just an opportunist."

"This was meant to be a private gathering. We better go warn someone."

"Agreed, but let's leave Jinseung out of this. Don't want to ruin his day. I'll tell Changsoo."

I didn't delay. I walked straight up to Jinseung's manager.

"Everything okay?" he asked.

I directed his attention to the man behind the tree, but by then someone else had already noticed. Mr. Kim strode out to confront the man, his laid-back appearance quickly turning intimidating. I didn't know what he said to the man, but whatever it was, the man looked stricken and fled the scene at once.

"*Omo*. Mr. Kim can be scary when he wants to be," I observed.

"He didn't climb all the way to his position by being a nice guy," Changsoo said. "At least it's taken care of."

Mr. Kim returned looking completely carefree and composed. Jinseung hadn't noticed a thing. He was still busy saying goodbyes, giving out hugs, and taking selfies with his friends.

Once Jinseung had worked his way around the entire party, the only person left he hadn't said goodbye to was me. I was beginning to think that he didn't even plan to say goodbye to me. Perhaps he thought that it went without saying. My bottom lip began to tremble and tears gathered in the corners of my eyes. I couldn't help it—I was so emotional about him leaving.

Is this it? Is this how we're going to part?

I was disappointed to say the least.

Jinseung stood near the gate, saying something to Changsoo. I was too far away to hear. He picked up his duffel bag.

I knew it. He's about to leave, and without even saying goodbye.

But he didn't leave. He grabbed something from his bag, pocketed it, then marched straight over to me and took my hand, intertwining his fingers with mine.

"For a moment there I thought you'd forgotten about me," I said, wiping my eyes.

He ruffled my hair. "You fool. Come with me."

"What? Where?"

"Anywhere. Away from here. Come on." He gently yanked my hand, guiding me towards a wooded area away from the road.

A faint dirt trail led into the shade of trees. We walked until we couldn't hear anything but the birds singing in the branches and the gentle rushing sound of a nearby stream. We were completely alone.

"Why couldn't you just say goodbye to me in front of everyone else?" I asked.

"Because then I wouldn't be able to do this." He swept me into his arms and sank his lips down onto mine.

I melted with a soft moan, yielding completely to his lips and tongue, allowing him to explore my mouth with all the urgency and passion of the moment. He held me tight while he kissed me, briefly breaking away to take my bottom lip between his teeth, biting me softly, then returning fully to my mouth, devouring me with such incredible heat and force, rendering me weak at my knees.

I felt his absence as soon as he parted from my lips, even as he still clung to me.

"Wow," I whispered.

Jinseung ran a hand over his head, looking sheepish. "On second thought, I better not get too excited."

I glanced downwards. "Too late. Those sweatpants don't leave much to the imagination."

"*Aish!*" He let go of me at once and stepped back to put some distance between us. "I'll need to give myself a few minutes to recover."

I giggled. "So, you wanted to kiss me? Is that the reason you took me out here?"

"Nah. That was spur of the moment. I actually brought you here because I wanted to give you something."

"Oh?"

He started to rummage in his jacket pocket.

My heart thumped against my ribs as I recalled what Jina said. Was she right? Did Jinseung intend to propose? *I can't believe this.*

He took something out of his pocket, covered by his hands. He approached me, and I half expected him to get down on one knee, but he did not. Instead, he took my hand, then pressed the object into my palm. Contrasting sharply with my expectation of a round and smooth metal item, it felt thin, plasticky, and rectangular. *What the heck?*

As soon as I looked down it was apparent what it was. A credit card.

"What's this for?" I asked, turning it over in my hands.

"My accountant will be taking care of all the usual expenses when I'm gone, but it occurred to me that you don't make much money, and I won't be around to gift you anything."

"You already pay for a lot, and my personal spending isn't much…"

"I know, but should anything come up…if there's anything you really want…I want you to have it."

I stared at the card in my hands.

"I trust you, Chloe, and I don't ever want you to struggle. That's why I'm giving you this. "

It wasn't a ring, but it still signified his feelings for me. I didn't need a proposal, anyway. It was too soon.

I leaned in and kissed him on the cheek. "Thank you. I appreciate this."

"Good. Make sure you use it too. Not like I'm going to be spending much while I'm in the army, so you might as well treat yourself to what you want."

"Okay, but I promise I won't go overboard."

"I know you won't."

I slipped the credit card into a zipped pocket in my coat. "I suppose we should go back. They'll think we disappeared into the woods for a quickie."

He smirked. "Let them think what they want."

"Then, one more kiss?"

"Yes, please."

I held him, revelling in the feel of his broad shoulders, strong arms, and hard chest. We found each other's lips and kissed each other, sweet and soft. He then burrowed his face into the crook of my neck, sighing with contentment.

"I love you," he murmured, breath prickling my skin.

"I love you too," I replied, cheek pressed to his chest.

I wished I could hold onto him forever, but after a while, I let my grip slacken. We simply stared at each other for a moment, taking everything in, savouring the mental image of one another.

He took my hand. "We better not leave them waiting much longer."

I knew he was right, but I still felt a pang of sorrow in my chest. Our last moment alone together was coming to an end.

We slowly walked back to the entry gate of the training centre, my heart sinking further with each step. When we arrived, Jinseung hugged me again, kissed me, wished me goodbye, and told me he loved me. Then he was by the gate, handed his backpack and duffel bag by Changsoo.

"Farewell, everyone," he said, waving goodbye, a charming smile upon his face masking the sadness.

Warm wishes of good luck shouted out from the crowd accompanied his walk, alone, through the gate. He turned back several times, waving and blowing kisses, but eventually he disappeared from view. I clutched at my chest, feeling like my heart was going to explode.

Chapter 10

I lay my head down, and when I opened my eyes, I realised with a jolt of panic that I was back in the dank basement apartment, surrounded by darkness except for the tiny barred window shining in the distance. Oh Sejung appeared before me, wraith-like, pale-faced, her limp black hair matted. She circled me, watching me with menacing eyes like a beast focused on its prey. Pure terror coursed through my veins.

"He doesn't love you," she taunted. "He left you all alone."

She entwined her skinny fingers around my neck, cold and clammy.

"He's not coming back," she whispered in my ear. "You'll never have him."

I shook my head. "That's not true."

"Oh, but it is. Don't believe me?" Her hands tightened.

I desperately tried to pry them away, but her vice-like grip held strong.

"Say goodbye, Chloe."

"No!"

"Insolent little bitch." She squeezed my neck so hard I thought it might snap.

Twisted visions of violent war scenes played in my head before everything went black, then I awoke coughing and spluttering, Oh Sejung's touch burnt on my neck.

"Jinseung-ah!" I gasped, reaching for him, but his side of the bed was empty, the place where his head lay still imprinted on the pillow from the night before.

I was confused for a moment, then everything flooded back. He had left for the army, and I was alone. Sejung's words echoed in my head.

"He left you all alone."

I groaned and clutched at my chest, an empty ache in my heart as I stared longingly at the vacant space next to me.

Jinseung...

I buried my face in his pillow, trying to comfort myself with the remnants of his scent.

Damn. I miss you so much already.

I stayed glued to his pillow until my muscles relaxed and my pounding heartbeat began to subside. When I had fully calmed down, I groped for my phone on the bedside table. 6:07 a.m. The countdown on my home screen read five hundred and ninety-nine days. I groaned. Perhaps setting that countdown was a mistake. A reminder that it would be so very long until Jinseung's return. I deleted the widget off the screen, vowing to put it back as soon as the number became easier to stomach.

I had two options—go back to sleep and risk having another nightmare, or get up and embrace the morning. It didn't take long for me to come to a decision.

Yawning loudly, I dragged myself to the kitchen and made a strong cup of coffee. When I started tinkering around looking for something to eat for breakfast, Buster stirred on his plush dog bed. He opened his little round black eyes and stood up, stretched, then came padding over to me.

"Do you want breakfast too?"

He yapped in reply, tail wagging.

"All right."

I plonked some dog food into his red paw-print-patterned bowl. He scoffed it quickly then licked the bowl for quite some time after.

I ate fruit—an apple and some grapes that looked like they might not have stayed fresh much longer, plus a handful of nuts.

"I'm up nice and early for once," I mused, staring out the window. The sun had yet to rise, but I could make out the silhouetted trees against the moonlit sky. "What should I do with all this time? Do you want to go for a walk, Buster?"

He leapt up in excitement.

"All right. Let's go."

I threw on a casual outfit, a coat, and a scarf, then grabbed Buster's lead. We headed out the door. Despite the lack of sunlight, the footpath was well-lit from the bright streetlamps. The air was brisk. I couldn't see anyone out and about—just the way I liked it.

Since revealing my relationship with Jinseung, I had been very cautious about being seen in public. So far, I had yet to run into any overzealous fans, and I planned to keep it that way.

I pulled up my scarf to cover the lower half of my face, just enough to obscure my identity. The neighbourhood was usually so quiet that I didn't have to worry too much about someone recognising me, not to mention the fact that most people who lived around here would be much more well-known than I was. It was that kind of post code.

For such a small dog, Buster was surprisingly powerful. He ran ahead of me until the lead was pulled tight. I had to jog a little to keep up.

The houses we passed were large, detached, and hidden behind tall fences. Whenever I walked around the neighbourhood, I liked to peer through the gaps in the fences or gates, take in the grandiose properties, and wonder about the people who lived there. I rarely saw my neighbours. Residents came and went in fancy cars with tinted windows. They kept to themselves.

The first person I came across on the walk was a woman out jogging, headphones on, clad head-to-toe in designer activewear. She passed me by without a hint of acknowledgement.

The next person I saw stopped me dead in my tracks. A dark figure emerging from a shadowed alleyway. That pale face, limp hair, callous eyes…

My breath caught. My blood ran cold.

No. It can't be!

I could hear my racing heart pound in my eardrums, beads of sweat running down my forehead. I felt dizzy, lightheaded. My vision blurred. An intense pain emanated from my head and I pressed my hands to my temples. My knees buckled. I crumpled down onto the hard pavement, groaning. I thought I might die, whether from Oh Sejung or the pain in my head.

No one came to my aid.

When the attack finally began to subside, I managed to properly open my eyes and look around. I was alone. No sign of the woman I thought was Oh Sejung.

Was she a vision?

My breath began to return. My heartbeat began to stabilise.

It was a hallucination. She wasn't real.

I got to my feet, body weak and trembling, a dull pain persistent in my head. That was when I realised Buster was gone. I must have dropped the lead. He probably got scared and ran away.

"Buster!" I cried out. "Buuuuster!"

He didn't come.

I couldn't muster enough energy to keep shouting his name or properly search for him, so I trudged back to my house, head hung in defeat.

One day without Jinseung and I have a panic attack and lose his precious dog. I can't believe this.

With a heavy heart, I opened the door and went inside. I had a little cry on my bed before recovering enough to call Yang Bora. She didn't pick up, but I left a message.

"Hey. It's me, Chloe. You know how you said that I can always rely on you with Jinseung gone? Well, I need your help. I just had a pretty bad panic attack. Call me back when you get this."

I left a similar message with Shin Jina.

After lying down for a while, I remembered the bottle of pills in the bathroom cabinet. My doctor gave them to me after my last panic attack—a similar episode which occurred when I had passed a random house which reminded me of the one where Oh Sejung had held me captive.

I took one pill with a tall glass of water and a piece of buttered toast. The effects were almost immediate. My body relaxed. My thoughts became blurry and indistinct. I went back to bed because I couldn't operate.

The next thing I knew, my phone was ringing—a sound loud and annoying enough to penetrate the thick fog in my brain. I groggily reached for it on the bedside table.

"Are you all right?" It was Yang Bora. She sounded concerned.

"I'm just…resting." I couldn't explain anything to her in my current state.

"Do you need me to come over?"

"You have to go to work, though."

"Yes, but Actor-nim has some appointments this afternoon that I don't need to be present for. I'm sure I'll be able to get away."

"If it's no trouble…"

"I'll come over as soon as I can. Call me again if you feel worse, okay?"

"Okay. Thank you."

Jina called me a little later.

"I'm so sorry, Chloe. I'm on a modelling shoot today. There's no way I can get out of it, and it will probably take some time. Not sure how long."

"It's okay. Bora is going to come over."

"Whew. Then at least I know you'll be in good hands. I'll call you again later."

Thank goodness for those two. Now all I had to do was stay calm and rest until Bora arrived. No work to do, so that was one good thing at least. In my mind, I started making a plan to go out and look for Buster, but I ended up falling asleep instead. Deep, dreamless sleep.

When I finally awoke, I felt much better—except when I passed

Buster's empty dog bed, reminding me of his absence. *I have to find him.*

I was at the door, putting my shoes on, when I found myself paralysed. Too scared to go back out in case I had another panic attack. *I better wait until Bora gets here.*

Fortunately, she arrived earlier than I anticipated. A ray of sunshine on my doorstep. She was in her work clothes—slim trousers, a cashmere turtleneck sweater with a blazer over the top. Her red-dyed hair in its usual style—half up in a high bun. Her eyes scanned me from behind her round, gold, wire-framed glasses, searching for answers.

"You came," I said lamely.

"Of course I did. Actor-nim was worried about you too. She insisted that I leave straight away to go check on you. What happened?"

"I was walking Buster this morning when I thought I saw…*her*. I had a panic attack and Buster ran away. I have no idea where he is."

She frowned sympathetically. "Oh dear. We better go look for him. Or if you don't feel up to it, I'll go on my own."

"I'll be okay if you're with me, but do you have time? Won't you have to get back to work?"

She shook her head. "It's okay. Actor-nim is with her assistant and they know I'll be a while. Come on, let's go."

So, Bora and I began our hunt for Buster. Our first stop, the place where I must have dropped his lead.

"It was in front of this alleyway that you had the panic attack?" Bora asked, looking down the narrow path.

"Yes." I averted my gaze from the exact spot I had seen the vision, even though daylight had chased away all the shadows.

"I can see how it would look scary in the dark. There's no streetlight here either. Do you know which way Buster ran?"

"I have no idea. I didn't even see him run away."

"Then let's just have a look around."

Both of us searched the immediate area, but there was no sign of him.

"He could be miles away by now," I grumbled. "I should have gone to look for him earlier."

"You couldn't have," Bora said. "And don't blame yourself. Jinseung *Oppa* wouldn't."

"Wouldn't he? He loves Buster."

"He loves *you* more."

"What about his parents? He was their dog too. His mother will have a fit."

"It's far too soon to abandon hope. We'll find him."

We widened our search area, checking every street and piece of land, and peering into yards he could have scrambled into.

"If we don't manage to find him, I'll make some posters," I resolved.

"And I'll check all the local social media groups," Bora said. "People who find pets usually post about it."

"Good idea."

"Oh!"

"What?"

"Over there, by those trees."

I glanced in the direction she pointed but couldn't see anything except the trees and patch of grass by a fence.

"I thought I saw movement," Bora said. "Maybe it was just the wind."

We continued our search, leaving no corner unexplored. When we ran into another woman walking her dog, Bora approached her.

"Excuse me, have you seen a little white dog walking alone around the neighbourhood?"

"No. Sorry."

"Ah. Thank you."

The woman strode away.

I was beginning to run out of hope. "Maybe we should head back? We've searched the area pretty thoroughly."

"Yeah," Bora agreed. "Looks like we'll have to move on to Plan B. Posters and social media."

I stared down at my feet. "I really hoped we'd find him."

"Someone's bound to have seen him. He's probably safe at someone's house right now, and once they see a missing poster, they'll contact you."

"Yes. That's got to be the case."

I thought about which photo of Buster to use on the poster. I'd have to crop Jinseung out if I used one with him in it.

"Do you get panic attacks often?" Bora asked as we walked back to my house.

"No. This was my second one. I think I was still half asleep when I left the house this morning. I had a nightmare last night. Maybe that's what set it off."

"You're still getting nightmares?"

"Yeah."

"I wish there was something I could do. You're all alone in that big house now."

"Maybe I should get a flatmate," I joked.

The words had barely escaped my mouth before it dawned on me. I didn't know why I hadn't thought of it sooner. Both of us looked at each other, and I knew she understood what I was thinking.

"Would *you* like to move in with me?" I asked.

"Seriously?"

"Of course. You could have your own room, you wouldn't need to pay any rent, and I'm sure Jinseung would agree to it. Just until he gets back from the military."

"Then, hell yes! I would absolutely like to move in with you."

"You're living with your parents now, right?"

She nodded. "I looked into apartments in town, but they were too expensive and I didn't want to have roommates. If it were you, though, that would be different."

"So you'd be able to move in straight away?"

"Yup. Pretty much. Maybe this weekend."

"Perfect!"

"*Omo*, this is going to be so great! I'm excited already."

I would have been excited too if it weren't for the fact that Buster was still missing. I wouldn't be able to celebrate properly until he returned.

"Well, here we are," I said when we reached the gate to my house. "We didn't find him."

"I'm sorry. Guess I'll head back to work if you think you'll be okay without me."

"I'm feeling better now, so I think I'll manage."

"*Omo!*" Bora clutched her chest.

"What is it?"

"Isn't that…?"

I followed Bora's gaze to the porch. Buster was sitting outside the front door, his little pink tongue poking out.

Chapter 11

"Does the agency know you're using their van as a moving truck?" I asked Bora when she pulled up in the driveway of my house three days later.

"Maybe," she said dismissively. She slid open the van door revealing a ton of boxes stuffed inside.

"I'll help you unpack," I offered.

"Living together is gonna be so much fun!" Bora said, heaving a large box to the door.

"I know! I'm so excited."

I grabbed two small boxes. Buster, curious as to what was going on, trailed at my feet as I carried them inside. Thank goodness he had turned up the other day. *Such a smart doggy.* He must have let himself in through a gap between the bars in the gate. *What a relief.* I promised myself that I'd never let him out of my sight again. Bora would be able to help look after him too, now that she'd be living here.

We marched back and forth between the van and Bora's new room —the largest guest room, complete with its own ensuite. I released a heavy box onto the floor with a loud thud.

"*Aigoo!* How much stuff do you have?"

"We're not even half done."

"At least there's plenty of space. There's the third bedroom too, if you wanna store some stuff in there as well. I don't use it for anything."

"I think this room will be big enough. I made it work with my old bedroom which was half the size, and I certainly didn't have my own bathroom."

It took several trips to empty the boxes from the van.

"Whew," I said, wiping a hand across my forehead when we were done. My body ached, and even in the cold I was sweating.

"Well, that's the easy part over and done with," Bora said. "Time to put everything away."

I gritted my teeth looking at all the boxes surrounding us, stacked almost to the ceiling. "Just give me a second to recover first. That was quite the workout."

"Yeah. Think I pulled my back muscle." She stretched her arms over her head, straightening her back with a series of tremendous clicks.

I cringed at the sound—worse than nails on a blackboard.

"Ah! Much better," she said, returning to her usual straight posture.

After a glass of water to refresh ourselves, we went back to the room to continue the job. I put myself in charge of storing Bora's clothing while she worked on everything else.

It turned out Bora had a lot of clothes, and my job was slow work because I kept stopping to examine each piece and gush over it.

"You have so many beautiful clothes!" I said, holding up a pretty plum-coloured wrap dress.

Bora grimaced. "Yeah, I know. Think I might have a shopping addiction. Ever since I got my promotion I've been spending up large. The first time in my life I've actually had disposable income and I've gone a bit crazy."

"That's to be expected. You'll get it under control once the novelty wears off."

"It's been over a year already! But you're right, hopefully the urge to shop will die down soon. In the meantime, if you ever want to borrow something to wear, feel free to raid my closet."

"Really? Thanks!" My excitement quickly faded, reminding myself that Bora was at least two sizes smaller than me. "Not that I could fit most of this stuff…"

"I'm sure some of it will work."

I picked up a pair of her shoes and lined them up against my feet. "Looks like we have the same shoe size."

"Then definitely borrow my shoes if you want. Some of them I've hardly even worn. There's my bags and accessories too."

As I went through the rest of her clothes and accessories, I checked each piece and made a mental note of items I'd like to borrow, which made the whole process much more fun.

When everything had finally been put away, we flattened all the boxes and stacked them in a pile to be recycled.

We stood back and admired our handiwork on the room. The sparse and uninspiring space had been transformed, injected full of Bora's personality by her sprawling collection of possessions. The bed was covered in her cushions and throws and her sheepskin rug tossed over the chair. Books, journals, photographs, and souvenirs filled shelves. Perfume bottles, candles, and jewellery boxes stood neatly arranged in vignettes on the dressing table.

"Wow," Bora said when she opened the wardrobe and the drawers in turn.

I had folded and arranged her clothing vertically so everything could be seen at a glance, and the wardrobe was organised by colour and length.

"It looks amazing!" Bora said. "Unfortunately I don't know how long I'll be able to keep it that way. I tend to keep my clothes on the bed or the floor most of the time."

"Haha. Don't worry. I'm not anal about tidiness. But maybe limit the mess to your bedroom, and not the living areas."

"Can do."

"All this hard work deserves a cold drink, don't ya think?"

"You read my mind."

We crashed on the couch with a couple of cans.

"Ahhh!" Bora leaned back and put her feet up on the ottoman.

"You're making yourself right at home," I noted.

"Yup! Gotta feel comfy, don't I?"

"Absolutely. Go for it."

"Hope you won't get sick of me now that we'll be seeing each other a whole lot more."

"It's not like you'll be here all the time, anyway. You work so much."

"True. You know I work strange hours. Sometimes I might not even come home at night if a shoot runs super late."

I nodded. "Jinseung used to have the same kind of schedule, if not worse. Promise me you'll text me, though, so I'm not worried about where you are."

"Yep. Same goes for you." She took a swig of beer then patted her stomach. "I'm starving. Got anything to eat?"

"I thought we could do a big grocery shop tomorrow. For now, let's get takeaway."

"I want pizza."

Just what I had been considering. "Great minds think alike."

I ordered from the delivery app on my phone. One large spicy Italian pizza to share. My tummy rumbled in anticipation.

While we waited for the pizza to arrive, Bora grabbed her tablet. I saw her check her work emails and Go Yoojin's schedule for the next day. She screwed her face up at something.

"What's wrong?" I asked.

"Actor-nim has to do another screen test tomorrow."

"Isn't that a good thing?"

"She's basically been given the role already. Didn't think she would need to do more. I wonder what the point is? Oh well. At least she's actually getting auditions, which is more than can be said for Jung Jen."

"Go Yoojin is more popular than Jung Jen now. That's so crazy when I think about it. Jen is practically a veteran actor compared to Yoojin."

"I know, right? Jen only gets minor roles these days. I've heard Mr. Kim is being super hard on her. She's always in his office for some reason or other. He's probably not happy with the situation. She's a liability."

"I feel so sorry for her. She seems pretty tired and stressed when I tutor her."

"She knew what she was risking when she two-timed San Seung. I don't blame her, though. Two gorgeous guys fawning over her…How could she choose? I'd probably do the same thing."

"Haha."

The intercom sounded, and the thought of hot, cheesy pizza overrode everything else in my head.

"That must be the pizza," I said.

"I'll go get it." Bora got to her feet.

I grabbed plates while she went outside to collect the pizza.

I could smell it even before she returned—mozzarella, olives, pepperoni. She waltzed in the doorway, bearing a square cardboard box stained with grease. What came next happened in slow motion. Buster scurried by her feet. She didn't see him, and as she stepped forward, she tripped over the little white furball. The pizza box left her grip and tipped over in the air, the lid falling partially open. The pizza went hurtling towards the floor.

"Noooo!" I cried, rushing over to try and save it.

Buster got to it before either me or Bora could salvage any pieces which didn't touch the floor.

"Oops," Bora said, rubbing her head sheepishly.

I folded my arms, both amused and peeved by the incident.

"What a waste."

Buster scoffed the pizza with loud chewing and licking noises. It made a terrible mess on the carpet.

"At least Buster is happy," Bora noted with a wry smile.

"I think he did that on purpose."

"Finds his own way home and works out how to get pizza. Smart dog."

Chapter 12

here is she? I looked up at the clock on the wall of the lesson room. 1:18 p.m. Go Yoojin was meant to arrive at one, and Bora had assured me that she'd be there as scheduled. I tapped my foot on the floor below the table, restless with impatience.

Another fifteen minutes passed before my phone started to ring, Yang Bora's name on the screen. I quickly picked up.

"Yes?"

"I am *so* sorry." Bora sounded flustered. "I know I told you this morning that Actor-nim would definitely make it today, but something has come up. She's not gonna be able to attend. Can we reschedule?"

"Sure, no problem."

At least I had confirmation. Now I could leave and get on with my day.

"I'll book another time in with you tonight," she said.

"Okay. Everything all right?"

"Yup. We ran into a famous producer and he invited us to lunch to talk about an upcoming project. Can't let a chance like this slip by."

"Ah. Well, see you tonight."

"Yep, see ya, *Unnie!*"

So much for coming into the office today. I packed up my things and left the lesson room.

At the elevator, I pressed the down button. The metal doors stuttered open momentarily. I caught the eyes of the single occupant—Mr. Kim. I froze for a second, startled to see him. He was sharply dressed in a navy suit and yellow silk tie. He smelled faintly of cigarettes and spicy cologne.

"Are you getting in?" he asked, holding the button down so the doors didn't close.

"Um, yes."

I entered the elevator and reached for the ground-floor button, but it wouldn't activate. I had been so flustered upon seeing Mr. Kim that I hadn't noticed the elevator's direction.

"Oh, it's going up. Whoops."

The doors had already closed.

"I've actually been meaning to speak with you," Mr. Kim said.

His comment took me by surprise.

"With me?" I asked incredulously.

Why would he want to speak with me? My status at KAM was so low, surely I wasn't more than a blip on his radar. Didn't he have other, much more important matters to attend to?

"Yes," he said, straightening his tie.

The elevator doors opened, and he stood between them, preventing them from closing.

"Will you come to my office?" he asked, face expressionless.

"Uh…okay."

I couldn't have said no even if I wanted to. Mr. Kim exuded that kind of power.

I followed him to his office, wondering the entire way what he was possibly going to speak with me about. Was it my working arrangement? My visa? Maybe it was something about Jinseung. Yes, that seemed like a strong possibility. Hopefully nothing bad had happened.

We entered his office, a spacious room full of shiny glass and black leather. A large bookcase occupied one wall, glossy volumes artfully arranged on its shelves. He closed the door behind us, and I thought I heard the click of a lock, or perhaps that was just my imagination.

"Take a seat," Mr Kim said, gesturing to the leather couch.

I sat down while Mr. Kim continued to stand, leaning against his desk. His bare ankles stuck out of his loafers.

I played with the hem of my shirt, waiting for him to speak.

"I've heard positive feedback about you from Go Yoojin and Jung Jen," he began. "It seems like you're doing a really good job with them, despite how little time they get to spend with you."

I lifted my head to meet his eyes, pleasantly surprised by the praise.

"Thank you, sir."

"English is becoming more and more important since we'd love our actors to work on international projects. We recently signed an agreement with an American agency. Through them, our portfolio of actors will be considered for any suitable roles which come their way and vice versa."

"I didn't know about that. Sounds like a good opportunity."

"Yes, it certainly is."

Maybe Jinseung would get to work on an American drama or film one day. Then again, his English was pretty poor so it seemed unlikely.

"In light of this, I was wondering if you would like some more hours," Mr. Kim said. "We have a couple of new recruits joining our ranks and I'd like you to tutor them in English."

I didn't need to think it over. I had little else to do with my time, anyway.

"Yes. Absolutely."

"Great. I'll put their managers in touch with you and you can sort something out with them." He stopped leaning against his desk.

Was that all he wanted to say? If so, what was the point of asking me to his office? I wasn't talent, and I didn't think he usually got involved with other staff matters. Did my relationship with Jinseung make me different? Perhaps that was why.

I gripped the handle of my bag, prepared to be dismissed from the room, but instead of going to the door, Mr. Kim dropped down beside me on the couch. I instinctively moved over so there was more space between us.

He turned to face me. From afar, he was quite a handsome man, but up close, I could see the pock marks on his upper cheeks and his nicotine-stained teeth.

"I also wanted to ask about how you're getting on without Shin Jinseung," he said. "I know it must be difficult to be on your own after the traumatic experience you went through."

"Yes, I mean, I'm going to miss him a lot, but I'll survive."

"Of course you will. You're a strong woman. I could tell that much from the first time I saw you."

"Oh, um, thanks."

"You'll survive, but I do wonder about Jinseung."

"What do you mean?"

"Announcing a relationship, taking a four-month hiatus, then joining the military. It's a lot to put himself through. Will his career ever recover?"

There it is. His usual disdain for me was peeking out.

"I don't see why it wouldn't," I returned. "None of those things should affect his ability to act."

He sniggered, and I could tell he thought I was naive for saying that.

"If only that was all that mattered," he said. "No, joining the military was to be expected, but usually people in the entertainment industry don't commit themselves to a relationship at such a young age. He has really sacrificed a lot to be with you."

My face burned.

"I know he has," I spluttered. "And I really, really appreciate everything he's done for me."

"And it's not just Jinseung who has taken a hit," he continued. "So has the agency as a whole. Jinseung was one of our top earners before, now he's one of our lowest."

I didn't know what to say to this, so I stayed silent, looking down at my feet and fiddling with my hands in my lap.

"And we even invented a role for you at the company just so you could come back to South Korea. We've really done a lot for the sake of you and Jinseung."

"I know you have. I'm so grateful…"

"If you recall, I was against your relationship from the beginning, but Jinseung convinced me to make a concession. To be honest, I'm still not entirely convinced I made the right move in allowing it."

I hadn't noticed him edge towards me until his leg brushed mine. There was no room for me to move away, I was already flush up against the arm of the couch. Uneasiness bloomed in the pit of my stomach, making me quiver.

"I'm not saying all this to make you feel bad," Mr. Kim said. "I just want to make sure you know the circumstances that we're facing. I'm on Jinseung's side. I'm fighting for him as best as I can, but how long can this continue? I don't know." He sighed and I could feel his hot, slightly rancid breath on my cheek. "Just think about what I've said, okay?" He patted me on the top of my leg.

I internally recoiled at his touch, yet on the outside I was frozen, too startled to do anything. What was he playing at?

His hand lingered against me. I stared at it like it was a cockroach.

"You're doing great work, but you could be doing more," he continued. "It's a simple matter of give and take. The agency has made sacrifices for your sake, so what can you offer us? Just think about it. That's all I'm asking."

He started to rub his hand up and down a little, stroking me.

For a moment I just sat there, paralysed, but I quickly came to my senses. I had to extract myself from this situation before it progressed.

"I-I've got to go now." I snapped to my feet, his hand limply falling away. "I have an appointment I need to get to."

"Of course. Go ahead." His voice was totally calm and steady, like there was nothing wrong with this situation at all.

I walked straight to the door, but when I pulled the handle, it was as I feared. The door was locked. A coldness washed over me, heart thrumming in my ears. I struggled with the door handle, causing a rattling sound as I tried to work out how to unlock it. My panic must have been palpable.

I didn't hear Mr. Kim come up behind me, but I felt his presence. I shuddered as he reached over my shoulder, his arm skimming the fabric of my shirt. In a quick, fluid motion, he unlatched the lock, then opened the door for me.

"Goodbye, Chloe," he said. "Enjoy the rest of your day."

I didn't turn around or say anything, I just marched straight out. I even took the stairs down instead of the elevator, not wanting to stand around a moment longer. As I made my way to the ground floor, I remembered Changsoo's words from the day that Jinseung entered the training centre.

He didn't climb all the way to his position by being a nice guy.

Now more than ever, those words resonated, and I wondered what exactly Mr. Kim was capable of.

Chapter 13

I replayed the encounter with Mr. Kim in my head over and over again as I drove home, so much that I began to question my interpretation of what had happened. His words—did they mean what I thought they meant? His touch—that wasn't supposed to be a comforting gesture, was it? He had locked the door, but then again, he had let me leave without a struggle.

I desperately wanted to give Mr. Kim the benefit of the doubt. Things would be much less complicated if he hadn't meant anything sordid by his actions. I wouldn't have to say anything to anyone. I wouldn't have to cause a stir...

I gripped the steering wheel, my knuckles white. *No.* I couldn't fool myself. My original instinct was definitely correct: Mr. Kim had propositioned me, asking me to do him a favour in payment for everything he'd done for me and Jinseung, and that favour was undeniably sexual in nature.

Sleazy bastard...

Jinseung would be furious if he found out, but what could he possibly do while he was so far away and with limited means to communicate? Was that why Mr. Kim had waited until he left for the military to make his move?

Yes, that must be it. Bastard!

I thumped my fist on the horn, the loud, sharp toot shocking me despite being my intention.

My mood hadn't calmed by the time I got home. I felt as weak as a feather, all jittery and fluttery. I couldn't think about anything else all afternoon. What could I do? Who should I tell? The only thing I knew for sure was that I'd spill everything to Bora. She'd listen to me. She would understand. I didn't want to call her, I wanted to speak with her face to face. I'd wait until she came home, no matter how late that was.

* * *

THE SMELLS of pork and vegetables, chilli peppers and soy sauce mingled in the air as the pot gently bubbled on the stove.

I heard Bora's voice before I saw her enter the room.

"Oooh. What's cooking? Smells soooo good!" Her cheery smile faded as soon as she set eyes on me. "*Unnie*, is something wrong?"

"Yes," I said.

"Oh no. Another panic attack?"

"No. Worse."

Her face fell even more. "Let's sit down. Tell me what happened."

"I'll tell you over dinner. It's ready now."

"Then you sit down, I'll serve it up."

I did as she said, pulling out a chair. Bora joined me after placing bowls of rice, dipping sauce, and meat and vegetables on the table. She served me a large portion, using her chopsticks to fill my plate before serving herself.

"I'm listening," Bora said from the chair opposite me. "Tell me everything."

I drew a deep breath before explaining what had happened, from the moment I saw Mr. Kim in the elevator, to the instant I left his office.

Bora didn't say anything, but her face grew paler and paler until she looked like she might faint. Her mouth was set in a deep frown.

She was shaking so much she couldn't control her chopsticks. I knew she'd be shocked, but her reaction was worse than I anticipated.

I finished my story, and still she said nothing. Did she need more time to fully digest what I told her?

"Well?" I prompted. "Say something. I need to hear your thoughts."

Bora bowed her head and mumbled something indistinct, averting her gaze from mine.

"Sorry, I couldn't hear you," I said.

"It can't be true," she repeated.

My heart dropped to the pit of my stomach.

"What?"

Surely she didn't mean what I thought she meant or else I must have misheard her.

"Are you certain you read the situation correctly?" she asked, still avoiding my eyes.

"Yes," I said, though a tiny bit of doubt crept in. "At least, I'm ninety percent certain."

"Ninety percent isn't enough. No one will believe you."

Her words stung like needles through my chest.

"Do *you* believe me?" I asked.

"...No."

It was a punch to my gut so hard I felt winded.

"I don't understand," I spluttered. "I thought you'd back me up on this."

"Well, you were wrong."

I felt angry now, my face burning, my hands fisted.

"Are you serious?" I spat. "You're the first person I've told because I thought I could trust you and I thought you'd be able to help me. Why are you being like this?"

"I can only help you when I believe what you're saying." Her voice was cold and harsh, yet weak at the same time.

"I'm telling you the truth!"

"But there's no way Mr. Kim would do such a thing. You've interpreted his actions wrong, that's the only valid explanation."

"But...but..."

Bora got to her feet, her eyes fixed firmly on the floor. "I need to go away and digest this."

"Where are you going?"

"Out." She turned and stormed out of the room and down the hall with heavy footsteps.

"When should I expect you back?" I called after her.

No answer. The front door slammed.

Left alone at the table with two plates of barely eaten food, I burst into tears.

I thought I could trust her. I thought she was my best friend. Why couldn't she believe me? Why would she take Mr. Kim's side instead? She wasn't behaving like her usual self. I didn't understand at all.

But maybe she was right.

Maybe I really did take my interpretation of events too far. It wasn't like he'd actually said or done anything that could outright constitute sexual harassment, had he?

"Arrrgggh," I groaned, clutching at the sides of my head feeling a massive headache coming on.

My phone began to ring and I reluctantly checked who was calling. *Jinseung.*

I picked up at once, unwilling to miss the opportunity to hear his voice, despite my inner turmoil.

"Hello," I answered.

"Hi," Jinseung said. "Are you okay? Are you upset about something?"

Trust him to extrapolate my feelings from just one word.

I swallowed my distress until it settled deep in my stomach.

"No, I'm fine. I just miss you, that's all."

His voice softened. "I miss you too."

I couldn't tell him the truth. I needed more time to properly assess the situation first. The moment I told him, he would definitely to do something rash, and I didn't want that.

"I can't believe it's already been three weeks since you left. How are you getting along?" I asked. "You must nearly be done with training now."

"Uh huh. I've been made the leader of my squadron too."

"What? Wow. That's amazing. Well done."

"Thanks."

"So, you're doing well?"

"Very well. Too well."

"Too well?"

"I see others struggling. Guys much younger than me. Guys who aren't used to self-discipline. Guys who are unfit and can't keep up with the drills. For me, it's like a walk in the park. I feel kinda guilty about that. It's easy for me."

"I'm just glad you're not one of the people who are struggling."

"Heh. I don't blame you for thinking that way."

"You never told me what the dorms are like. Are you comfortable?"

"Not really. They're big, sterile rooms full of rows of bunk beds. There's no privacy, even in the bathrooms."

"*Aigoo.* That must be hard for you."

"It was tough, especially in the beginning. Now the other guys are used to me being around. They've stopped staring at me and hounding me for autographs and photos."

"That's good."

"And you? Are you doing okay without me?"

"Well…" My voice broke. "It's hard."

"Are you lonely? I thought Bora moving in would have helped."

Her name stabbed me in the chest. I didn't comment.

"Why don't you give *Noona* a call? I'm sure she'd love to hang out with you."

"Maybe."

"Do it. And remember I gave you that credit card. Treat yourself."

"Are you encouraging me to go and waste your money on frivolous items?"

"Precisely."

"Be careful what you wish for."

Jinseung chuckled. "I better go. My parents are expecting me to call soon."

"All right. Talk again soon?"

"Of course. Love you."

"Love you too."

He hung up.

How long would I be able to keep my secret from him?

The food in front of me had long gone cold, but I shovelled in a few mouthfuls and swallowed them down, merely for sustenance.

Bora didn't come home that night, and I gave up waiting for her. I went to my room, and as I lifted the covers to crawl into bed, I felt sure that I was going to have another nightmare—only this time it wouldn't be about Oh Sejung.

Chapter 14

Bora didn't come back the next day, or the next day, or the day after that.

About to head off to work, I reached for my shoes on the small wooden shelf by the door but stopped short. A pair of Bora's shoes sat next to mine—pretty red slingback heels. I brushed a finger against the smooth leather, adoring the cute shoes and the woman who owned them.

We have the same shoe size...

A pang of regret squeezed my heart. Having Bora move in with me was the only good thing to come out of Jinseung's enlistment so far, and now look what had happened.

I slid on my ballet flats, remembering they were the pair Bora bought me for my birthday the previous year, which made my heart squeeze even tighter.

I desperately wanted to call her and beg for forgiveness, even though I knew it should be the other way around. She had wronged me. We had fought before but not like this. I couldn't bear it.

After lingering by the door lost in my thoughts for far longer than I should, I set out. My first trip to KAM HQ since *the incident*.

I hadn't seen or heard from Mr. Kim in the past few days, and I prayed it would stay that way.

When I arrived in the underground carpark, I had to take a few deep breaths to calm myself. I talked to my wary face in the rear-view mirror. *It's going to be okay. You won't see Mr. Kim and he won't see you. The run-in on the elevator was a one-off. It won't happen again.*

Despite my pep talk, I froze in front of the elevator door, my index finger mid-way to the call button. I decided to take the stairs instead. If anything, it would give me a good work-out.

I stopped at reception first to sign in, then continued up yet more stairs. Puffing slightly from the ascent, I settled down in the lesson room surrounded by walls covered in bright posters with English words on them.

Go Yoojin arrived shortly after me. The shock of her sudden entry caused me to spring from my seat.

"Actor-nim, you're here," I said, slightly flustered.

Go Yoojin undid her hair tie, letting her long black tresses fall to her waist. She wore amber-coloured contact lenses which made her eyes look even more intense and cat-like than usual.

"You seem surprised," she said, one perfect brow quirked.

"I wasn't sure whether to expect you or not," I explained.

"Didn't Manager-nim say I would come?"

"No, she didn't."

Bora had rescheduled the lesson in my online calendar without any other form of contact, and there had been no word from her since then. I just had to assume it was still going ahead.

"Oh. Well, I'm here," she said. "Surprise."

I chuckled sheepishly. "I'm glad. Take a seat."

The lesson plan for the day was to practice describing appearance and personality. We started by describing the pictures of people supplied in the workbook, then moved on to people in real life.

"Can you describe Yang Bora to me?" I asked in English, tensing slightly as the name rolled off my tongue.

Yoojin brought a finger decorated with intricate nail art to her lips in thought. "Umm…She is short and cute. She has long red hair."

"What else?"

"She have glasses."

"She *wears* glasses."

"She wears glasses. She wears nice clothes. She is pretty. Ummm."

"And her personality?"

"She is smart. She is strong. She is kind. She is…de-determin…"

"Determined?"

"Yes. Determined. And she is stubborn."

I nodded along. All those things were true, and hearing them said aloud made my chest ache with longing for my dearest friend. I still couldn't get over the fact that she didn't believe me, and the perfect angel was not as angelic as I had once thought.

I asked Yoojin to describe a few other people. She was doing well and I was about to move on to a different exercise when an idea struck me. There was another person we both knew, and I'd be interested to hear her take on him.

"Can you describe Mr. Kim?" I asked.

Yoojin's eyes widened.

I wondered if she was about to say she didn't want to talk about him, but then she opened her mouth and rattled off several familiar descriptors.

"He is average height and weight," she said. "He has short black hair and black eyes. He wears nice suits. He wears colourful shirts and ties."

"What is his personality like?"

"He is smart. He is funny. He is…" She used her hand to mime a talking mouth.

"Talkative, charismatic, extroverted," I offered.

"Charismatic," she repeated slowly, feeling out the sound in her mouth.

"Anything else?"

"Hmmm…He is scary. A little bit."

I snapped up straight in my seat. "Scary? Why is he scary?"

Yoojin shrugged. "I don't know. Manager Yang thinks so too."

"Yang Bora thinks he's scary?"

Yoojin nodded but struggled to form an explanation in English.

"Why does Yang Bora think he's scary?" I asked, reverting to Korean. I tried to keep my tone light-hearted while panic simmered in my stomach.

"I don't know. She just does. She doesn't let me meet with him alone."

The simmer turned up to a boil.

What does this mean? Does Bora fear Mr. Kim after all? Then why would she say she didn't believe me?

"Why is that?" I asked.

"I don't know. He's just a bit intimidating, don't you think? Even I don't dare talk back to him."

I suppressed my bubbling anxiety.

"Yes. I see," I said calmly.

If I continued this line of questioning, Yoojin would surely get suspicious. I had already pushed further than was reasonable, and I couldn't disguise this as part of the English lesson since we were speaking Korean now.

"Let's do another exercise," I suggested, going back to English.

Yoojin nodded, seeming eager to drop the previous subject.

The rest of the lesson went smoothly, and Yoojin even managed to stay until the end of our allotted time without the usual interruptions.

When I was ready to leave afterwards, I took the stairs again. I didn't expect to meet anyone in the grey, concrete stairwell, so the sound of approaching footsteps made me clench up inside. My initial instinct was to flee, but when I listened closely, they weren't the footsteps of a man. They were light and click-clacky, like a woman's heels. I continued my descent. The click-clack came to an abrupt stop. I looked down and saw Yang Bora. She averted her gaze and continued walking as if she hadn't seen me.

"Hello," I said when we met each other on the same flight of steps.

"Hi," she said in a voice several decibels weaker than her usual bright and lively tone.

We slowly passed each other by. I gave her one final glance over my shoulder and saw that she was still looking at me. She looked sad. Regretful. Then she cast her eyes away and hastily walked away before I could say anything.

Chapter 15

I woke in the middle of the night to a loud thud. I clutched at my chest, heart racing beneath my flannel pyjama top. *What the heck was that?*

Whatever it was had woken Buster too. I heard his paws thump as he scurried around barking his head off. Not a good sign. My ears pricked at another sound—the creak of floorboards. I gasped.

There is someone in the house.

I shook my head trying to wake myself up from what must have been a nightmare, but as my senses sharpened, all the noises became even clearer.

There is definitely someone in the house.

My pulse quickened. Beads of sweat prickled my forehead.

What do I do?

I was trapped between the idea of confronting whoever was in my house and cowering underneath my blankets.

A Sasaeng fan? How did they get through the gate and into the house without waking me sooner? Surely they would have set off the alarm.

Buster soon quietened, and the creaking trailed away to nothingness. Perhaps it really had been in my head, but I wouldn't be able to sleep until I knew for sure.

My self-defence kit keychain lay on the bedside table. I had got into a habit of leaving it there overnight—just in case. I grasped it in a white-knuckled hand and crept to my bedroom door. Racked with nerves, I slowly, carefully, opened the door, trying not to make a noise. I craned my neck out and looked both ways down the hallway.

All quiet, all still.

I tiptoed towards the kitchen. I was about to enter the doorway when I collided with someone.

I screamed and shone the mini flashlight in their eyes. The other person screamed as well—or more like a yelp of shock.

"Chloe! It's only me." Yang Bora squinted through the powerful beam of light, her open hands raised in the air.

I was so panic-stricken that it took a long moment to realise I wasn't in danger. Eventually, my breath returned and my heartbeat slowed down. I lowered the flashlight.

"I thought you were an intruder," I confessed.

"I tried not to wake you," Bora said.

"Well, you did, and you gave me the fright of my life. You know what I've been through. You should know better."

She cringed. "I'm sorry. I didn't think."

"What was that loud noise before?"

"I tripped over the step by the door."

I didn't bother to ask if she was okay. "Planning to sneak in, take your things, and leave again, were you?"

"No, I was going to stay here the night, and continue to stay here, if you'll let me."

Her answer surprised me. After the way she acted when we saw each other in the stairwell, I believed I'd lost her forever.

"So…you're back?" I needed further convincing.

"Yes." She was resolute.

I didn't let my relief show. I couldn't let her off the hook that easy after what she did to me.

"I can't live with someone who isn't on my side," I said.

"I *am* on your side." Her eyes were wide and pleading.

"Have you had a change of heart?"

"I've always been on your side. I was just too afraid to admit it."

She sounded so earnest. I couldn't stay angry at her. I was sure she had her reasons.

"Sounds like we better have a talk," I said.

Bora agreed with a sharp nod. "There's a lot to discuss."

We made hot drinks in the kitchen—the sweet contents of two coffee sachets mixed with freshly boiled water—then we sat opposite each other at the dining table, the room lit by a single floor lamp in the corner. Half of Bora's heart-shaped face glowed warmly in the dim light, the other half in shadow. She cradled her mug in her hands and sipped.

"So, you *do* believe me?" I asked again.

"Yes, I do. I believed you the moment you said what you did," she explained.

"Then...why?"

"Because I'm terrified, Chloe. Terrified of what it means. I've worked so hard to get to this point in my career. *So* hard. Has it all been based on a lie?"

"Why would it be?"

"Because I can't work for Mr. Kim if he does things like that. I can't work in the entertainment industry if this goes on and it's considered normal. I've heard stories, rumours, but I shut them out, preferring to believe that nothing like that could ever happen, but now..."

"Wait—have you heard other rumours about Mr. Kim?"

"Not about Mr. Kim—other staff, other companies. I was distanced enough not to let it affect me."

"But not anymore," I said softly, understanding dawning.

"Hearing what you said was overwhelming. I didn't want to accept it, even though I knew deep down you must be speaking the truth. I'm sorry." She looked down at the table with a strained expression on her face.

This must have been eating her up inside for the past few days.

"I think I understand you a bit better now, but I wish you told me this straight away."

"I know. I wouldn't blame you if you hated me right now."

She kept her head hung low, but I could still make out the anguish swirling in the depths of her eyes.

"I don't hate you. I could never hate you."

After all she had done for me over the course of our friendship, the least I could do was forgive her.

She lifted her head a little. "Really?"

"Of course."

I offered her a wry smile, coaxing one from her as well.

"I swear I'll never do something like that to you again. Can we still be best friends?"

"Absolutely."

Her bubbliness returned, filling the hollowness of her cheeks and making her eyes sparkle.

She was back, hopefully for good.

"The question is, what can we do about Mr. Kim?" she asked, suddenly serious again.

"The reason I told you in the first place was because I thought you might know what to do," I explained.

"I'm afraid you've overestimated me. I really have no idea. What he did was bad, but not bad enough that the police would do anything about it."

"What about HR? I could make an anonymous complaint."

"Mr. Kim is part owner of the agency. Filing a complaint against him wouldn't achieve anything."

"Then...the media? They're always looking for entertainment industry scandals to report on."

"A good idea in theory, but I wouldn't advise it. Mr. Kim would counter-attack. He'd get an article written about you which would be far worse. He'd drag your name through the mud to make you sound like a liar."

I sighed through gritted teeth. "You're right."

Bora adjusted her glasses. "We simply can't take on Mr. Kim by ourselves. He'll chew us up and spit us out. And then there's Shin Jinseung and Go Yoojin to consider."

I flinched at his name. "I haven't told Jinseung."

"I don't blame you. Who knows how he'd react? It's probably for the best—at least for now. We wouldn't want him to do anything rash. This is a complex issue. We need to think about it very carefully before taking action."

"And if Mr. Kim approaches me again in the meantime? Takes things a step further?"

"Then we'll have more ammunition to use against him."

My stomach lurched. "I don't know. That makes me feel uneasy."

"There *is* an alternative."

"What's that?"

"Quit working at KAM."

I shook my head. "I'd lose my visa. I'd have to leave the country."

"Exactly. You could leave all of this behind. Come back when Jinseung is discharged."

"I...don't know."

"Think about it."

Are those really my only two options? Both were untenable. Both made me feel ill.

"Well?" Bora asked, looking unsettled by my descent into deep and thoughtful silence.

"Let's play it by ear," I suggested.

Chapter 16

Face Mr. Kim or go back home. The choice plagued me for weeks until it began to feel irrelevant.

I hadn't seen Mr. Kim again since the initial incident. Time and space made me believe that perhaps I'd overreacted, perhaps he wasn't as dangerous as I'd built him up to be in my head. So I began to let my guard down.

The clock on the lesson room wall struck 7:30 p.m. I was halfway through a teaching session with Jung Jen, the first time I'd seen her in a long time because she had been busy shooting the medical drama, among other priorities.

Pink lipstick stood out against her ghostly white skin. Had she lost even more weight, or was she this skinny last time as well? I couldn't remember.

As I watched her silently work through an exercise, something Bora had said suddenly came back to me.

I've heard Mr. Kim is being particularly hard on her...She's always in his office for some reason or other...He's not happy with the situation...She's a liability...

I wondered what Jen thought of Mr. Kim. I had already asked Go Yoojin, perhaps now was my chance to question Jen.

She looked up at me. She must have sensed my enquiring stare.

"What is it?" she asked.

I was about to say, "Nothing," but changed my mind as soon as I opened my mouth.

I have to know.

"Actor-nim, Mr. Kim is your agent…"

Was that a slight flinch at his name?

She narrowed her eyes.

"What do you think of him?" I asked.

No games this time. No disguising it as a part of the lesson. Straight to the point.

She definitely flinched that time. She jolted back in her seat, eyes wide. "Why are you asking that?"

"Just…no reason."

I could hardly tell her the truth.

Her eyes flicked around the room. It looked like she was trying to find something. I followed her gaze but couldn't work out what she was looking at.

"I have no comments to make about him," she said, returning her focus to me.

A strange response, almost like she'd been instructed never to talk about him and it was the automatic reply she gave whenever someone asked. That was my impression, anyway.

"Huh. I see. Forget I said anything."

After that moment of weirdness, the rest of the lesson continued without a hitch.

"That's it for today," I said.

"Thank you, *Seonsaeng-nim*. I'll be going now." Jen tilted her head at me before leaving the room.

I stayed behind for a few minutes, jotting down notes on Jen's progress and ideas for what I could teach her in our next lesson.

Afterwards, I checked the time again, wondering if Bora would be finishing up soon too. It was getting pretty late, after all. Maybe she'd like a ride home. I sent her a text message, but she replied saying she was still held up with work.

I was half out of my chair when the lesson room door suddenly swung open. I was so startled that I gasped and dropped back down into my seat, clutching my heaving chest.

The woman who entered looked at me funny. She wore a plasticky apron and rubber gloves, tugging a cart of cleaning products behind her.

"Sorry," she said. "Should I come back later?"

"No. I'm leaving now." I gathered myself and left the room.

In my flustered state I forgot all about taking the stairs and automatically approached the elevator. As soon as I punched the button, I realised my mistake, but I decided that the chance of seeing Mr. Kim was slim. I'd take the risk.

I watched the floor number on the display panel descend, praying that I wouldn't see him inside. I tensed in anticipation when the metal door lurched open.

"Oh! Hey, Chloe."

I relaxed at the familiar voice. Seo Minjung stood inside the elevator, immaculately dressed as usual, a long trench coat over a sleek turtleneck and high-waisted trousers, her straight black hair secured with a chic tortoiseshell clip.

"Minjung-ssi!" I said, grateful to see her friendly face. "Finished for the day?"

"Yup."

"Me too."

"How are you? We don't bump into each other often."

"I know. I'm not here very often, so it's not surprising."

"Have you met the new recruits yet? I hear you'll be teaching them."

"New recruits?"

"You didn't know? Nam Sungjin and Do Junghwan just joined. Everyone in the office is talking about them."

Of course. Mr. Kim *did* say there would be new recruits. I had been so focused on other things that I hadn't absorbed it as fact.

"Oh! I remember now. Yes, I'm meant to be teaching them but I haven't heard anything from their managers yet."

"You'll probably hear soon. Hope the new actors won't be too much of a handful."

"I'm sure they'll be delightful."

We continued to chat as I walked to the touchscreen by the reception desk to sign out.

"Are you catching the subway?" Minjung asked.

"No. I'm parked downstairs. I don't take public transit anymore."

"Ah, that's right. I forget that you could get recognised these days. To me, you're—"

Her words faded into silence as soon as I saw Mr. Kim. He crossed the glossy floor carrying a black briefcase. He seemed to be moving in slow motion as I focused on him, everything else drowned out by his presence. I tried to avert my eyes but they were stuck to him.

Please, don't notice me...

As soon as I thought these words, his head turned and his eyes locked onto mine. Two cold, black eyes, soulless, just like Oh Sejung's. A bitter wave of dread seeped into my veins and crept through my body.

"Chloe..."

The voice was distant, as if I were underwater and someone were calling to me from the shore.

Mr. Kim no longer looked my way. Time sped back up as he strode purposefully towards the door.

"Chloe?"

Minjung waved a hand in front of me and I snapped out of my trance.

"Are you okay?"

"Yeah. Sorry, spaced out for a second there." *On the verge of another panic attack, more like.* "What were you saying?"

"Nothing, really. Just that I don't think of you as a celebrity, or the girlfriend of a celebrity, but knowing how hardcore some of the fans can be, you're right to avoid public outings when you can."

Little did she know that I had already had a dangerous encounter with one such "hardcore" fan.

"Anyway," she said. "I'm going to go home now. See you around."

"Okay. See you."

Mr. Kim had left the building through the main doors, which meant it would be safe to go down to the carpark.

I drove home thinking maybe Bora had been right. Maybe I should quit working at KAM. Avoidance tactics would only go so far, and I couldn't work in fear of seeing him again. I gnashed my teeth and grumbled. *What should I do?* Having to quit jobs and move was starting to become depressingly frequent, and the thought of going back to the UK was too bleak to bear. I wanted to stay in Korea so I could at least visit Jinseung whenever he had a break from the army. Ending up back at my parents' house in defeat like the other times was the last thing I wanted. My life was here, no matter what.

Buster was all over me as soon as I walked in the door, yapping and whining.

"Poor boy," I said, petting his fluffy head. "You've been waiting patiently for your dinner."

He followed me to the kitchen, where I filled his bowl with dog food and replenished his water.

After taking care of Buster's dinner, I turned my attention to preparing my own meal. I made enough for Bora as well, in case she didn't have time to eat at work, as was often the case.

I was about to serve the hot Japanese-style curry when I heard the front door open, followed by footsteps directly towards me.

Bora entered the room, a strange expression of determination mixed with concern on her face.

"Bora-ya! I thought you were going to be much later," I said. "There's plenty of food, if you want some."

"You've got to see this," she said. Her mind clearly wasn't on food.

"See what?"

She marched straight into the living room and turned the TV on.

"What is it?" I asked, watching the screen.

"You'll see."

A news programme played. A story about something to do with China's economy. I watched with a furrowed brow.

"Not this," Bora said. "I'm sure it will come on again soon."

After an ad break, the news anchor reappeared on camera.

"And back to tonight's top story," she read, "sexual abuse allegations have been made against a prominent executive in the entertainment industry."

Chapter 17

A lot of unusual things happened during my next lesson with Jung Jen. The first thing that shocked me was that Jen arrived early. No one ever arrived early. Tight schedules meant the actors were more likely to arrive late, or never, than on time, and especially not early.

The second thing that shocked me was that it looked like she'd been crying. Her eyes had a red tinge and were slightly swollen. Her makeup was blotchy, as if it had been ruined then haphazardly reapplied over the top.

"Hello," she said quietly, taking her seat opposite me.

I was so used to seeing the actors look sick and exhausted that I usually didn't ask "Are you okay?" even when I wanted to, but this time was different.

"Is everything okay?" I asked.

"Yes," she said.

I didn't believe her.

"I know I'm just your English tutor, but if there's something wrong, I'd like to try and help you. No matter what it is."

She smiled weakly. "Is it that obvious I've been crying?"

"Yes. I'm afraid it is."

She avoided my gaze, threading and unthreading her fingers together in her lap. "It's…really nothing. Just stress."

"Hmmm. I see."

There was something she wasn't telling me, but she was clammed up tight in her shell. I could tell she wasn't going to open up to me any time soon.

"If you don't want to talk about it, I'll get straight into the lesson, but if you change your mind, I'll listen to you. No one has to know that we just talked rather than doing the lesson."

She was adamant. "It's okay. Let's just get on with it."

It seemed pushing her wasn't going to get me anywhere.

"All right. Let's see…" I scanned the notes in front of me. "Last time we worked on the topic of shopping. Shall we start where we left off?"

"Okay. Oh—I did this." She rummaged in her bag and presented me with her workbook.

"Homework?" I asked, stunned.

"Yes."

My third shock of the lesson. She had never done homework before.

"Wow. You did this even though you're so busy and stressed?"

"Yes. Actually, it's less stressful to focus on homework than anything else. It's more like stress-relief."

"Can't say I've heard that before. Let's go through this first, then."

I reached for her workbook, but Jen abruptly slammed her hand down on the front cover before my fingertips could brush it.

"No," she said. "I mean, could you mark it after the lesson then go over it with me next time? I'd rather work on something else right now."

Her request made me raise an eyebrow but I went along with it.

"Sure. If that's what you want."

"Thanks." She looked me in the eyes as she pushed the book towards me. "By the way, I've marked some parts that I'm unsure about. Please pay attention to them."

Something felt odd about this request too. Perhaps it was the strange seriousness with which she spoke, or maybe it was just my imagination and I was reading too much into it. I'd been overthinking things a lot these days. That news story from the other day was case in point. Bora and I both had our suspicions, but the suspect had not been named, and Mr. Kim was still in his job, business as usual, so it couldn't really have been about him, could it?

"I will," I replied.

I filed her workbook away in my bag, making a mental note to check it as she'd asked.

With that out of the way, we carried on with the lesson. Jen's mood seemed to lift slightly, but she was still distracted and scatterbrained.

As time went on, the evidence of her past tears faded. No one would suspect a thing unless they looked very closely.

"*Omo!*" Jen gasped when her phone started to beep. She swiped at the screen. "I've got to go. Meeting with Mr. Kim."

"With Mr. Kim?" I repeated, unable to stop the words slipping from my mouth.

"Yes."

Could that be the reason why she was so upset? Stress about her upcoming meeting with Mr. Kim?

"With Mr. Kim…" I repeated, thinking it over.

Jen ignored me, grabbing her bag to leave.

"Be careful," I spluttered before she left the room.

She didn't turn back or acknowledge what I said.

I banged my fist on the table in frustration. *Shit!* This was eating me up inside. If there was even the smallest chance that my suspicions were right, I had to do something. But what?

I couldn't sit around any longer with the knowledge that something bad might happen in the back of my brain. Before I could talk myself out of it, I grabbed my things and rushed up the stairs to the fifth floor.

Chapter 18

I'd sworn to myself that I'd never visit the fifth floor alone again, yet here I was.

Being after hours, the reception desk was closed. I tiptoed through the corridors, my eyes and ears tuned in for signs of movement. I was shaking and my heart was beating loud in my ears. If anyone saw me sneaking around on the fifth floor, they'd surely question my intentions, and I wouldn't be able to provide an adequate explanation for why I was there. That was why I had to be careful not to get caught.

Very few offices occupied the floor. I assumed they all belonged to the company's top executives. Even the areas of the building which were dedicated to the company's talent weren't as posh as this floor, with its designer furniture pieces, framed paintings, and fancy light fittings, all set within a rich colour scheme of gold, aubergine, and dark wood.

I had only recently learned that KAM stood for Kim, Ahn, and Moon—the three founders of the agency. Mr. Moon had retired, but Mr. Kim and Mr. Ahn remained active, though Mr. Kim was much more visible.

I silently crept towards my target. Mr. Kim's office was situated down a long, windowless corridor, quite far apart from the rest of the offices. You wouldn't go past it unless it were your destination.

My ears pricked at the clang of the elevator doors opening, then footsteps. They sounded like they were heading in my direction. Heart beating furiously in my chest, I scurried around a corner, then pressed my back flush to the wall, trying not to make a sound.

The footsteps faded, and I thought I heard the creak of a door open and close. They must have gone into their office. *Whew.* I waited to catch my breath before moving on.

Mr. Kim's door was now in sight. Fists clenched into tight balls at my sides, I approached. The door was closed, of course, and so were the blinds of the internal window.

My mind raced. *I can't believe I'm doing this. Why am I even here? What good will this do?*

Breathing fast and heavy, I leaned close and pressed my ear to the wall. His office was most likely soundproofed, but I tried to listen anyway, straining my ears for just a hint of what might be going on inside.

It was no use. I couldn't hear anything. Pulling away in defeat, my gaze fell to where a crack of light shone beneath the door. That was when another idea struck me. *Worth a shot.* I knelt down with my ear almost to the carpet to try and listen through the crack. To my surprise, I could make out a voice—Mr. Kim's voice. But I couldn't exactly hear what he was saying. It seemed to be a one-sided conversation because I couldn't hear anyone else. Maybe he was on the phone?

This isn't any good...

I stood back up. What else could I do? Knock on the door? No, that was out of the question.

Looking around again, I suddenly became aware of all the security features of the door. It seemed to have some kind of electronic lock. Maybe an eye or fingerprint scanner. I hadn't paid attention when Mr. Kim took me to his office last time, so I couldn't remember how he unlocked it. I noticed the security cameras. It felt like all of them were trained directly on me. Perhaps I was being paranoid, but could there be a screen inside his office which showed who was outside? It was possible, though I couldn't recall ever seeing one when I was inside. I started to panic. *Arrggh.* I really hadn't thought this through properly. *Maybe I should just leave.*

I heard a sound. Movement behind the door. A clunking sound like the door was about to open.

Oh shit. What do I do? Run away?

There was no time. He'd see me.

Think, Chloe, think!

The door swung open and Mr. Kim appeared, partially silhouetted, dramatic shadows filling the hollows of his face. He looked down at me and didn't seem surprised.

He knew I was out here.

"Miss Gibson," he said. "What are you doing?" Despite his politeness, there was an undertone of malice in his voice.

"I, errr, sorry, Mr. Kim, I just…I just had a lesson with Jung Jen, and she left this with me." I fished for the workbook in my bag and held it out to him. "She told me she had a meeting with you, so I thought I'd try and catch her on her way out and give it to her."

Mr. Kim's eyes narrowed. "She told you she had a meeting with me?"

"Yes. That's what she said."

"Hmm."

"Is she there? Can I give it to her?" I craned my neck trying to peer into his office through the partially open door.

"She's not here."

From what I could see, he was telling the truth. His office appeared to be empty.

"Oh. That's strange."

"Yes, it is." His eyes lowered to the workbook in my hands. "I can take that and give it to her or her manager."

I dug my fingers into the book, clutching it much tighter than necessary. "No. That's fine. I'll give it to her."

"Suit yourself."

"I'll just be going then. Sorry to interrupt you." I turned away, eager to get away from him.

Mr. Kim's hand came firmly down on my shoulder.

I froze, with a shudder emanating from the point our bodies connected.

"Miss Gibson," he said.

"Yes?"

"Don't come to my office again unless I ask you to, or you've made an appointment through my secretary. You should know better."

"Yes, sir."

He dropped his hand and I walked away, resisting the urge to break into a run to escape. I heard his door lock with a click.

It wasn't until I was safely downstairs that I considered the situation. If Jung Jen wasn't with Mr. Kim, then where was she? Was she having a secret meeting with someone else? *Hmmm...*Maybe she just got her schedule confused. *Yeah.* That was more likely. Or maybe she was meeting someone else called Kim? Another likely scenario, considering the number of Kims in Korea. *Aggghh. What an idiot!* I put myself at risk and made a complete fool of myself in front of Mr. Kim for nothing. I should never have gotten involved.

Chapter 19

Another day, another English lesson, but as soon as I entered the lobby of KAM HQ, I knew something was wrong. A strange atmosphere pervaded the room. Everyone spoke in hushed tones with grave looks on their faces. I tried to listen to their conversations as I passed but couldn't hear anything except vague snatches. The words "devastating" and "tragic" stood out.

The receptionist, Minha, wore a similarly glum expression. I reached for the touch screen by the desk to sign myself in, when she stopped me.

"I don't think any of your lessons will be going ahead today," she said.

That was when I knew for sure that something serious was afoot. I was almost too scared to ask.

"Why not? Has something happened?"

She frowned. "Haven't you heard?"

"No. I just got here."

"We only found out a few minutes ago. It's terrible news. There's been a suicide."

My heart dropped and a sick taste filled my mouth.

"Who?" I asked, my throat dry.

I anticipated the answer before she said it.

"Jung Jen."

I felt faint. My head was spinning.

"No…" I choked. "Please, no. Not Jen. No."

"I'm afraid so."

"But I saw her just yesterday…"

"Yes. A lot of people saw her around the office yesterday. It's so tragic. Her manager discovered her body earlier this morning when he went to pick her up from her home. That's all I know—that's all anyone knows right now."

"Oh my God. I can't…" I pressed my hands to my temples and scrunched my eyes shut.

This wasn't happening. This was just another nightmare. *Yes. That must be it. A nightmare…*

"Are you all right?" Minha asked.

Flecks of light danced behind my eyelids. My legs felt weak. I was about to collapse.

"Whoa, there." She came out from behind the desk and rushed to provide a hand in support.

I clung to her arm, forcing myself to take slow and deep breaths until I recovered. "Thanks. I'm just so shocked."

"You should go home. Nobody will be getting much work done today."

"Yes, I will. Thank you for telling me."

"Will you be okay?"

"I think so."

No, not really, but I didn't want to cause a fuss.

She gently let me go and returned to her station.

I walked away, shivering despite the building's heating.

Jung Jen… The image of her in my head was so fresh and vivid. Long middle-parted hair framing an oval face with large eyes, an elegant nose, and fine lips. She was so lovely…so *young*…and now she was dead.

I paced the floor, the reality of the situation still sinking in. *I knew something weird was going on with Jen, and now this happens. I* couldn't help feeling like I was partially to blame for this horrible outcome.

Other people entered the building with the same confusion as I did before. I wondered whether Yang Bora and Go Yoojin were aware. Surely someone had told them. How were they dealing with the news? Right on cue, my phone began to ring. Yang Bora was calling.

I picked up and cut to the chase. "Did you hear?"

"I was about to ask you the same thing. So, both of us know." Her voice sounded weak and fragile, not the usual boisterous tone.

"Where are you?"

"I'm at Actor Go's house. She's absolutely distraught. Jung Jen was a good friend to her and she had no idea that something like this would happen."

"Bora-ya…" I needed to tell her what was on my mind.

"Yes?"

"When Jung Jen came to her lesson yesterday, it was obvious she'd been crying. I tried to talk to her but she wouldn't tell me anything. I feel so guilty…"

"Don't say that. It's not your fault."

"I feel like I could have done something. If only I had tried harder to reach her…"

"Everyone close to her will be feeling that way. We all knew she was going through a difficult time."

"I suppose…" I sighed deeply. "Will you be coming home? I don't really want to come back to an empty house right now."

"No. I need to stay with Actor-nim and keep an eye on her. You know what she's like. Who knows what she'd do, the state she's in."

"Ah. I see."

"But why don't you come over to her house?"

I perked up at her suggestion. "Would that be okay?"

"Just a sec. I'll ask."

I heard the muffled sound of her conversing with Yoojin in the background.

"Yes," she said, back on the line. "She says you can come over since you knew Jung Jen too. I'll text you the address."

"Thanks. I'll come soon."

I ended the call and made my way straight down to the carpark. The text message with the address came through and I typed it into the car's built-in GPS.

When I drove out of the carpark, the scene outside surprised me. The weather had been fine when I arrived. Now, thick grey clouds rolled across the sky and raindrops furiously pelted down, ricocheting off the asphalt. I flicked the windscreen wipers onto the highest setting.

Thoughts swirled in my head as I drove, paying attention to little else except the robotic voice of the GPS. I seemed to be catching every red traffic light, moving at a snail's pace in the heavy congestion as the relentless rain fell.

Something niggled in the back of my mind. Was it possible that Jung Jen took her life over something Mr. Kim did to her? Too many little things stacked up: Mr. Kim's behaviour towards me, the news report about a prominent entertainment industry executive, Jung Jen's reaction when I asked her about Mr. Kim, and the fact she said she was meeting him yesterday then seemingly didn't. Coincidences? Maybe…or maybe not.

Slowly but surely, the pieces came together like a jigsaw puzzle in my head. What if Jung Jen was the whistleblower who reported the executive? What if the consequences were too much for her to handle and she committed suicide? Or worse. What if it wasn't suicide at all? Mr. Kim's face, twisted and menacing, flashed in my mind.

Someone honked at me, and I realised I was first in the queue at the intersection. Without thinking, I pressed my foot on the accelerator, speeding up to get through before the light turned red, swinging the steering wheel around a little more sharply than necessary. A sickening screech rang out as the tyres skidded on the slippery-wet asphalt. I went careening wide around the corner, shock and panic engulfing me.

Chapter 20

I gripped the steering wheel, white-knuckled, heart pounding as my car hurtled towards the waiting traffic on the other side of the intersection. Time slowed down. I automatically moved my foot from the accelerator to the brake, trying not to slam down, pushing gently instead.

Please…

The car slid nearer to a collision. I braced myself, muscles tensing.

Time sped back up. It happened in a blur. My car missed the other car by a hair's breadth and emerged into the correct lane unscathed. Gulping mouthfuls of air, I regained full control and pulled over as soon as I could. Adrenaline pulsed through my body. I was shaking. I buried my face in my hands and sobbed.

Stupid. So stupid. I could have killed someone. I could have killed myself.

I never should have driven in my fragile mental state. I wasn't the best driver in the world to begin with, and I still wasn't used to the roads and traffic rules in Seoul. Add in the rain and my preoccupation with overanalysing the circumstances around Jung Jen's death and no wonder I nearly had an accident.

I didn't feel like driving the rest of the way, but I didn't really have a choice. According to the GPS, I was almost at Go Yoojin's house anyway. After taking a few more minutes to regain my composure, I pulled the seatbelt on and started the car up again, windscreen wipers reactivating with a swish and a thunk.

This time, I'd properly focus on driving, going slowly and cautiously. People could honk at me all they want.

I concentrated hard as I drove, emerging from a main shopping area onto a tree-lined street near the Han river, elegant low-rise apartment buildings tucked neatly behind fences and gates. Street-lights glowed dully through the dreariness. The rain had eased to a light drizzle.

"You have reached your destination," the pleasant female GPS voice told me.

This must be it.

To my right stood a modern five-storey building with a flat roof and balconies jutting out from its slate-grey exterior. I turned into the driveway, but a tall gate blocked the entrance. I called Bora and she opened the gate remotely. The iron bars clunked open. An outdoor light flicked on automatically as I rolled up towards the main doors of the building.

I put the car in park and turned the engine off.

Thank goodness. I made it.

I slumped forward over the steering wheel, heaving a sigh.

When I lifted my head, I saw Bora emerge from the building. I stumbled out of the car, rain spitting in my hair and on my shoulders.

"You made it," she said, coming to my side.

"Barely," I groaned.

She furrowed her brow, examining me. "It looks like you're in shock. You're pale as a ghost."

I rubbed my forehead. "I was shocked about Jung Jen, but I also nearly had a car accident on the way here. I'm still a bit shaken."

"Oh, dear. What happened?"

"My head was reeling with the news, and the rain was coming down so hard...It was my fault. I wasn't careful enough. I almost hit another car as I turned left at a traffic light."

"Thank God you're okay. I couldn't have taken any more bad news on top of all this. Come on. Let's get you inside."

She led the way through a second gate to the private entrance of Yoojin's ground-floor apartment and unlocked the door.

Spread over two levels, the actor's residence was much more extravagant and luxurious than Jinseung's old apartment. The bottom floor consisted of a large open-plan living area decorated in a glamorous, girly theme, with chandelier lighting and soft furnishings upholstered in velvet and faux fur.

"Want a hot drink?" Bora asked.

"Yes, please," I replied.

"Coffee?"

"Thanks."

"Take a seat and I'll bring it over."

I sat down on a tufted, velvety couch covered in fluffy cushions. A giant black-and-white portrait of Yoojin graced the opposite wall, her alluring pose in stark contrast to the pale and puffy-eyed figure crumpled in a heap on the chair across from me.

"Thank you for letting me come over to your house, Actor-nim," I said.

"She was my friend!" Yoojin wailed.

"I know. You must be very upset."

She sniffled and buried her head in the blanket over her lap.

I wasn't sure what else to say. She must have known Jung Jen much better than I did.

"*They* killed her," she moaned between sobs.

I straightened to attention. "They?"

"San Seung and Lee Changho's fans. The online bullying was too much. Must have driven her to it."

"Oh. I see."

"We don't know for sure that's the reason," Bora said, returning with a tray of three coffee mugs, then taking a seat beside me. "And perhaps we'll never know. She didn't leave a note, after all."

I sharply turned my head to her, surprised by this new tidbit. "Is that so? Where did you hear that?"

"Oh, I heard it from someone who heard it from Jung Jen's manager. Wait. No. Maybe I heard it from someone who *heard it from someone* who heard it from Jung Jen's manager. One of those."

"No note…" *How odd.*

Bora shook her head at me. "I know what you're thinking, but it definitely looked like a suicide. From what I heard, the police thoroughly investigated the scene and didn't find any signs of foul play. As for why she did it, well, there could have been a number of factors. Like Actor-nim said, bullying might have played a role, but she has also been under immense pressure to rebuild her career after the scandal. I wouldn't be surprised if that had something to do with it as well."

I took a sip of coffee. Upon reflection, my theory was a long shot compared to simple explanations like bullying, stress, and depression.

After finishing my drink, I took my mug to the kitchen to get a refill. Bora appeared behind me.

"What are you thinking?" she asked, looking into my eyes. "I can tell you have something on your mind."

"It's just…Well, it's silly, really."

"Nothing's silly. Tell me."

"I can't help thinking that Mr. Kim has something to do with all this."

I saw her swallow, a small lump bobbing in her throat.

"It's possible," she said.

"I recently asked her about him and she acted strangely. She was startled. She didn't end up saying anything bad about him, but still…"

"Mr. Kim was furious at her after the scandal. Everyone knows that. Yet he didn't drop her from the agency. I always found that strange."

"There was that story on the news. We both wondered if it could be about Mr. Kim. Well, what if we're right? And what if it was Jung Jen who reported him?"

Bora rubbed her chin. "I see what you mean, but there's too little information to jump to conclusions like that."

"Yesterday, Jen said she had a meeting with Mr. Kim after the lesson. I'm still not really sure why, but I went to Mr. Kim's office. To check on her, I suppose. I was afraid something might happen to her. But she wasn't there."

"She probably just got mixed up. Happens all the time."

"Yeah. That's what I thought too, but it's strange."

"I don't disagree. It seems there are a lot of unanswered questions."

We stood in silence for a minute, stewing in troubling thoughts. Then our phones made a sound at the same time.

"Huh?" I said.

Bora grabbed her phone first to check. "Oh! Here it is."

"What is it?"

"An announcement from Mr. Kim. Wait—I'll read it." She cleared her throat. "'To all KAM Entertainment staff, I have very sad news to share. Early this morning, our very own Jung Jen passed away in her home. I understand this is a difficult time for everyone who worked closely with Jung Jen. Anyone who feels they cannot work today is permitted to go home, and an on-site counsellor will be available for anyone who needs additional support. I ask that you all respect the privacy of Jung Jen's family. Do not speak to the media or speculate about the cause of death.'"

"I wonder how long it took him to get the phrasing just right," I mused.

"He's being deliberately vague, all right," Bora said.

"I don't know if I can trust a word from him anymore."

"Me too. And so much for not speculating."

I threw my head back with a sigh.

* * *

JINSEUNG and I talked on the phone for a long time that night.

"I feel numb," he said, voice raw.

The only time I recalled him sounding worse for wear was in the aftermath of my kidnapping.

I could hear other people in the background. Distant voices. Chatter and scattered laughter.

"Where are you right now?" I asked.

"In the lounge. It's communal, just as everywhere else is. I don't have the privacy to cry."

A vision of tears like shiny crystals on Jinseung's cheeks squeezed my heart.

"Do you *need* to cry?"

"Well, I'd like the option to without, y'know, drawing attention to myself."

"Hide somewhere."

This drew a hint of a chuckle from him.

"I will if I feel the sudden urge, but seriously, I think I'll be okay."

"Did you know Jen well?"

"We weren't particularly close or anything, but it's the shock of it. She was my colleague. My *seonbae*. Makes me think that it could have just as easily been me."

The very notion made my gut wrench.

"You've had those thoughts before?" I croaked.

He took a second to reply. "No. You wouldn't believe it, but I'm actually pretty terrified of dying."

There it was again—an air of lightheartedness despite the gravity of the situation.

"Is that a joke?"

"Sorta. Look, I recognise that I've been lucky. I've had it easy compared to others. Scandals haven't ruined me, and I've got you. So, no, I haven't thought about it."

He sounded serious now, so I believed him, relief sweeping over me.

"Just know that I'll always be there for you," I said. "You can tell me if you're feeling stressed out, or if you can't handle things, and I'll help you."

"I know. Thank you. And I'd do the same for you."

I felt a twinge of guilt again for holding back information from him, but I shook it off. Now wasn't the time.

"How are you holding up, anyway?" Jinseung asked. "You probably knew Jen even better than I did. All those one-on-one lessons…"

"We didn't talk much about our personal lives. Well, sometimes she mentioned her parents, but that's about it."

Maybe we should have talked more. Maybe I could have helped.

"Ah. Makes sense."

Buster stirred on my lap, and I stroked his snowy fur. His cuteness helped put me at ease. No wonder pets were considered a form of therapy.

"*Jagi*, I wish I could be with you right now," Jinseung said. "Talking on the phone isn't enough. I want to hug you. Kiss you better."

"Hearing you say that makes me miss you even more."

"Are you okay? Is Yang Bora with you?"

"Yes, she's here."

Go Yoojin's assistant had taken over for the night, so we were back home. Bora had already gone to bed.

"Good. Rest well, eat well—Bora too. Look after each other."

"We will."

"I love you."

"I love you too."

Then came the hardest part. I waited for him to hang up first because I couldn't do it. The end of the call was a short, sharp shock to my system. Our connection severed.

Chapter 21

When Mr. Kim made his speech at Jung Jen's memorial service a few days later, I couldn't help but notice the eye rolls in the audience. He stood behind a lectern, wearing a black suit, a sombre look on his face. The wall behind him was covered with pink and purple flowers and photographs of Jung Jen along with pages of handwritten messages to her.

As per the wishes of Jen's parents, a private funeral for family members only had recently been held. Today's memorial service was for friends and colleagues, as well as a specially selected media outlet to cover the event. I sat in a row in the audience with Changsoo, Bora, and Yoojin. We watched on with scepticism as Mr. Kim continued his speech.

"The loss of Miss Jung Jen—or Jung Seoyeon, as she was known to many—has been felt deeply by the team at KAM Entertainment," he said. "In this time of great sadness, it is a reminder that we must do all that we can to promote the mental health and wellbeing of our team members."

His words were in sharp contrast to a company-wide email he sent a day ago, which basically said that the time for mourning was over, and that everyone should get back to business as usual. The free counselling service had been dismantled before hardly anyone had the chance to use it. I could feel Bora twitch with suppressed rage on the seat next to me.

Fortunately, the rest of the speeches were much more heartfelt and sincere. The sound of people sniffling and wiping their tears filled the room. Yoojin even broke down and bawled at one point. She drew everyone's attention, but no one made a fuss. Bora quietly offered her a packet of tissues.

At the end of the service, we each took turns to kneel and pray at the shrine—a simple display consisting of a photo of Jen, a memorial tablet, and a written prayer, as well as offerings of food and drink laid out in a special arrangement on the table. When it was my turn, I bent down on my knees. I silently prayed that Jen's soul was resting in peace, then dipped my head to the floor in a deep bow.

When the formalities were over, everyone stood around conversing for a while before moving to an adjacent room with low tables set out. A buffet had been prepared where guests could help themselves to food and beverages. Our group grabbed a small table to ourselves.

"What about Mr. Kim's speech, eh?" Bora said. She looked around, making sure he wasn't nearby. "What a hypocrite."

"I agree," Changsoo said. "He certainly hasn't given the staff much time to recover from this tragedy."

Not to mention what he did to me.

Bora and I exchanged covert looks, acknowledging the extra information and suspicions we held.

Yoojin squirmed. "I gotta use the bathroom. Manager-nim?"

"Sure, I'll go with you," Bora said.

She got up to accompany her, leaving Changsoo and me alone at the table. Changsoo looked at me with unnerving pinpoint eyes.

"You're hiding something," he said, voice low.

"What do you mean?" I asked, unable to keep a hint of panic out of my voice.

"It's to do with Mr. Kim, isn't it? You flinch whenever anyone says his name. You can't look at him when he's in the same room."

He noticed that? Damn. The jig is up.

"Ugh. Nothing escapes you, does it?"

"Whatever it is, please tell me. Perhaps I can help."

I hesitated. *Can I trust him? What if he tells Jinseung? Worse—what if he tells Mr. Kim?*

"There's no use hiding things from me," he pressed. "I'll find out eventually. I'll ask Mr. Kim."

"No!" I stammered, accidentally raising my voice.

A quick glance around the room revealed I hadn't drawn attention to myself.

"Please don't," I said softly.

"Tell me then."

"I can't tell you *here*. In front of everyone."

"Then let's go outside and have a little talk, shall we?"

Why did I feel like a child about to get scolded?

"Fine," I said.

While Changsoo and I didn't always see eye to eye, I did know one thing for sure—he was on Jinseung's side and always would be. He wouldn't do anything that would make Jinseung hate him, and by proxy, that meant he wouldn't do anything to harm me.

I followed him outside to the carpark where he unlocked his car.

"Get in the passenger seat. No one will hear if we talk inside the car."

Unlike his work vehicle, Changsoo's personal car was messy inside and had a slight smell like stale sweat. I wanted to wind down the window but that would defeat the purpose of going in the car.

"Go on," he said, sitting in the driver seat. "Tell me what happened."

I told him about the incident in Mr. Kim's office—nothing more, nothing less. The plain truth.

Changsoo listened attentively, his mouth a straight line.

"So, that's about it," I finished.

"Mr. Kim hasn't done anything else since then?"

"No. He hasn't."

"Then let's not do anything hasty, especially since there's no proof except your word. Mr. Kim would destroy you if you came out with this. Ruthless bastard."

"I know."

"And better not tell Jinseung or he'll do something stupid."

I nodded.

"Thank you for telling me," Changsoo said. "I'll be careful about Mr. Kim from now on. Don't go meeting him on your own. If he ever requests to see you, I'll go with you."

Hearing Changsoo offer his help was actually very reassuring.

"Thanks. I'll definitely take you up on that if I need to."

"Shall we head back inside?"

"Yes. They'll be wondering where we went."

The post-ceremony celebration was in full swing by the time we returned, groups at the tables immersed in lively chatter, food and drinks flowing. To my relief, Mr. Kim was nowhere to be seen. Probably left early and went back to work. Wouldn't surprise me.

Bora and Yoojin had returned to the same table and were waiting for us. They hadn't started eating or drinking yet.

"There they are," Bora said.

"Who wants a drink?" Changsoo boomed.

Both Bora and Yoojin raised their hands enthusiastically. I followed suit.

"What was that about?" Bora asked when I had lowered myself onto the floor cushion opposite her and Changsoo was out of earshot.

"He worked out that something was going on," I explained.

"Did you tell him anything?"

"I had to."

"What did he say?"

"Not much. Just warned me not to do anything hasty. Said he can accompany me to meetings in future."

"Ah. That's okay, then."

"I think he's a bit worried."

"Unsurprising."

Go Yoojin began to get agitated from being left out of our private little whispered conversation.

"What are you two talking about?" she asked.

"It's stuff concerning Shin Jinseung," Bora improvised.

"What about him?"

Fortunately, Changsoo returned with shot glasses and bottles of soju, which took Yoojin's attention off the topic at hand. Since she would be turning twenty this year, she was legally allowed to drink with us. Changsoo poured shots for everyone around the table. Yoojin was the first to down hers.

"Don't drink too fast," Bora scolded.

Yoojin pouted. "You know how stressed I am. Barely get a moment to grieve, and I have to start filming tomorrow."

"All the more reason not to drink a lot. You won't want a hangover tomorrow."

Despite Bora's pleas, Yoojin continued to drink heavily throughout the afternoon. None of the rest of us could do anything—Bora was the only person with any semblance of control over her.

"I think you've had enough," Bora said, taking the glass from her.

"You're not the boss of me!" Yoojin screeched.

"Let's all calm down," Changsoo said, holding his hands up in gentle protest.

Yoojin got to her feet. "You didn't know Jung Jen like I did. You don't understand anything!" She turned to storm away.

People around the room gawked at her and murmured between themselves. Yoojin's behaviour was very disrespectful at such an event and unbecoming of someone with her celebrity status. Fortunately, the media crew weren't present.

"Wait!" Bora got up to follow her. "Where are you going?"

"Home!"

"Let me get you a taxi."

Yoojin left the room, Bora close behind her.

"*Aigoo*," Changsoo said, arms folded on the table. "Shin Jinseung never acted like this."

"Well, if anyone can handle her, Yang Bora can," I said.

"I agree"

Bora returned a few minutes later looking mildly exasperated.

"Is Yoojin okay?" I asked.

"She's still in a huff, but I got her safely into a taxi. If she's hungover tomorrow, she'll only have herself to blame."

"I'm going to head off now too." Changsoo said, getting up.

"Are you sure?" Bora asked.

"Yeah. Got work to do."

"All right. Guess I'll probably see you around tomorrow."

"Have a good night."

"See you," I said.

Changsoo quietly left the premises.

"Maybe we should get going soon as well," I said to Bora.

"Okay. I'll just finish this drink. Hey, since it's just the two of us now…" she leaned in close and spoke in a low voice, "have you noticed something strange?"

I paused for a second, scanning the room for a hint as to what she was talking about. "Something strange? No, I can't think of anything."

"Jung Jen's manager didn't attend today."

"Huh. That *is* strange."

"Of all the people Jung Jen worked with, he was the closest to her. He should have been here. Why wouldn't he come?"

"Too distraught?"

"It's okay to be distraught at a memorial, so that's not a good reason."

"Maybe he went to the actual funeral, so he didn't feel the need to come to the memorial."

"As far as I know, no one from work went to the funeral. It was a tiny service with only her close family members."

"Well, there's probably another simple explanation."

"Hmmm…"

"Why? What do you think it means?"

She was about to speak when Mr. Kim re-entered the room.

"Let's discuss it on the way home, shall we?" she said.

I nodded.

Outside, the sky had clouded over, causing the late afternoon to fall into premature darkness. We stood by a busy six-lane street, Bora poised to flag down the first passing taxi.

"So, what are you thinking about Jung Jen's manager?" I asked as soon as we were safely in the back seat of a cab heading home.

"Don't you think it's funny that there hasn't been a peep out of Manager Jeong since Jung Jen's death? No statement. Nothing. Everything I've heard has been second-hand information. I haven't even seen him around the office. He's the person who spent the most time with Jung Jen since her debut, and he was the one who discovered her body."

"So?"

She looked me in the eye. "What if he knows something? Something important about her death that he doesn't want anyone to know."

"Are you saying that you don't think this is a straightforward suicide case after all?"

"I don't know. I'm just conjecturing. Hey, you have Manager Jeong's number, don't you?"

"Yes."

"Try giving him a call."

"Why?"

"I suspect he won't answer."

"And if he does, what should I say?"

"Whatever you want. That you called the wrong person."

I took out my phone and scrolled through my list of contacts for his name. I wasn't quite sure what the point of this exercise was but called him anyway.

Phone pressed to my ear, I waited for him to pick up, but I was greeted by an automated message instead.

"The number you have called is not available."

Chapter 22

A realisation struck me when I awoke the next morning after a deep, dreamless sleep:

The nightmares had stopped.

I hadn't had a single dream about Oh Sejung since that fateful meeting with Mr. Kim. I had barely thought about her at all. Instead, my mind had been occupied by Mr. Kim, Jung Jen, Manager Jeong, and the mysterious unnamed entertainment industry executive who may or may not be involved in all of this.

Bora had gone straight to bed when we got home after the memorial, so we hadn't had a chance to discuss our thoughts and feelings about Manager Jeong much. I was still mulling it all over as I walked Buster the next day.

The sky was clear and the sun shone bright on the quiet, suburban street, but I paid little attention to the prettiness of my surroundings, focused on the thoughts swirling in my head instead.

Two possible reasons for Manager Jeong's absence from the memorial and work in general stuck out.

A. He was too distraught to face anyone or do anything.

Or B. He was hiding.

I couldn't help but zero in on option B, considering all kinds of theories as to why he'd be hiding. By the end of the walk, I had developed a dull headache from thinking about it too much.

By habit, I checked the letterbox when I reached the gate. A single white envelope graced the metal cavity. We didn't receive much mail at our house, for privacy reasons, but occasionally there would be something.

This was an official-looking envelope addressed to me. Something from a government agency? I tore open the envelope as I walked to the door and slipped out its contents.

A gasp escaped my mouth as soon as I saw the logo in the corner of the letter—*Seoul Central District Court.* I dropped the piece of paper in my shock and it fluttered to the ground.

* * *

"Oh Sejung's trial will be on the fifteenth of July," I told my mother over the phone.

The letter from court had revealed the date had been brought forward. Part of me was glad the waiting would be over soon, another part was anxious about the whole ordeal.

"We'll book our flights today," Mum said. "Is it okay if we come a few days early?"

"Of course, and don't worry about accommodation—there is a spare room at my house and plenty of space."

"Thank you, darling."

"I'm so glad you're going to be here."

I meant it. While my relationship with my parents was strained at times, we were family, after all, and I missed them.

"Of course we'll be there. What kind of parents would we be if we weren't there to support you?"

"Well, thank you. I know it's a long way to come, and you don't exactly love flying."

"I'd fly around the world ten times if I had to. I need to see you and make sure that vile woman gets sent to prison."

"My lawyer has been very reassuring. She said there's no reason to worry about the outcome."

"That's good to hear."

"When it's all over, maybe we could do some sightseeing?"

"I'd like that. It would be nice to see why you love that city so much."

"Let me know when you've booked the flights and what time you'll arrive. I can pick you up from the airport."

"I will. While I have you on the phone, is there anything else you want to talk about? We haven't spoken properly in a long time. What have you been up to?"

More than I could possibly tell you in one phone call.

I tried to keep my tone breezy. "Oh, you know, just life. Work. The usual. There's really not much to say."

I didn't feel bad about lying through omission. She'd overreact if I told her the truth.

"I've been following the news, you know." She sounded stern.

I shifted uncomfortably in my seat. What exactly had she found out?

"Oh yeah?"

"I saw that a girl from that KAM company died."

I cringed. So she knew that much.

"Yes, it's terrible," I said.

"Did you know her?"

"No. I didn't."

An outright lie this time.

"Oh. Well, it's not very nice, is it? So young. So much promise. I hope *you're* okay."

"I am, Mum. Don't worry about me."

"I can't help it. Bad things happened to you and I couldn't stop them."

"I'm an adult. I can't rely on you to take care of me anymore. I have to look after myself."

"I know, dear, it's just...*hard.* I think about you every day and how you're getting on. I still can't understand why you chose to go back after everything that happened."

I didn't respond. I didn't want to get into an argument and ruin what was supposed to be a constructive phone call.

"Anyway," she said after a pause and a sigh. "I can't wait to see you again."

"Me too."

"I'll let you go now then, if you've got nothing else to say. I'll be in touch soon."

"Okay. Goodnight. I mean, good morning."

"Bye, dear."

I put my phone down, feeling a confused mixture of guilt and relief. Not unlike every other phone call with my mother, I supposed.

Crunch. Crunch.

What the—?

I turned around to see Bora munching through a bag of honey butter chips.

"Was that your mother?" she asked.

"*Aigoo!* How long were you standing there? I didn't see you come in."

"You finally called her, did you?"

"I did."

"Good."

She tipped the remainder of the chips into a serving bowl so we could share them. I poured two glasses of wine.

"So, it's Yoojin's birthday in a few days," she explained.

"Is she doing anything for it?"

"Yep. Even with her busy filming schedule, she's been insistent on having a party. Frankly, I have little energy for parties right now."

"Are you going to go? Does a manager even get an invite?"

"Of course I'm invited. You know how close we are."

"So, you're going, then?"

"Yes. I think it will be a good opportunity." She fixed me with a pointed gaze.

"What do you mean?"

"I mean that a lot of the female talent from KAM have been invited. This will be one of the few times they're all together outside of headquarters and free from being constantly surrounded by staff."

I was beginning to catch her drift. *She must have a plan.*

"If any of them know something about Jung Jen, or about Mr. Kim, or anything, it could be the ideal time to get them to speak," she explained.

"You're going to play detective?"

"In a sense."

"You'd really do that?"

She nodded. "You've drawn me in and now I have to know."

Chapter 23

Bora was a lump under her duvet cover.

"Hey…Are you awake?" I asked, peering in from the doorway.

The lump stirred and groaned.

"Hangover?" I asked

Another groan.

"I take that as a yes."

In all our time as friends, I had never known Bora to get a hangover before.

There's a first time for everything, I guess.

Last night had been Go Yoojin's birthday party, and I wanted to know what had happened. Did Bora manage to find anything out? Unfortunately, she was hardly in a state to tell me anything.

"Rest up," I said softly, then closed the door, leaving her in peace.

I went about my morning routine as usual: had breakfast, got dressed, walked Buster, showered. After all that, Bora still wasn't up.

At eleven o'clock, I knocked softly before entering her room again, carrying a plate with peanut butter on toast and a drink I bought from the convenience store which purported to be a hangover cure.

"I brought you breakfast. Are you up to talking or shall I just leave it on the bedside table?"

Bora turned over and slowly lowered the cover off her face, squinting. Her eyes without glasses looked much smaller.

"Thank you," she said.

I sat down on the edge of her bed. "So...what happened at the party?"

"I didn't manage to find anything out, if that's what you want to know."

"So the mission was a failure, then?"

"All I managed to do was make people feel uncomfortable. No one had a negative word to say about Mr. Kim or Manager Jeong."

I hung my head. "Damn. I was so certain you'd uncover some kind of lead."

"Maybe we should look at this as a positive development. Perhaps there really is no foul play going on here."

"Perhaps..."

"Pass me that drink, will you?"

I handed her the brightly labelled bottle.

While she glugged it down, I checked my phone. I had one new work email—an email from Mr. Kim.

What's this?

I checked the message, and as soon as I realised what exactly it was, my blood turned cold.

"You okay?" Bora wiped her mouth with the sleeve of her PJ top.

"Mr. Kim wants to meet me tomorrow."

She grimaced. "Yikes."

I slipped my phone back in my pocket, unwilling to hit "accept" on the meeting invite, or even look at it a second longer. The moment I had been dreading had arrived. Soon I'd find out what Mr. Kim's true intentions really were.

Or would I?

I recalled Changsoo's offer.

"Maybe it will be okay. Manager Bong said he'd chaperone me."

Bora's forehead wrinkled in thoughtfulness. "Or...you could just go alone and see what happens."

I was so surprised, I shot up off the bed. "What? Why would I want to do that?"

"Plan A failed, so maybe it's time for Plan B." She reached for her glasses on the bedside table and put them on. That was how I knew she was about to get serious.

* * *

"Testing, testing."

I stood in an empty bathroom at KAM HQ, checking the hidden recording device attached to my bra. If it worked as it should, a recording should be saved to my phone and to the cloud.

I played back the short snippet. My voice came out through the phone's speaker loud and clear.

All right. There was no delaying it any further. The recording device that Bora set me up with worked perfectly.

Time to face Mr. Kim.

Waiting for the elevator to arrive and take me up to his office, my determination swiftly diminished. What if it went wrong? What if he worked out that I was recording him? What if I was putting myself in danger by going in alone? I didn't have any backup. Bora was on set with Yoojin. Changsoo didn't know anything about the plan—he'd definitely have talked me out of it. *Maybe he should have.*

The elevator doors opened and I hesitantly stepped inside. My throat was tight, my lips dry. I thought about backing out. It wasn't too late. I could tell him I felt sick and had to go home. The nauseous feeling in my stomach was real, after all.

The elevator climbed the levels without stopping. Two, three, four...

No. I have to do this.

So far, the most damning evidence we had against Mr. Kim was the suggestive remarks he'd made to me. If we were going to catch him out for anything, this was our best shot. If I was right about his true character, then I needed to stop him before he inevitably abused me or someone else in the future. I gritted my teeth and stepped out onto the fifth floor.

Since the meeting was within regular office hours, the receptionist was still on duty. He sat behind an arched desk, dressed in a suit and tie. Everything gleamed with immaculate cleanliness.

"I have a meeting with Mr. Kim," I reported.

"Your name, please?"

"Chloe Gibson."

He checked his computer screen before telling me to take a seat.

I twitched and fidgeted on the chair, an unsettled feeling in the pit of my stomach. How exactly was this going to play out? If nothing happened, I wouldn't catch him, but if something did happen…

"You may go through now," the receptionist said. He walked me to Mr. Kim's office despite the fact I already knew the way. The door was open, and he gestured for me to go inside. I gulped and crossed the threshold.

Mr. Kim stood by the bookcase, placing a file back on the shelf. He was dressed in a navy suit with a snazzy pineapple-patterned shirt underneath.

Before I knew it, the receptionist had disappeared, and I was alone in the office with Mr. Kim.

"Hello, Chloe. Please, sit down." Mr. Kim smiled in a way which would seem pleasant by most accounts. "This won't take long."

As I lowered my fluttery body onto the leather couch, he shut the door. My ears tuned in to hear the click of the lock. I didn't hear it, but I couldn't be certain.

To my relief, Mr. Kim didn't join me on the couch, preferring to lean casually against his desk instead. He looked totally cool and collected as usual.

"What is this meeting about?" I asked abruptly.

He didn't miss a beat. "I just wanted to address a few points I touched upon in our last meeting."

I swallowed the dry lump in my throat and croaked, "I see."

Here it comes.

"But first, how are you? Are you getting on okay while Jinseung is away? I can imagine it isn't easy for you."

"No, it's not. But I'm okay."

"Good. And has Jinseung been keeping in touch?"

"We talk most days"

"That's good to hear. Jinseung is doing well in the army, isn't he?"

"Yes, it seems so."

"I always knew he'd suit the army. He has the right personality for it. He must miss you a lot, though."

"It's the same for any couple at this age. You just have to deal with it."

"That's true."

I was beginning to wonder when we'd get down to the true subject at hand. Surely this meeting wasn't just to check in on me and exchange pleasantries.

A moment of awkward silence passed before Mr. Kim cleared his throat.

"Now, with, uh, *recent events*, I've been reminded that talent and employee wellbeing should be top priority in this agency," he said.

Hmmm. So far this was not what I expected to hear. I lifted my chin and watched him more directly, searching for clues in his unblinking eyes and relaxed demeanour.

"And upon reflection," he continued, "I realised that some of the things I said to you could be misconstrued."

What's this? An apology? An excuse?

"I don't want you to think that you owe me, or the agency, anything," he said. "Do you understand what I'm saying?"

No. Not really. I thought that was exactly what he'd meant. My expression must have looked bemused, but all I could say was, "I think so."

"I was trying to make a helpful suggestion, that's all. There *is* more work available for you to do if it suits, you just need to get in touch with HR and sort it out."

"I'll think about it."

"Good. Brilliant. You do that. Now, is there anything you'd like to say on the matter?"

"Wha…? Uh, no."

"Then you may leave and get on with your day. Thanks for your time."

"Thank—"

Wait a minute. He hadn't said anything that could be used against him. I had to get him to say something incriminating, or this whole set-up was for nothing. Drawing from the depths of my courage, I spoke up.

"Mr. Kim?"

"Yes?"

"In our last meeting, you…"

Was it just my imagination or did his eyes turn a shade darker?

"Go on," he said, daring me.

I braced myself as I let the words out. "You touched my leg."

"*Omo.*" He brought a hand to his chest, frowning. "Did I do that? I cannot recall."

"You did," I pressed.

"If you think so, then I sincerely apologise. Sometimes I do break with formality—that's just my style. You're probably not used to that from Korean men. Sorry if I made you feel uncomfortable. That was never my intention."

He sounded so sincere. So genuine. Part of me wanted to accept his apology—Were my memories wrong? Had it been a completely innocent gesture after all? An accidental touch? But I held my tongue.

"Is there anything else on your mind?" Mr. Kim asked.

"That's all," I said in defeat.

I didn't think anything I could say would force a confession out of him. He was far too resolute.

He opened the door for me. It wasn't locked after all.

I left feeling both relief and disappointment. Nothing bad happened to me, I was completely fine, and yet…Nothing Mr. Kim said could fully validate my memory of what happened. Somehow the whole meeting had flipped the situation on its head and made me feel like he was the good guy, and I was the unreasonable, irrational one.

I checked the recording when I got home. Everything had been captured, just how it had occurred, and it wasn't enough to implicate Mr. Kim in any way. Even his admission to touching my leg wasn't really an admission—"If you *think* so."

Bora arrived home early in the evening. We exchanged defeated looks as soon as we saw each other, and I knew that she must have already listened to the recording.

"Either Mr. Kim truly believes he's innocent or he's even more conniving than we thought," she said. "It's possible he knew you might try to record him and used that to his advantage."

"I don't know. Seems like a stretch."

"Nothing's a stretch. He's extremely clever, that's undeniable."

She wandered to the kitchen.

"I'm guessing you haven't thought of a Plan C yet?" I asked when she returned with a glass of water.

"Plan C? I don't know if there will be one. What more can we do?"

"I suppose so. It's just so…ugh…so frustrating."

"I know."

We sat down on the couch. I flicked the TV on just to take my mind off Mr. Kim.

"How's Go Yoojin doing?" I asked, changing the subject while ads played.

"Fantastically, considering how upset she was about Jung Jen not that long ago. Her scenes have all gone great and everything's still on schedule. If you can get through filming with at least four hours sleep each night, you know things are going well."

"That's a low standard."

"Says you who only works a few hours a week."

"You should try it sometime."

"No way. That would be far too boring."

We were still talking when the ads finished and the news came on. It took me a while to notice the ticker along the bottom of the screen, but when I did, I immediately tuned back in and turned up the volume.

"A recap of our leading news story this evening," the announcer said. "The entertainment company executive accused of sexual abuse can now be named. He is Byun Gimok, CEO of Moonbeam Entertainment."

Chapter 24

I decided once and for all to leave things alone. There was no conspiracy. It was all in my head. The executive under investigation was not Mr. Kim, and no evidence pointed to any misconduct except the memory in my head, which I questioned more and more each day. So I let go of my fear. If I bumped into Mr. Kim, it wouldn't matter. He hadn't done any of the bad things that I'd imagined he'd done…or so I told myself.

While I waited for Nam Sungjin to arrive, I opened my lesson notes. We'd be focusing on the future tense today.

As I tried to review my notes, something distracted me. The room was quiet except for a low buzzing noise. I hadn't noticed that sound ever before. Where was it coming from? I looked around the room, trying to locate its source. My eyes darted here and there until they landed upon a small electronic device up in the corner of the ceiling. A security camera, I realised, and it was pointing straight at me. Had that always been there? The buzzing sound was new, that was for sure. I didn't know whether I should be alarmed—how long had I been recorded in these private lessons? The thought was unsettling; then again, it wasn't unusual for companies to have a lot of security cameras in their buildings, especially in an entertainment company where the protection of the talent was paramount. I should have expected that I'd be on camera from the start.

I shrugged it off and started to turn my attention back to my notes when a memory suddenly struck me: the way Jung Jen's eyes had flicked around the room when I asked her about Mr. Kim. Had she been looking for a camera? Was that it? Was she too afraid to speak out because she knew she was being recorded? And did Mr. Kim know that I had been asking questions about him? Was that why he never acted upon his initial proposition? I ruminated on this idea for a while before reminding myself that I was done with conspiracy theories.

I'm not going to let myself get sucked into this again.

Trying to block these thoughts from my head, I returned to my notes.

Nam Sungjin arrived shortly. He was one of the new recruits at KAM. A nineteen-year-old boy, fresh out of high school, tall and skinny with floppy, blue-dyed hair and several piercings in each ear. He had a "bad boy" type image, but in reality he was attentive and hardworking, always turning up to his lessons and putting the effort in. It helped that his schedule wasn't as demanding as his *seonbaes*. It was largely made up of acting lessons and modelling work since he was too young for most major acting roles in K-dramas and movies.

"Good morning, *Seonsang-nim*," Sungjin said.

"Good morning, Actor-nim." I watched him get settled into his seat. "Do you have your workbook?"

"Yes." He fumbled in his messenger bag and retrieved it.

"Then let's get started where we left off last time—page 52"

"Oh, I already did some of that for homework."

"You did?"

None of the actors ever had time to do homework. Except...

I recalled my last lesson with Jung Jen. She'd done homework and I'd been so surprised. I never did get around to marking it. After her death, I had forgotten all about it; not that I needed to mark it now, anyway—what good would that do? But what was so strange was the way she'd acted on that day. She'd been so serious about the homework, as if it were really important. What did she say, again? *Hmmmm...*

It suddenly clicked.

Oh my God. How did I overlook this? I needed to get my hands on that homework as soon as possible.

"Seonsang-nim?" Sungjin asked, eyebrow raised.

I snapped back to attention. "Yes? Sorry."

"You okay?"

No. I wouldn't be able to think about anything else all lesson.

"There's something...something I need to do." My voice quavered.

Sungjin watched me with concern in his dark eyes. "Sounds serious."

I nodded.

He closed his workbook in a resolute motion. "You go do what you have to do."

I hesitated. "Are you sure?"

"Uh huh. Don't worry about it. We can reschedule."

"All right. Thank you." I didn't stick around any longer. I grabbed my things and left in a flurry.

I drove fast, throwing caution to the wind despite how recently I'd nearly had an accident. Every time I had to stop, my foot itched to press the accelerator again.

Come on...hurry up.

The traffic light turned green.

When at last I arrived home, I fumbled with the key trying to unlock the door. I was so desperate to get inside that I forgot to deactivate the security alarm, and it started blaring after the thirty-second grace period expired. *Damn it!* I raced back to the keypad by the door and input the code.

Now, where did I put Jung Jen's workbook?

I remembered separating it from the rest of my work stuff, and I was sure I hadn't thrown it away.

It must be here somewhere...

I searched my bedroom to no avail.

Did I put it in the office? Yes. It must be there.

I zoomed to the office and started pulling each drawer out of the desk one by one until I reached the bottom. I rifled through the last drawer, pulling out loose bits of paper and throwing them aside, creating a mess on the floor. A bit farther down the pile, I glimpsed it —Jung Jen's workbook, along with an assortment of other old teaching materials. Now I clearly remembered putting it there, out of the way so it wouldn't make me think of her. A critical mistake.

My heart pounded as I opened the book and flipped to the most recently filled-out section halfway through. My hands were shaking. I wasn't quite sure what I expected to find, yet I knew there must be some kind of key. That was why she'd done the homework. That was why she'd acted the way she had.

I began at the top of the page and quickly scanned down, waiting for something to jump out at me, but nothing did. My initial certainty began to wane. Maybe I was wrong. Maybe it was just plain old homework after all.

I reached the end of her writing with no new clues.

Should I just give up?

I clenched my teeth. *No.* Perhaps I was missing something.

Think, Chloe. Think...What did she say to me when she gave me her homework?

She'd been strangely serious—I remembered that much. She had wanted me to mark it after the lesson, meaning she didn't want to be around when I read it.

What else? Something about parts she wasn't sure about...What were her exact words? "Please pay attention to them"?

I opened the workbook again, and this time I read more slowly. There was definitely something weird about her answers. There were words scattered throughout that didn't quite make sense in the context of their paragraphs, and most of them were underlined. *Why? A code?* Maybe she didn't want anyone else to pick up the workbook and be able to see her message easily, in case they destroyed the evidence. *Yes. That's got to be it!*

I flipped back to the start of the exercise and went through and wrote down all the words she'd underlined. After the first couple of words, I knew my guess was correct.

Please help.

I frantically wrote down the rest of the words which strung together to form a crude message.

Please help me Kim black mail me take important document from safe in bedroom too won nine for

The first thing I did after reading the full message was call Bora. She answered swiftly. "Yes?"

My words came out in gibberish. "Found something…big…Jung Jen…"

"Okay. Calm down and say that again properly."

I took a breath. "Evidence. I've found evidence."

Bora paused. "Hold on. Let's talk about this at home. We need to keep this conversation private."

"How long will you be?"

"I don't know, but I'll be as fast as I can. Wait for me. Don't do anything until I get there."

"Got it."

Easier said than done.

How could I just sit around with such a big revelation dangling right in front of me? Mr. Kim was blackmailing Jung Jen, and she'd asked me to take an important document from her safe. I had to get that document. As soon as possible. Too bad there were a few obstacles in my way. I had no idea where her bedroom was, no way of accessing it, and wouldn't her belongings have been cleared out by now anyway? Was it too late? *Arrgh.*

I occupied myself by taking photos of the pages in Jen's workbook, then saving them to a USB drive, my cloud storage folder, and emailing them to myself as well. If something happened to the physical evidence, then I'd have backup.

With that done, I thought about how to get to the safe—assuming that it was still there in her bedroom. Some of the staff at KAM would surely know her address. So would the police. If she had any *sasaeng* fans, they'd be bound to know too. Bora would probably have some more ideas as well.

Eventually I gave up trying to keep myself occupied and waited on a chair outside with a view of the driveway. Buster came up to me with a bone-shaped chew toy in his mouth and dropped it beside me, so I lazily threw it for him. Who knew how many rounds of fetch passed before the gate clanged open and Bora's vehicle sped up the driveway. I rushed over to her.

"Right. Show me what you've got," she said.

We went inside and I showed her the workbook, at the same time explaining to her how I came to the conclusion that Jen had left a message for me.

"What about those random words at the end?" Bora asked. "Too won nine for? Oh, wait. Ha! That's the combination for the safe. Clever."

"It took me a few seconds to work that out as well."

"What do you think the message means? She left evidence in the safe in her bedroom?"

"Yes. That's exactly what I think it means."

"Then we have to get to that safe."

"I agree. Do you know where she lived?"

"No. Only Mr. Kim and a few of the key staff on her team would know."

"Well, we can't ask Mr. Kim."

"I don't think we can ask anyone at KAM. How suspicious would that look? Word would definitely get back to Mr. Kim."

"What about Go Yoojin? Would she know? She said they were friends. Maybe she's been to her house before."

"She might know, but then we'd have to drag her into this as well. Besides, even if we knew the address, how could we get inside?"

"Break in?" I surprised myself by even suggesting it.

Bora smirked. "I didn't expect to hear you say that."

"Neither did I."

"I admire your audacity, but I don't think it would be easy to break in. Celebrities take the security of their properties very seriously, as you know, and anyway, do we really want to risk doing something like that? No. I've got a better idea."

"All right. Spill."

"We call the police."

Somehow, I didn't feel very enthusiastic about this response, and I wavered. "I don't know. As soon as we get the police involved the investigation is outside our control. Jung Jen left the message for me, not the police, and I hate to say it, but can we trust the police? Especially with a high-powered individual like Mr. Kim involved."

"All valid concerns, but you're forgetting that we already have a contact in the police, and I think we can trust him." She pulled out her purse and rifled in it, producing a business card which she handed to me. I recognised the card immediately and reading the name confirmed it.

Officer Bae Sangwook.

Chapter 25

I never thought I'd have to see the inside of a police station again, yet here I was in the fluorescent-lit waiting room, a row of plastic chairs lining one end, the reception desk on the other side, and a water cooler in the corner which made a bubbling sound every so often. A few individuals waited restlessly, tapping their feet and fidgeting.

"What makes you so sure we can trust Officer Bae?" I had asked Bora when she suggested getting in touch with him.

She drew her brows together. "You're asking me that after everything he did for you?"

I shrugged. "I'm sure other police officers would have done the same."

"Actually, I bumped into Sangwook recently."

"Sangwook?"

Since when were they on given name basis?

"*Officer Bae.* We got chatting, and we've kinda kept in touch since then."

"Whoa. Why did I not know about this?"

"It's nothing, really. The odd message here and there. Moaning about how busy we are with our jobs and so on. Anyway, I'm a good judge of character, don't ya think? Officer Bae seems trustworthy."

"I don't know about Officer Bae but I know I trust you, so I'll take your word for it."

With my approval to proceed, she called him up straight away. He told us to come to the station during his office hours and file a report, so here we were.

Bora nudged me when the receptionist approached us.

"Officer Bae will see you now," the receptionist said.

I looked down at the half-finished report on the clipboard on my lap. "I haven't finished this yet."

"That's okay. Take it in with you now, and finish it afterwards." She directed us through a door into the main office area. I spotted Sangwook immediately, sitting at the same desk where we met him on the last occasion. He looked up at us and grinned.

His appearance had changed very little since the last time I saw him. He was a big, broad guy, but he had a soft, round face and kind eyes. His hair was short and tidy, and not a trace of facial hair to be seen. I'd guess his age at around thirty.

"*Oppa*," Bora said, a slight blush creeping onto her cheeks.

My eyes snapped to her like magnets. *Oppa?* So she called him that too. Just how close were they?

"Yang Bora-ssi, Miss Gibson," Sangwook said, addressing us with more formality.

He gestured to the two chairs opposite him and we sat down.

"I didn't expect you to have to file another report so soon after the last incident," Sangwook said. "You told me briefly over the phone that you have evidence of blackmail. Care to elaborate?"

I explained what had happened, starting with Mr. Kim's behaviour towards me and a plea to keep my name anonymous. Sangwook listened intently, but partway through my account, he stopped me.

"Let's go to a different room," he suggested.

We followed him down a corridor to a small, windowless room with beige walls which contained nothing apart from a small table, four chairs, and a security camera.

"I thought we'd better continue this somewhere more private," Sangwook said. "You're talking about someone who a lot of people would do anything to protect."

"Yes. This does seem wise," Bora said.

So even Bae Sangwook didn't trust other police staff.

"Please, go on," he said once we were all seated.

I continued from where I left off, through to discovering the message in Jung Jen's homework.

"And do you have this book with you?" Sangwook asked.

"I do." I retrieved it from my bag and passed it to him. I had bookmarked the relevant section with a pink sticky note.

He examined the book with interest. "I'm sure we'll be able to analyse the handwriting and prove that it belonged to her, but not the underlines—they could have been added by someone else later."

"I didn't—"

"I'm not accusing you of anything, but that's what someone could point out. It's moot anyway. The true test of the note's validity is the safe and the combination and the contents of that safe."

"Proof that Mr. Kim was blackmailing Jung Jen…"

Sangwook shook his head. "We don't know that much yet. The note only referred to 'Kim.' That could refer to half the population."

Bora scoffed. "You know as well as we do that he's the one she's referring to."

Sangwook didn't bite. "Let's get all our facts straight first. What matters most is the safe and the combination. If that checks out, then we've got a case."

"Was a safe recovered from her room after her death?" Bora asked.

"Possibly. A lot of celebrities have safes in their homes, after all. I'd have to find out." He rubbed his chin. "Though it seems strange she'd leave a safe containing an important document that she didn't want anyone to find except Chloe in her bedroom if she planned to end her life. She must have known that everything would get removed from her house."

"Maybe it's hidden somewhere secret in her room," I suggested.

"Then how would she expect you to be able to find it?"

"True."

He tapped his fingers on the table. "Her bedroom, of all places…"

"She rarely went anywhere on her own except her house," Bora pointed out, "so it makes sense in that way. Where else would she get time alone to store something in secret?"

"Hmmm. That's a good point. I wonder…Never mind. Enough speculating. The next step is to finish that report, including everything you just told me, and take it to reception—no, on second thought, you better fill it out now and give it straight to me. I wouldn't want it to mysteriously go missing. Rest assured, I'm going to personally see to it that this gets properly investigated."

"Thanks, Officer Bae," I said.

He waited with us in the room until I finished filling out the report. Bora read it over afterwards to check if I had missed anything. We didn't sign our names—neither of us were ready to go that far.

"It's finished," I said, passing the clipboard to Sangwook.

"This investigation is in my hands now," he said. "Leave it up to me and promise you won't do anything on your own. You could jeopardise the case, and at worst, you could put yourselves in serious danger."

"Yes, Officer Bae," Bora and I said in unison.

Chapter 26

I envied Bora. She was so busy with filming that she probably didn't have a spare moment to let her thoughts linger on the investigation; meanwhile, it was all I could think about. When was Officer Bae Sangwook going to find the safe and the evidence which could be used to press charges against Mr. Kim?

With each day that passed, I began to worry that it wasn't going to happen. Was Sangwook really as trustworthy as Bora seemed to think?

A knock on the front door shook me out of my melancholy mood. *What the...?* I wasn't expecting any visitors, and especially not someone who could let themselves in through the gate. Was it Bora? Had she forgotten her key? Buster was going crazy, yapping at full volume, tail wagging on fast forward. He raced to the front door, and I followed him to investigate. Peering through the peep hole, my heart jumped.

I flung open the door at once.

Jinseung stood in his camouflage army fatigues, tall and commanding, dashingly handsome. Despite his clean and tidy appearance, there was a ruggedness about him that he hadn't had before. Some of the former chubbiness in his face had gone. His shoulders seemed even broader. He had only been away for a few months, but he looked much older—in a good way—a sexy, mature, masculine way.

"Sergeant Shin Jinseung reporting for duty, ma'am," he said, grinning from ear to ear at my stunned reaction.

Every cell in my body radiated with delight. Here he was, right in front of me, his body within grasp. Solid. Real. Not just a dream. Not just a voice and an image on my phone.

"Jinseung-ah!" I gasped. "How…? Why…?"

"It's my first official break. I thought I'd surprise you."

"Well, I'm definitely surprised. Come here."

Unable to restrain myself any longer, I threw my arms around him. He hugged me back with the same urgency, pulling me flush to him, wrapping me tightly in his strong embrace. He felt so good in my arms. My hands clutched fistfuls of his uniform. I inhaled his smell—sweet and earthy and subtly spicy, like cinnamon.

"*Jagi*," he breathed, lips in my hair. "It's good to be back. I'm sorry I left you."

He brought a hand to my cheek and cradled my face, staring longingly into my eyes. His other hand came next, holding the opposite side. He pressed his forehead to mine. I could feel his breath, warm and ticklish on my chin.

Meanwhile, Buster jumped up his legs trying to get attention. Though Jinseung seemed intent on kissing me, it eventually proved too much of a distraction. He broke away to bend down and scoop Buster into his arms.

"Hey there, little buddy. Don't worry, I haven't forgotten about you."

We went inside. Jinseung coddled Buster, petting him, getting down on the hallway floor and letting him climb all over him, accepting his enthusiastic licks.

"Have you been managing okay while I've been away?" Jinseung asked me while Buster lay on his lap.

A bolt of panic shot through my spine. How much should I tell him? I didn't want to spoil the joy of this moment.

"Yes, for the most part," I said, trying not to let doubt pervade my voice.

"Any more nightmares? Panic attacks?"

"No."

Not recently, anyway.

"Thank goodness—Okay, Buster. That's enough."

He gently pushed the dog off, then led him out the back door and closed him outside. Buster stayed put on the doorstep, moaning and whimpering as if to say, "Let me back in!"

"Why'd you do that?" I asked as we crossed the hallway to the living room. "He was enjoying your attention."

"You deserve my attention too, don't you think?"

I smiled. "Well, yeah…"

He closed in on me, and suddenly I was up against the wall, trapped between his arms. Before I had time to react, his lips were on mine. He worked open my mouth and kissed me deeply, hungrily. We explored each other's mouths like new territory. It had been so long that he felt like a new lover, everything fresh and exciting.

My limbs felt weak. My mind was mush. I was so absorbed in kissing him that I didn't hear the car come up the driveway. Nor did I hear the front door open. I didn't notice anything at all until the startled "Oh!"

We broke apart. Bora stared at the scene in front of her, wide-eyed, red-cheeked.

"Bo-Bora-ssi," Jinseung stuttered.

Springing from her dumbfounded state, she sheepishly lifted a hand behind her head, grinning. "Don't mind me, guys. I'll just…make myself scarce."

"Wait—" I said, my hands thrust out in protest.

But she had already left the room. I heard her open the back door.

"Come on, Buster," she said. "Let's go for a walk. A nice, *long* walk."

"Should we try to stop her?" Jinseung asked. "I feel kinda bad. I totally forgot she lives here."

"She'll be fine. If she really wanted to stay, she'd stay."

"True."

I crossed my arms, sighing. "She certainly got an eyeful."

"Probably enjoyed it." He smirked.

"What makes you say that?"

"When she was my intern, she always used to get so excited whenever I had to shoot a kissing scene."

I laughed. "Sounds like her. I'm sure she's outgrown that by now, though."

"Does she have a boyfriend?"

An image of Bae Sangwook popped into my head. "No, but I suspect there's someone she likes."

"Oh? Interesting. I'll have to tease her about it later." He took my face in his hands. "Come on. Let's make the most of the time we have before she gets back."

He was so endearingly insistent that I couldn't do or say anything to stop him. Not that I wanted to.

We continued where we left off, kissing with all our pent-up energy from months spent apart.

But something wasn't right.

With every passing minute, the initial ecstasy of seeing Jinseung again wore off and reality sank in. The truth was going to come out soon. I wouldn't be able to keep lying to him through omission. I was in far too deep now. I had to tell him—but the thought of his reaction terrified me. Would he be annoyed at me for keeping things from him again? Scared about what could happen to his job? Would he even believe my story? He had a longer relationship with Mr. Kim than with me, after all.

Jinseung pulled back. "What's wrong?"

"Nothing."

"Don't lie to me. I can tell that something's bothering you. Did something happen?"

That was my cue. I sucked in a breath of air. "Actually, I…"

He squeezed my shoulder, his arm around me. "Hmm? Don't worry, you can tell me."

Where should I begin?

I opened my mouth to speak when the sound of Buster's yapping filled the room. Next, Bora burst in, flustered, breathless.

Back so soon? What's going on?

"I just had a call from Officer Bae," she said.

Chapter 27

Bora looked from me, to Jinseung, and back again with a strained expression on her face like she was bursting to say something but having to hold it in.

"Is something wrong?" Jinseung asked.

"Can I speak with Chloe alone?"

Jinseung opened his mouth in reaction, about to protest.

"It's okay," I cut in, exchanging a sombre glance with Bora. "I want to tell him."

No more secrets.

"Tell me what?" Jinseung asked with an edge of impatience in his tone.

"A lot has happened since you've been gone."

I felt jittery despite my resolve.

I'm really about to do this.

He softened with kindly concern. "Something *bad*?"

I nodded slowly.

"Look, I need to get this off my chest before anything else," Bora said. "The safe was empty, Chloe. He didn't find anything."

The safe was empty.

"What?" I spat. "How can that be?"

"According to Officer Bae, it had clearly been tampered with."

Now it made sense.

"Someone got to it before us."

"Exactly."

"What safe?" Jinseung asked, brow furrowed.

The moment couldn't be delayed any longer. The truth was about to come out.

"Let's sit down," I said. "I'll tell you everything."

"Me too," Bora said. "We're all involved in this."

The three of us settled around the dining room table and got down to business.

Thank goodness for Yang Bora. I didn't know how I could have managed without her there for support. She took it upon herself to do most of the explaining. She even shouldered the blame for encouraging me not to tell Jinseung what was going on.

As we recounted our story of what happened at KAM Entertainment in his absence, the expressions on his face said everything. Outrage. Confusion. Shock. Concern. Anger. His hands were clenched hard, making the veins in his arms pop out. At one point he shot up from his chair, trembling with rage.

"I'll kill him! I'll kill that bastard!"

Bora and I had to restrain him, his arm muscles bulging under our hands through his rolled-up sleeves.

"Try to stay calm," Bora said. "One reckless move could ruin everything."

"Let's leave it to the police," I said. "It's up to them now. We'll only get in the way."

Jinseung struggled against us a while longer before finally giving in, crumpling down on his seat in despair.

"I'll never forgive him for laying a finger on you," he growled, face in his hands.

Bora and I comforted him until he calmed down enough to let us engage in a rational conversation, even as he twitched with suppressed rage.

"So, the safe was empty. Now what?" I asked Bora.

"Sangwook—Officer Bae—is going to meet us and tell us what he knows face to face."

"I thought police officers weren't supposed to talk about ongoing investigations?"

"Strictly speaking. Luckily he's our friend, and a bit of begging and pleading was enough persuasion. Oh—and the promise that I'd buy him dinner."

Her admission ignited a little spark of glee, but I let it slip. There were more important things on my mind.

"When are we going to meet him?" I asked.

"He's coming here now."

"What?"

"Yep." She checked the dainty gold watch on her wrist. "He should arrive any minute now."

The intercom buzzed.

"Ah. That'll be him."

She went to open the gate.

"Bae Sangwook..." Jinseung stroked his chin. "That name sounds familiar."

"He was the main police officer involved with my case last year," I explained.

"Then we can trust him."

I nodded even though it was more of a comment than a question.

Bora re-entered the room with Bae Sangwook in tow. I noticed that his usual confident, upright demeanour had changed. He seemed battle-worn—face pallid, shoulders drooped, eyes tinged with red.

"Hello, Officer Bae," I said, getting to my feet and bowing slightly.

Jinseung did the same, reining in his residual fury to offer politeness.

"Good morning, Officer-nim."

Seeing Jinseung seemed to recharge Sangwook's battery, perking him up straight away.

"Wow. Shin Jinseung-ssi...Nice to meet you."

So, even a police officer wasn't immune to the charms of seeing a celebrity in the flesh.

"Thank you for helping Chloe. Again," Jinseung said.

"My pleasure. It's my duty, after all."

Jinseung took it upon himself to serve Sangwook a cold drink.

Sangwook spread out his notes on the table.

"I shouldn't really be doing this, you know," he said.

Bora ignored him, cutting to the chase. "First things first, how did you find the safe?"

"I'm curious about that too," I admitted.

Sangwook cleared his throat. "From the start, I suspected that Jung Jen wouldn't have really hidden important evidence—that she didn't want just anybody to find—in the bedroom at her house. That would be far too obvious. I had another idea."

"Which was?" I pressed.

"Don't we consider our childhood room at our parents' house to still be our bedroom?"

Understanding flashed on Bora's face. "Ah!"

"I interviewed her former intern and found out that Jung Jen had recently stayed at her parents' house in Daejeon, so that's where I went, and I was correct. I found the safe deep inside her wardrobe, hidden on a shelf behind her clothes."

"Why didn't she just put that in her message?" I asked. "I couldn't possibly have known..."

Sangwook shrugged. "She was probably in a fragile mental state when she wrote the message. Or maybe she expected you to work it out. Did she ever mention staying at her parents' house before?"

I skimmed through our last few meetings in my head. "Now that I think about it, perhaps she did."

"Did her parents know about the safe?" Bora asked Sangwook.

"No. They hadn't seen it before. I got the feeling that they were too heartbroken to go through her belongings. Everything looked like it was still in place exactly how she'd left it—like a shrine in her memory."

"Why didn't she simply leave the document for her parents to find instead of getting Chloe involved?" Bora asked.

"My guess is that she didn't want to endanger them for knowing too much. Or give them a heart attack—they're elderly."

"Jung Jen and I weren't that close," I mused, "but she knew that she could trust me because I had a bad experience with Mr. Kim as well—she must have worked that much out when I questioned her."

"Her lessons with you were one of the few times she had privacy from her manager and other KAM staff," Bora pointed out, "so that could be another reason as well."

"That's what I think too," Sangwook said.

While we discussed all these possibilities, Jinseung watched on in heavy silence. I could tell he wasn't really listening. He was still processing what I told him earlier.

Bora ran a finger back and forth around the rim of her glass of water. "I have another question."

"Fire away," Sangwook said.

"It seems like you worked out the location of the safe quite quickly, but why did it take you so long to go and get it?"

"Ah," he said, frowning, "that's another thing. Ever since I decided to start this investigation, road blocks have been put in my way. My workload on other cases spiked, and I had no time to visit Daejeon."

"Coincidence?"

"No. I don't think so."

I tensed, reading between the lines.

"Does Mr. Kim have friends in the police?" I asked.

"Mr. Kim has friends in all sorts of high places," Jinseung said, finally speaking up. "They visit his office at HQ all the time. If he doesn't know someone high up in the police, he knows someone who knows someone who does."

"In the end, I had to tell my subordinate, Officer Cha, to cover for me this morning so I could secretly go to Daejeon," Sangwook explained. "He's still covering for me now. Part of the reason I agreed to come here was in case...in case I couldn't continue the investigation. I wanted you to know what I had found out so far."

Suddenly his weary demeanour made a lot more sense. The case was causing trouble for him.

"Will you be okay?" Bora asked, face etched with concern.

Sangwook lifted his chin. "Don't worry. I'll be fine. I just didn't want to leave you in the lurch if they make me stop investigating."

A lot of questions had been answered, but there was still one major point we hadn't discussed.

"Any idea who accessed the safe and how they found out?" I asked.

Sangwook nodded. "It seems unlikely that anyone else knew about the coded message. The safe had been broken into by force, not with the combination."

"Very curious," Bora muttered.

"I think whoever found the safe knew that Jung Jen might have stored evidence at her parents' house and went there to check," Sangwook said. "They came across the safe and busted it open. I asked her parents who had visited their house since her death. Many people had —as expected. They came to pay their condolences."

"And they let people go into her bedroom?" Bora asked.

"Yes. People wanted to see her bedroom to bring back memories of her and have a moment of privacy to grieve, surrounded by her things."

"Did Mr. Kim visit?" I asked.

"Yes. He visited, but he didn't go into her bedroom as far as her parents could recall. There was someone else from the agency who did, though, and this is the person whom I suspect the most."

"Who?"

He threaded his fingers together and cracked his knuckles. "Jung Jen's manager, Jeong Daeshim."

Chapter 28

"Stop that!" Jinseung snapped.

His reaction to me apologising for the millionth time in three short days.

We lay in bed with a vast gulf between us. Our reunion was meant to be a happy occasion, but Jinseung had been on edge since he learned the truth.

"I can't help it," I retorted. "You're angry, and saying sorry is the only thing I can do. I want to make things better—"

"It's not you I'm angry at, it's *him*."

"I know, but—"

He closed the gap and pressed an aggressive kiss on my mouth, stopping any more words from passing my lips.

"Shhh…No more."

I obeyed, biting my tongue not to say sorry again.

He sighed and stretched his arms above his head, leaning his back against the headboard.

"As much as I hate to admit it, you were probably right not to tell me. I would have gone AWOL to confront Mr. Kim. I wouldn't have been able to control myself. I'm barely managing right now."

"Thanks for resisting. I know it's hard."

"I still want to punch him. God, I'm so mad. I don't know what I'll do if I have to see him again."

"Hopefully that won't be for a long time."

"I feel so powerless. I have to go back today. I have to leave you here to fend for yourself. You still work in the same building he does, pretending like everything's normal."

"It's a strange situation."

"I don't want anything bad to happen to you again. I want to protect you. I never want to lose you."

He cradled me in his arms. I could feel the desperation in the tightness of his embrace.

"Chloe, promise me you'll stay out of danger. You *and* Yang Bora. Stay out of danger no matter what."

"I promise."

He kissed me again, tenderly this time. We lay on our sides, our bodies close together, my hands around the back of his neck, his arms around my waist. He was warm. So warm. I sighed into his sweet kiss.

"I'm sorry I've been in a bad mood," he murmured with a voice like velvet.

I smirked. "Look at you. Now you're the one apologising."

"Let me make it up to you."

He flipped me onto my back, his perfectly flat and hard body on top of me. Our kissing became frantic, passionate.

"I forgive you," I gasped as I drew a breath.

"Don't let me off so easily," he said before crashing back to me.

* * *

WHEN WE EMERGED for a late breakfast, I didn't expect to find Changsoo standing in the middle of the kitchen, car keys dangling from his hand.

I stared at him, blinking drowsily. "Why are you here so early?"

"We'll need to head off shortly," he curtly replied, keys jingling.

The kettle boiled in the background. He was making an instant coffee.

Realising I was still in my dressing gown, I sheepishly pulled the tie to close the gap.

"Weren't you going to come in the afternoon?" I asked.

"It nearly is the afternoon, and I want to get a head start on the journey. I won't get back until nightfall as it is."

I crossed my arms in a huff.

Maybe I should have offered to drive Jinseung myself. Too late now.

"*Hyung*, I'll have something to eat, then we can go," Jinseung said, opening the fridge and peering at its contents. He grabbed some containers of last night's leftovers—*galbi*, seaweed salad, rice, and kimchi.

We ate at the dining table. Bora and Changsoo joined us, sipping from steaming coffee cups.

"It's so sad you have to go back today." Bora pouted at Jinseung. "I barely got to see you."

"*Ya!* The purpose of his trip was to see *me*," I lightheartedly retaliated.

"I didn't get to spend enough time with either of you," Jinseung mumbled, mouth half-full.

I ate slowly, thinking that if I stretched it out, it would delay the time Jinseung and Changsoo departed. But Jinseung finished eating before me, and he barely swallowed his last mouthful before Changsoo stood up, fumbling for his car keys again.

"Okay, guys, it's about time we get going," he said.

Jinseung rose from his chair. I clutched him protectively. Bora stuck out her bottom lip.

"Stop it," Changsoo said. "You all look like wide-eyed puppies staring at me like that."

Buster, who was lying under the table, barked at him.

"And *you* really are a wide-eyed puppy. Sorry, but we have to go."

Jinseung turned to me. "Remember what I said, okay? Keep safe."

I nodded.

He lifted a hand to my cheek and stroked it. "Goodbye, Chloe."

"Goodbye."

He softly kissed me on the lips, hugged me, then kissed me again on the cheek.

"Where's *my* goodbye hug?" Bora asked.

Jinseung grinned. "All right, you." He encircled her in a bear-like hug.

"And a kiss?" she asked, muffled by his chest.

I was sure she was only kidding, but Jinseung didn't object. He kissed her on the cheek, causing her to squeak like a startled mouse. If that had happened two years ago, she probably would have dropped dead.

"Look after Chloe for me," he said.

"I will."

He ruffled Buster's fur. "Bye, buddy."

"Right. Let's go," Changsoo said, standing in the doorway with his arms crossed, itching to get away.

Jinseung grabbed the backpack he'd packed the night before and tossed it over his shoulders. He squeezed my hand.

"See you on my next break. I'll give you a warning next time, promise."

"Love you," I said.

"Love you too."

The number of times we'd had to part for long periods like this was starting to rack up, but that didn't make it any easier. My stomach lurched as he turned to leave. I followed him as far as the front door, Buster at my heels. Jinseung stepped outside and kissed me one more time across the threshold before Changsoo closed the door behind them. I stood watching from the window until Changsoo's car disappeared out the gate.

"He's gone," I said, the familiar bitter emptiness in my heart from his absence.

"I'm sure he'll be back before you know it," Bora said, placing a comforting hand on my shoulder.

"More likely the days will drag on."

"Hey, it's not all bad. You have me."

"I s'pose."

"That was half-hearted," she goaded. "Maybe this will cheer you up —I'm free this evening. Let's go out, have a drink, chat like old times— nothing about all the crazy stuff going on."

I appreciated her effort, and it didn't sound like a bad idea at all.

"You know what? I think that *would* cheer me up."

She lightly slapped my back. "That's the spirit!"

* * *

THE BAR'S interior was all shiny black and purple neon. R&B music played at low volume lending a relaxed vibe and the ability to have a proper conversation without having to shout or strain your ears. A small handful of other patrons occupied the bar and the booths, quietly drinking and chatting.

As Bora's *unnie,* I ordered and paid for our drinks—two soju-based cocktails—and brought them back to our booth.

"Mmm. Looks delish!" Bora said, accepting her watermelon-infused drink.

"It has been a while since we went out like this, hasn't it?" I said.

"Yeah. I've been too busy to go out much ever since I became Actor Go's manager."

I rested my head in my hand, elbow on the table. "It's a shame that Shin Jina isn't here…"

"You're right. We should have invited her."

"Never mind. Next time. Whenever that will be."

"Hopefully soon."

We sipped our drinks.

"So, Jinseung looked well," Bora said after a pause. "Apart from how he took the news, I mean."

"Yeah. He hasn't had it that bad in the army, to my relief."

"If you're tough enough to excel in the entertainment industry, you're tough enough to excel in the army."

"That seems to be the case."

"He missed you, though. That was obvious." She smirked.

I recalled her walking in on us and blushed. "Sorry about, uh…"

"Don't worry about it. You two are just so cute! I wish someone would ravish me like that. *Aigoo.* I haven't had a boyfriend in years. What's it like?"

"With the amount of time we spend apart I'm starting to ask myself the same question."

"Pfft. You're so dramatic."

Talking about boyfriends piqued my interest and I couldn't help myself.

"About Bae Sangwook…"

Bora glared at me. "We promised we wouldn't talk about all that."

"I don't mean *that*. Do you like him?"

"I…*what?*"

"Come on. Don't deny it. I can tell."

She dismissed me. "I'm too busy to have a relationship."

"That didn't answer my question. Do you *like* him?"

"Well…" She turned the base of her cocktail glass in her fingers. "He's attractive, don't you think? Manly, fit, direct, and yet sensible and hardworking and smart. Y'know?"

"So you *do* like him."

She threw her hands up in the air. "I don't know. Yeah. I guess you could say that. *I like him.* Doesn't mean we have to date. I don't even know if he feels the same way about me."

"It's not like you to be shy about what you want."

"Who's shy? I don't know what I want."

"Hmm. If you say so."

Bora's phone started to ring and she grabbed it from her bag.

"Who's calling? Sangwook *Oppa?*" I chided.

She jabbed my shoulder. "Shut it, you. It's an unknown number. Better take it. Might be work-related." She answered the phone. "Oh, Sangwook-ssi, why are you calling from a different number?"

I was about to poke fun at her since it was Bae Sangwook after all, but her expression had turned dark.

"Understood," she said. "Just a minute."

She got up from the table, beckoning me to come with her. Leaving our half-finished drinks behind, I followed her towards the bathrooms. Bora scanned the area, making sure we were alone, before tugging me inside the disabled bathroom—a completely separate room unshared by other cubicles. She turned the lock.

"Chloe's with me too. I'm going to turn video on," she told Sangwook. "I don't think anyone will be able to hear through the door."

She pressed a button on the screen then put her phone down on the closed toilet lid. We crouched and huddled around it. Thankfully the room was nice and clean.

Sangwook appeared on the screen in what looked like a small, lamp-lit room with a whiteboard behind him which was covered with notes and pictures I suspected were related to Mr. Kim and Manager Jeong. He wore a serious expression on his tired face.

"Okay, I can see you," Bora said.

"I have an update," Sangwook said.

I prickled at the gravity of his voice.

"I have managed to locate Jeong Daeshim," he continued.

Bora and I looked at each other with a mixture of triumph and confusion.

"That's good news, isn't it?" I asked doubtfully.

"But I can't go. I'm positive now that someone's trying to stop this investigation."

"What happened?" Bora asked.

"I've been sent away to participate in a three-day conference."

"After the conference—"

"I have reason to believe that Jeong Daeshim is about to try to leave the country, and once that happens, it'll be much more difficult to track him down."

"Could you ask another police officer to go?" I asked.

"That would be the obvious solution, but the problem is that I don't know who I can trust to carry out the task, and anyone who tries will probably get stopped too."

"Officer Cha?"

"He's going to the conference as well."

"Then what can we do?"

"I'm sorry, but I think the best thing to do at this point is drop this lead and let it go—"

"No," Bora said. "I have an idea. Tell me where Jeong Daeshim is."

"Cheong—wait, you're not planning to go there yourself, are you?"

"...No."

"You are, aren't you? Please don't go. We have to drop this. We'll get another chance—"

"Tell me exactly where he's staying."

"No. Absolutely not."

"Then think of a way to catch him. We can't just let him go."

Sangwook drew a deep breath. "All right. I'll do what I can."

"Good."

Bora ended the call. She turned to me. "How do you feel about a trip to Cheongsando?"

Chapter 29

"I'm going. With or without you," Bora said, midway through packing her duffel bag. "Now, do you still have that recording stuff I lent you?"

"Please," I begged. "I promised Jinseung that we wouldn't put ourselves in any danger—"

"*You* promised Jinseung. *I* don't recall saying anything."

"And Bae Sangwook?"

"If he cared about me at all, he'd put up more of a fight to stop me from going. Can't he get out of that conference somehow? Will he be under surveillance nonstop?"

"He must have his reasons."

"Regardless, I'm going, and that's the end of it."

"You're being reckless—"

"So what? You don't have to come."

"But I can't let you go on your own!"

Bora zipped up her bag. "I'm leaving first thing tomorrow morning."

By the resolve in her voice, I knew that nothing I could say or do would stop her.

"Why are you so hung up on this?" I asked. "It's not like Mr. Kim did anything to *you*. It's not like Jung Jen asked for *your* help."

"I just…I have to do this."

"Why? What reason could you possibly have to do something as dangerous as this?"

She placed her packed duffel bag at the foot of the bed, ignoring me, but I wasn't going to leave her room until I had answers.

"Why?" I asked again.

"Leave me alone," she replied, a hitch in her voice. Her face was red. She turned her back to me, avoiding my eyes.

This was clearly a touchy subject. Now I was certain she was keeping something from me, and whatever it was, I had to know.

"There's something you haven't told me, isn't there?" I asked.

No response.

"I'm right, aren't I?" I pressed.

A stifled whimper.

I took her shoulders and turned her to face me. Tears were spilling from her eyes and rolling down her cheeks. My heart cracked like it was made of glass.

"What's wrong?" I asked, softening my tone. "Please, tell me."

"You might hate me if I tell you," she choked.

"I won't. I promise I won't. Come on, let's sit down. Tell me what happened. Did Mr. Kim do something to you as well?"

Bora shook her head. "No. Worse than that."

I wondered how it could possibly be worse.

I sat on the side of her bed and patted the space next to me on her cream duvet cover. Bora stared at the space for a few seconds, as if still weighing up whether she would tell me or not. At last, I felt the bed dip as she settled down.

"Have you ever wondered how I got my job as intern?" she asked, staring sombrely ahead at the wall.

"No, I can't say I have."

"A paid internship at an entertainment agency is a coveted position. There were hundreds of applicants—no, most likely thousands."

"You're so bright. I never would have thought to question it."

"Well, I didn't get the job just for being bright. There would have been so many others just like me, or better than me. I'm far from perfect."

"No one's perfect."

"You have to be pretty close to it."

"So, you didn't get the job on merit alone, is that what you're saying?"

She nodded, tears gathering in her eyes again. She brushed them away and took a moment to recover before continuing.

"The interviews were held over several days. I took mine in a group with two other applicants in front of a panel of three interviewers. I was so nervous. Long story short, it didn't go well for me. I was so sure I'd blown it. That's why after the interview I took the opportunity to sneak away and explore the building. I wouldn't get the internship, but at least I might get to see a celebrity. That was my thinking."

"You were pretty cheeky."

She cracked a faint smile. "Yeah, I was bold."

"And did you run into any celebrities?"

Her smile disappeared. "I did."

"Who?" I asked, even though I thought I might know the answer.

"Jung Jen."

"I see."

"I was lost in an area of the building that was like a maze, and no one was around," she explained. "But then I heard voices. Raised voices. Yelling. I was curious and followed the sound. I saw Jung Jen. She was still at the height of her fame back then. I would have been so excited if I had seen her in any other situation. She was in a room with Mr. Kim."

My stomach lurched.

"By the time I got there, they had stopped arguing." Her voice became strained.

"Take your time."

"He…Mr. Kim was…"

My heart was throbbing in my dry throat as I waited for her to gather her words.

"He was forcing himself on her," she said, unable to stifle a sob.

"Kissing her. His hands up her skirt. I was frozen in the doorway, watching, not knowing what to do."

I winced.

"Jung Jen's back was to me," she continued, "but Mr. Kim saw. He locked eyes with me for a second, then he pushed the door closed and I ran away."

I felt numb, unable to process the full extent of what she had just admitted to me. She knew about Mr. Kim's true character all along and kept it hidden from me, from everyone.

"Shortly after the incident, maybe a day or two, I got a call. I was asked to attend a second interview. I didn't expect to make it to the next round, so it took me by surprise. I turned up and found out that it was a one-on-one interview with the same man I saw with Jung Jen —Mr. Kim."

"What happened?" I croaked.

"To anyone listening, it was a totally normal job interview, but I knew differently. It was a test. Without saying anything aloud, he was checking to see if I'd bring up what I'd seen, or if I'd stay silent."

"You stayed silent."

"Yes."

"And you got the internship."

She looked down at the floor, her shame clearly displayed on wet hot cheeks and puffy eyes. "Yes."

"You knew all along."

"It's no excuse, but I made myself believe that what I saw was consensual—they were having an affair and it was none of my business. I convinced myself that was reality. It was the only way I could be happy working in my dream job, and I never witnessed or heard anything like that ever again, except—"

"When I told you what he did to me."

"I was in denial."

My fingers dug into the mattress. I was angry, and yet...What would I have done in the same situation? I knew exactly how hard, how *futile*, it was to speak up and do something, and then it was too late...

"I get it now—why you want to go and confront Manager Jeong," I said.

"I can't make up for what I've done, but I can at least do this."

"So there's no way I can stop you?"

She shook her head.

"Then I guess I'll have to go with you."

"You don't have to."

"No, I do. I'm coming."

"Then we'll leave tomorrow morning. Goodnight, Chloe."

"Wait, just answer me one question. How do you expect to find Manager Jeong? You only know the name of the town he's in and even that's a guess."

"Oh, I know where he is."

"How?"

"There were coordinates written on the whiteboard behind Officer Bae. I recorded the video and zoomed in a little."

Damn. Did those glasses give her superhuman eyesight or something? Still, I wasn't convinced.

"What will you do when you get there? Confront him head-on?"

"I'll make up some kind of story—a reason for being there."

"Hmmm."

Can she really pull this off?

I didn't like it, not one bit, but I simply couldn't let her do this without my help.

"I will go with you, but we're bringing backup."

"Who?"

The other member of our trio, Shin Jina, was the first person to come to mind—but no, I couldn't drag her into this. Jinseung would never forgive me for putting her in danger, as well as myself. I'd need someone else. Someone tough. Someone we could trust. Who else did I know? I racked my brain.

Yes...He'd be perfect.

"What about Jinseung's friend, Young Jae?" I suggested. "He'd make a good bodyguard, wouldn't he?"

I thought she'd protest, but she didn't.

"Do you think he'd agree to go with us?" she asked.

"He cares about Jinseung enough that he'd want to protect me, and he said to call him if I ever needed help while Jinseung's away."

She nodded. "All right. Call him."

Chapter 30

"You're crazy, you know that? Batshit crazy," Young Jae said the moment I opened the door.

It was five o'clock in the morning and Young Jae arrived just like he'd promised over the phone. He was wearing what I assumed was his old army uniform—a long-sleeve shirt and trousers in green-brown camouflage print. Appropriate clothing for the mission that lay ahead.

"Are you sure you still want to go ahead with this?" he asked, eyebrow cocked.

"Yes," Bora said, pulling her duffel bag over her shoulder beside me.

"Then am I right to believe that you have some kind of plan?"

"Of course."

I was much less confident, but I knew Bora wouldn't back down, so I had to forge ahead.

"Thank you for doing this," I said to Young Jae. "I know it's a lot to ask."

"I still haven't wrapped my head around what you told me last night. I just know that Jinseung would kill me if I let anything happen to you, so I gotta go along with it."

"Let's get a move on," Bora said. "We don't have time to lose."

"Need me to drive?" Young Jae asked.

"I was going to drive," I said, "but that's not a bad idea. Let's take your car. It will be less recognisable than Jinseung's."

"No problem."

We had already packed for the journey, including extra clothing in case we had to stay overnight. Young Jae carried our stuff to his car like it was weightless, and I felt relieved to have a guy that big and strong at our disposal.

I hopped in the front with Young Jae. Bora got in the back.

"Weren't you meant to be working today?" I asked Bora, suddenly remembering that this wasn't her day off. "How were you planning to get around that?"

"I asked Actor Go and the intern to cover for me," she replied. "They'll lie and say I'm out on set with them if asked."

"Wow. They've really got your back."

"Actor Go knows I wouldn't skip work unless I had an important reason."

"And you, Young Jae-ssi? Were you supposed to be working today?"

"Yeah. I'll just say I'm sick."

"Easy peasy."

The four-hour car ride was plenty of time to discuss our plan of attack. Bora was going to approach Manager Jeong, telling him that Mr. Kim had sent her. That would hopefully pique his interest enough to make him want to talk to her. Bora would try to gain his trust by saying that she was involved too—that Mr. Kim was also blackmailing Go Yoojin. From there she'd try to extract information from him. Anything that could be recorded and used against him. If she could find out what happened to Jung Jen's evidence, even better. Bora had nerves of steel, and I was confident that she'd be good enough at improvising to come up with a convincing act. Young Jae and I would be on standby, listening in, ready to come to her aid if she had any difficulties. Hopefully it wouldn't come to that.

The weather was patchy during the drive—pockets of heavy rain amidst long stretches of sunshine. I saw parts of South Korea I'd never seen before, but I was too focused on the mission ahead of us to properly take in the scenery. We didn't stop except for one toilet break halfway.

The final stretch of the journey to Cheongsando was aboard a passenger ferry from Wando. Once we'd parked the car below deck, we went up to the seating area. We didn't speak of our plan in front of the other passengers.

Fifty minutes later, we arrived at Cheongsando port. If I had come here under any other circumstances, I'd be excited to explore such a beautiful destination. The island was a tourist spot, known for its natural beauty and the slow way of living. I knew a couple of K-dramas that had been filmed in the area. I would have liked to do some sightseeing.

The atmosphere was tense in the car as we followed the directions on the GPS to Manager Jeong's hideout.

"How are you feeling?" I asked Bora, turning my head to the back seat.

"A bit nervous," she confessed.

"We don't have to go through with it if you're having second thoughts. We can cancel and turn back now. I wouldn't be mad at all."

"Oh, don't worry. I'm not having second thoughts."

But I am *worried.*

As we wound through quiet countryside dirt roads, steadily approaching our target destination, I secretly wished that it would be too late. Manager Jeong could have fled by now. He had already had a decent window of opportunity. I clung to this hope. If he had gone, we wouldn't need to put ourselves at risk.

"This must be it," Young Jae said as we passed a dilapidated two-storey house with peeling white paint on its exterior. A gated wooden fence sealed the perimeter, surrounded by an overgrown field scattered with colourful wildflowers. I would have found it pretty if not for the prospect that a dangerous man could be lurking inside.

Young Jae parked on a road a little farther away, out of sight from the house.

"Shall we go over the plan one more time?" he asked.

"It's simple, really," Bora said. "I'll approach the house and try to talk to Manager Jeong, secretly recording him. You two hide nearby and listen in on the audio stream. If the situation takes a turn for the worse, well, that's when you, Young Jae, might have to intervene."

"Understood."

"Let's check the equipment one more time," I suggested. "Is there a good signal out here?"

Bora attached the small microphone under her top, and we did a test run, Young Jae and me listening through earbuds. It worked perfectly.

"Have you got your self-defence kit?" I asked.

"Yes."

"All set, then?" Young Jae asked.

She nodded.

It wasn't cold but my teeth chattered uncontrollably as we left the car. Young Jae and I separated from Bora before the house came back into view. Bora walked along the side of the dusty road, while Young Jae and I crept up to the fence, crouching in the long grass. We watched from through the cracks in the splintered wooden fence as she unlatched the gate and approached the doorstep. Through our earbuds, we heard her quietly tell herself, "All right, here goes." She knocked on the door.

Chapter 31

I held my breath as I waited for someone to answer Bora's knock. Was he there? Would he answer? I pleaded to God the answer was no. As far as I was concerned, nothing we could possibly gain from this would be worth the risk.

Young Jae lay beside me in the tall, dry weeds, propped up by his elbows and forearms. He wore a serious expression, his eyes narrowed with intense focus.

No one answered the door.

Well, that's that. We came here for nothing. Let's go home—

Bora knocked again, louder this time.

The door opened straight away. I flinched in reaction to the sound, loud and clear through my headphones. Young Jae placed a hand on my back to still me.

"Manager Yang? What are you doing here?" He was out of view, but the voice was unmistakably Manager Jeong's. He had a distinct voice: monotone and a little bit nasal.

"Mr. Kim sent me," Bora confidently announced. "Can I come in?"

Manager Jeong paused, hesitant. "Why would he send *you*?"

"I think it's better if we discuss this inside."

"...All right. Come in."

They entered the house, door closing behind them. I heard rustling as Bora took off her shoes, then their light footsteps through the house, ending when they must have sat down in a nearby room. I couldn't see anything through the dusty window.

"Why did Mr. Kim send you?" Manager Jeong asked.

I clenched my muscles, anxious as to how Bora would proceed.

"He wanted me to get something from you," she explained. "He wouldn't tell me *what* exactly, but he believes you have some kind of document in your possession. Something he doesn't want anyone to get hold of."

Please work...please...

"And why should I trust you?" he asked.

"Because I'm involved in this too. I know what Mr. Kim has been doing to Actor Go, and I let him get away with it. If anything gets out, I don't know what I'd do."

"Go Yoojin?" He sounded shocked. "I didn't know..."

"This document that Mr. Kim wants—"

"I destroyed it."

"But you made copies, didn't you?"

I felt something crawling on my arm and looked down. A huge black beetle. I slammed a hand over my mouth to stifle a shriek. Young Jae calmly flicked the bug away.

"I can't believe Mr. Kim sent you of all people," Manager Jeong said.

I heard footsteps again and imagined him pacing the room, matching the rhythmic back and forth sound.

"You know very well that he can't come here himself," Bora said. "Who else would he send?"

Manager Jeong didn't comment.

"Where have you hidden the document?" Bora pressed. "Mr. Kim wants reassurance."

"I'll be out of the country tomorrow. That's all the reassurance I can give him."

"That's not good enough."

"How does he know about the document, anyway? I never told him about it."

"He's not stupid. So, where is it?"

"Like I said, I've destroyed it."

"And all the copies? I don't think he'd believe that. You must have them somewhere."

"As if I'd tell you." He had venom in his voice. "He should have sent someone else. I didn't even know you were a part of this."

"I know everything."

"And Mr. Kim is okay with that?"

"He trusts me."

"He has something on you?"

"You don't need to know the details."

A short silence, then Manager Jeong spoke. "You might as well leave. You're not going to get anything out of me."

"Mr. Kim won't rest until he knows those documents are destroyed. Even if you leave the country, he'll come after you."

"Hmmm."

"What's in them? Evidence? Testimony from Jung Jen about what exactly happened?"

"I'm not saying anything. Now leave."

"It must be evidence. That's why Mr. Kim doesn't want any chance of them being leaked. That's right, isn't it? Evidence that Jung Jen was being abused? And that's the reason she killed herself?"

Crap. She's really done it now.

Manager Jeong exploded. "That's enough! Get out of my house. Leave this island."

She had tested the limits of his patience to the brink. She was treading dangerous waters now. I wished she'd back down and get out of there. Young Jae shifted beside me, poised to rush in to her rescue if things went further south.

"All right," Bora said calmly. "I'll leave. But first, what should I tell Mr. Kim? I can't go back to him empty-handed."

Manager Jeong seemed to consider her point, then replied, "Tell him that the evidence has been destroyed."

"Fine. I will. He won't believe you, but that's what I'll tell him. I'll go—"

"Wait a minute."

My breath caught. Manager Jeong's tone of voice had changed. He sounded suspicious of her now.

"How did you get here?" he asked. "Where's your car?"

Bora hesitated. For the first time she seemed caught off-guard. "I-I was dropped off."

"By whom?"

"Local taxi driver."

"You didn't ask them to wait for you?"

"Wasn't sure how long this would take."

"Hmmm…"

He was thinking about this more clearly now. Bora had to get out before he deduced what was really going on.

"I'll just—be leaving now." Her voice wavered with a subtle note of panic.

Manager Jeong must have realised by now that something wasn't quite right. "How can I be so sure that Mr. Kim sent you? He didn't tell me anything."

Bora started to reply. "He-"

The sound cut out. I wondered if it was just me, but Young Jae looked at me like the same thing had happened to him.

"What should we do now?" I whispered.

"You stay here. I'm going to try and get closer to check everything's okay."

"And leave me here by myself?"

"It's the safest place."

I grabbed on to his shirt as he made to move away. "Be careful."

He nodded and I released him. He crawled on his hands and knees towards the gate. It had been left open, swinging slightly in the breeze. Bora must have left it unlatched on purpose.

I watched Young Jae through a gap in the fence as he stealthily approached the house, steering clear of windows. He pressed his back to the exterior wall and slowly moved around the outside.

Everything was quiet except for the sound of cicadas crying in the distance and my heavy breathing.

Young Jae crouched below a window, his face screwed up in concentration.

I didn't need the headphones to hear Bora's scream.

Chapter 32

Without thinking, I leapt from my hiding spot into plain view. I wanted to call her name at the top of my lungs. *Bora-ya! I'm coming!* The words were poised on the tip of my tongue, but Young Jae saw and shot me a warning glare in time to stop me. I ducked back under cover.

Young Jae silently approached the front door and tugged at the handle, but it wouldn't open. He gave up and crept around the exterior of the house again, leaving my field of vision.

I was wondering whether to move so I could get a better view when all of a sudden the front door swung open and Manager Jeong stepped onto the doorstep. He was sloppily dressed in baggy sweatpants and a threadbare t-shirt. Unshaven. A drastic change from his stylish work attire. His shifty eyes surveyed his surroundings.

Did he hear something? Is he onto us? Where is Bora?

He took one step down.

Then another.

Please, don't come towards me.

He reached the ground. Something piqued his attention, and he followed the direction Young Jae went, disappearing around the corner of the house.

I watched on, trembling uncontrollably in the tall grass. My heart was pounding so loud I thought he might be able to hear it.

If Manager Jeong caught Young Jae, what was I going to do? My instruction had been to run, take the car, and drive away to find help. But by then, would it be too late? What was Manager Jeong capable of?

Get a grip. Young Jae's got this.

Out of the two of them, Young Jae was bigger and stronger. He could take him on, no problem.

Young Jae emerged from the other side of the house, alone. His gaze was fixed on the front door, which Manager Jeong had left slightly ajar. He sneaked towards it, quickly, quietly. He barely made it inside before Manager Jeong reappeared.

Manager Jeong returned to the doorstep, where he stood and craned his neck from side to side, doing a final check. He appeared satisfied and turned to re-enter the house.

That was when I noticed it.

There was something sticking out of his back pocket. Something black, angular, possibly metal. *A gun?*

My blood ran cold.

Young Jae and Bora were still inside, and they couldn't possibly fight Manager Jeong if he had a gun. They needed more time to escape.

I had to do something. Something quick. Distract him. Create a diversion. Make a noise. Throw something.

Yes. That's what I'll do.

I scrounged on the ground until my fingertips brushed cool, jagged stone. I grasped the rock and crawled into position.

In one adrenaline-fuelled motion, I stuck my hand above the fence and flung the rock as hard as I could. It ricocheted off the side of the house and caused enough of a sound that it would have surely caught Manager Jeong's attention.

He came back out.

"Who's there?" he called, sneering.

I lay flat on the ground, unmoving. Not even breathing.

I thought he'd check the area where the rock had landed, but I was wrong. He walked straight towards the gate.

Oh, shit.

I hadn't thought this through. I had drawn too much attention to myself. If Young Jae and Bora didn't hurry up and come to my aid…

He was on the other side of the fence now, just metres from me.

Please, God, please…

I could no longer see him or hear his footsteps on the soft field.

I didn't know what to do. Stay put, hoping that Young Jae or Bora would come out and get his attention before he found me, or get up and make a run for it.

I stayed glued to the spot, mostly from indecision. I had to bite my tongue to stop my teeth from chattering.

No sign of Young Jae or Bora.

Manager Jeong was probably making his way around the outside of the fence, and any second now, he'd spot me.

This was it. I couldn't just lie there and wait for him to catch me. I had to run. If I could reach the car, I could get away from him. *As long as he doesn't shoot.* I got to my feet.

"*Ya!*" Manager Jeong called, spotting me instantly.

I kept my eyes ahead and ran for dear life, my feet thudding on soft earth.

Just…a bit…farther….

I tripped. My ankle rolled. A spike of pain shot up my leg and I screamed.

I didn't stop to recover, but I couldn't match his pace. I was limping. He was close now. I could hear his breath.

He reached out and grabbed me by the arm, his grip tight.

I should have been scared for my life, and yet…

Why does this feel so familiar?

Before I even registered what I was doing, I tore through the sequence of movements I learned in self-defence class and broke his grip.

Manager Jeong stumbled back, a stunned look on his face, and in his moment of confusion, I hurled a kick to his groin, released the can of pepper spray from my keychain, and sprayed it straight in his face.

I didn't anticipate the slight blowback.

As Manager Jeong buckled, shrieked, and wept in pain, my own eyes stung and watered. I gritted my teeth and endured the pain to keep my blurry eyes open a crack.

Now's my chance. I can make it to the car—

"Chloeeee!"

Bora's voice. She was close by. So was Young Jae. I stopped in my tracks. We came together in a triangle around Manager Jeong, who was still incapacitated on the ground.

"Thank God, you're safe," I said.

"Could say the same about you," Bora said.

Young Jae interrupted our reunion. "No time for chitchat. Let's get outta here."

"Not so fast!" Manager Jeong growled. He pulled his gun even as he writhed in pain, his slitted red eyes streaming moisture.

Young Jae gasped. Bora whimpered.

"Stay back," he warned, shakily getting to his feet. "Cooperate or I'll shoot."

There was no way he could aim properly in his condition, but even a random shot could be deadly.

I was numb. Unable to move. Unable to think properly. Even with my impaired vision, I registered the helplessness on Bora and Young Jae's pale, panic-stricken faces.

I shook myself out of my stupor.

There's got to be something we can do. It's three against one and he can barely open his eyes.

Bora must have been thinking the same thing, because she suddenly made a move. She ducked and lunged at Manager Jeong with full force, knocking him back to the ground.

A shot fired, cracking through the atmosphere.

Chapter 33

The acrid, burnt smell of gunpowder assaulted my nostrils.

I screamed. "Bora! Nooo!"

Nothing mattered now except saving her. Pulsing with adrenaline, I pounced at Manager Jeong. So did Young Jae. Together, we pinned him down and knocked the gun from his grasp.

In the flurry of it all, I couldn't tell if Bora was hurt.

A distant rumble grew louder. Tyres screeched, smelling of hot rubber. Dust filled the air.

Car doors flung open, and two men ran towards us through the field, silhouetted by bright sunlight behind them. Friends or foes? I didn't know. Either way, it would all be over soon.

"Weapons down!" one of the men shouted.

That was when I knew the balance had tipped dramatically in our favour. The voice was Officer Bae Sangwook's.

I heard Bora gasp beside me. So, she was conscious enough to know what was going on. *Thank goodness.*

Everything happened quickly from that point forward.

Sangwook instructed us to stand up, hands in the air. The other man, whom I recognised as Officer Cha, retrieved Manager Jeong's gun from the ground.

Manager Jeong had no chance to bolt. Sangwook was armed and ready to shoot if he did.

Bora, to my relief, looked okay. Shaken, but okay. Not a trace of blood to be seen. The gunshot must have missed her entirely.

"Jeong Daeshim-ssi, you're under arrest for withholding crucial evidence from the police," Sangwook said.

Manager Jeong's face twisted in disdain as Officer Cha handcuffed him.

"The rest of you, hands down. You're safe now," Sangwook said.

Tears streamed down Bora's cheeks. She ran towards Sangwook and flung her arms around him.

"Thank you. Thank you," she said between sobs.

Sangwook awkwardly patted her back.

Meanwhile, Officer Cha attended to Manager Jeong.

"You can work with us or against us now. I'd strongly suggest you cooperate if you want to get let off lightly."

"You can't do this! I haven't done anything!" Manager Jeong spluttered.

Bora broke away from Sangwook and stepped towards Manager Jeong, hands fisted at her sides.

"What you said in the house proves otherwise," she said. "You as good as admitted that you had seen evidence about what happened to Jung Jen!"

"You can't prove anything!"

I took my phone out of my pocket and played the recording on the highest volume, skipping to the part where Manager Jeong said, "Tell him that the evidence has been destroyed."

"Everything you said inside, everything you did, was recorded," I explained.

He didn't need to know that the recording cut out at one point. I stopped playing it before then.

Manager Jeong's face turned beetroot red. He flailed and growled, helpless against Officer Cha's restraint.

"Now, what can you tell us about Jung Jen's document?" Sangwook asked. "Where is it?"

"I'm not saying anything."

"Suit yourself. With or without it, the recording is enough to implicate you in this, and continuing to withhold information will ensure a much harsher sentence. Officer Cha, search the house."

Manager Jeong's flustered reaction was enough to reveal that he was, indeed, hiding something in there.

"You can't! You need a warrant."

Sangwook sniggered. "Do I? I've broken a lot of rules to come here. I'm okay with breaking more. Getting that evidence is more important. Officer Cha, proceed. I'll take care of Daeshim from here."

Officer Cha nodded. He made a stopover at the car before heading towards the gate, lugging a large case of what I assumed was equipment to aid the search.

Sangwook held on to Manager Jeong. "You're coming with me to the station."

"Wait! This is all a big mistake!"

"This is your last chance. Tell us where you've hidden the evidence and I'm sure the court will consider it in your favour."

"I...I..."

"Officer Cha will conduct a thorough search and find it regardless. Face it, there's no escaping your fate now, so you'd better fess up."

"..."

Sangwook yanked him towards the vehicle.

"I want immunity!" Manager Jeong spluttered.

Sangwook scoffed. "If you'd cooperated from the start that might have been an option. Too late now."

"...But they'll be lenient, right?"

"Yes, telling the truth is your best shot at leniency. Now, I'll ask you one more time. Where's the evidence?"

Manager Jeong dropped his head low. The tips of his ears were tinged red. He must have realised he was done for and had no choice but to relent.

"There's a USB drive taped inside a light fitting," he mumbled.

"All right. Lead us there. And don't even think about trying to run. There are other officers on standby around the island in case you attempt to flee." Sangwook let go of Manager Jeong's arm and jabbed him in the back towards the direction of the house.

Closely flanked by Sangwook and Young Jae, Manager Jeong silently proceeded through the gate and towards the front door of the house. Bora and I followed behind them, clinging to each other for physical and moral support.

"You're limping," Bora said. "And your eyes are red."

"I twisted my ankle and a little bit of pepper spray got in my eyes."

"*Omo.* Lean on me. You can close your eyes too. I'll guide you."

I wasn't in too much pain anymore, but I still took up her offer, relaxing my eyes and left foot.

"What about you?" I asked. "Are you okay? Did he hurt you?"

"I'm fine, just overwhelmed. My nerves are wrecked."

"I don't know what I would have done if you got injured—or worse."

"I took a calculated risk. One of us had to take action before the pepper spray wore off."

"You were extremely brave. What happened in the house? The sound cut out, then we heard you scream."

"I thought he was going to attack me, so I screamed to get your attention. Then he showed me his gun and told me to be quiet. I was powerless after that. He led me to a room where he locked me inside."

"So that's what happened. How did you get out?"

"Young Jae managed to pick the lock using one of the tools on his Swiss army knife."

"Clever."

"But time consuming. I was dreading what would happen if we got caught. Or if *you* got caught. I didn't know what was going on outside, but I knew there was a strong chance he'd find you."

"He did."

"But you managed to fight him off."

"I still can't believe it myself."

Bora sniffed back a fresh wave of tears. "I'm so sorry."

"For what?"

"Dragging you into this."

"We're equally responsible."

"You tried to talk me out of it. I didn't listen."

"Shhhh. What's done is done."

I opened my eyes again when we entered the house. The interior was dated, with scuffed floorboards, faded walls, and gaps in the window frames. A constant draft circulated. We entered the living room, large and high-ceilinged, sparsely furnished except for an empty bookcase, two worn-out couches, and a dusty floor lamp. Thick cobwebs occupied every corner. It seemed like the house had been vacant for a long time before Manager Jeong took refuge there, and he had done little to amend its state of disrepair.

Officer Cha was busy tearing into the couch cushions with a knife when Sangwook interrupted him. "Officer Cha, stop the search. Jeong Daeshim has agreed to lead us to the evidence."

"Yes, sir."

"Which light fitting is it?" Sangwook asked Manager Jeong.

"In the cupboard."

He led the way and opened the door to a dark and narrow utility closet with shelves full of old junk covered in a thick layer of dust.

Sangwook flicked the light switch but it didn't work. Officer Cha shone a flashlight inside.

"Is that it?" Officer Cha asked. He directed the flashlight at a bulb high up on the wall above the door.

"Yes," Manager Jeong said. "There's a stepladder in here."

Sangwook retrieved the ladder and positioned it under the bulb. He climbed up and twisted the bulb from its socket, then felt around inside the small cavity. I heard the sound of stubborn tape being peeled off in a quick motion, like a wax strip.

"Found it," he said, coming down the stepladder with the USB drive and the piece of black duct tape in his hand. "Officer Cha, go get the laptop."

We waited in strained anticipation for Officer Cha to return with the laptop so we could view the contents of the drive. My heart was racing. My mouth was dry. What were we about to see? What was so bad that Jung Jen died because of it? I was desperate to know, yet terrified of the answer.

Officer Cha came back and set up the laptop on the dining table. We all huddled around, except for Manager Jeong who stood apart, looking down at the floor. He seemed deeply ashamed of whatever was on there.

I held my breath as Officer Cha plugged the drive in and opened it up. An error sound played and a pop-up asked for a password.

"What's the password?" Sangwook asked.

Manager Jeong said nothing. He just shuffled on his feet.

"Tell us the password, or the digital forensics team will work it out, and you won't get any brownie points for helping."

"Three, two, nine, six, space, capital B."

Officer Cha typed the password in and pressed enter. I expected to hear another error sound, but none came. He had successfully opened the drive. I saw two lone files in the window—an MP4 and a PDF.

"A video?" Sangwook said, peering closely.

Before doing anything else, Officer Cha copied the files and made backups. With that taken care of, he double-clicked the icon of the MP4 file.

I shook to the rhythm of my hammering heart and fluttering stomach as the video loaded in the media player. This was it. The moment of truth.

Jung Jen appeared on the screen in a grainy video.

"If you're watching this, I'm probably dead by now," she began.

Chapter 34

Jung Jen was pale and hollow-eyed, a husk of her former self. She appeared to be sitting on a bed, but the low light conditions made it hard to tell. *Her bedroom at her parents' house?*

The five of us watched the screen with bated breath.

"Before I go, I have to explain what happened to me so that the people involved can be held responsible," Jen said, eyes downcast.

Her voice was so soft that Officer Cha had to turn the volume up full.

"This all started after my involvement with San Seung and Lee Changho," she said. "No—before then."

I remembered what Bora had told me—how she had witnessed Mr. Kim assault Jung Jen. If I had the timeline correct, that would have been quite a while before the scandal broke.

"I didn't realise it at the time, but I can see clearly now. Mr. Kim was grooming me from the very beginning, testing my boundaries, how far I would allow him to go without complaining."

I thought of Mr. Kim's hand on my leg and shivered with repulsion. Had he been testing my boundaries too?

"You have to understand that I come from a poor background," Jen explained. "Acting was my dream. I wasn't going to let anything stand in my way, not even a bit of sleazy behaviour. In fact, I considered it the norm. At least, that's what Mr. Kim made me think." She lowered her head. "Things took a turn for the worse after the scandal. I'm sure you've heard the story. My popularity plunged and I couldn't get big roles anymore, couldn't earn what I used to earn. That was a problem for me. My spending was out of control at the time. I had debt, and my parents had debt too—and expensive health issues. They were relying on me. I was in a lot of trouble financially...until Mr. Kim offered me a solution."

Bora and I exchanged wide-eyed glances of dread.

Jen continued. "All I had to do..." She stopped and sniffed and brushed the tears from her eyes. "I'm sorry. This is difficult. Just repeating it makes me feel sick." She took a deep breath. "All I had to do was have dinner with Jang Hojin, the CEO of Z-Tank Corp. Easy, right? He was a big fan and willing to pay handsomely for the pleasure of meeting me. So, I agreed." She shook her head and covered her eyes with her hands. "I was so stupid."

I braced myself for what she might say next, fending off the tightening grip of nausea around my stomach.

"Jang Hojin seemed like a nice man," she said. "Young and attractive. Rich beyond belief. He wouldn't have been short of female admirers. It pains me to admit it, but in a way, I was actually quite flattered. He chose me of all people.

"He was staying at a hotel in Gangnam, and he had booked a table in the hotel's restaurant. Only, when we got to the restaurant, we were told they had lost our booking—or they had never received it in the first place, more likely. They were fully booked all night and couldn't accommodate us. Hojin suggested we eat in his hotel room instead. I'm sure you know where this is going."

My hands clenched into fists. Bora held my arm tight.

Officer Cha paused the video.

"I can stop this now if you're uncomfortable," he said. "Officer Bae and I will review it at the station."

"No," I said. "We've come this far for the sake of finding out the truth, and now it's within our grasp."

"I agree," Bora said. "We've got to know, no matter how difficult it is."

"All right," Officer Cha said, "but if you change your mind, just give me the word."

He pressed play and the video continued.

"Jang Hojin is a very charming and charismatic man, and I was a little bit drunk" Jen said. "I didn't consider what happened to be rape at the time, but looking back, I do feel like I was pressured into it.

"Mr. Kim gave me the money the next day, and at that point it clicked that maybe sex had been the whole point all along, and I had basically just engaged in prostitution. I felt terrible." She stopped for another deep breath and to wipe her eyes. "Only a few days passed before Mr. Kim came to me with another *assignment* like the last one. I told him no. He said I had to, but I resisted—even if I lost my contract I wouldn't go through with it. That's when he showed me the video."

I felt a collective flinch travel through the room. All of us must have realised what she was going to say next. We already knew blackmail was involved, after all.

"I had no idea that I had been recorded that night in the hotel room," she explained between sobs. "Mr. Kim said he'd release the video if I didn't go along with what he wanted. I panicked. I was so scared of the video being leaked that I didn't dare tell anyone what was going on. I felt like I had no other option."

My heart broke for her. *What an unthinkable situation to be in.* My head reeled just trying to imagine what I'd do in her place.

"At first the men that Mr. Kim set me up with could be considered good-looking," Jen said. "Smart, successful, young...Obviously they weren't *good* guys, but they were palatable in some respects. I met them in fancy hotel rooms, ate at expensive restaurants. Some of them bought me extravagant gifts. But that didn't last long. Soon I was seeing much older men, men that most other women wouldn't go near with a barge pole. Cruel men. Powerful men. I was repulsed by them. No more fancy hotel suites either. Most of the encounters actually took place at KAM Headquarters itself."

Bora and I both gasped. *How could that be?*

"There's a secret room accessible from Mr. Kim's office, behind the bookcase," Jen explained. "I don't know if it was set up just for me, or if it has been used before for similar deeds."

I couldn't believe what I was hearing. This was the sort of thing that happened in TV dramas, not real life. Yet I clung to her words, and I knew they were the truth. I watched on, riveted and disturbed.

"At first my manager didn't know what was going on," Jen said, "but he found out pretty quickly and did little to stop it from happening. After a while, he actually started to help facilitate the abuse."

I heard a sputtering whimper from Manager Jeong, then he started to bawl his eyes out.

"I'm sorry, Actor-nim! I'm so sorry," he cried.

"Mr. Kim continued to pay me for what I was doing," Jen said. "I thought that if I could save up enough, I could run away and hide. Escape from everything and everyone. The only problem was my compulsive spending, and the stress of what was going on made it worse. It was a vicious cycle. He gave me money, I spent it, I needed more money. Mr. Kim knew I was fully dependent on him, and that's the way he liked it. Complete control."

"Bastard," Young Jae growled under his breath.

"That's it," Jen said, looking almost relieved. "That's what happened."

Finally having a chance to explain what happened to her must have been a weight off her shoulders.

"I've had enough," she said with a vague, defeated smile. "I can't go on like this and I can't live with that video out in the open. I just want to end it all. But before I do, I wanted to leave this message—secretly, so no one will be able to destroy it before it gets out."

She looked directly at me, a ghost behind a screen. Her gaze was so eerie I got chills.

"You're the one I've chosen, *Seonsaeng-nim*, because you seem to know that Mr. Kim is up to something. Maybe he's abusing you too. All I know is that I think I can trust you to bring this message to light. Please hurry, but be careful. Your life could be in danger if anyone knows you have this."

An indistinguishable noise in the background of the video caught her attention and she turned her head towards its source. Visibly startled, she reached out towards the camera, then the video cut out.

None of us said anything for a few minutes. We were all too shocked to speak. The only sound was Manager Jeong quietly sobbing in the corner behind us.

"That was…worse than I thought," I choked out at last. "I thought Mr. Kim was sexually abusing Jung Jen, but I had no idea he was pimping her out to other men."

"That creep," Bora uttered in plain disgust. "*Those* creeps."

"What about the other file?" Sangwook asked.

I had forgotten there was more. Officer Cha opened the PDF. A scanned document—a handwritten note. Names. Lots of names. They were separated into two categories labelled abusers and helpers. I understood those to mean people who directly participated in the abuse and those who helped to facilitate it.

"A list of all the people involved," Officer Cha muttered. "*Aigoo*… There are some high-up men on this."

"Wait—" Sangwook said. "Stop scrolling. There. Zoom in. Is that what I think it says?"

"You're right," Officer Cha said. He swallowed dryly. "That's him."

"Who?" I asked.

"Police Commissioner Ma Sungil," Sangwook said. "No wonder there were efforts to stop us from investigating this."

"This is big. Monumental," Officer Cha said. His hand was trembling over the mouse.

We descended into another long silence before Sangwook unplugged the drive and dropped it into a clear plastic bag.

"What will happen now?" Young Jae asked.

"We'll hand Jeong Daeshim over to the local police station," Sangwook said. "You three have your own vehicle, right? Follow us there. You're all involved in this, so we'll need your testimony as well."

"Come on, Daeshim-ssi, you're coming with us," Officer Cha said, grabbing his arm.

Manager Jeong didn't resist.

Bora, Young Jae, and I didn't say much as we drove to the station.

We followed all the necessary procedures with the police, filling in reports, stating everything that had happened. Not even the commissioner would be able to stop the course of events now. Manager Jeong was willing to speak and Jung Jen's video and note were far too compelling to ignore. Officer Cha had sent the files far and wide within the police force and prosecution offices so they couldn't be covered up anymore.

After a long day at the station, we sat down with Sangwook and Officer Cha at a small restaurant with plastic tables and chairs, peeling green wallpaper, and a drinks refrigerator that continually buzzed. We hadn't had the chance to eat all day, yet none of us could stomach much. The downtime served as an opportunity to discuss our unanswered questions, at least.

"How did you know we'd come here?" I asked Sangwook while I picked at the spicy pork-and-rice dish in front of me.

"I twigged pretty quickly," he said. "The coordinates were written on the board behind me during our call. I shouldn't have been so careless."

"It took you long enough to get here," Bora said, pouting. "I nearly thought you weren't going to."

I shot her a pointed look. "Wait—were you *expecting* Officer Bae to come?"

"I knew—I *hoped* he'd find a way to get out of the conference."

"Was that your plan all along?"

She shrugged. "More or less."

"You should have told us!"

"I didn't want us to rely on him coming, just in case he didn't actually show up. I was beginning to get doubtful myself."

"You put your life at risk hoping he'd come save you like some scene out of a drama?" Young Jae asked, incredulous.

"Well, I wouldn't quite put it that way."

"You were foolish and reckless," Sangwook scolded. "I'm disappointed in you."

"If we hadn't gone through with it then Jeong Daeshim might have gotten away," she snapped back. "We might never have found the evidence—"

"I've probably lost my job over this," Sangwook grumbled. "Going AWOL from the conference, arresting Jeong Daeshim, and searching the house without a warrant…"

"Surely not," Bora retorted. "If you manage to put Mr. Kim and the others behind bars, you should be rewarded, not fired."

"That may be so, but we're not quite out of the woods yet. No doubt the defence will say that Jung Jen was lying."

This dose of reality went down like a bucket of cold water being poured over us.

"But there's still more we can do," Officer Cha piped up. "There are a few missing pieces in the puzzle we should hopefully be able to recover."

"What missing pieces?" I asked.

"The secret room at KAM headquarters and the video which was used to blackmail Jung Jen," he explained. "With those two pieces, we can corroborate Jung Jen's testimony. With those two pieces, Mr. Kim won't stand a chance."

* * *

"Can I sleep in your room?" Bora asked, standing outside my door, eyes downcast and cheeks blazing. "I don't want to be alone tonight."

"Of course you can," I replied. "Come in."

To be honest, I felt the same way she did. Even with Bae Sangwook and Officer Cha staying on the same floor of the hotel, I was on high alert. My racing heart hadn't slowed since the confrontation in the field, and I kept seeing the grainy image of Jung Jen in my mind. I didn't think I'd be able to sleep.

Bora's slippered feet crossed the threshold. She was dressed in her blue gingham-print pyjama set and hotel robe. Her eyes looked significantly smaller lacking the usual addition of glasses.

"Huh? Your room's big," she noted.

"It is? Luck of the draw, I guess."

"Sorry. I wasn't complaining or anything."

The room *was* spacious—but basic. Everything was clean and white. I opened a cupboard containing a mini fridge and an electric kettle and boiled some water.

"Chamomile tea?" I asked. "It might help you relax."

"Yes, please."

She sat on the end of the bed, leaving the single chair at its foot available for me. She twiddled her thumbs, oddly quiet while I made the tea.

"How's your ankle?" she asked when I sat down.

"A little sore."

"Let me take a look."

I lifted my pyjama leg an inch then paused. "Really? You're not one of those people who are grossed out by feet?"

"Not at all."

"Okay, then."

I removed my slipper and raised my bare foot.

She took her glasses out of her robe's pocket and put them on to inspect the damage, peering closely, with a small crease between her brows.

"It looks fine. Slightly swollen, maybe."

I was about to lower my foot when she suddenly took it in her hands and began to massage my ankle.

"How does that feel?" she asked.

"Good. That's helping."

"Chloe…"

"Yes?"

"I'm sorry about today."

My usual instinct would be to respond, "It's okay," or, "It's not your fault," but this time, I stayed silent. A big part of me did blame her, after all.

"You already survived one life-threatening situation and I made you put your life in danger again," she said.

I wrenched my foot from her gentle grasp. "What's done is done.

We came out alive and helped spur major progress in the investigation."

"It wasn't worth it. I'm okay with sacrificing myself, but not you. Not after everything you've already been through. I should have gone by myself."

"No, you shouldn't have. You couldn't have done this on your own, and I wouldn't have let you."

She started to cry. Big, fat, juicy tears rolled down her cheeks and sploshed off her chin.

"I was scared," she spluttered. "Terrified."

Her tears sparked my tears. I moved to sit beside her on the bed and let her weep on my shoulder.

We stayed like that for a while, forgetting the cups of tea which sat cooling on the ledge by the TV.

"Are you going to tell Jinseung what happened?" Bora asked when she recovered from her crying enough to string a proper sentence together.

I nodded. "There's no way I could keep something like this a secret, and Young Jae will definitely tell him if I don't. But not tonight. I'm too tired. Tomorrow night when we're back home. I'll explain everything."

"Please, blame me all you want. Make sure he knows it was all my fault."

"I will. Can't have him thinking this was my idea."

She cracked a little smile.

Chapter 35

I looked around the busy ground floor of KAM HQ—staff members and visitors chatting, laughing, totally carefree except for the usual stress of their jobs.

All these people have absolutely no idea that all hell is about to break loose.

It felt strange, to say the least, going in to work and pretending as if nothing out of the ordinary had happened and that the police weren't going to bust in and perform a raid at any minute.

Throughout my lesson with Nam Sungjin I had my ears tuned in to catch a commotion from the corridors as police officers descended on the building—but nothing happened.

I went back down to the lobby at the end of the lesson. Nothing had changed. No sign of the police. What was going on?

Don't tell me that they still haven't got the warrants they need.

Even with all the evidence we had gathered, could red tape be holding up the process?

I signed out and made my way to the elevator.

Oh well. It'll be easier if I'm not here when it happens. I've already dealt with enough.

The elevator doors opened and I was about to step inside when I heard what sounded like a stampede, followed by a series of gasps and murmurs.

"What's going on?"

"Why are the police here?"

"Has something happened?"

And so it begins.

I stood and watched as the police swarmed the building and proceeded to block all exits. No one was allowed to leave while they searched the premises for more evidence and arrested all the suspects.

Some of the staff members around me asked if I knew what was going on. I shrugged and pretended like I didn't know. How could I possibly explain everything?

The first arrest was Mr. Kim's secretary. He went with the police, his head bowed in shame and his hands cuffed behind his back as they led him to a police car waiting outside the building. Onlookers stared at the spectacle, pointing, whispering, wide-eyed and mouths agape. A few others shuffled on their feet and fidgeted with their hands, eyes darting anxiously around the room, guilt written on their faces—whether over this or some other unknown crime.

The second arrest was the fifth-floor receptionist. A handful of other arrests followed, but notably, Mr. Kim was not one of them. Perhaps he wasn't in the building. Did he know this was going to happen? Had he already enacted an escape plan?

When we were finally allowed to leave, we were greeted by a chaotic scene outside—reporters, cameras, microphones. Police officers had to direct cars and foot traffic safely through the crowds of media and journalists. The tinted windows of Jinseung's car ensured my privacy as I drove out of the carpark. Now, to the secret rendezvous.

* * *

THIS CAN'T BE RIGHT, *can it?*

I stood outside a graffiti-covered metal door in a back alley, too afraid to knock. I fumbled in my bag, retrieved my phone, and scrutinised the email's directions.

Hmmm...Seems accurate.

I tentatively reached out and knocked, then deciding I had done it too softly, knocked again with more force, hurting my knuckles on the cold, hard, metal surface.

The door creaked open and a head popped out. To my relief, it was Young Jae. He wore a beanie and a pair of gold earrings. He smelled like cigarettes. If I didn't know him, I'd find him intimidating.

"Come in," he said.

"The entrance is a bit uninviting," I grumbled as he shut the door behind me and bolted it.

He smirked. "It's the back entry. Besides, it's my private studio. It doesn't need to look inviting. This way."

He guided me down the dimly lit hallway to a cramped, windowless room full of sound equipment and a microphone stand amidst a jumble of power cords on the floor. Four mismatched chairs were arranged in front of a guitar rack and a tower of amps. Bora was seated on one of them, legs crossed and arms folded.

"Officer Bae isn't coming," she said.

"Why not?" I asked, unable to mask my disappointment.

I desperately wanted to know how the case was progressing. After everything we had contributed, weren't we owed that much at least?

"He's tied down at the station. Must be pretty hectic."

"I heard some pretty serious shit went down at KAM HQ today," Young Jae said, taking a seat.

I nodded. "Yep. I was there. I'll tell you what happened."

"I have information too," Bora said. "Officer Bae might not be coming, but we've been talking through encrypted email. This meeting won't be for nothing. *Unnie*, you go first."

I shared my story, recounting every detail I could recall from the raid.

"Must have been pretty scary for everyone who had no idea what was going on," Bora said, biting her lip.

"There was a lot of panic and confusion."

"Imagine seeing five of your colleagues get arrested right in front of you," Young Jae said, "and more brought to the police station for questioning, wondering if you'll be next. That's pretty effed up."

"But not Mr. Kim," I pointed out.

"Why am I not surprised?" Bora said. "Clever bastard either worked it out on his own or someone tipped him off."

"What did you find out from Officer Bae?" I asked.

"Remember how Jung Jen described a secret room at KAM HQ?"

"Of course. How could I forget?"

"She wasn't lying. The police found it during the raid."

I swallowed the bile which suddenly rose in my throat.

"It was empty," Bora explained. "Whatever was in there had already been removed."

"Further evidence that Mr. Kim knew this was going to happen." I sighed.

"And what about the sex video?" Young Jae asked. "Have you heard anything about that?"

"It hasn't been recovered yet," Bora replied.

"Ah."

"Have there been any more arrests?" I asked. "Anyone out of the men on Jung Jen's list?"

Bora shook her head. "Not that I know of. I imagine the police are still gathering evidence."

We sat in silence for a moment. No doubt the others were sifting through their thoughts and feelings just like I was.

A blaring alarm intercepted the thoughtful quiet.

I winced. "What the—?"

The sound emanated from the vicinity of Bora.

"Sorry," she said. "It's my phone."

Not a ring tone or notification ping I was familiar with.

She fumbled in her pockets, grabbed her phone, then turned off the alarm.

"I set up an alert," she explained. "Any news articles mentioning KAM Entertainment and my phone rings and vibrates like crazy."

"Does this mean there's been a new development?" I asked.

"Let me see." She adjusted her glasses and peered closely at the screen.

Chapter 36

"What is it?" Young Jae asked. "What does it say?"

Both of us hunched over Bora's shoulders, trying to read her screen.

"There's been another arrest," she said.

"Who?" I asked.

"It doesn't say. But it's in connection to KAM Entertainment. They were arrested at Incheon Airport this morning, attempting to board a flight to Xiamen."

"My money's on Mr. Kim," Young Jae said.

"Mine too," I agreed. "Who else would try to escape the country?"

"I'm sure Sangwook can confirm one way or another," Bora said, "but I have a feeling you're both right."

I flopped onto my chair. "Thank goodness. I might actually be able to sleep tonight."

"It's over," Young Jae said.

Bora shook her head. "For us, maybe, but there's still so much more that needs to happen. We'll have to wait and see how things play out over the following weeks, months, maybe even years. Who knows how deep this corruption goes? There could be more victims, other entertainment agencies involved, a connection to Byun Gimok…"

"True," I said. "But the three of us have done all we can. The rest is up to the police."

"Back to normal life," Young Jae said with a tiny hint of regret.

"As normal as can be, given the circumstances," Bora said. "What's gonna happen to KAM Entertainment? What will happen to all the talent and staff who worked for Mr. Kim, including me and Chloe, Jinseung and Yoojin?"

Of course I was worried about that, but I wasn't thinking about myself, only Jinseung. What impact would this have on his career? Even if the agency survived, its reputation would be tarnished.

"Hopefully someone will step in to fill Mr. Kim's role," Young Jae suggested. "KAM Entertainment is a resilient beast. It won't crumble and fall that easily. "

"I suppose we'll just have to wait for the CEO to release a statement," Bora said, folding her arms.

We didn't have much left to say. Bora and I thanked Young Jae for his contribution once again, then left the studio.

Night had fallen in the meantime, blanketing the sky in darkness. We walked to where I had parked the car. Yawning, I opened the door to the driver side.

"Sleepy?" Bora asked. "Want me to drive?"

I shook my head. "It's just...been a long day. I'll be fine." I took the seat at the wheel and dropped my phone into the cup holder.

"Your phone's flashing," Bora said, pulling her seatbelt on.

I didn't pick it up since I had already started to back out of the carpark. "Want to check it for me?"

She swiped away the screensaver. "*Aigoo.* You have, like, ten missed calls."

I winced. "Oops. I had my phone on silent during the meeting. Is it Jinseung?"

"Yep."

Jinseung already knew what happened. I told him everything once we returned to Seoul. He was shaken, angry, but most of all, he was relieved that I was okay. He was probably calling now because he'd heard the news of what went down at KAM Entertainment and the arrests.

"Shall I call him back?" Bora asked. "I'll put it through the Bluetooth."

"Yes, please."

She connected my phone to the car speaker and made the call. Jinseung answered straight away.

"You finally pick up," he said.

"I'm so sorry! I was having a debrief with Bora and Young Jae and didn't notice you were calling."

"It's okay. What are you doing now?"

"Driving home with Bora."

"Am I on speaker?"

"Yep."

"Bora-ya, make sure Chloe gets home safe."

"Yes, sir!" Bora said. "I won't let you down."

"Good."

After taking full responsibility for what occurred in Cheongsando, Bora had promised Jinseung to be on her best behaviour.

"Changsoo told me what happened," Jinseung said. "The raid, the arrests...He didn't know if Mr. Kim had been apprehended or not, but he couldn't get through to him when he tried to call. In custody or in hiding, my guess."

"In custody," Bora said, looking at her phone. "Bae Sangwook has just sent through confirmation."

I heard Jinseung exhale. "That's a relief. I thought he might have got away."

"He did try to leave the country, but border security caught him."

Jinseung sighed. "What a weird feeling. I've known Mr. Kim for so many years and never imagined him capable of something like this. I'll probably never see him again."

"We'll see him at his trial," Bora reminded us.

His trial.

Her words echoed in my brain until it clicked and I gasped so hard

I made the car wobble. Bora stuck out her hand to stabilise the steering wheel.

"*Omo!*" I cried. "Oh Sejung's trial. It's soon, isn't it? What's today's date?"

"The twenty-fourth of June," Bora said.

"So…it's in three weeks, then. I'm not prepared. I've been so preoccupied by the situation—"

"Calm down," Jinseung said. "I've been in touch with your lawyer. She has everything under control, and you still have time to meet her again."

"Yes. You're right. Thank you for doing that."

"She's one of the best lawyers in the entertainment industry. Everything's going to be fine."

My hands tightened around the steering wheel. "Oh Sejung…"

"Are you scared about seeing her again?"

"I don't know. I haven't been thinking about it."

"Well, you'll have plenty of support. Your parents are coming, aren't they?"

"Yes. They are. And Han Seri and her parents too."

"And you'll have me. I've already arranged my leave."

"So…I'll see you again soon?"

"You will. Stay strong in the meantime, okay? I know you'll get through this."

Chapter 37

Three weeks later

The riot of butterflies inside my stomach intensified throughout the drive to court.

Today was the first day of the trial, the day I'd have to see Oh Sejung again.

The leather upholstery squeaked as I squirmed in the back of the taxi between my parents. Mum took my hand in hers.

"It's going to be okay," she cooed.

My lawyer, Ms. Yoon, sat in the front passenger seat. The elegant older woman wore a beautifully tailored suit, her grey hair pulled back in a strict bun and her lips painted red. An Hermès handbag rested on her lap and a fat leather briefcase by her feet.

The car slowed down. A nearby sign said Seoul Central District Court. We stopped.

Here we are. This is it.

I wound a lightweight silk scarf around my neck and pulled it up to cover the lower half of my face, then popped on a pair of oversized sunglasses.

So far, we had managed to keep the case a secret from the media, but Ms. Yoon had warned me of reporters lurking in and around the building. It was only a matter of time before someone scooped the story, especially once Jinseung arrived. Still, I wanted to protect my privacy as much as possible.

We emerged from the car and walked up a wide pathway surrounded by manicured lawns and leafy green trees to the stately building's arched entrance.

A security guard greeted us in the foyer. He motioned to me to lower my scarf and remove my sunglasses.

"ID?" he asked.

Once I had shown him my passport, he let me cover my face again.

He IDed Ms. Yoon and my parents as well, then we walked single file through a metal detector and received pat downs from the guard on the other side.

Mum assaulted Ms. Yoon with a barrage of questions as we navigated the large building. Ms. Yoon patiently reassured her, speaking in flawless English. Dad just listened and nodded along.

My nerves picked up again as we approached the designated courtroom. Soon I would come face to face with Oh Sejung once again. My stomach twisted so tight I thought it might pop.

"You two head through," Ms. Yoon told my parents. "I want to have a final word with Chloe in private."

Mum looked like she was about to protest, but Dad put a hand on her shoulder and guided her through the door into the courtroom.

I had no idea what Ms. Yoon wanted to tell me in private, but I followed her wordlessly down the corridor to a pair of closed double doors where another guard stood. He checked our IDs again then let us through.

"This is a VIP area," Ms. Yoon explained, "for high-profile court attendees such as yourself and Shin Jinseung."

My heart skipped a beat. "You mean...?"

She pushed a door open.

Jinseung rose to his feet in the plush waiting room. I ran to him with open arms.

"*Oppa!*"

"*Jagi*," he returned, welcoming me to his warm, hard chest.

"I'll just be outside," Ms. Yoon said. "I'll knock when it's time to go."

The door clicked shut.

Jinseung was dressed in formal military attire: a dark teal suit with gold buttons and a badge displaying his rank of sergeant. He looked as dashing and regal as a prince. *My* prince. Tall, lean, groomed to perfection. He smelled of soap and fresh laundry, with a hint of his own sweet spiciness underneath.

"How are you holding up?" he asked.

"Let's put it this way, I couldn't eat breakfast because I didn't think I'd be able to keep it down."

"You'll have your appetite back by lunchtime. I'll buy you something to eat."

"When did you get here?"

"Just a minute ago."

"You sure cut it fine."

"Sorry for the hold-up. I would've come last night if I could, but, you know, slight mix up. Their end, not mine."

"Never mind. Did you make it here without anyone seeing you?"

"I think so."

"Good."

A knock came from the other side of the door.

"Already?" I grumbled.

"*Jagi*, just one thing."

Jinseung grasped my chin, tilted my head up, and pressed his lips to mine.

"I'm so glad you're all right," he said.

He continued to hold my chin and gazed into my eyes so intently I blushed. After all this time, he still had the power to turn me to mush with little more than eye contact.

Another knock. Ms. Yoon peeked her head inside.

"It's time," she said.

I let out a shaky sigh before leaving the room, hand in hand with Jinseung, not caring who saw us at that point.

"Do you remember what you're going to say?" Ms. Yoon asked me on the short walk down the corridor.

"I think so."

"Just do your best. Be honest and give as much detail as possible."

I nodded.

"Here we are."

I gulped a quick breath of air before entering.

For some reason I expected to see Oh Sejung as soon as I walked in, but I only saw friendly faces. Yang Bora, Young Jae, Bae Sangwook, and Shin Jina sat together in a row near the front of the gallery. Behind them, Han Seri, her parents, and a young Caucasian man whom I recognised as her boyfriend, Adrian. Bong Changsoo sat farther back by himself. Jinseung's parents were there too, right up front near my own parents.

My heart instantly filled up and overflowed as tears in my eyes. All these people had come to support me. I couldn't be more grateful.

But there was no time for greetings and thank-yous.

Ms. Yoon walked me down the gently sloping wooden floor to our designated table positioned between the judge and jury areas.

The jury seats filled up.

On the defendant side, the seats remained largely empty, with just a couple of people occupying separate spaces. Friends or family of Oh Sejung, I didn't know.

My eyes wandered while I waited, tense with apprehension. The courtroom reminded me of a small lecture theatre, with white walls, dark wooden tables, and black chairs on a slanted floor. A Korean flag hung limply by the empty judge's table at the front.

I snapped my head around when I heard the door at the back of the room creak open. This was it. The moment I'd been dreading. Oh Sejung entered the room, flanked by a police officer and a suited man whom I assumed was her lawyer. She was pale and bony, wearing an orange jumpsuit, hands cuffed behind her back. Her hair had been chopped short. Her eyes were the same as I remembered—two bottomless black pits which could strike terror directly to the root of your soul. She didn't look at me, choosing to leer at Jinseung instead. He didn't give her the satisfaction of looking back.

"All rise," the clerk said.

We stood as the judge entered and took up residence at her table. It seemed like the trial was about to start, when two last stragglers entered the room—a young woman, her identity obscured by a headscarf and sunglasses, and a young man I didn't recognise. I couldn't work out who the woman was until she removed her glasses, revealing herself as Go Yoojin. The young man must have been her assistant or intern. I gave her a nod of acknowledgement and a thankful smile as she sat down near Changsoo.

The judge began the trial with a list of the charges brought towards Oh Sejung, including kidnapping, attempted murder, drugging, assault, stalking, harassment, and so many more I lost count. Next, the prosecutor made an opening statement, followed by the defence.

My moment had come. The judge called me forward to give my statement. A hush fell as I walked up to the stand. I could feel everyone's stares like hot lasers on my face.

For a moment, I just froze, completely overwhelmed.

Come on, Chloe. Get a grip. You can do this.

I reminded myself why I was there. Oh Sejung was going to get punished for what she did to me. Drumming up as much audacity as I could, I locked eyes with her, daring her to put up her best fight.

You're going down.

Chapter 38

The waiting felt like an eternity. As the hours crawled forward, doubt began to creep into the back of my mind. Had I done everything I could to convince the jury of Oh Sejung's guilt? What if she got a much lighter sentence than I felt she deserved? What if she didn't go to jail at all?

No. Now I'm just being silly.

Ms. Yoon must have sensed my unease.

"The verdict will be in our favour," she reassured. "We have too much evidence and witness testimony on our side to ignore. Just hold tight and you'll see."

The trial was in its fifth day, and the jury had been deliberating for four hours now. The courtroom was jam-packed. Word must have spread via the court reporters to the media at large, who flocked to view the spectacle—*Shin Jinseung's girlfriend versus the sasaeng fan.* They weren't allowed to take pictures, or even to name names, but I expected a lot of details would still leak out. It bugged me—though much less than my concerns about the outcome of the trial.

Everyone hushed when a man emerged from the jury room and conferred with the judge. I couldn't hear what they were saying, but the judge nodded and cleared her throat. He passed her something

—an envelope? Then he went back to the jury room and quickly returned, followed by the entire jury. They took their seats.

The judge hit her gavel.

"I would like to announce that a verdict has been reached," she said.

A buzz of anticipation rippled through the room. I held my breath, knuckles white as I clamped the edge of my chair.

Please...please...

Her voice rang out. "Oh Sejung-ssi, you have been found guilty on all charges. Sentencing will occur on the twentieth of August. Until then, you will be remanded in custody."

The weight lifted from my shoulders immediately. I felt so light I could've floated to the ceiling like a helium balloon.

As the police took a groaning, howling Sejung away, Ms. Yoon patted my back.

"Congratulations, Chloe," she said. "You won."

I won...I really won!

My friends and family swarmed to me with a whirlwind of hugs and congratulations.

"Well done," Han Seri said, hands on my shoulders. "You were so brave!"

Bora gave me a fist bump. "You nailed it!"

Jina took both my hands in hers. "That was epic. Congratulations!"

Changsoo simply smiled and nodded at me, though I detected the faint glimmer of a tear in one eye. My parents, on the other hand, were crying outright. They couldn't understand Korean, but they knew a guilty verdict when they saw it. Ms. Yoon had translated a lot for them during the breaks as well.

My attention turned to Jinseung, who stood alone in the aisle, shaking, on the verge of tears. The trial had been tough for him, reminding him of all the terrible things I went through that he couldn't protect me from. I approached him.

"It's okay. It's over now."

Ironic that I should be comforting him instead of the other way around.

"I'm sorry," he said over and over. "I'm so sorry. I'll never, ever, let something like that happen to you again. Even when I'm away in the army, I'll do everything I can to protect you."

"I know you will. Thank you. And thanks for hiring Ms. Yoon. She was fantastic, a total lifesaver."

Mrs. Woo stood up on a chair next to her worried-looking husband who held his arms out in case she fell. She waved her hand in the air to get everyone's attention.

"We will be having drinks and nibbles at Ji Soo Bar across the road. All friends and family invited! No media."

With that, our party relocated to the bar, which had been booked out in advance by Jinseung's parents in anticipation of a favourable verdict.

The evening was warm, and we sat outside on a rooftop courtyard lit by glowing lanterns dangling from potted green trees and fairy lights which snaked around an iron fence border. A perfect ending to a difficult few days.

Jinseung and I stopped by my parents' table first. They had never seemed impressed that I was dating a famous actor until this visit. Seeing the fabulous house Jinseung had bought for me and the beautiful neighbourhood I lived in had opened their eyes to his wealth. Then seeing him in person confirmed how handsome and charming he was, especially in his military attire. Mum hadn't stopped gawping at him since I introduced them. Dad was less obvious, but I could tell he was impressed as well.

We chatted for a while, me playing translator, until Mrs. Woo interrupted us with her husband in tow.

"You still haven't properly introduced us to your parents, Chloe. I'd like to talk to them, but I seem to have forgotten most of my English!"

"Of course, *Eomeonim.* Don't worry, I'll translate."

Seeing my parents with Jinseung's parents was odd, to say the least. The two couples couldn't be any more different. Jinseung's parents were in a class above mine, and the culture gap was clear—the elegant Korean couple and the unsophisticated British pair. Nevertheless, they exchanged polite greetings with my help as interpreter.

"Well, that was awkward," I whispered to Jinseung when his parents finally retreated.

"Come on. It wasn't that bad."

We moved on and chatted with Han Seri and her parents next.

"You have to come to Melbourne!" Seri said. "Adrian and I just bought a house. You're welcome to stay any time."

"Wow. That's amazing," I gushed. "I definitely want to come."

"Am I invited?" Jinseung asked.

"Of course!" Seri said. "Though I don't suppose you can while you're in service."

"True."

"What about you, *Abeonim, Eomeonim*?" I asked. "Do you visit Australia often?"

"We have only visited once," Mrs. Soo said, "but we are thinking about coming to live there once they get married."

"Married?!" I snapped my eyes to Seri.

She blushed. "*Eomma!* Aren't we getting ahead of ourselves?"

"Don't wait too long. You're already living together," Mrs. Soo said.

"We want grandchildren soon," Mr. Han added.

Seri turned a deeper shade of scarlet.

"What are you saying?" asked a confused Adrian in English.

"Oh…nothing…"

"They're talking marriage and children," I said, grinning.

"Oh!" He chuckled. "Why am I not surprised?"

After visiting every table, Jinseung and I settled down with Bora, Young Jae, and Sangwook, who were huddled close around a basket of fried chicken and fries. Jinseung nicked a chip straight away.

"And they join us at last!" Bora announced, swaying and slurring slightly. She seemed a little tipsy. Okay, *more* than a little tipsy. She leaned close to Sangwook, who touched her arm to steady her.

Young Jae held up a hand to signal a passing waiter. He ordered more drinks for the table.

"Sangwook *Oppa,* give them the update!" Bora said.

"Update?" I asked. "Do you have more news about the Mr. Kim case?"

He nodded.

"Let's hear it, then. If it's okay to tell us, I mean."

"First thing, Kim Sunwoo has been denied bail."

"Sunwoo?"

"Mr. Kim."

I sniggered. "Funny. I never knew his given name until now."

"Good news about the bail," Jinseung said.

"And what of the other suspects?" I asked.

"Jeong Daeshim has been allowed bail since he has been helping with the investigation," Sangwook explained. "We're still gathering the necessary evidence to arrest the others, but progress is being made, and the acting commissioner is fully on board with the investigation."

"And your job is safe?"

"Yes. I've been pardoned for my errors this time around."

"See? I knew you'd pull through," Bora teased, lightly jabbing him in the ribs.

He swatted her hand, though his sheepish smile gave his amusement away.

"What about the video?" I asked. "Did you find it?"

He shook his head. "At this point, I doubt it will ever be recovered. I suspect that, having no further use for it, Mr. Kim destroyed it upon her death."

"In a way, I'm kind of glad," I admitted. "More than anything, Jung Jen didn't want anyone to see that video."

"I agree," Bora said. "It's better left unseen."

"I'm confident we'll be able to obtain enough evidence without it," Sangwook said.

Jina appeared at our table, cheerful and effortlessly glam as usual in gold hoop earrings and a slinky black dress. "Hey, peeps! Mind if I join in?"

"Where were you?" I asked.

"Inside. I know the bartender here."

Young Jae moved over to make a space where she could pull up a chair. "*Noona*, long time no see."

"Thanks. Oooh…" She eyed Bora and Sangwook. "When did *this* happen?"

"This?" Bora asked, blushing.

"You're dating, right?"

"Well…"

My heart was beating fast on her behalf while I watched with curiosity as to how this would unfold.

"Yeah. Kind of," Sangwook said, making Bora blush harder. "I mean, we've been on dates."

"Those were dates?"

"I thought they were. Didn't you?"

"Yeah, I guess. So…we're dating now?"

"Any objections?" he replied, arms folded across his chest.

"…No."

"That settles it then."

Unable to contain ourselves, Jina and I simultaneously squealed in delight. We got up, grabbed each other's hands, and jumped up and down until we ran out of steam.

"So cuuuute!" Jina gushed.

Young Jae poured everyone refills then raised his glass. "To the new couple."

We all clinked glasses and cheered. I couldn't be more happy for Bora.

As the evening continued, numbers began to dwindle. My parents and Jinseung's parents left in taxis. Soon, only our table of six remained.

"How's everyone getting home?" Sangwook asked, always the responsible one.

"I'm taking Chloe home," Jinseung said.

"Want to share a taxi, Young Jae?" Jina asked. "Your place isn't far from mine."

"Actually, I thought I might go out," he replied. "My friend's DJing at The Sound Cave."

"Ooh. Can I come?"

"Sure. Anyone else…? No takers, huh? It'll just be us."

"Fine with me!"

That left the obvious pairing of Sangwook and Bora. They looked at each other, both slightly pink-cheeked.

"Then, shall we…?" Sangwook asked.

"Do you mind?" Bora replied.

"Not at all."

I couldn't wipe the smile off my face. Those two were adorable.

After thanking the bar staff, we exited and went our separate ways. I slumped into Jinseung's car and pulled the seatbelt on.

"Did you have fun?" Jinseung asked, taking the wheel.

"I'm just glad the trial is over."

"Yeah, me too."

I watched the city lights pass us by—a blur of colourful neon. Where would life take us next? Could I continue working at KAM Entertainment, waiting for Jinseung to be discharged? And what about Jinseung's career? Would his contract still get renewed amidst all the chaos? I let out a small sigh, my breath misting the window.

"Everything okay?" Jinseung asked.

"Just thinking about the future…"

"Thinking about what you're going to do now?"

"Mmhmm. And you. What will you do when you leave the army?"

"Don't worry about me. I'll figure something out."

"Even if your contract doesn't get renewed?"

"I don't know if I can stomach the idea of continuing to work for KAM Entertainment. The whole thing has left a sour taste in my mouth. Even if they do offer to renew my contract, I don't think I'll accept."

I gasped at his sudden declaration. "You won't renew?" I had to ask again, just to be sure.

He nodded, eyes staring straight ahead at the road. "That's right. I won't renew."

"Wow. That's a big deal. When did you decide this?"

"Recently. But I started thinking about it as soon as you told me what Mr. Kim did to you. I felt so betrayed."

I took a minute to consider the implications of his announcement, my fingers twisting the seatbelt. "Does this mean you'll quit acting?"

"No. Maybe I'll sign with a different agency. Or maybe I'll do something completely different. Either way, I feel excited about the opportunities out there."

As he spoke, I noticed the road sign signalling our exit, but we sped past it. "Hey—you missed the turn-off."

"Don't worry. We're going the right way."

"But—"

"We're not going home."

"Then…where are we going?"

The corner of his lips quirked up and he had a glint in his eyes. "Wait and see."

Chapter 39

I could only think of one reason why we would be driving to Namsan Mountain. The famous tourist attraction, N Seoul Tower, stood at its peak, lit up bright pink, its needle tip piercing the dark expanse of sky. But why would Jinseung take me to one of the busiest tourist locations in Seoul? Unlikely that he suddenly fancied a spot of sightseeing, I would have thought.

Jinseung parked in the carpark by the cable car ticket office. He had taken off his stiff jacket and replaced it with a soft hoodie. He wore the hood over his head, and a black fabric mask to cover the lower half of his face. I wrapped my silk scarf around my neck and burrowed my chin into it. The darkness provided the rest of our cover. A few people milled around the area, but I couldn't see a queue anywhere, and the cable car station was unlit and shut off, the ticket windows closed.

"Looks like the cable cars have stopped running for the night," I said.

"We'll walk up." Jinseung took my hand in his.

We walked side by side along a moonlit path through Namsan Park, lined by trees on both sides, gently sloping uphill towards the tower. Every now and then I caught glimpses of the city below through the branches, like dashes of glitter on a dark backdrop.

The crowds grew thicker until we reached the plaza at the base of the tower. I nervously glanced around.

"Is this okay? There are so many people..."

"We'll blend in," Jinseung said, adjusting his mask. "We're tourists, just like everyone else."

"If you say so."

Most of the shops in the plaza were closed, but the main attraction was the view. I rushed to the fence to lean over and gaze upon the sea of glimmering multi-coloured lights below.

"Wow..."

"It's beautiful, isn't it?" Jinseung said over my shoulder.

"Stunning."

"Have you ever been here before?"

"No, actually. I haven't."

"You never did the tourist stuff, huh?"

"No. So why did you bring me here?"

He smirked. "All will be revealed. First, we must go to the tower."

As he guided the way, we passed fences covered with colourful padlocks—love locks, just like the ones on the bridges across the Seine River in Paris. You could purchase the locks from several nearby vending machines.

"*Aigoo*. So overpriced," I said, peering through the glass at the garish novelty padlocks inside. "We're not going to do this, are we?"

Jinseung pouted. "Why not?"

"It's kind of tacky, isn't it?"

"Well, I guess I'm just a tacky sort of guy. Besides, secretly you want to, am I right?"

I scoffed, but a sheepish smile slipped out.

"There it is. You totally want to."

"Okay. You got me. It *is* kinda romantic."

He produced a bright pink padlock and a black permanent marker from his pocket. "Here's one I prepared earlier."

"*Aigoo*. You really thought of everything."

"Let's write our names." He passed me the marker.

I wrote C.A.G. In my neatest handwriting.

"What does the A stand for?" he asked.

"Alice. It's my middle name."

"I didn't know that!"

"Did I never mention it?"

"No. I would have remembered if you did. *Alice*. Cute."

He took the marker and wrote his own name in Hangul characters, plus a heart in the middle.

"Where shall we put it?" I asked.

"Let's find a good spot."

The fence was already completely covered. Locks were attached to locks that were attached to other locks. Eventually I clipped it onto a lock which seemed to belong to another multicultural couple—Ella and Taehwang. I guess I felt some kind of weird affinity for them.

"There." I stood back to admire it from a distance.

"Perfect."

We both took photos of the lock and a selfie with the two of us standing by the fence. I tried to imprint the exact location of the lock in my mind, hoping that I'd be able to find it if I ever returned.

A group of nearby girls started staring and whispering between themselves. I wondered if they had recognised Jinseung.

"Come on." Jinseung tugged me away before the girls could approach. He led me towards the tower with purposeful strides. I wondered what would await me when we got there. He clearly had something planned, but what?

My excitement turned to disappointment as we closed in on the tower entrance. The doors were shut, the lights were off, and security guards were turning people away.

I frowned. "It looks closed. I think we're too late."

"It *is* closed. To everyone but us, that is."

"What do you mean?"

"Patience, *jagi*." He approached one of the security guards, pulled down his mask, and passed him a folded-up document he had stored in his pocket. The guard unfolded the piece of paper, looked it over, then nodded. He unlocked the door and led us inside. The place was deserted except for a few staff members finishing up. All of the gift shops and cafes were closed and only a few dim lights remained turned on to guide our way through the building. We stepped into the elevator and the guard pressed the button for the observatory.

"I hope you're not scared of heights," Jinseung said.

"I think I'll be fine."

"Then you're in for a treat."

We got out at the third floor.

"Come back here when you've finished looking around." The guard gestured to us to go on ahead while he stationed himself beside the elevator.

The room was circular with windows along the outer wall providing a 360-degree panoramic view of central Seoul—a sparkling, kaleidoscopic paradise emitting a hazy glow into the sky. I pressed myself close to the cool glass. I felt like I was floating above the world.

"Oh, this is wonderful. Spectacular."

"Pretty special, isn't it?" Jinseung wrapped me in his arms from behind, his chin nestled beside my ear.

I admired the view for a while longer, staring down at the vibrant cityscape below.

"This must be the most romantic thing anyone's ever done for me."

"So, you like it?"

"I do. What made you think to do this?"

"I wanted this night to be as special…as *memorable* as possible."

"All this to celebrate the end of the trial? Wait—is it our anniversary or something?"

He chuckled. "Close your eyes."

I did so, anticipation rising in my chest like an oversized bubble. I heard a slight shuffling sound as he temporarily released me from his arms.

"Hold out your hand," he said.

I lifted my right hand and held it in front of me, palm facing up. My breathing hitched when he placed something there—a small box, smooth and heavy. He closed my fingers around it. "Now. Open your eyes."

I tried to keep my expectations low, but my heart was beating on overdrive. I cracked my eyes open a slit, and then fully, gazing at the box in my grasp—black and glossy with smooth rounded corners.

A jewellery box.

Was this really happening? Was this what I thought it was?

"Go ahead. Open it," Jinseung urged in a low, husky tone.

Hand shaking, I pushed the pin down and the box opened with a hefty click. There, nestled in a cushion of black velvet, was a ring. A gold ring with a single, multifaceted diamond.

"Is this…?" My voice was hoarse.

"Yes."

"Oh…" My breath came in short spurts as my eyes filled with tears.

Jinseung put his hands on my shoulders and turned me around to face him.

"Chloe." He stared deep into my eyes. "Will you marry me?" His voice wavered slightly, and his cheeks were tinged pink.

I didn't want to leave him hanging, but I couldn't speak because I was sobbing so hard. He had done it. He had proposed. The thing I had never allowed myself to even imagine had really happened. I was in a state of shock.

Eventually I managed to choke it out. "Yes! Yes, I will." I threw my arms around him and pulled him close.

He placed one hand on my cheek, the other on my chin, and tilted my face up so he could kiss me—a long, dreamy sigh of a kiss. His lips were soft, his mouth was comfortable and warm.

"Thank you," he whispered, before kissing me again with more passion, my back to the window.

Fully absorbed in the kiss, I nearly dropped the ring box. I had to break away and steady myself.

"I should put this on," I said, opening the box again.

"Allow me." He plucked the ring from its velvet bed, took my hand, and slid it onto my finger. "This ring belonged to my *halmoni*."

I held my hand in front of me, admiring the way the dim light reflected off the shiny stone. "It's beautiful. It fits perfectly."

Jinseung stroked my hand. "I planned to do this on the day I leave the army, but I couldn't wait."

"I think I'll be emotional enough that day without a surprise proposal. Then again, I'm pretty emotional today as well."

Jinseung chuckled before leaning in to plant kisses on my neck and cheek.

We enjoyed our privacy in the observatory for a while longer before heading back down to the plaza. The crowds had thinned out, likely due to the late hour.

"It's been an amazing night," I said, yawning, "but we better head home. I'm so tired."

Jinseung murmured in agreement. "It's way past bedtime."

As we slowly walked downhill, I found myself gazing at the ring again, entranced by its sparkling angles under the moonlight.

"My parents will be in for a surprise when they see this," I said.

"Your parents already know everything."

"What?"

"I told them yesterday. I asked their permission for your hand."

"Wow. So old-fashioned! How did you manage? Did you write it down in English and say it like a speech?"

"More or less. There were probably mistakes, but they still understood."

"That was very sweet of you. I can't imagine how my parents reacted."

"I think they were confused why I would ask but pleased at the same time."

"Right. What about your parents? Did you tell them as well?"

"Think I could rely on my mother to keep such a secret? No. They don't know. I'll tell them tomorrow—later today, I mean—it's past midnight."

I barely managed to stay awake on the drive home. As soon as we entered our room I dove onto the bed and landed in the soft blankets with a sigh.

"Gonna sleep in those clothes?" Jinseung asked with a smirk.

"No," I mumbled into the pillow.

"Then let me undress you."

I allowed him the task without protest. He removed my clothes with love and care and minimal disturbance to my resting form, then he pulled the covers over me. I felt the bed dip when he climbed in. He cuddled up to me, skin to skin, his hand stroking up and down my arm.

"When are you going back to the army?" I asked. He had told me before, but I blocked it out so I could pretend that he wouldn't be going back.

"Tomorrow afternoon," he replied.

"So soon…"

He began to massage my shoulders. "Chloe, once we marry, you won't have to worry ever again about whether you can stay in Korea. You'll be able to become a resident, if you want to."

"I know. That's a big relief."

"It's not the reason I proposed, of course, just an added bonus. And if you don't want to stay in Korea, that's an option too. We can go anywhere you like. I'm open to the possibilities. You probably don't know right now, but we can think about it. There's plenty of time."

"The only thing I know is that I want my life to be considerably less dramatic from now on. K-dramas are fun to watch on TV, not so much when they play out in real life."

I felt his amused smile against the back of my neck. "I feel the same way."

It had taken a long time, but it finally felt like we were on the same page. Sighing with contentment, I turned over and pulled the covers up closer to my chin.

"Goodnight, Jinseung-ah."

"Goodnight, *jagi.*"

My eyes fell closed straight away, and I lost consciousness of everything except the warmth of Jinseung's arms around me and the weight and feel of the smooth band of gold around my ring finger.

Glossary

- **-ah/-ya** — A casual title used when addressing a close friend
- **-nim** — An honorific used when addressing someone by their profession
- **-ssi** — A polite title used when addressing someone
- **Abeoji** — Father
- **Abeonim** — Father (formal)
- **Aegyo** — A display of cutesy gestures/behaviour
- **Agassi** — Polite way to address a young unmarried female
- **Aigoo** — An exclamation expressing surprise or exasperation
- **Aish** — An exclamation of displeasure
- **Ajumma** — A middle-aged woman
- **Ajussi** — A middle-aged man
- **Appa** — Dad
- **Banchan** — Side dish
- **Banmal** — Informal form of Korean language
- **Bibimbap** — Korean mixed rice dish
- **Bulgogi** — Korean marinated beef or pork
- **Daebak** — Awesome

- **Dongsaeng** — Younger sibling/friend
- **Eomeoni** — Mother
- **Eomeonim** — Mother (formal)
- **Eomma** — Mum
- **Galbi** — Korean grilled ribs
- **Gimbap** — Korean seaweed and rice roll
- **Hagwon** — Cram school
- **Halmoni** — Grandmother
- **Hanbok** — A traditional Korean dress
- **Hanok** — A traditional Korean house
- **Hwaiting** — An expression of encouragement
- **Hyung** — Used by males to address older brothers or older male friends
- **Jagi** — Darling/honey (can also mean myself/himself/herself depending on context)
- **Jajangmyeon** — Noodles in black bean sauce
- **Jjimjilbbang** — Bathhouse/sauna
- **Kkoolbbang** — A sweet made from bean paste inside fried dough
- **Maknae** — Youngest sibling or youngest team member
- **Noona** — Used by males to address older sisters or older female friends
- **Noraebang** — Karaoke venue
- **Oeguk saram** — foreigner
- **Omo** — An expression of shock or surprise
- **Oppa** — Used by females to address their older brother, older male friends, or boyfriend
- **PD** — The director of a TV programme
- **Pojangmacha** — A street food stall in a tent
- **Pororo** — The name of a kids' cartoon with a penguin character called Pororo
- **Ramyeon** — Ramen
- **Samgyupsal gui** — Grilled pork belly
- **Saranghae** — I love you (informal)
- **Sasaeng fan** — An obsessive fan

- **Seonbae** — Senior
- **Seonsaeng-nim** — Teacher
- **Sundae** — Blood sausage
- **Tteokbokki** — A dish of rice cakes in a spicy sauce
- **Unnie** — Used by females to address their older sisters or older female friends
- **Ya** — Hey, oi
- **Yeobo** — Darling/Honey
- **Yeoboseyo** — Used when you answer the phone
- **Yo** — Traditional Korean mattress